D0959193

A WHISPER
OF BLOOD

A WHISPER OF BLOOD

A Collection of Modern

Vampire Stories

Edited by Ellen Datlow

FALL
RIVER
PRESS

Originally published in two separate volumes as:
Blood Is Not Enough © 1989 by Ellen Datlow
A Whisper of Blood © 1991 by Ellen Datlow

This 2008 edition published by Fall River Press.

Permissions appear on page 605.

Fall River Press
122 Fifth Avenue
New York, NY 10011

ISBN-13: 978-1-4351-0962-9

Printed and bound in the United States of America

1 3 5 7 9 10 8 6 4 2

BLOOD IS
NOT ENOUGH

17 Stories of Vampirism

For my parents

Acknowledgments

I would like to thank the following people for help in putting together this book: Astrid Anderson Bear, Michael Swanwick, Ginjer Buchanan, Ed Bryant, Brian McCann, Pat Lobrutto, Brian Thomsen, Tom Disch, Bruce McAllister, Shelley Frier, Merrilee Heifetz, Jim Frenkel, David Hartwell. I'd also like to thank Greg Cox for letting me pick his brain over egg creams. And for giving me an early draft of his book from Borgo Press, *The Transylvanian Library: A Consumer's Guide to Vampire Fiction*. It was invaluable for background on the subject.

CONTENTS

INTRODUCTION

As an adolescent I was fascinated by the Dracula movies with the exotic Bela Lugosi and the sexy Christopher Lee, and later in college was repulsed by the original *Nosferatu the Vampire*—not a very sexy creature as far as I was concerned. But my first experience of the overt sex appeal of vampires came about by accident. I ran out to see Frank Langella on Broadway in *Dracula* because the set was designed by Edward Gorey, whose work I adore and collect. Wow! Langella was one sexy vampire. I forgot all about Gorey's sets by the end of the second act when Dracula carries Lucy unconscious to bed and leans over her neck. Curtain.

The play prompted me finally to read Bram Stoker's *Dracula*. Ordinarily, I am not a fan of gothic style but I was stunned by the story's power. This despite being jaded by overexposure to the mythic creatures in books, movies, and television. I can imagine the shock of Victorian readers at the book's blatant sexuality. The biting of the neck, the passivity of the victim (traditionally young and female and attractive), the loss of will, can all be taken as a cautionary metaphor for the power of unbound lust. Stoker's *Dracula* has set the standard against which every vampire novel or story written since is measured.

There has been a distinct evolution in vampire literature over the years. Many of the early stories and novels seemed to start from scratch—the characters knowing nothing about vampirism or the existence of vampires. As a result much of the action was taken up in identifying the cause of those strange little red marks on the throats of victims who mysteriously became listless and began to sleepwalk. These days, there is a self-awareness in vampire literature. Although some of the literature still insists that the characters remain adamantly ignorant of the vampire in their midst, I doubt today's reader finds this kind of material very believable. This new sophistication on the part of the reader's expectations has quite a positive effect on the literature. It forces writers to find new ways to interest and surprise and scare.

I know that the vampires I've always found most interesting are not just your ordinary bloodsuckers. One of my favorites is Miriam Blaylock, the tragic immortal of Whitley Strieber's *The Hunger,* who carries the remains of her human lovers with her over the centuries, doomed to a loneliness impossible to fully comprehend. Another fascinating protagonist is Suzy McKee Charnas's Dr. Edward Weyland of *The Vampire Tapestry,* who while trying to blend in with humans and undergoing forced psychotherapy, eventually becomes so co-opted by our race that he has difficulty seeing us as "prey," a perception necessary for a vampire to retain in order to survive. Then there is Michael McDowell's vampire in his story "Halley's Passing," who while retaining the brutal violence characteristic of vampires, has completely forgotten, and obviously outgrown, the original reason for his actions— the need for blood. What these vampires have in common is that they all have an inner life apart from their blood-taking. They are either plagued by ethics (or at least doubts) concerning their condition, or their condition has changed in ways that overwhelm and threaten their existence. Originally a supernatural creature which survived like an animal on instinct, without much thought and surely no self-reflection, the vampire has evolved into a being with some human characteristics, and an individuality the reader can relate to.

Now we can have ethical versus unethical vampires like those in George R. R. Martin's novel *Fevre Dream* or vampires as heroes as in Chelsea Quinn Yarbro's *The Saint-Germain Chronicles.* Books are written from the vampire's point of view (Anne Rice's trilogy); vampires are psychoanalyzed (the *Unicorn Tapestry* novella by Charnas); and writers delve into the actual ramifications of vampirism. As a result, the writers have a much larger canvas to work with and are able to produce in-depth portraits of vampires in more varied circumstances. Since I've always been interested in the unusual, the quirky, the perverse in all my reading, this kind of odd vampire led to my interest in the wider range of vampiric behavior and the broader concept of vampirism. In traditional vampire fiction, blood is the essence. When I talk about vampirism I mean the draining of energy, the sucking of the will, the life force itself. Or as William Burroughs writes in *The Adding Machine: Selected Essays:*

> They always take more than they leave by the basic nature of the vampiric process of inconspicuous but inexorable consumption. The vampire converts quality, live blood, vitality, youth, talent into quantity food and time, for himself. He perpetuates the most basic betrayal of the spirit, reducing all human dreams to his shit.

There have been quite a few anthologies on vampires, inevitably containing the occasional story of vampirism as well. *Vampires,* edited by Alan Ryan, does a nice job of putting the vampire story into an historical perspective. *Vamps,* edited by Martin H. Greenberg and Charles G. Waugh, collects stories exclusively about female vampires. These anthologies and others before them deal mostly with the taking of blood. But vampirism can go beyond black capes and teeth marks on the neck. In *Blood Is Not Enough* there are manipulative telepaths, life-sucking aliens, modern incubi, the resurrected dead. "Lazarus," by Leonid Andreyev, is the oldest story in the book, first published in the early 1900's, and only three others—"Try a Dull Knife" (1969), "The Girl With the Hungry Eyes" (1949), and Gahan Wilson's "The Sea Was Wet as Wet Can Be" (1967)—were published more than ten years ago. Many of the stories are original to this book, commissioned to explore this theme. Some came to me through my position as Fiction Editor of *Omni,* and a couple were recommended by colleagues in the field.

Some of the characters in these stories don't even realize they're vampires ("Return of the Dust Vampires," "Time-Lapse," "Lazarus," and "Dirty Work"). Others try to deny what they are, like the vampire in "The Silver Collar." Blood is shed often enough, but blood is not enough. The *raison d'être* of most of these vampires is the draining of energy, life, will. Somehow both the erotic and the horrific show through them. And it seems that vampirism becomes one of the main themes of our culture in this century.

Ellen Datlow,
New York

CARRION COMFORT

Dan Simmons

What attracts me to this story (and intrigues me) is the southern gentility of these human monsters as they reminisce over the parts they played in the death of innocents. Most people have the ability to manipulate others by psychological gamesmanship—but what if you could do it by sheer force of will? Simmons has since expanded the novelette into a novel, as yet unpublished.

Nina was going to take credit for the death of the Beatle, John. I thought that was in very bad taste. She had her scrapbook laid out on my mahogany coffee table, newspaper clippings neatly arranged in chronological order, the bald statements of death recording all of her Feedings. Nina Drayton's smile was radiant, but her pale-blue eyes showed no hint of warmth.

"We should wait for Willi," I said.

"Of course, Melanie. You're right, as always. How silly of me. I know the rules." Nina stood and began walking around the room, idly touching the furnishings or exclaiming softly over a ceramic statuette or piece of needle-point. This part of the house had once been the conservatory, but now I used it as my sewing room. Green plants still caught the morning light. The light made it a warm, cozy place in the daytime, but now that winter had come the room was too chilly to use at night. Nor did I like the sense of darkness closing in against all those panes of glass.

"I love this house," said Nina.

She turned and smiled at me. "I can't tell you how much I look forward to coming back to Charleston. We should hold all of our reunions here."

I knew how much Nina loathed this city and this house.

"Willi would be hurt," I said. "You know how he likes to show off his place in Beverly Hills—and his new girlfriends."

"And boyfriends," Nina said, laughing. Of all the changes and darkenings in Nina, her laugh has been least affected. It was still the husky but childish laugh that I had first heard so long ago. It had drawn me to her then—one lonely, adolescent girl responding to the warmth of another as a moth to a flame. Now it served only to chill me and put me even more on guard. Enough moths had been drawn to Nina's flame over the many decades.

"I'll send for tea," I said.

Mr. Thorne brought the tea in my best Wedgwood china. Nina and I sat in the slowly moving squares of sunlight and spoke softly of nothing important: mutually ignorant comments on the economy, references to books that the other had not gotten around to reading, and sympathetic murmurs about the low class of persons one meets while flying these days. Someone peering in from the garden might have thought he was seeing an aging but attractive niece visiting her favorite aunt. (I drew the line at suggesting that anyone would mistake us for mother and daughter.) People usually consider me a well-dressed if not stylish person. Heaven knows I have paid enough to have the wool skirts and silk blouses mailed from Scotland and France. But next to Nina I've always felt dowdy.

This day she wore an elegant, light-blue dress that must have cost several thousand dollars. The color made her complexion seem even more perfect than usual and brought out the blue of her eyes. Her hair had gone as gray as mine, but somehow she managed to get away with wearing it long and tied back with a single barrette. It looked youthful and chic on Nina and made me feel that my short artificial curls were glowing with a blue rinse.

Few would suspect that I was four years younger than Nina. Time had been kind to her. And she had Fed more often.

She set down her cup and saucer and moved aimlessly around the room again. It was not like Nina to show such signs of nervousness. She stopped in front of the glass display case. Her gaze passed over the Hummels and the pewter pieces and then stopped in surprise.

"Good heavens, Melanie. A pistol! What an odd place to put an old pistol."

"It's an heirloom," I said. "A Colt Peacemaker from right after the War Between the States. Quite expensive. And you're right, it *is* a silly place to keep it. But it's the only case I have in the house with a lock on it and Mrs. Hodges often brings her grandchildren when she visits—"

"You mean it's *loaded?*"

"No, of course not," I lied. "But children should not play with such things . . ." I trailed off lamely. Nina nodded but did not bother to conceal the condescension in her smile. She went to look out the south window into the garden.

Damn her. It said volumes about Nina that she did not recognize that pistol.

On the day he was killed, Charles Edgar Larchmont had been my beau for precisely five months and two days. There had been no formal announcement, but we were to be married. Those five months had been a microcosm of the era itself—naive, flirtatious, formal to the point of preciosity, and romantic. Most of all, romantic. Romantic in the worst sense of the word: dedicated to saccharine or insipid ideals that only an adolescent—or an adolescent society—would strive to maintain. We were children playing with loaded weapons.

Nina, she was Nina Hawkins then, had her own beau—a tall, awkward, but well-meaning Englishman named Roger Harrison. Mr. Harrison had met Nina in London a year earlier, during the first stages of the Hawkinses' Grand Tour. Declaring himself smitten—another absurdity of those times—the tall Englishman had followed her from one European capital to another until, after being firmly reprimanded by Nina's father (an unimaginative little milliner who was constantly on the defensive about his doubtful social status), Harrison returned to London to "settle his affairs." Some months later he showed up in New York just as Nina was being packed off to her aunt's home in Charleston in order to terminate yet another flirtation. Still undaunted, the clumsy Englishman followed her south, ever mindful of the protocols and restrictions of the day.

We were a gay group. The day after I met Nina at Cousin Celia's June ball, the four of us were taking a hired boat up the Cooper River for a picnic on Daniel Island. Roger Harrison, serious and solemn on every topic, was a perfect foil for Charles's irreverent sense of humor. Nor did Roger seem to mind the good-natured jesting, since he was soon joining in the laughter with his peculiar *haw-haw-haw*.

Nina loved it all. Both gentlemen showered attention on her, and although Charles never failed to show the primacy of his affection for me, it was understood by all that Nina Hawkins was one of those young women who invariably becomes the center of male gallantry and attention in any gathering. Nor were the social strata of Charleston blind to the combined charm of our foursome. For two months of that now-distant summer, no party was complete, no excursion adequately planned, and no occasion considered a success unless we four were invited and had chosen to attend. Our happy dominance of the youthful social scene was so pronounced that Cousins Celia and Loraine wheedled their parents into leaving two weeks early for their annual August sojourn in Maine.

I am not sure when Nina and I came up with the idea of the duel. Perhaps it was during one of the long, hot nights when the other "slept over"—creeping into the other's bed, whispering and giggling, stifling our laughter when the rustling of starched uniforms betrayed the presence of our colored maids moving through the darkened halls. In any case, the idea was the natural outgrowth of the romantic pretensions of the time. The picture of Charles and Roger actually dueling over some abstract point of honor relating to *us* thrilled both of us in a physical way that I recognize now as a simple form of sexual titillation.

It would have been harmless except for the Ability. We had been so successful in our manipulation of male behavior—a manipulation that was both expected and encouraged in those days—that neither of us had yet suspected that there was anything beyond the ordinary in the way we could translate our whims into other people's actions. The field of parapsychology did not exist then; or rather, it existed only in the tappings and knockings of parlor-game séances. At any rate, we amused ourselves for several weeks with whispered fantasies, and then one of us—or perhaps both of us—used the Ability to translate the fantasy into reality.

In a sense, it was our first Feeding.

I do not remember the purported cause of the quarrel, perhaps some deliberate misinterpretation of one of Charles's jokes. I cannot recall who Charles and Roger arranged to have serve as seconds on that illegal outing. I do remember the hurt and confused expression on Roger Harrison's face during those few days. It was a caricature of ponderous dullness, the confusion of a man who finds himself in a situation not of his making and from which he cannot escape. I remember Charles and his mercurial swings of mood—the bouts of humor, periods of black anger, and the tears and kisses the night before the duel.

I remember with great clarity the beauty of that morning. Mists were floating up from the river and diffusing the rays of the rising sun as we rode out to the dueling field. I remember Nina reaching over and squeezing my hand with an impetuous excitement that was communicated through my body like an electric shock.

Much of the rest of that morning is missing. Perhaps in the intensity of that first, subconscious Feeding, I literally lost consciousness as I was engulfed in the waves of fear, excitement, pride—of *maleness*—emanating from our two beaus as they faced death on that lovely morning. I remember experiencing the shock of realizing, *this is really happening,* as I shared the tread of high boots through the grass. Someone was calling off the paces. I dimly recall the weight of the pistol in my hand—Charles's hand, I think; I will never know for sure—and a second of cold clarity before an explosion broke the connection, and the acrid smell of gunpowder brought me back to myself.

It was Charles who died. I have never been able to forget the incredible quantities of blood that poured from the small, round hole in his breast. His white shirt was crimson by the time I reached him. There had been no blood in our fantasies. Nor had there been the sight of Charles with his head lolling, mouth dribbling saliva onto his bloodied chest while his eyes rolled back to show the whites like two eggs embedded in his skull.

Roger Harrison was sobbing as Charles breathed his final, shuddering gasps on that field of innocence.

I remember nothing at all about the confused hours that followed. The next morning I opened my cloth bag to find Charles's pistol lying with my things. Why would I have kept that revolver? If I had wished to take something from my fallen lover as a sign of remembrance, why that alien piece of metal? Why pry from his dead fingers the symbol of our thoughtless sin?

It said volumes about Nina that she did not recognize that pistol.

"Willi's here," announced Nina's amanuensis, the loathsome Miss Barrett Kramer. Kramer's appearance was as unisex as her name: short-cropped, black hair, powerful shoulders, and a blank, aggressive gaze that I associated with lesbians and criminals. She looked to be in her mid-thirties.

"Thank you, Barrett dear," said Nina.

Both of us went out to greet Willi, but Mr. Thorne had already let him in, and we met in the hallway.

"Melanie! You look marvelous! You grow younger each time I see you. Nina!" The change in Willi's voice was evident. Men continued to be overpowered by their first sight of Nina after an absence. There were hugs and kisses. Willi himself looked more dissolute than ever. His alpaca sport coat was exquisitely tailored, his turtleneck sweater successfully concealed the eroded lines of his wattled neck, but when he swept off his jaunty sports-car cap the long strands of white hair he had brushed forward to hide his encroaching baldness were knocked into disarray. Willi's face was flushed with excitement, but there was also the telltale capillary redness about the nose and cheeks that spoke of too much liquor, too many drugs.

"Ladies, I think you've met my associates, Tom Luhar and Jenson Reynolds?" The two men added to the crowd in my narrow hall. Mr. Luhar was thin and blond, smiling with perfectly capped teeth. Mr. Reynolds was a gigantic Negro, hulking forward with a sullen, bruised look on his coarse face. I was sure that neither Nina nor I had encountered these specific cat's-paws of Willi's before. It did not matter.

"Why don't we go into the parlor?" I suggested. It was an awkward procession ending with the three of us seated on the heavily upholstered chairs surrounding the Georgian tea table that had been my grandmother's. "More tea, please, Mr. Thorne." Miss Kramer took that as her cue to leave, but Willi's two pawns stood uncertainly by the door, shifting from foot to foot and glancing at the crystal on display as if their mere proximity could break something. I would not have been surprised if that had proved to be the case.

"Jense!" Willi snapped his fingers. The Negro hesitated and then brought forward an expensive leather attaché case. Willi set it on the tea table and clicked the catches open with his short, broad fingers. "Why don't you two see Mrs. Fuller's man about getting something to drink?"

When they were gone Willi shook his head and smiled apologetically at Nina. "Sorry about that, Love."

Nina put her hand on Willi's sleeve. She leaned forward with an air of expectancy. "Melanie wouldn't let me begin the Game without you. Wasn't that *awful* of me to want to start without you, Willi dear?"

Willi frowned. After fifty years he still bridled at being called Willi. In Los Angeles he was Big Bill Borden. When he returned to his native Germany—which was not often because of the dangers involved—he was once again Wilhelm von Borchert, lord of dark manor, forest, and hunt. But Nina had called him Willi when they had first met in 1931 in Vienna, and Willi he had remained.

"You begin, Willi dear," said Nina. "You go first."

I could remember the time when we would have spent the first few days of our reunion in conversation and catching up with one another's lives. Now there was not even time for small talk.

Willi showed his teeth and removed news clippings, notebooks, and a stack of cassettes from his briefcase. No sooner had he covered the small table with his material than Mr. Thorne arrived with the tea and Nina's scrapbook from the sewing room. Willi brusquely cleared a small space.

At first glance one might see certain similarities between Willi Borchert and Mr. Thorne. One would be mistaken. Both men tended to the florid, but Willi's complexion was the result of excess and emotion; Mr. Thorne had known neither of these for many years. Willi's balding was a patchy, self-consciously concealed thing—a weasel with mange; Mr. Thorne's bare head was smooth and unwrinkled. One could not imagine Mr. Thorne ever having *had* hair. Both men had gray eyes—what a novelist would call cold, gray eyes—but Mr. Thorne's eyes were cold with indifference, cold with a clarity coming from an absolute absence of troublesome emotion or thought. Willi's eyes were the cold of a blustery North Sea winter and were often clouded with shifting curtains of the emotions that controlled him—pride, hatred, love of pain, the pleasures of destruction.

Willi never referred to his use of the Ability as *Feedings*—I was evidently the only one who thought in those terms—but Willi sometimes talked of The Hunt. Perhaps it was the dark forests of his homeland that he thought of as he stalked his human quarry through the sterile streets of Los Angeles. Did Willi dream of the forest, I wondered. Did he look back to green wool hunting jackets, the applause of retainers, the gouts of blood from the dying boar? Or did Willi remember the slam of jack-boots on cobblestones and the pounding of his lieutenants' fists on doors? Perhaps Willi still associated his Hunt with the dark European night of the ovens that he had helped to oversee.

I called it Feeding. Willi called it The Hunt. I had never heard Nina call it anything.

"Where is your VCR?" Willi asked. "I have put them all on tape."

"Oh, Willi," said Nina in an exasperated tone. "You know Melanie. She's *so* old-fashioned. You know she wouldn't have a video player."

"I don't even have a television," I said. Nina laughed.

"Goddamn it," muttered Willi. "It doesn't matter. I have other records here." He snapped rubber bands from around the small, black notebooks. "It just would have been better on tape. The Los Angeles stations gave much coverage to the Hollywood Strangler, and I edited in the . . . Ach! Never mind."

He tossed the videocassettes into his briefcase and slammed the lid shut.

"Twenty-three," he said. "Twenty-three since we met twelve months ago. It doesn't seem that long, does it?"

"Show us," said Nina. She was leaning forward, and her blue eyes seemed very bright. "I've been wondering since I saw the Strangler interviewed on *Sixty Minutes*. He *was* yours, Willi? He seemed so—"

"*Ja, ja,* he was mine. A nobody. A timid little man. He was the gardener of a neighbor of mine. I left him alive so that the police could question him, erase any doubts. He will hang himself in his cell next month after the press loses interest. But this is more interesting. Look at this." Willi slid across several glossy black-and-white photographs. The NBC executive had murdered the five members of his family and drowned a visiting soap-opera actress in his pool. He had then stabbed himself repeatedly and written 50 SHARE in blood on the wall of the bathhouse.

"Reliving old glories, Willi?" asked Nina. "DEATH TO THE PIGS and all that?"

"No, goddamn it. I think it should receive points for irony. The girl had been scheduled to drown on the program. It was already in the script outline."

"Was he hard to Use?" It was my question. I was curious despite myself.

Willi lifted one eyebrow. "Not really. He was an alcoholic and heavily into cocaine. There was not much left. And he hated his family. Most people do."

"Most people in California, perhaps," said Nina primly. It was an odd comment from Nina. Years ago her father had committed suicide by throwing himself in front of a trolley car.

"Where did you make contact?" I asked.

"A party. The usual place. He bought the coke from a director who had ruined one of my—"

"Did you have to repeat the contact?"

Willi frowned at me. He kept his anger under control, but his face grew redder. "*Ja, ja.* I saw him twice more. Once I just watched from my car as he played tennis."

"Points for irony," said Nina. "But you lose points for repeated contact. If he were as empty as you say, you should have been able to Use him after only one touch. What else do you have?"

He had his usual assortment. Pathetic skid-row murders. Two domestic slayings. A highway collision that turned into a fatal shooting. "I was in the crowd," said Willi. "I made contact. He had a gun in the glove compartment."

"Two points," said Nina.

Willi had saved a good one for last. A once-famous child star had suffered a bizarre accident. He had left his Bel Air apartment while it filled with gas and then returned to light a match. Two others had died in the ensuing fire.

"You get credit only for him," said Nina.

"*Ja, ja.*"

"Are you absolutely sure about this one? It *could* have been an accident."

"Don't be ridiculous," snapped Willi. He turned toward me. "*This* one was very hard to Use. Very strong. I blocked his memory of turning on the gas. Had to hold it away for two hours. Then forced him into the room. He struggled not to strike the match."

"You should have had him use his lighter," said Nina.

"He didn't smoke," growled Willi. "He gave it up last year."

"Yes," smiled Nina. "I seem to remember him saying that to Johnny Carson." I could not tell whether Nina was jesting.

The three of us went through the ritual of assigning points. Nina did most of the talking. Willi went from being sullen to expansive to sullen again. At one point he reached over and patted my knee as he laughingly asked for my support. I said nothing. Finally he gave up, crossed the parlor to the liquor cabinet, and poured himself a tall glass of bourbon from father's decanter. The evening light was sending its final, horizontal rays through the stained-glass panels of the bay windows, and it cast a red hue on Willi as he stood next to the oak cupboard. His eyes were small, red embers in a bloody mask.

"Forty-one," said Nina at last.

She looked up brightly and showed the calculator as if it verified some objective fact. "I count forty-one points. What do you have, Melanie?"

"*Ja,*" interrupted Willi. "That is fine. Now let us see your claims, Nina." His voice was flat and empty. Even Willi had lost some interest in the Game.

Before Nina could begin, Mr. Thorne entered and motioned that dinner was served. We adjourned to the dining room—Willi pouring himself another glass of bourbon and Nina fluttering her hands in mock frustration at the interruption of the Game. Once seated at the long, mahogany table, I worked at being a hostess. From decades of tradition, talk of the Game was banned from the dinner table. Over soup we discussed Willi's new movie and the purchase of another store for Nina's line of boutiques. It seemed that Nina's monthly column in *Vogue* was to be discontinued but that a newspaper syndicate was interested in picking it up.

Both of my guests exclaimed over the perfection of the baked ham, but I thought that Mr. Thorne had made the gravy a trifle too sweet. Darkness had filled the windows before we finished our chocolate mousse. The refracted light from the chandelier made Nina's hair dance with highlights while I feared that mine glowed more bluely than ever.

Suddenly there was a sound from the kitchen. The huge Negro's face appeared at the swinging door. His shoulder was hunched against white hands and his expression was that of a querulous child.

". . . the hell you think we are sittin' here like goddamned—"The white hands pulled him out of sight.

"Excuse me, ladies." Willi dabbed linen at his lips and stood up. He still moved gracefully for all of his years.

Nina poked at her chocolate. There was one sharp, barked command from the kitchen and the sound of a slap. It was the slap of a man's hand—hard and flat as a small-caliber-rifle shot. I looked up and Mr. Thorne was at my elbow, clearing away the dessert dishes.

"Coffee, please, Mr. Thorne. For all of us." He nodded and his smile was gentle.

Franz Anton Mesmer had known of it even if he had not understood it. I suspect that Mesmer must have had some small touch of the Ability. Modern pseudosciences have studied it and renamed it, removed most of its power, confused its uses and origins, but it remains the shadow of what Mesmer discovered. They have no idea of what it is like to Feed.

I despair at the rise of modern violence. I truly give in to despair at times, that deep, futureless pit of despair that poet Gerard Manley Hopkins called carrion comfort. I watch the American slaughterhouse, the casual attacks on popes, presidents, and uncounted others, and I wonder whether there are many more out there with the Ability or whether butchery has simply become the modern way of life.

All humans feed on violence, on the small exercises of power over another. But few have tasted—as we have—the ultimate power. And without the Ability, few know the unequaled pleasure of taking a human life. Without the Ability, even those who do feed on life cannot savor the flow of emotions in stalker and victim, the total exhilaration of the attacker who has moved beyond all rules and punishments, the strange, almost sexual submission of the victim in that final second of truth when all options are canceled, all futures denied, all possibilities erased in an exercise of absolute power over another.

I despair at modern violence. I despair at the impersonal nature of it and the casual quality that has made it accessible to so many. I had a television set until I sold it at the height of the Vietnam War. Those sanitized snippets of death—made distant by the camera's lens—meant nothing to me. But I believe it meant something to these cattle that surround me. When the war and the nightly televised body counts ended, they demanded more, *more,* and the movie screens and streets of this sweet and dying nation have provided it in mediocre, mob abundance. It is an addiction I know well.

They miss the point. Merely observed, violent death is a sad and sullied tapestry of confusion. But to those of us who have Fed, death can be a *sacrament.*

"My turn! My turn!" Nina's voice still resembled that of the visiting belle who had just filled her dance card at Cousin Celia's June ball.

We had returned to the parlor. Willi had finished his coffee and requested a brandy from Mr. Thorne. I was embarrassed for Willi. To have one's closest associates show any hint of unplanned behavior was certainly a sign of weakening Ability. Nina did not appear to have noticed.

"I have them all in order," said Nina. She opened the scrapbook on the now-empty tea table. Willi went through them carefully, sometimes asking a question, more often grunting assent. I murmured occasional agreement although I had heard of none of them. Except for the Beatle, of course. Nina saved that for near the end.

"Good God, Nina, that was you?" Willi seemed near anger. Nina's Feedings had always run to Park Avenue suicides and matrimonial disagreements ending in shots fired from expensive, small-caliber ladies' guns. This type of thing was more in Willi's crude style. Perhaps he felt that his territory was being invaded. "I mean . . . you were risking a lot, weren't you? It's so . . . damn it . . . *so public.*"

Nina laughed and set down the calculator. "Willi *dear,* that's what the Game is *about,* is it not?"

Willi strode to the liquor cabinet and refilled his brandy snifter. The wind tossed bare branches against the leaded glass of the bay window. I do not like winter. Even in the South it takes its toll on the spirit.

"Didn't this guy . . . what's his name . . . buy the gun in Hawaii or someplace?" asked Willi from across the room. "That sounds like his initiative to me. I mean, if he was *already* stalking the fellow—"

"Willie dear." Nina's voice had gone as cold as the wind that raked the branches. "No one said he was *stable.* How many of yours are stable, Willi? But I made it *happen,* darling. I chose the place and the time. Don't you see the irony of the *place,* Willi? After that little prank on the director of that witchcraft movie a few years ago? It was straight from the script—"

"I don't know," said Willi. He sat heavily on the divan, spilling brandy on his expensive sport coat. He did not notice. The lamplight reflected from his balding skull. The mottles of age were more visible at night, and his neck, where it disappeared into his turtleneck, was all ropes and tendons. "I don't know." He looked up at me and smiled suddenly, as if we shared a conspiracy. "It could be like that writer fellow, eh, Melanie? It could be like that."

Nina looked down at the hands in her lap. They were clenched and the well-manicured fingers were white at the tips.

The Mind Vampires. That's what the writer was going to call his book.

I sometimes wonder if he really would have written anything. What was his name? Something Russian.

Willi and I received telegrams from Nina: COME QUICKLY YOU ARE NEEDED. That was enough. I was on the next morning's flight to New York. The plane was a noisy, propeller-driven Constellation, and I spent much of the flight assuring the overly solicitous stewardess that I needed nothing, that, indeed, I felt fine. She obviously had decided that I was someone's grandmother, who was flying for the first time.

Willi managed to arrive twenty minute before me. Nina was distraught and as close to hysteria as I had ever seen her. She had been at a party in lower Manhattan two days before—she was not so distraught that she forgot to tell us what important names had been there—when she found herself sharing a corner, a fondue pot, and confidences with a young writer. Or rather, the writer was sharing confidences. Nina described him as a scruffy sort with a wispy little beard, thick glasses, a corduroy sport coat worn over an old plaid shirt—one of the type invariably sprinkled around successful parties of that era, according to Nina. She knew enough not to call him a beatnik, for that term had just become passé, but no one had yet heard the term *hippie,* and it wouldn't have applied to him anyway. He was a writer of the sort that barely ekes out a living, these days at least, by selling blood and doing novelizations of television series. Alexander something.

His idea for a book—he told Nina that he had been working on it for some time—was that many of the murders then being committed were actually the result of a small group of psychic killers, he called them *mind vampires,* who used others to carry out their grisly deeds.

He said that a paperback publisher had already shown interest in his outline and would offer him a contract tomorrow if he would change the title to *The Zombie Factor* and put in more sex.

"So what?" Willi had said to Nina in disgust. "You have me fly across the continent for this? I might buy the idea myself."

That turned out to be the excuse we used to interrogate this Alexander somebody during an impromptu party given by Nina the next evening. I did not attend. The party was not overly successful according to Nina but it gave Willi the chance to have a long chat with the young would-be novelist. In the writer's almost pitiable eagerness to do business with Bill Borden, producer of *Paris Memories, Three on a Swing,* and at least two other completely forgettable Technicolor features touring the drive-ins that summer, he revealed that the book consisted of a well-worn outline and a dozen pages of notes.

He was sure, however, that he could do a treatment for Mr. Borden in five weeks, perhaps even as fast as three weeks if he were flown out to Hollywood to get the proper creative stimulation.

Later that evening we discussed the possibility of Willi simply buying an option on the treatment, but Willi was short on cash at the time and Nina was insistent. In the end the young writer opened his femoral artery with a Gillette blade and ran screaming into a narrow Greenwich Village side street to die. I don't believe that anyone ever bothered to sort through the clutter and debris of his remaining notes.

"It could be like that writer, *ja*, Melanie?" Willi patted my knee. I nodded. "He was mine," continued Willi, "and Nina tried to take credit. Remember?"

Again I nodded. Actually he had been neither Nina's nor Willi's. I had avoided the party so that I could make contact later without the young man noticing he was being followed. I did so easily. I remember sitting in an overheated little delicatessen across the street from the apartment building. It was over so quickly that there was almost no sense of Feeding. Then I was aware once again of the sputtering radiators and the smell of salami as people rushed to the door to see what the screaming was about. I remember finishing my tea slowly so that I did not have to leave before the ambulance was gone.

"Nonsense," said Nina. She busied herself with her little calculator. "How many points?" She looked at me. I looked at Willi.

"Six," he said with a shrug. Nina made a small show of totaling the numbers.

"Thirty-eight," she said and sighed theatrically. "You win again, Willi. Or rather, you beat *me* again. We must hear from Melanie. You've been so quiet, dear. You must have some surprise for us."

"Yes," said Willi, "it is your turn to win. It has been several years."

"None," I said. I had expected an explosion of questions, but the silence was broken only by the ticking of the clock on the mantelpiece. Nina was looking away from me, at something hidden by the shadows in the corner.

"None?" echoed Willi.

"There was . . . one," I said at last. "But it was by accident. I came across them robbing an old man behind . . . but it was completely by accident."

Willi was agitated. He stood up, walked to the window, turned an old straight-back chair around and straddled it, arms folded. "What does this mean?"

"You're quitting the Game?" Nina asked as she turned to look at me. I let the question serve as the answer.

"Why?" snapped Willi. In his excitement it came out with a hard *v*.

If I had been raised in an era when young ladies were allowed to shrug, I would have done so. As it was, I contented myself with running my fingers along an imaginary seam on my skirt. Willi had asked the question, but I stared straight into Nina's eyes when I finally answered, "I'm tired. It's been too long. I guess I'm getting old."

"You'll get a lot *older* if you do not Hunt," said Willi. His body, his voice, the red mask of his face, everything signaled great anger just kept in check. "My God, Melanie, you *already* look older! You look terrible. This is *why* we hunt, woman. Look at yourself in the mirror! Do you want to die an old woman just because you're tired of using *them?*" Willi stood and turned his back.

"Nonsense!" Nina's voice was strong, confident, in command once more. "Melanie's *tired*, Willi. Be nice. We all have times like that. I remember how *you* were after the war. Like a whipped puppy. You wouldn't even go outside your miserable little flat in Baden. Even after we helped you get to New Jersey you just sulked around feeling sorry for yourself. Melanie *made up* the Game to help you feel better. So quiet! *Never* tell a lady who feels tired and depressed that she looks terrible. Honestly, Willi, you're such a *Schwachsinniger* sometimes. And a crashing boor to boot."

I had anticipated many reactions to my announcement, but this was the one I feared most. It meant that Nina had also tired of the game. It meant that she was ready to move to another level of play.

It had to mean that.

"Thank you, Nina darling," I said. "I knew you would understand."

She reached across and touched my knee reassuringly. Even through my wool skirt, I could feel the cold of her fingers.

My guests would not stay the night. I implored. I remonstrated. I pointed out that their rooms were ready, that Mr. Thorne had already turned down the quilts.

"Next time," said Willi. "Next time, Melanie, my little love. We'll make a weekend of it as we used to. A week!" Willi was in a much better mood since he had been paid his thousand-dollar prize by each of us. He had sulked, but I had insisted. It soothed his ego when Mr. Thorne brought in a check already made out to WILLIAM D. BORDEN.

Again I asked him to stay, but he protested that he had a midnight flight to Chicago. He had to see a prizewinning author about a screenplay. Then he was hugging me good-bye, his companions were in the hall behind me and I had a brief moment of terror.

But they left. The blond young man showed his white smile, and the Negro bobbed his head in what I took as a farewell. Then we were alone.

Nina and I were alone.

Not quite alone. Miss Kramer was standing next to Nina at the end of the hall. Mr. Thorne was out of sight behind the swinging door to the kitchen. I left him there.

Miss Kramer took three steps forward. I felt my breath stop for an instant. Mr. Thorne put his hand on the swinging door. Then the husky little brunette opened the door to the hall closet, removed Nina's coat, and stepped back to help her into it.

"Are you sure you won't stay?"

"No, thank you, darling. I've promised Barrett that we would drive to Hilton Head tonight."

"But it's late—"

"We have reservations. Thank you anyway, Melanie. I *will* be in touch."

"Yes."

"I mean it, dear. We must talk. I understand *exactly* how you feel, but you have to remember that the Game is still important to Willi. We'll have to find a way to end it without hurting his feelings. Perhaps we could visit him next spring in Karinhall or whatever he calls that gloomy old Bavarian place of his. A trip to the Continent would do wonders for you, dear."

"Yes."

"I *will* be in touch. After this deal with the new store is settled. We need to spend some time together, Melanie . . . just the two of us . . . like old times." Her lips kissed the air next to my cheek. She held my forearms tightly. "Good-bye, darling."

"Good-bye, Nina."

I carried the brandy glass to the kitchen. Mr. Thorne took it in silence.

"Make sure the house is secure," I said. He nodded and went to check the locks and alarm system. It was only nine forty-five, but I was very tired. *Age,* I thought. I went up the wide staircase, perhaps the finest feature of the house, and dressed for bed. It had begun to storm, and the sound of the cold raindrops on the window carried a sad rhythm to it.

Mr. Thorne looked in as I was brushing my hair and wishing it were longer. I turned to him. He reached into the pocket of his dark vest. When his hand emerged a slim blade flicked out. I nodded. He palmed the blade shut and closed the door behind him. I listened to his footsteps recede down the stairs to the chair in the front hall, where he would spend the night.

I believe I dreamed of vampires that night. Or perhaps I was thinking about them just prior to falling asleep, and a fragment had stayed with me until morning. Of all mankind's self-inflicted terrors, of all its pathetic little monsters, only the myth of the vampire had any vestige of dignity. Like the humans it feeds on, the vampire must respond to its own dark compulsions. But unlike its petty human prey, the vampire carries out its sordid means to the only possible ends that could justify such actions—the goal of literal immortality. There is a nobility there. And a sadness.

Before sleeping I thought of that summer long ago in Vienna. I saw Willi young again—blond, flushed with youth, and filled with pride at escorting two such independent American ladies.

I remembered Willi's high, stiff collars and the short dresses that Nina helped to bring into style that summer. I remembered the friendly sounds of crowded *Biergartens* and the shadowy dance of leaves in front of gas lamps.

I remembered the footsteps on wet cobblestones, the shouts, the distant whistles, and the silences.

Willi was right; I had aged. The past year had taken a greater toll than the preceding decade. But I had not Fed. Despite the hunger, despite the aging reflection in the mirror, *I had not Fed.*

I fell asleep trying to think of that writer's last name. I fell asleep hungry.

Morning. Bright sunlight through bare branches. It was one of those crystalline, warming winter days that make living in the South so much less depressing than merely surviving a Yankee winter. I had Mr. Thorne open the window a crack when he brought in my breakfast tray. As I sipped my coffee I could hear children playing in the courtyard. Once Mr. Thorne would have brought the morning paper with the tray, but I had long since learned that to read about the follies and scandals of the world was to desecrate the morning. I was growing less and less interested in the affairs of men. I had done without a newspaper, telephone, or television for twelve years and had suffered no ill effects unless one were to count a growing self-contentment as an ill thing. I smiled as I remembered Willi's disappointment at not being able to play his video cassettes. He was such a child.

"It is Saturday, is it not, Mr. Thorne?" At his nod I gestured for the tray to be taken away. "We will go out today," I said. "A walk. Perhaps a trip to the fort. Then dinner at Henry's and home. I have arrangements to make."

Mr. Thorne hesitated and half-stumbled as he was leaving the room. I paused in the act of belting my robe. It was not like Mr. Thorne to commit an ungraceful movement. I realized that he too was getting old. He straightened the tray and dishes, nodded his head, and left for the kitchen.

I would not let thoughts of aging disturb me on such a beautiful morning. I felt charged with a new energy and resolve. The reunion the night before had not gone well but neither had it gone as badly as it might have. I had been honest with Nina and Willi about my intention of quitting the Game. In the weeks and months to come, they—or at least Nina—would begin to brood over the ramifications of that, but by the time they chose to react, separately or together, I would be long gone. Already I had new (and old) identities waiting for me in Florida, Michigan, London, southern France, and even in New Delhi. Michigan was out for the time being. I had grown unused to the harsh climate. New Delhi was no longer the hospitable place for foreigners it had been when I resided there briefly before the war.

Nina had been right about one thing—a return to Europe would be good for me. Already I longed for the rich light and cordial *savoir vivre* of the villagers near my old summer house outside of Toulon.

The air outside was bracing. I wore a simple print dress and my spring coat. The trace of arthritis in my right leg had bothered me coming down the stairs, but I used my father's old walking stick as a cane. A young Negro servant had cut it for father the summer we moved from Greenville to Charleston. I smiled as we emerged into the warm air of the courtyard.

Mrs. Hodges came out of her doorway into the light. It was her grandchildren and their friends who were playing around the dry fountain.

For two centuries the courtyard had been shared by the three brick buildings. Only my home had not been parceled into expensive town-houses or fancy apartments.

"Good morning, Miz Fuller."

"Good morning, Mrs. Hodges. A beautiful day, isn't it?"

"It is that. Are you off shopping?"

"Just for a walk, Mrs. Hodges. I'm surprised that Mr. Hodges isn't out today. He always seems to be working in the yard on Saturdays."

Mrs. Hodges frowned as one of the little girls ran between us. Her friend came squealing after her, sweater flying. "Oh, George is at the marina already."

"In the daytime?" I had often been amused by Mr. Hodges's departure for work in the evening, his security-guard uniform neatly pressed, gray hair jutting out from under his cap, black lunch pail gripped firmly under his arm.

Mr. Hodges was as leathery and bowlegged as an aged cowboy. He was one of those men who were always on the verge of retiring but who probably realized that to be suddenly inactive would be a form of death sentence.

"Oh, yes. One of those colored men on the day shift down at the storage building quit, and they asked George to fill in. I told him that he was too old to work four nights a week and then go back on the weekend, but you know George. He'll never retire."

"Well, give him my best," I said.

The girls running around the fountain made me nervous.

Mrs. Hodges followed me to the wrought-iron gate. "Will you be going away for the holidays, Miz Fuller?"

"Probably, Mrs. Hodges. Most probably." Then Mr. Thorne and I were out on the sidewalk and strolling toward the Battery. A few cars drove slowly down the narrow streets, some tourists stared at the houses of our Old Section, but the day was serene and quiet.

I saw the masts of the yachts and sailboats before we came in sight of the water as we emerged onto Broad Street.

"Please acquire tickets for us, Mr. Thorne," I said. "I believe I would like to see the fort."

As is typical of most people who live in close proximity to a popular tourist attraction, I had not taken notice of it for many years. It was an act of sentimentality to visit the fort now. An act brought on by my increasing acceptance of the fact that I would have to leave these parts forever. It is one thing to plan a move; it is something altogether different to be faced with the imperative reality of it.

There were few tourists. The ferry moved away from the marina and into the placid waters of the harbor. The combination of warm sunlight and the steady throb of the diesel caused me to doze briefly. I awoke as we were putting in at the dark hulk of the island fort.

For a while I moved with the tour group, enjoying the catacomb silences of the lower levels and the mindless singsong of the young woman from the Park Service. But as we came back to the museum, with its dusty dioramas and tawdry little trays of slides, I climbed the stairs back to the outer walls. I motioned for Mr. Thorne to stay at the top of the stairs and moved out onto the ramparts.

Only one other couple—a young pair with a cheap camera and a baby in an uncomfortable-looking papoose carrier—were in sight along the wall.

It was a pleasant moment. A midday storm was approaching from the west and it set a dark backdrop to the still-sunlit church spires, brick towers, and bare branches of the city.

Even from two miles away I could see the movement of people strolling along the Battery walkway. The wind was blowing in ahead of the dark clouds and tossing whitecaps against the rocking ferry and wooden dock. The air smelled of river and winter and rain by nightfall.

It was not hard to imagine that day long ago. The shells had dropped onto the fort until the upper layers were little more than protective piles of rubble. People had cheered from the rooftops behind the Battery. The bright colors of dresses and silk parasols must have been maddening to the Yankee gunners. Finally one had fired a shot above the crowded rooftops. The ensuing confusion must have been amusing from this vantage point.

A movement down below caught my attention. Something dark was sliding through the gray water—something dark and shark silent. I was jolted out of thoughts of the past as I recognized it as a Polaris submarine, old but obviously still operational, slipping through the dark water without a sound. Waves curled and rippled over the porpoise-smooth hull, sliding to either side in a white wake. There were several men on the tower. They were muffled in heavy coats, their hats pulled low. An improbably large pair of binoculars hung from the neck of one man, whom I assumed to be the captain. He pointed at something beyond Sullivan's Island. I stared. The periphery of my vision began to fade as I made contact. Sounds and sensations came to me as from a distance.

Tension. The pleasure of salt spray, breeze from the north, northwest. Anxiety of the sealed orders below. Awareness of the sandy shallows just coming into sight on the port side.

I was startled as someone came up behind me. The dots flickering at the edge of my vision fled as I turned.

Mr. Thorne was there. At my elbow. Unbidden. I had opened my mouth to command him back to the top of the stairs when I saw the cause of his approach. The youth who had been taking pictures of his pale wife was now walking toward me. Mr. Thorne moved to intercept him.

"Hey, excuse me, ma'am. Would you or your husband mind taking our picture?"

I nodded and Mr. Thorne took the proffered camera. It looked minuscule in his long-fingered hands. Two snaps and the couple were satisfied that their presence there was documented for posterity. The young man grinned idiotically and bobbed his head. Their baby began to cry as the cold wind blew in.

I looked back to the submarine, but already it had passed on, its gray tower a thin stripe connecting the sea and sky.

We were almost back to town, the ferry was swinging in toward the ship, when a stranger told me of Willi's death.

"It's awful, isn't it?" The garrulous old woman had followed me out onto the exposed section of deck. Even though the wind had grown chilly and I had moved twice to escape her mindless chatter, the woman had obviously chosen me as her conversational target for the final stages of the tour. Neither my reticence nor Mr. Thorne's glowering presence had discouraged her. "It must have been terrible," she continued. "In the dark and all."

"What was that?" A dark premonition prompted my question.

"Why, the airplane crash. Haven't you heard about it? It must have been awful, falling into the swamp and all. I told my daughter this morning—"

"What airplane crash? When?" The old woman cringed a bit at the sharpness of my tone, but the vacuous smile stayed on her face.

"Why last night. This morning I told my daughter—"

"Where? What aircraft are you talking about?" Mr. Thorne came closer as he heard the tone of my voice.

"The one last night," she quavered. "The one from Charleston. The paper in the lounge told all about it. Isn't it terrible? Eighty-five people. I told my daughter—"

I left her standing there by the railing. There was a crumpled newspaper near the snack bar, and under the four-word headline were the sparse details of Willi's death. Flight 417, bound for Chicago, had left Charleston International Airport at twelve-eighteen A.M. Twenty minutes later the aircraft had exploded in midair not far from the city of Columbia. Fragments of fuselage and parts of bodies had fallen into Congaree Swamp, where fishermen had found them. There had been no survivors. The FAA and FBI were investigating.

There was a loud rushing in my ears, and I had to sit down or faint. My hands were clammy against the green-vinyl upholstery. People moved past me on their way to the exits.

Willi was dead. Murdered. Nina had killed him. For a few dizzy seconds I considered the possibility of a conspiracy—an elaborate ploy by Nina and Willi to confuse me into thinking that only one threat remained. But no. There would be no reason. If Nina had included Willi in her plans, there would be no need for such absurd machinations.

Willi was dead. His remains were spread over a smelly, obscure marsh-land. I could imagine his last moments. He would have been leaning back in first-class comfort, a drink in his hand, perhaps whispering to one of his loutish companions.

Then the explosion. Screams. Sudden darkness. A brutal tilting and the final fall to oblivion. I shuddered and gripped the metal arm of the chair.

How had Nina done it? Almost certainly not one of Willi's entourage. It was not beyond Nina's powers to Use Willi's own cat's-paws, especially in light of his failing Ability, but there would have been no reason to do so. She could have Used anyone on that flight. It *would* have been difficult. The elaborate step of preparing the bomb. The supreme effort of blocking all memory of it, and the almost unbelievable feat of Using someone even as we sat together drinking coffee and brandy.

But Nina could have done it. Yes, she *could* have. And the timing. The timing could mean only one thing.

The last of the tourists had filed out of the cabin. I felt the slight bump that meant we had tied up to the dock. Mr. Thorne stood by the door.

Nina's timing meant that she was attempting to deal with both of us at once. She obviously had planned it long before the reunion and my timorous announcement of withdrawal. How amused Nina must have been. No wonder she had reacted so generously! Yet, she had made one great mistake. By dealing with Willi first, Nina had banked everything on my not hearing the news before she could turn on me. She knew that I had no access to daily news and only rarely left the house anymore. Still, it was unlike Nina to leave anything to chance. Was it possible that she thought I had lost the Ability completely and that Willi was the greater threat?

I shook my head as we emerged from the cabin into the gray afternoon light. The wind sliced at me through my thin coat. The view of the gangplank was blurry, and I realized that tears had filled my eyes. For Willi? He had been a pompous, weak old fool. For Nina's betrayal? Perhaps it was only the cold wind.

The streets of the Old Section were almost empty of pedestrians. Bare branches clicked together in front of the windows of fine homes. Mr. Thorne stayed by my side. The cold air sent needles of arthritic pain up my right leg to my hip. I leaned more heavily upon father's walking stick.

What would her next move be? I stopped. A fragment of newspaper, caught by the wind, wrapped itself around my ankle and then blew on.

How would she come at me? Not from a distance. She was somewhere in town. I knew that. While it is possible to Use someone from a great distance, it would involve great rapport, an almost intimate knowledge of that person. And if contact were lost, it would be difficult if not impossible to reestablish at a distance. None of us had known why this was so. It did not matter now. But the thought of Nina still here, nearby, made my heart begin to race.

Not from a distance. I would see my assailant. If I knew Nina at all, I knew that. Certainly Willi's death had been the least personal Feeding imaginable, but that had been a mere technical operation. Nina obviously had decided to settle old scores with *me,* and Willi had become an obstacle to her, a minor but measurable threat that had to be eliminated before she could proceed. I could easily imagine that in Nina's own mind her choice of death for Willi would be interpreted as an act of compassion, almost a sign of affection. Not so with me. I felt that Nina would want me to know, however briefly, that she was behind the attack. In a sense, her own vanity would be my warning. Or so I hoped.

I was tempted to leave immediately. I could have Mr. Thorne get the Audi out of storage, and we could be beyond Nina's influence in an hour—away to a new life within a few more hours. There were important items in the house, of course, but the funds that I had stored elsewhere would replace most of them. It would be almost welcome to leave everything behind with the discarded identity that had accumulated them.

No. I could not leave. Not yet.

From across the street the house looked dark and malevolent. Had *I* closed those blinds on the second floor? There was a shadowy movement in the courtyard, and I saw Mrs. Hodges's granddaughter and a friend scamper from one doorway to another. I stood irresolutely on the curb and tapped father's stick against the black-barked tree. It was foolish to dither so—I knew it was—but it had been a long time since I had been forced to make a decision under stress.

"Mr. Thorne, please check the house. Look in each room. Return quickly."

A cold wind came up as I watched Mr. Thorne's black coat blend into the gloom of the courtyard. I felt terribly exposed standing there alone. I found myself glancing up and down the street, looking for Miss Kramer's dark hair, but the only sign of movement was a young woman pushing a perambulator far down the street.

The blinds on the second floor shot up, and Mr. Thorne's face stared out whitely for a minute. Then he turned away, and I remained staring at the dark rectangle of window. A shout from the courtyard startled me, but it was only the little girl—what was her name?—calling to her friend. Kathleen, that was it. The two sat on the edge of the fountain and opened a box of animal crackers. I stared intently at them and then relaxed. I even managed to smile a little at the extent of my paranoia. For a second I considered using Mr. Thorne directly, but the thought of being helpless on the street dissuaded me. When one is in complete contact, the senses still function but are a distant thing at best.

Hurry. The thought was sent almost without volition. Two bearded men were walking down the sidewalk on my side of the street. I crossed to stand in front of my own gate. The men were laughing and gesturing at each other. One looked over at me. *Hurry.*

Mr. Thorne came out of the house, locked the door behind him, and crossed the courtyard toward me. One of the girls said something to him and held out the box of crackers, but he ignored her. Across the street the two men continued walking. Mr. Thorne handed me the large front-door key. I dropped it in my coat pocket and looked sharply at him. He nodded. His placid smile unconsciously mocked my consternation.

"You're sure?" I asked. Again the nod. "You checked all of the rooms?" Nod. "The alarms?" Nod. "You looked in the basement?" Nod. "No sign of disturbance?" Mr. Thorne shook his head.

My hand went to the metal of the gate, but I hesitated. Anxiety filled my throat like bile. I was a silly old woman, tired and aching from the chill, but I could not bring myself to open that gate.

"Come." I crossed the street and walked briskly away from the house. "We will have dinner at Henry's and return later." Only I was not walking toward the old restaurant. I was heading away from the house in what I knew was a blind, directionless panic. It was not until we reached the waterfront and were walking along the Battery wall that I began to calm down.

No one else was in sight. A few cars moved along the street, but to approach us someone would have to cross a wide, empty space. The gray clouds were quite low and blended with the choppy, white-crested waves in the bay.

The open air and fading evening light served to revive me, and I began to think more clearly. Whatever Nina's plans had been, they certainly had been thrown into disarray by my day-long absence. I doubted that Nina would stay if there were the slightest risk to herself. No, she would be returning to New York by plane even as I stood shivering on the Battery walk. In the morning I would receive a telegram, I could see it. MELANIE ISN'T IT TERRIBLE ABOUT WILLI? TERRIBLY SAD. CAN YOU TRAVEL WITH ME TO THE FUNERAL? LOVE, NINA.

I began to realize that my reluctance to leave immediately had come from a desire to return to the warmth and comfort of my home. I simply had been afraid to shuck off this old cocoon. I could do so now. I would wait in a safe place while Mr. Thorne returned to the house to pick up the one thing I could not leave behind. Then he would get the car out of storage, and by the time Nina's telegram arrived I would be far away. It would be *Nina* who would be starting at shadows in the months and years to come. I smiled and began to frame the necessary commands.

"Melanie."

My head snapped around. Mr. Thorne had not spoken in twenty-eight years. He spoke now.

"Melanie." His face was distorted in a rictus that showed his back teeth. The knife was in his right hand. The blade flicked out as I stared. I looked into his empty, gray eyes, and I knew.

"Melanie."

The long blade came around in a powerful arc. I could do nothing to stop it. It cut through the fabric of my coat sleeve and continued into my side. But in the act of turning, my purse had swung with me. The knife tore through the leather, ripped through the jumbled contents, pierced my coat, and drew blood above my lowest left rib. The purse had saved my life.

I raised father's heavy walking stick and struck Mr. Thorne squarely in his left eye. He reeled but did not make a sound. Again he swept the air with the knife, but I had taken two steps back and his vision was clouded. I took a two-handed grip on the cane and swung sideways again, bringing the stick around in an awkward chop. Incredibly, it again found the eye socket. I took three more steps back.

Blood streamed down the left side of Mr. Thorne's face, and the damaged eye protruded onto his cheek. The rictal grin remained. His head came up, he raised his left hand slowly, plucked out the eye with a soft snapping of a gray cord, and thew it into the water of the bay. He came toward me. I turned and ran.

I *tried* to run. The ache in my right leg slowed me to a walk after twenty paces. Fifteen more hurried steps and my lungs were out of air, my heart threatening to burst. I could feel a wetness seeping down my left side and there was a tingling—like an ice cube held against the skin—where the knife blade had touched me. One glance back showed me that Mr. Thorne was striding toward me faster than I was moving. Normally he could have overtaken me in four strides. But it is hard to make someone run when you are Using him. Especially when that person's body is reacting to shock and trauma. I glanced back again, almost slipping on the slick pavement. Mr. Thorne was grinning widely. Blood poured from the empty socket and stained his teeth. No one else was in sight.

Down the stairs, clutching at the rail so as not to fall. Down the twisting walk and up the asphalt path to the street. Pole lamps flickered and went on as I passed. Behind me Mr. Thorne took the steps in two jumps. As I hurried up the path, I thanked God that I had worn low-heel shoes for the boat ride. What would an observer think seeing this bizarre, slow-motion chase between two old people? There were no observers.

I turned onto a side street. Closed shops, empty warehouses. Going left would take me to Broad Street, but to the right, half a block away, a lone figure had emerged from a dark storefront. I moved that way, no longer able to run, close to fainting. The arthritic cramps in my leg hurt more than I could ever have imagined and threatened to collapse me on the sidewalk. Mr. Thorne was twenty paces behind me and quickly closing the distance.

The man I was approaching was a tall, thin Negro wearing a brown nylon jacket. He was carrying a box of what looked like framed sepia photographs.

He glanced at me as I approached and then looked over my shoulder at the apparition ten steps behind.

"Hey!" The man had time to shout the single syllable and then I reached out with my mind and *shoved*. He twitched like a poorly handled marionette. His jaw dropped, and his eyes glazed over, and he lurched past me just as Mr. Thorne reached for the back of my coat.

The box flew into the air, and glass shattered on the brick sidewalk. Long, brown fingers reached for a white throat. Mr. Thorne backhanded him away, but the Negro clung tenaciously, and the two swung around like awkward dance partners. I reached the opening to an alley and leaned my face against the cold brick to revive myself. The effort of concentration while Using this stranger did not afford me the luxury of resting even for a second.

I watched the clumsy stumblings of the two tall men for a while and resisted an absurd impulse to laugh.

Mr. Thorne plunged the knife into the other's stomach, withdrew it, plunged it in again. The Negro's fingernails were clawing at Mr. Thorne's good eye now. Strong teeth were snapping in search of the blade for a third time, but the heart was still beating and he was still usable. The man jumped, scissoring his legs around Mr. Thorne's middle while his jaws closed on the muscular throat. Fingernails raked bloody streaks across white skin. The two went down in a tumble.

Kill him. Fingers groped for an eye, but Mr. Thorne reached up with his left hand and snapped the thin wrist. Limp fingers continued to flail. With a tremendous exertion, Mr. Thorne lodged his forearm against the other's chest and lifted him bodily as a reclining father tosses a child above him. Teeth tore away a piece of flesh, but there was no vital damage. Mr. Thorne brought the knife between them, up, left, then right. He severed half the Negro's throat with the second swing, and blood fountained over both of them. The smaller man's legs spasmed twice, Mr. Thorne threw him to one side, and I turned and walked quickly down the alley.

Out into the light again, the fading evening light, and I realized that I had run myself into a dead end. Backs of warehouses and the windowless, metal side of the Battery Marina pushed right up against the waters of the bay. A street wound away to the left, but it was dark, deserted, and far too long to try.

I looked back in time to see the black silhouette enter the alley behind me.

I tried to make contact, but there was nothing there. Nothing. Mr. Thorne might as well have been a hole in the air. I would worry later how Nina had done this thing.

The side door to the marina was locked. The main door was almost a hundred yards away and would also be locked. Mr. Thorne emerged from the alley and swung his head left and right in search of me. In the dim light his heavily streaked face looked almost black. He began lurching toward me.

I raised father's walking stick, broke the lower pane of the window, and reached in through the jagged shards. If there was a bottom or top bolt I was dead. There was a simple doorknob lock and crossbolt. My fingers slipped on the cold metal, but the bolt slid back as Mr. Thorne stepped up on the walk behind me. Then I was inside and throwing the bolt.

It was very dark. Cold seeped up from the concrete floor and there was a sound of many small boats rising and falling at their moorings. Fifty yards away light spilled out of the office windows. I had hoped there would be an alarm system, but the building was too old and the marina too cheap to have one. I walked toward the light as Mr. Thorne's forearm shattered the remaining glass in the door behind me. The arm withdrew. A great kick broke off the top hinge and splintered wood around the bolt. I glanced at the office, but only the sound of a radio talk show came out of the impossibly distant door. Another kick.

I turned to my right and stepped to the bow of a bobbing inboard cruiser. Five steps and I was in the small, covered space that passed for a forward cabin. I closed the flimsy access panel behind me and peered out through the Plexiglas.

Mr. Thorne's third kick sent the door flying inward, dangling from long strips of splintered wood. His dark form filled the doorway. Light from a distant streetlight glinted off the blade in his right hand.

Please. Please hear the noise. But there was no movement from the office, only the metallic voices from the radio. Mr. Thorne took four paces, paused, and stepped down onto the first boat in line. It was an open outboard, and he was back up on the concrete in six seconds. The second boat had a small cabin. There was a ripping sound as Mr. Thorne kicked open the tiny hatch door, and then he was back up on the walkway. My boat was the eighth in line. I wondered why he couldn't just hear the wild hammering of my heart.

I shifted position and looked through the starboard port. The murky Plexiglas threw the light into streaks and patterns. I caught a brief glimpse of white hair through the window, and the radio was switched to another station. Loud music echoed in the long room. I slid back to the other porthole. Mr. Thorne was stepping off the fourth boat.

I closed my eyes, forced my ragged breathing to slow, and tried to remember countless evenings watching a bowlegged old figure shuffle down the street. Mr. Thorne finished his inspection of the fifth boat, a longer cabin cruiser with several dark recesses, and pulled himself back onto the walkway.

Forget the coffee in the thermos. Forget the crossword puzzle. Go look!

The sixth boat was a small outboard. Mr. Thorne glanced at it but did not step onto it. The seventh was a low sailboat, mast folded down, canvas stretched across the cockpit. Mr. Thorne's knife slashed through the thick material. Blood-streaked hands pulled back the canvas like a shroud being torn away. He jumped back to the walkway.

Forget the coffee. Go look! Now!

Mr. Thorne stepped onto the bow of my boat. I felt it rock to his weight. There was nowhere to hide, only a tiny storage locker under the seat, much too small to squeeze into. I untied the canvas strips that held the seat cushion to the bench. The sound of my ragged breathing seemed to echo in the little space. I curled into a fetal position behind the cushion as Mr. Thorne's leg moved past the starboard port. *Now.* Suddenly his face filled the Plexiglas strip not a foot from my head. His impossibly wide grimace grew even wider. *Now.* He stepped into the cockpit.

Now. Now. Now.

Mr. Thorne crouched at the cabin door. I tried to brace the tiny louvered door with my legs, but my right leg would not obey. Mr. Thorne fist slammed through the thin wooden strips and grabbed my ankle.

"Hey there!"

It was Mr. Hodges's shaky voice. His flashlight bobbed in our direction.

Mr. Thorne shoved against the door. My left leg folded painfully. Mr. Thorne's left hand firmly held my ankle through the shattered slats while the hand with the knife blade came through the opening hatch.

"Hey—" My mind shoved. Very hard. The old man stopped. He dropped the flashlight and unstrapped the buckle over the grip of his revolver.

Mr. Thorne slashed the knife back and forth. The cushion was almost knocked out of my hands as shreds of foam filled the cabin. The blade caught the tip of my little finger as the knife swung back again.

Do it. Now. Do it. Mr. Hodges gripped the revolver in both hands and fired. The shot went wide in the dark as the sound echoed off concrete and water. *Closer, you fool. Move!* Mr. Thorne shoved again and his body squeezed into the open hatch. He released my ankle to free his left arm, but almost instantly his hand was back in the cabin, grasping for me. I reached up and turned on the overhead light. Darkness stared at me from his empty eye socket. Light through the broken shutters spilled yellow strips across his ruined face. I slid to the left, but Mr. Thorne's hand, which had my coat, was pulling me off the bench. He was on his knees, freeing his right hand for the knife thrust.

Now! Mr. Hodges's second shot caught Mr. Thorne in the right hip. He grunted as the impact shoved him backward into a sitting position. My coat ripped, and buttons rattled on the deck.

The knife slashed the bulkhead near my ear before it pulled away.

Mr. Hodges stepped shakily onto the bow, almost fell, and inched his way around the starboard side. I pushed the hatch against Mr. Thorne's arm, but he continued to grip my coat and drag me toward him. I fell to my knees. The blade swung back, ripped through foam, and slashed at my coat. What was left of the cushion flew out of my hands. I had Mr. Hodges stop four feet away and brace the gun on the roof of the cabin.

Mr. Thorne pulled the blade back and poised it like a matador's sword. I could sense the silent scream of triumph that poured out over the stained teeth like a noxious vapor. The light of Nina's madness burned behind the single, staring eye.

Mr. Hodges fired. The bullet severed Mr. Thorne's spine and continued on into the port scupper. Mr. Thorne arched backward, splayed out his arms, and flopped onto the deck like a great fish that had just been landed. The knife fell to the floor of the cabin, while stiff, white fingers continued to slap nervelessly against the deck. I had Mr. Hodges step forward, brace the muzzle against Mr. Thorne's temple just above the remaining eye, and fire again. The sound was muted and hollow.

There was a first-aid kit in the office bathroom. I had the old man stand by the door while I bandaged my little finger and took three aspirin.

My coat was ruined, and blood had stained my print dress. I had never cared very much for the dress—I thought it made me look dowdy—but the coat had been a favorite of mine. My hair was a mess. Small, moist bits of gray matter flecked it. I splashed water on my face and brushed my hair as best I could. Incredibly, my tattered purse had stayed with me although many of the contents had spilled out. I transferred keys, billfold, reading glasses, and Kleenex to my large coat pocket and dropped the purse behind the toilet. I no longer had father's walking stick, but I could not remember where I had dropped it.

Gingerly I removed the heavy revolver from Mr. Hodges's grip. The old man's arm remained extended, fingers curled around air. After fumbling for a few seconds I managed to click open the cylinder. Two cartridges remained unfired. The old fool had been walking around with all six chambers loaded! *Always leave an empty chamber under the hammer.* That is what Charles had taught me that gay and distant summer so long ago when such weapons were merely excuses for trips to the island for target practice punctuated by the shrill shrieks of our nervous laughter as Nina and I allowed ourselves to be held, arms supported, bodies shrinking back into the firm support of our so-serious tutors' arms. *One must always count the cartridges,* lectured Charles, as I half-swooned against him, smelling the sweet, masculine shaving soap and tobacco smell rising from him on that warm, bright day.

Mr. Hodges stirred slightly as my attention wandered. His mouth gaped, and his dentures hung loosely. I glanced at the worn leather belt, but there were no extra bullets there, and I had no idea where he kept any. I probed, but there was little left in the old man's jumble of thoughts except for a swirling tape-loop replay of the muzzle being laid against Mr. Thorne's temple, the explosion, the—

"Come," I said. I adjusted the glasses on Mr. Hodges's vacant face, returned the revolver to the holster, and let him lead me out of the building.

It was very dark out. We had gone six blocks before the old man's violent shivering reminded me that I had forgotten to have him put on his coat. I tightened my mental vise, and he stopped shaking.

The house looked just as it had . . . my God . . . only forty-five minutes earlier. There were no lights. I let us into the courtyard and searched my overstuffed coat pocket for the key. My coat hung loose and the cold night air nipped at me. From behind lighted windows across the courtyard came the laughter of little girls, and I hurried so that Kathleen would not see her grandfather entering my house.

Mr. Hodges went in first, with the revolver extended. I had him switch on the light before I entered.

The parlor was empty, undisturbed. The light from the chandelier in the dining room reflected off polished surfaces. I sat down for a minute on the Williamsburg reproduction chair in the hall to let my heart rate return to normal. I did not have Mr. Hodges lower the hammer on the still-raised pistol. His arm began to shake from the strain of holding it. Finally, I rose and we moved down the hall toward the conservatory.

Miss Kramer exploded out of the swinging door from the kitchen with the heavy iron poker already coming down in an arc. The gun fired harmlessly into the polished floor as the old man's arm snapped from the impact. The gun fell from limp fingers as Miss Kramer raised the poker for a second blow.

I turned and ran back down the hallway. Behind me I heard the crushed-melon sound of the poker contacting Mr. Hodges's skull. Rather than run into the courtyard I went up the stairway. A mistake. Miss Kramer bounded up the stairs and reached the bedroom door only a few seconds after me. I caught one glimpse of her widened, maddened eyes and of the upraised poker before I slammed and locked the heavy door. The latch clicked just as the brunette on the other side began to throw herself against the wood. The thick oak did not budge. Then I heard the concussion of metal against the door and frame. Again.

Cursing my stupidity, I turned to the familiar room, but there was nothing there to help me. There was not as much as a closet to hide in, only the antique wardrobe. I moved quickly to the window and threw up the sash. My screams would attract attention but not before that monstrosity had gained access. She was prying at the edges of the door now. I looked out, saw the shadows in the window across the way, and did what I had to do.

Two minutes later I was barely conscious of the wood giving away around the latch. I heard the distant grating of the poker as it pried at the recalcitrant metal plate. The door swung inward.

Miss Kramer was covered with sweat. Her mouth hung slack, and drool slid from her chin. Her eyes were not human. Neither she nor I heard the soft tread of sneakers on the stairs behind her.

Keep moving. Lift it. Pull it back—all the way back. Use both hands. Aim it.

Something warned Miss Kramer. Warned Nina, I should say; there was no more Miss Kramer. The brunette turned to see little Kathleen standing on the top stair, her grandfather's heavy weapon aimed and cocked. The other girl was in the courtyard shouting for her friend.

This time Nina knew she had to deal with the threat. Miss Kramer hefted the poker and turned into the hall just as the pistol fired. The recoil tumbled Kathleen backward down the stairs as a red corsage blossomed above Miss Kramer's left breast. She spun but grasped the railing with her left hand and lurched down the stairs after the child. I released the ten-year-old just as the poker fell, rose, fell again. I moved to the head of the stairway. I had to see.

Miss Kramer looked up from her grim work. Only the whites of her eyes were visible in her spattered face. Her masculine shirt was soaked with her own blood, but still she moved, functioned. She picked up the gun in her left hand. Her mouth opened wider, and a sound emerged like steam leaking from an old radiator.

"Melanie . . ." I closed my eyes as the thing started up the stairs for me.

Kathleen's friend came in through the open door, her small legs pumping. She took the stairs in six jumps and wrapped her thin, white arms around Miss Kramer's neck in a tight embrace.

The two went over backward, across Kathleen, all the way down the wide stairs to the polished wood below.

The girl appeared to be little more than bruised. I went down and moved her to one side. A blue stain was spreading along one cheekbone, and there were cuts on her arms and forehead. Her blue eyes blinked uncomprehendingly.

Miss Kramer's neck was broken. I picked up the pistol on the way to her and kicked the poker to one side. Her head was at an impossible angle, but she was still alive. Her body was paralyzed, urine already stained the wood, but her eyes still blinked and her teeth clicked together obscenely. I had to hurry. There were adult voices calling from the Hodgeses' town house. The door to the courtyard was wide open. I turned to the girl. "Get up." She blinked once and rose painfully to her feet.

I shut the door and lifted a tan raincoat from the coatrack.

It took only a minute to transfer the contents of my pockets to the raincoat and to discard my ruined spring coat. Voices were calling in the courtyard now.

I kneeled down next to Miss Kramer and seized her face in my hands, exerting pressure to keep the jaws still. Her eyes had rolled upward again, but I shook her head until the irises were visible. I leaned forward until our cheeks were touching. My whisper was louder than a shout.

"I'm coming for you, Nina."

I dropped her head onto the wood and walked quickly to the conservatory, my sewing room. I did not have time to get the key from upstairs; so I raised a Windsor side chair and smashed the glass of the cabinet. My coat pocket was barely large enough.

The girl remained standing in the hall. I handed her Mr. Hodges's pistol. Her left arm hung at a strange angle and I wondered if she had broken something after all. There was a knock at the door, and someone tried the knob.

"This way," I whispered, and led the girl into the dining room.

We stepped across Miss Kramer on the way, walked through the dark kitchen as the pounding grew louder, and then were out, into the alley, into the night.

There were three hotels in this part of the Old Section. One was a modern, expensive motor hotel some ten blocks away, comfortable but commercial. I rejected it immediately. The second was a small, homey lodging house only a block from my home. It was a pleasant but nonexclusive little place, exactly the type I would choose when visiting another town. I rejected it also. The third was two and a half blocks farther, an old Broad Street mansion done over into a small hotel, expensive antiques in every room, absurdly overpriced. I hurried there. The girl moved quickly at my side. The pistol was still in her hand, but I had her remove her sweater and carry it over the weapon. My leg ached, and I frequently leaned on the girl as we hurried down the street.

The manager of the Mansard House recognized me. His eyebrows went up a fraction of an inch as he noticed my disheveled appearance. The girl stood ten feet away in the foyer, half-hidden in the shadows.

"I'm looking for a friend of mine," I said brightly. "A Mrs. Drayton."

The manager started to speak, paused, frowned without being aware of it, and tried again. "I'm sorry. No one under that name is registered here."

"Perhaps she registered under her maiden name," I said. "Nina Hawkins. She's an older woman but very attractive. A few years younger than I. Long, gray hair. Her friend may have registered for her . . . an attractive, young, dark-haired lady named Barrett Kramer—"

"No, I'm sorry," said the manager in a strangely flat tone. "No one under that name has registered. Would you like to leave a message in case your party arrives later?"

"No," I said. "No message."

I brought the girl into the lobby, and we turned down a corridor leading to the restrooms and side stairs. "Excuse me, please," I said to a passing porter. "Perhaps you can help me."

"Yes, ma'am." He stopped, annoyed, and brushed back his long hair. It would be tricky. If I was not to lose the girl, I would have to act quickly.

"I'm looking for a friend," I said. "She's an older lady but quite attractive. Blue eyes. Long, gray hair. She travels with a young woman who has dark, curly hair."

"No, ma'am. No one like that is registered here."

I reached out and grabbed hold of his forearm tightly. I released the girl and focused on the boy. "Are you sure?"

"Mrs. Harrison," he said. His eyes looked past me. "Room 207. North front."

I smiled. *Mrs. Harrison.* Good God, what a fool Nina was. Suddenly the girl let out a small whimper and slumped against the wall. I made a quick decision. I like to think that it was compassion, but I sometimes remember that her left arm was useless.

"What's your name?" I asked the child, gently stroking her bangs. Her eyes moved left and right in confusion. "Your name!"

"Alicia." It was only a whisper.

"All right, Alicia. I want you to go home now. Hurry, but don't run."

"My *arm* hurts," she said. Her lips began to quiver. I touched her forehead again and *pushed*.

"You're going home," I said. "Your arm does not hurt. You won't remember anything. This is like a dream that you will forget. Go home. Hurry, but do not run." I took the pistol from her but left it wrapped in the sweater. "Bye-bye, Alicia."

She blinked and crossed the lobby to the doors. I handed the gun to the bellhop. "Put it under your vest," I said.

"Who is it?" Nina's voice was light.

"Albert, ma'am. The porter. Your car's out front, and I'll take your bags down."

There was the sound of a lock clicking and the door opened the width of a still-secured chain. Albert blinked in the glare, smiled shyly, and brushed his hair back. I pressed against the wall.

"Very well." She undid the chain and moved back. She had already turned and was latching her suitcase when I stepped into the room.

"Hello, Nina," I said softly. Her back straightened, but even that move was graceful. I could see the imprint on the bedspread where she had been lying. She turned slowly. She was wearing a pink dress I had never seen before.

"Hello, Melanie." She smiled. Her eyes were the softest, purest blue I had ever seen. I had the porter take Mr. Hodges's gun out and aim it. His arm was steady. He pulled back the hammer and held it with his thumb. Nina folded her hands in front of her. Her eyes never left mine.

"Why?" I asked.

Nina shrugged ever so slightly. For a second I thought she was going to laugh. I could not have borne it if she had laughed—that husky, childlike laugh that had touched me so many times. Instead she closed her eyes. Her smile remained.

"Why Mrs. Harrison?" I asked.

"Why, darling, I felt I owed him *something*. I mean, poor Roger. Did I ever tell you how he died? No, of course I didn't. And you never asked." Her eyes opened. I glanced at the porter, but his aim was steady. It only remained for him to exert a little more pressure on the trigger.

"He *drowned*, darling," said Nina. "Poor Roger threw himself from that steamship—what was its name?—the one that was taking him back to England. So strange. And he had just written me a letter promising marriage. Isn't that a *terribly* sad story, Melanie? Why do you think he did a thing like that? I guess we'll never know, will we?"

"I guess we never will," I said. I silently ordered the porter to pull the trigger.

Nothing.

I looked quickly to my right. The young man's head was turning toward me. *I had not made him do that.* The stiffly extended arm began to swing in my direction. The pistol moved smoothly like the tip of a weather vane swinging in the wind.

No! I strained until the cords in my neck stood out. The turning slowed but did not stop until the muzzle was pointing at my face. Nina laughed now. The sound was very loud in the little room.

"Good-bye, Melanie *dear*," Nina said, and laughed again. She laughed and nodded at the porter. I stared into the black hole as the hammer fell. On an empty chamber. And another. And another.

"Good-bye, Nina," I said as I pulled Charles's long pistol from the raincoat pocket. The explosion jarred my wrist and filled the room with blue smoke. A small hole, smaller than a dime but as perfectly round, appeared in the precise center of Nina's forehead. For the briefest second she remained standing as if nothing had happened. Then she fell backward, recoiled from the high bed, and dropped face forward onto the floor.

I turned to the porter and replaced his useless weapon with the ancient but well-maintained revolver. For the first time I noticed that the boy was not much younger than Charles had been. His hair was almost exactly the same color. I leaned forward and kissed him lightly on the lips.

"Albert," I whispered, "there are four cartridges left. One must always count the cartridges, mustn't one? Go to the lobby. Kill the manager. Shoot one other person, the nearest. Put the barrel in your mouth and pull the trigger. If it misfires, pull it again. Keep the gun concealed until you are in the lobby."

We emerged into general confusion in the hallway.

"Call for an ambulance!" I cried. "There's been an accident. Someone call for an ambulance!" Several people rushed to comply. I swooned and leaned against a white-haired gentleman. People milled around, some peering into the room and exclaiming. Suddenly there was the sound of three gunshots from the lobby. In the renewed confusion I slipped down the back stairs, out the fire door, into the night.

Time has passed. I am very happy here. I live in southern France now, between Cannes and Toulon, but not, I am happy to say, too near St. Tropez.

I rarely go out. Henri and Claude do my shopping in the village. I never go to the beach. Occasionally I go to the townhouse in Paris or to my pensione in Italy, south of Pescara, on the Adriatic. But even those trips have become less and less frequent.

There is an abandoned abbey in the hills, and I often go there to sit and think among the stones and wild flowers. I think about isolation and abstinence and how each is so cruelly dependent upon the other.

I feel younger these days. I tell myself that this is because of the climate and my freedom and not as a result of that final Feeding. But sometimes I dream about the familiar streets of Charleston and the people there. They are dreams of hunger.

On some days I rise to the sound of singing as girls from the village cycle by our place on their way to the dairy. On those days the sun is marvelously warm as it shines on the small white flowers growing between the tumbled stones of the abbey, and I am content simply to be there and to share the sunlight and silence with them.

But on other days—cold, dark days when the clouds move in from the north—I remember the shark-silent shape of a submarine moving through the dark waters of the bay, and I wonder whether my self-imposed abstinence will be for nothing. I wonder whether those I dream of in my isolation will indulge in their own gigantic, final Feeding.

It is warm today. I am happy. But I am also alone. And I am very, very hungry.

I suspect that the vampire myth is as persistent, resilient, and satisfying as it is because there is a bit of the vampire in each of us. Much has been written about the blood symbolism in vampire tales, much about the latent erotic imagery, but little is said about the simple attraction of *control*. If you believe as I do that any exercise of power over another person is an incipient act of violence, then the vampire represents the ultimate violence—an extension of power over others to the grave and beyond.

"Carrion Comfort" has its genesis in a variety of places. There is a marvelous scene in the otherwise laughable 1931 *Dracula* where Bela Lugosi has a contest of wills with the aging Van Helsing. The old man staggers forward a few paces under the vampire's influence and then pulls back painfully, slowly, struggling against invisible bonds. "You have a strong vill, Van Helsing," smiles Lugosi. But we know who will win the contest in the end.

And of course any story or novel about extrasensory powers of control must recognize Frank M. Robinson's *The Power* (1956) as a seminal influence.

In the end, however, it was the simple image of these three old people meeting in pleasant reunion, sunlight moving across their aged skin and young eyes, that proved the prime mover for "Carrion Comfort." As many of us suspect, the road to success is littered with the brittle bones of our victims. After a while we do not notice.

We are what we devour.

Dan Simmons

THE SEA WAS WET AS WET COULD BE

Gahan Wilson

Lewis Carroll's Alice in Wonderland *and* Through the Looking Glass *are among my favorite works of fantasy. The books, in addition to being charming and entertaining, are deft commentaries on the economic, social, and political conditions of the times. And beneath some of the cute rhymes lurks genuine horror. So it is with "The Walrus and the Carpenter." Gahan Wilson's "The Sea Was Wet as Wet Could Be" is the story that prompted me to begin* Blood Is Not Enough.

I felt we made an embarrassing contrast to the open serenity of the scene around us. The pure blue of the sky was unmarked by a single cloud or bird, and nothing stirred on the vast stretch of beach except ourselves. The sea, sparkling under the freshness of the early morning sun, looked invitingly clean. I wanted to wade into it and wash myself, but I was afraid I would contaminate it.

We are a contamination here, I thought. We're like a group of sticky bugs crawling in an ugly little crowd over polished marble. If I were God and looked down and saw us, lugging our baskets and our silly, bright blankets, I would step on us and squash us with my foot.

We should have been lovers or monks in such a place, but we were only a crowd of bored and boring drunks. You were always drunk when you were with Carl. Good old, mean old Carl was the greatest little drink pourer in the world. He used drinks like other types of sadists used whips. He kept beating you with them until you dropped or sobbed or went mad, and he enjoyed every step of the process.

We'd been drinking all night, and when the morning came, somebody, I think it was Mandie, got the great idea that we should all go out on a picnic. Naturally, we thought it was an inspiration, we were nothing if not real sports, and so we'd packed some goodies, not forgetting the liquor, and we'd piled into the car, and there we were, weaving across the beach, looking for a place to spread our tacky banquet.

We located a broad, low rock, decided it would serve for our table, and loaded it with the latest in plastic chinaware, a haphazard collection of food and a quantity of bottles.

Someone had packed a tin of Spam among the other offerings and, when I saw it, I was suddenly overwhelmed with an absurd feeling of nostalgia. It reminded me of the war and of myself soldierboying up through Italy. It also reminded me of how long ago the whole thing had been and how little I'd done of what I'd dreamed I'd do back then.

I opened the Spam and sat down to be alone with it and my memories, but it wasn't to be for long. The kind of people who run with people like Carl don't like to be alone, ever, especially with their memories, and they can't imagine anyone else might, at least now and then, have a taste for it.

My rescuer was Irene. Irene was particularly sensitive about seeing people alone because being alone had several times nearly produced fatal results for her. Being alone and taking pills to end the being alone.

"What's wrong, Phil?" she asked.

"Nothing's wrong," I said, holding up a forkful of the pink Spam in the sunlight. "It tastes just like it always did. They haven't lost their touch."

She sat down on the sand beside me, very carefully, so as to avoid spilling the least drop of what must have been her millionth Scotch.

"Phil," she said, "I'm worried about Mandie. I really am. She looks so unhappy!"

I glanced over at Mandie. She had her head thrown back and she was laughing uproariously at some joke Carl had just made. Carl was smiling at her with his teeth glistening and his eyes deep down dead as ever.

"Why should Mandie be happy?" I asked. "What, in God's name, has she got to be happy about?"

"Oh, Phil," said Irene. "You pretend to be such an awful cynic. She's *alive*, isn't she?"

I looked at her and wondered what such a statement meant, coming from someone who'd tried to do herself in as earnestly and as frequently as Irene. I decided that I did not know and that I would probably never know. I also decided I didn't want anymore of the Spam. I turned to throw it away, doing my bit to litter up the beach, and then I saw them.

They were far away, barely bigger than two dots, but you could tell there was something odd about them even then.

"We've got company," I said.

Irene peered in the direction of my point.

"Look, everybody," she cried, "we've got company!"

Everybody looked, just as she had asked them to.

"What the hell is this?" asked Carl. "Don't they know this is my private property?" And then he laughed.

Carl had fantasies about owning things and having power. Now and then he got drunk enough to have little flashes of believing he was king of the world.

"You tell 'em, Carl!" said Horace.

Horace had sparkling quips like that for almost every occasion. He was tall and bald and he had a huge Adam's apple and, like myself, he worked for Carl. I would have felt sorrier for Horace than I did if I hadn't had a sneaky suspicion that he was really happier when groveling. He lifted one scrawny fist and shook it in the direction of the distant pair.

"You guys better beat it," he shouted. "This is private property!"

"Will you shut up and stop being such an ass?" Mandie asked him. "It's not polite to yell at strangers, dear, and this may damn well be *their* beach for all you know."

Mandie happens to be Horace's wife. Horace's children treat him about the same way. He busied himself with zipping up his windbreaker, because it was getting cold and because he had received an order to be quiet.

I watched the two approaching figures. The one was tall and bulky, and he moved with a peculiar, swaying gait. The other was short and hunched into himself, and he walked in a fretful, zigzag line beside his towering companion.

"They're heading straight for us," I said.

The combination of the cool wind that had come up and the approach of the two strangers had put a damper on our little group. We sat quietly and watched them coming closer. The nearer they got, the odder they looked.

"For heaven's sake!" said Irene. "The little one's wearing a square hat!"

"I think it's made of paper," said Mandie, squinting, "folded newspaper."

"Will you look at the mustache on the big bastard?" asked Carl. "I don't think I've ever seen a bigger bush in my life."

"They remind me of something," I said.

The others turned to look at me.

The Walrus and the Carpenter . . .

"They remind me of the Walrus and the Carpenter," I said.

"The who?" asked Mandie.

"Don't tell me you never heard of the Walrus and the Carpenter?" asked Carl.

"Never once," said Mandie.

"Disgusting," said Carl. "You're an uncultured bitch. The Walrus and the Carpenter are probably two of the most famous characters in literature. They're in a poem by Lewis Carroll in one of the *Alice* books."

"In *Through the Looking Glass*," I said, and then I recited their introduction:

"The Walrus and the Carpenter
Were walking close at hand
They wept like anything to see
Such quantities of sand . . ."

Mandie shrugged. "Well, you'll just have to excuse my ignorance and concentrate on my charm," she said.

"I don't know how to break this to you all," said Irene, "but the little one *does* have a handkerchief."

We stared at them. The little one did indeed have a handkerchief, a huge handkerchief, and he was using it to dab at his eyes.

"Is the little one supposed to be the Carpenter?" asked Mandie.

"Yes," I said.

"Then it's all right," she said, "because he's the one that's carrying the saw."

"He is, so help me, God," said Carl. "And, to make the whole thing perfect, he's even wearing an apron."

"So the Carpenter in the poem has to wear an apron, right?" asked Mandie.

"Carroll doesn't say whether he does or not," I said, "but the illustrations by Tenniel show him wearing one. They also show him with the same square jaw and the same big nose this guy's got."

"They're goddamn doubles," said Carl. "The only thing wrong is that the Walrus isn't a walrus, he just looks like one."

"You watch," said Mandie. "Any minute now he's going to sprout fur all over and grow long fangs."

Then, for the first time, the approaching pair noticed us. It seemed to give them quite a start. They stood and gaped at us and the little one furtively stuffed his handkerchief out of sight.

"We can't be as surprising as all that!" whispered Irene.

The big one began moving forward, then, in a hesitant, tentative kind of shuffle. The little one edged ;ahead, too, but he was careful to keep the bulk of his companion between himself and us.

"First contact with the aliens," said Mandie, and Irene and Horace giggled nervously. I didn't respond. I had come to the decision that I was going to quit working for Carl, that I didn't like any of these people about me, except, maybe, Irene, and that these two strangers gave me the honest creeps.

Then the big one smiled, and everything was changed.

I've worked in the entertainment field, in advertising and in public relations. This means I have come in contact with some of the prime charm boys and girls in our proud land. I have become, therefore, not only a connoisseur of smiles, I am a being equipped with numerous automatic safeguards against them. When a talcumed smoothie comes at me with his brilliant ivories exposed, it only shows he's got something he can bite me with, that's all.

But the smile of the Walrus was something else.

The smile of the Walrus did what a smile hasn't done for me in years— it melted my heart. I use the corn-ball phrase very much on purpose. When I saw his smile, I knew I could trust him; I felt in my marrow that he was gentle and sweet and had nothing but the best intentions. His resemblance to the Walrus in the poem ceased being vaguely chilling and became warmly comical. I loved him as I had loved the teddy bear of my childhood.

"Oh, I *say,*" he said, and his voice was an embarrassed boom, "I *do* hope we're not intruding!"

"I daresay we are," squeaked the Carpenter, peeping out from behind his companion.

"The, uhm, fact is," boomed the Walrus, "we didn't even notice you until just back then, you see."

"We were talking, is what," said the Carpenter.

> They wept like anything to see
> Such quantities of sand . . .

"About sand?" I asked.

The Walrus looked at me with a startled air.

"We *were*, actually, now you come to mention it."

He lifted one huge foot and shook it so that a little trickle of sand spilled out of his shoe.

"The stuff's impossible," he said. "Gets in your clothes, tracks up the carpet."

"Ought to be swept away, it ought," said the Carpenter.

> 'If seven maids with seven mops
> Swept it for half a year,
> Do you suppose,' the Walrus said,
> 'That they could get it clear?'

"It's too much!" said Carl.

"Yes, indeed," said the Walrus, eying the sand around him with vague disapproval, "altogether too much."

Then he turned to us again and we all basked in that smile.

"Permit me to introduce my companion and myself," he said.

"You'll have to excuse George," said the Carpenter, "as he's a bit of a stuffed shirt, don't you know?"

"Be that as it may," said the Walrus, patting the Carpenter on the flat top of his paper hat, "this is Edward Farr, and I am George Tweedy, both at your service. We are, uhm, both a trifle drunk, I'm afraid."

"We are, indeed. We are that."

"As we have just come from a really delightful party, to which we shall soon return."

"Once we've found the fuel, that is," said Farr, waving his saw in the air. By now he had found the courage to come out and face us directly.

"Which brings me to the question," said Tweedy. "Have you seen any *driftwood* lying about the premises? We've been looking high and low and we can't seem to find *any* of the blasted stuff."

"Thought there'd be piles of it," said Farr, "but all there is is sand, don't you see?"

"I would have sworn you were looking for oysters," said Carl.

Again, Tweedy appeared startled.

> 'O Oysters, come and walk with us!'
> The Walrus did beseech . . .

"Oysters?" he asked. "Oh, no, we've *got* the oysters. All we lack is the means to cook 'em."

" 'Course we could always use a few more," said Farr, looking at his companion.

"I suppose we *could*, at that," said Tweedy thoughtfully.

"I'm afraid we can't help you fellows with the driftwood problem," said Carl, "but you're more than welcome to a drink."

There was something unfamiliar about the tone of Carl's voice that made my ears perk up. I turned to look at him, and then had difficulty covering up my astonishment.

It was his eyes. For once, for the first time, they were really friendly.

I'm not saying Carl had fishy eyes, blank eyes—not at all. On the surface, that is. On the surface, with his eyes, with his face, with the handling of his entire body, Carl was a master of animation and expression. From sympathetic, heart-felt warmth, all the way to icy rage, and on every stop in-between, Carl was completely convincing.

But only on the surface. Once you got to know Carl, and it took a while, you realized that none of it was really happening. That was because Carl had died, or been killed, long ago. Possibly in childhood. Possibly he had been born dead. So, under the actor's warmth and rage, the eyes were always the eyes of a corpse.

But now it was different. The friendliness here was genuine, I was sure of it. The smile of Tweedy, of the Walrus, had performed a miracle. Carl had risen from his tomb. I was in honest awe.

"*Delighted*, old chap!" said Tweedy.

They accepted their drinks with obvious pleasure, and we completed the introductions as they sat down to join us. I detected a strong smell of fish when Tweedy sat down beside me but, oddly, I didn't find it offensive in the least. I was glad he'd chosen me to sit by. He turned and smiled at me, and my heart melted a little more.

It soon turned out that the drinking we'd done before had only scratched the surface. Tweedy and Farr were magnificent boozers, and their gusto encouraged us all to follow suit.

We drank absurd toasts and were delighted to discover that Tweedy was an incredible raconteur. His specialty was outrageous fantasy: wild tales involving incongruous objects, events, and characters. His invention was endless.

> 'The time has come,' the Walrus said,
>   'To talk of many things:
> Of shoes—and ships—and sealing-wax—
>   Of cabbages—and kings—
> And why the sea is boiling hot—
>   And whether pigs have wings.'

We laughed and drank, and drank and laughed, and I began to wonder why in hell I'd spent my life being such a gloomy, moody son of a bitch, been such a distrustful and suspicious bastard, when the whole secret of everything, the whole core secret, was simply to enjoy it, to take it as it came.

I looked around and grinned, and I didn't care if it was a foolish grin. Everybody looked all right, everybody looked swell, everybody looked better than I'd ever seen them look before.

Irene looked happy, honestly and truly happy. She, too, had found the secret. No more pills for Irene, I thought. Now that she knows the secret, now that she's met Tweedy who's given her the secret, she'll have no more need of those goddamn pills.

And I couldn't believe Horace and Mandie. They had their arms around each other, and their bodies were pressed close together, and they rocked as one being when they laughed at Tweedy's wonderful stories. No more nagging for Mandie, I thought, and no more cringing for Horace, now they've learned the secret.

And then I looked at Carl, laughing and relaxed and absolutely free of care, absolutely unchilled, finally, at last, after years of—

And then I looked at Carl again.

And then I looked down at my drink, and then I looked at my knees, and then I looked out at the sea, sparkling, clean, remote and impersonal.

And then I realized it had grown cold, quite cold, and that there wasn't a bird or a cloud in the sky.

> The sea was wet as wet could be,
>   The sands were dry as dry.
> You could not see a cloud, because
>   No cloud was in the sky:
> No birds were flying overhead—
>   There were no birds to fly.

That part of the poem was, after all, a perfect description of a lifeless earth. It sounded beautiful at first, it sounded benign. But then you read it again and you realized that Carroll was describing barrenness and desolation.

Suddenly Carl's voice broke through and I heard him say:

"Hey, that's a hell of an idea, Tweedy! By God, we'd love to! Wouldn't we, gang?"

The others broke out in an affirmative chorus and they all started scrambling to their feet around me. I looked up at them, like someone who's been awakened from sleep in a strange place, and they grinned down at me like loons.

"Come on, Phil!" cried Irene.

Her eyes were bright and shining, but it wasn't with happiness. I could see that now.

> 'It seems a shame,' the Walrus said,
>   'To play them such a trick . . .'

I blinked my eyes and stared at them, one after the other.

"Old Phil's had a little too much to drink!" cried Mandie, laughing.

"Come on, old Phil! Come on and join the party!"

"What party?" I asked.

I couldn't seem to get located. Everything seemed disorientated and grotesque.

"For Christ's sake, Phil," said Carl, "Tweedy and Farr, here, have invited us to join their party. There's no more drinks left, and they've got plenty!"

I set my plastic cup down carefully on the sand. If they would just shut up for a moment, I thought, I might be able to get the fuzz out of my head.

"Come *along*, sir!" boomed Tweedy jovially. "It's only a pleasant walk!"

> 'O oysters come and walk with us,'
>> The walrus did beseech.
> 'A pleasant walk, a pleasant talk,
>> Along the briny beach . . .'

He was smiling at me, but the smile didn't work anymore.

"You cannot do with more than four," I told him.

"*Uhm?* What's that?"

> '. . . we cannot do with more than four,
>> And give a hand to each.'

"I said, 'You cannot do with more than four.'"

"He's right, you know," said Farr, the Carpenter.

"Well, uhm, then," said the Walrus, "if you feel you really *can't* come, old chap . . ."

"What, in Christ's name, are you all talking about?" asked Mandie.

"He's hung up on that goddamn poem," said Carl. "Lewis Carroll's got the yellow bastard scared."

"Don't be such a party pooper, Phil!" said Mandie.

"To hell with him," said Carl. And he started off, and all the others followed him. Except Irene.

"Are you sure you really don't want to come, Phil?" she asked.

She looked frail and thin against the sunlight. I realized there really wasn't much of her, and that what there was had taken a terrible beating.

"No," I said. "I don't. Are you sure you want to go?"

"Of course I do, Phil."

I thought of the pills.

"I suppose you do," I said. "I suppose there's really no stopping you."

"No, Phil, there isn't."

And then she stooped and kissed me. Kissed me very gently, and I could feel the dry, chapped surface of her lips and the faint warmth of her breath.

I stood.

"I wish you'd stay," I said.

"I can't," she said.

And then she turned and ran after the others.

I watched them growing smaller and smaller on the beach, following the Walrus and the Carpenter. I watched them come to where the beach curved around the bluff, and watched them disappear behind the bluff.

I looked up at the sky. Pure blue. Impersonal.

"What do you think of this?" I asked it.

Nothing. It hadn't even noticed.

> 'Now, if you're ready, oysters dear,
>> We can begin to feed.'
> 'But not on us!' the oysters cried,
>> Turning a little blue,
> 'After such kindness, that would be
>> A dismal thing to do!'

A dismal thing to do.

I began to run up the beach, toward the bluff. I stumbled now and then because I had had too much to drink. Far too much to drink. I heard small shells crack under my shoes, and the sand made whipping noises.

I fell, heavily, and lay there gasping on the beach. My heart pounded in my chest. I was too old for this sort of footwork. I hadn't had any real exercise in years. I smoked too much and I drank too much. I did all the wrong things. I didn't do any of the right things.

I pushed myself up a little and then I let myself down again. My heart was pounding hard enough to frighten me. I could feel it in my chest, frantically pumping, squeezing blood in and spurting blood out.

Like an oyster pulsing in the sea.

'Shall we be trotting home again?'

My heart was like an oyster.

I got up, fell up, and began to run again, weaving widely, my mouth open and the air burning my throat. I was coated with sweat, streaming with it, and it felt icy in the cold wind.

'Shall we be trotting home again?'

I rounded the bluff and then I stopped and stood swaying, and then I dropped to my knees.

The pure blue of the sky was unmarked by a single bird or cloud, and nothing stirred on the whole vast stretch of the beach.

But answer came there none—
And this was scarcely odd, because . . .

Nothing stirred, but they were there. Irene and Mandie and Carl and Horace were there, and four others, too. Just around the bluff.

'We cannot do with more than four . . .

But the Walrus and the Carpenter had taken two trips.

I began to crawl toward them on my knees. My heart, my oyster heart, was pounding too hard to allow me to stand.

The other four had had a picnic, too, very like our own. They, too, had plastic cups and plates, and they, too, had brought bottles. They had sat and waited for the return of the Walrus and the Carpenter.

Irene was right in front of me. Her eyes were open and stared at, but did not see, the sky. The pure blue uncluttered sky. There were a few grains of sand in her left eye. Her face was almost clear of blood. There were only a few flecks of it on her lower chin. The spray from the huge wound in her chest seemed to have traveled mainly downward and to the right. I stretched out my arm and touched her hand.

"Irene," I said.

But answer came there none—
And this was scarcely odd, because
They'd eaten every one.

I looked up at the others. Like Irene, they were, all of them, dead. The Walrus and the Carpenter had eaten the oysters and left the shells.

The Carpenter never found any firewood, and so they'd eaten them raw. You can eat oysters raw if you want to.

I said her name once more, just for the record, and then I stood and turned from them and walked to the bluff. I rounded the bluff and the beach stretched before me, vast, smooth, empty, and remote.

Even as I ran upon it, away from them, it was remote.

I distrusted the *Alice* books from the start. My grown-ups tried to pretend they were children's books and that I should and would enjoy them, so they officially shuffled them in with the *Oz* and *Pooh* collection, but I knew better; I knew they were dangerous and I opened them only rarely and gingerly.

Of course Tenniel's Jabberwock leapt out at me from the start (as it has, I am sure, at many another innocent child), but there were many other horrors: the simultaneously fading and grinning cat; the impeccably cruel Duchess with her "little boy"; something about Bill the Lizard floating helplessly over the chimney; the crazed creatures at the Tea Party—the worst part of it was the thing that pervaded all those images and all the other images in the books (which I knew weren't about any "Wonderland" at all, but about the very world I was trying to grow up in, only seen from some terrifyingly sophisticated point of view); the weird convincingness of Carroll's horrible message that *nothing, nothing soever, made any sense at all!*

If it hadn't been for brave, stolid Alice (bless her stout, young, British heart), herself a child, I don't think I could have survived those goddamn books.

But there is no Alice in this story.

Gahan Wilson

THE SILVER COLLAR

Garry Kilworth

"The Silver Collar" is a departure for Garry, who usually writes contemporary or futuristic science fiction. It is the most traditional of the stories in this volume, a gothic fantasy in which the vampire main character is never on stage. It shows the folly of those who believe love can conquer all.

The remote Scottish island came into view just as the sun was setting. Outside the natural harbor, the sea was kicking a little in its traces and tossing its white manes in the dying light. My small outboard motor struggled against the ebbing tide, sometimes whining as it raced in the air as a particularly low trough left it without water to push against the blades of its propeller. By the time I reached the jetty, the moon was up and casting its chill light upon the shore and purple-heather hills beyond. There was a smothered atmosphere to this lonely place of rock and thin soil, as if the coarse grass and hardy plants had descended as a complete layer to wrap the ruggedness in a faded cover, hiding the nakedness from mean, inquisitive eyes.

As the agents had promised, he was waiting on the quay, his tall, emaciated figure stark against the gentle upward slope of the hinterland: a splinter of granite from the rock on which he made his home.

"I've brought the provisions," I called, as he took the line and secured it.

"Good. Will you come up to the croft? There's a peat fire going—it's warm, and I have some scotch. Nothing like a dram before an open fire, with the smell of burning peat filling the room."

"I could just make it out with the tide," I said. "Perhaps I should go now." It was not that I was reluctant to accept the invitation from this eremite, this strange recluse—on the contrary, he interested me—but I had to be sure to get back to the mainland that night, since I was to crew a fishing vessel the next day.

"You have time for a dram," his voice drifted away on the cold wind that had sprung up within minutes, like a breath from the mouth of the icy north. I had to admit to myself that a whisky, by the fire, would set me on my toes for the return trip, and his tone had a faintly insistent quality about it which made the offer difficult to refuse.

"Just a minute then—and thanks. You lead the way."

I followed his lean, lithe figure up through the heather, which scratched at my ankles through my seasocks. The path was obviously not well used and I imagined he spent his time in and around his croft, for even in the moonlight I could discern no other tracks incising the soft shape of the hill.

We reached his dwelling and he opened the wooden door, allowing me to enter first. Then, seating me in front of the fire, he poured me a generous whisky before sitting down himself. I listened to the wind, locked outside the timber and turf croft, and waited for him to speak.

He said, "John, is't it? They told me on the radio."

"Yes—and you're Samual."

"Sam. You must call me Sam."

I told him I would and there was a period of silence while we regarded each other. Peat is not a consistent fuel, and tends to spurt and spit colorful plumes of flame as the gases escape, having been held prisoner from the seasons for God knows how long. Nevertheless, I was able to study my host in the brief periods of illumination that the fire afforded. He could have been any age, but I knew he was my senior by a great many years. The same thoughts must have been passing through his own head, for he remarked, "John, how old are you? I would guess at twenty."

"Nearer thirty, Sam. I was twenty-six last birthday." He nodded, saying that those who live a solitary life, away from others, have great difficulty in assessing the ages of people they do meet. Recent events slipped from his memory quite quickly, while the past seemed so close.

He leaned forward, into the hissing fire, as if drawing a breath from the ancient atmospheres it released into the room. Behind him, the earthen walls of the croft, held together by rough timbers and unhewn stones, seemed to move closer to his shoulder, as if ready to support his words with confirmation. I sensed a story coming. I recognized the pose from being in the company of sailors on long voyages and hoped he would finish before I had to leave.

"You're a good-looking boy," he said. "So was I, once upon a time." He paused to stir the flames and a blue-green cough from the peat illuminated his face. The skin was taut over the high cheekbones and there was a wanness to it, no doubt brought about by the inclement weather of the isles—the lack of sunshine and the constant misty rain that comes in as white veils from the north. Yes, he had been handsome—still was. I was surprised by his youthful features and suspected that he was not as old as he implied.

"A long time ago," he began, "when we had horse-drawn vehicles and things were different, in more ways than one . . ."

A sharp whistling note—the wind squeezing through two tightly packed logs in the croft—distracted me. Horse-drawn vehicles? What was this? A second-hand tale, surely? Yet he continued in the first person.

". . . gas lighting in the streets. A different set of values. A different set of beliefs. We were more pagan then. Still had our roots buried in dark thoughts. Machines have changed all that. Those sort of pagan, mystical ideas can't share a world with machines. Unnatural beings can only exist close to the natural world and nature's been displaced.

"Yes, a different world—different things to fear. I was afraid as a young man—the reasons may seem trivial to you, now, in your time. I was afraid of, well, getting into something I couldn't get out of. Woman trouble, for instance—especially one not of my class. You understand?

"I got involved once. Must have been about your age, or maybe a bit younger since I'd only just finished my apprenticeship and was a journeyman at the time. Silversmith. You knew that? No, of course you didn't. A silversmith, and a good one too. My master trusted me with one of his three shops, which puffed my pride a bit, I don't mind telling you. Anyway, it happened that I was working late one evening, when I heard the basement doorbell jangle.

"I had just finished lighting the gas lamps in the workshop at the back, so I hurried to the counter where a customer was waiting. She had left the door open and the sounds from the street were distracting, the basement of course being on a level with the cobbled road. Coaches were rumbling by and the noise of street urchins and flower sellers was fighting for attention with the foghorns from the river. As politely as I could, I went behind the customer and closed the door. Then I turned to her and said, 'Yes madam? Can I be of service?'

"She was wearing one of those large satin cloaks that only ladies of quality could afford and she threw back the hood to reveal one of the most beautiful faces I have ever seen in my life. There was a purity to her complexion that went deeper than her flawless skin, much deeper. And her eyes—how can I describe her eyes?—they were like black mirrors and you felt you could see the reflection of your own soul in them. Her hair was dark—coiled on her head—and it contrasted sharply with that complexion, pale as a winter moon, and soft, soft as the velvet I used for polishing the silver.

"'Yes,' she replied. 'You may be of service. You are the silversmith, are you not?'

"'The journeyman, madam. I'm in charge of this shop.'

"She seemed a little agitated, her fingers playing nervously with her reticule.

"'I . . .' she faltered, then continued. 'I have a rather unusual request. Are you able to keep a secret, silversmith?'

"'My work is confidential, if the customer wishes it so. Is it some special design you require? Something to surprise a loved one with? I have some very fine filigree work here.' I removed a tray from beneath the counter. 'There's something for both the lady and the gentleman. A cigar case, perhaps? This one has a crest wrought into the case in fine silver wire—an eagle, as you can see. It has been fashioned especially for a particular customer, but I can do something similar if you require . . .'

"I stopped talking because she was shaking her head and seemed to be getting impatient with me.

"'Nothing like that. Something very personal. I want you to make me a collar—a silver collar. Is that possible?'

"'All things are possible.' I smiled. 'Given the time of course. A torc of some kind?'

"'No, you misunderstand me.' A small frown marred the ivory forehead and she glanced anxiously towards the shop door. 'Perhaps I made a mistake. . . ?

"Worried, in case I lost her custom, I assured her that whatever was her request I should do my utmost to fulfill it. At the same time I told her that I could be trusted to keep the nature of the work to myself.

"'No one shall know about this but the craftsman and the customer— you and I.'

"She smiled at me then: a bewitching, spellbinding smile, and my heart melted within me. I would have done anything for her at that moment—I would have robbed my master—and I think she knew it.

"'I'm sorry,' she said. 'I should have realized I could trust you. You have a kind face. A gentle face. One should learn to trust in faces.

"'I want you—I want you to make me a collar which will cover my whole neck, especially the throat. I have a picture here, of some savages in Africa. The women have metal bands around their necks which envelop them from shoulder to chin. I want you to encase me in a similar fashion, except with one single piece of silver, do you understand? And I want it to fit tightly, so that not even your . . .' She took my hand in her own small gloved fingers. 'So that not even your little finger will be able to find its way beneath.'

"I was, of course, extremely perturbed at such a request. I tried to explain to her that she would have to take the collar off quite frequently, or the skin beneath would become diseased. Her neck would certainly become very ugly.

"'In any case, it will chafe and become quite sore. There will be constant irritation . . .'"

"She dropped my hand and said, no, I still misunderstood. The collar was to be worn permanently. She had no desire to remove it, once I had fashioned it around her neck. There was to be no locking device or anything of that sort. She wanted me to seal the metal.

"'But?' I began, but she interrupted me in a firm voice.

"'Silversmith, I have stated my request, my requirements. Will you carry out my wishes, or do I find another craftsman? I should be loath to do so, for I feel we have reached a level of understanding which might be difficult elsewhere. I'm going to be frank with you. This device, well—its purpose is protective. My husband-to-be is not—not like other men, but I love him just the same. I don't wish to embarrass you with talk that's not proper between strangers, and personal to my situation, but the collar is necessary to ensure my marriage is happy—a limited happiness. Limited to a lifetime. I'm sure you *must* understand now. If you want me to leave your shop, I shall do so, but I am appealing to you because you are young and must know the pain of love—unfulfilled love. You are a handsome man and I don't doubt you have a young lady whom you adore. If she were suffering under some terrible affliction, a disease which you might contract from her, I'm sure it would make no difference to your feelings. You would strive to find a way in which you could live together, yet remain uncontaminated yourself. Am I right?'

"I managed to breathe the word 'Yes,' but at the time I was filled with visions of horror. Visions of this beautiful young woman being wooed by some foul creature of the night—a supernatural beast that had no right to be treading on the same earth, let alone touching that sacred skin, kissing— my mind reeled—kissing those soft, moist lips with his monstrous mouth. How could she? Even the thought of it made me shudder in revulsion.

"'Ah,' she smiled, knowingly. 'You want to save me from him. You think he is ugly and that I've been hypnotized, somehow, into believing otherwise? You're quite wrong. He's handsome in a way that you'd surely understand— and sensitive, kind, gentle—those things a woman finds important. He's also very cultured. His blood . . .'

"I winced and took a step backward, but she was lost in some kind of reverie as she listed his attributes and I'm sure was unaware of my presence for some time.

"'. . . his blood is unimpeachable, reaching back through a royal lineage to the most notable of European families. I love him, yet I do not want to become one of his kind, for that would destroy my love . . .'

"'And—he loves you of course,' I said, daringly.

"For a moment those bright eyes clouded over, but she replied, 'In his way. It's not important that we both feel the same *kind* of love. We want to be together, to share our lives. I prefer him to any man I have ever met and I *will not* be deterred by an obstacle that's neither his fault, nor mine. A barrier that's been placed in our way by the injustice of nature. He can't help the way he is—and I want to go to him. That's all there is to it.'

"For a long time neither of us said anything. My throat felt too dry and constricted for words, and deep inside me I could feel something struggling, like a small creature fighting the folds of a net. The situation was beyond my comprehension: that is, I did not wish to allow it to enter my full under-standing or I would have run screaming from the shop and made myself look foolish to my neighbors.

"'Will you do it, silversmith?'

"'But,' I said, 'a collar covers only the throat . . .' I left the rest unsaid, but I was concerned that she was not protecting herself fully: the other parts of her anatomy—the wrists, the thighs.

"She became very angry. 'He isn't an *animal*. He's a gentleman. I'm merely guarding against—against moments of high passion. It's not just a matter of survival with him. The act is sensual and spiritual, as well as—as well as—what you're suggesting,' there was a note of loathing in her tone, 'is tantamount to rape.'

"She was so incensed that I did not dare say that her lover must have satisfied his need *somewhere*, and therefore had compromised the manners and morals of a gentleman many times.

"'Will you help me?' The eyes were pleading now. I tried to look out of the small, half-moon window, at the yellow-lighted streets, at the feet moving by on the pavement above, in an attempt to distract myself, but they were magnetic, those eyes, and they drew me back in less than a moment. I felt helpless—a trapped bird—in their unremitting gaze of anguish, and of course, I submitted.

"I agreed. I just heard myself saying, 'Yes,' and led her into the back of the shop where I began the work. It was not a difficult task to actually fashion the collar, though the sealing of it was somewhat painful to her and had to be carried out in stages, which took us well into the night hours. I must have, subconsciously perhaps, continued to glance through the workshop door at the window, for she said once, very quietly, 'He will not come here.'

"Such a beautiful throat she had too. Very long, and elegant. It seemed a sacrilege to encase such beauty in metal, though I made the collar as attractive as I made any silver ornament which might adorn a pretty woman. On the outside of the metal I engraved centripetal designs and at her request, some representational forms: Christ on the cross, immediately over her jugular vein, but also Zeus and Europa, and Zeus and Leda, with the Greek god in his bestial forms of the bull and the swan. I think she had been seduced by the thought that she was marrying some kind of deity.

"When I had finished, she paid me and left. I watched her walk out, into the early morning mists, with a heavy guilt in my heart. What could I have done? I was just a common craftsman and had no right interfering in the lives of others. Perhaps I should have tried harder to dissuade her, but I doubt she would have listened to my impertinence for more than a few moments. Besides, I had, during those few short hours, fallen in love with her—utterly—and when she realized she had made a mistake, she would have to come back to me again, to have the collar removed.

"I wanted desperately to see her again, though I knew that any chance of romance was impossible, hopeless. She was not of my class—or rather, I was not of hers, and her beauty was more than I could ever aspire to, though I knew myself to be a good-looking young man. Some had called *me* beautiful—it was that kind of handsomeness that I had been blessed with, rather than the rugged sort.

"But despite my physical advantages, I had nothing which would attract a lady of quality from her own kind. The most I could ever hope for—the very most—was perhaps to serve her in some way.

"Three weeks later she was back, looking somewhat distraught.

"'I want it to come off,' she said. 'It must be removed.'

"My fingers trembled as I worked at cutting her free—a much simpler task than the previous one.

"'You've left him,' I said. 'Won't he follow?'

"'No, you're quite wrong.' There was a haunted look to her eyes which chilled me to the bone. 'It's not that. I was too mistrustful. I love him too much to withhold from him the very thing he desires. I must give myself to him—wholly and completely. I need him, you see. And he needs me—yet like this I cannot give him the kind of love he has to have. I've been selfish. Very selfish. I must go to him . . .'

"'Are you mad?' I cried, forgetting my position. 'You'll become like him—you'll become—'

"'How *dare* you! How dare you preach to *me?* Just do your work, silversmith. Remove the collar!'

"I was weak of course, as most of us are when confronted by a superior being. I cut the collar loose and put it aside. She rubbed her neck and complained loudly that flakes of skin were coming away in her hands.

"'It's ugly,' she said. 'Scrawny. He'll never want me like this.'

"'No—thank God!' I cried, gathering my courage.

"At that moment she looked me full in the eyes and a strange expression came over her face.

"'You're in love with me, aren't you? That's why you're so concerned, silversmith. Oh dear, I am so dreadfully sorry. I thought you were just being meddlesome. It was genuine concern for my welfare and I didn't recognize it at first. Dear man,' she touched my cheek. 'Don't look so sad. It cannot be, you know. You should find some nice girl and try to forget, because you'll never see me again after tonight. And don't worry about me. I know what I'm doing.'

"With that, she gathered up her skirts and was gone again, down toward the river. The sun was just coming up, since she had arrived not long before the dawn, and I thought: At least she will have a few hours more of natural life.

"After that I tried to follow her advice and put her out of my mind. I did my work, something I had always enjoyed, and rarely left the shop. I felt that if I could get over a few months without a change in my normal pattern of existence, I should be safe. There were nightmares of course, to be gone through after sunsets, but those I was able to cope with. I have always managed to keep my dreams at a respectable distance and not let them interfere with my normal activities.

"Then, one day, as I was working on a pendant—a butterfly requested by a banker for his wife—a small boy brought me a message. Though it was unsigned, I knew it was from her and my hands trembled as I read the words.

"They simply said, 'Come. I need you.'

"Underneath this request was scrawled an address, which I knew to be located down by one of the wharves, south of the river.

"She *needed* me—and I knew exactly what for. I touched my throat. I wanted her too, but for different reasons. I did not have the courage that she had—the kind of sacrificial courage that's produced by an overwhelming love. But I was not without strength. If there was a chance, just a chance, that I could meet with her and come away unscathed, then I was prepared to accept the risk.

"But I didn't see how that was possible. Her kind, as she had become, possessed a physical strength which would make any escape fraught with difficulty.

"I had no illusions about her being in love with me—or even fond of me. She wanted to use me for her own purposes, which were as far away from love as earth is from the stars. I remembered seeing deep gouges in the silver collar, the time she had come to have it removed. They were like the claw marks of some beast, incised into the trunk of a tree. No wonder she had asked to have it sealed. Whoever, *whatever,* had made those marks would have had the strength to tear away any hinges or lock. The frenzy to get at what lay beneath the silver must have been appalling to witness— *experience*—yet she had gone back to him, without the collar's protection.

"I wanted her. I dreamed about having her, warm and close to me. That she had become something other than the beautiful woman who had entered my shop was no deterrent. I knew she would be just as lovely in her new form and I desired her above all things. For nights I lay awake, running different schemes over in my mind, trying to find a path which would allow us to make love together, just once, and yet let me walk away safely afterward. Even as I schemed, I saw her beauty laid before me, willingly, and my body and soul ached for her presence.

"One chance. I had this one chance of loving a woman a dozen places above my station: a woman whose refined ways and manner of speech had captivated me from the moment I met her. A woman whose dignity, elegance, and gracefulness were without parallel. Whose form surpassed that of the finest silverwork figurine I had ever known.

"I had to find a way.

"Finally, I came up with a plan which seemed to suit my purposes, and taking my courage in both hands I wrote her a note which said, 'I'm waiting for you. *You* must come to *me.*' I found an urchin to carry it for me and told him to put it through the letter box of the address she had given me.

"That afternoon I visited the church and a purveyor of medical instruments.

"That evening I spent wandering the streets, alternately praising myself for dreaming up such a clever plan and cursing myself for my foolhardiness in carrying it through. As I strolled through the backstreets, stepping around the gin-soaked drunks and tipping my hat to the factory girls as they hurried home from a sixteen-hour day in some garment manufacturer's sweatshop, or a hosiery, I realized that for once I had allowed my emotions to overrule my intellect. I'm not saying I was an intelligent young man—not above the average—but I was wise enough to know that there was great danger in what I proposed to do, yet the force of my feelings was more powerful than fear. I could not deny them their expression. The heart has no reason, but its drive is stronger than sense dictates.

"The barges on the river ploughed slowly against the current as I leaned on the wrought-iron balustrade overlooking the water. I could see the gas lamps reflected on the dark surface and thought about the shadow world that lived alongside our own, where nothing was rigid, set, but could be warped and twisted, like those lights in the water when the ripples from the barges passed through them. Would it take me and twist me into something, not ugly, but insubstantial? Into something that has the appearance of the real thing, but which is evanescent in the daylight and can only make its appearance at night, when vacuous shapes and phantasms take on a semblance of life and mock it with their unreal forms?

"When the smell of the mud below me began to waft upward, as the tide retreated and the river diminished, I made my way homeward. There was a sharpness to the air which cut into my confidence and I was glad to be leaving it behind for the warmth and security of my rooms. Security? I laughed at myself, having voluntarily exposed my vulnerability.

"She came.

"There was a scratching at the casement windowpane in the early hours of the morning and I opened it and let her in. She had not changed. If anything, she was more beautiful than ever, with a paler color to her cheeks and a fuller red to her lips.

"No words were exchanged between us. I lay on the bed naked and she joined me after removing her garments. She stroked my hair and the nape of my neck as I sank into her soft young body. I cannot describe the ecstasy. It was—*unearthly*. She allowed me—encouraged me—and the happiness of those moments was worth all the risks of entering Hell for a taste of Heaven.

"Of course, the moment came when she lowered her head to the base of my throat. I felt the black coils of her hair against my cheek: smelled their sweet fragrance. I could sense the pulse in my neck, throbbing with blood. Her body was warm against mine—deliciously warm. I wanted her to stay there forever. There was just a hint of pain in my throat—a needleprick, no more, and then a feeling of drifting, floating on warm water, as if I had suddenly been transported to tropic seas and lay in the shallows of some sunbleached island's beaches. I felt no fear—only, *bliss*.

"Then, suddenly, she snorted, springing to her feet like no athlete I have ever seen. Her eyes were blazing and she spat and hissed into my face.

"'What have you done?' she shrieked.

"Then the fear came, rushing to my heart. I cowered at the bedhead, pulling my legs up to my chest in an effort to get as far away from her as possible.

"Again she cried, 'What have you done?'

"'Holy water,' I said. 'I've injected holy water into my veins.'

"She let out another wail which made my ears sing. Her hands reached for me and I saw those long nails, like talons, ready to slash at an artery, but the fear was gone from me. I just wanted her back in bed with me. I no longer cared for the consequences.

"'Please?' I said, reaching for her. 'Help me? I want you to help me.'

"She withdrew from me then and sprang to the window. It was getting close to dawn: The first rays of the sun were sliding over the horizon.

"'You fool,' she said, and then she was gone, out into the murk. I jumped up and looked for her through the window, but all I could see was the mist on the river, curling its way around the rotten stumps of an old jetty.

"Once I had recovered my common sense and was out of her influence, I remember thinking to myself that I would have to make a collar—a silver collar . . ."

The fire spat in the grate and I jerked upright. I had no idea how long Sam had been talking but the peat was almost all ashes.

"The tide," I said, alarmed. "I must leave."

"I haven't finished," he complained, but I was already on my feet. I opened the door and began to walk quickly down the narrow path we had made through the heather, to where my boat lay, but even as I approached it, I could see that it was lying on its side in the slick, glinting mud.

Angry, I looked back at the croft on the hillside. He must have known. He must have known. I was about to march back and take Sam to task, when I suddenly saw the croft in a new perspective. It was like most dwellings of its kind—timber framed, with sods of earth filling the cracks, and stones holding down the turf on the roof. But it was a peculiar shape—more of a mound than the normal four walls and a roof—and was without windows.

My mind suddenly ran wild with frightening images of wood, earth, and rocks. The wooden coffin goes inside the earth and the headstone weights it down. A mound—a burial mound. *He hadn't been able to stay away from her. The same trap that had caught her . . .*

I turned back to the boat and tried dragging it across the moonlit mud, toward the distant water, but it was too heavy. I could only inch it along, and rapidly became tired. The muscles in my arms and legs screamed at me. All the time I labored, one side of my mind kept telling me not to be so foolish, while the other was equally insistent regarding the need to get away. I could hear myself repeating the words. *"He couldn't stay away from her. He couldn't stay away."*

I had covered about six yards when I heard a voice at my shoulder—a soft, dry voice, full of concern.

"Here, John, let me help you . . ."

Sam did help me that day, more than I wished him to. I don't hate him for that, especially now that so many years have passed. Since then I have obtained this job, of night ferryman on the loch, helping young ladies like the one I have in the skiff with me now—a runaway, off to join her lover.

"Don't worry," I try to reassure her, after telling her my story, "we sailors are fond of our tales. Come and join me by the tiller. I'll show you how to manage the boat. Do I frighten you? I don't mean to. I only want to help you . . ."

Writers are so often asked where they get their ideas from and nine times out of ten I can't reply because I don't know myself. However, in this case I know exactly where it came from—my daughter's dream. A couple of nights before her wedding, Chantelle had a nightmare. She told me at breakfast the following morning that she dreamed she had discovered that Mark (her fiancé) was a vampire and that she had to wear a silver collar on their wedding night. So the main ingredient of the story was handed to me on a platter, the credit going to prenuptial nerves.

This is my first story involving the vampire myth. I'm not so much interested in the idea of the creatures themselves as I am in why we need them. Why do we invent blood-sucking monsters to feed our fascination? The idea that blood is a sacred substance, with properties of determining nobility or peasantry, racial superiority or inferiority, criminality or decency, goes back a long way and is still with us in various forms. Blue blood, *bad* blood, red-blooded youths. A whole mythological web has been woven out of this ordinary red, viscous fluid, that is important to us, but no more so than our kidneys. Anybody fancy writing a kidney-eating monster story? Ah, you laugh?

I think we need vampires, not because they drain our lifeblood, but because they change us into someone else and give us the gift of immortality. To live forever—now *there's* the rub.

Garry Kilworth

TRY A
DULL KNIFE

Harlan Ellison®

In my late teens I became an avid Ellison reader. I remember reading "Try a Dull Knife" in 1969 and the chill it gave me. It was one of the stories that helped formulate the concept behind this book. So here it appears, happily, in Blood Is Not Enough.

*I*t was *pachanga* night at The Cave. Three spick bands all going at once, each with a fat momma shaking her meat and screaming *¡Vaya!* The sound was something visible, an assault in silver lamé and screamhorn. Sound hung dense as smog-cloud, redolent as skunk-scent from a thousand roaches of the best shit, no stems or seeds. Darkness shot through with the quicksilver flashes of mouths open to show gold bridgework and dirty words. Eddie Burma staggered in, leaned against a wall and felt the sickness as thick as cotton wool in his throat.

The deep scar-burn of pain was bleeding slowly down his right side. The blood had started coagulating, his shirt stuck to his flesh, but he dug it: it wasn't pumping any more. But he was in trouble, that was the righteous truth. Nobody can get cut the way Eddie Burma'd been cut and not be in deep trouble.

And somewhere back out there, in the night, they were moving toward him, coming for him. He had to get through to—who? Somebody. Somebody who could help him; because only now, after fifteen years of what had been happening to him, did Eddie Burma finally know what it was he had been through, what had been done to him . . . what was *being* done to him . . . what they would certainly do to him.

He stumbled down the short flight of steps into The Cave and was instantly lost in the smoke and smell and twisting shadows. Ethnic smoke, Puerto Rican smells, lush shadows from another land. He dug it; even with his strength ebbing, he dug it.

That was Eddie Burma's problem. He was an empath. He felt. Deep inside himself, on a level most people never even know exists, he felt for the world. Involvement was what motivated him. Even here, in this slum night-club where intensity of enjoyment substituted for the shallow glamour and gaucherie of the uptown *boites*, here where no one knew him and therefore could not harm him, he felt the pulse of the world's life surging through him. And the blood started pumping again.

He pressed his way back through the crowd, looking for a phone booth, looking for a toilet, looking for an empty booth where he could hide, looking for the person or persons unknown who could save him from the dark night of the soul slipping toward him inexorably.

He caromed off a waiter, Pancho Villa moustache, dirty white apron, tray of draft beers. "Hey, where's the *gabinetto?*" he slurred the request. His words were slipping in their own blood.

The Puerto Rican waiter stared at him. Uncomprehending. "*¿Perdón?*"

"The toilet, the *pissoir*, the can, the head, the crapper. I'm bleeding to death, where's the potty?"

"Ohhh!" Meaning dawned on the waiter. "*¡Excusado . . . atavío!*" He pointed. Eddie Burma patted him on the arm and slumped past, almost falling into a booth where a man and two women were groping one another darkly.

He found the door to the toilet and pushed it open. A reject from a Cuban Superman film was slicking back his long, oiled hair in an elaborate pompadour before the foggy mirror. He gave Eddie Burma a passing glance and went back to the topography of his coiffure. Burma moved past him in the tiny room and slipped into the first stall.

Once inside, he bolted the door, and sat down heavily on the lidless toilet. He pulled his shirt up out of his pants, and unbuttoned it. It stuck to his skin. He pulled, gently, and it came away with the sound of mud squished underfoot. The knife wound ran from just below the right nipple to the middle of his waist. It was deep. He was in trouble.

He stood up, hanging the shirt on the hook behind the door, and pulled hanks of toilet paper from the gray, crackly roll. He dipped the paper in a wad, into the toilet bowl, and swabbed at the wound. Oh, God, *really* deep.

Then nausea washed over him, and he sat down again. Strange thoughts came to him, and he let them work him over:

This morning, when I stepped out the front door, there were yellow roses growing on the bushes. It surprised me; I'd neglected to cut them back last fall, and I was certain the gnarled, blighted knobs at the ends of the branches—still there, silently dead in reproach of my negligence—would stunt any further beauty. But when I stepped out to pick up the newspaper, there they were. Full and light yellow, barely a canary yellow. Breathing moistly, softly. It made me smile, and I went down the steps to the first landing, to get the paper. The parking lot had filled with leaves from the Eucalyptus again, but somehow, particularly this morning, it gave the private little area surrounding and below my secluded house in the hills a more lived-in, festive look. For the second time, for no sensible reason, I found myself smiling. It was going to be a good day, and I had the feeling that all the problems I'd taken on—all the social cases I took unto myself—Alice and Burt and Linda down the hill—all the emotional cripples who came to me for succor—would shape up, and we'd all be smiling by end of day. And if not today, then certainly by Monday. Friday, the latest.

I picked up the paper and snapped the rubber band off it. I dropped the rubber band into the big metal trash basket at the foot of the stairs, and started climbing back up to the house, smelling the orange blossoms and the fine, chill morning air. I opened the paper as I climbed, and with all the suddenness of a freeway collision, the morning calm vanished from around me. I was stopped in mid-step, one leg raised for the next riser, and my eyes felt suddenly grainy, as though I hadn't had enough sleep the night before. But I had.

The headline read: EDWARD BURMA FOUND MURDERED.

But . . . I was Eddie Burma.

He came back from memories of yellow roses and twisted metal on freeways to find himself slumped against the side of the toilet stall, his head pressed to the wooden wall, his arms hanging down, the blood running into his pants top. His head throbbed, and the pain in his side was beating, hammering, pounding with a regularity that made him shiver with fear. He could not sit there, and wait.

Wait to die, or wait for them to find him.

He knew they would find him. He knew it.

The phone. He could call . . .

He didn't know whom he could call. But there had to be someone. Someone out there who would understand, who would come quickly and save him. Someone who wouldn't take what was left of him, the way the others would.

They didn't need knives.

How strange that *that* one, the little blonde with the Raggedy Ann shoebutton eyes, had not known that. Or perhaps she had. But perhaps also the frenzy of the moment had overcome her, and she could not simply feed leisurely as the others did. She had cut him. Had done what they all did, but directly, without subtlety.

Her blade had been sharp. The others used much more devious weapons, subtler weapons. He wanted to say to her, "Try a dull knife." But she was too needing, too eager. She would not have heard him.

He struggled to his feet, and put on his shirt. It hurt to do it. The shirt was stained the color of teak with his blood. He could barely stand now.

Pulling foot after foot, he left the toilet, and wandered out into The Cave. The sound of "Mamacita Lisa" beat at him like gloved hands on a plate glass window. He leaned against the wall, and saw only shapes moving moving moving in the darkness. Were they out there? No, not yet; they would never look here first. He wasn't known here. And his essence was weaker now, weaker as he died, so no one in the crowd would come to him with a quivering need. No one would feel it possible to drink from this weak man, lying up against a wall.

He saw a pay phone, near the entrance to the kitchen, and he struggled toward it. A girl with long dark hair and haunted eyes stared at him as he passed, started to say something, then he summoned up strength to hurry past her before she could tell him she was pregnant and didn't know who the father was, or she was in pain from emphysema and didn't have doctor money, or she missed her mother who was still in San Juan. He could handle no more pains, could absorb no more anguish, could let no others drink from him. He didn't have that much left for his own survival.

My fingertips (he thought, moving) *are covered with the scars of people I've touched. The flesh remembers those touches. Sometimes I feel as though I am wearing heavy woolen gloves, so thick are the memories of all those touches. It seems to insulate me, to separate me from mankind. Not mankind from* me, *God knows, for they get through without pause or difficulty—but* me, *from mankind. I very often refrain from washing my hands for days and days, just to preserve whatever layers of touches might be washed away by the soap.*

Faces and voices and smells of people I've known have passed away, but still my hands carry the memories on them. Layer after layer of the laying-on of hands. Is that altogether sane? I don't know. I'll have to think about it for a very long time, when I have the time.

If I ever have the time.

He reached the pay phone; after a very long time he was able to bring a coin up out of his pocket. It was a quarter. All he needed was a dime. He could not go back down there, he might not make it back again. He used the quarter, and dialed the number of a man he could trust, a man who could help him. He remembered the man now, knew the man was his only salvation.

He remembered seeing him in Georgia, at a revival meeting, a rural stump religion circus of screaming and Hallelujahs that sounded like !H!A!L!L!E!L!U!J!A!H! with dark black faces or red necks all straining toward the seat of God on the platform. He remembered the man in his white shirtsleeves, exhorting the crowd, and he heard again the man's spirit message.

"Get right with the Lord, before *he* gets right with *you!* Suffer your silent sins no longer! Take out your truth, carry it in your hands, give it to me, all the ugliness and cesspool filth of your souls! I'll wash you clean in the blood of the lamb, in the blood of the Lord, in the blood of the truth of the word! There's no other way, there's no great day coming without purging yourself, without cleansing your spirit! I can handle all the pain you've got boiling around down in the black lightless pit of your souls! Hear me, dear God hear me . . . I am your mouth, your tongue, your throat, the horn that will proclaim your deliverance to the Heavens above! Evil and good and worry and sorrow, all of it is mine, I can carry it, I can handle it, I can lift it from out of your mind and your soul and your body! The place is here, the place is me, give me your woe! Christ knew it, God knows it, *I* know it, and now *you* have to know it! Mortar and trowel and brick and cement make the wall of your need! Let me tear down that wall, let me hear all of it, let me into your mind and let me take your burdens! I'm the strength, I'm the watering place . . . come drink from my strength!"

And the people had rushed to him. All over him, like ants feeding on a dead beast. And then the memory dissolved. The image of the tent revival meeting dissolved into images of wild animals tearing at meat, of hordes of carrion birds descending on fallen meat, of small fish leaping with sharp teeth at helpless meat, of hands and more hands, and teeth that sank into meat.

The number was busy.

It was busy again.

He had been dialing the same number for nearly an hour, and the number was always busy. Dancers with sweating faces had wanted to use the phone, but Eddie Burma had snarled at them that it was a matter of life and death that he reach the number he was calling, and the dancers had gone back to their partners with curses for him. But the line was still busy. Then he looked at the number on the pay phone, and knew he had been dialing himself all that time. That the line would always *always* be busy, and his furious hatred of the man on the other end who would not answer was hatred for the man who was calling. He was calling himself, and in that instant he remembered who the man had been at the revival meeting. He remembered leaping up out of the audience and taking the platform to beg all the stricken suffering ones to end their pain by drinking of his essence. He remembered, and the fear was greater than he could believe. He fled back to the toilet, to wait for them to find him.

Eddie Burma, hiding in the refuse room of a sightless dark spot in the netherworld of a universe that had singled him out for reality. Eddie Burma was an individual. He had substance. He had corporeality. In a world of walking shadows, of zombie breath and staring eyes like the cold dead flesh of the moon, Eddie Burma was a real person. He had been born with the ability to belong to his times; with the electricity of nature that some called charisma and others called warmth. He felt deeply; he moved through the world and touched; and was touched.

His was a doomed existence, because he was not only an extrovert and gregarious, but he was truly clever, vastly inventive, suffused with humor, and endowed with the power to listen. For these reasons he had passed through the stages of exhibitionism and praise-seeking to a state where his reality was assured. Was very much his own. When he came into a room, people knew it. He had a face. Not an image, or a substitute life that he could slip on when dealing with people, but a genuine reality. He was Eddie Burma, only Eddie Burma, and could not be confused with anyone else. He went his way, and he was identified as Eddie Burma in the eyes of anyone who ever met him. He was one of those memorable people. The kind other people who have no lives of their own talk about. He cropped up in conversations: "Do you know what Eddie said . . . ?" or "Guess what happened to Eddie?" And there was never any confusion as to who was the subject under discussion.

Eddie Burma was a figure no larger than life, for life itself was large enough, in a world where most of those he met had no individuality, no personality, no reality, no existence of their own.

But the price he paid was the price of doom. For those who had nothing came to him and, like creatures of darkness, amorally fed off him. They drank from him. They were the succubi, draining his psychic energies. And Eddie Burma always had more to give. Seemingly a bottomless well, the bottom had been reached. Finally. All the people whose woes he handled, all the losers whose lives he tried to organize, all the preying crawlers who slinked in through the ashes of their non-existence to sup at his board, to slake the thirsts of their emptiness . . . all of them had taken their toll.

Now Eddie Burma stumbled through the last moments of his reality, with the wellsprings of himself almost totally drained. Waiting for them, for all his social cases, all his problem children, to come and finish him off.

I live in a hungry world, Eddie Burma now realized.

"Hey, man! C'mon outta th'crapper!" The booming voice and the pounding on the stall door came as one.

Eddie trembled to his feet and unbolted the door, expecting it to be one of them. But it was only a dancer from The Cave, wanting to rid himself of cheap wine and cheap beer. Eddie stumbled out of the stall, almost falling into the man's arms. When the beefy Puerto Rican saw the blood, saw the dead pale look of flesh and eyes, his manner softened.

"Hey . . . you okay, man?"

Eddie smiled at him, thanked him softly, and left the toilet. The nightclub was still high, still screaming, and Eddie suddenly knew he could not let *them* find this good place, where all these good people were plugged into life and living. Because for *them* it would be a godsend, and they would drain The Cave as they had drained him.

He found a rear exit, and emerged into the moonless city night, as alien as a cavern five miles down or the weird curvature of another dimension. This alley, this city, this night, could as easily have been Transylvania or the dark side of the moon or the bottom of the thrashing sea. He stumbled down the alley, thinking . . .

They have no lives of their own. Oh, this poisoned world I now see so clearly. They have only the shadowy images of other lives, and not even real other lives—the lives of movie stars, fictional heroes, cultural clichés. So they borrow from me, and never intend to pay back. They borrow, at the highest rate of interest. My life. They lap at me, and break off pieces of me. I'm the mushroom that Alice found with the words EAT ME in blood-red on my id. They're succubi, draining at me, draining my soul. Sometimes I feel I should go to some mystical well and get poured full of personality again. I'm tired. So tired.

There are people walking around this city who are running on Eddie Burma's drained energies, Eddie Burma's life-force. They're putt-putting around with smiles just like mine, with thoughts I've second-handed like old clothes passed on to poor relatives, with hand-movements and expressions and little cute sayings that were mine, Scotch-taped over their own. I'm a jigsaw puzzle and they keep stealing little pieces. Now I make no scene at all, I'm incomplete, I'm unable to keep the picture coherent, they've taken so much already.

They had come to his party, all of the ones he knew. The ones he called his friends, and the ones who were merely acquaintances, and the ones who were using him as their wizard, as their guru, their psychiatrist, their wailing wall, their father confessor, their repository of personal ills and woes and inadequacies. Alice, who was afraid of men and found in Eddie Burma a last vestige of belief that males were not all beasts. Burt, the box-boy from the supermarket, who stuttered when he spoke, and felt rejected even before the rejection. Linda, from down the hill, who had seen in Eddie Burma an intellectual, one to whom she could relate all her theories of the universe. Sid, who was a failure, at fifty-three. Nancy, whose husband cheated on her. John, who wanted to be a lawyer, but would never make it because he thought too much about his clubfoot. And all the others. And the new ones they always seemed to bring with them. There were always so many new ones he never knew. Particularly the pretty little blonde with the Raggedy Ann shoebutton eyes, who stared at him hungrily.

And from the first, earlier that night, he had known something was wrong. There were too many of them at the party. More than he could handle . . . and all listening to him tell a story of something that had happened to him when he had driven to New Orleans in 1960 with Tony in the Corvette and they'd both gotten pleurisy because the top hadn't been bolted down properly and they'd passed through a snowstorm in Illinois.

All of them hung to his words, like drying wash on a line, like festoons of ivy. They sucked at each word and every expression like hungry things pulling at the marrow in beef bones. They laughed, and they watched, and their eyes glittered . . .

Eddie Burma had slowly felt the strength ebbing from him. He grew weary even as he spoke. It had happened before, at other parties, other gatherings, when he had held the attention of the group, and gone home later, feeling drained. He had never known what it was.

But tonight the strength did not come back. They kept watching him, seemed to be *feeding* at him, and it went on and on, till finally he'd said he had to go to sleep, and they should go home. But they had pleaded for one more anecdote, one more joke told with perfect dialect and elaborate gesticulation. Eddie Burma had begun to cry, quietly. His eyes were red-rimmed, and his body felt as though the bones and musculature had been removed, leaving only a soft rubbery coating that might at any moment cave in on itself.

He had tried to get up; to go and lie down; but they'd gotten more insistent, had demanded, had ordered, had grown nasty. And then the blonde had come at him, and cut him, and the others were only a step behind. Somehow . . . in the thrashing tangle that had followed, with his friends and acquaintances now tearing at one another to get at him, he had escaped. He had fled, he did not know how, the pain of his knifed side crawling inside him. He had made it into the trees of the little glen where his house was hidden, and through the forest, over the watershed, down to the highway, where he had hailed a cab. Then into the city . . .

See me! See me, please! Just don't always come and take. Don't bathe in my reality and then go away feeling clean. Stay and let some of the dirt of you rub off on me. I feel like an invisible man, like a drinking trough, like a sideboard dripping with sweetmeats . . . Oh God, is this a play, and myself unwillingly the star? How the hell do I get off stage? When do they ring down the curtain? Is there, please God, a man with a hook . . . ?

I make my rounds, like a faith healer. Each day I spend a little time with each one of them. With Alice and with Burt and with Linda down the hill; and they take from me. They don't leave anything in exchange, though. It's not barter, it's theft. And the worst part of it is I always needed that, I always let them rob me. What sick need was it that gave them entrance to my soul? Even the pack rat leaves some worthless object when it steals a worthless object. I'd take any thing from them: the smallest anecdote, the most used-up thought, the most stagnant concept, the puniest pun, the most obnoxious personal revelation . . . anything! But all they do is sit there and stare at me, their mouths open, their ears hearing me so completely they empty my words of color and scent . . . I feel as though they're crawling into me. I can't stand any more . . . really I can't.

The mouth of the alley was blocked.

Shadows moved there.

Burt, the box-boy. Nancy and Alice and Linda. Sid, the failure. John, who walked with a rolling motion. And the doctor, the jukebox repairman, the pizza cook, the used-car salesman, the swinging couple who swapped partners, the discothèque dancer . . . all of them.

They came for him.

And for the first time he noticed their teeth.

The moment before they reached him stretched out as silent and timeless as the decay that ate at his world. He had no time for self-pity. It was not merely that Eddie Burma had been cannibalized every day of the year, every hour of the day, every minute of every hour of every day of every year. The awareness dawned unhappily—in that moment of timeless time—that he had *let* them do it to him. That he was no better than they, only different. They were the feeders—and he was the food. But no nobility could be attached to one or the other. He *needed* to have people worship and admire him. He *needed* the love and attention of the masses, the worship of monkeys. And for Eddie Burma that was a kind of beginning to death. It was the death of his unself-consciousness; the slaughter of his innocence. From that moment forward, he had been aware of the clever things he said and did, on a cellular level below consciousness. He was aware. Aware, aware, aware!

And awareness brought them to him, where they fed. It led to self-consciousness, petty pretensions, ostentation. And that was a thing devoid of substance, of reality. And if there was anything on which his acolytes could not nourish, it was a posturing, phony, *empty* human being.

They would drain him.

The moment came to a timeless climax, and they carried him down under their weight, and began to feed.

When it was over, they left him in the alley. They went to look elsewhere.

With the vessel drained, the vampires moved to other pulsing arteries.

Though I have worked assiduously at living my life by Pasteur's dictum, "Chance favors the prepared mind," and consider it ludicrous and horrifying that the guy in the White House (as I sit writing this in May of 1988) is so loopy that he consults astrologers—a craziness we associate with utter derangement cases like Hitler, who maintained a staff stargazer—I nonetheless amuse myself with the harmless conceit that each of us possesses different kinds of "luck."

(Because I truly believe there is no such thing as "luck," but cannot deny both synchronicity and serendipity in the insensate universe, this is my childlike way of taking into account sheer randomness of circumstance that redounds to our benefit. And I'm not for a second truly serious about it.)

There are people who are "lucky" in love and people who are "lucky" in business and people who are "lucky" when they survive accidents. The kinds of "luck" that I possess are far less significant measured against the totality of my life. They are: parking-space luck; restaurant luck; bad-companion luck.

My friends (and ex-Executive Assistants) Linda Steele and Sarah Wood used to rage at my parking-space luck. It wouldn't matter if the destination was in the heaviest-traffic section of Westwood or Downtown L.A. As I neared the building in which I needed to transact my business, a parking place would open . . . usually smack in front of the entrance. There could be entire armadas of parked cars at my place of arrival . . . and someone would drive away just as we neared the most convenient spot. Linda and Sarah would revile me with splenic fervor, going so far as to bet me a buck it wouldn't happen *this* time.

I made a few dollars off that one.

Then there's restaurant luck. Trust me on this, I am systemically incapable of picking a bad eatery. Joints that look as though they've been selected for this year's Cockroach Party Conclave from the outside, invariably become secret dining treasures, to be whispered about only among my closest friends lest the word leak out and *they* invade the place, making it impossible for me to get a seat when I'm hungry. (We all know who *they* are: the uptown folks in Gucci loafers, with their rebuilt noses and friends who are big in debentures and real estate. You know the ones. They always need to push two tables together so they can scream at each other more conveniently.) I can be driving down an Interstate in a part of the country I've never visited before, and my head will come up and my nose (unrebuilt) will begin to twitch like a setter on point, and I'll say to my passengers, "If we take the next exit, turn right and go off in *that* direction, we'll find a sensational rib joint." They look at me with proper disbelief. So I do it, and we find a five-stool counter joint run by an ancient black man whose arcane abilities with baby-backs is strictly imperial. Never fails. Ask Silverberg. Ask Len Wein. Trust me on this.

But the most efficacious luck I command is the luck that keeps me away from deadbeats. Time-wasters, arrivistes, bums and mooches. The mooks of the world.

Now, I suppose, dealing with this pragmatically, it is only what Hemingway called "a built-in, shock-proof shit detector." The flawless functioning of the onboard computer that has been programmed with decades of experience and insight and body-language and tonal inflection and the behavior of sociopaths. Sherlock Holmes employed this methodology to scope a visitor to 221B Baker Street within moments of his/her arrival: deductive logic. That's what this "luck" must be, I'm certain of it.

Whatever the rationale, it works for me. I'm not about to say I've never been flummoxed—there was this lady I once married for 45 days, but that's another novel, for another time—yet the wool has been pulled very rarely. I can spot a twisto with the first sentence uttered. Lames and leaners and hustlers don't do very well with me. I seem to be creep-proof.

And so, almost all of the vast amount of trouble I've gotten myself into, has been no one's fault but my own. I cannot plead that I was "led astray by the wickedness of others." I am, in the Amerind sense of the phrase, absolutely responsible for my life and all the actions that have gone to construct that life. No accessory after the fact, I am precisely who I made me.

Yet in 1963–65, I "went Hollywood" for a while. Not so seriously that you might confuse me with William Holden's corpse floating in Gloria Swanson's swimming pool, but off-direction enough that I spent more time than I had to fritter away, in the company of people who drifted on the tide like diatoms. Some actors, some blue-sky entrepreneurs, some starlets, some taproots-in-Hell users and manipulators. I knew they were wrong the moment I opened the packages, but I'm no different from you: we all go to the zoo to watch the peculiar animals from faraway lands. Temporary fascination is not self-abuse, as long as one retains a sense of perspective; tip-toeing through the minefield satisfies our need for diversion and danger, as long as one doesn't lease a burrow and start buying furniture for permanent residency. As sheepish apologia, I offer the only explanation that ever seems acceptable for the peculiar things we do: it seemed like a good idea at the time.

And so, cute as a bug, I waded hip-deep in a social scene that bore as much relation to Living a Proper Life as Narnia bears to Ashtabula, Ohio. Which is to say, not a whole lot.

I was living in an actual treehouse at that time. A small, charming structure up a steep private road that ended in a parking lot below the house, a flat space surrounded by eucalyptus trees that totally hid the house from casual sight. It cost one hundred and thirty-five bucks a month, and had a small kitchen, a smaller bathroom, a decent-sized living room with a wood-burning fireplace, high beamed ceilings and paneled walls, and a "captain's cabin" bedroom that was, in truth, only a triangular-shaped walled-off section with old-fashioned bay windows all around. I loved that little place on Bushrod Lane.

To that eyrie, 1962–66, came an unending stream of odd types and casual liaisons. The house lay in the bosom of Beverly Glen, at that time a rich enclave of artistic and (what used to be called) bohemian intellects. Lee Marvin and Clint Eastwood, Robert Duvall and Harry Dean

Stanton, Robert Blake and Lenny Bruce . . . I knew them all, and a few of them became friends. The parties were intimate, because the house was so small; the fun was constant because it was poor folks fun, pizza and alla that smart chat, unimpaired by dope or booze because I don't do neither, and had no room for it in my environs.

In that venue, I stood off the son of the Detroit Mafia boss and two of his pistoleros with a Remington XP-100 pistol-rifle that fires enormous .221 Fireball cartridges, while I was ridiculously attired only in a bath towel around my waist. In that venue, I met and made friends with the dog Ahbhu, who still lives as Blood in "A Boy and His Dog." In that venue, I managed so fully to fulfill all my adolescent sex-fantasies that I was able to proceed with my life having flensed myself of the dopey dream-hungers that pursue men into middle-age.

And in that venue I wrote "Paingod" and " 'Repent, Harlequin!' Said the Ticktockman" and "Lonelyache" and "Soldier" and "Punky and the Yale Men" and "Pretty Maggie Moneyeyes" and "I Have No Mouth, and I Must Scream" and a great many other stories. It was in that venue that I conceived and began editing DANGEROUS VISIONS.

I partied, and I dissipated, and I screwed like a mad thing, but I always worked. Which is why I can look back on that time with pleasure and a smile. But were it not for having *done the writing*—the thing that has always saved me from becoming a bum—the years of my having "gone Hollywood" would reside in memory draped with a sense of loss, a coating of wasted time, a terror at how easily we can all be led astray.

"Try a Dull Knife" came out of that period.

It was the story that marked the end of my sojourn among the bad companions. What had been going on, had been going on for several years; and during that time I went from one bunch of gargoyles to another, with them mooching and leaning, wasting my nights and borrowing my money (of which there was damned little, despite my working steadily in TV, writing *Outer Limits* and *Burke's Law* and *Route 66* and dozens of other shows). I was constantly having to put people up in the tiny treehouse because they were being hunted by even deadlier types. When Bobby Blake needed a place to hide out so his producer couldn't find him, to force him to do retakes on a segment of *The Richard Boone Show* that Bobby had starred in, he went to ground in my living room. We shot a lot of pool in those days. A mountain lion leaped off the jungly hill that loomed over the treehouse and damned near ripped off my arm, right in the middle of a late night party.

And then, like drawing a deep breath, I sat down and wrote "Try a Dull Knife," and it was all over.

For me, the work has always been therapy. Writing and taking showers provides the spark of insight that informs my awareness of what the hell I'm doing in the Real World.

And the oddest part about "Try a Dull Knife" is that I had written the first two paragraphs sometime in 1963, had written those lines without any idea how they would proceed into a story, and had shoved the yellow second-sheet with those words on it into a drawer, and never went near it, never even remembered it, till 1965. Two years after the opening had been written, I was writing another story entirely. It started with the words "Somewhere back out there, in the night, they were moving toward him, coming for him." And as I wrote along, the story taking shape slowly, as slowly as was taking shape the realization that I was surrounded by, and being used by, a glittery species of emotional vampires . . . I realized that I had started the story in the wrong place. I'd begun the yarn at least one beat too late.

And I stopped writing, and without knowing why, I started rooting through that drawer full of odd pieces of snippets for stories that might never be written, that trash-bin of words and ideas that had foundered on the shoals of my lack of craft or insight. I found that yellow second-sheet, and I read what I had written, and I added the word "and" at the beginning of my current project, and . . . the pieces fit exactly.

The onboard computer was just beginning to learn what it needed to know, back in 1963. But the connection had been made, in 1965, and *I* learned a lesson I've never forgotten:

I trust my talent. Implicitly.

I may be a dolt, subject to all the idiocies and false beliefs and false starts to which we are all heir, but the talent knows what the hell it's doing. The talent protects itself. It knows it has to exist in this precarious liaison with a dolt, and it makes damned sure the envelope containing the message doesn't get postmarked to the Dead Letter Office.

"Try a Dull Knife" didn't get finished till 1968, but the writing of the first pages exploded the scene through which I was sloughing. It freed me, and within a week or so I was out in the open again, moving away from the blasted, creepy world in which I had spent my uneasy days and nights, locked in useless embrace with the vampires who abound in unknowing, innocent society.

"Try a Dull Knife" is a story about bloodsuckers. It is also a story about "luck."

Harlan Ellison®

VARICOSE WORMS

Scott Baker

The worms in this story drain the energy of their host and are the perfect representatives of their master. The story is also about magic, shamanism, and poetic justice. And it's a truly disgusting story, so don't try it before a meal.

*E*minescu Eliade's great good luck had been his last name, that and the fact that not only had he been a cultured cosmopolitan and intelligent man when he'd arrived in Paris (named Eminescu after his country's greatest nineteenth-century poet by parents who'd seen to it that he had a thorough classical education, he'd almost completed his studies as a veterinarian when he'd been forced to flee Romania as the result of an indiscretion with a rather highly placed local official's daughter) but that he'd arrived in Paris hungry, practically penniless and desperate. So desperate that when he'd seen a copy of Mircea Eliade's *Le Chamanisme et les techniques archaïques de l'extase* in a bookstore window on the rue St. Jacques, where it had been accompanied by a notice explaining that Professor Eliade had returned to Paris for a limited time to give a series of lectures at the Musée de l'Homme under the auspices of the Bollingen Foundation, he'd gone to the post office and spent what were almost the last of his few coins for two phone tokens. He called the museum with the first and somehow, despite his halting French and the implausibility of his story, convinced the woman who answered the phone to give him the phone number of the apartment in Montmartre where the professor was staying, then used the other token to call the professor himself and pretend to a family relationship that had as far as he knew no basis in fact.

His meeting with the professor a few days later resulted in nothing but an excellent hot meal and the chance to discuss his namesake's poetry in Romanian with a fellow exile, but the fact that he'd found a copy of the other's book on shamanism in a library and had read it carefully in preparation for the interview changed his life.

Because when, some weeks later, he found himself panhandling in back of the Marché St. Germain with all his clothes worn in thick layers to keep him warm and the rest of his few possessions in two plastic bags he kept tied to his waist with some twine he'd found, or sleeping huddled over the ventilation grating at the corner of the boulevard St. Germain and the rue de l'Ancienne Comédie where the hot dry air from the métro station underneath kept him warm, or under the Pont Neuf (the oldest bridge in Paris despite its name) on nights when it was raining and he couldn't get past the police who sometimes made sure no one got into the Odéon métro station without a ticket—in the weeks and months he spent standing with his fellow *clochards* sheltered from the wind against the urine-stained stone of the Église St. Sulpice, yelling and singing things at the passersby, or in alleyways passing the cheap red wine in the yellow-tinged green bottles with the fat stars standing out in bas-relief on their necks back and forth—he slowly came to realize that certain of his companions were not at all what they seemed, were in fact shamans—urban shamans—every bit as powerful, as fearsome and as wild as the long-dead Tungu shamans whose Siberian descendents still remembered them with such awe. Remembered them only, because long ago all the truly powerful shamans had left the frozen north with its starvation and poverty for the cities where they could put their abilities to better use, leaving only those whose powers were comparatively feeble or totally faked to carry on their visible tradition and be studied by scholars such as Professor Eliade.

And from his first realization of what he'd found and what it meant, it hadn't taken him all that long to put the knowledge to use and become what he'd been now for more than fifteen years: an internationally known French psychiatrist with a lucrative private practice in which the two younger psychiatrists with whom he shared his offices on avenue Victor Hugo were not his partners but his salaried employees. The diplomas hanging framed on his wall were all genuine despite the fact that the name on them—Julien de Saint-Hilaire—was false and that the universities in Paris and Geneva and Los Angeles that had issued them would have been appalled to learn just what he'd actually done to earn them. He had a twenty-two-room apartment in a private hotel overlooking the Parc Monceau that even the other tenants now thought had been in his family since the early sixteen hundreds, maids who were each and every one of them country girls from small villages in the provinces as maids were traditionally supposed to be, and a very beautiful blond-haired American wife, Liz, in her early twenties, who'd been a model for Cacharel before he'd married her and convinced her to give up her career.

He took two, and sometimes three, month-long business trips every year, leaving the routine care of his patients during his absences to Jean-Luc and Michel, both of whom were talented minor shamans though neither of them was as yet aware of just what it was that they did when they dealt with patients.

Last fall, for example, he'd left them with the practice while he attended a psychiatric congress in San Francisco where he and his fellow psychiatrists—or at least that sizable minority among them who were, like himself, practicing shamans—had gotten together in a very carefully locked and guarded auditorium, there to put on their shamanizing costumes so they could steal people's souls and introduce malefic objects into their bodies, thus assuring themselves and their less aware colleagues of an adequate supply of patients for the coming year. He'd learned quite a bit about the proper use of quartz crystals from two young aboriginal shamans attending their first international congress, but had done as poorly as usual in the competitions: The very gifts that made him so good at recovering souls no matter how well his colleagues hid them made it difficult for him to recognize those hiding places where they in turn would be unable to discover the souls *he* hid. But he'd had a good time drinking Ripple and Thunderbird and Boone's Farm Apple Wine from stained paper bags on street corners and in Golden Gate Park, where he and most of the other psychiatrists attending the congress had slept when the weather permitted, and by the time he'd returned to Paris Liz had lost all the weight she'd put on since the trip before.

But it was almost the end of March now, time to start readying himself for his next month-long separation from her and from his comfortable life as Julien de Saint-Hilaire. He had to retrieve the lost, strayed, and stolen souls of those he intended to cure, and damage or find new hiding places for the souls of those patients he intended to retain for further treatment.

And besides, Liz was starting to get fat again. It was a vicious circle: They both loved to eat but she couldn't keep up with him without putting on weight, and the fatter she got the more insecure she felt about her appearance, so the more she ate to comfort herself. She was already back to the stage where she was sneaking out to eat napoleons and lemon tarts and exotic ice creams and sherbets in three or four different tea salons every afternoon, doing it all so surreptitiously that if he didn't know beforehand where she was planning to go, it could take him a whole afternoon of searching to catch up with her; in another month or so she'd be getting worried enough to start looking to other men for reassurance again.

And that was something he couldn't, and wouldn't, allow. He had very precise plans for his heir, a boy whose soul was even now undergoing its third year of prenatal preparation in one of the invisible eagle's nests high up on the Eiffel Tower where since the turn of the century the most powerful French politicians and generals had received the training and charisma and made the contacts necessary to ready them for their subsequent roles. And after all the years he'd spent readying Liz to bear his son he wasn't going to let her negate his efforts with another man's seed. She had her pastries, her wines, cognacs, and sleeping pills, her clothing and her restaurants, her money and her social position, and she'd have to stay content with them for at least the next four years, until his son was born.

On the way to his office he stopped off at his second apartment. It was a one-room windowless garret on the rue de Condé that had obviously been somebody's attic at one time. It now boasted a tiny brick fireplace and chimney that he'd fitted with an elaborate and deadly labyrinth which enabled him to enter and leave as a bird without permitting entrance by any other shamans. He picked up some of the pills he kept for Liz. His supply was almost exhausted: He'd have to write the old Indian in Arizona (John Henry Two Feathers Thomas Thompson, whose father had toured with Buffalo Bill's Wild West Show before starting his own medicine show with a white barker for a front) again and get some more.

He put on his two caps—for something as trivial as what he was about to do he didn't really need the power the rest of is costume would have provided him with—and became a pigeon with orange eyes and naked pink legs. He negotiated the chimney maze, making sure the spirits who guarded it recognized him in the form he'd adopted, to emerge on the roof and fly back to his apartment overlooking the Pare Monceau. He and Liz had been up very late making love the night before, with only a brief pause at two in the morning for the cold buffet he'd had his catering service prepare them, and she was still asleep, even snoring slightly in the way she did when she'd had too much to drink or had taken too many sleeping pills the night before, all of which made things easier for him. As did the fact that he'd left the cage with the two mynah birds in it covered when he'd left the apartment. Liz had bought the birds at the Sunday bird market on the Île de la Cité while he'd been away on his last trip and the birds had never learned to tolerate his presence in any of the forms he took. But though they were alert enough to detect the fact that he wasn't what he seemed to be as either a bird or a man, they were too stupid to realize that despite their dark cage the night was over. So he didn't have to worry about the birds making enough noise to awaken Liz.

He slipped in through the window he'd left open in the master bedroom, plucked Liz's sleeping soul from her body and bruised it with his beak in a way he knew from experience would do her no lasting harm but which would give her migraines for the next few weeks. Then he returned her still-sleeping soul to her body and flew back to his garret, where he took off his caps and locked them away in the sky-blue steel steamer trunk he kept them in. He sprayed his hair with a kerosene-smelling children's delousing spray, to take care of the head-lice that made their home in the inner cap, then used a dry shampoo to get rid of both the spray and the smell from the cap itself. He finally locked the door behind him, making sure when he did so that the spirits guarding the apartment would continue to deny entry to anyone but himself, then went back down the five flights of stairs as Julien de Saint-Hilaire, checked with the concierge a moment, and caught a taxi to his office.

He checked with Jean-Luc and Michel when he arrived, but found that except for a matter concerning a long-time patient who was now more than a year behind on his bills and who showed no signs of being ready to pay (which wasn't their responsibility, anyway), they had everything more or less under control. Too much under control, even: Jean-Luc especially was doing those patients he worked with more good than Eminescu wanted them done, but there was no way to get the younger psychiatrist to stop curing them without explaining to him the true nature of his profession and just what it was he was really doing to get the results he was getting, and that was something Eminescu was not yet ready to let him know; perhaps in another twenty or twenty-five years, when he himself would have to begin thinking about conserving his force.

He sat down behind his desk, pretended to busy himself with one patient's case history while he thought about what to do to that patient who was refusing to pay and waited for Liz to phone him.

The call came perhaps half an hour later. She said she'd just awakened and all she could think about was how soon he was going to be going away, and did he know yet exactly when he was going to have to leave for Japan? He told her he'd received confirmation on his flights, and that he'd be leaving in another six days, on a Monday, very early in the morning. She told him that she had an awful headache, it had started as soon as she'd awakened and realized he was going to be leaving, and she asked him to bring her something for the pain, since it was obviously his fault she had the headache because he was going away and she always felt sick and tired and alone and unhappy whenever he left her for more than a few days. He said he'd bring her some of the painkillers he'd given her the last time, the ones that didn't leave her too groggy, and she said, fine, but try to make them a little stronger this time, Julien, even if they do make me a bit groggy. He said he would, but that if she was really feeling that bad perhaps it would be better if he came home early, he could cancel all his afternoon appointments. She said, no, that wouldn't be necessary, but if he'd meet her for lunch he could give her the pills then, she'd pick out the restaurant and make the reservations, come by to pick him up when it was time. About one o'clock?

He said that one o'clock would be perfect. When she arrived he gave her the first two of the old Indian's pills, and on the way to the restaurant soothed her headache. For that he didn't even need his caps, he had enough power left over from just having worn them earlier.

It was an excellent restaurant near the Comédie Française, on rue Richelieu, and he was enormously hungry—flying demanded a great deal of energy; the iron with which his bones had been reinforced and tied together after his initiatory dismemberment was heavy and hard to lift when he was a bird, for all that the iron-wrapped bones gave him the vitality and endurance of a much younger man when in human form—and both he and Liz enjoyed their meal. Afterward he dropped her off outside Notre Dame (where she had to meet some friends of her aunt's whom she'd been unable to get out of promising to show around), then went back to his apartment on the rue de Condé and put on his entire costume: the raccoon-skin cap with the snap-on tail that John Henry had given him and which he kept hidden under the over-large shapeless felt hat, the greasy false beard and hair (though in one sense they weren't really false at all, since they and the skin to which they were still attached had both been at one time his: more of the old Indian's work), the multiple layers of thermal underwear he wore under the faded work blues that were in turn covered by the old brown leather military trench coat with the missing buttons and half the left sleeve gone, the three pink plastic shopping bags from Monoprix filled with what looked like rags, but weren't, and the two pairs of crusted blue socks he wore under his seven-league work shoes (the ones he had specially made for him in Austria to look as though they were coming apart), so he could trace the pills' progress through Liz's system, and help them along when and if necessary.

It was raining by the time he'd completed his preparations and had begun beating his tambourine and hopping up and down, but he didn't feel like doing anything major about the weather even though he'd planned to go home as a pigeon again. So by the time he arrived back at the apartment he was very wet. But that gave him an excuse to remain perched there on the bedroom windowsill, ignoring the nasty looks the mynah birds were giving him while he ruffled his feathers and looked indignant.

Liz had already gotten rid of her aunt's friends, as he'd been sure she would; she was on the phone again, trying to find someone to go tea-salon hopping with her for the rest of the afternoon. She was having trouble: Very few of her woman friends could keep up with her pastry and sweets consumption and still look the way that Liz demanded the people she was seen with look, while Eminescu had for several years now made a practice of discouraging any and all of her male friends, even the homosexuals, who showed any tendency to spend too much, or even too attentive, time with her.

Not, of course, that he'd ever done so in any way that either Liz or her admirers could have ever realized had anything to do with her husband. The men in question just always had something go horribly wrong when they were with her—sudden, near fatal attacks of choking or vomiting; running into old wives or girlfriends they'd abandoned pregnant; being mistaken for notorious Armenian terrorists or Cypriot neo-nazi bombers by the CRS and so ending up clubbed unconscious and jailed incommunicado; other things of the same sort—with the result that Liz never had any *fun* with them, and began avoiding even those few hyper-persistent or genuinely lovestruck victims who kept trying to see her anyway.

Which reminded him: It was time for her to get her headache back. As a former veterinary student he was quite familiar with Pavlovian conditioning—had, in fact, been writing his thesis on the ways it had been used to train the attack dogs used by the government in quelling the then-recent Polish workers' insurrection when he'd been forced to flee Romania—and his spiritual experience in later years had proven to him how useful a correct application of its basic principles could be to a shaman like himself. Thus, whenever Liz did something he approved of he rewarded her for it, whenever she did something he disapproved of he punished her, but always in ways that would seem to her to be in some way the direct result of her behavior, and not of any interference or judgment on his part. And that, finally, was the rationale for the use of the pills he gave her whenever he went away: Not only did they keep her properly subdued in his absence and insure that she'd have taken off her excess weight by the time he returned and restored her to normal, but they made her so miserable that when he did return she equated his presence—the secondary stimulus—with the primary stimulus of her renewed health and vitality in the same way she'd learned to equate his absence with her misery.

It was all very rational and scientific, a fact on which he prided himself. Too many of his colleagues were little better than witch-doctors.

"You're my whole happiness," Liz had told him once. "My only reason for staying alive." And that, to be sure, was how he wanted things.

It had taken her five phone calls but she'd finally found someone: Marie-Claude had agreed to accompany her, and they were going to meet at the tea room they liked on the Île St. Louis where the ice cream was so good. And the sun was coming out again. He flew there to wait for them.

From his perch in the tree across the street from the tea salon he could see them easily enough as they entered together, though when they sat down away from the window he had to cock his head just right to watch them through the walls. They both ordered ice cream—Bertillon chocolate, coffee, and chestnut for Liz, the same for Marie-Claude but with coconut in place of the coffee—and while they were waiting for the waitress to bring it convinced each other that it would be all right to have some sherbets with their coffee afterward.

Eminescu waited until Liz's first few swallows of chocolate were reaching her stomach to cock his head at the angle that let him see what was going on inside her.

Her stomach acids and digestive enzymes had already dissolved the pills and liberated the encysted bladder worms, and these in turn were reacting to the acids and enzymes by evaginating—turning themselves inside out, as though they'd been one-finger gloves with the fingers pushed in, but with the fingers now popping out again. Once the young tapeworms (as he'd learned to call them at UCLA, and it was a better name for them than the French *vers solitaires*, because these worms at least were far from solitary) had their scolexes, head-sections, free they could use the suckers and hooks on them to attach themselves to the walls of Liz's intestines, there to begin growing by pushing out new anterior segments—though he'd be back to deal with them before any of the worms was more than five or so meters long, and thus before any of the worms had reached its full sexual maturity.

Three specimens each of three kinds of tapeworm—*Taenia solium, Taenia saginata,* and *Diphyllobothrium latum,* the pork, beef, and fish tapeworms, respectively—he allowed to hook and sucker themselves to Liz's intestinal walls, though not without first ensuring that the individuals he favored would all be fairly slow-growing, as well as unlikely to excrete excessive amounts of those toxic waste products peculiar to their respective species. The myriad other worms whose encysted forms the pills had contained he killed, reaching out from his perch in the tree to pluck them from her intestinal walls with his beak, pinch off and kill their voracious little souls. It was all very well controlled, all very scientific, with nothing left to chance.

He watched her the rest of the afternoon, at that and three other tea salons, to make sure the nine worms he'd selected for her would do her no more damage than he'd planned for them to do, and that none of the other worms the pills had contained had escaped his attention and survived.

When at last he returned to the apartment on the rue de Condé he was weak with hunger. He took a quick shower and ate a choucroute at a nearby brasserie before going back to his office to make sure nothing unexpected had come up in his absence.

And every day until the time came for him to leave, he checked Liz two or three times, to make sure the worms now growing so rapidly inside her would do no lasting harm. He valued Liz a great deal, enjoyed her youth and spontaneity fully as much as he valued the son she was going to bear him, and he had no desire to be unnecessarily cruel to her.

On the morning he'd chosen to leave he went to his second apartment and checked on her one last time as she showered—thinner already and beautiful for all the fatigue on her face and in her posture—then returned to the windowless room and resumed his human form. He was hungry, but for the next month he was Eminescu Eliade again, and there was no way he could use Julien de Saint-Hilaire's money to pay for as much as a merguez-and-fries sandwich from one of the window-front Tunisian restaurants on the rue St. André des Arts without destroying much of his costume's power.

The rat he was to follow was waiting for him as arranged at the bottom of the stairs, behind the trash cans. He put it in one of his plastic bags, where it promptly made a nest for itself out of the rags that weren't really rags. Then he went out to beg the money for the three things he'd need to get started: the bottles of wine he'd have to share with his fellow shamans as long as he remained aboveground, the first-class métro ticket he'd need to enter the labyrinths coexistent with the Parisian métro system, and the *terrine de foie de volailles au poivre vert* from Coesnon's which the rat demanded he feed it each time it guided him through the city's subway labyrinths.

There were a lot of clochards he didn't recognize behind the Marché and on the streets nearby, even a blond-haired threesome—two bearded young men and a girl with her hair in braids—who looked more like hitchhiking German or Scandinavian students temporarily short of money than like real clochards, for all that they seemed to know most of the others and be on good terms with them. What it added up to was an unwelcome reminder that he'd been spending too much time either abroad or as Julien de Saint-Hilaire, and not nearly enough staying in touch with his city and its spirit world—and that was an error that could well prove fatal to him unless he took steps to correct it. He'd have to stay in Paris that October after all, and miss the Australian congress that had had him so excited ever since he'd begun to learn the kinds of things one could do with quartz crystals.

It took him five days to get the money he needed: He was out of practice at begging and every few hours, of course, he had to put most of what he'd earned toward the wine he shared with the others. And Coesnon's had tripled their prices during the last year alone. But by the fifth evening he had what he needed, so he walked down the rue de l'Ancienne Comédie to the rue Dauphine, where he bought the four-hundred-and-fifty-franc terrine despite the staff's and other customers' horrified disapproval when he squeezed himself and his bulging sacks into the narrow charcuterie, knocking a platter of blood sausage with apples to the floor in the process, then spent another four hours listening to the mutterings and arguments of the future shamans awaiting birth in the hundreds of tiers of invisible pigeons' nests that completely covered the green bronze statue of Henri IV astride his horse, there on its pedestal atop the little fenced-off step pyramid on the Pont Neuf. But there was nothing useful to be heard—Tabarin and his pompous master Mondor arguing as usual in the nest they shared, Napoleon pleading to be rescued from the tiny statuette of himself that the overly zealous Bonapartist who'd been commissioned to cast Henri's statue had hidden in the king's right arm, thus inadvertently imprisoning his hero's spirit there until such time as someone should destroy the statuette or rescue him—and so after listening a while he proceeded on diagonally across the Île de la Cité to Chatelet where he entered the métro system.

He bought himself a first-class ticket and pretended to drop it as he went to insert it in the machine so he could release the rat. It scurried away from him through the thick crowds and he had to run after it as soon as the machine disgorged his enigmatically stamped ticket, plastic bags, rags and leather overcoat flapping as he ran. Four or five times he lost sight of the rat—once because some fifteen- or sixteen-year-olds thought it would be fun to trip him and see how long they could keep him from getting back to his feet before somebody stopped them—but each time he found the rat again and at last it led him in through one of the urinals to the first of the labyrinth's inner turnings. There he fed it the first half of the terrine and the stamped métro ticket.

The corridors were less crowded when he emerged from the urinal, the light dimmer and pinker, and with each subsequent turning away from the public corridors into the secret ways which led through the land of the dead there were more and more of the German shepherds whose powerful bodies housed the souls of those few dead who'd been granted leave of the Undercity for a day and a night in return for guarding Paris itself, fewer and fewer people, and those few only the dying and mentally ill, the North African blacks who worked as maintenance men and cleaners in the métro system, and shamans like himself—plus once a politician whose name he couldn't recall but to whom he'd made the proper ritual obeisances anyway.

When he regained his feet and wiped the filth from his forehead he found the corridor around him had changed yet again. The murky and polluted bottom waters of the Seine flowed sluggishly past and around him without touching him, and his guide now wore the baggy bright-red shorts with the two big gold buttons on the front that told him he'd finally escaped the outer world entirely and entered the land of the dead.

He fed the rat the rest of the terrine and began retracing the route he knew should take him back to the place where he'd hidden the soul of the first of those patients whom he intended to have make a miraculous recovery upon his return, a retired general suffering from the delusion that he was a young and bearded bouquiniste making his living selling subversive literature and antique pornographic postcards from a bookstall by the Seine.

But Hell had changed, changed radically and inexplicably in the year he'd spent away from it, and it took him almost seven weeks before he was able to escape it again by a route that led up and out through the sewer system. Because someone, somehow, had found his patients' souls where he'd buried them in the river mud and filth, had dug them up and left in their place small, vicious but somehow indistinct, creatures that had attacked him and tried to devour his soul. He'd been strong enough to fight them off, though they'd vanished before the mud cloud they'd stirred up had settled and he'd had a chance to get a closer look at them. But though he'd found his patients' souls and recovered them from their new hiding places without overmuch trouble, none of his usual contacts among the dead had been willing or able to tell him who his enemy was, or what the things that had attacked him had been.

He'd planned to stay Eminescu Eliade for a while after his return to the surface so he could try to locate his enemy where he knew the man had to be hiding, among the clochards who had not yet achieved professional recognition in a second identity (because while professional ethics allowed stealing other psychiatrists' patients' souls, even encouraged it as tending to keep everyone alert and doing their best, leaving creatures such as the things that had attacked him to devour a fellow psychiatrist's soul was specifically forbidden by the Ordre des médecins)—but when he took the form of a pigeon and returned to the apartment he shared with Liz to see how she was doing and make sure the tapeworms in her intestines hadn't done her any real harm in the extra weeks, ready to perhaps even kill one or two of them if they were getting a little too long, he saw that something further had gone wrong, horribly wrong.

Liz was in the kitchen in her striped robe, spooning chestnut purée from a one-kilo can frantically into her mouth as though she were starving, and his first impression was that he'd never before seen her looking so disgustingly fat and sloppy. But then he realized that though her belly was distended and she looked as though she'd neither slept nor washed in a few days she was if anything skinnier than she'd been when he'd seen her last. Much skinnier. And that the swollen puffiness that so disfigured her face came from the fact that she was crying, and that her legs—her legs that had always been so long and smooth and beautiful, so tawny despite her naturally ash-blond hair that she'd always refused to wear any sort of tinted or patterned stockings, even when her refusal had cost her work—her legs were streaked with long, twitching fat blue veins. Varicose veins, as though she were a fat and flaccid woman in her sixties.

He cocked his pigeon's head to the right and looked in through her abdominal walls to see what was happening within her intestines, in through the skin and muscles of her legs to understand what was going on there.

Only to find that the tapeworms had reached sexual maturity despite all the careful checking he'd done on them before his departure, and that not only had their intertwined ten-meter bodies almost completely choked her swollen and distended intestines, but that their hermaphroditic anterior segments had already begun producing eggs. And those eggs—instead of having been excreted as they should have been, to hatch only when and if stimulated by the distinctive digestive juices of the pigs, cows, or fish whose particular constellation of acids and enzymes alone could provide their species of worm with its necessary stimuli—those eggs were hatching almost immediately, while they were still within Liz's digestive tract, and the minute spherical embryos were anchoring themselves to the intestinal walls with the six long hooks they each sported, then boring through the walls to enter her bloodstream, through which they then let themselves be carried down into her legs. There, in the smaller vessels in her calves and thighs, they were anchoring themselves and beginning to grow, not encysting as normal tapeworm embryos would have done, but instead developing into myriads of long, filament-thin worms that were slowly climbing their way from their anchor points up through her circulatory system toward her heart as they lengthened.

His enemy, whoever his enemy was, had planned the whole farce with his patients' stolen but easily recoverable souls and the things that had been lying in wait for him in their place just to keep him occupied while *he* played around with the worms in Liz, modified them for his own purposes. He must have had her under observation long enough to have known about the fear of all other doctors but himself that Eminescu had long ago conditioned into her, known that he'd have a free hand with her until Eminescu got back. And if Eminescu'd stayed trapped in the secret ways even a few days longer she might well have lost her feet, perhaps even her legs, to gangrene and so been ruined as the potential mother of his son. A week or two beyond that and she could have been dead.

She was constantly moving her legs, twitching them as she gorged herself on the purée, kneading her calves and thighs. Keeping the circulation going as best she could despite the filament worms waving like strands of hungry kelp in her veins, the worms that had so far only impeded, and not yet blocked, the flow of blood through her legs.

It was all very scientific and precise, masterfully devised. Whoever'd done it could have easily killed her, done so with far less effort and imagination than he'd expended on producing her present condition. The whole thing was a challenge, could only be a challenge, traditional in intent for all that the way it had been done was new to him. And what the challenge said was, I want your practice and your position and everything else you have, and I can take it away from you, I've already proved that anything you can do I can do better, and I'm going to go ahead and do it unless you can stop me before I kill you. The challenge was undoubtedly on file with the Ordre des médecins, though there'd be no way for Eminescu to get a look at the records and learn who his challenger was:

The relevant laws were older than France or Rome, and were zealously enforced.

But what he could do was take care of Liz and keep her from being damaged any further while he tried to learn more about his opponent. He reached out with his beak, twisted the souls of the filament worms in Liz's legs dead. They were much tougher than he'd anticipated, surprisingly hard to kill, but when at last they were all dead he pulled them carefully free of the blood vessels in which they'd anchored themselves, pulled them out through Liz's muscles and skin without doing her any further damage, then patched the damaged veins and arteries with tissues he yanked from the legs of a group of Catholic schoolgirls who happened to be passing in the street. They were young: They'd recover soon enough. The stagnant and polluted blood, slimy with the worms' waste products, began to flow freely through her system again.

He watched Liz closely for a while to make sure the waste products weren't concentrated or toxic enough to be dangerous to her in the time it would take her liver or other organs to filter them from her blood. When he was sure that any harm they might do her would be trivial enough to be ignored he reached out to take and squeeze the souls of the tapeworms knotted together and clogging her intestines, snatched himself back just in time to save himself when he recognized them: the creatures that had attacked him in the land of the dead. But fearsome though they were on the spiritual plane—and now that he had a chance to examine them better he saw that their souls were not those of tapeworms but of some sort of lampreys, those long eel-like parasitic vertebrates whose round sucking mouths contain circular rows of rasping teeth with which they bore their way in through the scales of the fish they've attached themselves to, so as to suck out the fish's insides and eventually kill it in the process—physically they were still only tapeworms despite their modified reproductive systems. And that meant that he could destroy them by physical—medical—means. Quinacrine hydrochloride and aspidium oleoresin should be more than sufficient, if there hadn't been something better developed recently that he wasn't aware of yet. But to make use of any kind of medicine he'd have to resume his identity as Julien de Saint-Hilaire, if only long enough to return home, soothe Liz and prescribe for her, then make sure she was following the treatment he suggested and that it was working for her.

But before he did that he had to try to learn a little more about his challenger, so he returned to his apartment on the rue de Condé and resumed his human form. His efforts in the Undercity and just now as a bird had totally depleted his body's reserves of fat and energy; he was gaunt and trembling, so that those passersby he approached after making his way down the back stairs to the street who weren't frightened away by his diseased look were unusually generous. After he'd made the phone call that confirmed that, yes, an official challenge had been registered against Julien de Saint-Hilaire, he was able to buy not only the wine he needed to approach his fellow clochards but some food from the soup kitchen behind the Marché as well.

He slept that night in the métro, curled up on the benches with three other clochards, one of whom was a woman, though as much a shaman as himself or the other two. The woman had a bottle of cheap rosé; they passed it back and forth while they talked, and he listened to them while saying as little himself as possible, trying to find out if they knew anything about his enemy without revealing what he was doing, but either they knew nothing about his opponent or they were siding with him against Eminescu and keeping their knowledge hidden. Which was quite possible: He'd seen it happen that way a few times before, with older shamans who were particularly arrogant and disliked, though he'd never imagined it could happen to him.

The next day he spent sitting on a bench on the Pont Neuf, panhandling just enough to justify his presence there while he tried to learn something from the spirits in their nests on the statue of Henri IV. He even promised to free Napoleon from the statuette in which the former Emperor was trapped and promised him a place in one of the highest eagle's nests on the Eiffel Tower from which he'd be able to make a triumphant return to politics, if only he'd tell Eminescu his enemy's name or something that would help him find him. But Napoleon had been imprisoned there in the statuette in King Henri's statue's right arm pleading with and ranting at the shamans who refused to so much as acknowledge his existence for too many years and he'd become completely insane: He refused to reply to Eminescu's questions, continued his habitual pleas and promises even after Eminescu had begun hurting him and threatening to silence his voice forever unless he responded rationally.

Eminescu finally left him there, still ranting and pleading: It would have been pointless to waste any more of his forces in carrying out the threats he'd made. He had enough money to pay his entry to the Eiffel Tower, so he flew there as a pigeon, cursing the unaccustomed heaviness of his iron-wrapped bones, then transformed himself back into a clochard in the bushes and went up to the observation deck in the elevator, there found his son and General de Gaulle in their respective nests and asked their advice. De Gaulle—perhaps because the nest in which he was preparing his triumphal return was next to Eminescu's son's nest and the two had come to know each other fairly well— was always polite to Eminescu, wherein the other politicians and military men, able to sense the fact that he wasn't truly French and themselves chauvinistic to the core, refused to even speak to him.

But neither de Gaulle nor his son knew anything useful, and his son seemed weaker and less coherent than the last time Eminescu had spoken to him, as though the forces conspiring against his birth were already beginning to make him fade. Still, at least he was safe from any sort of direct attack: The invisible eagles that guarded his nest allowed no one not of their own kind to approach the tower in anything but human form, and would have detected and killed any mere shaman like Eminescu or his enemy who'd attempted to put on an eagle's form to gain entry.

He returned to the rue de Condé so he could beat his tambourine and sing and dance without danger of interruption, and thus summon the maximum possible power. It was night by the time he felt ready, so he took the form of an owl and returned to the apartment overlooking the Parc Monceau, perched outside the bedroom window, terrifying the mynah birds, and killed the tapeworm embryos that had made their way into Liz's bloodstream again. It was easier this time: He had a lot more strength available to him as an owl, though it was harder to hold the form and he paid for that strength later on, when he regained his humanity.

He examined the worms in Liz's intestines with the owl's sharper eyes to see if there was some way he could destroy them without harming Liz or risking his own safety, saw that even as an owl he didn't have enough concentrated spiritual strength at his disposal to destroy all the worms together. There would have been a way to do it with quartz crystals, replacing those sections of her intestines to which the tapeworms had anchored themselves with smooth crystal so they'd lose their purchase and be eliminated from her body, but he was far from skillful enough yet to carry out the operation without killing her, since loose quartz crystals in her body would be like just so many obsidian knives, and he lacked the experience needed to mold the quartz to her flesh and infuse it with her spirit so as to make it a living part of her.

He could have done it if he'd had a chance to go to that Australian convention he'd planned to attend in the fall. As it was he'd have to try to find another way.

That night he slept under the Pont Neuf on some sheets of cardboard a previous sleeper had left behind him, satisfying the tremendous hunger his efforts as an owl had awakened in him as best he could from the garbage cans behind Coesnon's and some of the other gourmet boutiques on the rue Dauphine.

The next morning he flew to his offices on Avenue Victor Hugo as a pigeon and spent a long time watching Jean-Luc and Michel. It had been months since he'd last been there as anything but Julien de Saint-Hilaire and he wanted to make sure that neither of them had developed the kind of power his challenger so obviously had. They were, after all, the two persons most likely to covet his position and the two most prepared to fill it when he was gone, despite the fact that a challenge from either of them would have been a clear violation of medical ethics and that his challenger had registered his challenge with the Ordre des médecins in thoroughly proper fashion.

He watched them working, soothing souls in pain, coaxing lost or strayed souls back to the bodies they'd left. They were both small, slim and dark, both immensely sincere, and they were both fumbling around blindly in the spirit realm for souls that they could have recovered in instants if they'd known what it was they were really doing. No, their instincts were good, but they were still just what he'd always thought them to be, talented amateurs with no idea of the true nature of their talents, even though those talents seemed to be growing, in Jean-Luc's case in particular.

Since he was there Eminescu used the opportunity to undo some of the good Michel had done a young schizophrenic he had no intention of seeing recover, then returned to the rue de Condé, and from there, as Julien de Saint-Hilaire, to his apartment overlooking the park, stopping only briefly on the way to buy and eat seven hundred and fifty grams of dark chocolates.

Liz was asleep, passed out half dressed on the living room sofa with a partially eaten meal cold on a tray on the table beside her. The kitchen was littered with empty and half-empty cans and bottles.

The servants were all gone and he knew Liz well enough to be sure she'd sent them away, unable to bear the idea of having anyone who knew her see what had happened to her legs, just as she would have been unable to face being examined by another doctor.

She twitched in her sleep, shifting the position of her legs on the sofa, then moved them back the way they'd been. The blue veins in her thighs and calves looked perhaps a little less fat and swollen than they'd seemed when he'd first found out what'd happened to her, but only slightly so: Even though he'd gotten rid of the worms in the veins themselves and replaced a tiny fraction of the damaged vessels it would take a long time for the rest to regain their elasticity. He might even have to replace them altogether.

He'd stopped at a pharmacy run by a minor shaman he knew on the way over to order the various medicines he'd need to deal with the tapeworms as well as a comprehensive selection of those sleeping and pain pills which Liz had a tendency to abuse when he failed to keep her under close enough supervision but which would serve now to keep her more or less anesthetized and incapable of worrying too much for the next few weeks, until his present troubles were over one way or another. And there was at least the consolation of knowing that if he did succeed in discovering his opponent's identity and destroying him, the other's attack on Liz would have served to further reinforce the way Eminescu'd conditioned her to associate his every absence with unhappiness and physical misery, his return with health and pleasure.

He picked up the phone, intending to awaken her with a faked call to the pharmacy so as to make it seem as though he'd just entered, taken one look at her lying there with her legs all swollen and marbled with twitching blue veins and had immediately and accurately diagnosed her condition and so known exactly what he'd have to do without needing to subject her to the indignity of further examinations or tests. It was what she expected of him: Liz had always had a childlike faith in doctors and medicine for all her fear of them. But at the last moment he put the phone down again and went back into the bedroom to take a careful look at the two mynah birds in their cage.

His presence alarmed them: They started hopping nervously back and forth between their perches, making little hushed cries of alarm as if afraid that if they were any louder they'd draw his attention to them. But hushed as their cries were they were still making more noise than he wanted them to, so he closed the heavy door behind him to cut off the sound and keep them from awakening Liz. Without his cap and costume he couldn't examine them to find out if they were just the rather stupid birds they appeared to be or if one or even both of them were spies for his enemy, perhaps that enemy himself in bird-form. (But could two shamans together challenge a third? He had the impression it was forbidden, but that there was perhaps a way for a challenger to make use of a second shaman's aid.) In any case, the mynah birds were living creatures over whom he exercised no control and which had been introduced into his home with neither his knowledge nor his permission at a time when he'd been away, and he couldn't trust them.

He opened the cage door, reached in quickly with both hands and grabbed the birds before they could escape or make more than one startled squeak apiece, then wrung their necks and threw them out the window, aiming the bodies far enough to the right so that Liz wouldn't see them if she just took a casual look out the window. He could retrieve them later and take them back with him to examine more closely at his other apartment before Liz'd had a chance to leave the house and discover them dead.

He left the cage door open and opened the window slightly, to provide an explanation for their absence when Liz noticed they were gone, then covered the cage to keep her from noticing it immediately.

He went back into the living room. Liz had turned over again and was scratching her right calf in her sleep, leaving angry red scratches all up and down it. He played out the scene he'd planned beforehand with the faked call to the pharmacy, reassured her as soon as the sound of his voice awakened her: He was back, he'd known what had happened to her as soon as he took one look at her, it was a side-effect of certain illegal hormones that people had been injecting dairy cows with recently and which had been showing up, for some as yet unexplained reason, in high concentrations only in certain crèmes pâtissières used in such things as napoleons and eclairs, and he knew how to cure her condition, it wasn't even really anything to worry about, she wouldn't need surgery and in a few weeks she'd be completely cured, there wouldn't be any scars or anything else to show for the episode but some unpleasant memories, her legs would be as beautiful as before and she shouldn't worry, she should just trust him.

She'd burst into tears as soon as she'd seen him there, was holding on to him and crying with relief by the time he'd finished telling her not to worry, that everything was going to be all right.

The bell rang: the pharmacy, one of the few in Paris willing to deliver, with the medicines he'd ordered. He paid the delivery man, tipping him extravagantly as always, then went back into the bedroom where Liz'd run to hide herself when she heard the bell and gave her two sleeping pills and a pain pill. Only when she was completely groggy and he'd tucked her into bed did he explain his absence, telling her about the two weeks he'd spent completely isolated in a tiny village in the mountains where the Japanese government was carrying out an experimental mental health program and from which it had been impossible to phone her, though he didn't understand how she could have failed to receive the long, long telegram he'd sent her from Tokyo after he'd tried so many times to get her on the phone without once succeeding.

She started nodding out near the end of the explanation, as he'd intended: She'd never remember exactly what it was that he'd told her but only that he'd explained things, and he could always modify his story later and then tell her that the modified story was exactly the same as the one he'd told her before. Though that was probably just an unnecessary precaution: She always believed even the most implausible stories he told her, just as she seemed to have believed his story about the hormones.

He got her to take the various pills, powders, and liquids he'd obtained to treat the tapeworms with—there'd been a number of new medicines he'd been totally unaware of on the market, yet another reminder of how out of touch he'd been allowing himself to become—then gave her two more sleeping pills to make sure she'd stay unconscious for a while. He waited until she was asleep and snoring raggedly, then left.

He retrieved the two mynah birds from the bushes, put them in a plastic sack and caught a taxi to his other apartment, where he put on his costume to examine them.

But the birds were just mynah birds, as far as he could tell when he took them apart, and when he returned once again to his other apartment as a pigeon and flew in through the bathroom window he'd left open for himself he saw that the medicines he'd used were having no effect whatsoever on the tapeworms—no effect, that is, except to stimulate them to a frantically accelerated production of new eggs.

Once again his enemy had anticipated him, known what his next move would be long before he himself had done so and had arranged to use it against him. He was being laughed at, played for a fool, a clown.

But for all the anger that knowledge awakened in him there was nothing he could do about it yet. He had to stay there beside Liz on the bed for hours, stalking nervously back and forth on his obscenely pink legs as he plucked embryo after embryo from her bloodstream and destroyed them, until he was so hungry and exhausted he could barely keep himself conscious. Then he had no choice but to return to his other apartment—resting every two or three blocks in a tree or on a window ledge—so he could resume his identity as Julien de Saint-Hilaire long enough to pay for a large meal in a restaurant.

He ate an immense meal at an Italian restaurant a few blocks away, followed it with a second, equally large, meal at a bad Chinese restaurant he usually avoided and felt better.

He tried telephoning John Henry Two Feathers Thomas Thompson but was told that the old Indian's number was no longer in service and that there was no new listing for him. Eminescu didn't know if that meant he was dead, or had moved, or had just obtained an unlisted number. But there was no one Eminescu could trust who lived near enough to his former teacher to contact him, and he didn't have the time to fly to America and try to find him himself, either as a bird or by taking a plane as Julien de Saint-Hilaire. So he sent the old Indian a long telegram, and hoped that he'd not only get it, but that he'd have something to say that would help Eminescu.

He bought a sandwich from a sidewalk stand and ate it on the way back to the rue de Condé apartment, then resumed his caps and costume and returned to the Parc Monceau apartment yet one more time as a pigeon to try to deal with the embryos, yet despite the huge meals he'd eaten and the hours he'd spent in his other identity he was still too hungry and too exhausted to keep it up for more than a few hours before the embryos started getting past him despite everything he could do. And the worms in Liz's intestines seemed to be producing their eggs ever faster now, as though the process he'd begun when he gave her the medicines was still accelerating.

Defeated and furious, he returned to his other apartment, passed out as soon as he regained his human form. When he reawakened he barely had enough strength to crawl over to the sink where he'd left the two dismembered mynah birds and strip the meat from their bones and devour it.

There was no way he could hope to save Liz if he continued the way he was going. All he was really doing was destroying himself, using up all the forces which he'd need to protect himself from his opponent when it finally came to a direct attack on him. For a moment he was tempted to just abandon Liz, give up his identity as Julien de Saint-Hilaire and let her die or be taken over by the challenger when he moved into the Julien de Saint-Hilaire role in Eminescu's place. But he'd come too far, was too close to the true power and security he knew his son would provide him with, the assurance that he himself would be born in one of the Eiffel Tower's eagles' nests, to abandon everything now. Besides, Liz still pleased him, though it wasn't just that, just the kind of sentimental weakness that he knew would destroy him if he ever let it get the upper hand. No, what mattered was that Liz was *his,* his to dispose of and no one else's, and his pride was such that he could never allow anyone else to take her away from him. That pride he knew for his strength, as all sentimentality was weakness: Without his pride he was nothing.

He had to save her life, but he couldn't do it as a pigeon, nor even as an owl. Yet they were in the heart of Paris; the only other animal forms he could put on safely—cats, perhaps ducks or other small birds, insects, rats, and mice—would be equally ineffectual. If he tried to put on an eagle's form the invisible eagles atop the Eiffel Tower would detect him and destroy him for his presumption, for all that he had a son they were raising as one of their own; if he put on a wolf's or a dog's form the dead who patrolled the city as German shepherds would bring him down, for only they were allowed to use canine form, and Paris had for centuries been forbidden to wolves. And if he tried to put on a bear's body—a bear's form would be ideal, as far as he knew he was the only shaman in France who knew how to adopt it and there'd be no way his enemy could have been prepared to deal with it, but there was also no way he could shamble the huge, conspicuous body across Paris undetected, nor anyone he could trust to transport it for him, and for all the force that being a bear would give him, the dogs would still be able to bring him down if they attacked as a pack, and he'd be vulnerable as well to humans with guns.

Unless he was willing to give up the complete separation of his two identities which he'd always maintained for his own protection, and took his costume and tambourine with him to the other apartment, and made the transformation there. The problem wasn't just the basically trivial difficulty of explaining his clochard-self's presence to Liz and the domestics (and that, anyway, would be no problem at all with the servants gone and Liz full of pills) but that the more people who knew he was both Eminescu Eliade and Julien de Saint-Hilaire, the less safe he was. Both identities were, of course, registered with the Ordre des médecins and there were a very few of his French psychiatric colleagues who knew him as both, though most knew only that he was both shaman and psychiatrist, but those few who did know were all men to whom he'd chosen to reveal himself because he was satisfied they posed no real threat to him, while at the same time they knew he in turn would never threaten them, thus rendering mutual trust possible. The clochards with whom he spent his time as Eminescu Eliade, of course, knew that he was a shaman, just as he knew which among them were also shamans, but though they knew that he had to have some sort of second identity, none of them, as far as he was aware, knew that that second identity was that of Julien de Saint-Hilaire. Thus none of them could attack him while he was in his psychiatrist's role, far from his caps, costume and drum, and so virtually defenseless.

It was Julien de Saint-Hilaire, and not Eminescu Eliade, who'd been challenged and who was under attack. Yet even so he knew that as long as he kept his unknown enemy from learning that the two were one and the same (and his opponent *couldn't* know that yet, or Eminescu would have already been dead) Eminescu Eliade would remain, if not safe, at least always free to escape to safety and anonymity. All of which would be lost if the other caught him taking his costume and drum to the other apartment.

Lost, unless he could destroy the worms in Liz and get his shamanizing aids back to the rue de Condé before the other realized what Eminescu was doing. Or unless he managed to kill the other before he'd had a chance to make use of the information he'd gained, and before he'd had a chance to reveal it to anyone else.

And Eminescu was tired of having to defend himself, of worrying about his safety, tired and very angry. He wanted to hurt his enemy, not just avoid him or survive his attacks. The other had to have a lot of his power—and that meant a lot of his soul—in the worms: If Eminescu could destroy them he might well cripple his enemy so that he could finish him off later, at his leisure. And too, this was the only way he could save Liz, and his unborn son.

He took his father's skull from the silver hatbox in the trunk, held it out at arm's length with both hands and asked it whether or not he'd succeed in saving Liz without betraying himself to his enemy. There was no reply, the skull became neither lighter nor heavier, but that proved nothing: His father rarely responded and those few times that the skull's weight had seemed to change Eminescu had been unable to rule out the possibility that the brief alteration in its heaviness he'd felt had been no more than the result of unconscious suggestion, like the messages he'd seen Liz seem to receive when she played with her Ouija board.

He put the skull and the rest of his shamanizing equipment back in the trunk and locked it, then went downstairs as Julien de Saint-Hilaire. He ate yet another two meals at nearby restaurants, then found the concierge's husband and got him to help move the heavy steamer trunk downstairs. Back at the other apartment he tipped the taxi driver who'd brought him there substantially extra to help carry the trunk up the rear stairs. When the driver left he dragged it into the apartment and locked it in the unused spare bedroom at the far end of the apartment, where Liz was least likely to be disturbed by the noise he'd make beating his tambourine and chanting, and where she was least likely to realize that a door to which she'd never had the key was now locked against her.

She was still in the bedroom, asleep. He called his catering service and asked them to deliver cold cuts for a party of fifteen in an hour, then went downstairs and bought a side of beef and a half dozen chickens from his butcher. The butcher and his two assistants helped him up the stairs and into the kitchen with the meat. When they were gone he dragged the beef into the spare bedroom, followed it with the chickens.

The caterers managed to deliver the cold cuts without waking Liz. He ate some of them, laid the others out where he'd be able to get at them easily when he made the transformation back to human, though since he wouldn't be flying he at least wouldn't have to waste the kinds of energy it took to get his iron-weighted body airborne. Then he locked all the doors and windows carefully and turned off the phone and doorbell, so as to make sure that nothing disturbed or awakened Liz before he was finished with her.

It was good to put his caps and costume on in the Parc Monceau apartment for the first time, good to beat his tambourine there in the spare room with the late-afternoon sun coming in through the curtains screening the window. Good to put on the bear's form after so many years of forcing himself to stay content with being no more than a pigeon or owl or rat.

It had been fifteen—no, seventeen—years since he'd last been a bear, there in that box canyon in Arizona with John Henry Two Feathers Thomas Thompson, and he'd forgotten what joy it was to be huge and shaggy and powerful, forgotten the bear's keen intelligence and cunning, the enormous reserves of strength its anger gave it.

Forgotten too the danger of losing himself in the bear, of letting the seeming inexhaustibility of the forces at his disposal seduce him into going too far beyond his limits, so that when the time came for him to resume his human form he'd lack the energy to animate his body and so die.

Outside a dog began to bark, and then another. He couldn't tell if they were just dogs barking, or some of the dead who'd detected his transformation, but even if they were just dogs they were a reminder that the longer he stayed a bear the more chance there was that his enemy would detect him, realize what he was doing and counterattack.

More dogs, a growing number of them living animals now, howling all around his building and even within it: He recognized the excited voices of the thirteen whippets the film distributor on the first floor kept, the sharp yapping of the old lady on the second floor's gray poodle and the deeper and stupider baying of her middle-aged daughter's obnoxious Irish setter. Lights were beginning to go on in other buildings. Which meant he had to hurry, leave the meat and chickens he'd planned to eat before he began for later, so he could get to Liz and soothe her immediately, before even drugged as she was the noise woke her.

Soothe her and then destroy the worms before the disturbance the dead were making brought his enemy. If he wasn't already here, or coming.

He'd left the door to the room he was using slightly ajar. Now he pushed it open with his snout, squeezed through the narrow doorway and shambled down the long hall toward the master bedroom. He was already hungry, though he still had some margin before he'd be in danger.

Halfway down the hall to the bedroom he knocked a tall glass lamp from a table. It hit the parquet floor and shattered loudly, and for a moment he was sure that the noise would be enough to awaken Liz after all: She metabolized her sleeping pills very rapidly and would already be beginning to get over the effects of the ones he'd given her. But when he reached the bedroom and poked his head in to check on her she was still asleep, though the howling outside and within the building was still getting louder and louder. There had to be fifty or sixty dogs out there by now, perhaps even more.

He shambled the rest of the way into the room, reared up and balanced himself on his hind legs at the foot of the bed, then reached out and plucked Liz's soul from her body, locked it away from all pain and sensation in her head. As though her skull were a mother's womb inside which she lay curled like a haggard but voluptuous foetus, her whole adult body there within her head, filling it and overflowing it slightly, one hand dangling from her right ear, a foot and ankle and short length of calf protruding from her half-open mouth.

He turned her over with his paws and made a quick incision in her belly with his long claws, pulled the flesh apart so he could reach in and flip her intestines free of her abdomen. He ripped them open and seized the worms in his teeth, ripped them free of her intestinal walls and then tore them apart, killing the scolexes and each and every segment before he swallowed them. It was easy, amazingly easy, like the time John Henry Two Feathers Thomas Thompson had taught him to flip trout from a stream with his paws, and though the tapeworms were lampreys as well as worms they couldn't get a grasp on his shaggy body with their sucking mouths, their concentric circles of razor-sharp rasping teeth, so it was only a matter of moments before he'd killed them all and devoured their dead bodies.

All eight of them, where there should have been nine.

He cursed himself for the way he'd let the noise the dogs were making outside the apartment rush him into beginning without examining Liz very, very carefully again first, realized that at no time since he'd returned from the Undercity had he thought to count the worms in her belly, that he'd just assumed that all nine were still there.

But there was no time now to try to solve the problem of the ninth worm's escape or disappearance; he had to try to get Liz's intestines back together and inside her and functioning before she bled to death, and before the hunger growing ever more insistent within him reached the point where it could be fatal.

He licked the insides of her intestines clean with his long tongue, making sure he got each and every egg and embryo and crushed the life out of them between his teeth before he swallowed them. Then he pushed the ripped intestines back into shape with his nose and tongue, licked them until they'd stopped bleeding and begun to heal, licked them a little more and then nosed them back into place in her abdominal cavity, licked the incision in her belly until it closed and healed, continued to lick it until no further trace of its presence remained.

Then he reached into her legs and bloodstream, pulled the embryos and filament worms he found there from her body, killed and devoured them.

And it had been easy, almost too easy. He would have thought the whole thing another diversion, only a means of luring him here in his shaman's self, had it not been for the fact that there was no one else in France who knew he was able to take on the form of a bear. There were very few people left anywhere in Europe who knew how to do so, and those few were all far to the North, in the Scandinavian countries.

Besides, there was still the missing tapeworm to consider.

Liz's soul still filled her head. He very carefully checked her body to make sure it was now free of worms, eggs, embryos, and toxins before he released her soul, let it begin slowly filtering down out of her head into the rest of her body.

The veins in her legs were still blue and fat, undoubtedly painful: The filament worms had damaged all the tiny valves in the vessels that kept the blood from pooling there. But all that was, now that the worms had been removed, was ordinary varicose veins; he should be able to heal them easily enough, and if they proved for some reason more difficult to deal with than he expected them to be he could always steal healthy veins from other people's legs for her. From that patient who was so late paying his bills, if his blood type was right and his circulatory system in good condition.

His hunger had passed the danger point, especially with his human form weakened as it was by his previous efforts, but he forced himself to go over the bedroom and both the attached bathrooms meticulously, looking for the ninth worm. It wasn't there. Perhaps the medicines he'd given Liz had destroyed it; perhaps the first worm's death had been the signal which had stimulated the other worms to their accelerated egg production. In any case, the worm was gone.

Liz was sleeping soundly now, would remain asleep for another five or six hours while her soul reintegrated itself with her body. More than long enough for him to change the bloodstained sheets and blankets and mattress cover.

He fell once on his way back through the corridor to the spare bedroom, got a good look at himself in the hall mirror as he was getting back up. He looked almost dead of starvation, a bit like a weasel or wolverine, but with neither the sleekness nor the grace.

He made it back into the spare bedroom and pushed the door closed behind him, though he had no way to lock it before he regained his human form. He devoured the cold cuts on their platter, ate the chickens and began ripping chunks of meat from the side of beef.

And when he'd cracked open the last bone and licked it clean of the last of the marrow it had contained he triggered his transformation.

He lay there, Eminescu Eliade, too tired to move or do anything else, just letting the strength begin flowing gently back into him from his caps and costume. There'd been enough energy in the food he'd eaten to keep him alive, just barely enough, but it would be a while before he'd be strong enough to pull his tambourine to him, tap out the rhythms on it he could use to summon the strength he'd need to get to his feet and change back into Julien de Saint-Hilaire, then get something more to eat from the kitchen and finally clean up Liz and the bed.

Everything was silent, completely silent, both within the apartment and outside. He had a throbbing pain in his head and he felt dizzy and a little nauseated and very hungry. The floor was too hard for him now that he'd lost the flesh that had formerly cushioned his bones and it hurt him even through his many layers of swaddling clothing. He'd have to find a way to explain to Liz the twenty kilos or more he'd lost so suddenly.

He lay there, half-dozing, letting the strength return to him.

And then he must have passed out, because when he opened his eyes again Liz was kneeling over him, still covered with dry blood but dressed now, her robe wrapped around her. He tried to tell her something, he wasn't sure quite what, but she shook her head and put her fingers to her lips. She was smiling, but it was a strange, tight-lipped smile and he felt confused.

The door opened behind him, letting in a current of cold air. Jean-Luc and Michel came in together, holding hands.

Liz snatched Eminescu's two caps from his head and put them on her own before he'd had a chance to realize what she was doing, and by then it was too late to even try to change himself back into a bear, or into anything else.

She motioned to Jean-Luc and Michel. They bent down to kiss her on both cheeks in greeting while she did the same to them, then took up their positions, Jean-Luc kneeling across from her on the opposite side of Eminescu's body, Michel down by his feet. Jean-Luc helped her strip Eminescu's leather coat from him while Michel took his seven-league shoes and his socks from his feet. Without his caps he had no strength with which to even try to resist them, and with each article and layer of clothing they stripped from him he was weaker still, until at the end he no longer had the strength to so much as lift his head.

When he was naked and shivering in the cold air Liz took off her robe and gave it to Jean-Luc to hold while she dressed herself in Eminescu's many layers of rags. Then together she and Jean-Luc wrapped him in her discarded robe while Michel picked up Eminescu's tambourine and began to beat it.

Naked and weakened as he was, he could sense nothing of the power they were summoning and using. He had never felt it, not even in the end, never detected in any of them the slightest sign of the power that had defeated and destroyed him, and in a way that was almost as bad as the fact of the defeat itself, that he would never know if Liz or one of the other two had been his true enemy, keeping his or her powers hidden from Eminescu in some way he would never now get the chance to understand, or if all three of them together had been only the instrument for some challenger whose identity he would never know.

Liz knelt down beside him again, pulled the beard from his face and put it on her own. She leaned over him then, began nuzzling his cheek and then kissing him on the mouth.

Without ceasing to kiss him she brought her hands up, jammed her fingers into his mouth and pried it wide, held his jaw open despite his feeble efforts to close it while she stuck her tongue in his mouth.

Her tongue explored his mouth, then uncoiled its flat, twelve-meter body and slid slowly down his throat into its new home.

"Varicose Worms" started as a title, inspired by the combination of someone I saw walking on the street and a long-standing fascination/revulsion for internal/intestinal parasites. Since I had been immersed in the Ashlu Cycle, in which I had been trying to treat shamanism with total seriousness, for a number of years, I felt like having some fun with the ideas I'd been using and treating them more ironically for a change.

Scott Baker

LAZARUS

Leonid Andreyev

The oldest story in Blood Is Not Enough, *"Lazarus" was published in the early 1900s. It's about what might have happened after Jesus Christ resurrected Lazarus, three days dead, who up to that point had been a normal man of his times. From this biblical miracle, Andreyev began an incredible story of existential horror, which is more in the eye of the beholder than in poor, undead Lazarus.*

When Lazarus left the grave, where for three days and three nights he had been under the enigmatical sway of death, and returned alive to his dwelling, for a long time no one noticed in him those sinister things which made his name a terror as time went on. Gladdened by the sight of him who had been returned to life, those near to him made much of him, and satisfied their burning desire to serve him, in solicitude for his food and drink and garments. They dressed him gorgeously, and when, like a bridegroom in his bridal clothes, he sat again among them at the table and ate and drank, they wept with tenderness. And they summoned the neighbors to look at him who had risen miraculously from the dead. These came and shared the joy of the hosts. Strangers from far-off towns and hamlets came and adored the miracle in tempestuous words. The house of Mary and Martha was like a beehive.

Whatever was found new in Lazarus' face and gestures was thought to be some trace of a grave illness and of the shocks recently experienced. Evidently the destruction wrought by death on the corpse was only arrested by the miraculous power, but its effects were still apparent; and what death had succeeded in doing with Lazarus' face and body was like an artist's unfinished sketch seen under thin glass. On Lazarus' temples, under his eyes, and in the hollows of his cheeks, lay a deep and cadaverous blueness; cadaverously blue also were his long fingers, and around his finger-nails, grown long in the grave, the blue had become purple and dark. On his lips, swollen in the grave the skin had burst in places, and thin reddish cracks were formed, shining as though covered with transparent mica. And he had grown stout. His body, puffed up in the grave, retained its monstrous size and showed those frightful swellings in which one sensed the presence of the rank liquid of decomposition. But the heavy corpselike odor which penetrated Lazarus' grave-clothes and, it seemed, his very body, soon entirely disappeared, the blue spots of his face and hands grew paler, and the reddish cracks closed up, although they never disappeared altogether. That is how Lazarus looked when he appeared before people, in his second life, but his face looked natural to those who had seen him in the coffin.

In addition to the changes in his appearance, Lazarus' temper seemed to have undergone a transformation, but this had attracted no attention. Before his death Lazarus had always been cheerful and carefree, fond of laughter and a merry joke. It was because of this brightness and cheerfulness, with not a touch of malice and darkness that the Master had grown so fond of him. But now Lazarus had grown grave and taciturn, he never jested, nor responded with laughter to other people's jokes; and the words which he very infrequently uttered were the plainest, most ordinary and necessary words, as deprived of depth and significance as those sounds with which animals express pain and pleasure, thirst and hunger. They were the words that one can say all one's life, and yet they give no indication of what pains and gladdens the depth of the soul.

Thus, with the face of a corpse, which for three days had been under the heavy sway of death, dark and taciturn, already appallingly transformed, but still unrecognized by anyone in his new self, he was sitting at the feast table among friends and relatives, and his gorgeous nuptial garments glittered with yellow-gold and bloody scarlet. Broad waves of jubilation, now soft, now tempestuously sonorous surged around him; warm glances of love were reaching out for his face, still cold with the coldness of the grave; and a friend's warm palm caressed his blue, heavy, hand. Music played—the tympanum and the pipe, the cithara and the harp. It was as though bees hummed, grasshoppers chirped, and birds warbled over the happy house of Mary and Martha.

One of the guests incautiously lifted the veil. By a thoughtless word he broke the serene charm and uncovered the truth in all its naked ugliness. Ere the thought formed itself in his mind, his lips uttered with a smile: "Why do you not tell us what happened yonder?"

All grew silent, startled by the question. It was as if it occurred to them only now that for three days Lazarus had been dead, and they looked at him, anxiously awaiting his answer. But Lazarus kept silence.

"You do not wish to tell us," wondered the man; "is it so terrible yonder?"

And again his thought came after his words. Had it been otherwise, he would not have asked this question, which at that very moment oppressed his heart with its insufferable horror. Uneasiness seized all present, and with a feeling of heavy weariness they awaited Lazarus' words, but he was sternly and coldly silent, and his eyes were lowered. As if for the first time, they noticed the frightful blueness of his face and his repulsive obesity. On the table, as if forgotten by Lazarus, rested his bluish-purple wrist, and to this all eyes turned, as if it were from it that the awaited answer was to come. The musicians were still playing, but now the silence reached them too, and even as water extinguishes scattered embers, so were their merry tunes extinguished in the silence. The pipe grew silent; the voices of the sonorous tympanum and the murmuring harp died away; and as if the strings had burst, the cithara answered with a tremulous, broken note. Silence.

"You do not wish to say?" repeated the guest, unable to check his chattering tongue. But the stillness remained unbroken, and the bluish-purple hand rested motionless. And then he stirred slightly and everyone felt relieved. He lifted up his eyes, and lo! straightway embracing everything in one heavy glance, fraught with weariness and horror, he looked at them—Lazarus who had arisen from the dead.

It was the third day since Lazarus had left the grave. Ever since then many had experienced the pernicious power of his eye, but neither those who were crushed by it forever, nor those who found the strength to resist in it the primordial sources of life, which is as mysterious as death, never could they explain the horror which lay motionless in the depth of his black pupils. Lazarus looked calmly and simply with no desire to conceal anything, but also with no intention to say anything; he looked coldly, as one who is infinitely indifferent to those alive. Many carefree people came close to him without noticing him, and only later did they learn with astonishment and fear who that calm stout man was that walked slowly by, almost touching them with his gorgeous and dazzling garments. The sun did not cease shining when he was looking nor did the fountain hush its murmur, and the sky overhead remained cloudless and blue. But the man under the spell of his enigmatical look heard no more the fountain and saw not the sky overhead. Sometimes he wept bitterly, sometimes he tore his hair and in a frenzy called for help; but more often it came to pass that apathetically and quietly he began to die, and so he languished many years, before everybody's eyes wasted away, colorless, flabby, dull, like a tree silently drying up in a stony soil. And of those who gazed at him, the one who wept madly sometimes felt again the stir of life; the others never.

"So you do not wish to tell us what you have seen yonder?" repeated the man. But now his voice was impassive and dull, and deadly gray weariness showed in Lazarus' eyes. And deadly gray weariness covered like dust all the faces, and with dull amazement the guests stared at each other and did not understand wherefore they had gathered here and sat at the rich table. The talk ceased. They thought it was time to go home, but could not overcome the weariness which glued their muscles, and they kept on sitting there, yet apart, and torn away from each other, like pale fires scattered over a dark field.

But the musicians were paid to play, and again they took their instruments, and again tunes full of studied mirth and studied sorrow began to flow and to rise. They unfolded the customary melody, but the guests harkened in dull amazement. Already they knew not why it is necessary, and why it is well, that people should pluck strings, inflate their cheeks, blow in thin pipes, and produce a bizarre, many-voiced noise.

"What bad music!" said someone.

The musicians took offense and left. Following them, the guests left one after another, for night was already come. And when placid darkness encircled them and they began to breathe with more ease, suddenly Lazarus' image loomed up before each one in formidable radiance; the blue face of a corpse, grave clothes gorgeous and resplendent, a cold look in the depths of which lay motionless an unknown horror. As though petrified, they were standing far apart, and darkness enveloped them, but in the darkness blazed brighter and brighter the supernatural vision of him who for three days had been under the enigmatical sway of death. For three days had he been dead: Thrice had the sun risen and set, but he had been dead. And now he is again among them, touches them, looks at them, and through the black disks of his pupils, as through darkened glass, stares the unknowable Yonder.

No one was taking care of Lazarus, for no friends, no relatives were left to him, and the great desert, which encircled the holy city, came near the very threshold of his dwelling. And the desert entered his house, and stretched on his couch, like a wife, and extinguished the fires. No one was taking care of Lazarus. One after the other, his sisters—Mary and Martha—forsook him. For a long while Martha was loath to abandon him, for she knew not who would feed him and pity him. She wept and prayed. But one night, when the wind was roaming in the desert and with a hissing sound the cypresses were bending over the roof, she dressed noiselessly, and secretly left the house. Lazarus probably heard the door slam; it banged against the sidepost under the gusts of the desert wind, but he did not rise to go out and look at her that was abandoning him. All the night long the cypresses hissed over his head and plaintively thumped the door, letting in the cold, greedy desert.

Like a leper he was shunned by everyone, and it was proposed to tie a bell to his neck, as is done with lepers, to warn people against sudden meetings. But someone remarked, growing frightfully pale, that it would be too horrible if by night the moaning of Lazarus' bell were suddenly heard under the pillows, and so the project was abandoned.

And since he did not take care of himself, he would probably have starved to death, had not the neighbors brought him food in fear of something that they sensed but vaguely. The food was brought to him by children; they were not afraid of Lazarus, nor did they mock him with naive cruelty, as children are wont to do with the wretched and miserable. They were indifferent to him, and Lazarus answered them with the same coldness; he had no desire to caress the black little curls, and to look into their innocent shining eyes. Given to Time and to the desert, his house was crumbling down, and long since had his famishing goats wandered away to the neighboring pastures. His bridal garments became threadbare. Ever since that happy day when the musicians played, he had worn them unaware of the difference of the new and the worn. The bright colors grew dull and faded; vicious dogs and the sharp thorns of the desert turned the tender fabric into rags.

By day, when the merciless sun slew all things alive, and even scorpions sought shelter under stones and writhed there in a mad desire to sting, he sat motionless under the sun's rays, his blue face and the uncouth, bushy beard lifted up, bathing in the fiery flood.

When people still talked to him, he was once asked, "Poor Lazarus, does it please you to sit thus and to stare at the sun?"

And he had answered: "Yes, it does."

So strong, it seemed, was the cold of his three days' grave, so deep the darkness, that there was no heat on earth to warm Lazarus, nor a splendor that could brighten the darkness of his eyes. That is what came to the mind of those who spoke to Lazarus, and with a sigh they left him.

And when the scarlet, flattened globe would lower, Lazarus would set out for the desert and walk straight toward the sun, as if striving to reach it. He always walked straight toward the sun, and those who tried to follow him and to spy upon what he was doing at night in the desert, retained in their memory the black silhouette of a tall stout man against the red background of an enormous flattened disk. Night pursued them with her horrors, and so they did not learn of Lazarus' doings in the desert, but the vision of the black on red was forever branded on their brains. Just as a beast with a splinter in its eye furiously rubs its muzzle with its paws, so they too foolishly rubbed their eyes, but what Lazarus had given was indelible, and Death alone could efface it.

But there were people who lived far away, who never saw Lazarus and knew of him only by report. With daring curiosity, which is stronger than fear and feeds upon it, with hidden mockery, they would come to Lazarus who was sitting in the sun and enter into conversation with him. By this time Lazarus' appearance had changed for the better and was not so terrible. The first minute they snapped their fingers and thought of how stupid the inhabitants of the holy city were; but when the short talk was over and they started homeward, their looks were such that the inhabitants of the holy city recognized them at once and said: "Look, there is one more fool on whom Lazarus has set his eye"; and they shook their heads regretfully, and lifted up their arms.

There came brave, intrepid warriors, with tinkling weapons; happy youths came with laughter and song; busy tradesmen, jingling their money, ran in for a moment, and haughty priests leaned their crosiers against Lazarus' door, and they were all strangely changed, as they came back. The same terrible shadow swooped down upon their souls and gave a new appearance to the old familiar world.

Those who still had the desire to speak, expressed their feelings thus:

"All things tangible and visible grew hollow, light and transparent, similar to lightsome shadows in the darkness of night;

"For that great darkness, which holds the whole cosmos, was dispersed neither by the sun nor by the moon and the stars, but like an immense black shroud enveloped the earth and like a mother embraced it;

"It penetrated all the bodies, iron and stone, and the particles of the bodies, having lost their ties, grew lonely; and it penetrated into the depth of the particles, and the particles of particles became lonely;

"For that great void, which encircles the cosmos, was not filled by things visible, neither by the sun, nor by the moon and the stars, but reigned unrestrained, penetrating everywhere, severing body from body, particle from particle;

"In the void, hollow trees spread hollow roots threatening a fantastic fall; temples, palaces, and houses loomed up and they were hollow; and in the void men moved about restlessly, but they were light and hollow like shadows;

"For time was no more, and the beginning of all things came near their end: the building was still being built, and builders were still hammering away, and its ruins were already seen and the void in its place; the man was still being born, but already funeral candles were burning at his head, and now they were extinguished, and there was the void in place of the man and of the funeral candles;

"And wrapped by void and darkness the man in despair trembled in the face of the horror of the infinite."

Thus spake the men who had still a desire to speak. But, surely, much more could those have told who wished not to speak, and died in silence.

At that time there lived in Rome a renowned sculptor. In clay, marble, and bronze he wrought bodies of gods and men, and such was their beauty that people called them immortal. But he himself was discontented and asserted that there was something even more beautiful, that he could not embody either in marble or in bronze. "I have not yet gathered the glimmers of the moon, nor have I my fill of sunshine," he was wont to say, "and there is no soul in my marble, no life in my beautiful bronze." And when on moonlight nights he slowly walked along the road, crossing the black shadows of cypresses, his white tunic glittering in the moonshine, those who met him would laugh in a friendly way and say:

"Are you going to gather moonshine, Aurelius? Why then did you not fetch baskets?"

And he would answer, laughing and pointing to his eyes:

"Here are the baskets wherein I gather the sheen of the moon and the glimmer of the sun."

And so it was: The moon glimmered in his eyes and the sun sparkled therein. But he could not translate them into marble, and therein lay the serene tragedy of his life.

He was descended from ancient patrician race, had a good wife and children, and suffered from no want.

When the obscure rumor about Lazarus reached him, he consulted his wife and friends and undertook the far journey to Judea to see him who had miraculously risen from the dead. He was somewhat weary in those days and he hoped that the road would sharpen his blunted senses. What was said of Lazarus did not frighten him: He had pondered much over Death, did not like it, but he disliked also those who confused it with life. "In this life are life and beauty," thought he; "beyond is Death, and enigmatical; and there is no better thing for a man to do than to delight in life and in the beauty of all things living." He had even a vainglorious desire to convince Lazarus of the truth of his own view and restore his soul to life, as his body had been restored. This seemed so much easier because the rumors, shy and strange, did not render the whole truth about Lazarus and but vaguely warned against something frightful.

Lazarus had just risen from the stone in order to follow the sun which was setting in the desert, when a rich Roman, attended by an armed slave, approached him and addressed him in a sonorous voice: "Lazarus!"

And Lazarus beheld a superb face, lit with glory, and arrayed in fine clothes, and precious stones sparkling in the sun. The red light lent to the Roman's face and head the appearance of gleaming bronze: That also Lazarus noticed. He resumed obediently his place and lowered his weary eyes.

"Yes, you are ugly, my poor Lazarus," quietly said the Roman, playing with his golden chain; "you are even horrible, my poor friend; and Death was not lazy that day when you fell so heedlessly into his hands. But you are stout, and, as the great Caesar used to say, fat people are not ill-tempered; to tell the truth, I don't understand why men fear you. Permit me to spend the night in your house; the hour is late, and I have no shelter."

Never had anyone asked Lazarus' hospitality.

"I have no bed," said he.

"I am somewhat of a soldier and I can sleep sitting," the Roman answered. "We shall build a fire."

"I have no fire."

"Then we shall have our talk in the darkness, like two friends. I think you will find a bottle of wine."

"I have no wine."

The Roman laughed.

"Now I see why you are so somber and dislike your second life. No wine! Why, then we shall do without it; there are words that make the head go round better than the Falernian."

By a sign he dismissed the slave, and they remained alone. And again the sculptor started speaking, but it was as if, together with the setting sun, life had left his words; and they grew pale and hollow, as if they staggered on unsteady feet, as if they slipped and fell down, drunk with the heavy lees of weariness and despair. And black chasms grew up between the worlds, like far-off hints of the great void and the great darkness.

"Now I am your guest, and you will not be unkind to me, Lazarus!" said he. "Hospitality is the duty even of those who for three days were dead. Three days, I was told, you rested in the grave. There it must be cold . . . and thence comes your ill habit of going without fire and wine. As to me, I like fire; it grows dark here so rapidly. . . . The lines of your eyebrows and forehead are quite, quite interesting: They are like ruins of strange palaces, buried in ashes, after an earthquake. But why do you wear such ugly and queer garments? I have seen bridegrooms in your country, and they wear such clothes—are they not funny?—and terrible? . . . But are you a bridegroom?"

The sun had already disappeared, a monstrous black shadow came running from the east, it was as if gigantic bare feet began rumbling on the sand, and the wind sent a cold wave along the backbone.

"In the darkness you seem still larger, Lazarus, as if you have grown stouter in these moments. Do you feed on darkness, Lazarus? I would fain have a little fire—at least a little fire. I feel somewhat chilly, your nights are so barbarously cold. Were it not so dark, I should say that you were looking at me, Lazarus. Yes, it seems to me you are looking. . . . Why, you are looking at me, I feel it—but there you are smiling."

Night came, and filled the air with heavy blackness.

"How well it will be, when the sun will rise tomorrow, anew. . . . I am a great sculptor, you know; that is how my friends call me. I create. Yes, that is the word . . . but I need daylight. I give life to the cold marble, I melt sonorous bronze in fire, in bright hot fire. . . . Why did you touch me with your hand?"

"Come," said Lazarus. "You are my guest."

They went to the house. And a long night enveloped the earth.

The slave, seeing that his master did not come, went to seek him, when the sun was already high in the sky. And he beheld his master side by side with Lazarus: In profound silence they were sitting right under the dazzling and scorching rays of the sun and looking upward. The slave began to weep and cried out: "My master, what has befallen you, master?"

The very same day the sculptor left for Rome. On the way Aurelius was pensive and taciturn, staring attentively at everything—the men, the ship, the sea, as if trying to retain something. On the high sea a storm burst upon them, and all through it Aurelius stayed on the deck and eagerly scanned the seas looming near and sinking with a dull boom.

At home his friends were frightened at the change which had taken place in Aurelius, but he calmed them, saying meaningly: "I have found it."

And without changing the dusty clothes he wore on his journey, he fell to work, and the marble obediently resounded under his sonorous hammer.

Long and eagerly he worked, admitting no one, until one morning he announced that the work was ready and ordered his friends to be summoned, severe critics and connoisseurs of art. And to meet them he put on bright and gorgeous garments, that glittered with yellow gold—and scarlet byssus.

"Here is my work," said he thoughtfully.

His friends glanced, and a shadow of profound sorrow covered their faces. It was something monstrous, deprived of all the lines and shapes familiar to the eye, but not without a hint at some new, strange image.

On a thin, crooked twig, or rather on an ugly likeness of a twig, rested askew a blind, ugly, shapeless, outspread mass of something utterly and inconceivably distorted, a mad heap of wild and bizarre fragments, all feebly and vainly striving to part from one another. And, as if by chance, beneath one of the wildly-rent salients a butterfly was chiseled with divine skill, all airy loveliness, delicacy, and beauty with transparent wings, which seemed to tremble with an impotent desire to take flight.

"Wherefore this wonderful butterfly, Aurelius?" said somebody falteringly.

But it was necessary to tell the truth, and one of his friends who loved him best said firmly: "This is ugly, my poor friend. It must be destroyed. Give me the hammer."

And with two strokes he broke the monstrous mass into pieces, leaving only the infinitely delicate butterfly untouched.

From that time on Aurelius created nothing. With profound indifference he looked at marble and bronze, and on his former divine works, where everlasting beauty rested. With the purpose of arousing his former fervent passion for work and awakening his deadened soul, his friends took him to see other artists' beautiful works, but he remained indifferent as before, and the smile did not warm up his tightened lips. And only after listening to lengthy talks about beauty, he would retort wearily and indolently: "But all this is a lie."

By day, when the sun was shining, he went into his magnificent, skill-fully built garden, and having found a place without a shadow, he exposed his bare head to the glare and heat. Red and white butterflies fluttered around; from the crooked lips of a drunken satyr, water streamed down with a splash into a marble cistern, but he sat motionless and silent, like a pallid reflection of him who, in the far-off distance, at the very gates of the stony desert, sat under the fiery sun.

And now it came to pass that the great, deified Augustus himself summoned Lazarus. The imperial messengers dressed him gorgeously, in solemn nuptial clothes, as if Time had legalized them, and he was to remain until his very death the bridegroom of an unknown bride. It was as if an old, rotting coffin had been gilded and furnished with new, gay tassels. And men, all in trim and bright attire, rode after him, as if in bridal procession indeed, and those foremost trumpeted loudly, bidding people to clear the way for the emperor's messengers. But Lazarus' way was deserted: His native land cursed the hateful name of him who had miraculously risen from the dead, and people scattered at the very news of his appalling approach. The solitary voice of the brass trumpets sounded in the motionless air, and the wilderness alone responded with its languid echo.

Then Lazarus went by sea. And his was the most magnificently arrayed and the most mournful ship that ever mirrored itself in the azure waves of the Mediterranean Sea. Many were the travelers aboard, but like a tomb was the ship, all silence and stillness, and the despairing water sobbed at the steep, proudly curved prow. All alone sat Lazarus exposing his head to the blaze of the sun, silently listening to the murmur and splash of the wavelets, and afar seamen and messengers were sitting, a vague group of weary shadows. Had the thunder burst and the wind attacked the red sails, the ships would probably have perished, for none of those aboard had either the will or the strength to struggle for life. With a supreme effort some mariners would reach the board and eagerly scan the blue, transparent deep, hoping to see a naiad's pink shoulder flash in the hollow of an azure wave, or a drunken gay centaur dash along and in frenzy splash the wave with his hoof. But the sea was like a wilderness, and the deep was dumb and deserted.

With utter indifference Lazarus set his feet on the street of the eternal city, as if all her wealth, all the magnificence of her palaces built by giants, all the resplendence, beauty, and music of her refined life were but the echo of the wind in the desert quicksand. Chariots were dashing, and along the streets were moving crowds of strong, fair, proud builders of the eternal city and haughty participants in her life; a song sounded; fountains and women laughed a pearly laughter; drunken philosophers harangued, and the sober listened to them with a smile; hoofs struck the stone pavements. And surrounded by cheerful noise, a stout, heavy man was moving, a cold spot of silence and despair, and on his way he sowed disgust, anger, and vague, gnawing weariness. Who dares to be sad in Rome? the citizens wondered indignantly, and frowned. In two days the entire city already knew *all* about him who had miraculously risen from the dead, and shunned him shyly.

But some daring people there were, who wanted to test their strength, and Lazarus obeyed their imprudent summons. Kept busy by state affairs, the emperor constantly delayed the reception, and seven days did he who had risen from the dead go about visiting others.

And Lazarus came to a cheerful Epicurean, and the host met him with laughter: "Drink, Lazarus, drink!" he shouted. "Would not Augustus laugh to see you drunk?"

And half-naked drunken women laughed, and rose petals fell on Lazarus' blue hands. But then the Epicurean looked into Lazarus' eyes and his gaiety ended forever. Drunkard remained he for the rest of his life; never did he drink, yet forever was he drunk. But instead of the gay revery which wine brings with it, frightful dreams began to haunt him, the sole food of his stricken spirit. Day and night he lived the poisonous vapors of his nightmares, and Death itself was not more frightful than its raving, monstrous forerunners.

And Lazarus came to a youth and his beloved, who loved each other and were most beautiful in their passions. Proudly and strongly embracing his love, the youth said with serene regret: "Look at us Lazarus, and share our joy. Is there anything stronger than love?"

And Lazarus looked. And for the rest of their life they kept loving each other, but their passion grew gloomy and joyless, like those funeral cypresses whose roots feed on the decay of the graves and whose black summits in a still evening hour seek in vain to reach the sky. Thrown by the unknown forces of life into each other's embraces, they mingled tears with kisses, voluptuous pleasures with pain, and they felt themselves doubly slaves, obedient slaves to life, and patient servants of the silent Nothingness. Ever united, ever severed, they blazed like sparks and like sparks lost themselves in the boundless Dark.

And Lazarus came to a haughty sage, and the sage said to him: "I know all the horrors you can reveal to me. Is there anything you can frighten me with?"

But before long the sage felt that the knowledge of horror was far from being the horror itself, and that the vision of Death was not Death. And he felt that wisdom and folly are equal before the face of Infinity, for Infinity knows them not. And it vanished, the dividing-line between knowledge and ignorance, truth and falsehood, top and bottom, and the shapeless thought hung suspended in the void. Then the sage clutched his gray head and cried out frantically: "I can not think! I can not think!"

Thus under the indifferent glance for him, who miraculously had risen from the dead, perished everything that asserts life, its significance and joys. And it was suggested that it was dangerous to let him see the emperor, that it was better to kill him, and having buried him secretly, to tell the emperor that he had disappeared no one knew whither. Already swords were being whetted and youths devoted to the public welfare prepared for the murder, when Augustus ordered Lazarus to be brought before him next morning, thus destroying the cruel plans.

If there was no way of getting rid of Lazarus, at least it was possible to soften the terrible impression his face produced. With this in view, skillful painters, barbers, and artists were summoned, and all night long they were busy over Lazarus' head. They cropped his beard, curled it, and gave it a tidy, agreeable appearance. By means of paints they concealed the corpselike blueness of his hands and face. Repulsive were the wrinkles of suffering that furrowed his old face, and they were puttied, painted, and smoothed; then, over the smooth background, wrinkles of good-tempered laughter and pleasant carefree mirth were skillfully painted with fine brushes.

Lazarus submitted indifferently to everything that was done to him. Soon he was turned into a becomingly stout, venerable old man, into a quiet and kind grandfather of numerous offspring. It seemed that the smile, with which only a while ago he was spinning funny yarns, was still lingering on his lips and that in the corner of his eye serene tenderness was hiding, the companion of old age. But people did not dare change his nuptial garments, and they could not change his eyes, two dark and frightful glasses through which the unknowable Yonder looked at men.

Lazarus was not moved by the magnificence of the imperial palace. It was as if he saw no difference between the crumbling house, closely pressed by the desert, and the stone palace, solid and fair, and indifferently he passed into it. The hard marble of the floors under his feet grew similar to the quicksand of the desert, and the multitude of richly dressed and haughty men became like void air under his glance. No one looked into his face, as Lazarus passed by, fearing to fall under the appalling influence of his eyes; but when the sound of his heavy footsteps had sufficiently died down, the courtiers raised their heads and with fearful curiosity examined the figure of a stout, tall, slightly bent old man, who was slowly penetrating into the very heart of the imperial palace. Were Death itself passing, it would be faced with no greater fear: For until then the dead alone knew Death, and those alive knew Life only—and there was no bridge between them. But this extraordinary man, although alive, knew Death, and enigmatical, appalling, was his cursed knowledge. "Woe!" people thought; "he will take the life of our great, deified Augustus"; and then sent curses after Lazarus, who meanwhile kept on advancing into the interior of the palace.

Already did the emperor know who Lazarus was, and prepared to meet him. But the monarch was a brave man, and felt his own tremendous, unconquerable power, and in his fatal duel with him who had miraculously risen from the dead he wanted not to invoke human help. And so he met Lazarus face to face.

"Lift not your eyes upon me, Lazarus," he ordered. "I heard your face is like that of Medusa and turns into stone whomsoever you look at. Now, I wish to see you and talk with you, before I turn into stone," he added in a tone of kingly jesting, not devoid of fear.

Coming close to him, he carefully examined Lazarus' face and his strange festal garments. And although he had a keen eye, he was deceived by his appearance.

"So. You do not appear terrible, my venerable old man. But the worse for us, if horror assumes such a respectable and pleasant air. Now let us have a talk."

Augustus sat, and questioning Lazarus with his eye as much as with words, started the conversation: "Why did you not greet me as you entered?"

Lazarus answered indifferently: "I knew not it was necessary."

"Are you a Christian?"

"No."

Augustus approvingly shook his head.

"That is good. I do not like Christians. They shake the tree of life before it is covered with fruit, and disperse its odorous bloom to the winds. But who are you?"

With a visible effort Lazarus answered: "I was dead."

"I had heard that. But who are you now?"

Lazarus was silent, but at last repeated in a tone of weary apathy: "I was dead."

"Listen to me, stranger," said the emperor, distinctly and severely giving utterance to the thought that had come to him at the beginning, "my realm is the realm of Life, my people are of the living, not of the dead. You are here one too many. I know not who you are and what you saw there; but, if you lie, I hate lies, and if you tell the truth, I hate your truth. In my bosom I feel the throb of life; I feel strength in my arm, and my proud thoughts, like eagles, pierce the space. And yonder in the shelter of my rule, under the protection of laws created by me, people live and toil and rejoice. Do you hear the battle cry, the challenge men throw into the face of the future?"

Augustus, as if in prayer, stretched forth his arms and exclaimed solemnly: "Be blessed, O great and divine Life!"

Lazarus was silent, and with growing sternness the emperor went on: "You are not wanted here, miserable remnant, snatched from under Death's teeth, you inspire weariness and disgust with life; like a caterpillar in the fields, you gloat on the rich ear of joy and belch out the drivel of despair and sorrow. Your truth is like a rusty sword in the hands of a nightly murderer, and as a murderer you shall be executed. But before that, let me look into your eyes. Perchance only cowards are afraid of them, but in the brave they awake the thirst for strife and victory; then you shall be rewarded, not executed . . . Now, look at me, Lazarus."

At first it appeared to the deified Augustus that a friend was looking at him, so soft, so tenderly fascinating was Lazarus's glance. It promised not horror, but sweet rest, and the Infinite seemed to him a tender mistress, a compassionate sister, a mother. But stronger and stronger grew its embraces, and already the mouth, greedy of hissing kisses, interfered with the monarch's breathing, and already to the surface of the soft tissues of the body came the iron of the bones and tightened its merciless circle, and unknown fangs, blunt, and cold, touched his heart and sank into it with slow indolence.

"It pains," said the deified Augustus, growing pale. "But look at me, Lazarus, look."

It was as if some heavy gates, ever closed, were slowly moving apart, and through the growing interstice the appalling horror of the Infinite poured in slowly and steadily. Like two shadows entered the shoreless void and the unfathomable darkness; they extinguished the sun, ravished the earth from under the feet, and the roof over the head. No more did the frozen heart ache.

Time stood still and the beginning of each thing grew frightfully near to its end. Augustus' throne, just erected, crumbled down, and the void was already in the place of the throne and of Augustus. Noiselessly did Rome crumble down, and a new city stood on its site and it too was swallowed by the void. Like fantastic giants, cities, states, and countries fell down and vanished in the void darkness, and with uttermost indifference did the insatiable black womb of the Infinite swallow them.

"Halt!" ordered the emperor.

In his voice sounded already a note of indifference, his hands dropped in languor, and in the vain struggle with the onrushing darkness his fiery eyes now blazed up, and now went out.

"My life you have taken from me, Lazarus," said he in a spiritless, feeble voice.

And these words of hopelessness saved him. He remembered his people, whose shield he was destined to be, and keen salutary pain pierced his deadened heart. "They are doomed to death," he thought wearily. "Serene shadows in the darkness of the Infinite," thought he, and horror grew upon him. "Frail vessels with living, seething blood, with a heart that knows sorrow and also great joy," said he in his heart, and tenderness pervaded it.

Thus pondering and oscillating between the poles of Life and Death, he slowly came back to life, to find in its suffering and in its joys a shield against the darkness of the void and the horror of the Infinite.

"No, you have not murdered me, Lazarus," said he firmly, "but I will take your life. Begone."

That evening the deified Augustus partook of his meats and drinks with particular joy. Now and then his lifted hand remained suspended in the air, and a dull glimmer replaced the bright sheen of his fiery eye. It was the cold wave of Horror that surged at his feet. Defeated, but not undone, ever awaiting its hour, that Horror stood at the emperor's bedside, like a black shadow all through his life, it swayed his nights but yielded the days to the sorrows and joys of life.

The following day, the hangman with a hot iron burned out Lazarus' eyes. Then he was sent home. The deified Augustus dared not kill him.

Lazarus returned to the desert, and the wilderness met him with hissing gusts of wind and the heat of the blazing sun. Again he was sitting on a stone, his rough, bushy beard lifted up; and the two black holes in place of his eyes looked at the sky with an expression of dull terror. Afar off the holy city stirred noisily and restlessly, but around him everything was deserted and dumb. No one approached the place where lived he who had miraculously risen from the dead, and long since his neighbors had forsaken their houses. Driven by the hot iron into the depth of his skull, his cursed knowledge hid there in an ambush. As if leaping out from an ambush it plunged its thousand invisible eyes into the man, and no one dared look at Lazarus.

And in the evening, when the sun, reddening and growing wider, would come nearer and nearer the western horizon, the blind Lazarus would slowly follow it. He would stumble against stones and fall, stout and weak as he was; would rise heavily to his feet and walk on again; and on the red screen of the sunset his black body and outspread hands would form a monstrous likeness of a cross.

And it came to pass that once he went out and did not come back. Thus seemingly ended the second life of him who for three days had been under the enigmatical sway of death, and rose miraculously from the dead.

L'CHAIM!

Harvey Jacobs

*A short, deft tale that came about as a result of a lunch I had with Harvey.
I mentioned the anthology and he was inspired . . . he says it's about yuppies.*

*D*elmore Grobit, who looked like a sponge with his cratered face
and yellow suntan, came early to the Tentacle Club. He settled
into his favorite chair, a leather throne near the window, found a *National
Geographic*, examined photographs of round Polynesian women, and waited
for James Guard. He looked up from time to time, observing other members
of the club who congregated around the fireplace under the hanging gold
symbol of the fraternity, a huge octopus. The same octopus symbol appeared
on drinking glasses, match book covers, napkins and on the blazers of more
dedicated souls. Delmore Grobit thought the octopus icon pretentious, ugly,
and bizarre.

Today was his birthday. The Tentacles would expect him to host a
dinner party later in the evening. The tradition bothered Delmore, not
because of the expense, which would come back to him in useless gifts, but
because the idea of marking the day one came wriggling and screaming into
the world made no sense. It was an occasion to forget, not sanctify.

Delmore looked forward to seeing James Guard. He didn't know if
James really liked him or if his young friend's affection over the years was
feigned. It could be merely gratitude. James had much to be grateful for.
Still, he did send thoughtful presents at Christmas and he surely would
bring some token tonight. He never forgot his benefactor's birthday.

The Tentacles' reading room seemed claustrophobic, a sure sign of impending spring. It was a winter room without question, ideal sanctuary on nights when the wind was a scream from a toothless mouth. In warmer months that room became oppressive.

As always, James Guard arrived on time and brought his own special energy. He radiated health and optimism. His assurance stopped just short of arrogance. Delmore appreciated his entrances. He saw a lot of himself in the young man.

"Happy birthday, Delmore," James said. "I brought you this small token."

"You shouldn't have, Jim. But thank you." Delmore's arthritic fingers had trouble but he managed to undo the green ribbon. He tore silver paper off a simple white box. Inside, lying on a bed of cotton, was a pair of cufflinks made from ancient Greek coins.

"Do you like them? They're authentic."

"They are very fine, Jim. Splendid."

"The least I could do."

"Ours has been a satisfying association," Delmore said. "I hope you feel the same."

"How else could I feel? You've given me everything. You've allowed me the best kind of life. I owe you more than I could ever think to repay."

"I'll never forget your face when I made you my offer."

"What could you expect? I was at rock bottom, miserable. I fit nowhere. Nobody wanted my paintings. I couldn't hold a job. I couldn't even afford the razor for suicide."

"Don't talk like that."

"Well, what's true is true. You found a loser and turned up a winner. Does that sound immodest?"

"Why be modest?"

"All that faith. All that money. Delmore, I've asked you many times. Why me?"

"Why indeed?"

"How did you find me? I know you said you'd heard about me. But looking back, I know that's impossible. My talent hadn't even begun to show. I was painting like a schoolboy. It had to be something else."

"Questions, questions. You could never just accept your luck."

"Do you know what I used to think? That you were my father. That my nun of a mother had one lapse."

"That's terrible."

"Why so terrible? At least it explained you."

"Nothing like that, Jim."

"What, then?"

Zachary, the perennial maître de of the Tentacles Club, shuffled to where they sat. He attempted a smile.

"Yes, Zachary?"

"I want to wish you felicitations, Mr. Grobit. Happy birthday and many, many more."

"Thank you."

"I've taken the liberty of arranging a small dinner party."

"Of course. Take care of the details."

"And the midnight toast?"

"Ah, yes. We must have the midnight toast."

"Certainly. As you know, it is expected . . ."

"I know the rules," Delmore said.

"I will bring the glasses, the Waterford crystal. As for the wine . . ."

"Zachary, we have time. I'm in conversation."

"Excuse me, sir. Forgive me."

"Excused. Forgiven."

Zachary turned slowly and walked toward the fireplace.

"Jim, I want to tell you a story. Many, many long years go, when I was your age, strange as it seems, my life was full of futures. I had begun my business career and I was about to marry a lovely girl of some means."

"I didn't even know you had a wife, Delmore."

"I did. A wife, a daughter, a house. And plans, dreams, goals. Like you, Jim. I bought a bottle of champagne on the day of my wedding. LaTouer '09, the finest wine I could find. I had planned to drink it on my wedding night, sharing the glorious vintage with my bride. But I didn't."

"Why not?"

"I don't know. I decided to save it for an even more special occasion. The birth of a child. Some triumph. I had nothing specific in mind, you see. A future special occasion. Well, there was a child and there were triumphs. But I saved the wine. Each time I decided to save the wine for future celebration. Even when my daughter gave birth to her first son I postponed opening that wine."

"I can understand. That bottle of wine was a guarantee for you, Delmore. As long as it remained unopened there would be a future."

"Exactly. Do you know when I finally opened it? On impulse. On a rainy night in the autumn of the year. I felt thirst. I uncorked the champagne. No special occasion. None were left. My wife was taken by the plague. My daughter and her child were random victims of some war. Do you know what I discovered when I opened the bottle? The wine had turned. It was syrupy and sour. The lovely bubbles were sludge. And I began to laugh. I laughed at the cosmic joke, Jim. I had the last laugh."

"The last laugh?"

"They found me dead in the morning."

"Beg pardon, Delmore?"

"It's rather complicated. A mere technicality. Besides, I had made provision."

"Provision for what?"

"Always questions, Jim. You have such a rapid mind. Provision for an ongoing. Lord knows, it didn't come cheap. They took the better part of my fortune."

"Who did?"

"The Tentacles, of course. They called it my initiation fee."

"I'm afraid I'm lost, Delmore."

"Wine has always interested me. I'm sure it's because of that cursed bottle of champagne. I'm quite an expert on the fruits of the grape, as they say. In fact, most of the Tentacles share that passion, or obsession. It's one of the few blessings of membership here. We spend countless hours talking of years, months, days, splendid crops, ecstatic harvests, orgasmic testings. I know it is an indulgence but I haven't many."

"Delmore, you don't need to apologize to me. If you enjoy a good wine, so be it. What harm done?"

"Which brings us to the toast. On midnight of one's birthday, it is customary that the birthday boy to provide a decanter of the finest wine for all the Tentacles to share. Tonight is my night."

"And I am very pleased that you asked me to join you here."

"I thought about my choice, Jim. And don't you know, I found myself thinking of a future special occasion. That is, I had a wine in mind but I decided to save it. Do we ever change? I realized that I'd already learned my lesson. No more waiting."

"Good. Live for the moment, Delmore."

"It's not only that. I was displaying selfishness. Frankly, Jim, I don't much enjoy this club. But it has become my family. It would be wrong to hold back on the membership. They demand the best one can offer."

"Then give it to them. There's always another bottle of wine. Think positively, Delmore. At this very moment, somewhere, new grapes are maturing. Maybe this will be a vintage year."

"I'm glad you share my feelings. Jim, you've had ten marvelous years."

"Because of you, Delmore. More than I could have expected of a lifetime."

"Yes. And the best thing is, you *know* it. You *appreciate.* So many of the youth are indifferent."

"I do appreciate."

Delmore reached over to embrace James Guard. The young man hugged him. They had never touched like that. Delmore felt a delicious warmth that reminded him of other embraces. He began to weep even as he cut the young man's throat with a quick slash of his silver pocket knife. Blood erupted from the violated neck. Delmore clapped his hands sharply. Zachary came toward them with the decanter but the waiter took forever. Delmore could not abide waste on such a scale.

"Hurry, hurry, for God's sake," Delmore yelled. "It is a minute to midnight. And what we have here is vintage 1955. December of 1955."

"Did you actually find a '55?" said one of the Tentacles. "A December?"

"I did," Delmore said. "I've kept it for a decade."

"This must be a very special occasion," the member said.

Zachary filled the decanter and corked the wound in James Guard's quivering corpse. Glasses were passed to the Tentacles who came to surround Delmore's chair.

"Actually," Delmore said, "it is just another birthday. Not a thousandth or ten thousandth. Just a birthday."

"Cheers," said Zachary, pouring fresh blood. "To Mr. Grobit."

"Drink hearty," Delmore said.

"I have a March, 1962," said another member. "I've kept her practically from birth. She's a social worker. Charming. I was going to save her for a while longer. But why? You've taught me something, Delmore. An occasion is made special if it is specially recognized."

Delmore had another sip. He felt better than he had in ages. The right wine is full of mystery. He could taste elusive ghosts. Tomorrow he would look for another bottle. And he would find it.

Ellen Datlow and I were lunching at a trendy bistro, and we began to speculate on the possibility of a new breed—the Yuppie Vampire. This upscale American vampire would need a whole new life-style (if that is the word) and a new literature to celebrate new standards of taste. To expect such a creature to be satisfied with old, established blood types was obviously wrong. *You eat what you are.* Or, in this case, drink. This insight caused a vessel to throb in Ms. Datlow's tempting neck and she said, "Write it, writer." Hence, "L'Chaim!," a toast to the nouvelle cuisine of the dark.

Harvey Jacobs

RETURN OF THE DUST VAMPIRES

S. N. Dyer

Dyer's story is one of several she's written that use her experiences as a medical doctor to great effect. The patient in the story is suffering from a mysterious, wasting disease. Written in 1980, "Return of the Dust Vampires" is a chillingly unintentional harbinger of the AIDS epidemic.

The man and woman ran across the burning sands, their faces surprisingly blank and unconcerned considering that they were being pursued by shambling, dust-colored monsters.

"I can't go on," the blonde cried.

Dr. Insomnia, leaning on the doorjamb, suggested, "Leave her." But the tall man paid no attention. He picked up the woman and stumbled onward, the creatures coming closer . . .

"Turkey," Dr. Todd remarked. "I'd've left her."

Dr. Insomnia looked in the newspaper. " 'Channel 16: *Desert Vampires*, 1955,'" she read. " 'One star'—I'd say they were being charitable."

"The actor there. Room 418."

She peered at the running man framed in long shot heading toward electric towers. "My guinea pig?" She left the call room and went to the nurses' station, skimmed 418's chart, then knocked on his door and entered without waiting. The patient lay in the patchy light from the neighboring research building. Dr. Insomnia woke him gently and introduced herself.

"Dr. Todd is watching one of your films."

"I'd heard interns suffered," he answered softly.

"Why should the patients be the only ones? We're going to switch your shots tonight—no more morphine. You'll get intravenous enkephalins for the pain."

"Enkeph . . . Do they work?"

"They're the body's own natural painkiller. But as one of my profs used to say, 'If enkephalins were any good, you could buy them on Delmar Street.' If you have any discomfort, make sure you tell me before we begin treatment tomorrow." She twirled her stethoscope. The man sighed and obligingly pulled himself into a seated position and unlaced his gown.

She compared the strong young figure on the TV to the frail dying man on the bed, thinking that neither could be the true him. The man had wasted away until he was sallow skin delineating bones. Despite his height, a single nurse could lift him. His body was consuming itself, cannibalizing the muscles. His cheeks and temples were hollowed, and even the essential fat in the eye sockets was going, making the dark eyes recede into the skull.

"Breathe, Mr. Dutcher."

"Call me Rich."

Dr. Insomnia removed the earpieces and stared into the shadowed eyes. "Rich Dutcher—wait. 'Time Seekers'?"

The man nodded.

"Well, all right! You were Commander Stone. I had a crush on you that was unbelievable." She smiled with one side of her mouth. "It's taken twenty years, but I've finally got Commander Stone naked and in my clutches."

He said weakly, "Cue up diabolical laughter and fade to cut."

I enter my office and Jason is in the comfortable chair, light glinting from his wedding band. Hugging him, I don't let go while he empties a bag of take-out food. Tousling his hair while he steals all the water chestnuts and I say, "It's nice of you to visit. It can't be very convenient, since you're dead," and he says, "Did you return my library books?"

Dr. Insomnia poured a cup of departmental coffee, then went to her own cubbyhole where she looked about the stacked journals, offprints, and half-full mugs, expecting to see Chinese food packets. *The dream's after-glow,* she thought. Slowly she drifted into full wakefulness, to alternate this state with one of zombielike exhaustion for sixteen more hours until her daily three or four hours of sleep.

She ripped yesterday from the desk calendar, half smiling as she remembered the luncheon date with Sean. *Only lunchtime affairs for the weary.* The phone rang.

"I'll be right there," she told the project technicians, pouring another mug of coffee. A cartoon on the office wall showed Dr. Insomnia holding an IV bottle and line in one hand, a Foley catheter and bag in the other, labeled respectively "Caffeine In" and "Caffeine Out."

She read the morning paper as the patients were brought in and interfaced, patient and doctor linked by the machine. At eleven Dutcher was wheeled in—a skeleton, swimming inside an expensive robe.

"You understand what we're doing?"

He nodded. "Grasping at straws."

"You're candid."

"I read the informed-consent information, though I didn't really understand most of it. 'Somatic self-image'—you intend to convince me that I'm healthy?" He laughed weakly. "That'll take some convincing."

"The imager reads off a template—in this case, me—and sets up resonant signals in your body. It's related to the placebo effect and to 'faith-healing.'" The technician began applying the patient's monitoring and invasive electrodes. Dr. Insomnia waved with her unwired hand and continued. "I haven't eaten in twenty-four hours. We'll begin by convincing your body that it also is hungry and can handle food. We can't step up your immune response and start fighting those metastases until you're in positive nutritional balance."

He shrugged. "It all sounds like the doubletalk in 'Time Seekers' or those fifties sci-fi flicks—*The Jellyfish from Hell.*"

"Hey, I saw that," the technician said, threading Dutcher's IV line into the imaging machine. He handed Dr. Insomnia her headphones, then stepped toward the patient, holding another pair.

Dr. Insomnia winked. "Close your eyes, lie still—and think of the British Empire."

She watched as Dutcher relaxed under the tranquilizer injection, the tensed muscles that clothed his skeleton gradually losing their harsh definition. The electroencephalograph showed increasing low-voltage slow waves. The pulsing blue light of his heart monitor slowed toward the steady rhythm of Dr. Insomnia's monitor.

The doctor gazed at an article and found the print slightly blurred. She closed the journal. Familiarity made dissection of the sensations difficult. There was the taste of metal, the itch of electrodes, the tingling of fingers and toes, the warm skin flush of blood dissipating heat acquired in passage through the analyzer. Dr. Insomnia felt as if her intellect were fuzzy; her mind seemed poised on the edge of a flood of memories.

She focused on a brief printout of her own EEG—some decreased alpha, increased beta, a hint of theta waves. She was hovering on the border between wakefulness and stage-one sleep.

"Too much feedback?" she asked the tech, her voice deep and isolated under the headphones.

He scanned the gauges, then wrote on a pad, "Everything checks at this end. You've been working all morning. Maybe you're just sleepy."

The blue pulses of the heart monitor synchronized.

Dr. Insomnia tossed the journal onto the floor to join the pile. She turned off the lights, closed her eyes, and concentrated on the patterns made by the random firing of retinal neurons. She imagined a tree, a glacier, a bear skiing down the ice. She thought of less and and then nothing, suddenly shuddered, and leaped back from the edge of sleep.

"Oh shit," she said, as she had nightly for ten years. "I've *got* to get some sleep." Her bed was striped with moonlight through the blinds. She heard the roar of cars on the busy street below, like surf against the beach, the omnipresent rumble becoming briefly silent as traffic moved on the cross street.

She groped for the TV controls. The picture grew out from the center in an expanding presence of light.

An Aztec priest rants on over a supine, writhing woman in a temple which is a redress of a set from *Flash Gordon*, which is in turn a redress from *Green Hell. You can't fool the doctor.* The entire Aztec nation is a half-dozen extras in loincloths.

"No no no," the woman shrieks preparatory to the sacrifice; suddenly conquistadors enter and rescue her. The dying priest is dragged off by acolytes to be mummified—

"Mummified? An Aztec?"

Jump cut to the 1950s present. A small Mexican archaeologist is talking to a tall American one. "Hey, 418!" It is Dutcher, a head taller than anyone else in the movie, his face young but with the important lines already set in. His head is bent in a perpetual tilt to see his fellow actors.

Everything is formula and predictable. The mummified priest walks around disposing of bit players. It's really trying to get at Dutcher's love-interest, who is:

(a) the older archaeologist's daughter, and

(b) the reincarnation of the princess who was rescued before the first commercial.

"Millions for defense. Not one penny for script," Dr. Insomnia mutters. The spooky part is seeing Dutcher frozen in youth and health. Dr. Insomnia's eyelids drift southward as the hero wonders how to electrocute the mummy.

"Throw in a radio while it's bathing," she suggests, and sleeps.

Mother says, "Eat. There are children starving in Europe." Dinner writhes like a sacrificial victim and melts. I'm running outside into rain, steaming ground like a tropical jungle, snakes in the banana, papaya, pineapple trees. Screeching monkey laughter. Green hell?

"*Aztec Doom* was on last night," she remarked around the hovering technician.

"One of mine?" Rich asked.

"You weren't very good."

"For what they paid, why bother?"

Again the body snapped convulsively as sleep neared. Again the sad grope for the TV controls.

"It's like nothing I've ever seen before," Rich says over the sheet-draped, desiccated corpse. People disappear from the small desert town for another half hour. Then some teen-agers are trapped and barely escape the monster, an actor in a dust-colored mask and bodysuit. Events limp forward. Rich carries the young blonde to the electric towers while the dust vampires pursue, bent on stealing moisture, flesh, life . . .

Dr. Insomnia sat back, feet on her desk, and contemplated her standard morning exhaustion. Her eyes were red as Christopher Lee's in *Satanic Rites of Dracula*. She'd forgotten the last night's dream before she could add it to her journal, but she had vague memories that it had been slow-going, like a Russian novel, or introductory chemistry for humanities majors. A plodding, sinking feeling.

"Quagmired in a marshmallow sea," she said aloud, pleased to have found the proper metaphor. She examined her breakfast doughnut once more, rotating it a full 360 degrees, staring at the multicolored sprinkles in the icing. She tossed it in the trash can, a perfect hook shot. Then she attended a departmental meeting, nodding sagely when necessary, and adopting an interested expression until her facial muscles ached. She felt as Rich must have, filming *Desert Vampires*, enduring take after take of trying to look concerned while other actors stumbled over their lines and speculated endlessly about the corpse.

Rich's handshake was firmer. "I think it's working," he said. "Look, I'm even drinking juice between meals."

She smiled. Never tell the patient he's fooling himself. What had she accomplished with the other five? Some improved appetite, less nausea—marijuana might do the same. At best, they now had better attitudes.

"I saw *Desert Vampires* last night."

"Not too selective."

"Channel 16 from Las Pulgas will run anything. Sometimes I think aliens have determined that TV waves are bad for us—they'll depopulate the earth or turn us into zombies or something. So the aliens buy up UHF stations all over and beam out vacuous nonsense twenty-four hours a day, even though no one's watching."

He looked thoughtful. "I think I was in that one. Fifty-eight. I played second lead to Gerald Mohr."

She hits the jackpot. A rerun of *Time Seekers*.

"It only lasted one season. No one syndicates shows that lasted one season." She lifts one corner of her mouth, her smile self-conscious even when she's alone with the TV. "No one? Channel 16 must take that as a challenge."

Dr. Insomnia loves the show. How can she not? It begins in Time Seekers' top-secret future headquarters. A beehive-hairdoed woman screams. The sun is preparing to go nova. Dr. Meter—she remembers the runt scientist from her youth—whips out his slide rule—(slide rule!)—and announces that they only have 14 hours, 58 minutes and 32.5 seconds left to live.

But as it continues, Dr. Insomnia forgets the camp, early sixties futurism. She falls back into her adolescence, when it was only the reassuring presence of *Time Seekers* every Wednesday that gave her purpose, like a tree pointing out a hidden path in an endless plain or a pyramid standing inflexible against erosion.

The hero, blue-eyed and cleft-chinned, fights off various fiends, eventually arriving at headquarters. Dr. Meter says, "Quick, Rusty. Commander Stone needs you."

Dr. Insomnia holds her breath as the door swings open to the commander's office. The past, especially an adolescent crush, is embarrassing. She always flinches at Herman's Hermits albums or the execrable acting of one of her teen idols. But Stone is a pleasant surprise. Rich is as he should be, face with definite planes and seams in the black and white. Forty-five is kind to him—the lines and shadowed hollows giving character, while the chin is only starting to fall, the stomach to grow, the hair to disappear. His expression is a studied blank, every word and movement minimal but perfectly correct.

"Shit. He can act," she says, quite pleased that she need not be embarrassed.

He sits behind the desk—"Naturally; he's taller than Rusty"—and rattles through the exposition. The hero is almost out the door when Stone's gravelly voice says, offhanded, "Oh, and, Rusty?" Dr. Insomnia says the words along with him. "All time and space depend on you."

The rest of the show is Rusty's heroics through Tudor England and some primitive jungle planet, as he fights thugs and repeatedly rescues a kidnap-prone woman. Insomnia waits for these scattered moments when they cut back to Time Seekers' headquarters. Dr. Meter paces anxiously. Stone sits on the edge of his desk.

"Time is running out."

"I know. We can only hope Rusty succeeds."

And the tag scene: "You did it, Rusty. The Time president wants to thank you."

"He'll have to wait." Sparkle. "I've got a heavy date in Elizabethan England and I don't want to keep the lady waiting." Sprightly music as he winks and leaves. Stone looks furious but, as Dr. Meter shrugs fondly, Stone's expression melts into a rueful grin. Fadeout.

Fog and drums. A row of conga drummers along the lower border of Hippie Hill in Golden Gate Park. Am I a kid again or—no, I'm me. Hare Krishna chanters. Marijuana smoke overlying eucalyptus scent. Someone playing with soap bubbles; a large one floats over the trees toward Haight Street, unseen behind, the bubble growing and swallowing the park inside it. Standing at the edge of the bubble, translucent, pulsing, rippling with colors like oil on a wet street. A man sits outside the bubble, his back familiar. I must reach him, reach out, reach through the soap wall . . .

"Sorry we're running late. I overslept," she said, marveling at the words.

Rich grinned. "I get to go out in the sun today. I've got some energy to burn." Enthusiasm seemed strange coming from the still cadaverously thin white-haired man.

"Dr. Todd says you're putting away four-course dinners now."

"First course awful, second course dreadful, third . . ."

"In other words, typical hospital food. I'll see if we can have some better meals sent in. Jeeves?" The technician rolled his eyes at the summons and turned on the machinery. White noise welled up in the headphones. Brains grew still in a semblance of sleep . . .

She wheeled Dutcher back to his room. His voice was huskier and slower than Commander Stone's, but it was sounding closer every day. "The best I can say for *Time Seekers* is that it was work. My first steady acting job after I lost the contract with the studio—I was too tall. Didn't make it as a leading man and they couldn't have a character actor dwarfing the romantic lead. Then I did that awful monster stuff and then TV, villains mostly. I've snuffed more people than Baby Face Nelson.

"*Time Seekers* was just an excuse to let them use their back lot and old props. Mongol Horde with Enfield rifles—that sort of stuff. My wife would wake me from a dead sleep and I'd say, 'Time and space depend on you, Rusty.' The hardest part of acting is keeping a straight face."

"Well, you kept one very well," she said. He barely needed help getting from the wheelchair to his bed. Stone had always seemed in control, sitting impassively as the universe about him rocked with chaos. She remembered adolescent nights, lying in the dark inventing a background for the character, fantasies explaining his imperturbability. She laughed aloud. "You know, I don't think I recognize you except when you're in the background, half in shadow and slightly out of focus."

"That's because the star's contract specified that he be the one in focus."

She went to the doorway and stopped. "Another cherished mystery bites the dust. Thanks a lot."

Dr. Insomnia's body did not rest. Like every body, it ceaselessly respired, digested, filtered, metabolized, excreted. And it served as mercenary soldier for six other unwell bodies. One night it looked at short strands of nucleic acids and responded with interferon. Another night a hapten inspired B cells to gear up into plasma cells and churn out immunoglobins. Or a tuberculin test awoke the cell-mediated immunity and marshaled the killer T-cells.

Dr. Insomnia's body went to war while Dr. Insomnia's brain watched *Time Seekers* and then slept. The roar of traffic subsided on the busy street. Solitary trucks rumbled by, shaking the apartment house. The sun rose over the mountains, illuminating the promise of another smog-filled San Yobebe morning. Light slid in between the slats of the Venetian blinds. The traffic built back up to surflike regularity.

Dr. Insomnia still slept.

Desert Vampires as it should be, hopeless and terrifying. We're shot down on
some desert planet, Time Seeker uniforms ragged and torn, waiting to die
of the cruel heat or alien marauders or indigenous monsters. Commander
Stone leads us, torn shirt, scraped cheek, mussed hair. He looks delicious. I'm
wearing medic clothes; the others are extras; people from work. "Keep walking," Stone orders, threatens, cajoles. "Toward the hills." What's in the hills?
More rock and sand and hopelessness. Someone lags behind and disappears
with a scream, us too tired to react. Only ashes. They pick us off one by one
in the daylight. Jason dies again. Sean stands there with an astonished wide-
eyed look and crumbles as sand. He's layers collapsing one by one, while I
hide my face in the tatters of Stone's uniform and his gravelly voice says,
"Don't worry. I won't let them get you." Screaming: "They've gotten everyone
else!" After all my hopes and expectations, I'm only a screamer needing to
be rescued and feeling disappointed with myself. But he seems to expect, to
like my helplessness. He says gravely, "They can't get me. I'm a regular . . ." In
a circle around us, the sand animates, pushing up into the figures of humans
and then shambling forward, solidifying, reaching toward us . . .

She awoke with the blankets on the floor, the sheet's indentations across her face, and the twenty-four hour flu in her gut.

The antibody test results came back later that week. "Just plain old influenza virus, last season's variety," Sean, her lunchtime lover, reported in a disappointed voice. "Any flu capable of downing Dr. Insomnia ought to be a brave new strain."

"I should be able to fight something so prosaic."

"Maybe you're tired."

She shook her head. "Maybe I'm not tired enough."

Two of the six patients were dead. Three more merely hung on. Dr. Insomnia fought skirmishes, delayed implacable besiegers who would sooner or later burn, starve, dig them out. Every day, as dessert, they wheeled in Rich Dutcher, looking healthier with each session. Dr. Insomnia looked forward to him as she used to look forward to *Time Seekers,* a joyful cap to a train of miserable events.

"You need more sun," Rich said. "You're pale."

"Thanks, doctor." She coughed and felt a stab of guilt and anxiety. *Mellow out,* she told herself. *It's not like he's immunosuppressed. In fact, right now his reticuloendothelial system is probably a damn sight healthier than yours.* Aloud she said, "Bit of a cold."

They interfaced with the machine. White noise swallowed the remainder of the morning. She blinked, returning to awareness in the warm noon light.

That evening she reviewed Dutcher's chart. Hemoglobin normal. Lymphocyte count high normal. Weight increasing. Radiology noted no new growths, the old ones decreasing to small scars. On the bottom of one page the intern had scribbled, "Query—remission?" The word was sunbursting through clouds.

Rich was awake and cynically watching one of his own movies. "Giant cockroaches," he said. "I had real ones in my apartment while I was making this turkey. They gave me the creeps—my wife had to kill them. But here I am zapping fifty-foot ones with an electric fly swatter."

"Are you implying it's unrealistic?"

He snorted, an old man scowling at himself. "Look at me. That's not acting, it's sleepwalking. I'll never be able to live it down. Fifty years after I'm dead they'll be showing this dreck on the late late show."

"Yeah. Like now, you can watch TV and fall in love with Bogart thirty years after he died."

He looked at her sharply, dark eyes in a pool of light. "Do you always get entranced by flickering images?"

She sighed. "It's so much easier to love people who don't exist. Safer too." She shook her head as if waking to the situation. "Revelations at this early hour? I came in to give you some good news."

He listened gravely as she described his progress. "I'm the only one on whom it's really worked?"

"You know what I think it is? Ego. Only someone with a colossal ego could will himself to health. No offense?"

He laughed. "Don't worry. Von Sternberg said actors are cattle, but we're special cattle. We have charisma. We project. We're immortal. Flies in amber."

She hooked a thumb at the TV. "That's more like a dinosaur in a tar pit. Cattle?" She muttered, "Grade A government-inspected beefcake," glancing obliquely at the screen. Rich, stripped to the waist, was climbing another electric tower. The old actor chuckled and left for his therapeutic walk down the hall and back. Dr. Insomnia watched the tiny man scramble about the tower trying to avoid a huge cockroach.

During the commercial she noticed a spiral-bound notebook on the nightstand. She opened it at random.

I'm outside, running in the rain. Trees—banana, pineapple. (Pineapple on trees?) Screaming noises.

She flipped a page.

The doctor is yelling—she can't make it. I'm shouting "The hills!"
Another.

. . . beside some endless translucent film, and a hand begins to push through . . .

Outside the room, Rich was speaking to a nurse. Inside, in the tube, he questioned a soldier. He was in stereo.

I'm attached by an umbilical IV line to the project machine, swinging the cord like a jump rope. Commander Stone sits in a corner, just staring at me. "Quit it," I say. "Knock it off." His eyes are recessed deep under his brow, like Rich's. The technician sits at the interfaced control—player piano, ragtime. Then he stands and flakes away as sand. The cord begins pulling me into the machine. Commander Stone reaches out and he's a dust monster, crudely sculpted sand in a Time Seeker's costume. He reaches out, stops, pulls back his hand, and I'm going into the machine, all gaping darkness . . .

The new clock radio read 5:33 in luminescent figures. It was set to go off at seven. She hadn't needed an alarm clock for over a decade. Her skin felt like burning sand. She stretched to find a good position to return to sleep and felt something warm against her back. A body. She was not alone. A dust monster!

She crawled out slowly, anxious not to awaken the quiet life-vampire, then went into the kitchen and put up water for instant coffee. She was afraid to return to bed.

"It's not a dust monster," she said, mouth dry with fever. "It's Sean, it's got to be Sean. Right?" She was unable to go and check the hypothesis.

The teapot screamed and it was every black-and-white thirty-frames-per-second terrified woman screaming for rescue. It was Dr. Insomnia.

They met in the corridor, doctor and patient both wearing robes and slippers. The walls were the same industrial green as Time Seekers' headquarters. He held up his IV bottle. "I'm searching for an honest man."

She hoisted her bottle. "I'll see your isotonic saline and raise you five percent glucose."

Voice suddenly full of concern, he asked, "Do they know what it is?"

"Not yet. More tests," she replied.

He said, "I'm being discharged soon. Mind if I come visit?"

"I'll be here." *I'll never leave.* The walk from her room to the nurses' station and back exhausted her. She lay down and was asleep.

Running across sand dunes toward the electric towers. The dune forms into a hand that grabs my ankle. I fall. Rolling down the dune into more sand that becomes arms grabbing, holding, smothering . . . Jason, there is no answer . . . All time and space depend on you Time. Time is the dust vampire.

As to an afterword—well, I don't know what to say. In high school my friends and I were vampire buffs; we watched *Dark Shadows*, read Bram Stoker, slept under Bela Lugosi posters. Since then I've changed, realizing that vampires aren't tall, dark strangers who will rescue you from mundane adolescent angst and introduce you to the hidden worlds of love, power, and cosmic wonder. Now, I guess I think of vampires as the things that keep you from love, power, and wonder—jobs, responsibility, mortality, and all the other baggage we accumulate by growing up. Maybe I was happier before . . .

On a different note, I wrote the story six years ago, in early medical school. While the jargon is no less accurate than the scientific details in most science fiction, it is a bit embarrassing from my current level of knowledge. But that's just more accumulations too.

S.N. Dyer

GOOD
KIDS

Edward Bryant

I've found that giving Ed an assignment is the best way to get him to finish a new story. It's worked at OMNI, *and it's worked here.*

It's tough for kids growing up in New York City—the world is a dangerous place and so they become tough themselves.

"*T*hat blood?" said Donnie, appalled. "That's grossss."

Angelique was peeking over her shoulder at the lurid paperback vampire novel. "Don't draw out your consonants. You sound like a geek."

"I'm not a geek," said Donnie. "I'm only eleven years old, you jerk. I get to draw out my esses if I want to."

"We're all too goddamned bright," said Camelia gloomily. "The last place I went to school, everybody just played with dolls or talked all day about crack."

"Public schools," Angelique snorted.

Donnie flipped the page and squinted. "Yep, he's lapping up her menstrual blood, all right. This vampire's a real gink."

"Wonderful. So her arching, lily-white swan throat wasn't enough," said Cammie. "Oh boy. I can hardly wait til *I* start having my period."

The lights flashed and the four of us involuntarily glanced up. Ms. Yukoshi, one of the Center's three night supervisors, stood framed in the doorway. "Okay, girls, lights out in three. Put away the book. Hit those bunks. Good night, now." She started to exit, but then apparently changed her mind. "I suppose I ought to mention that this is my last night taking care of you."

Were we supposed to clap? I wondered. Maybe give her a four-part harmony chorus of "Thank you, Ms. Yukoshi"? What was appropriate behavior?

"No thanks are necessary," said Ms. Yukoshi. "I just know I need a long, long vacation. Lots of R and R." We could all see her sharp, white teeth gleaming in the light from the overhead. "You'll have a new person to bedevil tomorrow night. His name is Mr. Vladisov."

"So why don't we ever get a good WASP?" Cammie whispered.

The other two giggled. I guess I did too. It's easy to forget that Camelia is black.

Ms. Yukoshi looked at us sharply. Donnie giggled again and dog-eared a page before setting the vampire book down. "Good night, girls." Ms. Yukoshi retreated into the hall. We listened to the click and echo of her stylish heels moving on to the next room, the next island of kids. Boys in that one.

"I wonder what Mr. Vladisov will be like," Donnie said.

Angelique smiled. "At least he's a guy."

"Good night, girls." Donnie mimicked Ms. Yukoshi.

I snapped off the lamp. And that was it for another fun evening at the renovated brownstone that was the Work-at-Night Child Care Center and Parenting Service. Wick Pus, we called it, all of us who had night-shift parents with no other place to put their kids.

"Good night," I said to everybody in general. I lay back in the bunk and pulled the covers up to my chin. The wool blanket scratched my neck.

"I'm hungry," said Angelique plaintively. "Cookies and milk aren't enough."

"Perhaps you want some blooood?" said Donnie, snickering.

"Good night," I said again. But I was hungry too.

The next day was Wednesday. Hump day. Didn't matter. No big plans for the week—or for the weekend. It wasn't one of the court-set times for my dad to visit, so I figured probably I'd be spending the time reading. That was okay too. I like to read. Maybe I'd finish the last thousand pages of Stephen King's new novel and get on to some of the stuff I needed to read for school.

We were studying urban legends and old wives' tales—a side issue was the class figuring out a nonsexist term for the latter.

We'd gone through a lot of the stuff that most of us had heard—and even believed at one time—like the hook killer and the Kentucky Fried Rat and the expensive car that was on sale unbelievably cheap because nobody could get the smell out of the upholstery after the former owner killed himself and the body wasn't discovered for three hot days. Then there was the rattlesnake in the K-Mart jeans and the killer spiders in the bouffant. Most of that didn't interest me. What I liked were the older myths, things like keeping cats out of the nursery and forbidding adults to sleep in the presence of children.

Now I've always liked cats, so I know where my sympathy lies with that one. Kitties love to snuggle up to warm little faces on chilly nights. No surprise, right? But the bit about sucking the breath from babies' lungs is a load of crap. Well, most of the time. As for the idea that adults syphon energy from children, that's probably just a cleaner way of talking about the incest taboo.

It's a way of speaking metaphorically. That's what the teacher said.

I can see why adults would want to steal kids' energy. Then they could rule the world, live forever, win all the Olympics. See what I mean? So maybe some adults do. You ever feel just how much energy is generated by a roomful of hyper kids? *I* know. But then, I'm a kid. I expect I'll lose it all when I grow up. I'm not looking forward to that. It'll be like death. Or maybe undeath.

It all sounds sort of dull gray and drab, just like living in the book *1984*.

The thing about energy is that what goes out has to come in first. Another lesson. First Law of Thermodynamics. Or maybe the Second. I didn't pay much attention that day. I guess I was too busy daydreaming about horses, or maybe sneaking a few pages of the paperback hidden in my vinyl binder.

Don't even ask what I'm going to do when I grow up. I've got lots of time to figure it out.

Mr. Vladisov had done his homework. He addressed us all by name. Evidently he'd sucked Ms. Yukoshi dry of all the necessary information.

"And you would be Shauna-Laurel Andersen," he said to me, smiling faintly.

I felt like I ought to curtsy at least. Mr. Vladisov was tall and courtly, just like characters in any number of books I'd read. His hair was jet-black and fixed in one of those widow's peaks. Just like a novel. His eyes were sharp and black too, though the whites were all bloodshot. They didn't look comfortable. He spoke with some kind of Slavic accent. Good English, but the kind of accent I've heard actors working in restaurants goofing around with.

Shauna-Laurel, I thought. "My friends call me SL," I said.

"Then I hope we shall be friends," said Mr. Vladisov.

"Do we have to call you 'sir'?" said Angelique. I knew she was just being funny. I wondered if Mr. Vladisov knew that.

"No." His gaze flickered from one of us to the next. "I know we shall *all* be very close. Ms. Yukoshi told me you were all . . ." He seemed to be searching for the correct phrase. ". . . good kids."

"Sure," said Donnie, giggling just a little.

"I believe," said Mr. Vladisov, "that it is customary to devour milk and cookies before your bedtime."

"Oh, that's not for a while yet," said Angelique.

"Hours," chimed in Donnie.

Our new guardian consulted his watch. "Perhaps twenty-three minutes?" We slowly nodded.

"SL," he said to me, "will you help me distribute the snacks?"

I followed Mr. Vladisov out the door.

"Be careful," said Angelique so softly that only I could hear. I wondered if I really knew what she meant.

Mr. Vladisov preceded me down the corridor leading to the playroom and then to the adjacent kitchenette. Other inmates looked at us through the doorways as we passed. I didn't know most of their names. There were about three dozen of them. Our crowd—the four of us—was pretty tight.

He slowed so I could catch up to his side. "Your friends seem very nice," he said. "Well behaved."

"Uh, yes," I answered. "They're great. Smart too."

"And healthy."

"As horses."

"My carriage," mused Mr. Vladisov, "used to be pulled by a fine black team."

"Beg pardon?"

"Nothing," he said sharply. His tone moderated. "I sometimes slip into the past, SL. It's nothing."

"Me," I said. "I love horses. My dad says he'll get me a colt for my graduation from middle school. We'll have to stable it out in Long Island."

Mr. Vladisov didn't comment. We had reached the closetlike kitchenette. He didn't bother to turn on the light. When he opened the refrigerator and took out a carton of milk, I could see well enough to open the cabinet where I knew the cookies were stored.

"Chocolate chip?" I said. "Double Stuf Oreos?"

Mr. Vladisov said, "I never eat . . . cookies. Choose what you like."

I took both packages. Mr. Vladisov hovered over the milk, assembling quartets of napkins and glasses. "Don't bother with a straw for Donnie," I said. "She's not supposed to drink through a straw. Doctor's orders."

Mr. Vladisov nodded. "Do these things help you sleep more soundly?"

I shrugged. "I 'spose so. The nurse told me once that a high-carb snack before bed would drug us out. It's okay. Cookies taste better than Ritalin anyway."

"Ritalin?"

"An upper that works like a downer for the hypers."

"I beg your pardon?"

I decided to drop it. "The cookies help us all sleep."

"Good," said Mr. Vladisov. "I want everyone to have a good night's rest. I take my responsibility here quite seriously. It would be unfortunate were anyone to be so disturbed she woke up in the early morning with nightmares."

"We all sleep very soundly," I said.

Mr. Vladisov smiled down at me. In the dim light from the hall, it seemed to me that his eyes gleamed a dusky red.

I passed around the Double Stuf Oreos and the chocolate-chip cookies. Mr. Vladisov poured and distributed the glasses of milk as solemnly as if he were setting out communion wine.

Cammie held up her milk in a toast. "We enjoyed Ms. Yukoshi, but we know we'll like you much better."

Mr. Vladisov smiled without parting his teeth and raised an empty hand as though holding a wine glass. "A toast to you as well. To life everlasting, and to the dreams which make it bearable."

Angelique and I exchanged glances. I looked at Donnie. Her face was saying nothing at all. We all raised our glasses and then drank. The milk was cold and good, but it wasn't the taste I wished. I wanted chocolate.

Mr. Vladisov wished us a more conventional good night, then smoothly excused himself from the room to see to his other charges. We listened hard but couldn't hear his heels click on the hallway tile.

"Slick," said Angelique, nibbling delicately around the edge of her chocolate-chip cookie.

"Who's he remind me of?" mused Cammie. "That old guy—I saw him in a play once. Frank Langella."

"I don't know about this," said Donnie.

"What don't you know?" I said.

"I don't know whether maybe one of us ought to stay up all night on watch." Her words came out slowly. Then more eagerly, "Maybe we could take turns."

"We all need our rest," I said, "It's a school night."

"I sure need all the energy *I* can get," said Cammie. "I've got a geography test tomorrow. We're supposed to know all the capitals of those weird little states west of New Jersey."

I said, "I don't think we have anything to worry about for a while. Mr. Vladisov's new. It'll take him a little while to settle in and get used to us."

Cammie cocked her head. "So you think we got ourselves a live one?"

"So to speak." I nodded. "Metaphorically speaking . . ."

So I was wrong. Not about what Mr. Vladisov was. Rather that he would wait to get accustomed to how things ran at Wick Pus. He must have been very hungry.

In the morning, it took Donnie forever to get up. She groaned when Cammie shook her, but didn't seem to want to move. "I feel shitty," she said, when her eyes finally opened and started to focus. "I think I've got the flu."

"Only if bats got viruses in their spit," said Cammie grimly. She gestured at Donnie's neck, gingerly zeroing in with her index finger.

Angelique and I leaned forward, inspecting the throat.

Donnie's brown eyes widened in alarm. "What's wrong?" she said weakly.

"What's wrong ain't pimples," said Cammie. "And there's two of them."

"Damn," said Angelique.

"Shit," said Donnie.

I disagreed with nobody.

The four of us agreed to try not to get too upset about all of this until we'd had time to confer tonight after our parents dropped us off at the Center. Donnie was the hardest to convince. But then, it was her throat that showed the pair of matched red marks.

Mrs. Maloney was the morning-shift lady who saw us off to our various buses and subways to school. Mr. Vladisov had gone off duty sometime before dawn. Naturally. He would return after dark. Double naturally.

"I'm gonna tell my mom I don't want to come back to the Center tonight," Donnie had said.

"Don't be such a little kid," said Cammie. "We'll take care of things."

"It'll be all right," Angelique chimed in.

Donnie looked at me as though begging silently for permission to chicken out. "SL?"

"It'll be okay," I said as reassuringly as I could. I wasn't so sure it would be that okay. Why was everyone staring at me as though I were the leader?

"I trust you," Donnie said softly.

I knew I was blushing. "It'll be all right." I wished I knew whether I was telling the truth.

At school, I couldn't concentrate. I didn't even sneak reads from my Stephen King paperback. I guess I sort of just sat there like a wooden dummy while lessons were talked about and assignments handed out.

I started waking up in the afternoon during my folklore class.

"The thing you should all remember," said Mrs. Dancey, my teacher, "is that myths never really change. Sometimes they're garbled and they certainly appear in different guises to different generations who recount them. But the basic lessons don't alter. We're talking about truths."

The truth was, I thought, I didn't know what we were all going to do about Mr. Vladisov. That was the long and short of it, and no urban myth Mrs. Dancey tempted me with was going to take my mind off that.

Time. Things like Mr. Vladisov, they figured they had all the time in the world, so they usually seemed to take things easy. Given time, we'd figure something out. Cammie, Donnie, Angelique, and me. We could handle anything. Always had.

"Shauna-Laurel?" It was Mrs. Dancey. Talking to me.

I didn't know what she had asked. "Ma'am?" I said. "Sorry."

But it was too late. I'd lost my chance. Too much daydreaming. I hoped it wouldn't be too late tonight.

Donnie's twin red marks had started to fade when the four of us huddled in our room at the Center to talk.

"So maybe they *are* zits," said Cammie hopefully.

Donnie irritably scratched at them. "They itch."

I sat on the edge of the bunk and swung my legs back and forth. "Don't scratch. They'll get infected."

"You sound like my mother."

"Good evening, my good kids." Mr. Vladisov filled the doorway. He was all dark clothing and angular shadows. "I hope you are all feeling well tonight?"

"Aren't you a little early?" said Angelique.

Mr. Vladisov made a show of consulting his watch. It was the old-fashioned kind, round and gold, on a chain. It had hands. I glanced out the window toward the street. The light had gone while we were talking. I wondered where Mr. Vladisov spent his days.

"Early? No. Perhaps just a bit," he corrected himself. "I find my position here at the Center so pleasant, I don't wish to be late." He smiled at us. We stared back at him. "What? You're not all glad to see me?"

"I have the flu," said Donnie dully.

"The rest of us will probably get it too," Angelique said.

Cammie and I nodded agreement.

"Oh, I'm sorry," said Mr. Vladisov. "I see why this should trouble you. Perhaps I can obtain for you an elixir?"

"Huh?" That was Cammie.

"For your blood," he said. "Something to strengthen your resistance. Tomato juice, perhaps? or V-8? Some other healthful beverage?"

"No," said Donnie. "No thank you. I don't think so. No." She hiccupped.

"Oh, you poor child." Mr. Vladisov started forward. Donnie drew back.

"Is there something I can do?" he said, checking himself in midstride. "Perhaps I should call for a doctor?" His voice sounded *so* solicitous. "Your parent?"

"No!" Donnie came close to shouting.

"She'll be okay," said Cammie.

Mr. Vladisov looked indecisive. "I don't know . . ."

"We do," I said. "Everything will be fine. Donnie just needs a good night's sleep."

"I'm sure she will get that," said Mr. Vladisov. "The night is quiet." Then he excused himself to fetch our milk and cookies. This time he didn't ask for volunteer help.

Cammie was stroking Donnie's hair. "We'll see nothin' happens. You'll be just fine."

"That's right," said Angelique. "We'll all stay up."

"No need," I said. "We can take turns. No use everybody killing themselves."

"Bad phrasing," said Cammie. "Taking turns sounds good to me."

I volunteered, "I'll take the first watch."

"Yeah." Cammie grinned. "That way the rest of us got to stay up in the scariest part of the night."

"Okay, so you go first and wake me up later."

"Naw. Just kidding."

I liked being friends with Cammie and the others. But then we were so much alike. More than you might think.

The daughter of a widowed Harlem mortician.

The daughter of the divorced assistant French consul.

The daughter of an ambitious off-Broadway director.

The daughter of a divorced famous novelist.

All of us denied latch-keys and dumped at Wick Pus. Handier than boarding school if a parent wanted us. But still out of their hair.

One of us used to love drugs. One of us was thinking about loving God. Another was afraid of being the baby of the group. And another just wanted peace and a horse. I smiled.

Donnie actually did look reassured.

After a while, Mr. Vladisov came back with our nightly snacks. He seemed less exuberant. Maybe he was catching on to the fact that we were on to him. Maybe not. It's hard to tell with adults.

At any rate, he bid us all a good evening and that was the last we saw of him until he came around to deliver a soft, "Lights out, girls. Sleep well. Sleep well, indeed."

We listened for his footsteps, didn't hear any, heard him repeating his message to the boys down the hall. Finally we started to relax just a little.

Through the darkness, Cammie whispered, "Three hours, SL. That's it. Don't knock yourself out, okay? Wake me up in three hours."

"Okay."

I heard Donnie's younger, softer whisper. "Thanks, guys. I'm glad you're all here. I'm even going to try to sleep."

"Want a ghost story first?" That was Angelique.

"No!" Donnie giggled.

We were all silent.

I listened for steady, regular breathing. I waited for anything strange. I eventually heard the sounds of the others sleeping.

I guess I really hadn't expected them to drift off like that.

And then I went to sleep.

I hadn't expected that either.

I woke up sweaty, dreaming someone was slapping me with big slabs of lunch meat. Someone *was* slapping me. Cammie.

"Wake up, you gink! She's gone!"

"Who's gone?" The lamp was on and I tried to focus on Cammie's angry face.

"Donnie! The honky blood-sucker stole her."

I struggled free of the tangled sheet. I didn't remember lying down in my bed. The last thing I recalled was sitting bolt upright, listening for anything that sounded like Mr. Vladisov skulking around. "I think he—he put me to sleep." I felt terrible.

"He put us all to sleep," said Angelique. "No time to worry about that. We've got to find Donnie before he drains her down to those cute little slippers." Donnie had been wearing a pair of plush Felix the Cat foot warmers.

"Where we gonna look?" Cammie looked about ready to pull Mr. Vladisov apart with her bare fingers with their crimson painted nails.

"Follow running blood downhill," I said.

"Jeez," Cammie said disgustedly.

"I mean it. Try the basement. I bet he's got his coffin down there."

"Traditionalist, huh?"

"Maybe. I hope so." I pulled on one Adidas, wound the laces around my ankle, reached for the other. "What time is it, anyway?"

"Not quite midnight. Sucker didn't even wait for the witching hour."

I stood up. "Come on."

"What about the others?" Angelique paused by the door to the hall.

I quickly thought about that. We'd always been pretty self-sufficient. But this wasn't your ordinary situation. "Wake 'em up," I said. "We can use the help." Cammie started for the door "But be quiet. Don't wake up the supervisors."

On the way to the door, I grabbed two Oreos I'd saved from my bedtime snack. I figured I'd need the energy.

I realized there were thirty or thirty-five kids trailing just behind as my roommates and I found one of Donnie's Felix slippers on the landing in the fire stairs. It was just before the final flight down to the dark rooms where the furnace and all the pipes were. The white eyes stared up at me. The whiskers didn't twitch.

"Okay," I said unnecessarily, "come on. Hurry!"

Both of them were in a storage room, just up the corridor from the place where the furnace roared like some giant dinosaur. Mr. Vladisov sat on a case of toilet paper. It was like he was waiting for us. He expected us. He sat there with Donnie cradled in his arms and was already looking up at the doorway when we burst through.

"SL . . ." Donnie's voice was weak. She tried to reach out toward me, but Mr. Vladisov held her tightly. "I don't want to be here."

"Me neither," muttered Cammie from beside me.

"Ah, my good kids," said Mr. Vladisov. "My lambs, my fat little calves. I am sorry that you found me."

It didn't sound like he was sorry. I had the feeling he'd expected it, maybe even wanted it to happen. I began to wonder if this one was totally crazy. A psychotic. "Let Donnie go," I said, trying for a firmness I don't think was really showing in my voice.

"No." That was simple enough.

"Let her go," I repeated.

"I'm not . . . done," he said, baring his fangs in a jolly grin.

I said, "Please?"

"You really don't understand." Mr. Vladisov sighed theatrically. "There are two dozen or more of you and only one of me; but I am a man of some power. When I finish snacking on this one, I will kill most of the rest of you. Perhaps all. I'll kill you and I will drink you."

"Horseshit," said Cammie.

"You will be first," said Mr. Vladisov, "after your friend." He stared directly at me, his eyes shining like rubies.

"Get fucked." I surprised myself by saying that. I don't usually talk that way.

Mr. Vladisov looked shocked. "Shauna-Laurel, my dear, you are not a child of *my* generation."

I definitely wasn't. "Let. Her. Loose," I said distinctly.

"Don't be tiresome, my child. Now be patient. I'll be with you in just a moment." He lowered his mouth toward Donnie's throat.

"You're dead," I told him.

He paused, smiling horribly. "No news to me."

"I mean *really* dead. For keeps."

"I doubt that. Others have tried. Rather more mature specimens than all of you." He returned his attention to Donnie's neck.

Though I didn't turn away from Mr. Vladisov, I sensed the presence of the other kids behind me. We had all crowded into the storage room, and now the thirty-odd of us spread in a sort of semicircle. If Mr. Vladisov wondered why none of us was trying to run away, he didn't show it. I guess maybe like most adults, he figured he controlled us all.

I took Cammie's hand with my right, Angelique's with my left. All our fingers felt very warm. I could sense us starting to relax into that fuzzy-feeling receptive state that we usually only feel when we're asleep. I knew we were teaming up with the other kids in the room.

It's funny sometimes about old folktales (we'd finally come up in class with a nonsexist term). Like the one forbidding adults to sleep in the same room with a child. They had it right. They just had it backwards. It's *us* who suck up the energy like batteries charging . . .

Mr. Vladisov must have felt it start. He hesitated, teeth just a little ways from Donnie's skin. He looked at us from the corners of his eyes without raising his head. "I feel . . ." he started to say, and then trailed off. "You're taking something. You're feeding—"

"Let her go." I shouldn't even have said that. It was too late for making bargains.

"My . . . blood?" Mr. Vladisov whispered.

"Don't be gross," said Cammie.

I thought I could see Donnie smile wanly.

"I'm sorry," said Angelique. "I thought you were going to work out okay. We wouldn't have taken much. Just enough. You wouldn't have suspected a thing. Finally you would have moved on and someone else would have taken your place."

Mr. Vladisov didn't look well. "Perhaps—" he started to say. He looked like he was struggling against quicksand. Weakly.

"No," I said. "Not on your life."

And then we fed.

There's a story I've wanted to write for years. It's about the nasty allegation that cats left alone in a nursery with an infant will suck the breath right from the little tyke's lungs. Twice now I've tried to adapt that aleurophobic slander into a story. Twice I've veered away from the original concept and done something else entirely. Fortunately, both those tangential tales have worked out fine.

The first time was with a story that eventually came to be called "The Baku." That ended up as a script for the CBS series, *The Twilight Zone*. The finished script was at first rejected; then it was heavily rewritten (by me) just in time for the news of the series' cancellation. What's a writer to do? I turned the unproduced script into a novelette for my collection of original fiction in *Night Visions 4*.

Then I decided to use the kitty cat terror angle for a story aimed at the book you hold in your hands, Ellen Datlow's vampirism collection. It didn't take long before the cats in "Good Kids" assumed a rather minimal role.

Maybe the third time'll be a charm.

I hope so. I think cats make terrific characters; and I'm excited about the cutting edge of contemporary dark fantasy that seems to be slicing away the middling paunch of traditional horror.

In the meantime, thanks to the cats who never did appear on stage in "Good Kids," I got acquainted with SL, Donnie, Cammie, and Angelique. I rather like them and suspect they'll return in at least another story. Maybe one of them'll get a cat.

Ed Bryant

THE GIRL WITH
THE HUNGRY EYES

Fritz Leiber

"The Girl with the Hungry Eyes," published in 1949, is a classic and will probably never become dated. The advertising industry is still searching for "The Look" to sell products to the great American maw. And with new technology continually being developed, the industry becomes more and more adept at insinuating itself into our lives.

All right, I'll tell you why the Girl gives me the creeps. Why I can't stand to go downtown and see the mob slavering up at her on the tower, with that pop bottle or pack of cigarettes or whatever it is beside her. Why I hate to look at magazines any more because I know she'll turn up somewhere in a brassiere or a bubble bath. Why I don't like to think of millions of Americans drinking in that poisonous half-smile. It's quite a story—more story than you're expecting.

No, I haven't suddenly developed any long-haired indignation at the evils of advertising and the national glamour-girl complex. That'd be a laugh for a man in my racket, wouldn't it? Though I think you'll agree there's something a little perverted about trying to capitalize on sex that way. But it's okay with me. And I know we've had the Face and the Body and the Look and what not else, so why shouldn't someone come along who sums it all up so completely, that we have to call her the Girl and blazon her on all the billboards from Times Square to Telegraph Hill?

But the Girl isn't like any of the others. She's unnatural. She's morbid. She's unholy.

Oh it's 1948, is it, and the sort of thing I'm hinting at went out with witchcraft? But you see I'm not altogether sure myself what I'm hinting at, beyond a certain point. There are vampires and vampires, and not all of them suck blood.

And there were the murders, if they were murders.

Besides, let me ask you this. Why, when America is obsessed with the Girl, don't we find out more about her? Why doesn't she rate a *Time* cover with a droll biography inside? Why hasn't there been a feature in *Life* or the *Post?* A Profile in *The New Yorker?* Why hasn't *Charm* or *Mademoiselle* done her career saga? Not ready for it? Nuts!

Why haven't the movies snapped her up? Why hasn't she been on *Information, Please?* Why don't we see her kissing candidates at political rallies? Why isn't she chosen queen of some sort of junk or other at a convention?

Why don't we read about her tastes and hobbies, her views of the Russian situation? Why haven't the columnists interviewed her in a kimono on the top floor of the tallest hotel in Manhattan and told us who her boyfriends are?

Finally—and this is the real killer—why hasn't she ever been drawn or painted?

Oh, no she hasn't. If you knew anything about commercial art you'd know that. Every blessed one of those pictures was worked up from a photograph. Expertly? Of course. They've got the top artists on it. But that's how it's done.

And now I'll tell you the *why* of all that. It's because from the top to the bottom of the whole world of advertising, news, and business, there isn't a solitary soul who knows where the Girl came from, where she lives, what she does, who she is, even what her name is.

You heard me. What's more, not a single solitary soul ever *sees* her— except one poor damned photographer, who's making more money off her than he ever hoped to in his life and who's scared and miserable as hell every minute of the day.

No, I haven't the faintest idea who he is or where he has his studio. But I know there has to be such a man and I'm morally certain he feels just like I *said.*

Yes, I might be able to find her, if I tried. I'm not sure though—by now she probably has other safeguards. Besides, I don't want to.

Oh, I'm off my rocker, am I? That sort of thing can't happen in this Year of our Atom 1948? People can't keep out of sight that way, not even Garbo?

Well I happen to know they can, because last year I was that poor damned photographer I was telling you about. Yes, last year, in 1947, when the Girl made her first poisonous splash right here in this big little city of ours.

Yes, I knew you weren't here last year and you don't know about it. Even the Girl had to start small. But if you hunted through the files of the local newspapers, you'd find some ads, and I might be able to locate you some of the old displays—I think Lovelybelt is still using one of them. I used to have a mountain of photos myself, until I burned them.

Yes, I made my cut off her. Nothing like what that other photographer must be making, but enough so it still bought this whisky. She was funny about money. I'll tell you about that.

But first picture me in 1947. I had a fourth-floor studio in that rathole the Hauser Building, catty-corner from Ardleigh Park.

I'd been working at the Marsh-Mason studios until I'd got my bellyful of it and decided to start in for myself. The Hauser Building was crummy— I'll never forget how the stairs creaked—but it was cheap and there was a skylight.

Business was lousy. I kept making the rounds of all the advertisers and agencies, and some of them didn't object to me too much personally, but my stuff never clicked. I was pretty near broke. I was behind on my rent. Hell, I didn't even have enough money to have a girl.

It was one of those dark gray afternoons. The building was awfully quiet—even with the shortage they can't half rent the Hauser. I'd just finished developing some pix I was doing on speculation for Lovelybelt Girdles and Buford's Pool and Playground—the last a faked-up beach scene. My model had left. A Miss Leon. She was a civics teacher at one of the high schools and modeled for me on the side, just lately on speculation too. After one look at the prints, I decided that Miss Leon probably wasn't just what Lovelybelt was looking for—or my photography either. I was about to call it a day.

And then the street door slammed four storeys down and there were steps on the stairs and she came in.

She was wearing a cheap, shiny black dress. Black pumps. No stockings. And except that she had a gray cloth coat over one of them, those skinny arms of hers were bare. Her arms are pretty skinny, you know, or can you see things like that any more?

And then the thin neck, the slightly gaunt, almost prim face, the tumbling mass of dark hair, and looking out from under it the hungriest eyes in the world.

That's the real reason she's plastered all over the country today, you know—those eyes. Nothing vulgar, but just the same they're looking at you with a hunger that's all sex and something more than sex. That's what everybody's been looking for since the Year One—something a little more than sex.

Well, boys, there I was, along with the Girl, in an office that was getting shadowy, in a nearly empty building. A situation that a million male Americans have undoubtedly pictured to themselves with various lush details. How was I feeling? Scared.

I know sex can be frightening. That cold, heart-thumping when you're alone with a girl and feel you're going to touch her. But if it was sex this time, it was overlaid with something else.

At least I wasn't thinking about sex.

I remember that I took a backward step and that my hand jerked so that the photos I was looking at sailed to the floor.

There was the faintest dizzy feeling like something was being drawn out of me. Just a little bit.

That was all. Then she opened her mouth and everything was back to normal for a while.

"I see you're a photographer, mister," she said. "Could you use a model?"

Her voice wasn't very cultivated.

"I doubt it," I told her, picking up the pix. You see, I wasn't impressed. The commercial possibilities of her eyes hadn't registered on me yet, by a long shot. "What have you done?"

Well she gave me a vague sort of story and I began to check her knowledge of model agencies and studios and rates and what not and pretty soon I said to her, "Look here, you never modeled for a photographer in your life. You just walked in here cold."

Well, she admitted that was more or less so.

All along through our talk I got the idea she was feeling her way, like someone in a strange place. Not that she was uncertain of herself, or of me, but just of the general situation.

"And you think anyone can model?" I asked her pityingly.

"Sure," she said.

"Look," I said, "a photographer can waste a dozen negatives trying to get one halfway human photo of an average woman. How many do you think he'd have to waste before he got a real catchy, glamorous pix of her?"

"I think I could do it," she said.

Well, I should have kicked her out right then. Maybe I admired the cool way she stuck to her dumb little guns. Maybe I was touched by her underfed look. More likely I was feeling mean on account of the way my pix had been snubbed by everybody and I wanted to take it out on her by showing her up.

"Okay, I'm going to put you on the spot," I told her. "I'm going to try a couple of shots of you. Understand, it's strictly on spec. If somebody should ever want to use a photo of you, which is about one chance in two million, I'll pay you regular rates for your time. Not otherwise."

She gave me a smile. The first. "That's swell by me," she said.

Well, I took three or four shots, close-ups of her face since I didn't fancy her cheap dress, and at least she stood up to my sarcasm. Then I remembered I still had the Lovelybelt stuff and I guess the meanness was still working in me because I handed her a girdle and told her to go behind the screen and get into it and she did, without getting flustered as I'd expected, and since we'd gone that far I figured we might as well shoot the beach scene to round it out, and that was that.

All this time I wasn't feeling anything particular in one way or the other except every once in a while I'd get one of those faint dizzy flashes and wonder if there was something wrong with my stomach or if I could have been a bit careless with my chemicals.

Still, you know, I think the uneasiness was in me all the while.

I tossed her a card and pencil. "Write your name and address and phone," I told her and made for the darkroom.

A little later she walked out. I didn't call any good-byes. I was irked because she hadn't fussed around or seemed anxious about her poses, or even thanked me, except for that one smile.

I finished developing the negatives, made some prints, glanced at them, decided they weren't a great deal worse than Miss Leon. On an impulse I slipped them in with the pix I was going to take on the rounds next morning.

By now I'd worked long enough so I was a bit fagged and nervous, but I didn't dare waste enough money on liquor to help that. I wasn't very hungry. I think I went to a cheap movie.

I didn't think of the Girl at all, except maybe to wonder faintly why in my present womanless state I hadn't made a pass at her. She had seemed to belong to a, well, distinctly more approachable social stratum than Miss Leon. But then of course there were all sorts of arguable reasons for my not doing that.

Next morning I made the rounds. My first step was Munsch's Brewery. They were looking for a "Munsch Girl." Papa Munsch had a sort of affection for me, though he razzed my photography. He had a good natural judgment about that, too. Fifty years ago he might have been one of the shoestring boys who made Hollywood.

Right now he was out in the plant pursuing his favorite occupation. He put down the beaded can, smacked his lips, gabbled something technical to someone about hops, wiped his fat hands on the big apron he was wearing, and grabbed my thin stack of pix.

He was about halfway through, making noises with his tongue and teeth, when he came to her. I kicked myself for even having stuck her in.

"That's her," he said. "The photography's not so hot, but that's the girl."

It was all decided. I wondered now why Papa Munsch sensed what the girl had right away, while I didn't. I think it was because I saw her first in the flesh, if that's the right word.

At the time I just felt faint.

"Who is she?" he asked.

"One of my new models." I tried to make it casual.

"Bring her out tomorrow morning," he told me. "And your stuff. We'll photograph her here. I want to show you."

"Here, don't look so sick," he added. "Have some beer."

Well I went away telling myself it was just a fluke, so that she'd probably blow it tomorrow with her inexperience, and so on.

Just the same, when I reverently laid my next stack of pix on Mr. Fitch, of Lovelybelt's rose-colored blotter, I had hers on top.

Mr. Fitch went through the motions of being an art critic. He leaned over backward, squinted his eyes, waved his long fingers, and said, "Hmmm. What do you think, Miss Willow? Here, in this light. Of course the photograph doesn't show the bias cut. And perhaps we should use the Lovelybelt Imp instead of the Angel. Still, the girl. . . . Come over here, Binns." More finger-waving. "I want a married man's reaction."

He couldn't hide the fact that he was hooked.

Exactly the same thing happened at Buford's Pool and Playground, except that Da Costa didn't need a married man's say-so.

"Hot stuff," he said, sucking his lips. "Oh, boy, you photographers!"

I hot-footed it back to the office and grabbed up the card I'd given to her to put down her name and address.

It was blank.

I don't mind telling you that the next five days were about the worst I ever went through, in an ordinary way. When next morning rolled around and I still hadn't got hold of her, I had to start stalling.

"She's sick," I told Papa Munsch over the phone.

"She at a hospital?" he asked me.

"Nothing that serious." I told him.

"Get her out here then. What's a little headache?"

"Sorry, I can't."

Papa Munsch got suspicious. "You really got this girl?"

"Of course I have."

"Well, I don't know. I'd think it was some New York model, except I recognized your lousy photography."

I laughed.

"Well look, you get her here tomorrow morning, you hear?"

"I'll try."

"Try nothing. You get her out here."

He didn't know half of what I tried. I went around to all the model and employment agencies. I did some slick detective work at the photographic and art studios. I used up some of my last dimes putting advertisements in all three papers. I looked at high school yearbooks and at employee photos in local house organs. I went to restaurants and drugstores, looking for waitresses, and to dime stores and department stores, looking at clerks. I watched the crowds coming out of movie theatres. I roamed the streets.

Evenings I spent quite a bit of time along Pick-up Row. Somehow that seemed the right place.

The fifth afternoon I knew I was licked. Papa Munsch's deadline—he'd given me several, but this was it—was due to run out at six o'clock. Mr. Fitch had already canceled.

I was at the studio window, looking out at Ardleigh Park.

She walked in.

I'd gone over this moment so often in my mind that I had no trouble putting on my act. Even the faint dizzy feeling didn't throw me off.

"Hello," I said, hardly looking at her.

"Hello," she said.

"Not discouraged yet?"

"No." It didn't sound uneasy or defiant. It was just a statement.

I snapped a look at my watch, got up and said curtly, "Look here, I'm going to give you a chance. There's a client of mine looking for a girl your general type. If you do a real good job you may break into the modeling business.

"We can see him this afternoon if we hurry." I said. I picked up my stuff. "Come on. And next time, if you expect favors, don't forget to leave your phone number."

"Uh, uh," she said, not moving.

"What do you mean?" I said.

"I'm not going to see any client of yours."

"The hell you aren't," I said. "You little nut, I'm giving you a break."

She shook her head slowly. "You're not fooling me, baby, you're not fooling me at all. They *want* me." And she gave me the second smile.

At the time I thought she must have seen my newspaper ad. Now I'm not so sure.

"And now I'll tell you how we're going to work," she went on. "You aren't going to have my name or address or phone number. Nobody is. And we're going to do all the pictures right here. Just you and me."

You can imagine the roar I raised at that. I was everything—angry, sarcastic, patiently explanatory, off my nut, threatening, pleading.

I would have slapped her face off, except it was photographic capital.

In the end all I could do was phone Papa Munsch and tell him her conditions. I know I didn't have a chance, but I had to take it.

He gave me a really angry bawling out, said "no" several times and hung up.

It didn't faze her. "We'll start shooting at ten o'clock tomorrow," she said.

It was just like her, using that corny line from the movie magazines.

About midnight Papa Munsch called me up.

"I don't know what insane asylum you're renting this girl from," he said, "but I'll take her. Come around tomorrow morning and I'll try to get it through your head just how I want the pictures. And I'm glad I got you out of bed!"

After that it was a breeze. Even Mr. Fitch reconsidered and after taking two days to tell me it was quite impossible, he accepted the conditions too.

Of course you're all under the spell of the Girl, so you can't understand how much self-sacrifice it represented on Mr. Fitch's part when he agreed to forego supervising the photography of my model in the Lovelybelt Imp or Vixen or whatever it was we finally used.

Next morning she turned up on time according to her schedule, and we went to work. I'll say one thing for her, she never got tired and she never kicked at the way I fussed over shots. I got along okay except I still had the feeling of something being shoved away gently. Maybe you've felt it just a little, looking at her picture.

When we finished I found out there were still more rules. It was about the middle of the afternoon. I started down with her to get a sandwich and coffee.

"Uh uh," she said, "I'm going down alone. And look, baby, if you ever try to follow me, if you ever so much as stick your head out that window when I go, you can hire yourself another model."

You can imagine how all this crazy stuff strained my temper—and my imagination. I remember opening the window after she was gone—I waited a few minutes first—and standing there getting some fresh air and trying to figure out what could be back of it, whether she was hiding from the police, or was somebody's ruined daughter, or maybe had got the idea it was smart to be temperamental, or more likely Papa Munsch was right and she was partly nuts.

But I had my pix to finish up.

Looking back it's amazing to think how fast her magic began to take hold of the city after that. Remembering what came after, I'm frightened of what's happening to the whole country—and maybe the world. Yesterday I read something in *Time* about the Girl's picture turning up on billboards in Egypt.

The rest of my story will help show you why I'm frightened in that big general way. But I have a theory, too, that helps explain, though it's one of those things that's beyond that "certain point." It's about the Girl. I'll give it to you in a few words.

You know how modern advertising gets everybody's mind set in the same direction, wanting the same things, imagining the same things. And you know the psychologists aren't so sceptical of telepathy as they used to be.

Add up the two ideas. Suppose the identical desires of millions of people focused on one telepathic person. Say a girl. Shaped her in their image.

Imagine her knowing the hiddenmost hungers of millions of men. Imagine her seeing deeper into those hungers than the people that had them, seeing the hatred and the wish for death behind the lust. Imagine her shaping herself in that complete image, keeping herself as aloof as marble. Yet imagine the hunger she might feel in answer to their hunger.

But that's getting a long way from the facts of my story. And some of those facts are darn solid. Like money. We made money.

That was the funny thing I was going to tell you. I was afraid the Girl was going to hold me up. She really had me over a barrel, you know.

But she didn't ask for anything but the regular rates. Later on I insisted on pushing more money at her, a whole lot. But she always took it with that same contemptuous look, as if she were going to toss it down the first drain when she got outside.

Maybe she did.

At any rate, I had money. For the first time in months I had money enough to get drunk, buy new clothes, take taxicabs. I could make a play for any girl I wanted to. I only had to pick.

And so of course I had to go and pick—

But first let me tell you about Papa Munsch.

Papa Munsch wasn't the first of the boys to try to meet my model but I think he was the first to really go soft on her. I could watch the change in his eyes as he looked at her pictures. They began to get sentimental, reverent. Mama Munsch had been dead for two years.

He was smart about the way he planned it. He got me to drop some information which told him when she came to work, and then one morning he came pounding up the stairs a few minutes before.

"I've got to see her, Dave," he told me.

I argued with him, I kidded him. I explained he didn't know just how serious she was about her crazy ideas. I pointed out he was cutting both our throats. I even amazed myself by bawling him out.

He didn't take any of it in his usual way. He just kept repeating, "But, Dave, I've got to see her."

The street door slammed.

"That's her," I said, lowering my voice. "You've got to get out."

He wouldn't, so I shoved him in the darkroom. "And keep quiet," I whispered. "I'll tell her I can't work today."

I knew he'd try to look at her and probably come busting in, but there wasn't anything else I could do.

The footsteps came to the fourth floor. But she never showed at the door. I got uneasy.

"Get that bum out of there!" she yelled suddenly from beyond the door. Not very loud, but in her commonest voice.

"I'm going up to the next landing," she said, "And if that fat-bellied bum doesn't march straight down to the street, he'll never get another pix of me except spitting in his lousy beer."

Papa Munsch came out of the darkroom. He was white. He didn't look at me as he went out. He never looked at her pictures in front of me again.

That was Papa Munsch. Now it's me I'm telling about. I talked about the subject with her, I hinted, eventually I made my pass.

She lifted my hand off her as if it were a damp rag.

"Nix, baby," she said. "This is working time."

"But afterward . . ." I pressed.

"The rules still hold." And I got what I think was the fifth smile.

It's hard to believe, but she never budged an inch from that crazy line. I mustn't make a pass at her in the office, because our work was very important and she loved it and there mustn't be any distractions. And I couldn't see her anywhere else, because if I tried to, I'd never snap another picture of her—and all this with more money coming in all the time and me never so stupid as to think my photography had anything to do with it.

Of course I wouldn't have been human if I hadn't made more passes. But they always got the wet-rag treatment and there weren't any more smiles.

I changed. I went sort of crazy and light-headed—only sometimes I felt my head was going to burst. And I started to talk to her all the time. About myself.

It was like being in a constant delirium that never interfered with business. I didn't pay attention to the dizzy feeling. It seemed natural.

I'd walk around and for a moment the reflector would look like a sheet of white-hot steel, or the shadows would seem like armies of moths, or the camera would be a big black coal car. But the next instant they'd come all right again.

I think sometimes I was scared to death of her. She'd seem the strangest, horriblest person in the world. But other times . . .

And I talked. It didn't matter what I was doing—lighting her, posing her, fussing with props, snapping my pix—or where she was—on the platform, behind the screen, relaxing with a magazine—I kept up a steady gab.

I told her everything I knew about myself. I told her about my first girl. I told her about my brother Bob's bicycle. I told her about running away on a freight and the licking Pa gave me when I came home. I told her about shipping to South America and the blue sky at night. I told her about Betty. I told her about my mother dying of cancer. I told her about being beaten up in a fight in an alley behind a bar. I told her about Mildred. I told her about the first picture I ever sold. I told her how Chicago looked from a sailboat. I told her about the longest drunk I was ever on. I told her about Marsh-Mason. I told her about Gwen. I told her about how I met Papa Munsch. I told her about hunting her. I told her about how I felt now.

She never paid the slightest attention to what I said. I couldn't even tell if she heard me.

It was when we were getting our first nibble from national advertisers that I decided to follow her when she went home.

Wait, I can place it better than that. Something you'll remember from the out-of-town papers—those maybe-murders I mentioned. I think there were six.

I say "maybe" because the police could never be sure they weren't heart attacks. But there's bound to be suspicion when heart attacks happen to people whose hearts have been okay, and always at night when they're alone and away from home and there's a question of what they were doing.

The six deaths created one of those "mystery poisoner" scares. And afterward there was a feeling that they hadn't really stopped, but were being continued in a less suspicious way.

That's one of the things that scares me now.

But at that time my only feeling was relief that I'd decided to follow her.

I made her work until dark one afternoon. I didn't need any excuses, we were snowed under with orders. I waited until the street door slammed, then I ran down. I was wearing rubber-soled shoes. I'd slipped on a dark coat she'd never seen me in, and a dark hat.

I stood in the doorway until I spotted her. She was walking by Ardleigh Park toward the heart of town. It was one of those warm fall nights. I followed her on the other side of the street. My idea for tonight was just to find out where she lived. That would give me a hold on her.

She stopped in front of a display window of Everly's department store, standing back from the glow. She stood there looking in.

I remembered we'd done a big photograph of her for Everly's, to make a flat model for a lingerie display. That was what she was looking at.

At the time it seemed all right to me that she should adore herself, if that was what she was doing.

When people passed she'd turn away a little or drift back farther into the shadows.

Then a man came by alone. I couldn't see his face very well, but he looked middle-aged. He stopped and stood looking in the window.

She came out of the shadows and stepped up beside him.

How would you boys feel if you were looking at a poster of the Girl and suddenly she was there beside you, her arm linked with yours?

This fellow's reaction showed plain as day. A crazy dream had come to life for him.

They talked for a moment. Then he waved a taxi to the curb. They got in and drove off.

I got drunk that night. It was almost as if she'd known I was following her and had picked that way to hurt me. Maybe she had. Maybe this was the finish.

But the next morning she turned up at the usual time and I was back in the delirium, only now with some new angles added.

That night when I followed her she picked a spot under a street lamp, opposite one of the Munsch Girl billboards.

Now it frightens me to think of her lurking that way.

After about twenty minutes a convertible slowed down going past her, backed up, swung in to the curb.

I was closer this time. I got a good look at the fellow's face. He was a little younger, about my age.

Next morning the same face looked up at me from the front page of the paper. The convertible had been found parked on a side street. He had been in it. As in the other maybe-murders, the cause of death was uncertain.

All kinds of thoughts were spinning in my head that day, but there were only two things I knew for sure. That I'd got the first real offer from a national advertiser, and that I was going to take the Girl's arm and walk down the stairs with her when we quit work.

She didn't seem surprised. "You know what you're doing?" she said.

"I know."

She smiled. "I was wondering when you'd get around to it."

I began to feel good. I was kissing everything good-bye, but I had my arm around hers.

It was another of those warm fall evenings. We cut across into Ardleigh Park. It was dark there, but all around the sky was a sallow pink from the advertising signs.

We walked for a long time in the park. She didn't say anything and she didn't look at me, but I could see her lips twitching and after a while her hand tightened on my arm.

We stopped. We'd been walking across the grass. She dropped down and pulled me after her. She put her hands on my shoulders. I was looking down at her face. It was the faintest sallow pink from the glow in the sky. The hungry eyes were dark smudges.

I was fumbling with her blouse. She took my hand away, not like she had in the studio. "I don't want that," she said.

First I'll tell you what I did afterward. Then I'll tell you why I did it. Then I'll tell you what she said.

What I did was run away. I don't remember all of that because I was dizzy, and the pink sky was swinging against the dark trees. But after a while I staggered into the lights of the street. The next day I closed up the studio.

The telephone was ringing when I locked the door and there were unopened letters on the floor. I never saw the Girl again in the flesh, if that's the right word.

I did it because I didn't want to die. I didn't want the life drawn out of me. There are vampires and vampires, and the ones that suck blood aren't the worst. If it hadn't been for the warning of those dizzy flashes, and Papa Munsch and the face in the morning paper, I'd have gone the way the others did. But I realized what I was up against while there was still time to tear myself away. I realized that wherever she came from, whatever shaped her, she's the quintessence of the horror behind the bright billboard. She's the smile that tricks you into throwing away your money and your life. She's the eyes that lead you on and on, and then show you death. She's the creature you give everything for and never really get. She's the being that takes everything you've got and gives nothing in return. When you yearn toward her face on the billboards, remember that. She's the lure. She's the bait. She's the Girl.

And this is what she said, "I want you. I want your high spots. I want everything that's made you happy and everything that's hurt you bad. I want your first girl. I want that shiny bicycle. I want that licking. I want that pinhole camera. I want Betty's legs. I want the blue sky filled with stars. I want your mother's death. I want your blood on the cobblestones. I want Mildred's mouth. I want the first picture you sold. I want the lights of Chicago. I want the gin. I want Gwen's hands. I want your wanting me. I want your life. Feed me, baby, feed me."

I originally wrote "The Girl with the Hungry Eyes" for the first issue of a magazine Donald Wollheim was trying to publish. That project didn't work out but instead, the story was published in Avon's original anthology, called *The Girl with the Hungry Eyes* (1949), edited by Wollheim. Marshall McLuhan quoted from the story in his early (and negatively reviewed) book on advertising, *The Mechanical Bride*. I later wrote a story called "The Mechanical Bride" as a kind of joke, in response.

Fritz Leiber

THE JANFIA
TREE

Tanith Lee

Vampirism is a recurring theme in Lee's work. In this graceful, ambiguous tale, a woman with no hope invokes a dark god who may or may not exist, just to conquer her own indifference to life. Vampires often mesmerize their victims with their gaze. In a neat little twist the Janfia tree gives off a seductive, overpowering fragrance as a lure.

After eight years of what is termed "bad luck," it becomes a way of life. One is no longer anything so dramatic as unhappy. One achieves a sort of state of what can only be described as de-happiness. One expects nothing, not even, actually, the worst. A certain relaxation follows, a certain equilibrium. Not flawless, of course. There are still moments of rage and misery. It is very hard to give up hope, that last evil let loose from Pandora's box of horrors. And it is always, in fact, after a bout of hope, springing without cause, perishing not necessarily at any fresh blow but merely from the absence of anything to sustain it, that there comes a revulsion of the senses. A wish, not exactly for death, but for the torturer at least to step out of the shadows, to reveal himself, and his plans. And to this end one issues invitations, generally very trivial ones, a door forgetfully unlocked, a stoplight driven through. Tempting fate, they call it.

"Well, you do look tired," said Isabella, who had met me in her car, in the town, in the white dust that veiled and covered everything.

I agreed that perhaps I did look tired.

"I'm so sorry about—" said Isabella. She checked herself, thankfully, on my thanks. "I expect you've had enough of all that. And this other thing.

That's not for a while, is it?"

"Not until next month."

"That gives you time to take a break at least."

"Yes."

It was a very minor medical matter to which she referred. Any one of millions would have been glad, I was sure, to exchange their intolerable suffering for something twice as bad. For me, it filled the quota quite adequately. I had not been sleeping very well. Isabella's offer of the villa had seemed, not like an escape, since that was impossible, yet like an island. But I wished she would talk about something else. Mind-reading, "Look at the olives, aren't they splendid?" she said, as we hurtled up the road. I looked at the olives through the blinding sun and dust. "And there it is, you see? Straight up there in the sky."

The villa rose, as she said, in the hard sky above; on a crest of gilded rock curtained with cypress and pine. The building was alabaster in the sun, and, like alabaster, had a pinkish inner glow where the light exchanged itself with the shade. Below, the waves of the olives washed down to the road, shaking to silver as the breeze ruffled them. It was all very beautiful, but one comes in time to regard mortal glamours rather as the Cathars regarded them, snares of the devil to hide the blemishes beneath, to make us love a world which will defile and betray us.

The car sped up the road and arrived on a driveway in a flaming jungle of bougainvillaea and rhododendrons.

Isabella led me between the stalks of the veranda, into the villa, with all the pride of money and goodwill. She pointed out to me, on a long immediate tour, every excellence, and showed me the views, which were exceptional, from every window and balcony.

"Marta's away down the hill at the moment, but she'll be back quite soon. She says she goes to visit her aunt, but I suspect it's a lover. But she's a dulcet girl. You can see how nicely she keeps everything here. With the woman who cooks, that's just about all, except for the gardeners, but they won't be coming again for a week. So no one will bother you."

"That does sound good."

"Save myself of course," she added. "I shall keep an eye on you. And tomorrow, remember, we want you across for dinner. Down there, beyond those pines, we're just over that spectacular ridge. Less than half a mile.

Indeed, if you want to you can send us morse signals after dark from the second bathroom window. Isn't that fun. So near, so far."

"Isabella, you're really too kind to me."

"Nonsense," she said. "Who else would be, you pessimistic old sausage." And she took me into her arms, and to my horror I shed tears, but not many. Isabella, wiping her own eyes, said it had done me good. But she was quite wrong.

Marta arrived as we were having drinks at the east end of the veranda. She was a pretty, sunlit creature, who looked about fourteen and was probably eighteen or so. She greeted me politely, rising from the bath of her liaison. I felt nothing very special about her, or that. Though I am often envious of the stamina, youth, and health of others, I have never wanted to be any of them.

"Definitely, a lover," said Isabella, when the girl was gone. "My God, do you remember what it was like at her age. All those clandestine fumblings in gray city places."

If that had been true for her, it had not been true of me, but I smiled.

"But here," she said, "in all this honey heat, these scents and flowers. Heaven on earth—arcadia. Well, at least I'm here with good old Alec. And he hands me quite a few surprises, he's quite the boy now and then."

"I've been meaning to ask you," I said, "that flowering tree along there, what is it?"

I had not been meaning to ask, had only just noticed the particular tree. But I was afraid of flirtatious sexual revelations. I had been denied in love-desire too long, and celibate too long, to find such a thing comfortable. But Isabella, full of intrigued interest in her own possessions, got up at once and went with me to inspect the tree.

It stood high in a white and terracotta urn, its stem and head in silhouette against a golden noon. There was a soft pervasive scent which, as I drew closer, I realized had lightly filled all the veranda like a bowl with water.

"Oh yes, the fragrance," she said. "It gets headier later in the day, and at night it's almost overpowering. Now what is it?" She fingered dark glossy leaves and found a tiny slender bloom, of a somber white. "This will open after sunset," she said. "Oh lord, what *is* the name?" She stared at me and her face cleared, glad to give me another gift. "Janfia," she said. "Now I can tell you all about it. Janfia—it's supposed to be from the French, *Janvier.*" It was a shame to discourage her.

"January. Why? Does it start to bloom then?"

"Well perhaps it's supposed to, although it doesn't. No. It's something to do with January, though."

"Janus, maybe," I said, "two-faced god of doorways. You always plant it by a doorway or an opening into a house? A guardian tree." I had almost said, a tree for good luck.

"That might be it. But I don't think it's protective. No, now isn't there some story. . . . I do hope I can recall it. It's like the legend of the myrtle—or is it the basil? You know the one, with a spirit living in the tree."

"That's the myrtle. Venus, or a nymph, coming out for dalliance at night, hiding in the branches by day. The basil is a severed head. The basil grows from the mouth of the head and tells the young girl her brothers have murdered her lover, whose decapitum is in the pot."

"Yum, yum," said Isabella. "Well Alec will know about the Janfia. I'll get him to tell you when you come to dinner tomorrow."

I smiled again. Alec and I made great efforts to get along with each other, for Isabella's sake. We both found it difficult. He did not like me, and I, reciprocating, had come to dislike him in turn. Now our only bond, aside from Isabella, was natural sympathy at the irritation endured in the presence of the other.

As I said good-bye to Isabella, I was already wondering how I could get out of the dinner.

I spent the rest of the afternoon unpacking and organizing myself for my stay, swimming all the while in amber light, pausing frequently to gaze out across the pines, the sea of olive groves. A little orange church rose in the distance, and a sprawling farm with Roman roofs. The town was already well-lost in purple shadow. I began, from the sheer charm of it, to have moments of pleasure. I had dreaded their advent, but received them mutely. It was all right, it was all right to feel this mindless animal sweetness. It did not interfere with the other things, the darkness, the sword hanging by a thread. I had accepted that, that it was above me, then why trouble with it.

But I began to feel well, I began to feel all the chances were not gone. I risked red wine and ate my supper greedily, enjoying being waited on.

During the night, not thinking to sleep in the strange bed, I slept a long while. When I woke once, there was an extraordinary floating presence in the bedroom. It was the perfume of the Janfia tree, entering the open shutters from the veranda below. It must stand directly beneath my window. Mine was the open way it had been placed to favor. How deep and strangely clear was the scent.

When I woke in the morning, the scent had gone, and my stomach was full of knots of pain and ghastly nausea. The long journey, the heat, the rich food, the wine. Nevertheless, it gave me my excuse to avoid the unwanted dinner with Isabella and Alec.

I called her about eleven o'clock. She commiserated. What could she say? I must rest and take care, and we would all meet further along the week.

In the afternoon, when I was beginning to feel better, she woke me from a long hot doze with two plastic containers of local yogurt, which would apparently do wonders for me.

"I'll only stay a moment. God, you do look pale. Haven't you got something to take for it?"

"Yes. I've taken it."

"Well. Try the yogurt, too."

"As soon as I can manage anything, I'll try the yogurt."

"By the way," she said, "I can tell you the story of the Janfia now." She stood in the bedroom window, looking out and down at it. "It's extremely sinister. Are you up to it, I wonder?"

"Tell me, and see."

Although I had not wanted the interruption, now it had arrived, I was oddly loath to let her go. I wished she would have stayed and had dinner with me herself, alone. Isabella had always tried to be kind to me. Then again, I was useless with people now. I could relate to no one, could not give them any quarter. I would be better off on my own.

"Well it seems there was a poet, young and handsome, for whose verses princes would pay in gold."

"Those were the days," I said idly.

"Come, it was the fifteenth century. No sewers, no antibiotics, only superstition and gold could get you by."

"You sound nostalgic, Isabella."

"Shush now. He used to roam the countryside, the young poet, looking for inspiration, doubtless finding it with shepherdesses, or whatever they had here then. One dusk he smelled an exquisite fragrance, and searching for its source, came on a bush of pale opening flowers. So enamoured was he of the perfume, that he dug up the bush, took it home with him, and planted it in a pot on the balcony outside his room. Here it grew into a tree, and here the poet, dreaming, would sit all afternoon, and when night fell and the moon rose, he would carry his mattress on to the balcony, and go to sleep under the moon-shade of the tree's foliage."

Isabella broke off. Already falling into the idiom, she said, "Am I going to write this, or are you?"

"I'm too tired to write nowadays. And anyway, I can't sell anything. You do it."

"We'll see. After all the trouble I had with that cow of an editor over my last—"

"And meantime, finish the story, Isabella."

Isabella beamed.

She told me, it began to be noticed that the poet was very wan, very thin, very listless. That he no longer wrote a line, and soon all he did was to sit all day and lie all night long by the tree. His companions looked in vain for him in the taverns and his patrons looked in vain for his verse. Finally a very great prince, the lord of the town, went himself to the poet's room. Here, to his dismay, he found the poet stretched out under the tree. It was close to evening, the evening star stood in the sky and the young moon was shining in through the leaves of the Janfia tree upon the poet's white face which was now little better than a beautiful skull. He seemed near to death, which the prince's physicians, being called in, confirmed. "How," cried the prince, in grief, "have you come to this condition?" Then, though it was not likely to restore him, he begged the poet to allow them to take him to some more comfortable spot. The poet refused. "Life is nothing to me now," he said. And he asked the prince to leave him, for the night was approaching and he wished to be alone.

The prince was at once suspicious. He sent the whole company away, and only he returned with stealth, and hid himself in the poet's room, to see what went on.

Sure enough, at midnight, when the sky was black and the moon rode high, there came a gentle rustling in the leaves of the Janfia. Presently there stepped forth into the moonlight a young man, dark-haired and pale of skin, clothed in garments that seemed woven of the foliage of the tree itself. And he, bending over the poet, kissed him, and the poet stretched up his arms. And what the prince then witnessed filled him with abysmal terror, for not only was it a demon he watched, but one which performed acts utterly proscribed by mother church. Eventually overcome, the prince lost consciousness. When he roused, the dawn was breaking, the tree stood scentless and empty, and the poet, lying alone, was dead.

"So naturally," said Isabella, with relish, "there was a cry of witchcraft, and the priests came and the tree was burned to cinders. All but for one tiny piece that the prince found, to his astonishment, he had broken off. Long after the poet had been buried, in unhallowed ground, the prince kept this little piece of the Janfia tree, and eventually thinking it dead, he threw it from his window out into the garden of his palace."

She looked at me.

"Where it grew," I said, "watered only by the rain, and nurtured only by the glow of the moon by night."

"Until an evening came," said Isabella, "when the prince, overcome by a strange longing, sat brooding in his chair. And all at once an amazing perfume filled the air, so mysterious, so irresistible, he dared not even turn his head to see what it portended. And as he sat thus, a shadow fell across his shoulder on to the floor in front of him, and then a quiet, leaf-cool hand was laid upon his neck."

She and I burst out laughing.

"Gorgeous," I said. "Erotic, gothic, perverse, Wildean, Freudian. Yes."

"Now tell me you won't write it."

I shook my head. "No. Maybe later, sometime. If you don't. But your story still doesn't explain the name, does it?"

"Alec said it might be something to do with Janus being the male form of the name Diana—the moon and the night. But it's tenuous. Oh," she said, "you do look so much better."

Thereby reminding me that I was ill, and that the sword still hung by its hair, and that all we had shared was a derivative little horror story from the back hills.

"Are you sure you can't manage dinner?" she said.

"Probably could. Then I'd regret it. No, thank you. Just for now, I'll stick to that yogurt, or it to me, whatever it does."

"All right. Well, I must dash. I'll call you tomorrow."

I had come to the villa for solitude in a different climate, but learned, of course, that climate is climate, and that solitude too is always precisely and only that. In my case, the desire to be alone was simply the horror of not being so. Besides, I never was alone, dogged by the sick, discontented, and unshakable companions of my body, my own restless mind.

The sun was wonderful, and the place was beautiful, but I quickly realized I did not know what to do with the sun and the beauty. I needed to translate them, perhaps, into words, certainly into feelings, but neither would respond as I wished. I kept a desultory journal, then gave it up. I read and soon found I could not control my eyes enough to get them to focus on the pages. On the third evening, I went to dinner with Isabella and Alec, did my best, watched Alec do his best, came back a little drunk, more ill in soul than in body. Disgraced myself in private by weeping.

Finally, the scent of the Janfia tree, coming in such tides into the room, drew me to the window.

I stood there, looking down at the veranda, the far-away hills beyond described only by starlight, the black tree much nearer, with here and there its moonburst of smoky white, an open flower.

And I thought about the poet, and the incubus that was the spirit of the tree. It was the hour to think of that. A demon which vampirized and killed by irresistible pleasures of the flesh. What an entirely enchanting thought. After all, life itself vampirized, and ultimately killed, did it not, by a constant equally irresistible, administration of the exact reverse of pleasure.

But since I had no longer any belief in God, I had lost all hopes of anything supernatural abroad in the universe. There was evil, naturally, in its abstract or human incarnations, but nothing artistic, no demons stepping from trees by night.

Just then, the leaves of the Janfia rustled. Some night breeze was passing through them, though not, it seemed, through any other thing which grew on the veranda.

A couple of handsome, shy wild cats came and went at the villa. The woman who cooked left out scraps for them, and I had seen Marta, one morning, leaving a large bowl of water in the shade of the cypress they were wont to climb. A cat then, prowling along the veranda rail, was disturbing the tree. I tried to make out the flash of eyes. Presently, endeavoring to do this, I began to see another thing.

It was a shadow, cast from the tree, but not in the tree's shape. Nor was there light, beyond that of the stars above the hills, to fashion it. A man then, young and slender, stood below me, by the Janfia, and from a barely suggested paleness, like that of a thin half moon, it seemed he might be looking up toward my room.

A kind of instinct made me move quickly back, away from the window. It was a profound and primitive reaction, which startled me, and refreshed me. It had no place on the modern earth, and scarcely any name. A kind of panic—the pagan fear of something elemental, godlike, and terrible. Caught up in it, for a second, I was no longer myself, no longer the one I dreaded most in all the world. I was no one, only a reaction to an unknown matter, more vital than sickness or pessimism, something from the days when all ills and joys were in the charge of the gods, when men need not think, but simply *were*.

And then, I did think. I thought of some intruder, something rational, and I moved into the open window again, and looked down, and there was nothing there. Just the tree against the starlight.

"Isabella," I said to her over the telephone, "would you mind if I had that tree carried up to my bedroom?"

"Tree?"

I laughed brightly. "I don't mean one of the pines. The little Janfia. It's funny, but you know I hadn't been sleeping very well—the scent seems to help. I thought, actually in the room, it would be about foolproof. Nonstop inhalations of white double brandies."

"Well, I don't see why not. Only, mightn't it give you a headache, or something? All that carbon monoxide—or is it dioxide—plants exude at night. Didn't someone famous suffocate themselves with flowers? One of Mirabeau's mistresses, wasn't it? No, that was with a charcoal brazier—"

"The thing is," I said, "your two gardeners have arrived this morning after all. And between them, they shouldn't have any trouble getting the urn upstairs. I'll have it by the window. No problems with asphyxia that way."

"Oh well, if you want, why not?" Having consented, she babbled for a moment over how I was doing, and assured me she would "pop in" tomorrow. Alec had succumbed to some virus, and she had almost forgotten me. I doubted that I would see her for the rest of the week.

Marta scintillantly organized the gardeners. Each gave me a narrow look. But they raised the terracotta and the tree, bore them grunting up to the second floor, plonked them by the window as requested. Marta even followed this up with a can of water to sprinkle the earth. That done, she pulled two desiccated leaves off the tree with a coarse functional disregard. It was part of the indoor furnishings now, and must be cared for.

I had been possessed by a curious idea, which I called, to myself, an experiment. It was impossible that I had seen anything, any "being," on the veranda. That was an alcoholic fantasy. But then again, I had an urge to call the bluff of the Janfia tree. Because it seemed to me responsible, in its own way, for my mirage. Perhaps the blooms were mildly hallucinogenic. If so, I meant to test them. In lieu of any other social event or creative project, an investigation of the Janfia would have to serve.

By day it gave, of course, very little scent; in the morning it had seemed to have none at all. I sat and watched it a while, then stretched out for a siesta. Falling asleep, almost immediately I dreamed that I lay bleeding in a blood-soaked bed, in the middle of a busy city pavement. People stepped around me, sometimes cursing the obstacle. No one would help me. Somebody—formless, genderless—when I caught at a sleeve, detached me with a good-natured, Oh, you'll be all right.

I woke up in a sweat of horror. Not a wise measure any more, then, to sleep by day. Too hot, conducive to the nightmare. . . . The dream's psychological impetus was all too obvious, the paranoia and self-pity. One was expected to be calm and well-mannered in adversity. People soon got tired of you otherwise. How not, who was exempt from distress?

I stared across the room at the Janfia tree, glossy with its health and beauty. Quite unassailable it looked. Was it a vampire? Did it suck away the life of other things to feed its own? It was welcome to mine. What a way to die. Not messily and uncouthly. But ecstatically, romantically, poignantly. They would say, they simply could not understand it, I had been a little under the weather, but *dying*—so very odd of me. And Isabella, remembering the story, would glance at the Janfia fearfully, and shakily giggle the notion aside.

I got up, and walked across.

"Why don't you?" I said. "I'm here. I'm willing. I'd be—I'd be only too glad to die like that, in the arms of something that needed me, held, in pleasure—not from some bloody slip of a careless uncaring knife, some surgeon with a hangover, whoops, lost another patient today, oh dear what a shame. Or else to go on with this bloody awful misery, one slap in the teeth after another, nothing going right, nothing, nothing. Get out, to oblivion hopefully, or get out and start over, or if there's some bearded old damnable God, he couldn't blame me, could he? 'Your honor,' I'd say, 'I was all for keeping going, suffering for another forty years, whatever your gracious will for me was. But a demon set on me. You know I didn't stand a chance.' So," I said again to the Janfia tree, "why not?"

Did it hear? Did it attend? I reached out and touched its stems, its leaves, the fruited, tight-coiled blossoms. All of it seemed to sing, to vibrate with some colossal hidden force, like an instrument still faintly thrumming after the hand of the musician has left it, perhaps five centuries ago.

"Christ, I'm going crazy," I said, and turned from the tree with an insulting laugh. See, the laugh said, I know all that is a lie. So, I *dare* you.

There was a writing desk in the room. Normally, when writing, I did not employ a desk, but now I sat at it and began to jot some notes on the legend of the tree. I was not particularly interested in doing this, it was only a sort of sympathetic magic. But the time went swiftly, and soon the world had reached the drinks hour, and I was able with a clear conscience to go down with thoughts of opening a bottle of white wine. The sun burned low in the cypress tree, and Marta stood beneath it, perplexed, a dish of scraps in her hand.

"Cats not hungry today?" I asked her.

She cast me a flashing look.

"No cats. Cats runs off. I am say, Where you go give you better food? Mrs. Isabella like the cats. Perhaps they there. Thing scares them. They see a monster, go big eyes and then they runs."

Surprising me with my surprise, I shivered.

"What was it? That they saw?"

Marta shrugged.

"Who's know? I am see them runs. Fat tail and big eyes."

"Where was it?"

"This minute."

"But where? Down here?"

She shrugged a second time.

"Nothing there. They see. I am go along now. My aunt, she is waits for me."

"Oh yes. Your aunt. Do go."

I smiled. Marta ignored my smile, for she would only smile at me when I was serious or preoccupied, or ill. In the same way, her English deteriorated in my presence, improved in Isabella's. In some fashion, it seemed to me, she had begun to guard herself against me, sensing bad luck might rub off.

I had explained earlier to everyone that I wanted nothing very much for dinner, some cheese and fruit would suffice, such items easily accessible. And they had all then accordingly escaped, the cook, the cats, and Marta. Now I was alone. Was I?

At the third glass I began to make my plans. It would be a full moon tonight. It would shine in at my bedroom window about two in the morning, casting a white clear light across the room, the desk, so that anything, coming between, would cast equally a deep shadow.

Well, I would give it every chance. The Janfia could not say I had omitted anything. The lunar orb, I at the desk, my back to night and moon and tree. Waiting.

Why was I even contemplating such a foolish adolescent act? Naturally so that tomorrow, properly stood up on my date with delicious death, I could cry out loudly: The gods are dead! There is nothing left to me but *this,* the dunghill of the world.

But I ought to be fairly drunk. Yes, I owed the situation that. Drink, the opening medicine of the mind and heart, sometimes of the psyche.

The clean cheeses and green and pink fruits did not interrupt the spell of the wine. They stabilized my stomach and made it only accommodating.

Tomorrow I would regret drinking so much, but tomorrow I was going to regret everything in any case.

And so I opened a second bottle, and carried it to the bath with me, to the ritual cleansing before the assignation or the witchcraft.

I fell asleep, sitting at the desk. There was a brief sealike afterglow, and my notes and a book and a lamp and the bottle spread before me. The perfume of the Janfia at my back seemed faint, luminous as the dying of the light. Beginning to read, quite easily, for the wine, interfering itself with vision, made it somehow less difficult to see or guess correctly the printed words, I weighed the time once or twice on my watch. Four hours, three hours, to moonrise.

When I woke, it was to an electric stillness. The oil lamp which I had been using in preference, was burning low, and I reached instantly and turned down the wick. As the flame went out, all the lit darkness came in about me. The moon was in the window, climbing up behind the jet-black outline of the Janfia tree.

The scent was extraordinary. Was it my imagination?—it seemed never to have smelled this way before, with this sort of aching, chiming note. Perhaps the full moon brought it out. I would not turn to look. Instead, I drew the paper to me and the pen. I wrote nothing, simply doodled on the pad, long spirals and convolutions; doubtless a psychiatrist would have found them most revealing.

My mind was a blank. A drunken, receptive, amiable blank. I was amused, but exhilarated. All things were supposed to be possible. If a black specter could stalk me through eight years, surely then phantoms of all kinds, curses, blessings, did exist.

The shadow of the Janfia was being thrown down now all around me, on the floor, on the desk and the paper: the lacy foliage and the wide-stretched blooms.

And then, something else, a long finger of shadow, began to spill forward, across everything. What was it? No, I must not turn to see. Probably some freak arrangement of the leaves, or even some simple element of the room's furniture, suddenly caught against the lifting moon.

My skin tingled. I sat as if turned to stone, watching the slow forward movement of the shadow which, after all, might also be that of a tall and slender man. Not a sound. The cicadas were silent. On the hills not a dog barked. And the villa was utterly dumb, empty of everything but me, and perhaps of this other thing, which itself was noiseless.

And all at once the Janfia tree gave a little whispering rustle. As if it laughed to itself. Only a breeze, of course only that, or some night insect, or a late flower unfolding . . .

A compound of fear and excitement held me rigid. My eyes were wide and I breathed in shallow gasps. I had ceased altogether to reason. I did not even feel. I waited. I waited in a type of delirium, for the touch of a cruel serene hand upon my neck—for truth to step at last from the shadow, with a naked blade.

And I shut my eyes, the better to experience whatever might come to me.

There was then what is known as a lacuna, a gap, something missing, and amiss. In this gap, gradually, as I sank from the heights back inside myself, I began after all to hear a sound.

It was a peculiar one. I could not make it out.

Since ordinary sense was, unwelcome, returning, I started vaguely to think, Oh, some animal, hunting. It had a kind of coughing, retching, whining quality, inimical and awesome, something which would have nothing to do with what basically it entailed—like the agonized female scream of the mating fox.

The noises went on for some time, driving me ever further and further back to proper awareness, until I opened my eyes, and stood up abruptly. I was cold, and felt rather sick. The scent of the Janfia tree was overpowering, nauseating, and nothing at all had happened. The shadows were all quite usual, and rounding on the window, I saw the last of the moon's edge was in it, and the tree like a cutout of black-and-white papers. Nothing more.

I swore, childishly, in rage, at all things, and myself. It served me right; fool, fool, ever to expect anything. And that long shadow, what had that been? Well. It might have been anything. Why else had I shut my eyes but to aid the delusion, afraid if I continued to look I must be undeceived.

Something horrible had occurred. The night was full of the knowledge of that. Of my idiotic invitation to demons, and my failure, their refusal.

But I really had to get out of the room, the scent of the tree was making me ill at last. How could I ever have thought it pleasant?

I took the wine bottle, meaning to replace it in the refrigerator downstairs, and going out into the corridor, brought on the lights. Below, I hit the other switches rapidly, one after the other, flooding the villa with hard modern glare. So much for the moon. But the smell of the Janfia was more persistent, it seemed to cling to everything—I went out on to the western veranda, to get away from it, but even here on the other side of the house the fragrance hovered.

I was trying, very firmly, to be practical. I was trying to close the door, banish the element I had summoned, for though it had not come to me, yet somehow the night clamored with it, reeked of it. What was it? Only me, of course. My nerves were shot, and what did I do but essay stupid flirtations with the powers of the dark. Though they did not exist in their own right, they do exist inside every one of us. I had called my own demons. Let loose, they peopled the night.

All I could hope for now was to go in and make a gallon of coffee, and leaf through and through the silly magazines that lay about, and stave off sleep until the dawn came. But there was something wrong with the cypress tree. The moon, slipping over the roof now in pursuit of me, caught the cypress and showed what I thought was a broken bough.

That puzzled me. I was glad of the opportunity to go out between the bushes and take a prosaic look.

It was not any distance, and the moon came bright. All the night, all its essence, had concentrated in that spot, yet when I first looked, and first saw, my reaction was only startled astonishment. I rejected the evidence as superficial, which it was not, and looked about and found the tumbled kitchen stool, and then looked up again to be sure, quite certain, that it was Marta who hung there pendant and motionless, her engorged and terrible face twisted away from me. She had used a strong cord. And those unidentifiable sounds I had heard, I realized now, had been the noises Marta made, as she swung and kicked there, strangling to death.

The shock of what had happened was too much for Isabella, and made her unwell. She had been fond of the girl, and could not understand why Marta had not confided her troubles. Presumably her lover had thrown her over, and perhaps she was pregnant—Isabella could have helped, the girl could have had her baby under the shelter of a foreign umbrella of bank notes. But then it transpired Marta had not been pregnant, so there was no proper explanation. The woman who cooked said both she and the girl had been oppressed for days, in some way she could not or did not reveal. It was the season. And then, the girl was young and impressionable. She had gone mad. God would forgive her suicide.

I sat on the veranda of the other villa, my bags around me and a car due to arrive and take me to the town, and Alec and Isabella, both pale with convalescence, facing me over the white iron table.

"It wasn't your fault," said Alec to Isabella. "It's no use brooding over it. The way they are here, it's always been a mystery to me." Then, he went in, saying he felt the heat, but he would return to wave me off.

"And poor poor you," said Isabella, close to tears. "I tell you to come here and rest, and this has to happen."

I could not answer that I felt it was my fault. I could not confess that it seemed to me that I, invoking darkness, had conjured Marta's death. I did not understand the process, only the result. Nor had I told Isabella that the Janfia tree seemed to have contracted its own terminal disease. The leaves and flowers had begun to rot away, and the scent had grown acid. My vibrations had done that. Or it was because the tree had been my focus, my burning-glass. That would reveal me then as my own enemy. That powerful thing which slowly destroyed me, that stalker with a knife, it was myself. And knowing it, naming it, rather than free me of it, could only give it greater power.

"Poor little Marta," said Isabella. She surrendered and began to sob, which would be no use to Marta at all, or to herself, maybe.

Then the car, cheerful in red and white, came up the dusty road, tooting merrily to us. And the driver, heaving my luggage into the boot, cried out to us in joy, "What a beautiful day, ah, what a beautiful day!"

Invited to say something about the genesis or content of this story, I'm afraid that all I *can* say is that it was based in part on a dream. Perhaps, in the light of the material itself, this is more than enough.

Tanith Lee

A CHILD OF
DARKNESS

Susan Casper

Sue has written several vampire stories, including one about a fat vampire. "A Child of Darkness" is a more serious study of a young girl so entranced by the myth of the vampire that she longs to be one, despite all evidence that there is no such creature.

The air is damp and tainted with the odors of tobacco, sweat, and urine. What light there is comes from a small bulb in the ceiling, its plastic cover green with ancient grime. Voices echo, re-echo along the concrete walls of the corridor until they sound like an old recording. It is Daria's only contact with the world outside of her little cell and she is torn between a nervous desire to shut it all out, and a need to listen greedily.

Far away a woman begins to sing an old gospel song. Her voice is thin and slightly off key; it gives Daria a shiver. *It makes my blood run cold,* she thinks, then laughs bitterly at the idea. Hers is not the only laughter. From somewhere in the depths comes the cackle of a mad woman—and then another voice joins in, slurred, unsteady, taunting. "That singin' won't help you none, bitch. God knows what you are. Whore of Babylon, that's what *you* are."

The singing stops. "What the hell do you know?" a Spanish accent replies.

"Ain't what I know that counts, bitch. It's what God knows. God knows you're a sinner. He's gonna get you, girl."

The accent protests. She prays, sobs, moans, repents, accuses, but her anguished voice is softer, and weaker, and somehow more frightening than the others.

Suddenly, a shrill, soprano, scream cuts across all the other noises. "Oh, the pain. Oh my God, the pain. I'm dying. Somebody please . . . help me."

"Hey, you, knock it off down there," a cold male voice replies.

Daria can see nothing from her cell but the stained gray wall across the corridor which seems to go on forever, but she finds that if she presses herself into the corner, she can just make out the place where the hallway ends on one side. A guard is sitting there. He is eating a sandwich that he peels from a wax-paper bag as if it were a banana. A Styrofoam cup is perched on the floor by his side. Another cop comes by. She can see him briefly as he passes through her narrow channel of vision, but he must have stopped to talk, because the first man's face splits into a grin and then she can see his lips move. His thumb points down her corridor and he begins to laugh.

Lousy bastard, she thinks.

The Kool-Aid looked a lot like wine in her mother's good stemware. Especially when the light shone through it, making the liquid glow like rubies, or maybe the glorious seeds of an autumn pomegranate. She lifted the glass, pinky raised in a grotesque child's parody, and delicately sipped the liquid. *Wine must taste a lot like this,* she thought, swirling the sugary drink in her mouth. This was what it would be like when she was a lady. She would pile her hair high atop her head in curls and wear deliciously tight dresses, her shoulders draped in mink. Just like Marilyn Monroe.

"Ha, ha, Dary's drinking wi-ine. Dary's drinking wi-ine," Kevin sang as he raced back and forth across the kitchen floor.

"It's not either wine," she said, more embarrassed than frightened at being caught by her little brother.

"If it's not wine then prove it," he said, snatching the glass from her hand. He held it tightly in his fist, one pinky shooting straight out into the air, mocking her already exaggerated grip. He sipped it, then made a face, eyes bugged and whirling. "Ugh, it is wine," he said, looking at her impishly. "I must be drunk." He began to stagger about, flinging himself around the room. Daria saw it coming. She wanted to cry out and stop him, or at least to cover her eyes so that she couldn't see the disaster, but it happened before she could do any of those things. Kevin tripped over the leg of a chair and went down in a crash of shattered crystal.

Her first thought was for the glass. That was one of the things that she hated herself for later. All she could think about was how it was Kevin's fault that the glass was broken, but she would be the one who got the spanking for it. Especially the way he was howling. Then she saw the blood all over her brother's arm. Already there was a small puddle on the floor. She knew that she should get a bandage, or call the emergency number that her mother always kept near the phone, or at the very least, run and get a neighbor, but she couldn't move. She couldn't take her eyes off of the bright-red stain. It was not as if she had never seen blood before, but suddenly she was drawn to it as she had never been drawn to anything before. Without knowing what she was doing, she found herself walking toward her brother, taking his arm in her hands and pulling it slowly toward her face. And then she could taste the salt and copper taste as she sucked at her brother's wound, filling a need that she hadn't even known existed. It was a hunger so all-consuming that she could not be distracted even by Kevin's fists flailing away at her back, or the sound of her mother's scream when she entered the room.

Daria realizes that she has wedged her face too tightly between the bars and the cold metal is bruising her cheeks. She withdraws into the dimness. There is a metal shelf bolted to the wall. It has a raised edge running around its sides and was obviously designed to hold a mattress that is long since gone. There are cookie-sized holes in the metal, placed with no discernible pattern along its length. Words have been scratched into this cot frame with nail files, hair pins, paper clips—mostly names like Barbara and Mike, and Gloria S. There are many expletives and an occasional statement about the "pigs," but no poems or limericks to occupy her attention for even a brief time. The metal itself is studded with rock-hard lumps of used chewing gum, wadded bits of paper and who knows what else. It is uncomfortable to sit on even without these things—too wide. Her skirt is too tight for her to sit cross-legged, and so if she sits back far enough to lean against the wall, the metal lip cuts sharply into the back of her calves. Already, there are bright-red welts on her legs, and so she lies on her side with her knees drawn up and her head pedestaled on her arm, the holes in the metal leaving rings along the length of her body. She pulls a crumpled package of cigarettes out of her pocket and stares at them longingly. Only three left. With a sigh, she puts them back. It is going to be a long night.

The doctor's name was printed in thick black letters on the frosted glass. Who knew what horrors waited for her on the other side. She knew that she had promised her mother that she would behave, but it was all too much for her. With tears streaming down her cheeks, she tried to pull free from her mother's grasp.

"No! Please. No, Mommy! I'll be a good girl, I promise."

Her mother grabbed her by both shoulders and stooped down until she could look into her daughter's eyes. With trembling fingers she brushed the child's hair. "Dary, honey, the doctor won't hurt you. All he wants to do is have a little talk with you. That's all. You can talk with the nice doctor, can't you?"

Daria sniffed and wiped her eyes with the backs of her hands. She knew what kind of people went to see psychiatrists. Crazy people. And crazy people got "put away" in the nuthouse. She allowed her mother to lead her into the doctor's office, a queen walking bravely to the gallows.

The waiting room was supposed to look inviting. One whole side was set up as a playroom, with a child-sized table and two little chairs, an open toybox with dolls and blocks spilling out of the top. A lady in starched white greeted them at the door and pointed Daria toward the corner, but she was not the least interested in playing. Instead, she hoisted herself onto a large wooden chair and sat there in perfect stillness, her hands folded across her lap. There she could hear some of the words that passed between her mother and the nurse. Their voices were hushed and they were quite far away, but she could hear enough to tell that her mother was ashamed to tell the white lady what Daria had done. She could hear the word "crazy" pass back and forth between them just as she had heard it pass between her father and her mother all the last week. And she could tell, even though she could only see the back of her head, that her mother was crying.

Suddenly, the door opened up behind the nurse's desk and Daria's mother disappeared through it. The nurse tried to talk to the sullen little girl, but Daria remained motionless, knowing that she would wait there forever, if necessary, but she would not move from that spot until her mother returned.

Then, like a miracle, her mother was back. Daria forgot all about her resolve to stay in the seat. She rushed to her mother's side. She would go anywhere, even inside the doctor's room if only her mother wouldn't leave her again. When her mother opened the door to the doctor's office and waved Daria through, the child went without hesitation, but then, her mother shut the door without following, and Daria was more frightened than ever.

"You must be Daria," Doctor Wells said without moving from his desk. He reminded Daria of the stuffed walrus in the museum, and he smelled of tobacco and Sen-Sen and mustache wax. He smiled, and it was a pleasant smile. "Your mother tells me that you're very smart and that you like to do puzzles. I have a puzzle here that's very hard. Would you like to try and do my puzzle?"

Daria nodded, but she did not move from her place near the door. Dr. Wells got up and walked over to a shelf and removed a large wooden puzzle. It was a cow. A three-dimensional puzzle. Daria had never seen anything like it before. He placed the puzzle on a little table that was a twin to the one in the waiting room and went back behind his desk.

"Well, you don't have to do it if you don't want to," he said after a minute, and then began to look through some papers on his desk, ignoring her. Soon, Daria's curiosity got the better of her and she found herself standing at the table looking at the puzzle, taking it apart.

Daria had expected the doctor would talk to her, but he didn't really seem interested in talking. He seemed content to watch her play with the puzzles and toys and he asked her very few questions. By the time she left his office, Daria had decided that she liked Dr. Wells very much.

She wakes slowly, unsure whether minutes or hours have passed. Her eyes are weeping from the cold of the metal where her head has been resting, and her muscles ache with stiffness. Her neck and chest, still covered with crusted blood that the arresting officers had refused to let her wash away, have begun to itch unmercifully. She sits up and realizes that her bladder is full. There is a toilet in the cell. It is a filthy affair with no seat, no paper, no sink, and no privacy from the eyes of the policemen who occasionally stroll up and down the corridor. She will live with the pain a while longer.

Suddenly, she realizes what it is that has woken her up. Silence. It is a silence as profound as the noise had been earlier. No singing, no taunting voices, nobody howling in pain. It is so quiet that she can hear the rustling newspaper of the guard at the end of the hall. She feels that she ought to be grateful not to have to listen to the racket, but instead, she finds the silence frightening.

Once again, she pulls the crumpled pack of cigarettes from her pocket. This time she cannot resist. She pulls one from the pack and straightens its bent form, then holds it between her lips for a long time before she begins the finalizing act of lighting it. She lets out the smoke in a long plume, pleased by the hominess of its smell. A familiar scent in this alien world.

"Can you spare one . . . please?" a soft voice calls from the next cell. "Please?" it asks again. The noise acts like a trigger as the tiny gospel singer starts in once more. A hand pokes through the bars in the corner of the cell. It is black and scarred and shaking with the strain of the reach. It is easily the largest hand she has ever seen. Large even for a man. Daria stares at the two cigarettes remaining in her pack. What the hell, she figures, they'll be gone soon anyway. She removes one and places it in the hand. It squeezes her own gently and withdraws.

"So, it has happened again, Daria?" Dr. Wells asked. The child nodded, looking down at her feet. "After three years we had great hope that it wouldn't happen again. But now that you are a little older, perhaps you can tell me what went on in your mind. What were you thinking when it happened? Do you have any idea why you did it?"

"I don't remember thinking anything. I don't even remember doing it. It was like a dream. They had us all lined up outside for gym. We were going to play field hockey. Tanya and Melinda were playing and Tanya hit her with her stick. I only wanted to help, but there was blood all over everything. I remember being afraid. I remember doing it, but it was almost more like watching television, when the camera's supposed to be you. The next thing I knew, Mrs. Rollie was holding me down and there were people everywhere." There was a long pause. "None of the other girls will talk to me now. They called me . . ." The child burst into tears. "They called me a vampire," she said.

"And how do you feel about that?" Dr. Wells goaded her.

"I don't know. Maybe it's true. It must be true, else why would I do what I do?" Tears streamed down her cheeks and she blotted them with a tissue.

"What do you know about vampires, Daria?"

"That they sleep in coffins and hate the sun . . . I know, but maybe it's only partly true. I do hate the sunlight. It hurts my eyes. And garlic, too. It makes me sick. Even the smell of it. Maybe the legends aren't quite right. Maybe I'm just a different kind of vampire. Why else would I do what I do?"

"Do you want to be a vampire, Daria?" Dr. Wells asked softly.

"No!" she shouted, the tears streaming down her face unimpeded, then again more softly, "no. Do you think I'm a vampire?" she asked.

"No, Daria. I don't believe in vampires. I think you're a young lady with a problem. And . . . I think if we work together, we can find out why you have this problem and what we can do about it."

There is the jingle of keys and the crisp sound of heavy feet. The dying woman has begun her plea for help again and Daria wonders if they are finally coming to see what is wrong, but the footsteps stop in front of her own cell. She looks up and sees the policeman consulting a piece of paper. "Daria Stanton?" he asks. She nods. He makes her back up, away from the door of the cell before he opens it. He tells her to turn around and put her hands behind her back. He handcuffs her and makes her follow him.

She is surprised to see there is only one cell between hers and the main corridor, something that she hadn't noticed on the way in. The cop she saw earlier is still sitting there, still eating, or perhaps eating again. She wants to ask him why he doesn't at least check on the woman who is screaming, but he doesn't look up at her as she passes. She is taken down an endless maze of corridors, all covered with the same green tile, except where they branch out into hallways full of cells. Eventually, she is taken to a room where her cuffs are removed and she is told to wait. He is careless shutting the door behind him and she can see that it isn't locked, but she makes no move to go through it. What difference can it make. Her fate was decided long ago.

"Daria Stanton? Please sit down, I have some questions to ask you."

Even after six months it still felt strange, coming to this new building, walking down a new corridor. She still missed Dr. Wells and hated him for dying that way, without any warning, as though it had been an act against her, personally. This new doctor didn't feel like a doctor at all; letting her call him Mark. And there should be a law against anyone's shrink being so cute, with all those new-fangled ideas. She paused outside the door, pulled off her mirrored sunglasses, and adjusted her hair and makeup in the lenses.

"Morning, Mark," she said as she seated herself in his green padded chair by the window. She couldn't bring herself to lie down on the couch, because all she could think of was how much she wanted him lying there with her. Seated where she was, she could watch the street outside while they talked. Two boys were standing around the old slide-bolt gum machine that had stood outside Wexler's Drug Store for as long as she could remember. It was easy to tell by their attitude that they were up to something. The dark-haired boy looked around furtively several times, then started sliding the bolt back and forth.

"I have some news for you this morning," Dr. Bremner told her. "Good news, I hope." The blond child kicked the machine and tried the bolt again. "The reports of your blood workup are back and I've gone over them with Dr. Walinski. Your blood showed a marked anemia of a type known as iron-deficiency porphyria. Now, ordinarily, I wouldn't be telling a patient that it was good news that she was sick, but in your case, it could mean that your symptoms are purely physical." A woman walked down the street. The two boys stopped tampering with the machine, turned and stared into the drug-store window until she had passed. ". . . a very rare disease. It is even more unusual for it to evince the symptoms that you have, but . . . it has been known to happen. Your body craves the iron porphyrins that it can't produce, and somehow, it knows what *you* don't . . . that whole blood is a source." The boys went back to the machine. One of them pulled a wire from his pocket and inserted it into the coin slot. "I've also talked with Dr. Ruth Tracey at the Eilman Clinic for Blood Disorders. She says your sensitivity to light and to garlic are all tied up in this too. For one thing, garlic breaks down old red blood cells. Just what a person with your condition can't afford to have happen." Once again the boys were interrupted and once again they removed themselves to the drugstore window. "Do you understand what all this means?"

Daria nodded morosely.

"How does it feel to know that there is a physiological cause for your problem?"

"I don't see what difference it makes," she said, brushing a wisp of straight black hair back from her forehead in irritation. "Insanity, vampirism, porphyria? What difference does it make what name you put on it? Even my family barely speaks to me any more. Besides, it's getting worse. I can't even stand to go out during the day anymore, and look at this." She pulled the sunglasses from her face to show him the dark circles under her eyes.

"Yes, I know, but Dr. Tracey can help you. With the right medications your symptoms should disappear. Imagine a time when you can see someone cut themself without being afraid of what you'll do. You'll be able to go to the beach and get a suntan for Chrissake."

Daria looked back out the window, but the boys were gone. She wasn't sure whether the half-empty globe had been full of gumballs a moment ago.

Hours—weeks—years later they bring her back to her cell. Though she has only been there since early evening, already it is like coming home. The chorus has changed. Two drunken, giggling voices have been added and someone is drumming on the bars with ringed fingers. The taunter still goads the gospel singer even though she has stopped singing and the dying woman is still dying, with a tough new voice telling her to do it already and shut up. Daria slumps back on her slab of metal, her back against the wall with her straight skirt hiked up so that her legs can be folded in front of her. She no longer cares what anybody sees. She has been questioned, photographed, and given one phone call. Mark will be there for the arraignment. He will see about getting her a lawyer. She has been told not to worry, that everything will be all right—but she is not worried . . . she knows that nothing will ever be all right for her again.

She stares at the dim and dirty green light that is always on and wonders if prison will be worse. From what she has read about penal institutions, she will not last very long once they send her away. A vampire in prison. She laughs at the thought and wonders what Dracula would do.

The fire was warmth seeping into her body, making her feel alive for the first time in years. She inched herself a little closer to the hearth. Mark came into the room holding a pair of cocktail glasses. He placed one by her elbow and joined her on the rug.

"Daria, there are things I wanted to tell you. So many things that I just couldn't say while you were my patient. You do understand why I couldn't go on treating you? Not the way I felt."

She reached out and squeezed his hand, reluctant to turn her face away from the fire for even the time it would have taken to look at him. He stroked her hair. Why did it make her feel like purring? She wanted him to take her in his arms, but she was afraid. Unlike most twenty-year-old women, she had no idea what to do; how to react. The boys that she met had often told her that she was beautiful, flirted, made passes or asked her out, but the moment they found out anything about her, they always became frightened and backed off. Mark was different. He already knew everything, even though he didn't choose to believe it all.

He took her face in his hands and kissed her. At first she wanted to pull away, but soon a burning started inside of her that made the fireplace unnecessary.

Daria can no longer stand the boredom. She climbs on the bars of her cell just for something to do. It is morning. She can tell by the shuffling of feet and slamming of doors that comes from the main corridor. She can tell by the food trays being brought down the hall, though none comes to her, and by the fact that the man in the chair has been replaced by a sloppy matron. She wonders if Mark is in the building yet. Probably. He has been in love with her since the first day she walked into his office, though she is convinced it is her condition and not herself that he loves. She would like to love him back, but though she needs him and wants him, truly enjoys his intimacy, she is sure that love is just another emotion that she cannot feel.

A different policeman stops outside her cell. He is carrying handcuffs, but he does not take them from his belt as he opens her cell door. "Time for your arraignment," he says cheerfully. Docile, she follows him down the same, and then a different, set of corridors. They take a long ride in a rickety elevator and when the doors open they are standing in a paneled hall. Spears of morning light stab through the windows making Daria cover her eyes. In the distance she can see a courtroom packed with people. Mark is there. He is standing by the double doors that lead inside. Someone is with him. Even on such short notice, he has found a lawyer—a friend of a friend. Mark takes her hand and they go through the double doors together. There are several cases to wait through before her name is called and he whispers reassurances to her while they sit there.

Finally, it is her turn, but the lawyer and Mark have taken that burden from her and she has no need to speak. Instead, she watches the judge. His face is puffy from sleep as he reads down the list of charges, aggravated assault, assault and battery . . . the list is long and Daria is surprised that they haven't thrown in witchcraft. The judge has probably slept through many such arraignments, but Daria knows that he will not sleep through this one. Indeed, she sees his eyes grow wide as the details of her crime are discussed. Interfering at the scene of an accident, obstructing the paramedics . . . there is no mercy in that face for her.

Then Mark begins to talk. Lovingly, he tells of her condition, of the work that Dr. Tracey is doing, of the hope for an imminent cure. He is so eloquent that for the very first time *she* is almost willing to believe that she is merely "sick." The judge's face softens. Illness is another matter. Daria has been so resigned to her fate that she is surprised to find that she has been freed. Released on her own recognizance until her trial. No bail. Mark throws his arms around her, but she is too stunned to hug him back.

"I love you," Mark tells her as he leads her out of the courtroom. He has brought glasses to shield her eyes from the sun.

A vein in his neck is throbbing.

"I love you too," she answers automatically. She tries not to stare at the throbbing vein. *This is a compulsion caused by illness,* she tells herself, *a chemical imbalance in the blood. It can be cured.*

"Daria, we're going to fight this. First we'll get you off on those ridiculous charges, and then Dr. Tracey is going to make you well. You'll see. Everything's going to be all right." He puts his arm around her shoulders, but something inside makes her stiffen and pull away.

Once again she looks at the throbbing vein and wonders what it will be like not to feel this hunger. All it will take is just the right compound stabbed into her arm with a little glass needle. A second of pain.

No, she thinks to herself in the crowded aloneness of the jailhouse steps. She finds inside herself a well of resolve, of acceptance, that she has never tapped before. She will no longer be put off by bottles of drugs, by diets that don't work, by hours of laborious talk. She will be what she is, the thing that makes her different, the thing that makes her herself. She is not just a young woman with a rare blood disease; she is a vampire, a child of darkness, and she had been fighting it for way too long.

Allowing her expression to soften to a smile, she turns to Mark and places her hand gently on his neck, feeling the pulse of the vein under her thumb. "Yes, Mark, you're right," she says softly. "You *will* have to get me off on these charges." So many little blue veins in so many necks. She will have to stay free if she is to feed.

This story stems, in part, from personal experience. (It was a bum rap, honest!) I remember reading an article in one of the science magazines which discussed porphyria as a medical rationale for vampirism. The article stated that this disease could very well explain an aversion to sunlight and garlic as well as a desire to drink blood. For a long time I had been thinking about doing a story about a girl who thought she was a vampire when it was actually more reasonable to believe that she was not. I thought of the seductive pull of vampires as they are expressed in pop culture and the appeal that they might have on a sensitive person who was ostracized because she was different. The prison experience seemed like a good hook to hang it all on.

Susan Casper

NOCTURNE

Steve Rasnic Tem

I wanted to use Sylvia Plath's poem "Daddy" but was stymied by the unrealistic demands of the Plath estate. So, on Ed Bryant's recommendation, I asked his fellow Coloradan Steve Rasnic Tem for a poem on the psychology of some arrested male-female relationships. "Nocturne" is his response.

Under neon patina,
    her eyes shift toward yellow.
The city enfolds them,
electric hum depleting
the rations of love.
"Do you even care?"
she asks, and still he's speechless,
seething because she cannot believe his rage,
because he cannot love
however much he makes love,
because one woman is never enough,
because he needs the dead visions
of women in pornographic prayerbooks,
raging because he needs.

She closes her eyes,
so he can stand inside her skin.
She feels him inside her,
his fingertips greeting

each inner wall.
kissing her unseen flesh.
He fills her outline completely,
like a balloon,
forcing out her own breath,
pressing out any sense.
She's emptied trying to fill him,
and still he won't be filled.

If she were dead she could not resist.
If she were dead she might fill.

A child, he'd played with dead mice.
He's sick for her smell.
He's sick for her life,
all his potency gone
into rusted etchings of consumed cars,
the slow-motion collapse of abandoned homes,
the sure specters of his childhood play,
the glossy feel of dead women.
Raging at the absence of love,
he burns over the wife he's made his mother,
whom he cannot repay with love,
whom he can only consume.

Her eyes shift toward red,
the taste of her like roasted seed.
He's drained her of sleep;
he's sapped her dreams.
Teeth and tongue to nape,
"You're so sweet," he says,
in hungry infant's voice,
"I could just eat you up,"
imitating mama.
He gives her lines to say.

She's slow to sleep
as pale and lazy as the sheets.
Tasting her like a baby,
using tongue for eyes,
his life becomes so still,
his life becomes so dark.

His breath rank with desire.
His aquiline face, lean nose,
his heavy eyebrows.
Ruddy lips and anemic ears.
He could become a wolf,
if he wanted to;
he could pass beneath a door.
He might speak with waxen beasts
and other neighbors of the night.

If she'd just let him feed.

One of the things poetry does best is to explore the gray areas: the ill-defined regions between genre expectations, those thematic realms which disturb while leaving us inarticulate about exactly what it is that disturbs us. Poetry is a form permitting us to grapple head-on with that inarticulateness, encouraging work about that very grasping after meaning. An ideal form for darker sorts of fantasy, I think.

And an appropriate form for capturing my own feelings about vampirism. On the one hand, admit it, it's a pretty silly idea—a Rudolph Valentino clone in an outdated suit, posturing melodramatically, mascara applied generously to heighten the color. The horror in that figure escapes me much of the time, it seems so far removed from my own apprehensions. But go beyond that—most of us have been in relationships which left us unaccountably drained, have known people whose very presence somehow left us weakened, edgy. People feed off each other. That's not necessarily bad; maybe it's just a natural consequence of having a brain that can aspire, and yearn. But like anything else, some people will take it too far.

Steve Rasnic Tem

Down Among the Dead Men

⁓

Gardner Dozois and Jack Dann

This story was first published in Oui *magazine because initially none of the fantasy or science fiction magazines (including* OMNI*) would take it. It was too "tough" and possibly "tasteless" a subject. There is an actual vampire in this story, and in a world where humans are monstrous to each other is he any worse a monster?*

*B*ruckman first discovered that Wernecke was a vampire when they went to the quarry that morning.

He was bending down to pick up a large rock when he thought he heard something in the gully nearby. He looked around and saw Wernecke huddled over a *Musselmänn*, one of the walking dead, a new man who had not been able to wake up to the terrible reality of the camp.

"Do you need any help?" Bruckman asked Wernecke in a low voice.

Wernecke looked up, startled, and covered his mouth with his hand, as if he were signing to Bruckman to be quiet.

But Bruckman was certain that he had glimpsed blood smeared on Wernecke's mouth. "The Musselmänn, is he alive?" Wernecke had often risked his own life to save one or another of the men in his barracks. But to risk one's life for a Musselmänn? "What's wrong?"

"Get away."

All right, Bruckman thought. Best to leave him alone. He looked pale, perhaps it was typhus. The guards were working him hard enough, and Wernecke was older than the rest of the men in the work gang. Let him sit for a moment and rest. But what about that blood? . . .

"Hey, you, what are you doing?" one of the young SS guards shouted to Bruckman.

Bruckman picked up the rock and, as if he had not heard the guard, began to walk away from the gully, toward the rusty brown cart on the tracks that led back to the barbed-wire fence of the camp. He would try to draw the guard's attention away from Wernecke.

But the guard shouted at him to halt. "Were you taking a little rest, is that it?" he asked, and Bruckman tensed, ready for a beating. This guard was new, neatly and cleanly dressed—and an unknown quantity. He walked over to the gully and, seeing Wernecke and the Musselmänn, said, "Aha, so your friend is taking care of the sick." He motioned Bruckman to follow him into the gully.

Bruckman had done the unpardonable—he had brought it on Wernecke. He swore at himself. He had been in this camp long enough to know to keep his mouth shut.

The guard kicked Wernecke sharply in the ribs. "I want you to put the Musselmänn in the cart. Now!" He kicked Wernecke again, as if as an afterthought. Wernecke groaned, but got to his feet. "Help him put the Musselmänn in the cart," the guard said to Bruckman; then he smiled and drew a circle in the air—the sign of smoke, the smoke which rose from the tall gray chimneys behind them. This Musselmänn would be in the oven within an hour, his ashes soon to be floating in the hot, stale air, as if they were the very particles of his soul.

Wernecke kicked the Musselmänn, and the guard chuckled, waved to another guard who had been watching, and stepped back a few feet. He stood with his hands on his hips. "Come on, dead man, get up or you're going to die in the oven," Wernecke whispered as he tried to pull the man to his feet. Bruckman supported the unsteady Musselmänn, who began to wail softly. Wernecke slapped him hard. "Do you want to live, Musselmänn? Do you want to see your family again, feel the touch of a woman, smell grass after it's been mowed? Then *move*." The Musselmänn shambled forward between Wernecke and Bruckman. "You're dead, aren't you Musselmänn," goaded Wernecke. "As dead as your father and mother, as dead as your sweet wife, if you ever had one, aren't you? Dead!"

The Musselmänn groaned, shook his head, and whispered, "Not dead, my wife . . ."

"Ah, it talks," Wernecke said, loud enough so the guard walking a step behind them could hear. "Do you have a name, corpse?"

"Josef, and I'm not a Musselmänn."

"The corpse says he's alive," Wernecke said, again loud enough for the SS guard to hear. Then in a whisper, he said, "Josef, if you're not a Musselmänn, then you must work now, do you understand?" Josef tripped, and Bruckman caught him. "Let him be," said Wernecke. "Let him walk to the cart himself."

"Not the cart," Josef mumbled. "Not to die, not—"

"Then get down and pick up stones, show the fart-eating guard you can work."

"Can't. I'm sick, I'm . . ."

"Musselmänn!"

Josef bent down, fell to his knees, but took hold of a stone and stood up.

"You see," Wernecke said to the guard, "it's not dead yet. It can still work."

"I told you to carry him to the cart, didn't I," the guard said petulantly.

"Show him you can work," Wernecke said to Josef, "or you'll surely be smoke."

And Josef stumbled away from Wernecke and Bruckman, leaning forward, as if following the rock he was carrying.

"Bring him *back!*" shouted the guard, but his attention was distracted from Josef by some other prisoners, who, sensing the trouble, began to mill about. One of the other guards began to shout and kick at the men on the periphery, and the new guard joined him. For the moment, he had forgotten about Josef.

"Let's get to work, lest they notice us again," Wernecke said.

"I'm sorry that I—"

Wernecke laughed and made a fluttering gesture with his hand—smoke rising. "It's all hazard, my friend. All luck." Again the laugh. "It was a venial sin," and his face seemed to darken. "Never do it again, though, lest I think of you as bad luck."

"Carl, are you all right?" Bruckman asked. "I noticed some blood when—"

"Do the sores on your feet bleed in the morning?" Wernecke countered angrily. Bruckman nodded, feeling foolish and embarrassed. "And so it is with my gums. Now go away, unlucky one, and let me live."

At dusk, the guards broke the hypnosis of lifting and grunting and sweating and formed the prisoners into ranks. They marched back to the camp through the fields, beside the railroad tracks, the electrified wire, conical towers, and into the main gate of the camp.

Josef walked beside them, but he kept stumbling, as he was once again slipping back into death, becoming a Musselmänn. Wernecke helped him walk, pushed him along. "We should let this man become dead," Wernecke said to Bruckman.

Bruckman only nodded, but he felt a chill sweep over his sweating back. He was seeing Wernecke's face again as it was for that instant in the morning. Smeared with blood.

Yes, Bruckman thought, we should let the Musselmänn become dead. We should all be dead. . . .

Wernecke served up the lukewarm water with bits of spoiled turnip floating on the top, what passed as soup for the prisoners. Everyone sat or kneeled on the rough-planked floor, as there were no chairs.

Bruckman ate his portion, counting the sips and bites, forcing himself to take his time. Later, he would take a very small bite of the bread he had in his pocket. He always saved a small morsel of food for later—in the endless world of the camp, he had learned to give himself things to look forward to. Better to dream of bread than to get lost in the present. That was the fate of the Musselmänner.

But he always dreamed of food. Hunger was with him every moment of the day and night. Those times when he actually ate were in a way the most difficult, for there was never enough to satisfy him. There was the taste of softness in his mouth, and then in an instant it was gone. The emptiness took the form of pain—it *hurt* to eat. For bread, he thought, he would have killed his father, or his wife. God forgive me, and he watched Wernecke— Wernecke, who had shared his bread with him, who had died a little so he could live. He's a better man than I, Bruckman thought.

It was dim inside the barracks. A bare light bulb hung from the ceiling and cast sharp shadows across the cavernous room. Two tiers of five-foot-deep shelves ran around the room on three sides, bare wooden shelves where the men slept without blankets or mattresses. Set high in the northern wall was a slatted window, which let in the stark white light of the kliegs.

Outside, the lights turned the grounds into a deathly imitation of day; only inside the barracks was it night.

"Do you know what tonight is, my friends?" Wernecke asked. He sat in the far corner of the room with Josef, who, hour by hour, was reverting back into a Musselmänn. Wernecke's face looked hollow and drawn in the light from the window and the light bulb; his eyes were deep-set and his face was long with deep creases running from his nose to the corners of his thin mouth. His hair was black, and even since Bruckman had known him, quite a bit of it had fallen out. He was a very tall man, almost six feet four, and that made him stand out in a crowd, which was dangerous in a death camp. But Wernecke had his own secret ways of blending with the crowd, of making himself invisible.

"No, tell us what tonight is," crazy old Bohme said. That men such as Bohme could survive was a miracle—or, as Bruckman thought—a testament to men such as Wernecke who somehow found the strength to help the others live.

"It's Passover," Wernecke said.

"How does he know that?" someone mumbled, but it didn't matter how Wernecke knew because he *knew*—even if it really wasn't Passover by the calendar. In this dimly lit barrack, it *was* Passover, the feast of freedom, the time of thanksgiving.

"But how can we have Passover without a *seder*?" asked Bohme. "We don't even have any *matzoh*," he whined.

"Nor do we have candles, or a silver cup for Elijah, or the shankbone, or *haroset*—nor would I make a *seder* over the *traif* the Nazis are so generous in giving us," replied Wernecke with a smile. "But we can pray, can't we? And when we all get out of here, when we're in our own homes in the coming year with God's help, then we'll have twice as much food—two *afikomens*, a bottle of wine for Elijah, and the *haggadahs* that our fathers and our fathers' fathers used."

It *was* Passover.

"Isadore, do you remember the four questions?" Wernecke asked Bruckman.

And Bruckman heard himself speaking. He was twelve years old again at the long table beside his father, who sat in the seat of honor. To sit next to him was itself an honor. "How does this night differ from all other nights?

On all other nights we eat bread and *matzoh;* why on this night do we eat only *matzoh?*

"*M'a nisht' ana halylah hazeah. . . .*"

Sleep would not come to Bruckman that night, although he was so tired that he felt as if the marrow of his bones had been sucked away and replaced with lead.

He lay there in the semidarkness, feeling his muscles ache, feeling the acid biting of his hunger. Usually he was numb enough with exhaustion that he could empty his mind, close himself down, and fall rapidly into oblivion, but not tonight. Tonight he was noticing things again, his surroundings were getting through to him again, in a way that they had not since he had been new in camp. It was smotheringly hot, and the air was filled with the stinks of death and sweat and fever, of stale urine and drying blood. The sleepers thrashed and turned, as though they fought with sleep, and as they slept, many of them talked or muttered or screamed aloud; they lived other lives in their dreams, intensely compressed lives dreamed quickly, for soon it would be dawn, and once more they would be thrust into hell. Cramped in the midst of them, sleepers squeezed in all around him, it suddenly seemed to Bruckman that these pallid white bodies were already dead, that he was sleeping in a graveyard. Suddenly it was the boxcar again. And his wife Miriam was dead again, dead and rotting unburied. . . .

Resolutely, Bruckman emptied his mind. He felt feverish and shaky, and wondered if the typhus were coming back, but he couldn't afford to worry about it. Those who couldn't sleep couldn't survive. Regulate your breathing, force your muscles to relax, don't think. Don't think.

For some reason, after he had managed to banish even the memory of his dead wife, he couldn't shake the image of the blood on Wernecke's mouth.

There were other images mixed in with it: Wernecke's uplifted arms and upturned face as he led them in prayer; the pale strained face of the stumbling Musselmänn; Wernecke looking up, startled, as he crouched over Josef . . . but it was the blood to which Bruckman's feverish thoughts returned, and he pictured it again and again as he lay in the rustling, fart-smelling darkness, the watery sheen of blood over Wernecke's lips, the tarry trickle of blood in the corner of his mouth, like a tiny scarlet worm. . . .

Just then a shadow crossed in front of the window, silhouetted blackly for an instant against the harsh white glare, and Bruckman knew from the shadow's height and its curious forward stoop that it was Wernecke.

Where could he be going? Sometimes a prisoner would be unable to wait until morning, when the Germans would let them out to visit the slit-trench latrine again, and would slink shamefacedly into a far corner to piss against a wall, but surely Wernecke was too much of an old hand for that. . . . Most of the prisoners slept on the sleeping platforms, especially during the cold nights when they would huddle together for warmth, but sometimes during the hot weather, people would drift away and sleep on the floor instead; Bruckman had been thinking of doing that, as the jostling bodies of the sleepers around him helped to keep him from sleep. Perhaps Wernecke, who always had trouble fitting into the cramped sleeping niches, was merely looking for a place where he could lie down and stretch his legs . . .

Then Bruckman remembered that Josef had fallen asleep in the corner of the room where Wernecke had sat and prayed, and that they had left him there alone.

Without knowing why, Bruckman found himself on his feet. As silently as the ghost he sometimes felt he was becoming, he walked across the room in the direction Wernecke had gone, not understanding what he was doing nor why he was doing it. The face of the Musselmänn, Josef, seemed to float behind his eyes. Bruckman's feet hurt, and he knew, without looking, that they were bleeding, leaving faint tracks behind him. It was dimmer here in the far corner, away from the window, but Bruckman knew that he must be near the wall by now, and he stopped to let his eyes readjust.

When his eyes had adapted to the dimmer light, he saw Josef sitting on the floor, propped up against the wall. Wernecke was hunched over the Musselmänn. Kissing him. One of Josef's hands was tangled in Wernecke's thinning hair.

Before Bruckman could react—such things had been known to happen once or twice before, although it shocked him deeply that *Wernecke* would be involved in such filth—Josef released his grip on Wernecke's hair. Josef's upraised arm fell limply to the side, his hand hitting the floor with a muffled but solid impact that should have been painful—but Josef made no sound.

Wernecke straightened up and turned around. Stronger light from the high window caught him as he straightened to his full height, momentarily illuminating his face.

Wernecke's mouth was smeared with blood.

"My God," Bruckman cried.

Startled, Wernecke flinched, then took two quick steps forward and seized Bruckman by the arm. "Quiet!" Wernecke hissed. His fingers were cold and hard.

At that moment, as though Wernecke's sudden movement were a cue, Josef began to slip down sideways along the wall. As Wernecke and Bruckman watched, both momentarily riveted by the sight, Josef toppled over to the floor, his head striking against the floorboards with a sound such as a dropped melon might make. He had made no attempt to break his fall or cushion his head, and lay now unmoving.

"My *God*," Bruckman said again.

"Quiet, I'll explain," Wernecke said, his lips still glazed with the Musselmänn blood. "Do you want to ruin us all? For the love of God, be *quiet.*"

But Bruckman had shaken free of Wernecke's grip and crossed to kneel by Josef, leaning over him as Wernecke had done, placing a hand flat on Josef's chest for a moment, then touching the side of Josef's neck. Bruckman looked slowly up at Wernecke. "He's dead," Bruckman said, more quietly.

Wernecke squatted on the other side of Josef's body, and the rest of their conversation was carried out in whispers over Josef's chest, like friends conversing at the sickbed of another friend who has finally fallen into a fitful doze.

"Yes, he's dead," Wernecke said. "He was dead yesterday, wasn't he? Today he had just stopped walking." His eyes were hidden here, in the deeper shadow nearer to the floor, but there was still enough light for Bruckman to see that Wernecke had wiped his lips clean. Or licked them clean, Bruckman thought, and felt a spasm of nausea go through him.

"*But you*," Bruckman said, haltingly. "You were. . . ."

"Drinking his blood?" Wernecke said. "Yes, I was drinking his blood."

Bruckman's mind was numb. He couldn't deal with this, he couldn't understand it at all. "But *why*, Eduard? Why?"

"To live, of course. Why do any of us do anything here? If I am to live, I must have blood. Without it, I'd face a death even more certain than that doled out by the Nazis."

Bruckman opened and closed his mouth, but no sound came out, as if the words he wished to speak were too jagged to fit through his throat. At last he managed to croak, "A vampire? You're a vampire? Like in the old stories?"

Wernecke said calmly, "Men would call me that." He paused, then nodded. "Yes, that's what men would call me. . . . As though they can understand something simply by giving it a name."

"But Eduard," Bruckman said weakly, almost petulantly. "The Musselmänn . . ."

"Remember that he *was* a Musselmänn," Wernecke said, leaning forward and speaking more fiercely. "His strength was going, he was sinking. He would have been dead by morning anyway. I took from him something that he no longer needed, but that I needed in order to live. Does it matter? Starving men in lifeboats have eaten the bodies of their dead companions in order to live. Is what I've done any worse than that?"

"But he didn't just die. You *killed* him. . . ."

Wernecke was silent for a moment, and then said, quietly, "What better thing could I have done for him? I won't apologize for what I do, Isadore; I do what I have to do to live. Usually I take only a little blood from a number of men, just enough to survive. And that's fair, isn't it? Haven't I given food to others, to help them survive? To you, Isadore? Only very rarely do I take more than a minimum from any one man, although I'm weak and hungry all the time, believe me. And never have I drained the life from someone who wished to live. Instead I've helped them fight for survival in every way I can, you know that."

He reached out as though to touch Bruckman, then thought better of it and put his hand back on his own knee. He shook his head. "But these Musselmänner, the ones who have given up on life, the walking dead—it is a favor to them to take them, to give them the solace of death. Can you honestly say it is not, *here?* That it is better for them to walk around while they are dead, being beaten and abused by the Nazis until their bodies cannot go on, and then to be thrown into the ovens and burned like trash? Can you say that? Would *they* say that, if they knew what was going on? Or would they thank me?"

Wernecke suddenly stood up, and Bruckman stood up with him. As Wernecke's face came again into the stronger light, Bruckman could see that his eyes had filled with tears. "You have lived under the Nazis," Wernecke said. "Can you really call me a monster? Aren't I still a Jew, whatever else I might be? Aren't I *here*, in a death camp? Aren't I being persecuted, too, as much as any other? Aren't I in as much danger as anyone else? If I'm not a Jew, then tell the Nazis—they seem to think so." He paused for a moment, and then smiled wryly. "And forget your superstitious boogey tales. I'm no night spirit. If I could turn myself into a bat and fly away from here, I would have done it long before now, believe me."

Bruckman smiled reflectively, then grimaced. The two men avoided each other's eyes, Bruckman looking at the floor, and there was an uneasy silence, punctured only by the sighing and moaning of the sleepers on the other side of the cabin. Then, without looking up, in tacit surrender, Bruckman said, "What about *him?* The Nazis will find the body and cause trouble...."

"Don't worry," Wernecke said. "There are no obvious marks. And nobody performs autopsies in a death camp. To the Nazis, he'll be just another Jew who had died of the heat, or from starvation or sickness, or from a broken heart."

Bruckman raised his head then and they stared eye to eye for a moment. Even knowing what he knew, Bruckman found it hard to see Wernecke as anything other than what he appeared to be: an aging, balding Jew, stooping and thin, with sad eyes and a tired, compassionate face.

"Well, then, Isadore," Wernecke said at last, matter-of-factly. "My life is in your hands. I will not be indelicate enough to remind you of how many times your life has been in mine."

Then he was gone, walking back toward the sleeping platforms, a shadow soon lost among other shadows.

Bruckman stood by himself in the gloom for a long time, and then followed him. It took all of his will not to look back over his shoulder at the corner where Josef lay, and even so Bruckman imagined that he could feel Josef's dead eyes watching him, watching reproachfully as he walked away abandoning Josef to the cold and isolated company of the dead.

Bruckman got no more sleep that night, and in the morning, when the Nazis shattered the gray predawn stillness by bursting into the shack with shouts and shrill whistles and barking police dogs, he felt as if he were a thousand years old.

They were formed into two lines, shivering in the raw morning air, and marched off to the quarry. The clammy dawn mist had yet to burn off, and marching through it, through a white shadowless void, with only the back of the man in front of him dimly visible, Bruckman felt more than ever like a ghost, suspended bodiless in some limbo between Heaven and Earth. Only the bite of pebbles and cinders into his raw, bleeding feet kept him anchored to the world, and he clung to the pain as a lifeline, fighting to shake off a feeling of numbness and unreality. However strange, however outré, the events of the previous night had *happened.* To doubt it, to wonder now if it had all been a feverish dream brought on by starvation and exhaustion, was to take the first step on the road to becoming a Musselmänn.

Wernecke is a vampire, he told himself. That was the harsh, unyielding reality that, like the reality of the camp itself, must be faced. Was it any more surreal, any more impossible than the nightmare around them? He must forget the tales that his grandmother had told him as a boy, "boogey tales" as Wernecke himself had called them, half-remembered tales that turned his knees to water whenever he thought of the blood smeared on Wernecke's mouth, whenever he thought of Wernecke's eyes watching him in the dark. . . .

"Wake up, Jew!" the guard alongside him snarled, whacking him lightly on the arm with his rifle butt. Bruckman stumbled, managed to stay upright and keep going. Yes, he thought, wake up. Wake up to the reality of this, just as you once had to wake up to the reality of the camp. It was just one more unpleasant fact he would have to adapt to, learn to deal with. . . .

Deal with how? he thought, and shivered.

By the time they reached the quarry, the mist had burned off, swirling past them in rags and tatters, and it was already beginning to get hot. There was Wernecke, his balding head gleaming dully in the harsh morning light. He didn't dissolve in the sunlight—there was one boogey tale disproved. . . .

They set to work, like golems, like ragtag clockwork automatons.

Lack of sleep had drained what small reserves of strength Bruckman had, and the work was very hard for him that day. He had learned long ago all the tricks of timing and misdirection, the safe way to snatch short moments of rest, the ways to do a minimum of work with the maximum display of effort, the ways to keep the guards from noticing you, to fade into the faceless crowd of prisoners and not be singled out, but today his head was muzzy and slow, and none of the tricks seemed to work.

His body felt like a sheet of glass, fragile, ready to shatter into dust, and the painful, arthritic slowness of his movements got him first shouted at, and then knocked down. The guard kicked him twice for good measure before he could get up.

When Bruckman had climbed back to his feet again, he saw that Wernecke was watching him, face blank, eyes expressionless, a look that could have meant anything at all.

Bruckman felt the blood trickling from the corner of his mouth and thought, *the blood . . . he's watching the blood . . .* and once again he shivered.

Somehow, Bruckman forced himself to work faster, and although his muscles blazed with pain, he wasn't hit again, and the day passed.

When they formed up to go back to camp, Bruckman, almost unconsciously, made sure that he was in a different line than Wernecke.

That night in the cabin, Bruckman watched as Wernecke talked with the other men, here trying to help a new man named Melnick—no more than a boy—adjust to the dreadful reality of the camp, there exhorting someone who was slipping into despair to live and spite his tormentors, joking with old hands in the flat, black, bitter way that passed for humor among them, eliciting a wan smile or occasionally even a laugh from them, finally leading them all in prayer again, his strong, calm voice raised in the ancient words, giving meaning to those words again. . . .

He keeps up together, Bruckman thought, he keeps us going. Without him, we wouldn't last a week. Surely that's worth a little blood, a bit from each man, not even enough to hurt. . . . Surely they wouldn't even begrudge him it, if they knew and really understood. . . . No, he is a good man, better than the rest of us, in spite of his terrible affliction.

Bruckman had been avoiding Wernecke's eyes, hadn't spoken to him at all that day, and suddenly felt a wave of shame go through him at the thought of how shabbily he had been treating his friend. Yes, his friend, regardless, the man who had saved his life . . . Deliberately, he caught Wernecke's eyes, and nodded, and then somewhat sheepishly, smiled. After a moment, Wernecke smiled back, and Bruckman felt a spreading warmth and relief uncoil his guts. Everything was going to be all right, as all right as it could be, here. . . .

Nevertheless, as soon as the inside lights clicked off that night, and Bruckman found himself lying alone in the darkness, his flesh began to crawl.

He had been unable to keep his eyes open a moment before, but now, in the sudden darkness, he found himself tensely and tickingly awake. Where was Wernecke? What was he doing, whom was he visiting tonight? Was he out there in the darkness even now, creeping closer, creeping nearer? ... Stop it, Bruckman told himself uneasily, forget the boogey tales. This is your friend, a good man, not a monster. ... But he couldn't control the fear that made the small hairs on his arms stand bristlingly erect, couldn't stop the grisly images from coming. ...

Wernecke's eyes, gleaming in the darkness ... was the blood already glistening on Wernecke's lips, as he drank? ... The thought of the blood staining Wernecke's yellowing teeth made Bruckman cold and nauseous, but the image that he couldn't get out of his mind tonight was an image of Josef toppling over in that sinister boneless way, striking his head against the floor. ... Bruckman had seen people die in many more gruesome ways during this time at the camp, seen people shot, beaten to death, seen them die in convulsions from high fevers or cough their lungs up in bloody tatters from pneumonia, seen them hanging like charred-black scarecrows from the electrified fences, seen them torn apart by dogs ... but somehow it was Josef's soft, passive, almost restful slumping into death that bothered him. That, and the obscene limpness of Josef's limbs as he sprawled there like a discarded rag doll, his pale and haggard face gleaming reproachfully in the dark. ...

When Bruckman could stand it no longer, he got shakily to his feet and moved off through the shadows, once again not knowing where he was going or what he was going to do, but drawn forward by some obscure instinct he himself did not understand. This time he went cautiously, feeling his way and trying to be silent, expecting every second to see Wernecke's coal-black shadow rise up before him.

He paused, a faint noise scratching at his ears, then went on again, even more cautiously, crouching low, almost crawling across the grimy floor.

Whatever instinct had guided him—sounds heard and interpreted subliminally, perhaps?—it had timed his arrival well. Wernecke had someone down on the floor there, perhaps someone he seized and dragged away from the huddled mass of sleepers on one of the sleeping platforms, someone from the outer edge of bodies whose presence would not be missed, or perhaps someone who had gone to sleep on the floor, seeking solitude or greater comfort.

Whoever he was, he struggled in Wernecke's grip, but Wernecke handled him easily, almost negligently, in a manner that spoke of great physical power. Bruckman could hear the man trying to scream, but Wernecke had one hand on his throat, half-throttling him, and all that would come out was a sort of whistling gasp. The man thrashed in Wernecke's hands like a kite in a child's hands flapping in the wind, and, moving deliberately, Wernecke smoothed him out like a kite, pressing him slowly flat on the floor.

Then Wernecke bent over him, and lowered his mouth to his throat.

Bruckman watched in horror, knowing that he should shout, scream, try to rouse the other prisoners, but somehow unable to move, unable to make his mouth open, his lungs pump. He was paralyzed by fear, like a rabbit in the presence of a predator, a terror sharper and more intense than any he'd ever known.

The man's struggles were growing weaker, and Wernecke must have eased up some on the throttling pressure of his hand, because the man moaned "Don't . . . please don't . . ." in a weaker, slurred voice. The man had been drumming his fists against Wernecke's back and sides, but now the tempo of the drumming slowed, slowed, and then stopped, the man's arms falling laxly to the floor. "Don't . . ." the man whispered; he groaned and muttered incomprehensively for a moment or two longer, then became silent. The silence stretched out for a minute, two, three, and Wernecke still crouched over his victim, who was now not moving at all. . . .

Wernecke stirred, a kind of shudder going through him, like a cat stretching. He stood up. His face became visible as he straightened up into the full light from the window, and there was blood on it, glistening black under the harsh glare of the kliegs. As Bruckman watched, Wernecke began to lick his lips clean, his tongue, also black in this light, sliding like some sort of sinuous ebony snake around the rim of his mouth, darting and probing for the last lingering drops. . . .

How smug he looks, Bruckman thought, like a cat who has found the cream, and the anger that flashed through him at the thought enabled him to move and speak again. "Wernecke," he said harshly.

Wernecke glanced casually in his direction. "You again, Isadore?" Wernecke said. "Don't you ever sleep?" Wernecke spoke lazily, quizzically, without surprise, and Bruckman wondered if Wernecke had known all along that he was there. "Or do you just enjoy watching me?"

"Lies," Bruckman said. "You told me nothing but lies. Why did you bother?"

"You were excited," Wernecke said. "You had surprised me. It seemed best to tell you what you wanted to hear. If it satisfied you, then that was an easy solution to the problem."

"Never have I drained the life from someone who wanted to live," Bruckman said bitterly, mimicking Wernecke. "Only a little from each man! My God—and I believed you! I even felt sorry for you!"

Wernecke shrugged. "Most of it was true. Usually I only take a little from each man, softly and carefully, so that they never know, so that in the morning they are only a little weaker than they would have been anyway. . . ."

"Like Josef?" Bruckman said angrily. "Like the poor devil you killed tonight?"

Wernecke shrugged again. "I have been careless the last few nights, I admit. But I need to build up my strength again." His eyes gleamed in the darkness. "Events are coming to a head here. Can't you feel it, Isadore, can't you sense it? Soon the war will be over, everyone knows that. Before then, this camp will be shut down, and the Nazis will move us back into the interior—either that, or kill us. I have grown weak here, and I will soon need all my strength to survive, to take whatever opportunity presents itself to escape. I *must* be ready. And so I have let myself drink deeply again, drink my fill for the first time in months. . . ." Wernecke licked his lips again, perhaps unconsciously, then smiled bleakly at Bruckman. "You don't appreciate my restraint, Isadore. You don't understand how hard it has been for me to hold back, to take only a little each night. You don't understand how much that restraint has cost me. . . ."

"You are gracious," Bruckman sneered.

Wernecke laughed. "No, but I am a rational man; I pride myself on that. You other prisoners were my only source of food, and I have had to be very careful to make sure that you would last. I have no access to the Nazis, after all. I am trapped here, a prisoner just like you, whatever else you may believe—and I have not only had to find ways to survive here in the camp,

I have had to procure my own food as well! No shepherd has ever watched over his flock more tenderly than I."

"Is that all we are to you—sheep? Animals to be slaughtered?"

Wernecke smiled. "Precisely."

When he could control his voice enough to speak, Bruckman said, "You're worse than the Nazis."

"I hardly think so," Wernecke said quietly, and for a moment he looked tired, as though something unimaginably old and unutterably weary had looked out through his eyes. "This camp was built by the Nazis—it wasn't my doing. The Nazis sent you here—not I. The Nazis have tried to kill you every day since, in one way or another—and I have tried to keep you alive, even at some risk to myself. No one has more of a vested interest in the survival of his livestock than the farmer, after all, even if he does occasionally slaughter an inferior animal. I have given you food—"

"Food you had no use for yourself. You sacrificed nothing!"

"That's true, of course. But *you* needed it, remember that. Whatever my motives, I have helped you to survive here—you and many others. By doing so I also acted in my own self-interest, of course, but can you have experienced this camp and still believe in things like altruism? What difference does it make what my reason for helping was—I still helped you, didn't I?"

"Sophistries!" Bruckman said. "Rationalizations! You twist words to justify yourself, but you can't disguise what you really are—a monster!"

Wernecke smiled gently, as though Bruckman's words amused him, and made as if to pass by, but Bruckman raised an arm to bar his way. They did not touch each other, but Wernecke stopped short, and a new quivering kind of tension sprung into existence in the air between them.

"I'll stop you," Bruckman said. "Somehow I'll stop you, I'll keep you from doing this terrible thing—"

"You'll do nothing," Wernecke said. His voice was hard and cold and flat, like a rock speaking. "What can you do? Tell the other prisoners? Who would believe you? They'd think you'd gone insane. Tell the *Nazis*, then?" Wernecke laughed harshly. "They'd think you'd gone crazy, too, and they'd take you to the hospital—and I don't have to tell you what your chances of getting out of there alive are, do I? No, you'll do *nothing*."

Wernecke took a step forward; his eyes were shiny and black and hard, like ice, like the pitiless eyes of a predatory bird, and Bruckman felt a sick rush of fear cut through his anger. Bruckman gave way, stepping backward involuntarily, and Wernecke pushed past him, seeming to brush him aside without touching him.

Once past, Wernecke turned to stare at Bruckman, and Bruckman had to summon up all the defiance that remained in him not to look uneasily away from Wernecke's agate-hard eyes. "You are the strongest and cleverest of all the other animals, Isadore," Wernecke said in a calm, conversational voice. "You have been useful to me. Every shepherd needs a good sheepdog. I still need you, to help me manage the others, and to help me keep them going long enough to serve my needs. This is the reason why I have taken so much time with you, instead of just killing you outright." He shrugged. "So let us both be rational about this—you leave me alone, Isadore, and I will leave you alone also. We will stay away from each other and look after our own affairs. Yes?"

"The others. . . ." Bruckman said weakly.

"They must look after themselves," Wernecke said. He smiled, a thin and almost invisible motion of his lips. "What did I teach you, Isadore? Here everyone must look after themselves. What difference does it make what happens to the others? In a few weeks almost all of them will be dead anyway."

"You *are* a monster," Bruckman said.

"I'm not much different from you, Isadore. The strong survive, whatever the cost."

"I am *nothing* like you," Bruckman said, with loathing.

"No?" Wernecke asked, ironically, and moved away; within a few paces he was hobbling and stooping, vanishing into the shadows, once more the harmless old Jew.

Bruckman stood motionless for a moment, and then, moving slowly and reluctantly, he steppped across to where Wernecke's victim lay.

It was one of new men Wernecke had been talking to earlier in the evening, and, of course, he was quite dead.

Shame and guilt took Bruckman then, emotions he thought he had forgotten—black and strong and bitter, they shook him by the throat the way Wernecke had shaken the new man.

Bruckman couldn't remember returning across the room to his sleeping platform, but suddenly he was there, lying on his back and staring into the stifling darkness, surrounded by the moaning, thrashing, stinking mass of sleepers. His hands were clasped protectively over his throat, although he couldn't remember putting them there, and he was shivering convulsively. How many mornings had he awoken with a dull ache in his neck, thinking it was no more than the habitual bodyaches and strained muscles they had all learned to take for granted? How many nights had Wernecke fed on *him?*

Every time Bruckman closed his eyes he would see Wernecke's face floating there in the luminous darkness behind his eyelids . . . Wernecke with his eyes half-closed, his face vulpine and cruel and satiated . . . Wernecke's face moving closer and closer to him, his eyes opening like black pits, his lips smiling back from his teeth . . . Wernecke's lips, sticky and red with blood . . . and then Bruckman would seem to feel the wet touch of Wernecke's lips on *his* throat, feel Wernecke's teeth biting into *his* flesh, and Bruckman's eyes would fly open again. Staring into the darkness. Nothing there. Nothing there *yet.* . . .

Dawn was a dirty gray imminence against the cabin window before Bruckman could force himself to lower his shielding arms from his throat, and once again he had not slept at all.

That day's work was a nightmare of pain and exhaustion for Bruckman, harder than anything he had known since his first few days at the camp. Somehow he forced himself to get up, somehow he stumbled outside and up the path to the quarry, seeming to float along high off the ground, his head a bloated balloon, his feet a thousand miles away at the end of boneless beanstalk legs he could barely control at all. Twice he fell, and was kicked several times before he could drag himself back to his feet and lurch forward again. The sun was coming up in front of them, a hard red disk in a sickly yellow sky, and to Bruckman it seemed to be a glazed and lidless eye staring dispassionately into the world to watch them flail and struggle and die, like the eye of a scientist peering into a laboratory maze.

He watched the disk of the sun as he stumbled towards it; it seemed to bob and shimmer with every painful step, expanding, swelling, and bloating until it swallowed the sky. . . .

Then he was picking up a rock, moaning with the effort, feeling the rough stone tear his hands. . . .

Reality began to slide away from Bruckman. There were long periods when the world was blank, and he would come slowly back to himself as if from a great distance, and hear his own voice speaking words that he could not understand, or keening mindlessly, or grunting in a hoarse, animalistic way, and he would find that his body was working mechanically, stooping and lifting and carrying, all without volition. . . .

A Musselmänn, Bruckman thought, I'm becoming a Musselmänn . . . and felt a chill of fear sweep through him. He fought to hold onto the world, afraid that the next time he slipped away from himself he would not come back, deliberately banging his hands into the rocks, cutting himself, clearing his head with pain.

The world steadied around him. A guard shouted a hoarse admonishment at him and slapped his rifle butt, and Bruckman forced himself to work faster, although he could not keep himself from weeping silently with the pain his movements cost him.

He discovered that Wernecke was watching him, and stared back defiantly, the bitter tears still runneling his dirty cheeks, thinking, *I won't become a Musselmänn for you, I won't make it easy for you, I won't provide another helpless victim for you* . . . Wernecke met Bruckman's gaze for a moment, and then shrugged and turned away.

Bruckman bent for another stone, feeling the muscles in his back crack and the pain drive in like knives. What had Wernecke been thinking behind the blankness of his expressionless face? Had Wernecke, sensing weakness, marked Bruckman for his next victim? Had Wernecke been disappointed or dismayed by the strength of Bruckman's will to survive? Would Wernecke now settle upon someone else?

The morning passed, and Bruckman grew feverish again. He could feel the fever in his face, making his eyes feel sandy and hot, pulling the skin taut over his cheekbones, and he wondered how long he could manage to stay on his feet. To falter, to grow weak and insensible, was certain death; if the Nazis didn't kill him, Wernecke would. . . . Wernecke was out of sight now, on the other side of the quarry, but it seemed to Bruckman that Wernecke's hard and flinty eyes were everywhere, floating in the air around him, looking out momentarily from the back of a Nazi soldier's head, watching him from the dulled iron side of a quarry cart, peering at him from a dozen different angles. He bent ponderously for another rock, and when he had pried it up from the earth he found Wernecke's eyes beneath it, staring unblinkingly up at him from the damp and pallid soil. . . .

That afternoon there were great flashes of light on the eastern horizon, out across the endless flat expanse of the steppe, flares in rapid sequence that lit up the sullen gray sky, all without sound. The Nazi guards had gathered in a group, looking to the east and talking in subdued voices, ignoring the prisoners for the moment. For the first time Bruckman noticed how disheveled and unshaven the guards had become in the last few days, as though they had given up, as though they no longer cared. Their faces were strained and tight, and more than one of them seemed to be fascinated by the leaping fires on the distant edge of the world.

Melnick said that it was only a thunderstorm, but old Bohme said that it was an artillery battle being fought, and that that meant that the Russians were coming, that soon they would all be liberated.

Bohme grew so excited at the thought that he began shouting, "The Russians! It's the Russians! The Russians are coming to free us!" Dichstein, another one of the new prisoners, and Melnick tried to hush him, but Bohme continued to caper and shout—doing a grotesque kind of jig while he yelled and flapped his arms—until he had attracted the attention of the guards. Infuriated, two of the guards fell upon Bohme and beat him severely, striking him with their rifle butts with more than usual force, knocking him to the ground, continuing to flail at him and kick him while he was down, Bohme writhing like an injured worm under their stamping boots. They probably would have beaten Bohme to death on the spot, but Wernecke organized a distraction among some of the other prisoners, and when the guards moved away to deal with it, Wernecke helped Bohme to stand up and hobble away to the other side of the quarry, where the rest of the prisoners shielded him from sight with their bodies as best they could for the rest of the afternoon.

Something about the way Wernecke urged Bohme to his feet and helped him to limp and lurch away, something about the protective, possessive curve of Wernecke's arm around Bohme's shoulders, told Bruckman that Wernecke had selected his next victim.

That night Bruckman vomited up the meager and rancid meal that they were allowed, his stomach convulsing uncontrollably after the first few bites. Trembling with hunger and exhaustion and fever, he leaned against the wall and watched as Wernecke fussed over Bohme, nursing him as a man might nurse a sick child, talking gently to him, wiping away some of the blood that still oozed from the corner of Bohme's mouth, coaxing Bohme to drink a few sips of soup, finally arranging that Bohme should stretch out on the floor away from the sleeping platforms, where he would not be jostled by the others. . . .

As soon as the interior lights went out that night, Bruckman got up, crossed the floor quickly and unhesitantly, and lay down in the shadows near the spot where Bohme muttered and twitched and groaned.

Shivering, Bruckman lay in the darkness, the strong smell of the earth in his nostrils, waiting for Wernecke to come. . . .

In Bruckman's hand, held close to his chest, was a spoon that had been sharpened to a jagged needle point, a spoon he had stolen and begun to sharpen while he was still in a civilian prison in Cologne, so long ago that he almost couldn't remember, scraping it back and forth against the stone wall of his cell every night for hours, managing to keep it hidden on his person during the nightmarish ride in the sweltering boxcar, the first few terrible days at the camp, telling no one about it, not even Wernecke during the months when he'd thought of Wernecke as a kind of saint, keeping it hidden long after the possibility of escape had become too remote even to fantasize about, retaining it then more as a tangible link with the daydream country of his past than as a tool he ever actually hoped to employ, cherishing it almost as a holy relic, as a remnant of a vanished world that he otherwise might almost believe had never existed at all. . . .

And now that it was time to use it at last, he was almost reluctant to do so, to soil it with another man's blood. . . .

He fingered the spoon compulsively, turning it over and over; it was hard and smooth and cold, and he clenched it as tightly as he could, trying to ignore the fine tremoring of his hands.

He had to kill Wernecke. . . .

Nausea and an odd feeling of panic flashed through Bruckman at the thought, but there was no other choice, there was no other way. . . . He couldn't go on like this, his strength was failing; Wernecke was killing him, as surely as he had killed the others, just by keeping him from sleeping. . . . And as long as Wernecke lived, he would never be safe: always there would be the chance that Wernecke would come for him, that Wernecke would strike as soon as his guard was down. . . . Would Wernecke scruple for a second to kill *him,* after all, if he thought that he could do it safely? . . . No, of course not. . . . Given the chance, Wernecke would kill him without a moment's further thought. . . . No, he must strike *first.* . . .

Bruckman licked his lips uneasily. Tonight. He had to kill Wernecke *tonight.* . . .

There was a stirring, a rustling: Someone was getting up, working his way free from the mass of sleepers on one of the platforms. A shadowy figure crossed the room toward Bruckman, and Bruckman tensed, reflexively running his thumb along the jagged end of the spoon, readying himself to rise, to strike—but at the last second, the figure veered aside and stumbled toward another corner. There was a sound like rain drumming on cloth; the man swayed there for a moment, mumbling, and then slowly returned to his pallet, dragging his feet, as if he had pissed his very life away against the wall. It was not Wernecke.

Bruckman eased himself back down to the floor, his heart seeming to shake his wasted body back and forth with the force of its beating. His hand was damp with sweat. He wiped it against his tattered pants, and then clutched the spoon again. . . .

Time seemed to stop. Bruckman waited, stretched out along the hard floorboards, the raw wood rasping his skin, dust clogging his mouth and nose, feeling as though he were already dead, a corpse laid out in the rough pine coffin, feeling eternity pile up on his chest like heavy clots of wet black earth. . . . Outside the hut, the kliegs blazed, banishing night, abolishing it, but here inside the hut it was night, here night survived, perhaps the only pocket of night remaining on a klieg-lit planet, the shafts of light that came in through the slatted windows only serving to accentuate the surrounding darkness, to make it greater and more puissant by comparison. . . . Here in the darkness, nothing ever changed . . . there was only the smothering heat, and the weight of eternal darkness, and the changeless moments that could not pass because there was nothing to differentiate them one from the other. . . .

Many times as he waited Bruckman's eyes would grow heavy and slowly close, but each time his eyes would spring open again at once, and he would find himself staring into the shadows for Wernecke. Sleep would no longer have him, it was a kingdom closed to him now; it spat him out each time he tried to enter it, just as his stomach now spat out the food he placed in it. . . .

The thought of food brought Bruckman to a sharper awareness, and there in the darkness he huddled around his hunger, momentarily forgetting everything else. Never had he been so hungry. . . . He thought of the food he had wasted earlier in the evening, and only the last few shreds of his self-control kept him from moaning aloud.

Bohme did moan aloud then, as though unease were contagious. As Bruckman glanced at him, Bohme said, "Anya," in a clear calm voice; he mumbled a little, and then, a bit more loudly, said, "Tseitel, have you set the table yet?" and Bruckman realized that Bohme was no longer in the camp, that Bohme was back in Dusseldorf in the tiny apartment with his fat wife and his four healthy children, and Bruckman felt a pang of envy go through him, for Bohme, who had escaped.

It was at that moment that Bruckman realized that Wernecke was standing there, just beyond Bohme.

There had been no movement that Bruckman had seen. Wernecke had seemed to slowly materialize from the darkness, atom by atom, bit by incremental bit, until at some point he had been solid enough for his presence to register on Bruckman's consciousness, so that what had been only a shadow a moment before was now unmistakably Wernecke as well, however much a shadow it remained.

Bruckman's mouth went dry with terror, and it almost seemed that he could hear the voice of his dead grandmother whispering in his ears. Boogey tales . . . Wernecke had said *I'm no night spirit.* Remember that he had said that. . . .

Wernecke was almost close enough to touch. He was staring down at Bohme; his face, lit by a dusty shaft of light from the window, was cold and remote, only the total lack of expression hinting at the passion that strained and quivered behind the mask. Slowly, lingeringly, Wernecke stooped over Bohme. "Anya," Bohme said again, caressingly, and then Wernecke's mouth was on his throat.

Let him feed, said a cold remorseless voice in Bruckman's mind. It will be easier to take him when he's nearly sated, when he's fully preoccupied and growing lethargic and logy . . . growing *full.* . . .

Slowly, with infinite caution, Bruckman gathered himself to spring, watching in horror and fascination as Wernecke fed. He could hear Wernecke sucking the juice out of Bohme, as if there were not enough blood in the foolish old man to satiate him, as if there were not enough blood in the whole camp . . . or perhaps, the whole world. . . . And now Bohme was ceasing his feeble struggling, was becoming still. . . .

Bruckman flung himself upon Wernecke, stabbing him twice in the back before his weight bowled them both over. There was a moment of confusion as they rolled and struggled together, all without sound, and then Bruckman found himself sitting atop Wernecke, Wernecke's white face turned up to him. Bruckman drove his weapon into Wernecke again, the shock of the blow jarring Bruckman's arm to the shoulder. Wernecke made no outcry; his eyes were already glazing, but they looked at Bruckman with recognition, with cold anger, with bitter irony and, oddly, with what might have been resignation or relief, with what might almost have been pity. . . .

Bruckman stabbed again and again, driving the blows home with hysterical strength, panting, rocking atop his victim, feeling Wernecke's blood spatter against his face, wrapped in the heat and steam that rose from Wernecke's torn-open body like a smothering black cloud, coughing and choking on it for a moment, feeling the steam seep in through his pores and sink deep into the marrow of his bones, feeling the world seem to pulse and shimmer and change around him, as though he were suddenly seeing through new eyes, as though something had been born anew inside him, and then abruptly he was *smelling* Wernecke's blood, the hot organic reek of it, leaning closer to drink in that sudden overpowering smell, better than the smell of freshly baked bread, better than anything he could remember, rich and heady and strong beyond imagining.

There was a moment of revulsion and horror, and he tried to wonder how long the ancient contamination had been passing from man to man to man, how far into the past the chain of lives stretched, how Wernecke himself had been trapped, and then his parched lips touched wetness, and he was drinking, drinking deeply and greedily, and his mouth was filled with the strong clean taste of copper.

The following night, after Bruckman led the memorial prayers for Wernecke and Bohme, Melnick came to him. Melnick's eyes were bright with tears. "How can we go on without Eduard? He was everything to us. What will we do now? . . ."

"It will be all right, Moishe," Bruckman said. "I promise you, everything will be all right." He put his arm around Melnick for a moment to comfort him, and at the touch sensed the hot blood that pumped through the intricate network of the boy's veins, just under the skin, rich and warm and nourishing, waiting there inviolate for him to set it free.

This story started out as a sentence I jotted down in my story-idea notebook: "vampire in death camp, during Second World War."

It stayed in that form for a couple of years, until one night when Jack Dann was down in Philadelphia for a visit—my calendar shows that it was March 6, 1981—and we were sitting in my living room in my rundown old apartment on Quince Street, kicking around potential ideas for collaborative stories. I got my notebook out and started throwing ideas from it out at Jack; one of them was the vampire sentence. Jack took fire with that idea at once. We talked about the overall plot for a half hour or so, brainstorming, kicking it back and forth, and then Jack got up, sat down behind my ancient, massive Remington office-model standup standard typewriter, which lived on one side of my somewhat-unsteady kitchen table, and started writing the story. He wrote like a madman for a few hours, and by the time he stood up again, he had finished a rough draft of about the first nine manuscript pages, carrying the story through the brilliant Passover scene, which was entirely of his own devising. Then he left, headed back to Binghamton, and the ball was in my court. I worked pretty extensively on the story for a solid week (obviously, I work much more slowly than Jack!), and then worked on it off and on for the next couple of months, with one hurried story conference with Jack at that year's Nebula Banquet to hammer out a plot problem, and the passing back and forth by mail of several different drafts of one particularly difficult scene toward the story's end. The story was finished on May 9, 1981. It bounced around for a while, and finally sold to *Oui*. It was reprinted in *The Magazine of Fantasy and Science Fiction*, where its appearance prompted a major horror writer to remark that it was the most morally offensive story he'd ever read. We were quietly proud.

At the core of the story, it seems to me, is the question of identity. In spite of being a supernatural monster, Wernecke is *perceived* by the Nazis as a Jew, and so that's the way they treat him, no better or worse than the other prisoners. To some extent, we are what other people think we are, whether we want to be or not. For me, the real meat of the story is in the two conversations between Wernecke and Bruckman, and in some ways those were the most difficult scenes to write.

I'd always wanted to call a story "Down Among the Dead Men," a line from an old English folksong, and the title certainly seemed to fit the story well enough, so that's what we called it.

Gardner Dozois

A noted writer of genre horror once complained that this story was in bad taste, as it depicted a concentration camp internee as a vampire. It is our opinion, however, that in order to rise above genre cookie patterns, fiction must take chances and try to reflect that which really *is* the dark side of human nature.

It has been said that the events of the holocaust were so terrible in themselves that they are beyond any kind of fictive telling. Note some of the statistics: In five years the Nazis exterminated nine million people. Six million were Jews. The efficiency of the concentration camps was such that twenty thousand people could be gassed in a day. The Nazis at Treblinka boasted that they could "process" the Jews who arrived in the cattle cars in forty-five minutes.

In 1943 six hundred desperate Jews revolted and burned Treblinka to the ground. These men were willing to martyr themselves so that a few might live to "testify" and tell a disbelieving world of the atrocities committed in the camps, lest those who had died be forgotten . . . lest *we* forget those events which are too terrible to contemplate.

Out of the six hundred, forty survived to tell their story.

"Down Among the Dead Men," like the companion story "Camps," is our attempt to testify, to bring the terror and horror and discomfort to another generation of readers in the only way we know how. Perhaps through the metaphoric and symbolic medium of horror—of the fantastic—we might catch a dark reflection of that terrible event. Even if it is impossible to grasp the terrible reality of what happened in the camps, still, we must try.

In order to survive, the prisoners had to take part in the "process" of killing other prisoners; that was one of the greatest attrocities of the concentration camps. It became a maxim of the survivors—those who did not let themselves be reduced to *Musselmänner,* the walking, living dead—that "first you save yourself, then you save yourself, and then, and only then, can you try to save others." Prisoners could survive only against almost impossible odds, and the guilt was impossible to escape. It was built into the Nazi extermination system . . . into the new technology of genocide.

To live, you had to help kill.

The vampire is . . . *us!*

Indeed, the vampire is a horrifying metaphor. It would have been much more palatable if we had made him one of the Nazis. But perhaps by testifying, by taking chances, by leaning over the edge of what might be construed as "bad taste," we can keep the memory of what happened alive.

It is too easy to forget our history.

But as the philosopher George Santayana said, "Those who cannot remember the past are condemned to repeat it."

God forbid. . . .

Jack Dann

...To Feel
Another's Woe

Chet Williamson

The sharklike intensity necessary to succeed in the highly competitive New York theater scene is a given. Williamson has obviously brushed against the life or he wouldn't have written the following piece about those who will do anything to make it.

I had to admit she looked like a vampire when Kevin described her as such. Her face, at least, with those high model's cheekbones and absolutely huge, wet-looking eyes. The jet of her hair set off her pale skin strikingly, and that skin was perfect, nearly luminous. To the best of my knowledge, however, vampires didn't wear Danskin tops and Annie Hall flop-slacks, nor did they audition for Broadway shows.

There must have been two hundred of us jammed into the less than immaculate halls of the Ansonia Hotel that morning, with photo/résumés clutched in one hand, scripts of *A Streetcar Named Desire* in the other. John Weidner was directing a revival at Circle in the Square, and every New York actor with an Equity card and a halfway intelligible Brooklyn dialect under his collar was there to try out. Stanley Kowalski had already been spoken for by a new Italian-American film star with more *chutzpah* than talent, but the rest of the roles were open. I was hoping for Steve or Mitch, or maybe even a standby, just something to pay the rent.

I found myself in line next to Kevin McQuinn, a gay song-and-dance man I'd done Jones Beach with two years before. A nice guy, not at all flouncy. "Didn't know this was a musical," I smiled at him.

"Sure. You never heard of the Stella aria? And he sang softly, "I'll never stop saying Steh-el-*la* . . ."

"Seriously. You going dramatic?"

He shrugged. "No choice. Musicals these days are all rock or opera or rock opera. No soft shoes in *Sweeney Todd.*"

"*Sweeney Todd* closed ages ago."

"That's 'cause they didn't have no soft shoes."

Then she walked in holding her P/R and script, and sat on the floor with her back to the wall as gracefully as if she owned the place. I was, to Kevin's amusement, instantly smitten.

"Forget it," he said. "She'd eat you alive."

"I wish. Who is she?"

"Name's Sheila Remarque."

"Shitty stage name."

"She was born with it, so she says. Me, I believe her. Nobody'd *pick* that."

"She any good?"

Kevin smiled, a bit less broadly than his usually mobile face allowed. "Let's just say that I've got twenty bucks that says she'll get whatever part she's after."

"Serious?"

"The girl's phenomenal. You catch *Lear* in the park last summer?" I nodded. "She played Goneril."

"Oh *yeah.*" I was amazed that I hadn't recalled the name. "She *was* good."

"You said good, I said phenomenal. Along with the critics."

As I thought back, I remembered the performance vividly. Generally Cordelia stole the show from Lear's two nasty daughters, but all eyes had been on Goneril at the matinee I'd seen. It wasn't that the actress had been upstaging, or doing anything to excess. It was simply (or complexly, if you're an actor) that she was so damned *believable.* There'd been no trace of *acting,* no indication shared between actress and audience, as even the finest performers will do, no self-consciousness whatsoever, only utterly true emotion. As I remembered, the one word I had associated with it was *awesome.* How stupid, I thought, to have forgotten her name. "What else do you know about her?" I asked Kevin.

"Not much. A mild reputation with the boys. Love 'em and leave 'em. A Theda Bara vampire type."

"Ever work with her?"

"Three years ago. *Oklahoma* at Allenberry. I did Will Parker, and she was in the chorus. Fair voice, danced a little, but lousy presence. A real poser, you know? I don't know what the hell happened."

I started to ask Kevin if he knew where she studied, when he suddenly tensed. I followed his gaze, and saw a man coming down the hall carrying a dance bag. He was tall and thin, with light-brown hair and a nondescript face. It's hard to describe features on which not the slightest bit of emotion is displayed. Instead of sitting on the floor like the rest of us, he remained standing, a few yards away from Sheila Remarque, whom he looked at steadily, yet apparently without interest. She looked up, saw him, gave a brief smile, and returned to her script.

Kevin leaned closer and whispered. "You want to know about *Ms.* Remarque, *there's* the man you should ask, not me."

"Why? Who is he?" The man hadn't taken his eyes from the girl, but I couldn't tell whether he watched her in lust or anger. At any rate, I admired her self-control. Save for that first glance, she didn't acknowledge him at all.

"Name's Guy Taylor."

"The one who was in *Annie?*"

Kevin nodded. "Three years here. One on the road. Same company I went out with. Used to drink together. He was hilarious, even when he was sober. But put the drinks in him and he'd make Eddie Murphy look like David Merrick. Bars would fall apart laughing."

"He went with this girl?"

"Lived with her for three, maybe four months, just this past year."

"They split up, I take it."

"Mmm-hmm. Don't know much about it, though." He shook his head. "I ran into Guy a week or so ago at the *Circle of Three* auditions. I was really happy to see him, but he acted like he barely knew me. Asked him how his lady was—I'd never met her, but the word had spread—and he told me he was living alone now, so I didn't press it. Asked a couple people and found out she'd walked out on him. Damn near crushed him. He must've had it hard."

"That's love for you."

"Yeah. Ain't I glad I don't mess with women."

Kevin and I started talking about other things then, but I couldn't keep my eyes off Sheila Remarque's haunting face, nor off the vacuous features of

Guy Taylor, who watched the girl with the look of a stolid, stupid guard dog. I wondered if he'd bite anybody who dared to talk to her.

At ten o'clock, as scheduled, the line started to move. When I got to the table, the assistant casting director, or whatever flunky was using that name, looked at my P/R and at me, evidently approved of what he saw, and told me to come back at two o'clock for a reading. Kevin, right beside me, received only a shake of the head and a "thank you for coming."

"Dammit," Kevin said as we walked out. "I shouldn't have stood behind you in line, then I wouldn't've looked so un-macho. I mean, didn't they *know* about Tennessee Williams, for crissake?"

When I went back to the Ansonia at two, there were over thirty people already waiting, twice as many men as women. Among the dozen or so femmes was Sheila Remarque, her nose still stuck in her script, oblivious to those around her. Guy Taylor was also there, standing against a wall as before. He had a script open in front of him, and from time to time would look down at it, but most of the time he stared at Sheila Remarque, who, I honestly believe, was totally indifferent to, and perhaps even ignorant of, his perusal.

As I sat watching the two of them, I thought that the girl would make a stunning Blanche, visually at least. She seemed to have that elusive, fragile quality that Vivien Leigh exemplified so well in the film. I'd only seen Jessica Tandy, who'd originated the role, in still photos, but she always seemed too horsey-looking for my tastes. By no stretch of the imagination could Sheila Remarque be called horsey. She was exquisite porcelain, and I guess I must have become transfixed by her for a moment, for the next time I looked away from her toward Guy Taylor, he was staring at me with that same damned expressionless stare. I was irritated by the proprietary emotion I placed on his face, but found it so disquieting that I couldn't glare back. So I looked at my script again.

After a few minutes, a fiftyish man I didn't recognize came out and spoke to us. "Okay, Mr. Weidner will eliminate some of you without hearing you read. Those of you who make the final cut, be prepared to do one of two scenes. We'll have the ladies who are reading for Blanche and you men reading for Mitch first. As you were told this morning, ladies, scene ten, guys six. Use your scripts if you want to. Not's okay too. Let's go—"

Seven women and fifteen men, me and Guy Taylor among them, followed the man into what used to be a ballroom. At one end of the high-ceilinged room was a series of raised platforms with a few wooden chairs on them. Ten yards back from this makeshift stage were four folding director's chairs. Another five yards in back of these were four rows of ten each of the same rickety wooden chairs there were on the stage. We sat on these while Weidner, the director, watched us file in. "I'm sorry we can't be in the theater," he said, "but the set there now can't be struck for auditions. We'll have to make do here. Let's start with the gentlemen for a change."

He looked at the stage manager, who read from his clipboard, "Adams."

That was me. I stood up, script in hand. Given a choice, I always held book in auditions. It gives you self-confidence, and if you try to go without and go up on the lines, you look like summer stock. Besides, that's why they call them readings.

"Would someone be kind enough to read Blanche in scene six with Mr. Adams?" Weidner asked. A few girls were rash enough to raise their hands and volunteer for a scene they hadn't prepared, but Weidner's eyes fell instantly on Sheila Remarque. "Miss Remarque, isn't it?" She nodded. "My congratulations on your Goneril. Would you be kind enough to read six? I promise I won't let it color my impressions of your scene ten."

Bullshit, I thought, but she nodded graciously, and together we ascended the squeaking platform.

Have you ever played a scene opposite an animal or a really cute little kid? If you have, you know how utterly impossible it is to get the audience to pay any attention to you whatsoever. That was exactly how I felt doing a scene with Sheila Remarque. Not that my reading wasn't good, because it was, better by far than I would have done reading with a prompter or an ASM, because she gave me something I could react to. She made Blanche so real that I had to be real too, and I was good.

But not as good as her. No way.

She used no book, had all the moves and lines down pat. But like I said of her Goneril, there was no *indication* of acting at all. She spoke and moved on that cheapjack stage as if she were and had always been Blanche DuBois, formerly of Belle Rêve, presently of Elysian Fields, New Orleans in the year 1947. Weidner didn't interrupt after a few lines, a few pages, the way directors usually do, but let the scene glide on effortlessly to its end, when, still holding my script, I kissed Blanche DuBois on "her forehead and her eyes and finally her lips," and she sobbed out her line, " 'Sometimes—there's God—so quickly!' " and it was over and Blanche DuBois vanished, leaving Sheila Remarque and me on that platform with them all looking up at us soundlessly. Weidner's smile was suffused with wonder. But not for me. I'd been good, but she'd been great.

"Thank you, Mr. Adams. Thank you very much. Nice reading. We have your résumé, yes. Thank you," and he nodded in a gesture of dismissal that took me off the platform. "Thank you too, Miss Remarque. Well done. While you're already up there, would you care to do scene ten for us?"

She nodded, and I stopped at the exit. Ten was a hell of a scene, the one where Stanley and the drunken Blanche are alone in the flat, and I had to see her do it. I whispered a request to stay to the fiftyish man who'd brought us in, and he nodded an okay, as if speaking would break whatever spell was on the room. I remained there beside him.

"Our Stanley Kowalski was to be here today to read with the Blanches and Stellas, but a TV commitment prevented him," Weidner said somewhat bitchily. "So if one of you gentlemen would be willing to read with Miss Remarque . . ."

There were no idiots among the men. Not one volunteered. "Ah, Mr. Taylor," I heard Weidner say. My stomach tightened. I didn't know whether he'd chosen Taylor to read with her out of sheer malevolence, or whether he was ignorant of their relationship, and it was coincidence—merely his spotting Taylor's familiar face. Either way, I thought, the results could be unpleasant. And from the way several of the gypsies' shoulders stiffened, I could tell they were thinking the same thing. "Would you please?"

Taylor got up slowly, and joined the girl on the platform. As far as I could see, there was no irritation in his face, nor was there any sign of dismay in Sheila Remarque's deep, wet eyes. She smiled at him as though he were a stranger, and took a seat facing the "audience."

"Anytime," said Weidner. He sounded anxious. Not impatient, just anxious.

Sheila Remarque became drunk. Just like that, in the space of a heartbeat. Her whole body fell into the posture of a long-developed alcoholism. Her eyes blurred, her mouth opened, a careless slash across the ruin of her face, lined and bagged with booze. She spoke the lines as if no one had ever said them before, so any onlooker would swear that it was Blanche DuBois's liquor-dulled brain that was creating them, and in no way were they merely words that had existed on a printed page for forty years, words filtered through the voice of a performer.

She finished speaking into the unseen mirror, and Guy Taylor walked toward her as Stanley Kowalski. Blanche saw him, spoke to him. But though she spoke to Stanley Kowalski, it was Guy Taylor who answered, only Guy Taylor reading lines, without a trace of emotion. Oh, the *expression* was there, the nuances, the rhythm of the lines and their meaning was clear. But it was like watching La Duse play a scene with an electronic synthesizer. She destroyed him, and I thought back, hoping she hadn't done the same to me.

This time Weidner didn't let the scene play out to the end. I had to give him credit. As awful as Taylor was, *I* couldn't have brought myself to deny the reality of Sheila Remarque's performance by interrupting, but Weidner did, during one of Stanley's longer speeches about his cousin who opened beer bottles with his teeth. "Okay, fine," Weidner called out. "Good enough. Thank you, Mr. Taylor. I think that's all we need see of you today." Weidner looked away from him. "Miss Remarque, if you wouldn't mind, I'd like to hear that one more time. Let's see . . . Mr. Carver, would you read Stanley, please." Carver, a chorus gypsy who had no business doing heavy work, staggered to the platform, his face pale, but I didn't wait to see if he'd survive. I'd seen enough wings pulled off flies for one day, and was out the door, heading to the elevator even before Taylor had come off the platform.

I had just pushed the button when I saw Taylor, his dance bag over his shoulder, come out of the ballroom. He walked slowly down the hall toward me, and I prayed the car would arrive quickly enough that I wouldn't have to ride with him. But the Ansonia's lifts have seen better days, and by the time I stepped into the car he was a scant ten yards away. I held the door for him. He stepped in, the doors closed, and we were alone.

Taylor looked at me for a moment. "You'll get Mitch," he said flatly.

I shrugged self-consciously and smiled. "There's a lot of people to read."

"But they won't read Mitch with *her*. And your reading *was* good."

I nodded agreement. "She helped."

"May I," he said after a pause, "give you some advice?" I nodded. "If they give you Mitch," he said, "turn them down."

"Why?" I asked, laughing.

"She's sure to be Blanche. Don't you think?"

"So?"

"You heard me read today."

"So?"

"Have you seen me work?"

"I saw you in *Annie*. And in *Bus Stop* at ELT."

"And?"

"You were good. Real good."

"And what about today?"

I looked at the floor.

"Tell me." I looked at him, my lips pinched. "Shitty," he said. "Nothing there, right?"

"Not much," I said.

"She did that. Took it from me." He shook his head. "Stay away from her. She can do it to you too."

The first thing you learn in professional theater is that actors are children. I say that, knowing full well that I'm one myself. Our egos are huge, yet our feelings are as delicate as orchids. In a way, it stems from the fact that in other trades, rejections are impersonal. Writers aren't rejected—it's one particular story or novel that is. For factory workers, or white-collars, it's lack of knowledge or experience that loses jobs. But for an actor, it's the way he looks, the way he talks, the way he moves that make the heads nod yes or no, and that's rejection on the most deeply personal scale, like kids calling each other Nickel-nose or Fatso. And often that childish hurt extends to other relationships as well. Superstitious? Imaginative? Ballplayers have nothing on us. So when Taylor started blaming Sheila Remarque for his thespian rockslide, I knew it was only because he couldn't bear to admit that it was *he* who had let his craft slip away, not the girl who had taken it from him.

The elevator doors opened, and I stepped off. "Wait," he said, coming after me. "You don't believe me."

"Look, man," I said, turning in exasperation, "I don't know what went on between you and her and I don't care, okay? If she messed you over, I'm sorry, but I'm an actor and I need a job and if I get it I'll *take* it!"

His face remained placid. "Let me buy you a drink," he said.

"Oh Jesus . . ."

"You don't have to be afraid. I won't get violent." He forced a smile. "Do you think I've *been* violent? Have I even raised my voice?"

"No."

"Then please. I just want to talk to you."

I had to admit to myself that I *was* curious. Most actors would have shown more fire over things that meant so much to them, but Taylor was strangely zombielike, as if life were just a walk-through. "All right," I said, "all right."

We walked silently down Broadway. By the time we got to Charlie's it was three thirty, a slow time for the bar. I perched on a stool, but Taylor shook his head. "Table," he said, and we took one and ordered. It turned out we were both bourbon drinkers.

"Jesus," he said after a long sip. "It's cold."

It was. Manhattan winters are never balmy, and the winds that belly through the streets cut through anything short of steel.

"All right," I said. "We're here. You're buying me a drink. Now. You have a story for me?"

"I do. And after I tell it you can go out and do what you like."

"I intend to."

"I won't try to stop you," he went on, not hearing me. "I don't think I could even if I wanted to. It's your life, your career."

"Get to the point."

"I met her last summer. June. I know Joe Papp, and he invited me to the party after the Lear opening, so I went. Sheila was there with a guy, and I walked up and introduced myself to them, and told her how much I enjoyed her performance. She thanked me, very gracious, very friendly, and told me she'd seen me several times and liked my work as well. I thought it odd at the time, the way she came on to me. Very strong, with those big, wet, bedroom eyes of hers eating me up. But her date didn't seem to care. He didn't seem to care about much of anything. Just stood there and drank while she talked, then sat down and drank some more. She told me later, when we were together, that he was a poet. Unpublished, of course, she said. She told me that his work wasn't very good technically, but that it was very emotional. 'Rich with feeling,' were the words she used.

"I went to see her in Lear again, several times really, and was more impressed with each performance. The poet was waiting for her the second time I went, but the third, she left alone. I finessed her into a drink, we talked, got along beautifully. She told me it was all over between her and the poet, and that night she ended up in my bed. It was good, and she seemed friendly, passionate, yet undemanding. After a few more dates, a few more nights and mornings, I suggested living together, no commitments. She agreed, and the next weekend she moved in with me.

"I want you to understand one thing, though. I never loved her. I never told her I loved her or even suggested it. For me, it was companionship and sex, and that was all. Though she was good to be with, nice to kiss, to hold, to share things with, I never loved her. And I know she never loved me." He signaled the waiter and another drink came. Mine was still half full. "So I'm not a . . . a victim of unrequited love, all right? I just want you to be sure of that." I nodded and he went on.

"It started a few weeks after we were living together. She'd want to play games with me, she said. Theater games. You know, pretend she was doing something or say something to get a certain emotion out of me. Most of the time she didn't let me know right away what she was doing. She'd see if she could get me jealous, or mad, or sullen. Happy too. And then she'd laugh and say she was just kidding, that she'd just wanted to see my reactions. Well, I thought that was bullshit. I put it down as a technique exercise rather than any method crap, and in a way I could understand it—wanting to be face-to-face with emotions to examine them—but I still thought it was an imposition on me, an invasion of my privacy. She didn't do it often, maybe once or twice a week. I tried it on her occasionally, but she never bit, just looked at me as if I were a kid trying to play a man's game.

"Somewhere along the line it started getting kinky. While we were having sex, she'd call me by another name, or tell me about something sad she'd remembered, anything to get different reactions, different rises out of me. Sometimes . . ." He looked down, drained his drink. "Sometimes I'd . . . come and I'd cry at the same time."

The waiter was nearby, and I signaled for another round. "Why did you stay with her?"

"It wasn't . . . she didn't do this all the time, like I said. And I *liked* her. It got so I didn't even mind it when she'd pull this stuff on me, and she knew it. Once she even got me when I was stoned, and a couple of times after I'd had too much to drink. I didn't care. Until winter came.

"I hadn't been doing much after the summer. A few industrials here in town, some voice-over stuff. Good money, but just straight song and dance, flat narration, and no reviews. So the beginning of December Harv Piersall calls me to try out for *Ahab*. The musical that closed in previews? He wanted me to read for Starbuck, a scene where Starbuck is planning to shoot Ahab to save the Pequod. It was a good scene, a strong scene, and I got up there and I couldn't do a thing with it. Not a goddamned thing. I was utterly flat, just like in my narration and my singing around a Pontiac. But there it hadn't mattered—I hadn't had to put out any emotion—just sell the product, that was all. But *now*, when I had to feel something, had to express something, I couldn't. Harv asked me if anything was wrong, and I babbled some excuse about not feeling well, and when he invited me to come back and read again I did, a day later, and it was the same.

"That weekend I went down to St. Mark's to see Sheila in an OOB production—it was a new translation of *Medea* by some grad student at NYU—and she'd gotten the title role. They'd been rehearsing off and on for a month, no pay to speak of, but she was enthusiastic about it. It was the largest and most important part she'd done. Papp was there that night, someone got Prince to come too. The translation was garbage. No set, tunics for costumes, nothing lighting. But Sheila . . ."

He finished his latest drink, spat the ice back into the glass. "She was . . . superb. Every emotion was real. They should have been. She'd taken them from me.

"Don't look at me like that. I thought what you're thinking too, at first. That I was paranoid, jealous of her talents. But once I started to think things through, I knew it was the only answer.

"She was so loving to me afterward, smiled at me and held my arm and introduced me to her friends, and I felt as dull and lifeless as that poet I'd seen her with. Even then I suspected what she'd done, but I didn't say anything to her about it. That next week when I tried to get in touch with the poet, I found out he'd left the city, gone home to wherever it was he'd come from. I went over to Lincoln Center, to their videotape collection, and watched *King Lear*. I wanted to see if I could find anything that didn't jell, that wasn't quite *right*. Hell, I didn't know what I was looking for, just that I'd know it when I saw it."

He shook his head. "It was ... incredible. On the tape there was no sign of the performance I'd seen her give. Instead I saw a flat, lifeless, amateurish performance, dreadfully bad in contrast to the others. I couldn't believe it, watched it again. The same thing. Then I knew why she never auditioned for commercials, or for film. It didn't ... *show up* on camera. She could fool people, but not a camera.

"I went back to the apartment then, and told her what I'd found out. It wasn't guessing on my part, not a theory, because I *knew* by then. You see, I *knew.*"

Taylor stopped talking and looked down into his empty glass. I thought perhaps I'd made a huge mistake in going to the bar with him, for he was most certainly paranoid, and could conceivably become violent as well, in spite of his assurances to the contrary. "So what ..." My "so" came out too much like "sho," but I pushed on with my question while he flagged the waiter, who raised an eyebrow, but brought more drinks. "So what did she say? When you told her?"

"She ... verified it. Told me that I was right. 'In a way,' she said. In a way."

"Well ..." I shook my head to clear it. "... didn't she probably mean that she was just studying you? That's hardly, hardly *stealing* your emotions, is it?"

"No. She stole them."

"That's silly. That's still silly. You've still got them."

"No. I wanted ... when I knew for sure, I wanted to kill her. The way she smiled at me, as though I were powerless to take anything back, as though she had planned it all from the moment we met—that made me want to kill her." He turned his empty eyes on me. "But I didn't. Couldn't. I couldn't get angry enough."

He sighed. "She moved out. That didn't bother me. I was glad. As glad as I could feel after what she'd done. I don't know *how* she did it. I think it was something she learned, or learned she had. I don't know whether I'll ever get them back or not, either. Oh, not from *her.* Never from her. But on my own. Build them up inside me somehow. The emotions. The feelings. Maybe someday."

He reached across the table and touched my hand, his fingers surprisingly warm. "So much I don't know. But one thing I do. She'll do it again, find someone else, *you* if you let her. I saw how you were looking at her today." I pulled my hand away from his, bumping my drink. He grabbed it before it spilled, set it upright. "Don't," he cautioned. "Don't have anything to do with her."

"It's absurd," I said, half stuttering. "Ridiculous. You still . . . show emotions."

"Maybe. Maybe a few. But they're only outward signs. Inside it's hollow." His head went to one side. "You don't believe me."

"N—no . . ." And I didn't, not then.

"You should have known me before."

Suddenly I remembered Kevin at the audition, and his telling me how funny and wild Guy Taylor had gotten on a few drinks. My own churning stomach reminded me of how many we had had sitting here for less than an hour, and my churning mind showed me Sheila Remarque's drunk, drunk, perfectly drunk Blanche DuBois earlier that afternoon. "You've had . . ." I babbled, ". . . how many drinks have you had?"

He shrugged.

"But . . . you're not . . . showing any *signs* . . ."

"Yes. That's right," he said in a clear, steady, sober voice. "That's right."

He crossed his forearms on the table, lowered his head onto them, and wept. The sobs were loud, prolonged, shaking his whole body.

He wept.

"There!" I cried, staggering to my feet. "There, see? See? You're *crying,* you're *crying!* See?"

He raised his head and looked at me, still weeping, still weeping, with not one tear to be seen.

When the call came offering me Mitch, I took the part. I didn't even consider turning it down. Sheila Remarque had, as Kevin, Guy Taylor, and I had anticipated, been cast as Blanche DuBois, and she smiled warmly at me when I entered the studio for the first reading, as though she remembered our audition with fondness. I was pleasant, but somewhat aloof at first, not wanting the others to see, to suspect what I was going to do.

I thought it might be difficult to get her alone, but it wasn't. She had already chosen me, I could tell, watching me through the readings, coming up to me and chatting at the breaks. By the end of the day she'd learned where I lived, that I was single, unattached, and straight, and that I'd been bucking for eight years to get a part this good. She told me that she lived only a block away from my building (a lie, I later found out), and, after the rehearsal, suggested we take a cab together and split the expense. I agreed, and the cab left us out on West 72nd next to the park.

It was dark and cold, and I saw her shiver under her down-filled jacket. I shivered too, for we were alone at last, somewhat hidden by the trees, and there were no passersby to be seen, only the taxis and buses and cars hurtling past.

I turned to her, the smile gone from my face. "I know what you've done," I said. "I talked to Guy Taylor. He told me all about it. And warned me."

Her face didn't change. She just hung on to that soft half smile of hers, and watched me with those liquid eyes.

"He said . . . you'd be after me. He told me not to take the part. But I had to. I had to know if it's true, all he said."

Her smile faded, she looked down at the dirty, ice-covered sidewalk, and nodded, creases of sadness at the corners of her eyes. I reached out and did what I had planned, said what I had wanted to say to her ever since leaving Guy Taylor crying without tears at the table in Charlie's.

"Teach me," I said, taking her hand as gently as I knew how. "I'd be no threat to you, no competition for roles. In fact, you may need me, need a man who can equal you on stage. Because there aren't any now. You can take what you want from me as long as you can teach me how to get it back again.

"Please. Teach me."

When she looked up at me, her face was wet with tears. I kissed them away, neither knowing nor caring whose they were.

A decade ago I was a member of Actors' Equity, active in stock and regional theater. But when I endured the audition process in New York for a few months, I decided that I preferred those individual writer's rejections that my character Adams speaks of to the blanket rejections that are the lot of actors. I have sat in the halls of the Ansonia, as well as on the other side of the audition table (as a writer and producer of industrial shows), and watched the people bare their souls while contradictorily sheltering their fragile egos. I've seen a few grow old, lose their talents, and eerily vanish from an occupation so unstable that, when people ask me why I became a freelance writer, I can honestly answer, "for the security."

The realities of the acting life can be a far more chilling horror story than the one that arises from Sheila Remarque's odd gift.

Chet Williamson

TIME LAPSE

Joe Haldeman

A father's loss triggers an obsession that ends up violating the trust needed within families. A powerful poem by Joe Haldeman, who is primarily a science fiction writer, "Time Lapse" perfectly captures the need that becomes vampirism in a tortured relationship.

At first a pink whirl
        there on the white square:
the girl too small to stay still.

        After a few years, though
        (less than a minute),
        her feet stay in the same place.

Her pink body vibrates with undiscipline;
her hair a blond fog. She grows now
perceptibly. Watch . . . she's seven,
eight, nine: one year each twelve seconds.

            Always, now, in the audience,
            a man clears his throat.
            Always, a man.

Almost every morning
for almost eighteen years,

she came to the small white room,
put her bare feet on the cold floor,
on the pencilled H's,
and stood with her hands palms out
while her father took four pictures:
both profiles, front, rear.

It was their secret. Something
they did for Mommy in heaven,
a record of the daughter
she never lived to see.

By the time she left (rage and something
else driving her to the arms of a woman)
he had over twenty thousand
eight-by-ten glossy prints of her
growing up, locked in white boxes.

He sought out a man with a laser
who some called an artist
(some called a poseur),
with a few quartets of pictures,
various ages: baby, child, woman.
He saw the possibilities.
He paid the price.

It took a dozen Kelly Girls
thirty working hours apiece
to turn those files of pretty pictures
into digits. The artist,
or showman,
fed the digits into his machines,
and out came a square
of white where
in more than three dimensions

a baby girl
grows into a woman
in less than four minutes.

Always a man clears his throat.
The small breasts bud
and swell in seconds. Secret
places grow blond stubble, silk;
each second a spot of blood.

Her stance changes
as hips push out
and suddenly
she puts her hands on her hips.
For the last four seconds,
four months;
a gesture of defiance.

The second time you see her
(no one watches only once),
concentrate on her expression.
The child's ambiguous flicker
becomes uneasy smile,
trembling thirty times a second.
The eyes, a blur at first,
stare fixedly
in obedience
and then
(as the smile hardens)
the last four seconds,
four months:

Time Lapse

a glare of rage

All unwilling,
she became the most famous
face and figure of her age.
Everywhere stares.
As if Mona Lisa, shawled,
had walked into the Seven/Eleven . . .

No wonder she killed her father.

The judge was sympathetic.
The jury wept for her.
They studied the evidence
from every conceivable angle:

Not guilty,
by reason of insanity.

So now she spends her days
listening quietly, staring
while earnest people talk,
trying to help her grow.

But every night she starts to scream
and has to be restrained, sedated,
before she'll let them take her back

to rest

in her small white room.

I carried this idea around for almost seventeen years. I remember mentioning the notion of this creepily exploitative father to my brother when his daughter was born. I wrote it a few months after taking her downtown to get her first driver's license.

Why so long a gestation period? Maybe it's because I was thinking of it in too conventional a way. As a plain short story, it couldn't jell, because plot and character were subordinate to the single visual image that's at the center of the story. Written as a narrative poem, though, the story can "radiate" from the image. That's my theory, anyhow. It was fun to write.

Joe Haldeman

DIRTY WORK

Pat Cadigan

Deadpan Allie, the pathosfinder, is a character familiar to Pat Cadigan fans, who've followed Allie's career through several science fiction stories (a few of which appeared in OMNI*) and the sf novel* Mindplayers *(Bantam). Because of my fondness for the character and because so many of her "cases" seemed to verge on the subject of vampirism, I asked Pat to write a Deadpan Allie story for this book.*

Com 1879625-JJJDeadpanAllie
TZT-Tijuaoutlie
XQWithheld

NelsonNelson
NelsonNelsonMindplayAgency
TZT-Easct.Njyman
XQ.2717.06X0661818JL

GO

So, NN, how's the family? Ah, sorry, I mean the agency. Of course. Yes, of course. I'm sending you this instead of coming back myself. Sorry to cut into your Bolshoi Ballet viewing time like this. I won't be transmitting a vocal. I haven't spoken for, I'm not sure, days. Lots of days. Something's happened to my speech center. I'd have to put a socket in my head to vocalize and there doesn't seem to be a surgeon handy. Anyway, I know how much you hate sockets. Then, too, I don't speak any Romance language. But just about all the merchants sign, so I make my needs known that way. I used to sign a lot back at J. Walter Tech when I was getting my almost worthless education and learning to read Emotional Indexes—Indices?—and I'd forgotten how much I enjoyed it. You know, NN, I like it so much, I'm thinking about just letting my speech center go. I haven't sustained complete damage to language. I can write, and I can read what I've written for as long as my short-term memory cares to hold it. It's a capricious thing, short-term memory. Where was I? Oh. Ever hear of that kind of damage before? I don't know if I can understand anything said to me because I haven't heard any English or Mandarin since I got here. But then, maybe I wouldn't know if I had. I hear them talking here in their own language and it doesn't sound right, it doesn't sound like language. It sounds like noise. Clang-clang, clang-clang. Being a mute may be unnecessary in this day, but it's hardly a handicap in my profession. People talk too goddam much.

You wouldn't see it that way. *You* talked me into this job. Big bonus, you said. Buy the apartment I've been scouting, you said. Just a job, where's my professionalism, you said, and you said, and you said. Nothing wrong with *your* speech center.

But you know it—you would love me if you could see me now. Because one of the other effects of this half-assed aphasia I've got is my facial muscles are paralyzed. You'd never ask me again if they called me Deadpan Allie for nothing.

That's what you asked me when you talked me into this. I can remember. I've got one eye out and I'm plugged into the memory boost (all the equipment's here, I wouldn't want it to fall into the wrong hands. Like yours.) Left eye. I tried the other eye but I don't think my left hemisphere wants to talk to you because I can't type and remember at the same time plugged in on that side. Typing lefthanded, too. I guess I've got enough language on that side of the brain.

I'm meandering. You'll have to bear with me.

I told you when you talked me into this I don't do dirty work. People like me because I'm clean. I was clean with the fetishist, I was clean with the mindsuck composer, I was clean with your son-in-law and he pushed me. But you wanted me to do this one. Do you remember what I said or do you need a boost for it? I told you anyone who insisted on working with an empath didn't need me.

Fine. It's a silly prejudice. Maybe I wouldn't want anyone to get that close to me without the decency of a machine between us. It's my right to feel that way. Why did you send me when you knew I felt that way? Professionalism. I know that. Don't try getting in touch with me to tell me something I already know. Fine. They asked for me. They asked for me. Fine. They asked for me. They asked for me. Fine. They asked for—

Excuse. I got a bounce on that, a real ricochet. I'm not myself today. Or maybe I am, for the first time in a long time.

I'd always thought of the entourage as a thing of the past. Not just entourage, but Entourage, as in the people who tend to accumulate around someone who happens to be Somebody. Now, I've seen performance artists who keep an audience on retainer so they can hone work as they go but an Entourage is a lot more than that, and a lot less, too. Caverty had a whole houseful of Entourage—highly unusual for a holo artist, I thought—and there was a hell of a lot of house. I'd already been told how it was with him—hell, I knew about the empath, didn't I?—but that didn't mean I could anticipate the experience of opening the front door and finding them all there.

Yes, I did open the front door myself. Noisy crowd, they didn't hear me ring so I tried the controls and the door swung open to the entry hall. All those done-over mansions in the Midwest retained the original entry halls, complete with chandelier. Yesterday's gentility, today's bright idea. This one was tiled in a black-and-white compass pattern. When you came in, you could see you were standing just slightly east of true north, if that sort of thing mattered to you. The Compass hasn't permeated everything the way the Zodiac has, but then it's a pretty new idea. Personally, I think *What's your direction?* will always be as dumb a question as *What's your sign?* None of the half-dozen people standing around in the entry hall asked me either question, or anything else, including *Need some help?* as I unloaded my baggage from the flyer. The pilot watched from the front seat; she was union and definitely not a baggage handler, as she'd told me several times on the trip out.

It wasn't until I had all my system components piled up on the center of the compass—excuse, Compass, I mean (they'd want it that way)—that someone broke loose from the group and came over. To examine the boxes, as it turned out. She refused to notice me until she heard the whiny hum of the flyer as it lifted off outside.

"Are these for Caverty?" she asked, putting one hand on top of the pile proprietarily.

I put my own hand atop the pile, even with hers. "Not exactly. I'm the pathosfinder."

The silver-and-gold-weave eyebrows went up. In the middle of the day, they gave her the look of someone who hasn't yet gone home from last night's party. So did the rest of her outfit, which seemed to be a collection of swatches from this season's best fabrics or something, predominantly silver and gold with the textures varying. Some people I know would have tried to buy it right off her back.

"Pathosfinder," she said, tasting the word uncertainly. "I don't think—" she shrugged. "I'm sorry, I don't remember us ordering a pathosfinder." She turned to the other people still clustered over near the foot of a curving marble-and-ebony staircase. "Anyone put in an order for a pathosfinder?"

"Caverty did," I said before any of them could answer. "You should ask him."

The gray eyes widened; not biogems, I noticed, but eyes that looked like eyes. It seemed kind of out of character for her. "Oh, no," she said. "Caverty works with an empath, everybody knows that."

"He still works with an empath," I said, "only he's also going to be working with me temporarily."

The woman shrugged again. "I'm sorry, I don't think you understand how things are. If Caverty ordered some equipment from you, I'm sure he means to use it himself somehow, but I know that he didn't order you to come with it. You can leave the equipment here and I'll see that he gets it and sends your company a receipt but—" She was starting to show me the egress when the chandelier said, in a cheery, female voice, "You're a lousy doorman, Priscilla, you should stick to partying. I'm coming right down."

For several moments, all Priscilla did was gape up at the chandelier with her mouth open. I stole a look at the little group by the stairs; the Emotional Indices ranged from apprehension to mild indignation to somewhat malicious satisfaction. I felt myself going over a mental speed bump. The milieu here was going to be a bitch to get around, and it would no doubt be reproduced in some way in Caverty's mind. Terrific, I thought. As if the job weren't already hard enough, I had a complicated social structure to clamber around on. *NN, you old bastard.*

Then another woman came trotting down the staircase. "Ah, here we are. The pathosfinder. Alexandra Haas, right? Deadpan Allie?" Somehow her hitting the foot of the stairs shooed everyone, including Priscilla, away; they flowed off into a room to the left, or west, according to the Compass.

"Sorry about that," said the woman. She was all business, tailored, no frills, brown all over, including her eyes, which were some kind of artificial gem the color of oak. "Sometimes the Entourage gets a little out of hand around here. I'm Harmony. At least, Caverty hopes I am." She laughed. "I'm kind of the general factotum, grand scheduler, traffic director, hall monitor. I try to keep things harmonious. I'm the one who contacted your agency about you. I've done quite a lot of research on pathosfinders; I'm really happy you were able to take the job."

I nodded. "Thanks. I need a place to stash my equipment and then I'd like to meet Caverty."

"I've had a room prepared for you upstairs, away from the general foofooraw and infighting—"

"Somewhere close to Caverty, I hope?" I said, as she tried to herd me toward the stairs. "I like to be as available and accessible to a client as possible."

Harmony's face clouded slightly. "Oh. Well. I, uh, I'd really have to check that out with Caverty. He has his own section of the house where no one else stays, out of respect to his need for a private working environment. You're experienced with creative people, so I guess you know how that is."

"I understand completely. However, clients sometimes feel that they have to see me right away, in the middle of the night or whatever. I need to be easily available."

Harmony smiled with indulgence. "There's nowhere you can go in this house where you would not be available to Caverty on a moment's notice or less. Everyone here understands that. It *is* his house, after all."

I opened my mouth, thought quickly, and shut it again. Trying to explain to her that I was not just another body added to the general Entourage population wasn't going to penetrate; I could tell. She was sure she knew the kind of people who stayed in Caverty's house, she was one of them. "My system—" I said, gesturing at the stack of components still sitting in the center of the Compass.

"I've already taken care of that. It'll be moved up to your room for you."

"I'll just wait here, then, until I see everything moved."

The professional mask almost slipped. She caught herself before she could sigh and spoke into her brown bracelet instead. "Entry hall right *now*." Four people with straps and handtrucks emerged from a door half hidden by the start of the curve of the staircase. They weren't exactly in uniform but there was a sameness to them and I knew immediately from their posture that they weren't Entourage. They were employees.

"We don't do that much heavy lifting and moving large objects around here," Harmony said as the hired help labored along behind us with my system. "The people who come and go here tend to travel light, although we haven't actually had anyone leave for a long time. Leave permanently, I mean. Which is good. For all of Caverty's—oh, I don't know what you'd call it, wildness of heart or freedom of spirit, I guess—for all that, he really needs a stable living situation. And things have really stabilized here. It's good. I think you'll see that while you're here."

Even though I was getting short of breath on those damned stairs I had to do breathing exercises to maintain the deadpan. She was making my skin crawl.

Whoa. Have to stop sometimes. That boost. Too vivid sometimes. I don't know why I'm reliving this for you anyway, NN. I mean, can you appreciate it? What do I think I'm doing, making art or something? I'm no artist, not in that sense. But I'm the best pathosfinder in the hemisphere. Right? You made me the best pathosfinder in the hemisphere, remember? You did it. And you know, that was nothing compared to what some people can do to you.

I know what you're saying right now. I went into it with a bad attitude. Isn't that what you're saying? I know it is, even though—chuckle, chuckle—I doubt I could actually understand you if I were there right now and you were saying it to me. Clang-clang, clang-clang.

Um, bad attitude. Yes, you'd say I'd gone into it with a bad attitude. Now what kind of a thing is that for someone trading on the name Deadpan Allie, and my reputation and all. Well, I'll tell you. It's knowing when you're in a bad situation. I wanted to pack up and go right then. Leaving aside the skin crawling and that stuff (interesting mental image, there, pack up and go and leave aside the skin crawling; there I go meandering again, bear with me, it happens, did I mention that? I guess I did but it's too late to go back and see if I really did because I can't read that part any more). So. Even if my skin hadn't been crawling like a lizard, like a million little tiny lizards, I should have seen it was already too hard. Pathosfinding you need privacy for. Go down and root around in somebody's soul like that; the client gets embarrassed in front of *me* sometimes. Facing someone else can be impossible. Caverty should have known that, he was a professional, he'd worked with a pathosfinder years before, before he'd discovered his empath.

So that was mainly why I stayed, you know. I wanted to check that out, see this empath and Caverty, get a feel for how they worked and why Caverty wanted to work that way. But I think I must have had it in the back of my mind that I was going to leave after that, unless Caverty could disentangle himself from his empath and his Harmony and the rest of the Entourage. So I could work him properly.

Disentangle? Did I really say that?

I don't know. I can't read it any more.

Harmony gave me the house tour. Done-over mansion, the usual things overdone as well as done over. Ten thousand rooms, not counting bedrooms. Ballrooms, dining rooms, sitting rooms, room rooms, an art gallery, a theatre where Caverty showed his holos if he felt like it. That last wasn't the way Harmony put it but that was the general idea, or so I gathered from her Emotional Index.

Reading the Emotional Index of someone who is trying like hell to give you the best impression can be amusing or annoying, depending on your mood. Occasionally I found myself feeling one way or the other about it but mostly I felt uneasy. She'd fallen into some kind of PR ramadoola that she was running on me. Silliness; you don't give a pathosfinder PR because she finds out what the truth is right away. But Harmony was straining to make me happy or get some kind of approval from me. Maybe because she thought then I'd do a better job with her boss?

No, that wasn't it. She was trying to *sell* me something.

Or convert me.

Oh, yes. Once I saw it, there was no way not to see it. But never mind. Sooner or later, I'd get to Caverty and I wouldn't have to bother with Harmony or Priscilla the Party Baby or anyone else in the Entourage.

"I need to see Caverty as soon as possible," I told Harmony as she led me down yet another upstairs hall toward yet another room she thought she had to show me. "He *is* my client, I have to let him know I've arrived."

Harmony turned to look at me with mild surprise. "But—were you thinking of starting work today?"

"If Caverty wanted to start in five minutes, I'd do my best to be ready."

"He won't want to start today, I'm positive. And I'm sure someone must have told him you're here." The smile turned a little hard. "Perhaps Priscilla. Anyway, wouldn't you like to get comfortable, settle in a little, get to know the place? Not to mention all of us. Caverty's group. I know he'd like you to feel like you're a part of things. I mean, if you're going to be here awhile—"

"I don't actually know how long I'll be here. I won't have any idea until Caverty and I begin working together, and even then it'll be hard to say. Pathosfinding isn't a simple business. And that doesn't even come into it. Some extremely complicated jobs have taken less than a day to complete while others that were more straightforward took weeks." I resisted the temptation to look apologetic; not hard, really, because they *don't* call me Deadpan Allie for nothing, but her proselytizing was working at me, trying to find a way in, at least to my politeness sympathies. "I really must speak to Caverty, whether we begin working today or two weeks from now. He's my client."

Harmony spread her hands and then clasped them together with a little sigh. Her nails were also painted brown, I noticed. That shouldn't have seemed bizarre. "Well. If you must, you must. Could I at least phone him and tell him we're coming? Is that all right?"

"Of course."

She stepped into a room which seemed to be a souvenir gallery of some kind—still holos alongside flat pictures promoting one or other of Caverty's works, things that might have been awards, props, or just items he (or someone) had wanted to keep for sentimental reasons. Not a junk room; it was all neat and very organized. I glanced around while Harmony used a talk-only phone on a seven-tiered ceramic table. She didn't say much and she didn't say it to Caverty, I was pretty sure. The Entourage has a completely different way of talking to the Man (or Woman) than they do to each other, and for each other, they had their own pecking order that was never quite congruent with the Man's idea of who was over whom. Harmony was talking to an equal, without a doubt and, without a doubt, that wasn't the empath.

"He says come right up," Harmony said, replacing the phone. "Caverty lives at the top of the house; starting on this floor, there are elevators so we don't have to climb a million stairs." The smile was forced now, though I wouldn't have been able to tell if I hadn't known how to read an Emotional Index. She really hadn't wanted to take me to Caverty today at all and I couldn't figure that out. She'd chosen me (according to her, anyway); her own comfort was contingent on my helping the Man but she was reluctant to let me near him. Not completely reluctant—just for today. Tomorrow. Mañana, no problem. Entourages could be funny things. I had a passing thought that Caverty had better turn out to be worth it after the obstacle course I was having to run to get to him.

Well, of course, he had the whole top floor of the house, though the main room where he did most of his living and working was a big studio at the rear of the building, where he could look out a fan-shaped, floor-to-ceiling window at cultivated rolling country. He was sitting at the window when Harmony led me in—I was never going to walk with Harmony, I saw, she was always going to lead—off to the left side, looking away from the sunset, which was visible through another much smaller window behind him. A woman was sitting at his feet, one hand resting casually on his ankle. I could just barely hear their voices in quiet conversation. Harmony looked around, saw no one else and nearly panicked.

"I talked to Langtree, *he* told me to come up," she said, ostensibly to me but actually so Caverty would hear and know that she hadn't just taken it upon herself to barge in. Whatever happened to *Caverty says come right up,* I wondered.

"It's all right, Harmony," Caverty called out. There was a slight echo off the mostly empty walls. "I sent Langtree out."

"Oh," she breathed, pretending to fan herself relievedly with one brown-tipped hand, "that's good, I'm glad I wasn't interrupting anything important—"

"You weren't," Caverty said good-naturedly. He had one of those voices that would sound good-natured all the time, even when it was chewing someone out. "You're okay, Harmony, thanks for everything. You can go now, too, take a break, get some rest. Have a drink, have kinky sex, whatever you want."

Harmony gave one of those full-bodied *ha-ha-ha* laughs and sort of backed out of the room, looking from me to Caverty and the woman on the floor and back again.

"The pathosfinder," Caverty said to me.

"The pathosfinder. Yes." I looked around. The holo equipment was in an untidy pile in the righthand corner nearest the door. Except for one of the cameras and a couple of colored lights, it all looked as though it hadn't been touched for a long time, not even to be cleaned. For me, that will always be what a creative block really looks like, in the mind or in the world: a pile of mostly unused equipment, gathering dust.

Caverty didn't get up. "Come closer," he said. "Please."

I walked across the room slowly enough to have time to look at both of them. Caverty was a solidly built man, more good-looking than he really needed to be. Sculpture, of course; these days everyone's from Mt. Olympus, with bone structure to die for (which, of course, you have to pay for and only the filthoid rich can pay for custom designs like the one Caverty had). But on Caverty, there was a sense of overkill about his attractiveness, too many nice things crammed into one place.

The same could not be said about the woman sitting on the floor. There was a naturalness about her that was also very expensive, except she hadn't bought her looks. She stopped short of being delicate—*fine* was the way that old bastard NN would have put it. Aquamarine eyes; the facets in the pupils glittered like tears. Thick, dark straight hair cut ragamuffin-style. Thin as a ballet dancer but without any sense of a dancer's litheness. I realized belatedly that she had stolen my attention away from Caverty completely.

Caverty looked up at me with the start of a smile. "My empath, Madeleine." He pronounced it *Mad-a-LAYNE*. "We were just enjoying some quiet moments at the end of the day. No matter what I'm doing I try to take time to enjoy those few moments before the daylight fades." He shifted position slightly, adjusting his caftan. It was gray, very thick and heavily textured, mimicking a handweave. "Although we never watch the sunset. I don't believe in such things of course but Harmony says that west is definitely not my direction. I'm northeast. Which is why this house is perfect for me. According to the Compass, I mean, if you believe such things. I don't imagine pathosfinders put any more stock in them than holo artists." He looked at Madeleine. "Or empaths?"

She gave a short, breathy laugh. "We've known each other far too long for you to have to ask that."

"How long is that?" I asked conversationally.

They had to look at each other before they could answer me. "Fifteen years," Caverty said, while Madeleine nodded. "That is, we've known each other for fifteen years; we've been working together for eight. Of course, just knowing Madeleine affected me deeply, even before we began working together. Affected my work. So perhaps we have been working together the whole time we've known each other. She's been working *on* me, anyway." He chuckled, looking at his empath fondly while she sat under his praise smiling demurely at her knees.

"Before that, how often did you work with a pathosfinder?" I asked.

They both looked up at me with mild surprise. "Maybe once, twice a year," Caverty said. "It isn't the sort of thing you can do all the time. Why?"

"I was just wondering. For the sake of the job. It can help before we start if I know a little about your last mindplay experience."

"Bless me, Allie, for I have sinned. It has been eight years since my last mindplay experience. With a pathosfinder. I can barely remember it now, it seems."

Madeleine gave him a soft pat on the leg.

"Could I ask why you feel the need to work with one now after all these years?"

Caverty took a deep breath. "I need something different. My work needs something different. Have you seen any of my holos?"

"I've seen all of them, including your last release, *Dinners Between Dinners*."

"Retitled *Food Fight* by the critics," he said with a hint of hurt feelings. "Not that there wasn't something to what some of them said. There is no easy way to look at yourself and see that you're getting stale. Especially when you were considered an innovator early in your career. You have no idea how excruciating it is to have to give up the position of Promising Young Turk because all your Promising Young Turk stuff has become an old story. People begin to recognize the devices you fall back on as, well, the devices you fall back on. I thought it was time to explore some different things."

"And what about you?" I said to the empath.

She sat up slightly, blinking. "What do you mean?"

"What will you be doing?"

"When?"

"While Caverty's exploring these different things?"

"Why, what I always do. I'll be empathizing." Her tiny smile grew even tinier. "Won't I?" She looked to Caverty.

He leaned over to say something to her, paused, and frowned up at me. "Won't she?"

Time for the tightrope walk fifty yards above the glass net. "There are, I'm sure, pathosfinders who will work with a tandem of any kind. And there are pathosfinders who work with empaths—"

"Is there something wrong with empaths?" she asked. Not a bit defensive, either; her Emotional Index was devoid of any hostility. She just wanted to know. I felt myself relax a little.

"Well, when you're mindplaying, the system facilitating the contact between minds imposes a certain amount of order on the encounter—there's a medium for the minds to interact within, strict boundary conditions that keep separate entities truly separate so that there isn't any confusion as to whose thoughts are whose, and a certain amount of protocol that reinforces the personal sense of security."

She nodded. "Yes."

"Yes." I waited and she waited with me. "I mean, that's it. That's what it is."

She looked at me doubtfully. "That's what's wrong with empaths?" Caverty's posture changed very subtly to a protective position.

"I'm sorry, I didn't actually mean there was anything wrong with empaths. What I mean is—well, that's why I don't work with empaths. I thought the agency made that clear."

Caverty rubbed his chin with two fingers. "They didn't."

"I'm surprised. My agency has always been careful to spell out exactly what the mindplayers do. And don't do."

"Well, that's all right anyway," Caverty said, warmth flowing into his voice from somewhere deep inside. "You don't have to work with an empath. *I* work with an empath. That will do."

"Will it do for you not to work with an empath while you're working with me?"

Caverty's smile shrank somewhat. "You mean while we're hooked in together or the whole time you're here?"

I didn't look at Madeleine. "The whole time I'm here."

"Oh . . ." He slumped back in his chair and stared intently at the toes of his slippers. Doeskin slippers, possibly synthetic but then again, perhaps not. This was the home of the filthoid rich, after all. "I—I'm not sure."

Madeleine reached out to put a hand on his knee and then changed her mind, showing me that she was letting him make his own decision this time.

"I'm not sure I'm capable of doing that," he said. "Madeleine and I—we've been together for so long—not working with Madeleine is—it would be like not working with air."

"Oh, Caverty," Madeleine said. "You have to do what is best for your work."

I wasn't sure I could take the sudden emotional charge pressurizing the room. All at once, there seemed to be a heaviness on my solar plexus, the way you feel when you barge in on some kind of intimate scene, or perhaps when it barges in on you. But they don't call me Deadpan Allie for nothing. (For fun, maybe, hey, NN? Depends on your idea of fun.) I waited it out; Caverty and the empath rode it out. Without moving, either.

Presently, she said, "You should try it, Caverty. You have to try it, you owe it to yourself, you owe it to your work. We both know you've gotten stale—"

"Don't say that too loud, the critics might have the place bugged." They smiled sadly at each other in lieu of laughing.

"Try it," she said. "It'll be . . . different. You need something different. Something besides me."

Did she think I was completely stupid? Or just stupid enough not to know how to read an Emotional Index? Hers said she believed he needed nothing of the sort, that she would continue to be the one and only thing he needed, work or no work.

But then, she was an empath. Maybe it wasn't her Emotional Index I was reading but his.

I resisted the urge to blink several times and maintained as much neutrality as I could, which, under the circumstances, wasn't really very much. Just by being there I was pitting myself against her, forcing a choice between us.

She got up suddenly. "Try it now. Just here, just the two of you."

He reached out for her, about to protest.

"No. I insist. This is your *career*, Caverty. It's all right, I'm not going anywhere except out of the room. You know I'll always be here for you."

She gave me a quick, level, professional-to-professional smile as she passed me on her way out. Caverty looked after her with dismay, fear, and guilt fighting it out for dominance on his handsome face. He stared at the door for a long time after she shut it. Then finally his attention came over to me.

"And now what?" he asked, spreading his hands. They were shaking a little.

"Now not so much. I thought we might talk. Get acquainted. I don't like to go cold into contact with someone's mind and I'm sure you wouldn't want to, either."

"Oh, no, certainly not." He shifted position in the chair, trying to get comfortable. It was a very comfortable chair, not one of those living contour things that adjusts itself to your every little move, just a very receptive inanimate, but it was impossible for him now that Madeleine was out of the room. "What, ah, do you need to know? Oh, dinner's coming up. We don't want to miss dinner. The meals around here are *prima*."

The sun had gone down and, as it had grown progressively darker outside, the lights had come up in perfect equilibrium with the fading sunlight so that you almost didn't notice the change.

"We won't miss any meals. Pathosfinding doesn't require that anyone starve for their art." I wanted to go over to him but I had no intention of sitting at his feet. I looked around for another chair, spotted one near the pile of equipment and dragged it over so I could sit across from him.

"That's good," he said, stealing a glance at the door again. "I doubt that I could, any more. I've grown too used to eating regularly and well." Pause, and then a rueful smile. "That being why I called you in."

"At this point, you wouldn't starve if you never worked up another holo. It's a different kind of need now."

He squinted at me with thoughtful surprise. "You *know*."

"Yes, I know. I've worked with many, many artists of many different kinds." *And empaths aren't the only ones who know how other people feel,* I added to myself. "You can do lots of things to keep from starving, but only one thing to produce your art."

"Absolute. Just absolute." He nodded, feeling comfortable for all of three seconds. "That's the truth." He put his hand on his stomach. "Was that me? Did you hear that? My stomach just roared like a wild animal. I think I can smell dinner from here."

Let him go, said some small part of my mind. Probably the last shred of my common sense. Let him go, let him cling to his empath and later you can hook in with him and fail and go home none the worse for wear.

"I need to be able to look at any holos you have available for viewing around here."

"Oh. Certainly."

"And it would be best if we could look at them together."

"Oh. . . . Yes, I guess it would."

"But we don't have to do that before dinner."

"After dinner?" He looked a little pale.

"Tomorrow will be soon enough. I did just get here, after all."

Now he really came to life. "Oh, of course, this is really thoughtless of me, keeping you here when you'd probably like to get some rest and you must be hungry, too—"

He babbled both of us out of the room. I broke away and made a stop at my quarters before heading down to the dining room, which in any other place would have been known as a banquet hall.

Now, NN, I *know*, I just *know* you're picking up on my hostility toward the empath. The poor innocent empath. What on earth have I got against empaths? And how can I be so unprofessional as to show it?

Hang me, shoot me—emotional criminal!

I told you, I didn't work with empaths. It feels indecent, doing something like that without a machine.

Hang me, shoot me—emotional prude! You just can't win in this business. I always knew that.

But I'll tell you what else I don't like about empaths. I know all about empathy; you know that, you taught me everything I know, right? You do still claim that, don't you? Sure you do, I know you. Yah, I know all about empathy; empaths are something else.

There's something about empaths touching you—not even touching you, being around you. You just know they're soaking it all up, whatever it is. They're always just—soaking it all up. Drinking you in. You're supposed to feel such kinship with them. You're not alone any more, someone knows exactly how you feel, someone's walked a mile in your moccasins. But what's that for, anyway? Yah, I know, so you feel you're not alone any more, right, we said that, didn't we. Didn't I, excuse me, I'm doing all of the semitalking. But what's it really for? What possible survival value can that have? For you, I mean—you the regular person. What's the survival value of feeling such kinship with someone, of not feeling alone any more emotionally. Pretend you're a regular person instead of a dried-up old bastard just for the sake of example, okay, NN? The survival value of, yes, empaths in terms of you, the regular person. Well, there is none. Not for you.

It's all for the empath. When you know exactly how anyone— *everyone*—feels, that's a pretty powerful survival tool. In fact, you'd probably end up doing a lot more than just surviving with it. Survive and thrive, yah; and soaking it all up all the time, you'd get terribly—*accustomed* to it, more than accustomed, *addicted*. Except that's not quite the word. I mean, are you *addicted* to air?

Yah, so what's in it for you, the regular person? (You pretend like you're a regular person, okay, NN, or have I already asked you to do that?) What's in it for you? I mean, shouldn't you get something out of this? Well, sure you should, and you do.

You get to *like* having someone crawling around in your emotions, feeling them with you, and letting you feel other emotions from other people.

Except maybe *like* is the wrong word.

Do you *like* air?

Caverty had thirty pairs of moccasins, by the way, and Mad-a-LAYNE had had her sensitive little soles in every one of them.

It was a banquet hall, but the type of place where you sat down in one spot only if you really wanted to, if you were tired or something. Most of the Entourage were gypsy diners, the type of people who seem to be reluctant to light anywhere even semipermanently, in case they should see a better place to sit. So they were all cruising around, plates or cups or whatever in hand, cocktail-party style, working at enjoying themselves.

I'd stopped off at my room for a change of clothes and a dose of solitude so I could refortify myself. There wasn't time for even the quickest mental exercise with the system, unless I wanted to miss a good portion of the dinnertime dynamics and something told me I didn't want to miss very much in this house.

I managed to arrive in the dining room before both Caverty and Madeleine, which meant dinner was not quite underway. You could tell that by the general demeanor of the room. The entire Entourage was in a waiting mode.

Quite a mixed bag, this Entourage. There had to be at least thirty of them, acting out their inner lives. A few were dressed after certain animals; bears or lions seemed to be the fashion, though I spotted a couple of chicken people. At least, they looked like chicken people to me. A peacock might have been appropriate in some cases but no one cared to be quite that obvious. There was an umbrella woman who took up a lot of space; at various times, her umbrella skirt would open or shut for some private reason of her own, following no pattern I could see. I saw Priscilla with her little group; she'd changed some of the swatches on her outfit and polished her metallics so that she twinkled under the chandeliers. The members of her group were now each wearing an outfit made from one of her swatches. You might have briefly mistaken them for the focal point of the Entourage. On second glance, they'd have reminded you of nothing so much as some kind of in-house organization. Like security guards. It would figure, I thought, helping myself to a bowl of something fragrant. If definite job assignments weren't made, individuals within the Entourage would automatically fall into certain roles, depending on their personalities. Priscilla was a natural for the cops.

I was looking around for a place to sit when someone finally chose to notice me. I'd noticed him wading along behind me as I'd made my way to the buffet. It would have been hard not to notice him. He was at least six-three and bulky and where he wasn't bulky, he was hairy; the kind of person who makes you feel crowded just by being nearby. I'd figured I'd mix in among everyone as though there were nothing unusual about my being there but he planted himself in front of me, cutting off most of my view of the room and said, "You're new here."

His tone was politely matter-of-fact, not accusatory at all; wherever he fit in here, he wasn't the cops. "Yes, I am," I said, shifting position so a woman in a harlequinesque outfit could pass behind me.

"Did you come to join?" he asked, reaching around me for a bowl of the same stuff I had. His arms were so long he barely had to move.

"No, I'm—"

"Didn't think so." He smiled cheerily. "I always know when someone's coming in to join. Hasn't happened in an awfully long time. Came alone, didn't you?"

I nodded. "I was just upstairs talking to Caverty and Mad-a-Layne."

His eyebrows went up very slightly. "It's a good group here. Good balance of all different kinds." Priscilla cruised by closely enough to hear what we were saying. My bulky friend looked at her for a few moments with mild hostility on his dark furry face. "Mostly a good balance. When you've got all kinds, you've got *all* kinds. But as long as they serve their purpose and don't just take up space and eat up all the food, you can tolerate just about anyone." He looked down at me again. "Of course, we're all on the same side here," he added quickly. "There may be a slob here and there, but they're *our* slobs. If you get what I mean."

"Couldn't be clearer."

"I'm Arlen. Some people call me The Bear, but not to my face." He chuckled into his beard. "Of course, they don't know *I* started them calling me The Bear. Planted the name myself. I figured if they were going to be calling me something, I might as well have some say over what it was."

"Is that name insulting to you?" I asked.

"Hell, no. But *they* think it is." He laughed again. "Some people, if they think they're insulting you, it's all they need to know. And that's how you survive in an Entourage." He herded me a few feet away from the buffet table. "What's your name and what are you planning to do here besides survive?"

"Allie. Deadpan Allie, actually, and I'm a pathosfinder."

I'd finally managed to rumple his smooth. "Pathosfinder?" He actually stepped back from me. "For *who?* Not Caverty?"

A white-blond woman in a shimmering blue Japanese-style kimono turned around. "Pathosfinder?" The word echoed, flowing out into the people immediately around us and I found myself in the middle of a minor group within the group instead of just being among them.

"Who called you?" the Nordic-looking woman asked, worry large on her luminous face. "Is it *my* fault?"

Arlen The Bear patted her shoulder gently with a huge pawlike hand. "That's not quite the right question, Lina. Poor Lina thinks any time something goes wrong around here, she's somehow to blame for not spotting the problem early enough."

"For some people, sensitivity has to be cultivated, worked on every moment, waking *and* sleeping," the woman explained to me anxiously. "Otherwise, they get hardened to everything without ever realizing it because being *in*sensitive is their natural state of mind. And it can be contagious, too, insensitivity can. It can spread from just one person to infect a whole group and pretty soon you can have a whole population incapable of feeling for their fellow human being."

"Yes," I said, "but—"

"So that's why I asked if our needing a pathosfinder was my fault." She looked up at Arlen with begging eyes. Icy-blue eyes, I noticed. "*Is* it me, Arlen? You'd tell me, wouldn't you?"

Arlen's laugh was kindly as he gave her a gentle hug. "Sure I would, but by the time I did, you'd already have been told several times by everyone else. Stop worrying. She isn't here because of anything you've done wrong. But she hasn't yet said why she *is* here." His expression was a little less kindly now; I'd upset one of their own. God knew how they were going to receive the fact that I was going to be messing with the entourage's *raison d'être*. But we can't lie to anyone directly involved with a client, whether it's a friend, enemy, parent, Entourage or something even more baroque. Not unless it's to save someone's life. *Suppose it's your own life?* I'd once asked NN. *Don't be silly*, he'd said. *Who'd want to kill you?*

I thought about that as I said, "I'm here for Caverty."

Nobody said anything. A third of my audience backed off.

"Caverty called you?" Arlen asked finally. "He must have. I can't believe it. All these years with Madeleine and now—" He shook his head a little. "What are you going to—I mean, are you—"

"I'm not replacing Mad-a-LAYNE permanently." I could hear the sighs of relief above the general chatter in the room. "I really hadn't meant to create a disturbance," I said, glancing to my right, where the umbrella woman was getting the news that there was a pathosfinder at large from a waifish type in black secondskins. "I'm going to do some work with Caverty and when it's done, I'll be leaving and life will go on."

"Maybe you won't want to leave," said a chubby man in a pouch suit, ordinary except for the fact that it seemed to be padded to make him even chubbier.

"Yah. You might really get to like it here," said the Nordic woman. "That happens."

"I have some things to go back to that are very important to me," I said politely.

"What?" asked The Bear with what seemed to be genuine curiosity.

"Ah . . ." Something told me they weren't going to perceive my career as suitably important. I seized the first thing that came into my head. "There's Nelson Nelson."

"An important *someone?*" asked the Nordic woman.

"Ask him to come here. He might like it," the Bear suggested.

"I, uh, no, I couldn't."

"It's up to you," said the man in the pouch suit. "But don't count it out completely, staying here. You just might. You never know."

The general babble in the room changed its tone and I knew without even looking that Caverty had come in.

Immediately, their attention went directly to him, allowing me to slide out of the spotlight and into the general crowd. Slipping between derelicts and duchess types, I made my way over to a small raised area containing a few small tables where I could sit and regroup. A few chiffon fanciers lingered by the steps up to the area; I managed to pass them unnoticed, in spite of the fact that I'd dipped the corner of somebody's scarf in my dish. If he didn't care, I didn't.

Relieved to be out of the general crowd, I didn't see that there was someone else sitting at the table I'd chosen until I was about to sample the night's entree.

"You're new here," he said.

I paused with my spoon nearly at my lips.

"Only the new people choose to sit up here. The very new and the very old." He smiled with the left half of his mouth; his diamond eyes twinkled. Diamond biogems are seldom a good choice but his olive skin kept him from looking too much like a willing victim of blindness. He was older than someone you'd expect to find in an Entourage, and not as done over as the average citizen. The nose had been broken at least once, but the effect wasn't homely. He'd have reminded you of your father, if that was your orientation. It wasn't mine. To me, he looked only like a graying, older man in comfortably baggy shirt and pants, too sensible to be here but staying anyway for some reason of his own.

"It's Madeleine they're all so worried about," he continued, watching as the room rearranged itself around Caverty's presence.

"Not Caverty?"

"Oh, of course, Caverty. Both of them, really. We don't have one without the other here, as you must know. But they're worried about Caverty in terms of Madeleine and what you mean for her. I know. I've been here with the Entourage since before it was formally an Entourage. I may have founded the Entourage. Or helped found it. I came to him, others came. Then we were a caravan." He paused to watch a woman wearing a jewel-encrusted cage over her face and neck make her way through the room. One of the chicken people stopped her and they embraced warmly.

"I know all their dynamics, small and large. I direct the domestic drama here. At one time or another, I've gotten all of them to play at least some small part. Caverty finds it amusing, I think, to watch other people besides himself have problems, even if they're just staged. And once he based a holo on one of my scenarios—*Dinners Between Dinners*, after my scenario, *Food Fight*."

"You don't say."

"That was the only instance, though. Usually I cribbed from him now and then. As a kind of tribute to his work. And as a kind of tribute to being fresh out of ideas at the time, too." He fell silent, watching Caverty moving among his Entourage.

The Entourage both moved aside for him and crowded around him all at once. It was as though a new element had been dropped into simmering waters. Caverty slipped among them much more easily than I'd been able to, maneuvering effortlessly, balancing socializing and finger food. He ate a little, held court, ate a little more, held a little more court—a reception, I realized. Every night, the Entourage gave him a reception of the type he'd probably gotten on the debut of a new holo. Not so unusual, really. Performers become addicted to applause quite easily. But Caverty had found a way to get a fix of applause every day—more often than that, if he wanted—without having to go through the tiresome business of working for it.

"Get it direct, from producer to consumer," I muttered.

"Pardon?"

I shrugged. "Just a stray thought."

The man got up with a smile and tossed a cloth napkin onto the table. "Well, I should go say 'good evening' to the great man."

"Do you always do this?"

"Every night, dinner's an occasion here. Didn't they tell you?"

"I mean, you personally going over to pay your respects."

Mildly troubled frown. "I stay here by his good graces. I eat his food, take up space, ply my trade, all by virtue of his hospitality. Once a day, I can let the man know how I feel." He paused, studying me for a moment. "You have to mean something here, you know. Whether you stay or not." Then he looked toward Caverty, prepared a friendly smile, and moved away, straightening his clothes.

It took him over a minute to make his way through the cluster around Caverty, not because it was so crowded, really, but because some of the *couture* was voluminous, like the umbrella lady, and because they were all deferring to each other as well as socializing among themselves, while Caverty favored each person who reached him with more than just token conversation. Didn't the novelty ever wear off, for any of them?

Off to one side, I saw that Harmony had appeared amid the near-fringe of the ragged circle around "the great man" and was subtly directing traffic, moving people along so they could greet Caverty in turn and moving those who'd already spoken to him away without seeming to. Caverty was facing in her general direction, reinforcing the idea of them getting in line for him. It might have been engineered, but it had the look and feel of incidental choreography—they'd fallen into doing things this way and as long as it worked they'd keep doing it.

I tried to catch the expression on each face as the Entourage members paid their respects and turned away but I wasn't close enough to see them all. The ones I could see looked content, or satisfied, or, I don't know— appeased, somehow, the way children look when they all go home from the party with a gift. Which was probably the case.

Caverty looked the same way; a little drawn and besieged, perhaps, but generally content. Appeased. Happy, even.

He shouldn't have been. He should have felt tired and put upon and too in demand. *But then,* I thought, *if he's not giving any of himself to his work, he has plenty left to give to his Entourage. Right, Allie?*

No, wrong—he supposedly wasn't doing any work because he didn't have any inside him, so he shouldn't have had anything to offer this live-in applause machine. So what exactly was he giving them and where was it coming from?

I scanned the room again and found her at last. She was at the opposite end of an invisible straight line that ran from Harmony through Caverty. That look. She could have been in religious trance; she could have been gazing at her firstborn child; she could have been dreaming of a lover or fantasizing a murder behind that look. Her Emotional Index shifted, melted, segued through a thousand different states in less time than it took to think about it.

The food, I noticed, had been completely forgotten. Or maybe not so much forgotten as dropped, like any other pretense.

All right, NN, three quick choruses of *What's It All About?* and if you haven't figured it out by then, you're a candidate for brain salad.

Yah, well, what do you think I did after that? I got the hell out of there and went off to my room, my luxuriously appointed room with the singing, vibrating bed and custom-built lavabo and tried to compose a message which would convey beautifully and inarguably why the Entourage had to leave as soon as they could pack themselves up. Halfway through the start of the sixth draft, I plugged into a memory boost and relived the scene for myself, for reinforcement, so I could make it more—I don't know, urgent? Real? Immediate? So he could see it as I saw it. And then I realized he couldn't see it as I saw it and not be too alienated to work with me. I was already separating him and Mad-a-LAYNE. Madeleine. But I kept thinking of her in that exaggerated way. Mad-a-LAYNE. Mad-a-LAYNE. Mad-a-LAYNE in PAIN falls MAINly in your BRAIN.

I'd started yawning midway through the second holo. By the start of the third, I had to ask Caverty for coffee. He roused himself from the stupor I'd nearly fallen into and dialed some up from the bar near the projection booth.

"Am I supposed to ask you what you think?" he said as we perched on antique stools together.

"I really don't know what you're *supposed* to do."

Caverty laughed a little. "Neither do I, most of the time. As you can probably guess. Actually, I don't have to ask. I was comatose from boredom myself."

"Your own boredom with your work isn't much of a barometer. However you feel about your work is tied up in the difficulties you're having right now, so you're not a terribly reliable judge."

He glanced over his shoulder briefly and I squelched the urge to tell him Madeleine wasn't there. Today he was a bit less uncomfortable in her absence but he was still looking around for her. "Maybe not, but I used to know when the work was good. At least, I thought I did. Now I'm beginning to think I spent close to two decades fooling myself." He stared gloomily into his coffee cup.

We'd watched one holo from his beginning phase and one from his experimental. Both had been narrative pieces, the stories simple while the embellishment was complex, especially in the experimental work. He'd been very young when he'd done that one, though it had come after the previous piece. He'd just been discovering how much fun it was to break the rules and from time to time, ghost images of himself with his holocam had drifted through the piece, recording other ghost images as well as the central scene in progress. It was the sort of thing most artists do sooner or later and usually it's a bad choice but somehow, Caverty had made it work, either through luck or sheer talent, or perhaps a combination of the two. It left an aftertaste in the brain; your memory kept returning to it, going over the core story—boy meets self, boy gets self, boy loses self, boy buys new self—while the trimmings drifted around as vividly in memory as they'd been in the holo itself.

The interesting part was that Caverty had used minimal sound—no dialog, no musical scoring, few sound effects except as a kind of punctuation here and there, and yet you tended to remember more sound than he'd used. While I wasn't sure that I really liked it, it did seem to summarize all of Caverty's strong points as an artist. I didn't want to ask him how autobiographical it was; artists never really know exactly how autobiographical any of their work is. I could find out later if I really wanted to know.

"You're very quiet," Caverty said. "That, uh, well . . . *scares* me."

"I'm not a critic. You have to stop thinking of me as some kind of master evaluator."

"But you are, aren't you? Evaluating my talent, how you can help me. *If* you can help me." Pause while he drained his coffee. "*Can* you help me? How bad off *is* this patient, doctor?"

"How bad off do you feel?"

"If you're going to tell me it's all up to me—"

"Not exactly. It's a matter of how much help you're willing to accept; then it's a matter of how much help you'll be able to accept. Plus a lot of other things." I pushed my coffee aside. "This isn't something I discuss in detail with my clients, as it tends to make them far too self-conscious. I don't want you getting in your own way."

He nodded absently, glancing over his shoulder again. "Well. How many more holos did you want to see?"

"One representative piece from each stage of your career would be fine. And if there are any others you want me to look at, that's fine, too."

He nodded again but his gaze was on some point off to my right, as though he were daydreaming or suddenly remembering something very pleasant, or perhaps getting a new idea for a holo. For a moment, I was uncertain as to whether it was any of those things but then I realized, and just as I did, it touched me.

It was a very light touch, a brush that might have been accidental. A pathosfinder's mind isn't at all receptive to casual telepathy or an empath just cruising; it's all that self-definition and controlled concentration we engage in during the course of mindplay. After a while, it becomes second nature. It's going on all the time somewhere in your mind, an engine on idle. Madeleine brushed up against me and passed on, like someone who'd accidentally knocked on the wrong door and didn't wait for an answer. She was gone before I could sense how close she was.

Caverty sighed cheerfully and then looked down at his hands resting on his thighs. "It's just good to know she's there."

"I can't have that."

"Pardon?" He didn't look up.

"I can't have her coming in like that. Especially when we're hooked in together."

"Oh, she knows that, I asked her to look in on me, as it were. Just so I'd know she was there."

"You'll have to ask her not to do it."

"She knows that, too." His hands came together, gripping each other tightly and I realized she hadn't quite left yet. I let him be until he raised his head and I could see that the faraway look on his face was gone. "She understands, she really does. I know she does."

"Good. I'm glad. We can look at the next holo."

We looked at six more—a couple of display pieces normally presented on loop for continuous exhibition, a juvenile piece that had been badly received, and a thematic trilogy having to do with growing older. The juvenile piece was negligible in terms of his work as a whole—he no longer had any idea what it was like to be a child. The trilogy was interesting as a precursor of his present state; after viewing it, you might have thought he was having difficulty accepting the fact that he himself was growing older. But while he'd alluded to that earlier, I didn't think that was the bulk of his problem.

It was close to suppertime when we finished, so I let him go, pleaded fatigue for myself and headed for my room so I could review/relive everything on boost.

The last thing I had expected her to do was to come to me. How could Caverty possibly cope with his Entourage without her somewhere in the room doing whatever it was she did—I still hadn't figured out exactly what her function was, but whatever it was, she was good at it.

She didn't even knock. Knocking wasn't customary in this house, apparently. I was taking a semimeditative breather from boosted reviewing and she slipped into the room like a bit of cloth blown in by an errant draft.

"Hi," she said shyly, standing with her back against the door.

I gestured at one of the pudgy spot chairs. Not the closest one. She sank into it gingerly, keeping her hands on the sides of the cushions as though she might have to launch herself out of it on short notice.

"I know you must be wondering why I'm not at dinner," she said. "I don't always go. Sometimes I take a night off, eat in my room. But Caverty loves his public."

"Do you think a private Entourage qualifies as a 'public'?"

"In Caverty's case, yes, I think so. Public as opposed to the privacy of his mind."

I didn't feel like arguing it with her so I let it go.

"We live a very balanced life here. You may not think so but it is. Every element is carefully balanced against every other element. The Entourage population stabilized a little while ago and it provides Caverty with the security he needs to be able to work."

"But he isn't able to work."

"Well, no, not now but before he hit this rough patch in his creativity, he was able to work very well."

"You're the second person, I think, who's told me that the Entourage has 'stabilized.'"

She nodded. "And?"

"I wouldn't call it stabilization."

"What, then?"

"I'd call it entropy."

She drew back slightly, as though I'd taken a swipe at her.

"Or stagnation. I'm sorry if that hurts your feelings."

Mad-a-LAYNE laughed. "*My* feelings?"

"Or whomever's you've got."

Still smiling, she leaned forward. "I could have anybody's. Everybody's. You know us empaths. Especially those of us with a stronger telepathic bent than most."

I felt that brush against my mind again; she didn't persist.

"You're resistant, though. I guess most mindplayers are. All that holding yourself together that you do when you're in contact with someone else's mind. Holding your identity together. Holding tight to what you are. Isn't that the way they put it in mindplayer school, or wherever it is you go to learn how to handle those *machines?* Hold tight to what you are, am I right?"

I had the sensation of the room rearranging itself around us so that we were squared off against each other. Beside me, my system was assembled, the optic nerve connections capped but primed and ready for use.

"*Am* I right? Hold tight to what you are?"

"Generally the client isn't trying to get *at* what you are. So it isn't really necessary to go around clenched like a fist."

"Then why do you?"

"I'm sure it must seem that way to you, having such free access to all the people around here. But I'm really quite normal."

"Normal in whose terms? Them, out there in the world, where you use that *can opener* to break into people's minds?"

I shook my head. "I think I'd better go."

"What?" A look of panic, now. "Wait—why?"

Half out of my own chair, I paused. "*Why?* You must know."

"No, I don't. I *would* know if you didn't shut me out."

I saved my laugh for later, on the trip home. "It's not the sort of thing you need empathic powers to know."

"For me, it is."

I started to disassemble the system. "He's going to know. Caverty, I mean. He'll know what's happened between us just now and he won't be able to work with me."

She got up and came over to me, intending to put her hand on my arm; I stepped away from the system quickly. "Sorry," she said, putting the hand behind her back. "I wasn't thinking. I just wanted you to stop that. You mustn't leave."

"I don't think there's much choice any more."

"I really didn't mean to do this, to try to force you out of here. I was just—" She blew out a frustrated breath. "I'm sorry. I don't even know how to begin to try to explain it to you, I'm so used to just letting people know how I feel. Especially when the feeling is so complex. Do you know how that is, to feel so many different things at one moment?" She paused. "Or is that not being properly *deadpan?*"

She wiped both hands over her face and through her hair, turning away from me. "So many misunderstandings because *words* get in the way. People unable to imagine how other people feel because you can't explain to someone with just *words* a feeling of jealousy and gladness mixed up with the desire to see a loved one succeed."

I refrained from pointing out that she just had. "Just because you don't have emotional access to me doesn't mean that I have no understanding. I don't *have* to feel exactly what you feel to know what it is." I shrugged. "In any case, I still have to leave."

"No. Please don't. Caverty would never forgive me."

"Sure he would."

She allowed herself a tremulous, momentary smile. "Yes, he would. But I don't want to put him through the effort. *I* would never forgive *myself*, and the effect of that on Caverty would be horrible. I agreed to your conditions voluntarily, I urged Caverty to go along with them. If I sabotage everything, Caverty won't have a chance."

"Of course he will," I said quietly, though I tended to doubt it.

She looked over at me sharply. "I meant he won't have a chance to find out whether this could have worked for him or not."

"Oh. Yes, that *is* different."

"You see? Another misunderstanding because of *words*. If you'd been open to me, you would have understood what I meant instantly."

I did not tell her I didn't see why that was necessarily a better arrangement than the usual conversational mode of imparting information, emotional or otherwise. Not to mention the fact that there wouldn't have been a misunderstanding had there been *enough* words. NN, I thought, was going to give me a medal for self-control when he reviewed my report.

"Anyway," she said, softening, "you mustn't leave. Please. I promise I won't interfere any more."

"It's not that," I said. "It's that Caverty's going to know what happened between us."

"You'd tell him?"

"No. But you would. You couldn't help yourself."

She drew herself up. "Yes, I can. I can hold as tight to my own as you can to yours. I can keep feelings from him or allow them out as I choose. And I promised not to touch him while you're working with him, so I won't even have to make the effort. I *will* keep from touching him. And you. I *will*." She paused. "Stay?"

I nodded, without words.

I could tell he'd slept well and it surprised me. I'd have thought the prospect of meeting me in his studio/sanctorum shortly after dawn without Mad-a-LAYNE would have kept him on the thin edge of wakefulness for most of the night. It must have been a terrific dinner for him, the whole Entourage love-bombing him with lots of acclaim and reassurance. Either that or Mad-a-LAYNE had been with him after all, in spite of her protests to me. As I worked at reassembling the system, I found myself hoping she had. I would hook in with Caverty, discover she'd lied, disconnect, and go home. End of story.

The way I was wanting forever to get out of there, you'd have thought I'd have done just that, said to hell with it all and risked whatever NN's professional wrath would have brought. If anything. I'd turned down jobs before and NN hadn't sued me. I'd even cut some short and NN had seen the correctness of my action. But I'd never backed out of one and I just wasn't sure how the old bastard would take that. Of course, I hadn't wanted it in the first place but I'd allowed myself to be talked into it—my own fault, really. Which I guess was why I kept reassembling the system in Caverty's studio, and primed the optic nerve connections and got him all settled and comfortable on a chaise and removed his beautiful biogem eyes and hooked him into a building-colors relaxation exercise. It had been my own idea to skip the real-time outside exercises. Somehow a round of *What Would You Do?* or *What Do You Hear In These Pictures?* just didn't seem right for him. There were a couple of others I might have tried with him, including *Finish the Following*, which NN himself had invented for visual artists, involving real-time completion of a partial image but no doubt that would have made him feel as though I were forcing his hand. As it were. Besides, I felt the more time he could spend getting accustomed to being inward without Mad-a-LAYNE, the easier it would be to work with him.

I had the system run continuous checks on his vitals while I prepared myself to meet him mind-to-mind. He showed no signs of panicking or disintegrating so I took my time. I had to; there were a lot of feelings to put away.

He'd been in the relaxation exercise for nearly half an hour before I felt prepared enough to remove my own eyes and slip them into solution and a little longer after I hooked myself up to the system before I allowed it to bring my consciousness and his together.

The contact was gradual. I chose a new color as a vehicle and slipped in among the others he had been forming. He sensed me immediately and accepted the contact just as quickly. The colors cleared out, leaving us in a visualization not of his studio but of the banquet hall where dinner were celebrated every night.

Well, he said, *here we are.*

Is this where you keep your holos?

No. It's where I keep myself. My self, I mean.

What do you do here?

He looked around and I looked with him. The room seemed pretty much as it was in realife, down to the buffet tables, except he had not visualized food on them. I saw the area where I had sat with the domestic actor the first night I'd been there; it too was empty. I was about to repeat my question when the room began to darken, first in the corners and then spreading out in waves of shadows.

This is what I do here, he said. *I don't be alone here.*

I don't be alone is an awkward verbalization of what it was and not quite what he said but that was the way I received it. Before I could get meaning around it, the shadows had formed themselves into images of the Entourage, ghostly and nowhere near as substantial as our own representations but somehow no less present. Immediately they were cluttering up everything, hanging all over us as though we were underwater with a lot of rags and scarves.

Come on now, I coaxed, holding my patience. *You can clear them all out.*

A ghost of the umbrella woman flowed over his face. *Yes, I can,* he said.

I waited and he waited to see what I was waiting for. I felt the warm brush of someone's presence and for a moment I was nose to nose with the woman who'd had a cage on her head. Admiration, envy, a sense of accomplishment . . . the emotions belonged to several different people. I brushed her away.

Caverty?

If I want to. That's what it is, you see. I can clear them all out if I want to. But I don't want to. I don't want to! I! DON'T! WANT! TO!

It was a mental blast that blew me into the center of the room. I flew through the ghosts, tasting a thousand different emotions in a second, the admiration, the desire to be close, the envy, the sorrow, the loneliness, the gladness, the fatigue of routine followed by the sense of security, the euphoria, the craving that is addiction and most of all the appeasement that came both from having received something and having had something taken, the sweet need of being increased, the even sweeter need of being diminished.

They meant to pin me but ghosts can't really do anything, not even mental ones. I spread them out easily, clearing an area around myself big enough to accommodate myself and Caverty's ego.

I know you don't want to, Caverty, I said, calling to him through the wraiths wrapping themselves around his face, *but if you're willing to join me here, you can and it won't be me forcing you to do anything. Understand?*

Understand, they all said, Caverty and all of them together. *Don't want to, though!*

Then that's it, I said. *We don't have anything more to do.*

Arlen The Bear floated over me with his big arms held out. *Are you sure about that?* he asked with Caverty's mental voice.

I pulled all the way into myself so they—*he, Caverty,* I reminded myself—so he wouldn't feel my anger for the time and effort wasted when he'd never intended to try working with me. For several mental moments,

I was aware only of composing myself. When I came out of it to face Caverty again, he was much closer than before, almost intrusive. My alarm nearly showed; after eight years without any mindplaying, he shouldn't have had that much skill at creeping up on me. Time to go, I thought, threw myself out of the visualization into the relaxation exercise. Caverty followed me and the colors caught him like quicksand and held him.

Even so, the taste of his consciousness seemed slow to fade out of my own mind, as though he were still chasing me anyway. My problem, I thought; sometimes the most unlikely people can get a hook into you and it's hell to get out. When I got home, I'd have myself dry-cleaned. And at NN's expense.

I disconnected from the system the moment it told me I could do so without trauma, groped for my eyes and couldn't contain the sigh of relief at finding them still in the container. I popped them back in and just sat for several minutes in Caverty's comfortable chair, rocking back and forth and breathing my way down to a calm state.

We were alone in the room. I hadn't expected us to be. I'd expected to come out and find them all there, waiting, wanting to—I forced the thought away before my heartrate could increase again.

Caverty lay on his chaise, completely relaxed. I had a strong urge to just leave him like that, limp and blind and harmless, and sneak out of the house and run all the way back to the agency. We hadn't even touched on ideas or holos or creativity or anything vaguely related. I hadn't even found any *memories*—just that damned Entourage, as present in his brain as it was outside of it.

Except for Mad-a-LAYNE, I realized. I hadn't felt her in there anywhere. As though she didn't exist.

I shook away my questions. Ask later; get out now. *Now.* But it was another minute before I could bring myself to touch Caverty even just to disconnect him from the system and put his eyes back in.

"Jesus," he said, sitting up slowly. He rubbed his forehead in a dazed way. "I didn't realize that—I didn't realize." He looked up at me pleadingly. "I don't know what to say to you."

I capped his connections and slipped them into a drawer in the system. "You don't have to say anything. I'll be going now."

"We aren't going to try again?"

"I don't think we can. Not until you do something about the general population in there."

He touched his forehead again. "They are all in there, aren't they?"

"Oh, yes."

"And I think if you hooked in with each of them, you'd find me in every single one."

"That's right."

"Madeleine?"

I nodded. "Prolonged empathy."

A slow smile spread across his face. "Sometimes I was afraid it hadn't worked. But Madeleine was right." His eyes narrowed. "And that's why you don't want to try again. Because I like it."

"Not the only reason, but that's part of it."

"And you *don't* like it."

I shrugged. "If you like it, it doesn't make much difference about me."

Without saying anything, he got up, stretched, and walked over to the pile of unused holo equipment. I paused for a moment, watching him, and then capped the set of connections I'd used. "I'd appreciate it if Harmony or someone would call me a flyer." No response. He didn't even look at me. "As for your fee, my agency may give you a partial refund. Minus expenses and time spent in the system." Still no response. I couldn't even get a clear reading of his Emotional Index. Maybe he was thinking about what it meant to give up the art for the audience. I didn't know and I really didn't want to. I moved around to the other side of the system to run a three-second diagnostic before disassembling the components and turned my back to him. It was the dumbest thing I ever did.

Coming to from a state of unconsciousness when you're hooked into the system is like going from death to a dream. For a while, you don't even know you're conscious and when you finally do realize it, the vertigo is furious. You fall in every direction at once, through every idea and thought you have. It seems like you'll fall forever and then you grab onto something, some concept, some belief, some identity thing, and you hold as tight as you can for a long time. And then, a mental century later, you feel steady enough to look around and see where you are and why and who else is there, if anyone.

I was back in the banquet room again, except this one was *my* banquet room, not the one in Caverty's mind, and there was no one there but me. At the moment. I could sense him nearby, though, waiting for me to tell him to come in.

I don't work that way, Caverty, I said and strode to the door. It was a big wooden antique with a shiny carved handle. *I'm coming out to you.*

I yanked at the handle. It wouldn't budge. Smoothing out the panic ripples, I stepped back from the door and gathered my strength into my hands, making them big, even bigger than Arlen The Bear's, and took hold of the handle again, intending to crush it. It swelled to fit my palms and even as I pressed on it, my hands were shrinking.

I jumped back, looking around for another way out.

Forget it, said the chandelier. Harmony. *You don't want to leave. You don't know what it's like to feel that way, to not want to leave. If you did, you'd feel differently.*

I didn't want to deal with that absurdity, nor did I want them to sense how trapped I felt. *All right,* I said, *standoff. I don't get out and you don't get in.*

Wrong.

Softer than a whisper; quieter than a brush against you in passing. She stood in the center of the empty room, very small. Delicate, even; a delicate vessel filled with so many feelings. She came toward me. I tried to back away but the floor shifted under me, keeping me in the same spot but still letting her approach.

They'll know how you feel and you'll know how they feel, she said gently. Cracks appeared in the wall behind her. *Without a word needing to be spoken.* Her arms reached for me.

Somehow, I managed to pull back a little. The cracks in the wall grew larger; faces showed through. Not ghosts this time.

We're all here now. We thought it could work made contact with Caverty after you hooked in together, but we were wrong. Your concentration would allow only limited contact. We were all ghosts and I couldn't even appear. You didn't even recognize us as being present. So I made contact with Caverty and then we hooked you in with him. Much better. It's working now.

She did not quite have me, though; she couldn't quite reach through the layers of deadpan to my core.

Every relationship is something like this, she said, trying to pull me closer. *People feed on each other whether it's lover to lover, friend to friend, audience to artist. We consume, we are consumed. You couldn't live otherwise. We've just refined it, made it more efficient—more satisfying. You'll see. Dinner here is always an Event. Especially when we finally get something new in. A nice change, to have variety in the menu. It's been a long time since the last one.*

I struggled back a little more, gaining ground even though the cracks in the walls were opening wider. *The only problem is I'm not willing.*

And as soon as I said it, I knew *that* was the dumbest thing I'd ever done. Admitting to it, admitting to anything at all gave her the lever she needed to pry off the last of Deadpan, leaving naked Allie.

The walls, as they say, came tumbling down while Mad-a-LAYNE lowered me to the floor. They swelled around her, blocking out the light with their faces.

Unwillingness, she said, face close to mine, *is a feeling. We know how you feel.*

And they did, every single one of them, while she directed traffic. Caverty. Harmony. Arlen The Bear, the chubby man, the domestic drama guy. The Nordic blonde in the kimono. The umbrella woman, the chicken people. Even Priscilla. Even Priscilla. Over and over again. Over and over and over.

Maybe it went on for days. Maybe only hours. When Mad-a-LAYNE disconnected me, I was asleep. In Caverty's studio. They were all gone. Sleeping it off themselves. I staggered around and when my vision cleared, I figured out how to pack my system up.

They should have caught me going down the stairs with it. Priscilla the cop, you know. I got to the bottom of the stairs and that Compass and I thought I *was* caught because someone came out from behind the staircase. I didn't recognize the face but I remembered the style of dress and the manner. Employee. That's when I found out I couldn't talk, right then, because I was going to beg for mercy and nothing came out. Like the record skipped the groove. You remember records. He didn't say anything, either. He just took one look at me and went over to the panel near the front door and pressed a button. I was too fried to run for it so I just waited for them all to come swooping down on me but the house stayed quiet. A little later— I don't know how little, my sense of time was still gone—I heard the flyer land outside. Completely automated, no pilot. I looked through the navigator program and found a picture of a place I liked. Not telling you what it looked like. I just punched for it and off I went and here I am and that's about all.

Yah, so maybe they meant to let me go? Could be. Maybe they figured I'd be too disoriented to turn up anywhere. I guess maybe they didn't want to keep me because they'd *stabilized,* you see. They were all so proud of having *stabilized,* they didn't need a new item on the menu permanently. Just for a change of pace.

Yah, so. I could let you find me and you could get them, right. I mean, this is big-time mindcrime here.

So you go ahead and go get them.

But you're not getting me.

It's peaceful now. I won't ever have to hook in with anyone again or talk, ever. I like that idea. It appeals to my basic deadpan nature, see. I don't want to know how anyone feels anymore. And I don't want anyone knowing how I feel, either. Caverty's Entourage, they're not the only ones who feed off each other's emotions. Everybody does it, even just a little bit. I'm not taking any chances anymore. Nobody else is going to feed off me. They all know how I feel and that's enough. That's enough.

Clang-clang. Clang-clang.

Ever since the first story about Deadpan Allie, "The Pathosfinder," appeared in 1981, there's been the potential for a story involving vampirism. "Dirty Work" was, in fact, the second story I set out to write, but after two pages, I put it away. It was too soon. Five years later, Ellen Datlow began putting together this nontraditional vampirism anthology and we both agreed Allie was a natural.

Ellen got upset with me for what happened to Allie. "How could you do that to her, you creep?" she said. I thought, *gosh, maybe I should have given Allie more of a break—maybe I've been entirely too merciless.*

And then I thought, *Naaah.*

Pat Cadigan

A WHISPER
OF BLOOD

18 More Tales of Vampirism

In memory of Blue

Acknowledgments

I'd like to thank the following people for helping to make this anthology possible: Merrilee Heifetz, David Hartwell, Rob Killheffer, Ginjer Buchanan, Don Keller, and, as always, all the contributors.

CONTENTS

INTRODUCTION

*I*n *Blood Is Not Enough,* I wanted to extend the boundaries of what a vampire is—expand the bloodsucker image into the concept of vampirism. I believe I succeeded. With *A Whisper of Blood,* I had intended to see just *how* far I could take the concept without any actual bloodsucking. But my editor, and certain avid fans of the vampire-as-entity who had read and enjoyed the first volume, expressed dismay that I planned to include no actual vampires. So . . . here and there among these metaphorical bloodsuckers lurks a vampire or two. You'll know them when you see them.

Admittedly, some of the stories are a stretch—at least three posit *situations* as vampiric in nature. In "The Pool People," the act of rape has drained the victim of her essential selfhood, she no longer trusts herself or others; in "Teratisms," a family's human monster, and a promise, have robbed the siblings of their own lives, their hopes, even their selves; and in "Folly for Three," the bizarre means of keeping a relationship alive not only drains the participants of any love they may feel for each other but ultimately destroys them as well. "Do I Dare to Eat a Peach?" is about the "State" stealing a man's soul, and in both "The Moose Church" and "Mrs. Rinaldi's Angel," dreams have an enervating effect on the dreamer.

The concept of vampirism can be seen as a metaphor for negative relationships. In these stories, our ideas of love and devotion and loyalty—parental, spousal, friendly, student/teacher, employer/employee—are all perverted in some way, and betrayals abound. The factor of betrayal seems inherent in the idea of the vampire: After all, by showing one hospitality (inviting one into your house) you get bitten. By looking for love (seduction), you get bitten and infected (how appropriate in today's sexual climate). And not only is just one person infected, but the contagion spreads—physically, in the case of the vampire; metaphorically, in other sorts of vampirism—one person's perversion, as in "Teratisms," can corrupt the whole family structure; the ripples of faithlessness in "Infidel" can, it is hinted, spread heresy throughout Christendom; the ruling class's desire to maintain the status quo in "Requiem" forces stagnation upon the entire world.

Anyone picking up this book will have encountered the vampire in fiction before—at least, will have seen *Dracula* or *The Lost Boys*—and so will have already developed some ideas or feelings relating to vampirism. For some, the vampire inspires fear, horror, or terror; for others, the vampire is a seductive creature and promises sex, freedom from ordinary restraint, and immortality. Tapping into the preexisting emotional context that the reader brings to the concept of vampirism, the stories gain an extra dimension, an added edge.

The focus is on the negative relationships themselves, and, in most of the stories here, on the victim. Because of this emphasis on the victim's reaction to the rape, the reader doesn't care about the psychology of the rapist—whether he was abused as a child; or if the dependent aged parent is a ravening monster, the plight of the child in devoting herself to his care is highlighted, rather than the misery of the parent—at least for the duration of the storytelling.

On a panel at the World Fantasy Convention one year, Doug Winter claimed that most horror published today supports the status quo and makes us feel safe. He wasn't wrong. He was talking about *bad* horror fiction. Complacency is, to me, the antithesis of good horror. Effective horror should disturb, perhaps disgust, and, hopefully, linger in the mind of the reader, and like all the best fiction should provoke the reader's self-examination. It can do this by using supernatural elements or psychological ones. The supernatural used to be a comforting way of looking at evil. It came from outside of us and so we weren't responsible for it. I think that the real world has become a much more frightening place, and to many people today it seems easier to believe in the monstrosity of man (after Hitler and Hiroshima) than it is to believe in outside devils who made them/us do it. The prominence of the serial killer in real life and in fiction (particularly the ground-breaking novels by Thomas Harris, *Red Dragon* and *The Silence of the Lambs*) has produced a rash of "psycho-killer" novels and stories. Man has become the monster/demon.

I'm a nonbeliever in the supernatural, which doesn't mean I can't be temporarily frightened by good supernatural fiction. Whether horror can accomplish its purpose is of course dependent on the effectiveness of the storytelling. When I was younger, I was more easily influenced and impressed by the fiction I read: I read and reread Fowles's *The Magus* and Hesse's *Steppenwolf.* They told me things about myself that I might have been better off not knowing but I loved them anyway for making me think. I find there is very little so-called mainstream fiction that can still do that for me. But great weird fiction or horror can occasionally accomplish that. For me, the best horror fiction (or any fiction) works on more than one level—the melody first, to get my attention, the middle and lower ranges to hold it, and to force me to reevaluate the story and, far more rarely, the way I live my life. Horror fiction is meant to disturb complacency and challenge assumptions and I hope the stories in *A Whisper of Blood* will do that for all of you.

Ellen Datlow,
New York

NOW I LAY ME
DOWN TO SLEEP

Suzy McKee Charnas

Charnas's reluctant vampire, Rose, is a far cry from her famous Professor Weyland. She is not aggressive and means no harm. Despite this, her motivation for becoming a vampire is the same as most other vampires—the desire to cheat death and claim immortality for oneself. Although Rose is one of the few actual vampires in this anthology, she is not by nature a predator and this story is a somewhat gentle piece to soothe the reader into the horror to come.

After Rose died, she floated around in a nerve-wracking fog for a time looking for the tunnel, the lights, and other aspects of the near-death experience as detailed in mass-media reports of such events.

She was very anxious to encounter these manifestations since apparently something loomed in the offing, in place of the happy surcease of consciousness her father had insisted on as the sequel to death. The older she had grown, the more inclined Rose had been to opt for Papa Sol's opinion. Maybe he would show up now trying to explain how he was right even though he was wrong, a bewildered figure of light along with Mom and Nana and everybody?

It would be nice to see a familiar face. Rose felt twinges of panic laced with a vague resentment. Here she was with the gratifyingly easy first step taken, and nothing was going on. Since she was still conscious, shouldn't there be something to exercise that consciousness on?

A siren wailed distantly. Suddenly she found herself walking on—or almost on, for her feet made only the memory of contact—the roof of her apartment building with its expensive view eastward across Central Park.

She hadn't been to the park in years, nor even outside her own apartment. Her minute terrace had provided quite enough contact with the streets below. As far as Rose was concerned, these streets were not the streets she had grown up in. She preferred the comfortable security of her own apartment.

Being on the roof felt very odd, particularly since it seemed to be broad daylight and cold out. Far below in the street she could see one of the doormen waving down a cab; he wore his overcoat with the golden epaulets on the shoulders. Rose could have sworn she had taken her carefully hoarded pills late at night, in the comfortable warmth of 14C. Why else would she be wearing her blue flannel nightgown?

Turning to go back to the refuge of her own place, she found an Angel standing close behind her. She knew him—it?—at once by its beautifully modeled, long-toed feet, the feet of a Bernini Angel she had seen in an Italian church on a tour with Fred. Indeed, the entire form was exactly that of the stone Angel she remembered, except that the exposed skin was, well, skin-toned, which she found unsettling. Like colorizing poor old Humphrey Bogart.

"Leave me alone," she said. "I don't want to go."

"You'll go," the Angel said in a drifting, chiming voice that made her ears itch. "Eventually. Everyone does. Are you sure you want to stand out there like that? I wouldn't say anything, but you're not really used to it yet."

Rose looked down and discovered that she had unwittingly backed off or through or over the parapet and now hovered nineteen stories above the street. She gasped and flailed about, for though she had no body to fall—nor for that matter arms to flail or breath to gasp with—sensory flashes still shot along her shadowy, habitual nerve pathways.

Thus the Angel's fingers closed, cool and palpable, on hers and lifted her lightly back onto the roof. She snatched her hand back at once. No one had touched her in years except her doctor, and that didn't count.

But it was not really the Angel's touch she feared.

"I don't want to go anywhere," she said, unable to bring herself to mention by name the anywhere she did not wish to go. "I'm a suicide. I killed myself."

"Yes," the Angel said, clasping its hands in front of its chest the way Dr. Simkin always used to do when he was about to say something truly outrageous. But it said nothing more.

"Well, how does—how do you, um, all feel about that, about people who kill themselves?" She knew the traditional answer, but dared to hope for a different one.

The Angel pursed its perfect lips. "Grouchy," it replied judiciously.

Unwillingly Rose recalled instances from the Old Testament of God's grouchiness. Actually there had been no Bible in her parents' house. She had read instead a book of Bible stories slipped to her one birthday by Nana and kept hidden from Papa Sol. Even watered down for kids, the stories had been frightening. Rose trembled.

"I was brought up an atheist," she said faintly.

The Angel answered, "What about the time you and Mary Hogan were going to run away and enter a convent together?"

"We were kids, we didn't know anything," Rose objected. "Let me stay here. I'm not ready."

"You can't stay," the Angel said. Its blank eyes contrasted oddly with its earnest tone of voice. "Your soul without its body is light, and as memories of the body's life fade, the spirit grows lighter, until you'll just naturally rise and drift."

"Drift? Drift where?" Rose asked.

"Up," the Angel said. Rose followed the languid gesture of one slender hand and saw what might to living eyes seem just a cloud bank. She knew it was nothing of the kind. It was a vast, angry, looming presence of unmistakable portent.

She scuttled around trying to put the Angel between herself and the towering form. At least the face of cloud was not looking at her. For the moment. Luckily there was lots else to look down disapprovingly at in New York City, most of it a good deal more entertaining than Rose Blum.

She whispered urgently to the Angel, "I changed my mind, I want to go back. I can see now, there are worse things than having your cats die and your kids plan to put you away someplace for your own good. Let them, I'll go, they can have my money, I don't care."

"I'm sorry," the Angel said, and Rose suddenly saw herself from above, not her spirit self but her body, lying down there in the big white tub. The leaky old faucets still dribbled in a desultory way, she noted with an exasperated sigh. Her "luxury" building had high ceilings and the rooms were sizable, but the plumbing was ancient.

Her pale form lay half submerged in what looked like rust-stained water. Funny, she had forgotten entirely that after the pills she had taken the further step of cutting her wrists in the bath. The blue nightgown was an illusion of habit.

Not a bad body for her age, she reflected, though it was essentially an Old World model, chunky flesh on a short-boned frame. The next generation grew tall and sleek, a different species made for playing tennis and wearing the clothes the models in the magazines wore. Though her granddaughter Stephanie, now that she thought of it, was little, like Rose herself; petite, but not so wide-hipped, an improved version of the original import with a flavor of central Europe and probably an inclination to run to fat if allowed.

Good heavens, somebody was in there, also looking at her—two men, Bill the super and Mr. Lum the day concierge! Rose recoiled, burning with shame. Her vacated body couldn't even make the gestures of modesty.

They were talking, the two of them. She had given them generous holiday tips for years to repay them for helping her organize a life that had never required her to leave her apartment after Fred's death and the consequent money squabbles in the family.

Bill said, "Two mil at least, maybe more on account of the terrace."

Mr. Lum nodded. "Forgot the terrace," he said.

She wished she hadn't tipped them at all. She wished her body didn't look so—well—dead. Definitively dead.

"Okay, I can't go back," she admitted to the Angel, relieved to find herself alone with it on the roof again. "But there must be something I can do besides go—you know." She shuddered, thinking of the monstrous shape lowering above her—a wrathful, a terrible, a vengeful God. She needed time to get used to the idea, after Papa Sol and a lifetime of living in the world had convinced her otherwise. Why hadn't somebody told her?

Well, somebody besides Mary Hogan, who had been a Catholic, for crying out loud.

"Well," the Angel said, "you can postpone."

"Postpone," Rose repeated eagerly. "That's right, that's exactly what I had in mind. How do I postpone?"

The Angel said, "You make yourself a body out of astral material: this." Its slim hand waved and a blur of pale filaments gathered at the tapered fingertips.

"Where did that stuff come from?" Rose said nervously. Was the Angel going to change form or disintegrate or do something nasty like something in a horror movie?

"It's all around everybody all the time," the Angel said, "because the physical world and the nonphysical world and everything in between interpenetrate and occupy the same space and time interminably."

"I don't understand physics," Rose said.

"You don't need to," the Angel said. "Astral sculpting is easy, you'll get the hang of it. With a body made of this, you can approach living people and ask them to help you stay. At night, anyway—that's when they'll be able to see you."

Rose thought of Bill and Mr. Lum standing there talking about the value of her apartment. Then she thought of her kids whom she hadn't liked for quite a while and who didn't seem to like her either. Not much use asking them for anything. Maybe Frank, the elevator man? He had always struck her as decent.

"Help, how?" she asked.

"By letting you drink their blood," said the Angel.

Appalled, Rose said nothing for a moment. Down below, a taxi pulled in at the awning and disgorged a comically foreshortened figure. Rose watched this person waddle into the building. "Drink their blood," she said finally. "I'm supposed to go around drinking blood, like Dracula?"

The Angel said, "You need the blood to keep you connected with the physical world. But you can't take it against a person's will, you have to ask. That's the meaning of the business about having to be invited into the donor's house. The house is a metaphor for the physical shell—"

"I'm a vampire?" Rose cried, visions of Christopher Lee and Vampirella and the rest from late-night TV flashing through her stunned mind.

"You are if you want to put off going up," the Angel said with a significant glance skyward. "Most suicides do."

Rose didn't dare look up and see if the mighty cheek of cloud had turned her way.

"That's why suicides were buried at crossroads," the Angel went on, "to prevent their return as vampires."

"Nobody gets buried at a crossroad!"

"Not now," the Angel agreed, "and cremation is so common; but ashes don't count. It's no wonder there's a vampire craze in books and movies. People sense their presence in large numbers in the modern world."

"This is ridiculous," Rose burst out. "I want to see somebody senior to you, I want to talk to the person in—"

She stopped. The Person in charge was not likely to be sympathetic.

The Angel said, "I'm just trying to acquaint you with the rules."

"I'm dead," Rose wailed. "I shouldn't have rules!"

"It's not all bad," the Angel said hastily. "You can make your astral body as young as you like, for instance. But sunlight is a problem. Living people have trouble seeing astral material in sunlight."

For the first time in years she wished Fred were around, that con man. He could have found a way out of this for her if he'd felt like showing off.

"It's not fair!" Rose said. "My G— Listen, what about crosses? Am I supposed to be afraid of crosses?"

"Well," the Angel said, "in itself the cross is just a cross, but there's the weight of the dominant culture to consider, and all its symbols. When western people see a cross, what are they most likely to think of, whether they're personally Christians or not?"

Rose caught herself in time to avoid glancing upward at the shadow giant in the sky. Little changes of terror ran through her so that she felt herself ripple like a shower curtain in a draft. No poor scared dead person would be able to hold her astral self together under that kind of stress.

The Angel began to move away from her, pacing solemnly on the air over the street where a cab trapped by a double-parked delivery truck was honking dementedly.

"Wait, wait," Rose cried, ransacking her memory of *Dracula*, which she and her sister had read to each other at night by flashlight one winter. "What about crossing water? Is it true that a vampire can't cross water?"

"Running water can disorient you very severely," the Angel said over its exquisite shoulder. "You could find yourself visiting places you never meant to go to instead of the ones you did."

Water flows downhill, Rose thought. Down. Hell was down, according to Mary Hogan, anyway. She made a shaky mental note: Don't cross running water.

"How am I supposed to remember all this?" she wailed.

The Angel rose straight into the air without any movement of the translucent wings she now saw spreading from its back. "Just think of the movies," it said. "Film is the record of the secret knowledge of the cultural unconscious."

"You sound like Dr. Simkin, that terrible shrink my daughter sent me to," Rose accused the floating figure.

"I was Harry Simkin," the Angel replied. "That's why I'm doing your intake work." It folded its aristocratic hands and receded rapidly toward the high, rolling clouds.

"My God, you were a young man," Rose called after it. "Nobody told me you died."

The door onto the roof burst open with a crash and two boys lugging heavily weighted plastic bags tumbled out, shouting. Ignoring Rose, they rushed to the parapet. Each one took a spoiled grapefruit out of one of the bags and leaned out into space, giggling and pointing, choosing a passing car roof to aim for.

Rose sidled up to the smaller one and cleared her throat. As loudly as she could she said, "Young man, how would you like to meet a real vampire?"

He lobbed a grapefruit and ducked behind the parapet, howling in triumph at the meaty sound of impact from below but apparently deaf to Rose's voice. Revolting child. Rose bent over and tried to bite his neck. He didn't seem to notice. But she couldn't unwrap the scarf he wore, her fingers slipped through the fabric. So she aimed for a very small patch of exposed skin, but she had no fangs that she could discover and made no impression on his grimy neck.

The whole thing was a ludicrous failure. Worse, she couldn't imagine how it could work, which did not augur well for her future as a vampire. Maybe the Angel had lied. Maybe it was really a devil in disguise. She had never trusted that Simkin anyway.

Worst of all, she was continually aware of the looming, ever-darkening presence, distant but palpable to her spirit, of Him Whom Papa Sol had scoffed at with good socialist scorn. It was all so unfair! Since He was up there after all, why didn't He do something about these horrible boys instead of harassing a poor dead old woman?

Rose didn't want Him witnessing her ineptitude, which might inspire Him to drag her up there to face Him right now. She gave up on the grape-fruit-hurling boys and drifted back down to 14C.

It gave her some satisfaction to sift under the sealed apartment door in the form of an astral mist. She floated around admiring the handsomely appointed rooms; she had always had excellent taste.

In the bathroom the tub was empty and reeked of pine-scented disinfectant. Someone had already made off with her silver-backed hairbrush, she noted. But what did that matter, given that her strides were unusually long and slightly bounding, as if she were an astronaut walking on the moon? This could only mean that she was lightening up, just as the Angel had warned.

Frantically she clawed astral material out of the air and patted it into place as best she could, praying that in the absence of blood this astral gunk itself might help to hold her down until somebody came and consented to be a—donor. Her children would come, if only to calculate the considerable value of her things. She was determined to greet them as herself, or as near to that as she could get, to cushion the shock of her request for their donations.

She couldn't see herself in the mirror to check the likeness or to inspect her mouth for fangs. Astral material had a number of limitations, it seemed, among them inability to cast a reflection. She couldn't even turn on the television; her astral fingers wouldn't grip the switch. She couldn't pick up things, the Chinese figurines and fine French clocks that she had brought back from travel and had converted into lamps. Very nice lamps, too. Fred had done his import deals or whatever had been really going on—half the time she had thought him a secret arms trader—but Rose was the one who had had the eye.

My God, she'd been a shopper!

How light she was, how near to drifting—up. No wonder vampires were so urgent about their hunger. By the time Bill the super showed up with two yuppies in tow, Rose felt that for the first time she understood what her daughter Roberta used to mean by that awful phrase "strung out."

Bill was saying, "—first refusal on the lease, that's the law, but if nobody in the old lady's family wants to take it up, then—"

He saw her—the windowpanes, Rose noted, were now dark—and turned red. "I don't know how you got in here, lady, but you'll have to leave."

He didn't seem to recognize her. Of course he wasn't expecting her. Maybe she hadn't done such a hot job with the astral stuff?

She said firmly, "Bill, I have every right to be here, and if these are prospective new tenants you've sneaked in for bribe money, they ought to know that I'm staying."

The young woman said, "Excuse me, but who is this?"

The color drained from Bill's face. He said hoarsely, "What are you doing here, Mrs. Blum? You were dead in the tub, I found you." He waved his arms. "You can't stay here!"

"Let's cut the crap, all right?" the young man said. He thrust money at Rose. Several fifties and three of his fingers went through her forearm.

"Ted, she's a ghost," the woman said, clutching at his coat. "She must be the ghost of the woman who died here."

"Well," Ted said, letting his extended hand float slowly back down to his side. "Tiffany, honey, I think you're right. So, uh, what would you think about living in a haunted, I mean, co-occupying with, um? I'm sure we could work something out, a sort of time-share arrangement? I mean, look at the height of these ceilings."

Rose said, "Sure, we can fix it. All I need is for you to let me drink a little blood now and then. You could take turns."

"Ah, Jesus," sobbed Bill.

Tiffany's eyes bulged. "It's not a ghost," she gasped. "It's a vampire."

"How much blood, exactly?" Ted said, pale but still game.

"I don't exactly know," Rose said. "We'd have to experiment a little at first—"

They fled.

"That's a ten-thousand-dollar finder's fee you cost me!" howled Bill the super, lunging at her.

His breath reached her before he did, and Rose felt her careful astral assemblage fly apart. He had been eating garlic, and the fumes acted on her new body like acid. Her consciousness bounced around like a beach ball in the slipstream of a speeding truck as her body dissolved.

Bill jammed his fist into his mouth and ran, slamming the door so hard behind him that a very nice French Empire miniature fell off the wall.

"Garlic," said a familiar voice. "It's a remarkable food. Completely dissolves the cohesability of astral material."

Grabbing for errant parts of her body, Rose grumbled, "Why didn't you tell me?"

"I tried to cover everything," the Angel said.

"Listen, Dr. Simkin," Rose said. "I can't do this. I'm no vampire. I'm a nice Jewish girl."

"A nice Jewish radical girl, not religious at all," the Angel reminded her. "You named your first cat Emma Goldman."

"We were all freethinkers in those days, but so what? A Jew is a Jew, and Jews don't have vampires. I can't do this blood-drinking thing. It's not natural."

The Angel sighed. "It's your choice, of course, but you'll have to go up. Your life review is overdue as it is."

Rose thought of God reviewing her life. "What about you?" she said desperately. "You must be drinking blood yourself, to be sticking around driving me crazy like this. You could spare me some."

"Oh, no," the Angel said, "I do all my work strictly on the astral, nothing physical at all. I don't need weight."

"Why do you look like that?" Rose said. "Harry Simkin didn't look like that, don't think I don't remember."

"Well, I like it," the Angel answered rather shyly. "And I thought it would reassure you. You always had a good eye for art, Mrs. Blum."

"A lot of good it does me now," she said. "Listen, I want to talk to Fred. You know Fred, my husband?"

The Angel cocked its head to one side and rolled its blank eyes. Then it said, "Sorry, he's not available. He's finished his processing and moved on to another stage."

"What stage?" Rose said, feeling a surprising twinge of apprehension for Fred. She remembered all those *New Yorker* cartoons showing fat-bellied businessmen making glum quips to each other in hell, with pitchfork-toting devils leering in the background.

"Don't you think you have enough to deal with as it is?" the Angel countered. "You're bobbing, you know, and your head isn't on straight. It won't be long at this rate."

"I'll find somebody," Rose said quickly. "I need more time to get used to the idea."

"Don't take too long," the Angel said. "Isn't it interesting? This is the first time you've asked me about anybody who's come before you."

"What?" said Rose. "Anybody, who? Who should I ask about? I've been on my own for twenty years. Who cares for an old woman, so who should I care for?"

The Angel, inspecting its fingernails again, drifted silently out through the pane of the closed window.

It was very quiet in the apartment. The walls in these old buildings were very thick, with real plaster. Rose had peace and quiet in which to reassemble herself. It wasn't much fun—no point in making yourself look like, say, Marilyn Monroe if you couldn't see yourself in the mirror—and it wasn't easy, either. At one point she looked down and realized she had formed up the shape of her most recent cat, Mimsy, on a giant scale.

She was losing contact with her physical life, and nobody was likely to come around and help her reestablish it again for a while. Maybe never, if Bill the super went gibbering about what he'd seen in the apartment.

She hovered in front of the family photographs on the wall over the living-room mantel. The light was hard to see by, odd and watery—was it day or night?—but she knew who was who by memory: Papa Sol and Mama; Auntie Lil with that crazed little dog of hers, Popcorn was its name (God, she missed Mimsy, and the others); the two Kleinfeldt cousins who had gone to California and become big shots in television production; Nana in her old-fashioned bathing suit at Coney Island; Uncle Herb; more cousins. She had completely lost track of the cousins.

There was one picture of Fred, and several of the two cute babies who had turned into Mark and Roberta. I should have stuck to shopping and skipped the kids, she thought.

Two pictures showed Rose herself, once amid the cousins now scattered to their separate marriages and fates, and once with two school friends, girls whose names now escaped her. As everything seemed bent on escaping her. She sat in the big wing chair and crossed her astral arms and rocked herself, whispering, "Who cares for an old woman?"

There was no help, and no safe place. She had to hold on to the arms of her chair to keep from floating several inches off the seat. If she didn't get some blood to drink soon, she would float up before that huge, angry face in the sky and be cast into hell on a bolt of black thunder—

The door opened cautiously and a man walked into the apartment. It was her lawyer, Willard.

"Oh, my God," he murmured, looking straight at her. "They told me the place was haunted. Mrs. Blum, is that you?"

"Yes," she said. "What time is it, Willard?"

"Seven-thirty," he said, still staring. "I stayed late at the office."

Seven-thirty on a November evening; of course he could see her. She hoped her head was on straight and that it was her own head and not Mimsy's.

"Oh, Willard," she said, "I've been having the most terrible time." She stopped. She had never talked to anyone like that, or at least not for a very long time.

"No doubt, no doubt," he said, steadying himself against the hall table and putting his briefcase down carefully on the floor. "Do you still keep scotch in the breakfront?"

She did, for the occasional visitor, of which scant number Willard had been one. He poured himself a drink with shaking hands and gulped it, his eyes still fixed on Rose. He poured himself another. "I think I'd better tell you," he said in a high, creaky tone very unlike him, "this haunting business could have serious repercussions on the disposition of your estate."

"It's not haunting, exactly," Rose said, gliding toward him. She told him what it was, exactly.

"Ha, ha, you're kidding, Mrs. Blum," Willard said, smiling wildly and turning a peculiar shade of yellow. He staggered backward against the edge of the couch, turned, and fell headlong. His glass rolled across the carpet and clinked against the baseboard. Rose saw a pale mist drift out of the top of Willard's head as his body threshed briefly in the throes of what she immediately recognized as a heart attack like the one that had killed Fred.

"Willard, wait," she cried, seeing that his foggy spirit stuff was rapidly escaping upward into the ceiling. "Don't leave me!"

But he did.

Rose knelt by the body, unable to even attempt to draw its still and cooling blood. The Angel didn't show. Willard Carnaby must have gone directly wherever he was headed. She felt abandoned and she cried, or something like it, not for Willard, who had known, as usual, where to go and how to get there with a minimum of fuss, but for herself, Rose the vampire.

After they took the body away nobody came for days. Rose didn't dare to go out. She was afraid she would get lost in the uncertain light; she was afraid she would run into the outwash from some restaurant kitchen and be blasted to such smithereens by garlic fumes that she would never be able to get herself together again; she was afraid of water running in the gutters and crosses on churches. She was afraid of the eyes of God.

She was bumping helplessly against the bedroom ceiling in a doomed panic when someone did arrive. Not Roberta (as she at first thought because of the honey-gold hair) but Stephanie, from the next generation; her granddaughter, who wanted to be—what? An actress. She was certainly pretty enough, and so young. Rose blinked hungrily at her.

Someone was with her, a boy. Stephanie pulled back the curtains and daylight streamed in. She would not be able to see Rose, maybe not even hear her.

Rose noticed something new—a shimmer of color and motion around Stephanie, and another around this boy. If she concentrated hard, while floating after them as they strolled through the place giggling and chatting with their heads together, Rose could see little scenes like bits of color TV taking place within the aura of each of the young people: quick little loops of the two of them tangled in each other's arms in his, and a rapid wheel of scenes in Stephanie's aura involving this boy dancing with her, applauding from an excited audience, showing her off to important people.

Their hopes and dreams were visible to Rose, like sit-com scenes without sound. The walking-on-the-beach scene, a comfortable winter beach with gray skies and green sea and no sand fleas, Rose recognized at once. She had had the same fantasy about Fred.

While he was having, no doubt, fantasies like this boy's, of sex, sex, and more sex; and sex with another girl, some friend of Stephanie's—

"Dump him, Stephanie, he's nothing but a wolf," she said indignantly, out loud.

The boy was too rapt in his hormones to hear. Stephanie frowned and glanced sharply around the room.

"Come on," the boy said. "Who'd know? It would be exciting." Good grief, he was proposing that the two of them make love right here—on the floor, on Rose's antique Chinese carpet! Rose saw the little scene clearly in his aura.

Stephanie hesitated. Then she tossed her honey hair and called him an idiot and tugged him out of the place by the hand. But she came back. She came back alone after dark and without turning on the lights she sat down quietly in the big wing chair by the window.

"I heard you, Gramma Rose," she said softly, looking wide-eyed around the room. "I heard what you said to me about Jeff, and you're right, too. I know you're here. The stuff about the apartment being haunted is true, isn't it? I know you're here, and I'm not scared of you. You can come out, you can talk to me. Really. I'd like it."

Rose hung back, timid and confused now that her moment had come. After all, did she really want her grandchild's presumably fond memories of Gramma Rose replaced with the memory of Rose the vampire?

Stephanie said, "I won't go until you come talk to me, Gramma Rose."

She curled up on Rose's empty bed and went to sleep.

Rose watched her dreams winking and wiggling in her aura. Such an appealing mixture of cynicism and naïveté, so unlike her mother. Fascinated, Rose observed from the ceiling where she floated.

Involuntarily reacting to one of the little scenes, she murmured, "It's not worth fighting with your mother; just say yes and go do what you want."

Stephanie opened her eyes and looked directly up. Her jaw dropped. "Gramma Rose," she squeaked. "I see you! What are you doing up there?"

"Stephanie darling," Rose said in the weak, rusty voice that was all she could produce now, "you can help me. Will you help me?"

"Sure," Stephanie said, sitting up. "Didn't you stop me from making an utter idiot of myself with Jeff Stanhope, which isn't his real name of course, and he has a gossip drive on him that just won't quit. I don't know what I was thinking of, bringing him up here, except that he's cute of course, but actors are mostly cute. It's his voice, I think, it's sort of hypnotic. But you woke me up, just like they say, a still, small voice. So what can I do for you?"

"This will sound a little funny," Rose said anxiously—to have hope again was almost more than she could bear—"but could you stand up in the bed and let me try to drink a little blood from your neck?"

"Ew." Stephanie stared up at her. "You're kidding."

Rose said, "It's either that or I'm gone, darling. I'm nearly gone as it is."

"But why would it help to, ugh, suck a person's blood?"

"I need it to weigh me down, Stephanie. You can see how high I'm drifting. If I don't get some blood to anchor me, I'll float away."

"How much do you need?" Stephanie said cautiously.

"From you, darling, just a little," Rose assured her. "You have a rehearsal in the morning, I don't want to wear you out. But if you let me take a little,

I can stay, I can talk to you."

"You could tell me all about Uncle Herb and whether he was gay or not," Stephanie said, "and whether Great-Grandpa really left Hungary because of a quarrel with a hussar or was he just dodging the draft like everybody else—all the family secrets."

Rose wasn't sure she remembered those things, but she could make up something appropriate. "Yes, sure."

"Is this going to hurt?" Stephanie said, getting up on her knees in the middle of the mattress.

"It doesn't when they do it in the movies," Rose said. "But, Stephanie, even if there's a little pinprick, wouldn't that be all right? Otherwise I have to go, and, and I don't want to."

"Don't cry, Gramma Rose," Stephanie said. "Can you reach?" She leaned to one side and shut her eyes.

Rose put her wavery astral lips to the girl's pale skin, thinking, FANGS. As she gathered her strength to bite down, a warm sweetness flowed into her mouth like rich broth pouring from a bowl. She stopped almost at once for fear of overdoing it.

"That's nice," Stephanie murmured. "Like a toke of really good grass."

Rose, flooded with weight and substance that made her feel positively bloated after her recent starvation, put her arm around Stephanie's shoulders and hugged her. "Just grass," she said, "right? You don't want to poison your poor old dead gramma."

Stephanie giggled and snuggled down in the bed. Rose lay beside her, holding her lightly in her astral arms and whispering stories and advice into Stephanie's ear. From time to time she sipped a little blood, just for the thrill of feeling it sink through her newly solid form, anchoring it firmly to her own familiar bed.

Stephanie left in the morning, but she returned the next day with good news. While the lawyers and the building owners and the relatives quarreled over the fate of the apartment and everything in it (including the ghost that Bill the super wouldn't shut up about), Stephanie would be allowed to move in and act as caretaker.

She brought little with her (an actress has to learn to travel light, she told Rose), except her friends. She would show them around the apartment while she told them how the family was fighting over it, and how it was haunted, which made everything more complicated and more interesting, of course. Rose herself was never required to put in a corroborating appearance. Stephanie's delicacy about this surprised and pleased Rose.

Still, she preferred the times when Stephanie stayed home alone studying her current script, which she would declaim before the full-length mirror in the bedroom. She was a terrible show-off, but Rose supposed you had to be like that to be on the stage.

Rose's comments were always solicited, whether she was visible or not. And she always had a sip of blood at bedtime.

Of course this couldn't go on forever, Rose understood that. For one thing, at the outer edges of Stephanie's aura of thoughts and dreams she could see images of a different life, somewhere cool and foggy and hemmed in with dark trees, or city streets with a vaguely foreign look to them. She became aware that these outer images were of likely futures that Stephanie's life was moving toward. They didn't seem to involve staying at Rose's.

She knew she should be going out to cultivate alternative sources for the future—vampires could "live" forever, couldn't they—but she didn't like to leave in case she couldn't get back for some reason, like running water, crosses, or garlic.

Besides, her greatest pleasure was coming to be that of floating invisibly in the air, whispering advice to Stephanie based on foresight drawn from the flickering images she saw around the girl:

"It's not a good part for you, too screechy and wild. You'd hate it."

"That one is really ambitious, not just looking for thrills with pretty actresses."

"No, darling, she's trying to make you look bad—you know you look terrible in yellow."

Rose became fascinated by the spectacle of her granddaughter's life shaping itself, decision by decision, before her astral eyes. So that was how a life was made, so that was how it happened! Each decision altered the whole mantle of possibilities and created new chains of potentialities, scenes and sequences that flickered and fluttered in and out of probability until they died or were drawn in to the center to become the past.

There was a young man, another one, who came home with Stephanie one night, and then another night. Rose, who drowsed through the days now because there was nothing interesting going on, attended eagerly, and invisibly, on events. The third night Rose whispered, "Go ahead, darling, it wouldn't be bad. Try the Chinese rug."

They tumbled into the bed after all; too bad. The under rug should be used for something significant, it had cost her almost as much per yard as the carpet itself.

Other people's loving looked odd. Rose was at first embarrassed and then fascinated and then bored: bump bump bump, squeeze, sigh, had she really done that with Fred? Well, yes, but it seemed very long ago and sadly meaningless. The person with whom it had been worth all the fuss had been—whatsisname, it hovered just beyond memory.

Fretful, she drifted up onto the roof. The clouds were there, the massive form turned toward her now. She cringed but held her ground. No sign from above one way or the other, which was fine with her.

The Angel chimed, "How are you, Rose?"

Rose said, "So what's the story, Simkin? Have you come to reel me in once and for all?"

"Would you mind very much if I did?"

Rose laughed at the Angel's transparent feet, its high, delicate arches. She was keenly aware of the waiting form of the cloud-giant, but something had changed.

"Yes," she said, "but not so much. Stephanie has to learn to judge things for herself. Also, if she's making love with a boy in the bedroom knowing I'm around, maybe she's taking me a little for granted. Maybe she's even bored by the whole thing."

"Or maybe you are," the Angel said.

"Well, it's her life," Rose said, feeling as if she were breaking the surface of the water after a deep dive, "not mine."

The Angel said, "I'm glad to hear you say that. This was never intended to be a permanent solution."

As it spoke, a great throb of anxiety and anger reached Rose from Stephanie.

"Excuse me," she said, and she dropped like a plummet back to her apartment.

The two young people were sitting up in bed facing each other with the table lamp on. The air vibrated with an anguish connected with the telephone on the bed table. In the images dancing in Stephanie's aura Rose read the immediate past: There had been a call for the boy, a screaming voice raw with someone else's fury. He had just explained to Stephanie, with great effort and in terror that she would turn away from him. The girl was indeed filled with dismay and resentment. She couldn't accept this dark aspect of his life because it had all looked so bright to her before, for both of them.

Avoiding her eyes, he said bitterly, "I know it's a mess. You have every right to kick me out before you get any more involved."

Rose saw the pictures in his aura, some of them concerned with his young sister who went in and out of institutions and, calamitously, in and out of his life. But many showed this boy holding Stephanie's hand, holding Stephanie, applauding Stephanie from an audience, sitting with Stephanie on the porch of a wooden house amid dark, tall trees somewhere—

Rose looked at Stephanie's aura. This boy was all over it. Invisible, Rose whispered in Stephanie's ear, "Stick with him, darling, he loves you and it looks like you love him, too."

At the same moment she heard a faint echo of very similar words in Stephanie's mind. The girl looked startled, as if she had heard this, too.

"What?" the boy said, gazing at her with anxious intensity.

Stephanie said, "Stay in my life. I'll try to stay in yours."

They hugged each other. The boy murmured into her neck, where Rose was accustomed to take her nourishment, "I was so afraid you'd say no, go away and take your problems with you—"

Seeing the shine of tears in the boy's eyes, Rose felt the remembered sensation of tears in her own. As she watched, their auras slowly wove together, flickering and bleeding colors into each other. This seemed so much more intimate than sex that Rose felt she really ought to leave the two of them alone.

The Angel was still on the roof, or almost on it, hovering above the parapet.

Rose said, "She doesn't need me anymore; she can tell herself what to do as well as I can, probably better."

"If she'll listen," the Angel said.

Rose looked down at the moving lights of cars on the street below. "All right," she said. "I'm ready. How do I get rid of the blood I got from Stephanie this morning?"

"You mean this?" The Angel's finger touched Rose's chest, where a warm red glow beat in the place where her heart would have been. "I can get rid of it for you, but I warn you, it'll hurt."

"Do it," Rose said, powered by a surging impatience to get on with something of her own for a change, having been so immersed in Stephanie's raw young life—however long it was now. Time was much harder to divide intelligibly than it had been.

The Angel's finger tapped once, harder, and stabbed itself burningly into her breast. There came a swift sensation of what it must feel like to have all the marrow drawn at once from your bones. Rose screamed.

She opened her eyes and looked down, gasping, at the Angel. Already she was rising like some light, vaned seed on the wind. She saw the Angel point downward at the roof with one glowing, crimson finger. One flick and a stream of bright fire shot down through the shadowy outline of the building and landed—she saw it happen, the borders of her vision were rushing away from her in all directions—in the kitchen sink and ran away down the drain.

Stephanie turned her head slightly and murmured, "What was that? I heard something."

The boy kissed her temple. "Nothing." He gathered her closer and rolled himself on top of her, nuzzling her. What an appetite they had, how exhausting!

Other voices wove in and out of their murmuring voices. Rose could see and hear the whole city as it slowly sank away below her, a net of lights slung over the dark earth.

But above her—and she no longer needed to direct her vision to see what was there but saw directly with her mind's eye—the sky was thick with a massed and threatening darkness that she knew to be God: still waiting, scowling, implacable, for His delayed confrontation with Rose.

Despite the panic pulsating through her as the inevitable approached, she couldn't help noticing that there was something funny about God. The closer she got, the more His form blurred and changed, so that she caught glimpses of tiny figures moving, colors surging, skeins of ceaseless activity going on all at once and overlapping inside the enormous cloudy bulk of God.

She recognized the moving figures: Papa Sol, teasing her at the breakfast table by telling her to look, quick, at the horse on the windowsill, and grabbing one of the strawberries from her cereal while she looked with eager, little-girl credulity; Roberta, crying and crying in her crib while grown-up Rose hovered in the hallway torn between exhaustion and rage and love and fear of doing the wrong thing no matter what she did; Fred, sparkling with lying promises he'd never meant to keep, but pleased to entertain her with them; Stephanie, with crooked braids and scabby knees, counting the pennies from the penny jar that Rose had once kept for her. And that was the guy, there, Aleck Mills, one of Fred's associates, with whom love had felt like love.

If she looked beyond these images, Rose realized that she could see, deeper in the maze, the next phase of each little scene, and the next, the whole spreading tangle of consequences that she was here to witness, to comprehend, and to judge.

The web of her awareness trembled as it soared, curling in on itself as if caught in a draught of roasting air.

"Simkin, where are you?" she cried.

"Here," the Angel answered, bobbing up alongside of her and looking, for once, a bit flustered with the effort of keeping up. "And you don't need me anymore. Guardian angels don't need guardian angels."

"Now I lay me down to sleep," Rose said, remembering that saccharine Humperdinck opera she had taken Stephanie to once at Christmas time, years ago, because it was supposed to be for kids. "A bunch of vampires watch do keep?"

"You could put it that way," the Angel said.

"What about Dracula?" Rose said. "Could I have done that instead?"

"Sure," the Angel said. "There's always a choice. Who do you think it is who goes around making deals for the illusion of immortal life? And the price isn't anything as romantic as your soul. It's just a little blood, for as long as you're willing."

"And when you stop being willing?"

The Angel flashed its blank eyes upward. "Your life will wait as long as it has to."

"I'm scared of my life," Rose confessed. "I'm scared there's nothing worthwhile in it, nothing but furniture, and statuettes made into lamps."

"Kid," the Angel said, "you should have seen mine."

"Yours?"

"Full of people I tried to make into furniture, all safe and comfortable, with lots of dust cuzzies stuck underneath."

"What's in mine?" Rose said.

"Go and see," the Angel said gently.

"I am, I'm going," Rose said. In her heart she moaned, This will be hard, this is going to be so hard.

But she was heartened by a little scene flickering high up where God's eye would have been if there had been a god instead of this mountain of Rose's own life, and in that scene Stephanie and the boy did walk together on a winter beach. By the way they hugged and turned up their collars and hurried along, it was cold and windy there; but they kept close together and made blue-lipped jokes about the cold.

Beyond them, beyond the edges of the cloud-mountain itself, Rose could make out nothing yet. Perhaps there was nothing, just as Papa Sol had promised. On the other hand, she thought, whirling aloft, so far Papa Sol had been 100 percent dead wrong.

I never expected to write another vampire story after *The Vampire Tapestry*, but Ellen said, "C'mon, c'mon," and after a while something started (as a story about people walking their dogs, actually, but that's one reason I am so slow to produce work—everything starts somewhere else and the real story has to be teased out into the light). And pretty soon I was working on the old bloodsucker concept with a different perspective than that which produced Dr. Weyland, my 1980 model of the beast.

For one thing, I'm fifty years old and more inclined than I was to contemplate last things. Also, like many of my generation I have numerous elderly relatives, most of them (though not all) female, most of them living alone; so maybe it's not at all surprising that this story became Rose's story. I'm glad it did.

And then, too, the more clearly one recognizes that what's frightening about life in the world is the destructive flailings of people's fears, and the more sophisticated those fears become in a sophisticated age, the more quaintly baroque become such fusty old creatures of superstition as vampires; and one's approach alters accordingly.

On the other hand (not for nothing am I a Libra), I recently did a collaboration with Quinn Yarbro for the purposes of which I woke up Weyland. Now he won't lie down again, and he is a bit light in the quaint and endearing department. So who knows what coloring my next outing into this territory may take (if indeed there is a next outing that is fit to see print)? That's the nice thing about the career of making up stories—you can always change your mind and tell it the *other* way next time.

Suzy McKee Charnas

THE SLUG

Karl Edward Wagner

Here is a rather harsh view of those who interrupt the artist at work—
I wouldn't even want to speculate as to how close this story is to the author's
heart. . . .

Martine was hammering away to the accompaniment of Lou
Reed, tapedeck set at stun, and at first didn't hear the
knocking at her studio door. She set aside hammer and chisel, put Lou Reed
on hold, and opened the door to discover Keenan Bauduret seated on her
deck rail, leaning forward to pound determinedly at her door. The morning
sun shone bright and cheery through the veil of pines, and Keenan was
shit-faced drunk.

"Martine!" He lurched toward her. "I need a drink!"

"What you need is some coffee." Martine stood her ground. At six feet
and change she was three inches taller than Keenan and in far better shape.

"Please! I've got to talk to someone." Keenan's soft brown eyes implored.
He was disheveled and unshaven in baggy clothes that once had fit him, and
Martine thought of a stray spaniel, damp and dirty, begging to be let in. And
Keenan said: "I've just killed someone. I mean, some thing."

Martine stepped inside. "I can offer gin and orange juice."

"Just the gin."

Keenan Bauduret collapsed onto her wooden rocking chair and mopped
at his face with a crumpled linen handkerchief, although the morning was
not yet warm. Now he reminded her of Bruce Dern playing a dissolute
southern lawyer, complete with out-of-fashion and rumpled suit; but in fact

Keenan was a writer, although dissolute and southern to be sure. He was part of that sort of artist/writer colony that the sort of small university town such as Pine Hill attracts. Originally he was from New Orleans, and he was marking time writing mystery novels while he completed work on the Great Southern Novel. At times he taught creative writing for the university's evening college.

Martine had installed a wet bar complete with refrigerator and microwave in a corner of her studio to save the walk back into her house when she entertained here. She sculpted in stone, and the noise and dust were better kept away from her single-bedroom cottage. While Keenan sweated, she looked for glasses and ice.

"Just what was it you said that you'd killed?"

"A slug. A gross, obscene, mammoth, and predatory slug."

"Sounds rather like a job for Orkin. Did you want your gin neat?"

"Just the naked gin."

Martine made herself a very light gin screwdriver and poured a double shot of Tanqueray into Keenan's glass. Her last name was still McFerran, and she had her father's red hair, which she wore in a long ponytail, and his Irish blue eyes and freckled complexion. Her mother was Scottish and claimed that her side of the family was responsible for her daughter's unexpected height. Born in Belfast, Martine had grown up in Pine Hill as a faculty brat after her parents took university posts here to escape the troubles in Northern Ireland. Approaching the further reaches of thirty, Martine was content with her bachelorhood and her sculpture and had no desire to return to Belfast.

"Sure you don't want orange juice?" She handed the glass to Keenan.

Keenan shook his head. "To your very good health." He swallowed half the gin, closed his eyes, leaned back in the rocker and sighed. He did not, as Martine had expected, tip over.

Martine sat down carefully in her prized Windsor chair. She was wearing scuffed Reeboks, faded blue jeans, and a naturally torn university sweatshirt, and she pushed back her sleeves before tasting her drink.

"Now, then," she said, "tell me what really happened."

Keenan studied his gin with the eye of a man who is balancing his need to bolt the rest of it against the impropriety of asking for an immediate refill. Need won.

"Don't get up." He smiled graciously. "I know the way."

Martine watched him slosh another few ounces of gin into his glass, her own mood somewhere between annoyance and concern. She'd known Keenan Bauduret casually for years, well before he'd hit the skids. He was a few years older than she, well read and intelligent, and usually fun to be around. They'd never actually dated, but there were the inevitable meetings at parties and university town cultural events, lunches and dinners and a few drinks after. Keenan had never slept over, nor had she at his cluttered little house. It was that sort of respectful friendship that arises between two lonely people who are content within their self-isolation, venturing forth for non-threatening companionship without ever sensing the need.

"I've cantelope in the fridge," Martine prompted.

"Thanks. I'm all right." Keenan returned to the rocker. He sipped his gin this time. His hands were no longer shaking. "How well do you know Casper Crowley?"

"Casper the Friendly Ghost?" Martine almost giggled. "Hardly at all. That is, I've met him at parties, but he never has anything to say to anyone. Just stands stuffing himself with chips and hors d'oeuvres—I've even seen him pocket a few beers as he's left. I'm told he's in a family business, but no one seems to know what that business is—and he writes books that no one I know has ever read for publishers no one has heard of. He's so dead dull boring that I always wonder why anyone ever invites him."

"I've seen him at your little gatherings," Keenan accused.

"Well, yes. It's just that I feel sorry for poor boring Casper."

"Exactly." Keenan stabbed a finger and rested his case. "That's what happened to me. You won't mind if I have another drink while I tell you about it?"

Martine sighed mentally and tried not to glance at her watch.

His greatest mistake, said Keenan, was ever to have invited Casper Crowley to drop by in the first place.

It began about two years ago. Keenan was punishing the beer keg at Greg Lafollette's annual birthday bash and pig-picking. He was by no means sober, or he never would have attempted to draw Casper into conversation. It was just that Casper stood there, wrapped in his customary loneliness, mechanically feeding his face with corn chips and salsa, washing it down with great gulps of beer, as expressionless as a carp taking bread crumbs from atop a pool.

"How's it going, Casper?" Keenan asked harmlessly.

Casper shaved his scalp but not his face, and he had bits of salsa in his bushy orange beard. He was wearing a tailored tweed suit whose vest strained desperately to contain his enormous beer gut. He turned his round, bland eyes toward Keenan and replied: "Do you know much about Aztec gods?"

"Not really, I suppose."

"In this book I'm working on," Casper pursued, "I'm trying to establish a link between the Aztecs and Nordic mythology."

"Well, I do have a few of the usual sagas stuck away on my shelves." Keenan was struggling to imagine any such link.

"Then would it be all right if I dropped by your place to look them over?"

And Casper appeared at ten the following morning, while Keenan was drying off from his shower, and he helped himself to coffee and doughnuts while Keenan dressed.

"Hope I'm not in your way." Casper was making a fresh pot of coffee.

"Not at all." Keenan normally worked mornings through the afternoon, and he had a pressing deadline.

But Casper plopped down on his couch and spent the next few hours leafing without visible comprehension through various of Keenan's books, soaking up coffee, and intermittently clearing his throat and swallowing horribly. Keenan no longer felt like working after his guest had finally left. Instead he made himself a fifth rum and Coke and fell asleep watching *I Love Lucy*.

At ten the following morning, Keenan had almost reworked his first sentence of the day when Casper phoned.

"Do you know why a tomcat licks his balls?"

Keenan admitted ignorance.

"Because he can!"

Casper chuckled with enormous relish at his own joke, while Keenan scowled at the phone. "How about going out to get some barbecue for lunch?" Casper then suggested.

"I'm afraid I'm really very busy just now."

"In that case," Casper persisted, "I'll just pick us up some sandwiches and bring them on over."

And he did. And Casper sat on Keenan's couch, wolfing down barbecue sandwiches with the precision of a garbage disposal, dribbling gobbets of sauce and cole slaw down his beard and belly and onto the upholstery. Keenan munched his soggy sandwich, reflecting upon the distinction between the German verbs, *essen* (to eat) and *fressen* (to devour). When Casper at last left, it was late afternoon, and Keenan took a nap that lasted past his usual dinnertime. By then the day had long since slipped away.

He awoke feeling bloated and lethargic the next morning, but he was resolved to make up for lost time. At ten-thirty Casper appeared on his doorstep, carrying a bag of chocolate-covered raspberry jelly doughnuts.

"Do you know how many mice it takes to screw in a light bulb?" Casper asked, helping himself to coffee.

"I'm afraid I don't."

"Two—but they have to be real small!" Jelly spurted down Casper's beard as he guffawed. Keenan had never before heard someone actually guffaw; he'd always assumed it was an exaggerated figure of speech.

Casper left after about two in the afternoon, unsuccessful in his efforts to coax Keenan into sharing a pizza with him. Keenan returned to his desk, but inspiration was dead.

And so the daily routine began.

"Why didn't you just tell him to stay away and let you work?" Martine interrupted.

"Easy enough to say," Keenan groaned. "At first I just felt sorry for him. OK, the guy is lonely—right? Anyway, I really was going to tell him to stop bugging me every day—and then I had my accident."

A rain-slick curve, a telephone pole, and Keenan's venerable VW Beetle was grist for the crusher. Keenan fared rather better, although his left foot would wear a plaster sock for some weeks after.

Casper came over daily with groceries and bottles of beer and rum. "Glad to be of help," he assured Keenan as he engulfed most of a slice of pepperoni-and-mushroom pizza. Sauce obscured his beard. "Must be tough having to hobble around day after day. Still, I'll bet you're getting a lot of writing done."

"Very little," Keenan grudgingly admitted. "Just haven't felt up to it lately."

"Guess you haven't. Hey, do you know what the difference is between a circus and a group of sorority girls out jogging?"

"I give up."

"Well, one is a cunning array of stunts!" Casper chortled and wiped red sauce from his mouth. "Guess I better have another beer after that one!"

Keenan missed one deadline, and then he missed another. He made excuses owing to his accident. Deadlines came around again. The one novel he did manage to finish came back with requests for major revisions. Keenan worked hard at the rewrite, but each new effort was only for the worse. He supposed he ought to cut down on his drinking, but the stress was keeping him awake nights, and he kept having nightmares wherein Casper crouched on his chest and snickered bad jokes and dribbled salsa. His agent sounded concerned, and his editors were losing patience.

"Me," said Casper, "I never have trouble writing. I've always got lots of ideas."

Keenan resisted screaming at the obese hulk who had camped on his sofa throughout the morning. Instead he asked civilly: "Oh? And what are you working on now?"

"A follow-up to my last book—by the way, my publisher really went ape-shit over that one, wants another like it. This time I'm writing one that traces the rise of Nazi Germany to the Druidic rites at Stonehenge."

"You seem to be well versed in the occult," observed Keenan, repressing an urge to vomit.

"I do a lot of research," Casper explained. "Besides, it's in my blood. Did I ever tell you that I'm related to Aleister Crowley?"

"No."

"Well, I am." Casper beamed with secret pride.

"I should have guessed."

"Well, the name, of course."

Keenan had been thinking of other similarities. "Well, I really do need to get some work done now."

"Sure you don't need me to run you somewhere?"

"No, thank you. The ankle is a little sore, but I can get around well enough."

At the door, Casper persisted: "Sure you don't want to go get some barbecue?"

"Very sure."

Casper pointed toward the rusted-out Chevy wagon in Keenan's driveway. "Well, if that heap won't start again, just give me a call."

"I put in a new battery," Keenan said, remembering that the mechanic had warned him about the starter motor. Keenan had bought the clunker for three hundred bucks—from a student. He needed wheels, and wheels were about all that did work on the rust-bucket. His insurance hadn't covered replacement for his antique Beetle.

"Heard you had to return your advance on that Zenith contract."

"Where'd you hear that?" Keenan wanted to use his fists.

"My editor—your old editor—brought it up when we were talking contract on my new book the other day. She said for me to check out how you were getting along. Sounded concerned. But I told her you were doing great, despite all the talk."

"Thanks for that much."

"Hey, you know the difference between a sorority girl and a bowling ball?"

Keenan did not trust himself to speak.

"No? Well, you can't stuff a sorority girl into a bowling ball!"

After the university informed Mr. Bauduret that his services would no longer be required as instructor of creative writing at the evening college, Keenan began to sell off his books and a few antiques. It kept the wolves at arm's length, and it paid for six-packs. Editors no longer phoned, and his agent no longer answered his calls.

Casper was sympathetic, and he regularly carried over doughnuts and instant coffee, which he consumed while drinking Keenan's beer.

"Zenith gobbled up *Nazi Druids*," he told Keenan. "They can't wait for more."

The light in Keenan's eyes was not the look of a sane man. "So, what's next?"

"I got an idea. I've discovered a tie-in between flying saucers and the Salem witch burnings."

"They hanged them. Or pressed them. No burnings in this country."

"Whatever. Anyway, I bought a bunch of your old books on the subject at the Book Barn the other day. Guess I won't need to borrow them now."

"Guess not."

"Hey, you want some Mexican for lunch? I'll pay."

"Thank you, but I have some work to do."

"Good to see you're still slugging away."

"Not finished yet."

"Guess some guys don't know when they're licked."

"Guess not."

"Hey"—Casper chugged his beer—"you know what the mating cry of a sorority girl is?"

Keenan gritted his teeth in a hideous grin.

Continued Casper in girlish falsetto: "Oh, I'm so-o-o drunk!" His belly shook with laughter, although he wasn't Santa. "Better have another beer on that one!"

And he sat there on the couch, methodically working his way through Keenan's stock of beer, as slowly mobile and slimy gross as a huge slug feasting its way across the garden. Keenan listened to his snorts and belches, to his puerile and obscene jokes, to his pointless and inane conversation, too drained and too weak to beg him to leave. Instead he swallowed his beer and his bile, and fires of loathing stirred beneath the ashes of his despair.

That night Keenan found the last bottle of rum he'd hidden away against when the shakes came at dawn, and he dug out the vast file of typed pages, containing all the fits and starts and notes and revisions and disconnected chapters that were the entirety of his years' efforts toward the Great Southern Novel.

He had a small patio, surrounded by a neglected rock garden and close-shouldering oak trees, and he heaped an entire bag of charcoal into the barbecue grill that rusted there. Then Keenan sipped from the bottle of Myers's, waiting for the coals to take light. When the coals had reached their peak, Keenan Bauduret fed his manuscript, page by crumpled page, onto the fire; watched each page flame and char, rise in dying ashes into the night.

"That was when I knew I had to kill Casper Crowley."

Martine wasn't certain whether she was meant to laugh now. "Kill

Casper? But he was only trying to be your friend! I'm sure you can find a way to ask him to give you your space without hurting his feelings."

Keenan laughed instead. He poured out the last of her gin. "A friend? Casper was a giant grotesque slug! He was a gross leech that sucked out my creative energy! He fed off me and watched over me with secret delight as I wasted away!"

"That's rather strong."

"From the first day the slug showed up on my doorstep, I could never concentrate on my work. When I did manage to write, all I could squeeze out was dead, boring, lifeless drivel. I don't blame my publishers for sending it back!"

Martine sighed, wondering how to express herself. She did rather like Keenan; she certainly felt pity for him now. "Keenan, I don't want to get you upset, but you have been drinking an awful lot this past year or so. . . ."

"Upset?" Keenan broke into a wild grin and a worse laugh, then suddenly regained his composure. "No need for me to be upset now. I've killed him."

"And how did you manage that?" Martine was beginning to feel uneasy.

"How do you kill a slug?"

"I thought you said he was a leech."

"They're one and the same."

"No they're not."

"Yes they are. Gross, bloated, slimy things. Anyway, the remedy is the same."

"I'm not sure I'm following you."

"Salt." Keenan seemed in complete control now. "They can't stand salt."

"I see." Martine relaxed and prepared herself for the joke.

Keenan became very matter-of-fact. "Of course, I didn't forget the beer. Slugs are drawn to beer. I bought many six-packs of imported beer. Then I prepared an enormous barbecue feast—chickens, ribs, pork loin. Casper couldn't hold himself back."

"So you pushed his cholesterol over the top, and he died of a massive coronary."

"Slugs can't overeat. It was the beer. He drank and drank and drank some more, and then he passed out on the patio lounge chair. That was my chance."

"A steak through the heart?"

"Salt. I'd bought dozens of bags of rock salt for this. Once Casper was snoring away, I carried them out of my station wagon and ripped them open. Then, before he could awaken, I quickly dumped the whole lot over Casper."

"I'll bet Casper didn't enjoy that."

"He didn't. At first I was afraid he'd break away, but I kept pouring the rock salt over him. He never said a word. He just writhed all about on the lounge chair, flinging his little arms and legs all about, trying to fend off the salt."

Keenan paused and swallowed the last of the gin. He wiped his face and shuddered. "And then he began to shrivel up."

"Shrivel up?"

"The way slugs do when you pour salt on them. Don't you remember? Remember doing it when you were a kid? He just started to shrivel and shrink. And shrink and shrink. Until there was nothing much left. Just a dried-out twist of slime. No bones. Just dried slime."

"I see."

"But the worst part was the look in his eyes, just before they withered on the ends of their stalks. He stared right into my eyes, and I could sense the terrible rage as he died."

"Stalks?"

"Yes. Casper Crowley sort of changed as he shriveled away."

"Well. What did you do then?"

"Very little to clean up. Just dried slime and some clothes. I waited through the night, and this morning I burned it all on the barbecue grill. Wasn't much left, but it sure stank."

Keenan looked at his empty glass, then glanced hopefully at the empty bottle. "So now it's over. I'm free."

"Well," said Martine, ignoring his imploring gaze, "I can certainly see that you've regained your imagination."

"Best be motivating on home now, I guess." Keenan stood up, with rather less stumbling than Martine had anticipated. "Thanks for listening to my strange little story. Guess I didn't expect you to believe it all, but I had to talk to someone."

"Why not drive carefully home and get some sleep," Martine advised, ushering him to the door. "This has certainly been an interesting morning."

Keenan hung on to the door. "Thanks again, Martine. I'll do just that.

Hey, what do you say I treat you to Chinese tomorrow for lunch? I really feel a whole lot better after talking to you."

Martine felt panic, then remorse. "Well, I am awfully busy just now, but I guess I can take a break for lunch."

Martine sat back down after Keenan had left. She was seriously troubled, wondering whether she ought to phone Casper Crowley. Clearly Keenan was drinking far too heavily; he might well be harboring some resentment. But harm anyone . . . No way. Just some unfunny attempt at a shaggy dog story. Keenan never could tell jokes.

When she finally did phone Casper Crowley, all she got was his answering machine.

Martine felt strangely lethargic—her morning derailed by Keenan's bursting in with his inane patter. Still, she thought she really should get some work done on her sculpture.

She paused before the almost finished marble, hammer and chisel at ready, her mind utterly devoid of inspiration. She was working on a bust of a young woman—the proverbial artist's self-portrait. Martine squared her shoulders and set chisel to the base of the marble throat.

As the hammer struck, the marble cracked through to the base.

Not much need be said, actually. Every writer—every creative person—lives in dread of those nagging and inane interruptions that break the creative flow. A sentence perfectly crystallized, shattered by a stupid phone call, never regained. A morning filled with inspiration and energy, clogged by an uninvited guest, the day lost. The imaginative is the choice prey of the banal, and uncounted works of excellence have died stillborn thanks to junk phone calls and visits from bored associates.

After all, a writer doesn't have a real job. Feel free to crash in at any time. Probably wants some company.

Nothing in this story is in any way a reflection upon this one writer's various friends, nor does it in any way resemble any given actual person or composite of any persons known to the author. It is entirely a fictitious work and purely the product of the author's imagination.

It has taken me five days to scribble out this afterword.

There's the door....

Karl Edward Wagner

WARM MAN

Robert Silverberg

This story, the first of many that Robert Silverberg sold to Fantasy &
Science Fiction *magazine, juxtaposes Aickmanesque tone and subtlety with
a satire of suburban manners. In it, he explores the dangerous addiction of
an empath.*

No one was ever quite sure just when Mr. Hallinan came to live in
New Brewster. Lonny Dewitt, who ought to know, testified that
Mr. Hallinan died on December 3, at 3:30 in the afternoon, but as for the
day of his arrival no one could be nearly so precise.

It was simply that one day there was no one living in the unoccupied
split-level on Melon Hill, and then the next *he* was there, seemingly having
grown out of the woodwork during the night, ready and willing to spread
his cheer and warmth throughout the whole of the small suburban
community.

Daisy Moncrieff, New Brewster's ineffable hostess, was responsible for
making the first overtures toward Mr. Hallinan. It was two days after she
had first observed lights on in the Melon Hill place that she decided the
time had come to scrutinize the newcomers, to determine their place in
New Brewster society. Donning a light wrap, for it was a coolish October
day, she left her house in the early forenoon and went on foot down
Copperbeech Road to the Melon Hill turnoff, and then climbed the sloping
hill till she reached the split-level.

The name was already on the mailbox: DAVID HALLINAN. That probably
meant they'd been living there a good deal longer than just two days, thought

Mrs. Moncrieff; perhaps they'd be insulted by the tardiness of the invitation? She shrugged and used the doorknocker.

A tall man in early middle age appeared, smiling benignly. Mrs. Moncrieff was thus the first recipient of the uncanny warmth that David Hallinan was to radiate throughout New Brewster before his strange death. His eyes were deep and solemn, with warm lights shining in them; his hair was a dignified gray-white mane.

"Good morning," he said. His voice was deep, mellow.

"Good morning. I'm Mrs. Moncrieff—*Daisy* Moncrieff, from the big house on Copperbeech Road. You must be Mr. Hallinan. May I come in?"

"Ah—please, no, Mrs. Moncrieff. The place is still a chaos. Would you mind staying on the porch?"

He closed the door behind him—Mrs. Moncrieff later claimed that she had a fleeting view of the interior and saw unpainted walls and dust-covered bare floors—and drew one of the rusty porch chairs for her.

"Is your wife at home, Mr. Hallinan?"

"There's just me, I'm afraid. I live alone."

"Oh." Mrs. Moncrieff, discomforted, managed a grin nonetheless. In New Brewster *everyone* was married; the idea of a bachelor or a widower coming to settle there was strange, disconcerting . . . and just a little pleasant, she added, surprised at herself.

"My purpose in coming was to invite you to meet some of your new neighbors tonight—if you're free, that is. I'm having a cocktail party at my place about six, with dinner at seven. We'd be so happy if you came!"

His eyes twinkled gaily. "Certainly, Mrs. Moncrieff. I'm looking forward to it already."

The *ne plus ultra* of New Brewster society was impatiently assembled at the Moncrieff home shortly after 6, waiting to meet Mr. Hallinan, but it was not until 6:15 that he arrived. By then, thanks to Daisy Moncrieff's fearsome skill as a hostess, everyone present was equipped with a drink and a set of speculations about the mysterious bachelor on the hill.

"I'm sure he must be a writer," said Martha Weede to liverish Dudley Heyer. "Daisy says he's tall and distinguished and just *radiates* personality. He's probably here only for a few months—just long enough to get to know us all, and then he'll write a novel about us."

"Hmm. Yes," Heyer said. He was an advertising executive who commuted to Madison Avenue every morning; he had an ulcer, and was acutely aware of his role as a stereotype. "Yes, then he'll write a sizzling novel exposing suburban decadence, or a series of acid sketches for *The New Yorker.* I know the type."

Lys Erwin, looking desirable and just a bit disheveled after her third martini in thirty minutes, drifted by in time to overhear that. "You're *always* conscious of *types,* aren't you darling? You and your gray flannel suit?"

Heyer fixed her with a baleful stare but found himself, as usual, unable to make an appropriate retort. He turned away, smiled hello at quiet little Harold and Jane Dewitt, whom he pitied somewhat (their son Lonny, age 9, was a shy, sensitive child, a total misfit among his playmates), and confronted the bar, weighing the probability of a night of acute agony against the immediate desirability of a Manhattan.

But at that moment Daisy Moncrieff reappeared with Mr. Hallinan in tow, and conversation ceased abruptly throughout the parlor while the assembled guests stared at the newcomer. An instant later, conscious of their collective faux pas, the group began to chat again, and Daisy moved among her guests, introducing her prize.

"Dudley, this is Mr. Davis Hallinan. Mr. Hallinan, I want you to meet Dudley Heyer, one of the most talented men in New Brewster."

"Indeed? What do you do, Mr. Heyer?"

"I'm in advertising. But don't let them fool you; it doesn't take any talent at all. Just brass, nothing else. The desire to delude the public, and delude 'em good. But how about you? What line are you in?"

Mr. Hallinan ignored the question. "I've always thought advertising was a richly creative field, Mr. Heyer. But, of course, I've never really known at firsthand—"

"Well, I have. And it's everything they say it is." Heyer felt his face reddening, as if he had had a drink or two. He was becoming talkative, and found Hallinan's presence oddly soothing. Leaning close to the newcomer, Heyer said, "Just between you and me, Hallinan, I'd give my whole bank account for a chance to stay home and *write.* Just write. I want to do a novel. But I don't have the guts; that's my trouble. I know that come Friday there's a $350 check waiting on my desk, and I don't dare give that up. So I keep writing my novel up here in my head, and it keeps eating me away down here in my gut. *Eating.*" He paused, conscious that he had said too much and that his eyes were glittering beadily.

Hallinan wore a benign smile. "It's always sad to see talent hidden, Mr. Heyer. I wish you well."

Daisy Moncrieff appeared then, hooked an arm through Hallinan's, and led him away. Heyer, alone, stared down at the textured gray broadloom.

Now why did I tell him all that? he wondered. A minute after meeting Hallinan, he had unburdened his deepest woe to him—something he had not confided in anyone else in New Brewster, including his wife.

And yet—it had been a sort of catharsis, Heyer thought. Hallinan had calmly soaked up all his grief and inner agony, and left Heyer feeling drained and purified and warm.

Catharsis? Or a blood-letting? Heyer shrugged, then grinned and made his way to the bar to pour himself a Manhattan.

As usual, Lys and Leslie Erwin were at opposite ends of the parlor. Mrs. Moncrieff found Lys more easily, and introduced her to Mr. Hallinan.

Lys faced him unsteadily, and on a sudden impulse hitched her neckline higher. "Pleased to meet you, Mr. Hallinan. I'd like you to meet my husband, Leslie. *Leslie!* Come here, please?"

Leslie Erwin approached. He was twenty years older than his wife, and was generally known to wear the finest pair of horns in New Brewster—a magnificent spread of antlers that grew a new point or two almost every week.

"Les, this is Mr. Hallinan. Mr. Hallinan, meet my husband, Leslie."

Mr. Hallinan bowed courteously to both of them. "Happy to make your acquaintance."

"The same," Erwin said. "If you'll excuse me, now—"

"The louse," said Lys Erwin when her husband had returned to his station at the bar. "He'd sooner cut his throat than spend two minutes next to me in public." She glared bitterly at Hallinan. "I don't deserve that kind of thing, do I?"

Mr. Hallinan frowned sympathetically. "Have you any children, Mrs. Erwin?"

"Hah! He'd never give me any—not with *my* reputation! You'll have to pardon me; I'm a little drunk."

"I understand, Mrs. Erwin."

"I know. Funny, but I hardly know you and I like you. You seem to *understand*. Really, I mean." She took his cuff hesitantly. "Just from looking at you, I can tell you're not judging me like all the others. I'm not really *bad*, am I? It's just that I get so *bored*, Mr. Hallinan."

"Boredom is a great curse," Mr. Hallinan observed.

"Damn right it is! And Leslie's no help—always reading his newspapers and talking to his brokers! But I can't help myself, believe me." She looked around wildly. "They're going to start talking about us in a minute, Mr. Hallinan. Every time I talk to someone new they start whispering. But promise me something—"

"If I can."

"Someday—someday soon—let's get together? I want to *talk* to you. God, I want to talk to someone—someone who understands why I'm the way I am. Will you?"

"Of course, Mrs. Erwin. Soon." Gently he detached her hand from his sleeve, held it tenderly for a moment, and released it. She smiled hopefully at him. He nodded.

"And now I must meet some of the other guests. A pleasure, Mrs. Erwin."

He drifted away, leaving Lys weaving shakily in the middle of the parlor. She drew in a deep breath and lowered her décolletage again.

At least there's one decent man in this town now, she thought. There was something *good* about Hallinan—good, and kind, and understanding.

Understanding. That's what I need. She wondered if she could manage to pay a visit to the house on Melon Hill tomorrow afternoon without arousing too much scandal.

Lys turned and saw thin-faced Aiken Muir staring at her slyly, with a clear-cut invitation on his face. She met his glance with a frigid, wordless *go to hell.*

Mr. Hallinan moved on, on through the party. And, gradually, the pattern of the party began to form. It took shape like a fine mosaic. By the time the cocktail hour was over and dinner was ready, an intricate, complex structure of interacting thoughts and responses had been built.

Mr. Hallinan, always drinkless, glided deftly from one New Brewsterite to the next, engaging each in conversation, drawing a few basic facts about the other's personality, smiling politely, moving on. Not until after he moved on did the person come to a dual realization: that Mr. Hallinan had said quite little, really, and that he had instilled a feeling of warmth and security in the other during their brief talk.

And thus while Mr. Hallinan learned from Martha Weede of her paralyzing envy of her husband's intelligence and of her fear of his scorn, Lys Erwin was able to remark to Dudley Heyer that Mr. Hallinan was a remarkably kind and understanding person. And Heyer, who had never been known to speak a kind word of anyone, for once agreed.

And later, while Mr. Hallinan was extracting from Leslie Erwin some of the pain his wife's manifold infidelities caused him, Martha Weede could tell Lys Erwin, "He's so gentle—why, he's almost like a saint!"

And while little Harold Dewitt poured out his fear that his silent 9-year-old son Lonny was in some way subnormal, Leslie Erwin, with a jaunty grin, remarked to Daisy Moncrieff, "That man must be a psychiatrist. Lord, he knows how to talk to a person. Inside of two minutes he had me telling him all my troubles. I feel better for it, too."

Mrs. Moncrieff nodded. "I know what you mean. This morning, when I went up to his place to invite him here, we talked a little while on his porch."

"Well," Erwin said, "if he's a psychiatrist he'll find plenty of business here. There isn't a person here riding around without a private monkey on his back. Take Heyer, over there—he didn't get that ulcer from happiness. That scatterbrain Martha Weede, too—married to a Columbia professor who can't imagine what to talk to her about. And my wife Lys is a very confused person, too, of course."

"We all have our problems," Mrs. Moncrieff sighed. "But I feel much better since I spoke with Mr. Hallinan. Yes: *much* better."

Mr. Hallinan was now talking with Paul Jambell, the architect. Jambell, whose pretty young wife was in Springfield Hospital slowly dying of cancer. Mrs. Moncrieff could well imagine what Jambell and Mr. Hallinan were talking about.

Or rather, what Jambell was talking about—for Mr. Hallinan, she realized, did very little talking himself. But he was such a *wonderful* listener! She felt a pleasant glow, not entirely due to the cocktails. It was good to have someone like Mr. Hallinan in New Brewster, she thought. A man of his tact and dignity and warmth would be a definite asset.

When Lys Erwin woke—alone, for a change—the following morning, some of the past night's curious calmness had deserted her.

I have to talk to Mr. Hallinan, she thought.

She had resisted two implied, and one overt, attempts at seduction the night before, had come home, had managed even to be polite to her husband. And Leslie had been polite to her. It was most unusual.

"That Hallinan," he had said. "He's quite a guy."

"You talked to him, too?"

"Yeah. Told him a lot. Too much, maybe. But I feel better for it."

"Odd," she had said. "So do I. He's a strange one, isn't he? Wandering around that party, soaking up everyone's aches. He must have had half the neuroses in New Brewster unloaded on his back last night."

"Didn't seem to depress him, though. More he talked to people, more cheerful and affable he got. And us, too. You look more relaxed than you've been in a month, Lys."

"I *feel* more relaxed. As if all the roughness and ugliness in me was drawn out."

And that was how it felt the next morning, too. Lys woke, blinked, looked at the empty bed across the room. Leslie was long since gone, on his way to the city. She knew she had to talk to Hallinan again. She hadn't got rid of it all. There was still some poison left inside her, something cold and chunky that would melt before Mr. Hallinan's warmth.

She dressed, impatiently brewed some coffee, and left the house. Down Copperbeech Road, past the Moncrieff house where Daisy and her stuffy husband Fred were busily emptying the ashtrays of the night before, down to Melon Hill and up the gentle slope to the split-level at the top.

Mr. Hallinan came to the door in a blue checked dressing gown. He looked slightly seedy, almost overhung, Lys thought. His dark eyes had puffy lids and a light stubble sprinkled his cheeks.

"Yes, Mrs. Erwin?"

"Oh—good morning, Mr. Hallinan. I—I came to see you. I hope I didn't disturb you—that is—"

"Quite all right, Mrs. Erwin." Instantly she was at ease. "But I'm afraid I'm really extremely tired after last night, and I fear I shouldn't be very good company just now."

"But you said you'd talk to me alone today. And—oh, there's so much more I want to tell you!"

A shadow of feeling—*pain? fear?* Lys wondered—crossed his face. "No," he said hastily. "No more—not just yet. I'll have to rest today. Would you mind coming back—well, say Wednesday?"

"Certainly, Mr. Hallinan. I wouldn't want to disturb you."

She turned away and started down the hill, thinking: *He had too much of our troubles last night. He soaked them all up like a sponge, and today he's going to digest them—*

Oh, what am I thinking?

She reached the foot of the hill, brushed a couple of tears from her eyes, and walked home rapidly, feeling the October chill whistling around her.

And so the pattern of life in New Brewster developed. For the six weeks before his death, Mr. Hallinan was a fixture at any important community gathering, always dressed impeccably, always ready with his cheerful smile, always uncannily able to draw forth whatever secret hungers and terrors lurked in his neighbors' souls.

And invariably Mr. Hallinan would be unapproachable the day after these gatherings, would mildly but firmly turn away any callers. What he did, alone in the house on Melon Hill, no one knew. As the days passed, it occurred to all that no one knew much of anything about Mr. Hallinan. He knew *them* all right, knew the one night of adultery twenty years before that still racked Daisy Moncrieff, knew the acid pain that seared Dudley Heyer, the cold envy glittering in Martha Weede, the frustration and loneliness of Lys Erwin, her husband's shy anger at his own cuckoldry—he knew these things and many more, but none of them knew more of him than his name.

Still, he warmed their lives and took from them the burden of their griefs. If he chose to keep his own life hidden, they said, that was his privilege.

He took walks every day, through still-wooded New Brewster, and would wave and smile to the children, who would wave and smile back. Occasionally he would stop, chat with a sulking child, then move on, tall, erect, walking with a jaunty stride.

He was never known to set foot in either of New Brewster's two churches. Once Lora Harker, a mainstay of the New Brewster Presbyterian Church, took him to task for this at a dull party given by the Weedes.

But Mr. Hallinan smiled mildly and said, "Some of us feel the need. Others do not."

And that ended the discussion.

Toward the end of November a few members of the community experienced an abrupt reversal of their feelings about Mr. Hallinan— weary, perhaps, of his constant empathy for their woes. The change in spirit was spearheaded by Dudley Heyer, Carl Weede, and several of the other men.

"I'm getting not to trust that guy," Heyer said. He knocked dottle vehemently from his pipe. "Always hanging around soaking up gossip, pulling out dirt—and what the hell for? What does *he* get out of it?"

"Maybe he's practicing to be a saint," Carl Weede remarked quietly. "Self-abnegation. The Buddhist Eightfold Path."

"The women all swear by him," said Leslie Erwin. "Lys hasn't been the same since he came here."

"*I'll* say she hasn't," said Aiken Muir wryly, and all of the men, even Erwin, laughed, getting the sharp thrust.

"All I know is I'm tired of having a father-confessor in our midst," Heyer said. "I think he's got a motive back of all his goody-goody warmness. When he's through pumping us he's going to write a book that'll put New Brewster on the map for good."

"You always suspect people of writing books," Muir said. "*Oh, that mine enemy would write a book . . . . !*"

"Well, whatever his motives I'm getting annoyed. And that's why he hasn't been invited to the party we're giving on Monday night." Heyer glared at Fred Moncrieff as if expecting some dispute. "I've spoken to my wife about it, and she agrees. Just this once, dear Mr. Hallinan stays home."

It was strangely cold at the Heyers' party that Monday night. The usual people were there, all but Mr. Hallinan. The party was not a success. Some, unaware that Mr. Hallinan had not been invited, waited expectantly for the chance to talk to him, and managed to leave early when they discovered he was not to be there.

"We should have invited him," Ruth Heyer said after the last guest had left.

Heyer shook his head. "No. I'm glad we didn't."

"But that poor man, all alone on the hill while the bunch of us were here, cut off from us. You don't think he'll get insulted, do you? I mean, and cut us from now on?"

"I don't care," Heyer said, scowling.

His attitude of mistrust toward Mr. Hallinan spread through the community. First the Muirs, then the Harkers, failed to invite him to gatherings of theirs. He still took his usual afternoon walks, and those who met him observed a slightly strained expression on his face, though he still smiled gently and chatted easily enough, and made no bitter comments.

And on December 3, a Wednesday, Roy Heyer, age 10, and Philip Moncrieff, age 9, set upon Lonny Dewitt, age 9, just outside the New Brewster Public School, just before Mr. Hallinan turned down the school lane on his stroll.

Lonny was a strange, silent boy, the despair of his parents and the bane of his classmates. He kept to himself, said little, nudged into corners, and stayed there. People clucked their tongues when they saw him in the street.

Roy Heyer and Philip Moncrieff made up their minds they were going to make Lonny Dewitt say something, or else.

It was *or else.* They pummeled him and kicked him for a few minutes; then, seeing Mr. Hallinan approaching, they ran, leaving Lonny weeping silently on the flagstone steps outside the empty school.

Lonny looked up as the tall man drew near.

"They've been hitting you, haven't they? I see them running away now."

Lonny continued to cry. He was thinking, *There's something funny about this man. But he wants to help me. He wants to be kind to me.*

"You're Lonny Dewitt, I think. Why are you crying? Come, Lonny, stop crying! They didn't hurt you that much."

They didn't, Lonny said silently. *I like to cry.*

Mr. Hallinan was smiling cheerfully. "Tell me all about it. Something's bothering you, isn't it? Something big, that makes you feel all lumpy and sad inside. Tell me about it, Lonny, and maybe it'll go away." He took the boy's small cold hands in his own, and squeezed them.

"Don't want to talk," Lonny said.

"But I'm a friend. I want to help you."

Lonny peered close and saw suddenly that the tall man told the truth. He wanted to help Lonny. More than that: he *had* to help Lonny. Desperately. He was pleading. "Tell me what's troubling you," Mr. Hallinan said again.

OK, Lonny thought. *I'll tell you.*

And he lifted the floodgates. Nine years of repression and torment came rolling out in one roaring burst.

I'm alone and they hate me because I do things in my head and they never understood and they think I'm queer and they hate me I see them looking funny at me and they think funny things about me because I want to talk to them with my mind and they can only hear words and I hate them hate them hate hate hate—

Lonny stopped suddenly. He had let it all out, and now he felt better, cleansed of the poison he'd been carrying in him for years. But Mr. Hallinan looked funny. He was pale and white-faced, and he was staggering.

In alarm, Lonny extended his mind to the tall man. And got:

Too much. Much too much. Should never have gone near the boy. But the older ones wouldn't let me.

Irony: the compulsive empath overloaded and burned out by a compulsive sender who'd been bottled up.

. . . like grabbing a high-voltage wire . . .

. . . he was a sender, I was a receiver, but he was too strong . . .

And four last bitter words: *I . . . was . . . a . . . leech. . . .*

"Please, Mr. Hallinan," Lonny said out loud. "Don't get sick. I want to tell you some more. Please, Mr. Hallinan."

Silence.

Lonny picked up a final lingering wordlessness, and knew he had found and lost the first one like himself. Mr. Hallinan's eyes closed and he fell forward on his face in the street. Lonny realized that it was over, that he and the people of New Brewster would never talk to Mr. Hallinan again. But just to make sure he bent and took Mr. Hallinan's limp wrist.

He let go quickly. The wrist was like a lump of ice. *Cold*—burningly cold. Lonny stared at the dead man for a moment or two.

"Why, it's dear Mr. Hallinan," a female voice said. "Is he—"

And feeling the loneliness return, Lonny began to cry softly again.

It was January, 1957: my God, a whole lifetime ago. I was in my very early twenties, had just won a Hugo as the best new writer of the year, was producing stories with insane prolificacy, two or three a week. (My ledger entry for that month shows seventeen titles, 85,000 words, and I was just warming up for the *really* productive times a couple of years down the line.)

A phenomenon, I was. And one who took notice of it was Anthony Boucher, the urbane and sophisticated editor of *Fantasy & Science Fiction*. He was a collector at heart, who wanted one of everything for his magazine—including a story by this hypermanic kid from New York who seemed to be able to turn one out every hour. But he wasn't going to relax his high standards simply for the sake of nailing me for his contents page; and so, although he told me in just about so many words that he'd be delighted to publish something of mine, he turned down the first few that I sent him, offering great regrets and hope for the future. What I had to do in order to sell one to him, I told myself, was break free of the pulp-magazine formulas that I had taken such trouble to master, and write something about and for adults. (Not so easy, when I had barely made it to voting age—twenty-one, then—myself!)

The specific genesis of "Warm Man" was a moment at the first Milford Writers' Conference in September, 1956, where Harlan Ellison and I, the two hot young new writers of the moment, were mascots, so to speak, for a galaxy of masters of the field—Theodore Sturgeon, James Blish, Frederik Pohl, Damon Knight, Lester del Rey, C. M. Kornbluth, Fritz Leiber—everyone who was anyone, all of them discussing their lives and their crafts in the most astonishingly open way. During one workshop session involving a Kornbluth story, Cyril had some sort of epiphany about his writing and suddenly cried out in a very loud voice, "Warm!" What that signified to him, I never knew; he declined to share his insight with anyone, though it was obviously a very powerful one. Somehow it set something working in me, though, which very likely had nothing at all to do with whatever passed through Cyril's mind, and out came, a few months later, this tale of psychic vampirism. I sent it to Boucher (who I think had been present at Milford also) and by return mail across the continent came his expression of delight that I had broken the ice at last with him. He ran the story a few months later—May 1957—and put my name on the cover, a signal honor for a newcomer. Boucher was the best kind of editor—a demanding one, yes, but also the kind who is as pleased as you are that you have produced something he wants to publish. He (and a few others back then) helped to teach me the difficult lesson that quantity isn't as effective, in the long run, as quality. Which is demonstrated by this story's frequent reappearance in print over the span of more than three decades since it was written.

Robert Silverberg

TERATISMS

Kathe Koja

Kathe Koja has been building a solid reputation with her enigmatic science fiction and dark fantasy stories for the last few years.

"Teratisms" is a quirky and brutal piece about how even innocence can be ugly and how one family member can enslave or even suck the life out of the others. The family in this story seems cut from the same cloth as the pseudo-family in the film Near Dark.

"*B*eaumont." Dreamy, Alex's voice. Sitting in the circle of the heat, curtains drawn in the living room: laddered magenta scenes of birds and dripping trees. "Delcambre. Thibodaux." Slow-drying dribble like rusty water on the bathroom floor. "Abbeville," car door slam, "Chinchuba," screen door slam. Triumphant through its echo, "Baton Rouge!"

Tense hoarse holler almost childish with rage: "Will you shut the fuck *up?*"

From the kitchen, woman's voice, Randle's voice, drawl like cooling blood: "Mitch's home."

"You're damn right Mitch is home." Flat slap of his unread newspaper against the cracked laminate of the kitchen table, the whole set from the Goodwill for thirty dollars. None of the chairs matched. Randle sat in the cane-bottomed one, leg swinging back and forth, shapely metronome, making sure the ragged gape of her tank top gave Mitch a good look. Fanning herself with four slow fingers.

"Bad day, big brother?"

Too tired to sit, propping himself jackknife against the counter. "They're all bad, Francey."

"Mmmm, forgetful. My name's Randle now."

"Doesn't matter what your name is, you're still a bitch."

Soft as dust, from the living room: "De Quincy. Longville." Tenderly, "Bewelcome."

Mitch's sigh. "Numbnuts in there still at it?"

"All day."

Another sigh, he bent to prowl the squat refrigerator, let the door fall shut. Half-angry again, "There's nothing in here to eat, Fran—Randle."

"So what?"

"So what'd you eat?"

More than a laugh, bubbling under. "I don't think you really want to know." Deliberately exposing half a breast, palm lolling beneath like a side-show, like a street-corner card trick. Presto. "Big brother."

His third sigh, lips closed in decision. "I don't need this," passing close to the wall, warding the barest brush against her, her legs in the chair as deliberate, a sluttish spraddle but all of it understood: an old, unfunny family joke; like calling names; nicknames.

The door slamming, out as in, and in the settling silence of departure: "Is he gone?"

Stiff back, Randle rubbing too hard the itchy tickle of sweat. Pushing at the table to move the chair away. "You heard the car yourself, Alex. You know he's gone."

Pause, then plaintive, "Come sit with me." Sweet; but there are nicknames and nicknames, jokes and jokes; a million ways to say I love you. Through the raddled arch into the living room, Randle's back tighter still, into the smell, and Alex's voice, bright.

"Let's talk," he said.

Mitch, so much later, pausing at the screenless front door, and on the porch Randle's cigarette, drawing lines in the dark like a child with a sparkler.

"Took your time," she said.

Defensively, "It's not that late."

"I know what time it is."

He sat down, not beside her but close enough to speak softly and be heard. "You got another cigarette?"

She took the pack from somewhere, flipped it listless to his lap. "Keep 'em. They're yours anyway."

He lit the cigarette with gold foil matches, JUDY'S DROP-IN. An impulse, shaming, to do as he used to, light a match and hold it to her fingertips to see how long it took to blister. No wonder she hated him. "Do you hate me?"

"Not as much as I hate him." He could feel her motion, half a head-shake. "Do you know what he did?"

"The cities."

"Besides the cities." He did not see her fingers, startled twitch as he felt the pack of cigarettes leave the balance of his thigh. "He was down by the grocery store, the dumpster. Playing. It took me almost an hour just to talk him home." A black sigh. "He's getting worse."

"You keep saying that."

"It keeps being true, Mitch, whether you want to think so or not. Something really bad's going to happen if we don't get him—"

"Get him what?" Sour. No bitter. "A doctor? A *shrink*? How about a one-way ticket back to Shitsburg so he—"

"Fine, that's fine. But when the cops come knocking I'll let you answer the door," and her quick feet bare on the step, into the house. Tense unconscious rise of his shoulders: Don't slam the door. Don't wake him up.

Mitch slept, weak brittle doze in the kitchen, head pillowed on the Yellow Pages. Movement, the practiced calm of desire. Stealth, until denouement, a waking startle to Alex's soft growls and tweaks of laughter, his giggle and spit. All over the floor. All over the floor and his hands, oh God Alex your *hands*—

Showing them off the way a child would, elbows turned, palms up. Showing them in the jittery bug-light of the kitchen in the last half hour before morning, Mitch bent almost at the waist, then sinking back, nausea subsiding but unbanished before the immensity, the drip and stutter, there was some on his mouth too. His chin, Mitch had to look away from what was stuck there.

"Go on," he said. "Go get your sister."

And waited there, eyes closed, hands spread like a medium on the Yellow Pages. While Alex woke his sister. While Randle used the washcloth. Again.

Oxbow lakes. Flat country. Randle sleeping in the back seat, curled and curiously hot, her skin ablush with sweat in the sweet cool air. Big creamy Buick with all the windows open. Mitch was driving, slim black sunglasses like a cop in a movie, while Alex sat playing beside him. Old wrapping paper today, folding in his fingers, disappearing between his palms. Always paper. Newsprint ink under his nails. Glossy foilwrap from some party, caught between the laces of his sneakers. Or tied there. Randle might have done that, it was her style. Grim droll jokery. Despite himself he looked behind, into the back seat, into the stare of her open eyes, so asphalt blank that for one second fear rose like a giant waiting to be born and he thought, Oh no, oh not her too.

Beside him Alex made a playful sound.

Randle's gaze snapped true into her real smile; bared her teeth in burlesque before she rolled over, pleased.

"Fucking bitch," with dry relief. With feeling.

Alex said, "I'm hungry."

Mitch saw he had begun to eat the paper. "We'll find a drive-through somewhere," he said, and for a moment dreamed of flinging the wheel sideways, of fast and greasy death. Let someone else clean up for a change.

There was a McDonald's coming up, garish beside the blacktop; he got into the right lane just a little too fast. "Randle," coldly, "put your shirt on."

Chasing the end of the drive-through line, lunchtime and busy and suddenly Alex was out of the car, leaned smiling through the window to say, "I want to eat inside." And gone, trotting across the parking lot, birthday paper forgotten on the seat beside.

"Oh God," Mitch craning, tracking his progress, "go after him, Randle," and Randle's snarl, the bright slap of her sandals as she ran. Parking, he considered driving off. Alone. Leaving them there. Don't you ever leave them, swear me. You have to swear me, Michie. Had she ever really said that? Squeezed out a promise like a dry log of shit? I hope there is a hell, he thought, turning off the car, I hope it's big and hot and eternal and that she's in it.

They were almost to the counter, holding hands. When Randle saw him enter, she looked away; he saw her fingers squeeze Alex's, twice and slow. What was it like for her? Middleman. Alex was staring at the wall menu as if he could read. "I'll get a booth," Mitch said.

A table, instead; there were no empty booths. One by one Alex crumbled the chocolate-chip cookies, licked his fingers to dab up the crumbs. Mitch drank coffee.

"That's making me sick," he said to Randle.

Her quick sideways look at Alex. "What?" through half a mouthful, a tiny glob of tartar sauce rich beside her lower lip.

"That smell," nodding at her sandwich. "Fish."

Mouth abruptly stretched, chewed fish and half-smeared sauce, he really was going to be sick. Goddamned *bitch*. Nudging him under the table with one bare foot. Laughing into her Coke.

"Do you always have to make it worse?"

Through another mouthful, "It can't get any worse." To Alex, "Eat your cookies."

Mitch drank more coffee; it tasted bitter, boiled. Randle stared over his head as she ate: watching the patrons? staring at the wall? Alex coughed on cookie crumbs, soft dry cough. Gagged a little. Coughed harder.

"Alex?" Randle put down her sandwich. "You okay? Slap his back," commandingly to Mitch, and he did, harder as Alex kept coughing, almost a barking sound now and heads turned, a little, at the surrounding tables, the briefest bit of notice that grew more avid as Alex's distress increased, louder whoops and Randle suddenly on her feet, trying to raise him up as Mitch saw the first flecks of blood.

"Oh *shit*," but it was too late, Alex spitting blood now, spraying it, coughing it out in half-digested clots as Randle, frantic, working to haul him upright as Mitch in some stupid reflex swabbed with napkins at the mess. Tables emptied around them. Kids crying, loud and scared, McDonald's employees surrounding them but not too close, Randle shouting, "*Help* me, you asshole!" and Mitch in dumb paralysis watched as a tiny finger, red but recognizable, flew from Alex's mouth to lie wetly on the seat.

Hammerlock, no time to care if it hurts him, Randle already slamming her back against the door to hold it open and Alex's staining gurgle hot as piss against his shoulder, Randle screaming, "Give me the keys! Give me the keys!" Her hand digging hard into his pocket as he swung Alex, white-faced, into the back seat, lost his balance as the car jerked into gear and fell with the force of motion to his temple, dull and cool, against the lever of the seat release.

And lay there, smelling must and the faint flavor of motor oil, Alex above collapsed into silence, lay a long time before he finally thought to ask, "Where're we going?" He had to ask it twice to cut the blare of the radio.

Randle didn't turn around. "Hope there's nothing in that house you wanted."

Night, and the golden arches again. This time they ate in the car, taking turns to go inside to pee, to wash, the rest rooms small as closets. Gritty green soap from the dispenser. Alex ate nothing. Alex was still asleep.

Randle's lolling glance, too weary to sit up straight anymore. "You drive for a while," she said. "Keep on I-10 till you get—"

"I know," louder than he meant; he was tired too. It was a chore just to keep raising his hand to his mouth. Randle was feeling for something, rooting slowly under the seat, in her purse. When he raised his eyebrows at her she said, "You got any cigarettes?"

"Didn't you just buy a pack?"

Silence, then, "I left them at the house. On the back of the toilet," and without fuller warning began to weep, one hand loose against her mouth. Mitch turned his head, stared at the parking lot around them, the fluttering jerk of headlights like big fat clumsy birds. "I'm sick of leaving stuff places," she said. Her hand muffled her voice, made it sound like she spoke from underwater, some calm green place where voices could never go. "Do you know how long I've been wearing this shirt?" and before he could think if it was right to give any answer, "Five days. That's how long. Five fucking days in this same fucking shirt."

From the back seat Alex said, "Breaux Bridge," in a tone trusting and tender as a child's. Without turning, without bothering to look, Randle pistoned her arm in a backhand punch so hard Mitch flinched watching it.

Flat-voiced, "You just shut up," still without turning, as if the back seat had become impossible for her. "That's all you have to do. Just shut up."

Mitch started the car. Alex began to moan, a pale whimper that undercut the engine noise. Randle said, "I don't care what happens, don't wake me up." She pulled her T-shirt over her head and threw it out the window.

"Randle, for God's sake! At least wait till we get going."

"Let them look." Her breasts were spotted in places, a rashy speckle strange in the greenish dashlight, like some intricate tattoo the details of which became visible only in hard daylight. She lay with her head on his thigh, the flesh beneath her area of touch asleep before she was. He drove for almost an hour before he lightly pushed her off.

And in the back seat the endless sound of Alex, his rustling paper, the marshy odor of his tears. To Mitch it was as if the envelope of night had closed around them not forever but for so long there was no difference to be charted or discerned. Like the good old days. Like Alex staggering around and around, newspaper carpets and the funnies especially, vomiting blood that eclipsed the paler smell of pigeon shit from the old pigeon coop. Pigeonnier. Black dirt, alluvial crumble and sprayed like tarot dust across the blue-tiled kitchen floor. Wasn't it strange that he could still remember that tile, its gaudy Romanesque patterns? Remember it as he recalled his own nervous shiver, hidden like treasure behind the mahogany boards. And Randle's terrified laughter. Momma. Promises, his hands between her dusty palms; they were so small then, his hands. Alex wiping uselessly at the scabby drip of his actions, even then you had to watch him all the time. Broken glasses, one after another. Willow bonfires. The crying cicadas, no, that was happening now, wasn't it? Through the Buick's open windows. Through the hours and hours of driving until the air went humid with daylight and the reeking shimmer of exhaust, and Randle stirring closed-eyed on the front seat beside him and murmuring, anxious in her sleep, "Alex?"

He lay one hand on her neck, damp skin, clammy. "Shhhh, he's all right. It's still my turn. He's all right."

And kept driving. The rustle of paper in the back seat. Alex's soft sulky hum, like some rare unwanted engine that no lack of fuel could hamper, that no one could finally turn off.

And his hands on the wheel as silent as Randle's calmed breathing, as stealthy as Alex's cities, the litany begun anew: Florien, Samtown, Echo, Lecomte, drifting forward like smoke from a secret fire, always burning, like the fires on the levees, like the fire that took their home. Remember that? Mouth open, catching flies his mother would have said. Blue flame like a gas burner. What color does blood burn?

And his head hanging down as if shamefaced, as if dunned and stropped by the blunt hammer of anger, old anger like the fires that never burned out. And his eyes closing, sleeping, though he woke to think, Pull over, had to, sliding heedless as a drunken man over to the shoulder to let himself fall, forehead striking gentle against the steering wheel as if victim of the mildest of accidents. Randle still asleep on the seat beside. Alex, was he still saying his cities? Alex? Paper to play with? "Alex," but he spoke the word without authority, in dreams against a landscape not welcome but necessary: in which the rustle of Alex's paper mingled with the slower dribble of his desires, the whole an endless pavane danced through the cities of Louisiana, the smaller, the hotter, the better. And he, and Randle too, were somehow children again, kids at the old house where the old mantle of protection fell new upon them, and they unaware and helpless of the burden, ignorant of the loss they had already and irrevocably sustained, loss of life while living it. You have to swear me, Michie. And Randle, not Randle then, not Francey but Marie-Claire, that was her name, Marie-Claire promising as he did, little sister with her hands outstretched.

The car baked slow and thorough in the shadeless morning, too far from the trees. Alex, grave as a gargoyle chipped cunningly free, rose, in silence the back door handle and through the open windows his open palms, let the brownish flakes cascade down upon Mitch and Randle both, swirling like the glitter-snow in a paperweight, speckles, freckles, changing to a darker rain, so lightly they never felt it, so quiet they never heard. And gone.

The slap of consciousness, Randle's cry, disgust, her hands grubby with it, scratching at the skin of her forearms so new blood rose beneath the dry. Scabbed with blood, painted with it. Mitch beside her, similarly scabbed, brushing with a detached dismay, not quite fastidious, as if he were used to waking covered with the spoor of his brother's predilections.

"I'm not his mother!" Screaming. She was losing it, maybe already had. Understandable. Less so his own lucidity, back calm against the seat; shock-free? Maybe he was crazier than she was. Crazier than Alex, though that would be pushing it. She was still screaming, waves of it that shook her breasts. He was getting an erection. Wasn't that something.

"I'm sick of him being a monster. I can't—"

"We have to look for him."

"You look! You look! I'm tired of looking!" Snot on her lips. He grabbed her by the breasts, distant relish, and shoved her very hard against the door. She stopped screaming and started crying, a dry drone that did not indicate if she had actually given in or merely cracked. Huh-huh-huh. "Put your shirt on," he said, and remembered she didn't have one, she had thrown it away. Stupid bitch. He gave her his shirt, rolled his window all the way down. Should they drive, or go on foot? How far? How long had they slept? He remembered telling her it was his turn to watch Alex. Staring out the window. Willows. Floodplain. Spanish moss. He had always hated Spanish moss. So *hot*, and Randle's sudden screech, he hated that too, hated the way her lips stretched through mucus and old blood and new blood and her pointing finger, pointing at Alex. Walking toward them.

Waving, extravagant, exuberant, carrying something, something it took both hands to hold. Even from this distance Mitch could see that Alex's shirt was soaked. Saturated. Beside him Randle's screech had shrunk to a blubber that he was certain, this time, would not cease. Maybe ever. Nerves, it got on his nerves, mosquito with a dentist's drill digging at your ear. At your brain. At his fingers on the car keys or maybe it was just the itch of blood as he started the car, started out slow, driving straight down the middle of the road to where he, and Randle, and Alex, slick and sticky to the hairline, would intersect. His foot on the gas pedal was gentle, and Alex's gait rocked like a chair on the porch as he waved his arms again, his arms and the thing within.

Randle spoke, dull through a mouthful of snot. "Slow down," and he shook his head without looking at her, he didn't really want to see her at this particular moment.

"I don't think so," he said as his foot dipped, elegant, like the last step in a dance. Behind Alex, the diagonal shadows of willow trees, old ones; sturdy? Surely. There was hardly any gas left in the car, but he had just enough momentum for all of them.

I am uncomfortable with afterwords, forewords, and so on because to me a story is useless if it doesn't speak solely for itself. That said, I will note that "Teratisms" is about love, and hunger, and one of the many districts where they intersect.

Kathe Koja

M IS FOR THE
MANY THINGS

Elizabeth Massie

Here is another story about a family, although this one is strictly structured in contrast to the chaos of Koja's, and is voluntary. Well, mostly. A perfect example of the adage the road to hell is paved with good intentions.

*M*other was dying. Her forehead was splotched and red, and her hair was brittle and dry on the pillow. She sweated without relief, her body like a huge hot cloud on a summer's day, raining steadily, the water collecting in the creases of her flesh and dripping to the folds of the sheet beneath her. The sweat smelled of Vicks VapoRub, and the soiled linens, piled in the corner of Mother's room, added a scent of urine and diarrhea. It was Barbara's job to do the linens, but they were dirtied so quickly now that she had a hard time keeping up.

Grace, feeling ill herself, dabbed Mother's body with the edge of a towel. Mother's breathing had been labored for two days. She was dying. The sense of impending loss and despair roiled in Grace's bowels. Emotions of which she could make no sense were tangled in her chest, causing her lungs to hurt. She shuddered, and wiped the length of Mother's collarbone.

Greg, Grace's brother, came into the room. He stepped lightly on his bare feet, and sat beside Grace on a low chair. Grace gave him the towel. He dabbed Mother's arm. He said nothing. Grace knew he was waiting for her to decide if she could talk about this, or wanted to leave it in silence.

Pain squeezed Grace's vocal cords, and she said, "How can I bear this?"

Greg didn't look at Grace, nor touch her. None of the brothers and sisters knew how to comfort each other. That was Mother's duty. He lifted

Mother's massive hand and gently dabbed the moist places between each finger. Then he said, "Stay strong if you can. I've been through this before, and I know what I'm saying. Stay strong."

Grace swallowed, and it hurt.

"Why don't you go to dinner?" Greg said. He put Mother's hand down, then wiped her breast. "I'll take my turn. Mary has made a nice stew. She's upset that no one was on time to the dining hall tonight."

Grace closed her eyes. Several heavy tears joined the sweat on the bed. Then she rose and left the room.

Outside the door, Grace slipped on her clothes and stepped into her shoes. She walked along the hall to the top of the staircase, passing the two open doors of the girls' rooms and the closed door of the nursery. A soft squeak emanated from behind the nursery door, and Grace let her hand touch the wood briefly as she went by. It was Grace's job to do the hourly feeding, but it was only six-thirty. From below was the bland aroma of Mary's cooking, and the sound of Eldon buffing the living-room floor.

At the top of the stairs, Grace's kitten lay in a weak ball. Grace picked it up and squeezed it tightly. It was a shame; this kitty was no good. It had been a nice, healthy animal when Grace had found it in the backyard, but now it was thin and weak and its fur was coming out. Just like all the other kittens Grace had tried to keep as pets. They had been playful and cute and full of energy. Then they each got sick and died. Grace had loved them greatly. And they all died.

Suddenly Grace was flushed with the need to go back to Mother. She dropped the kitten and grabbed the top of the banister, her jaws clenching. Then the sensation passed. Greg was with Mother, it was his turn. And Grace did need to eat. It was almost twenty minutes past dinnertime.

Downstairs, Mary stood in the dining hall, arms crossed, bushy eyebrows a furious dragon across the top of her face. She was the oldest of the children, nearly thirty-nine. She was usually the cook, and always the assigner of chores. She was the rememberer of the rules and the doler of punishments. Mary was the only one of the children to have a room to herself. No one argued with Mary; they complained about her under their breaths at work or in the darkness on their cots at night.

"You're last," Mary told Grace. "You'll have dish duty, then."

Grace said, "That's all right." She slumped to her assigned seat at the long wooden table, poured herself a glass of milk from the carton, and picked up her spoon.

Mary took up a rumpled cotton napkin and looked at it steadily, then sat down across from Grace. "How is Mother?"

"The same."

Mary sighed. "Maybe I'll help you with the dishes," she said. "It will keep me from thinking."

Grace ate a piece of carrot. It caught in her throat. "I wish I'd had time in the infirmary, Mary. Don't you? Maybe then we would know what to do."

Mary shook her head. "Nobody worked in the infirmary, and you don't wish you had. It was bad in there, a lot of sickness we could have caught. Don't you remember Celia Duncan? She died in the infirmary, Grace. Some awful disease. They were right not to let us in there unless we were sick ourselves."

Grace nodded and chewed a bit of cubed beef. Mary cooked just as good as Mrs. Griffith used to. But tonight the food seemed to have no taste.

"You've only been with us a year," said Mary. She paused, then scratched her graying hair. The sound of the buffer stopped, and there was the bumping and scraping as Eldon put the machine back into the front hall closet. "You'll be all right."

Grace wiped her mouth on the cloth napkin and put it back into her lap. "You don't have to help me with dishes."

"Suit yourself."

"Who has devotions tonight?"

"Paul."

"I don't think I can eat all this."

"You don't eat it you get no snack."

Grace sighed and brought another spoonful of stew to her lips. Eldon came into the dining hall. He was just three years Mary's junior, but appeared much older. He was skinny and ugly, with ears that pointed forward like fleshy megaphones and white hair shaved close to his bony head.

"Whole downstairs is done," he announced. There was a pride in his voice. "Could skate on it. Could see your own face if you looked close enough. But I won't be doing upstairs...." He trailed off, then blinked and looked away from Mary and Grace. "Could I at least buff the nursery?" he asked softly.

"No," said Mary.

Eldon's shoulders went up, then down.

Mary said, "Shake the rugs?"

Eldon said, "Yes. All done."

"Barbara and Al and Paul will be in soon from their after-dinner chores. We'll have devotions. A special one for Mother. Why don't you wait in the living room for us, and find a nice verse for Mother in the Bible?"

"But Paul has devotions tonight, don't he?"

Mary frowned, and Eldon became immediately submissive. "Okay," he said. He pulled at one huge ear. "A long verse or a short one?"

"Long," said Grace. Her stew bowl was empty. She held it up and Mary said, "Better."

Grace took her dishes into the small kitchen at the back of the house, and washed the pile that waited there for her. They were nearly all dried and put away when Paul and Al came in the front door. Grace carried the bowl she was drying to the kitchen door and leaned against the frame.

Paul shed his Windbreaker and hung it in the closet between the dining hall and living room. He was thirty-three, with short black hair and brown skin hardened to parchment by the outdoor work he and Al did to earn money for the others. Al stood beside Paul with his hands in his jeans pockets. Al never wore a coat, even in the coldest weather. He kept the sleeves of his T-shirts cut off, and he sported a constant sunburn.

"Mother?" asked Al.

"The same, I think," said Mary. "Greg is with her."

Grace ran the dry rag around and around in the bowl.

Paul set his jaw and his eyes hitched. "Devotions in a few minutes," he said. He turned and went into the living room.

"Barbara out back?" asked Al.

Mary nodded. "Hanging out sheets," she said. "Lots of sheets this past week."

"Want me to get her?"

"That's fine, Al. Tell her it's devotion time, the sheets'll wait."

Al walked past Grace into the kitchen. Grace took the bowl to the cabinet and put it in with the others. Al opened the door leading to the backyard, causing the blinds on the door's window to clap noisily against the glass. He stepped out to the stoop and called for Barbara to come inside.

Grace hurried upstairs for a quick seven o'clock feeding, then came back down to the living room. It was a long, narrow room with a single window facing the street. There were pots of plants that Barbara tried to keep, but most of them were dead or nearly so. The room was kept shaded, because Mary did not like the view of the street. She did not like seeing all the people going about their busy business in their frantic ways; she did not like the bustle of the independents, nor the stiflingly close vicinity of the neighbors. Grace knew Mary kept the shade down so she could imagine she was still at the Home. Mary liked to dust the empty bookshelves and sew up sock holes and think about the Home she had been forced to leave when she was eighteen, twenty years ago.

"Greg going to come down?" asked Paul. He was seated on the flowered sofa beneath the mantel. The Bible was in his lap. Beside him, Eldon pulled at his ear.

"Greg!" called Mary from the base of the steps. "Devotions. Come on, now."

Al sat down beside Eldon. Grace took the floor beside the broken recliner. Barbara, her thin brown ponytail blown askew by the backyard wind, sat on the straight-backed wooden chair by the door, across from the sofa. Mary sat on the recliner.

They all waited in silence, Eldon holding on to his ear, Barbara twisting the end of her ponytail, Paul strumming the pages of the Bible, Grace picking lint from the rug. They did not look at each other.

Greg came downstairs, buttoning his shirt. He entered the living room. "Mother moved a little," he offered, but said no more. He sat on the floor beneath the window.

Paul cleared his voice. "Verses first," he said, and he began. " 'Ye shall find the babe wrapped in swaddling clothes, lying in a manger.'"

Eldon said, " 'Jesus wept.'"

Al said, " 'A bone of his shall not be broken.'"

" 'They came round about me daily like water,'" said Greg.

" 'Jesus wept,'" said Grace.

Paul said, "Nope, already used."

Grace crossed her arms, frustrated. She could barely think. Then she said, " 'I will open my mouth in a parable.'"

" 'And he was with them coming in and going out at Jerusalem,'" said Mary from her chair.

" 'How much then is a man better than a sheep,'" said Barbara. This was one of the few verses that Grace liked, and that she understood. When she heard it she thought of pictures in her Sunday school class long ago, little baby sheep suckling Mother sheep, with Jesus standing by.

Verses done, they all looked at Paul. He opened the Bible to a little torn scrap of paper marking a place. "I found something to read in honor of Mother," he said. He sighed heavily. Nobody liked to be in charge of devotions. But Mary was stern; each took his or her turn. Paul's voice was awkward with the words, and embarrassed. " 'Therefore we are buried with him by baptism into death: that like as Christ was raised up from the dead by the glory of the Father, even so we also should walk in newness of life.'"

Grace listened as intently as she could, hoping this time she might find something that would make sense.

" 'For if we have been planted together in the likeness of his death, we shall be also in the likeness of his resurrection.'"

Paul read on another five minutes. Grace sat and heard the Scriptures, and it was as it had always been, a jumble of old words, a ritual of ancient babble. She did not need to ask the others to know it was the same for them as well. But they were trained to sit and read and quote and listen. In that repetition was the only small sense of calm.

Grace let her gaze wander to the photos and certificates on the mantel over the sofa. There was a picture of Mary back at the Baptist Home, no more than fifteen, wearing an apron and a wan smile, in the huge, smoky kitchen with Mrs. Griffith standing behind her. There was another picture of Al and Paul, twelve and thirteen, just old enough to be allowed to do grounds work, Al sitting on the seat of the Home's tractor, Paul standing on the grass. Behind Paul and Al were George Brennen and Ricky Altis, both fourteen at the time. Both George and Ricky had gone on from the Home, gotten jobs, and had married. They had become independents. They had been able to. Most of the children who had grown up in the Home had been able to. To the right of Al and Paul's snapshot was a photo that had been posed for inclusion in the Home's annual fund drive brochure. In it, a ten-year-old Barbara and an eight-year-old Grace were holding hands and running across the lawn in front of the Administration Building. There were no photos of Eldon. He hated to have his picture taken, and always hid when the Baptist Home board of trustees came out on excursions with their cameras.

"Amen," said Paul.

"Amen," repeated the others.

"Tonight, we'll each have a shorter time with Mother," said Mary. "No more than three minutes each, you hear me? Now, who was first last night?"

Eldon wiggled his hand.

"Then it's you, Barbara," said Mary. "Let's go upstairs."

The seven filed up the steps.

Barbara took off her clothes and went into Mother's room, closing the door behind her. Time with Mother was private, and respected. The others sat on the floor in the hallway. This was the most favored time of the day, yet Mother's illness had given it an urgent touch, and Grace sat quietly, trying to prepare herself. Usually Grace told Mother about her day as she snuggled and sucked on the great white breasts. Tonight, however, Grace thought that she, like Mother, would be without a voice.

They sat and waited. Mary went into the nursery for a minute, then came out and sat down again. The kitten rose from its spot at the top of the stairs and stumbled toward the gathering, then fell several feet short, panting and mewling. Grace didn't want the cat now, she wanted Mother, and so she let the cat lie.

Paul went in after Barbara. Grace had wondered what the boys did in the room alone with Mother, but would never ask. Before Grace had come to live with her brothers and sisters, she had tried to be an independent. She had lived with a man, and he had made her do awful things, like suckle him. She had tried to please him but could not do it, and he beat her. When she tried to kill him, the state put her into a home. Not a good place like the Home, but an ugly place where she had no chores and no devotions and they wanted to talk about her feelings. Grace wondered if Paul and Al and Eldon wanted Mother to suckle them as Grace's man had wanted.

Mary took her turn, and when she came out, her face was ashen. "Not long," she whispered as she zippered her skirt and sat beside Barbara. "She won't eat." Barbara put her head down on her arms. Mary stared at her fingers.

Grace went into Mother's room. As required, she went to the nightstand and chose a nice piece of candy for Mother. She mashed it in her fingers to make it easy for Mother to take, then leaned over the huge, naked body and pressed the candy to the sick lips. Mother did not take the candy, nor acknowledge that it was there. Her eyes did not open. Grace blinked and waited, hoping Mother would awaken and take the offering. But she did not.

Grace dropped the candy to the floor, and crawled onto the mattress with Mother. The cold dampness of Mother's sweat on the sheet made Grace's skin tighten and crawl.

"Today I began a picture of a cat," Grace said, pulling herself more tightly into the body. "It will be a nice one, a picture for you, and you can hang it up in your room." Grace looked up at the wall above Mother's head. On it were sketches that she had done with pencils and crayon crumbs. Pictures of sheep and their babies and Jesus and children doing chores and reading Bible verses and mowing lawns and saying prayers at cot-side and eating meals in the dining hall.

"It is a picture of the kitty I have now. She was a nice kitty, but not so nice anymore. But the picture is what she looked like when I first got her. Gray and white. You'll like it, I think."

Mother said nothing.

Grace closed her eyes and continued with her tale of the day. "Mary made stew, and it was good. Sometimes I wish we could have candy, but candy is sweet for sweet Mothers."

Mother did not move, but Grace could feel a pulse in her huge arm. Grace straddled Mother, and took a breast into her mouth. For a few minutes she suckled in silence. Peace settled on her and she lost awareness of the smell and the sweat and the fact that Mother was dying. Grace's body calmed. This was Mother. This was what they all had wanted. The others had banded together after they left the Home, forming a Home again in this house. They lived as they had learned, doing as they had been taught. But Greg had decided a Mother was the missing element. They had all needed a Mother for so long. After Grace's release from the hospital, she had called the Home and got Mary's new address. She was accepted into the Home of her long-ago brothers and sisters, and into a family that had at last, thanks be to Greg, a Mother.

Grace let go of the nipple, then rolled off the bed. As a parting gesture, she offered another piece of candy, and again, Mother did not take it. Grace stroked Mother's arm and thigh.

Suddenly Mother arched her back and her eyes flew open.

"Mother?"

Mother did not seem to recognize Grace, nor focus on anything. She trembled violently and her throat rumbled. The soft but strong terry towel restraints that were tied about her ankles and neck and shoulders drew taut and caused the bedposts to groan. Mother's mouth dropped open, and she grunted. The massive woman fought the cords. Her eyes spasmed.

She is dying certainly, Grace thought.

Then Mother slumped down again to the bed, and her eyes closed. She was silent, and the shuddering breathing resumed.

Grace went out into the hall. She put on her clothes. Al took his turn with Mother, closing the door behind him.

When the turns were done, Mary directed Eldon to take first watch with Mother during the night while the others slept. She did not believe Mother would last until morning, and it would be wrong for her to be alone when she died.

Mary told the others to brush their teeth and say their prayers and be off to bed. Grace washed her hands for the eight o'clock feeding.

Mary joined Grace at the nursery door. She said, "Why don't I help you this time?"

Grace shrugged. "You don't have to."

"I know I don't. But we'll do it together tonight."

Grace said, "All right."

Grace opened the door and the two went quietly inside.

There was a bed in the center of the nursery, a bedside table, and the rest of the room was bare. No one stayed in this room long enough to need a chair. This room was strictly business. It was a room for tending and cleaning and monitoring. It was dark and quiet and busy, like a little chamber in a honeybee comb.

Mary and Grace moved to the bed. Grace opened the box of candy on the bedside table. She smashed the chocolate between her fingers and held it out.

The figure on the bed strained and caught the candy. Then the mouth opened for more. Grace smiled slightly, then looked at Mary for approval.

"This is good," said Mary. "She's healthy and she eats."

Grace held out more mashed candy, and it was gobbled up. Even Grace's fingers were mouthed clean when she held them close enough.

Grace wiped her hand on her hip, then looked down at the woman on the bed. The woman was filling out nicely. With hourly feedings of good, sweet candy and soft drinks, she was beginning to look like a Mother, with soft, fleshy side rolls and arms like foam pillows. Soon she would be big enough to cuddle, large enough to hide in, soft enough to suckle. This woman, like Mother, was secured to her bed. This woman, also like Mother, had no voice. This was Greg's idea. He was the one to find the women and bring them home; and he was the one who said it was best to remove the tongues. This way, each in turn would be a good Mother. A good Mother who would listen and not scold.

Grace touched the woman's arm. The woman looked at Grace. Her eyes were alive and sparkling, as if mad tears swirled in them. She grunted and pulled at her restraints. Mary smacked her soundly.

"She'll learn," said Mary.

Grace picked another piece of candy from the box and looked at it. Candy tasted good, but Mother's breasts were sweeter. Mother's love was peace.

Grace crushed the candy. She offered it to the woman on the bed, who took it even as her eyes spilled and then brimmed over again.

At two the next morning, Mother died.

My husband, Roger, grew up in a children's home. He and three of his four brothers were put there when their mother died. Roger was six. His brothers were all younger. Roger lived there until he went to college at age eighteen.

Although the children's home was not a nightmare orphanage, the grounds were well maintained, the cottages clean, and counselors were on the payroll, there lacked the warmth and affection and support one would hope to have in a family. The house parents maintained strict discipline and inflexible rules. They never hugged the kids. They never told the kids that they loved them, or even liked them. The children grew up without adult affection, leaving them to either gain it from each other or not at all.

So I imagined that there would certainly be a number of people who, having grown up in this type of institution, would never be able to get beyond the routines and the security of the control the place had over them. And yet, out in the world, trying to re-create what they had known as children, they would also seek the adult tenderness they had never known.

Hey, the search for love is universal, right?

Too bad that search is sometimes deadly.

Elizabeth Massie

FOLLY FOR THREE

Barry N. Malzberg

Malzberg's science fiction has often been tinged with horror, so this story, with its minimalist style, should come as no surprise to those who have been reading him regularly over his career. It effectively conveys the fear of losing control— of a situation, and of one's life.

Good, he said again, this is very good. Just turn a little, let the light catch you. I want to see you in profile, against the light. There, he said, that's good. That's what I want. His voice had thickened, whether with passion or contempt she had no idea. They were still at that tentative state of connection where all moves were suspect, all signals indeterminate.

Ah, he said, you're a piece all right. That's what you are.

I've never done this before, she said. I've never done anything like this before. I want you to know that. She looked out the window, the grey clouds on the high floor hammering at the panes. Way, way up now. For everything there's a first time, she said.

Right, he said, humoring her. Whatever you say. I'm your first. Best in the world. Anything for a hump. He backed against a chair, crouched, fell into the cushions, stared at her from that angle, looking upward intently, checking out her crotch, then the high angle of her breasts, pulled upward within the brassiere, arching. He muttered something she could not hear and raised a hand.

What is it? she said. What do you want?

Come here. I want you to come here right now.

Tell me why.

I don't want games, he said. We'll have time for that later. You want to fool around, play with yourself. Come over here. Move it.

Can't you be a little kinder? I told you, I've never done anything like this before.

You want a commendation? he said. A Congressional Medal of Honor? He cleared his throat, looked at her with an odd and exacting impatience. Everybody has to have a first time, he said. Even I did once. I got through it. You'll get through it too. But you have to close your eyes and jump. Move it over here now.

This isn't the way I thought it would be, she said.

How did you think it would be? Flowers and wine? Tchaikovsky on the turntable? White Russians with straws? This is the setup, he said, this is what a nooner feels like. You don't hang out in bars midday if you're not looking for a nooner.

She looked at him, almost as if for the first time, noting the age spots on his arms, the fine, dense wrinkling around the eyes, which she had not noticed in the bar. Could she back out now? No, she thought, she couldn't. This was not the way it was done. That was all behind her now. I'm on the forty-eighth floor and that's all there is to it and no one in the world except this man knows I'm here. Not the kids, not Harry, not the cops. Okay, she said, I'm coming. She went toward him, trying to make her stockings glide, trying to move the way they moved in this kind of scene on *Dallas*. Maybe she could break him on the anvil of desire. Maybe she could quit him. Maybe—

There was a pounding on the door. Open up, someone in the hall said, open it! Open it now! The voice was huge, insistent.

For God's sake, she said, who is that?

He was trembling. I don't know, he said, what have you put us into? Detectives? Photographers? You got me into this, bitch. He backed away from her. His lips moved but there was no sound.

The noises in the hall were enormous, like nothing she had ever heard. The hammering was regular, once every three or four seconds now, an avid panting just beyond earshot. Like fucking, that's how it sounded. Last chance, the voice said, you open that goddamned door or we break it down.

What have you done? she said to the man. Stunned, absolutely without response, he ran his hands over his clothing, looked stupidly at the belt. This wasn't supposed to happen, she said. This wasn't part of it. *Who is out there?*

Nothing. He had nothing to say. He brought his clothing against him helplessly in the thin off-light in which she had so recently posed. She heard the sound of keys in the hallway. They were going to open the door.

An hour earlier in the bar she had said, Let's go now. I have a room in the Lenox around the corner.

Fast mover, he had said. His briefcase was on his lap, concealing an erection she supposed, one elbow draped over it awkwardly, clutching the briefcase there, the other hand running up and down her bare arm. She could feel the tremor in his fingers. He wanted her. Well, that was *his* problem.

I can be fast when I want, she said. Other times I can be slow. Whatever you say, big boy, I'm on your side. Who can believe these lines? she thought. This is what it's come to now.

Okay, he said. Just let me finish this drink. He raised the cocktail glass. I paid for it, he said, it's mine, I ought to have it.

She pressed his arm. You only think you're paying, she said. *I'm* paying. All the way, up and down the line. In his face she could see the pallor of acknowledgment, a blush of realization. *I've got a hot one here,* that face was saying. Well, that's the idea all right.

Let's go, friend, she said. She pushed away her own glass, clung to him for an instant, then pulled him upright. Let's see how fast you are where it counts. Out in the clean fresh air and then forty-eight stories *up*, that's the right place to put it.

He released her, yanked upright from the stool, took out a twenty, and put it on the bar. We'll see how fast I am, he said. He took the briefcase against his side, gripped the handle. Now, he said. The lust on his face seemed to struggle for just a moment with doubt, then faded to a kind of bleakness as she reached out again and stroked him. Now and now. He rose gravely to her touch. For God's sake, he said. For God's sake—

Now, she said.

They struggled toward the door. The man on the stool nearest the entrance looked up at them, his glasses dazzling in the strobe and said, You too? Every one of you?

She stared. She had never seen this man in her life. Of course, she reminded herself, the salesman with the briefcase was new also. Two strangers, one maybe as good as the other when she had walked in but the salesman was the one she had picked and in whom the time had been invested. No looking back. She said nothing, started toward the door.

Fornicators, the seated man said, infidels. Desolate lost angels of the Lord. Have you no shame? No hope?

Out on the street, the salesman said, Another bar, another crazy. They're all over the place. This city—

I don't want to hear about the city, she said. Please. Just take me to the hotel. Right now. She was appalled by the thought that the man at the bar would come after them. The thought was crazy but there it was. To the hotel, she said. I'm burning up, can't you tell. She yanked at his wrist. Now, she said, let's go.

She began to tug at him, he broke into a small trot. Hey, he said, hey look, it's all right. We've got all afternoon. I'm not going anywhere, we have hours. We have—

I'm afraid he's following us, she said. There, it was out, be done with it. I'm afraid he's going to come after us.

Who? The guy from the bar?

His footsteps, she said, I know them. He's coming up behind us. She turned and pointed, ready for a confrontation right there but of course there was nothing. A couple of secretaries giggling, a man with a dog, a beggar with a sign saying I AM BLIND, that was all. Quickly, she said, before he finds us. I know he's on the way.

She moved rapidly then, dropping her grip, striding out, making the salesman race. Let him struggle, she thought. Let him chase her a little. She was afraid of the man in the bar whether or not he was coming. Desolate lost angels of the Lord. Fornicators, she thought. We're all fornicators but some of us know more than others. There was something to come to terms with in this but she simply could not. All she wanted to do was get to the forty-eighth floor of the Hotel Lenox, take him into that room, get it over with, take him as deep as her brains. Make it happen, make it done. Get it into her. She was burning. Burning.

That morning in the kitchen he had said, I don't know how late I'll be. There's a conference midday and then I have to go out with the accounts exec again. I could be tied up till midnight with this guy, he's a professional drunk. If that's it I'll just get a room in the city and sleep in.

That's nice, she said. That's the third time I've heard that this month. Why bother coming home at all?

Hey, he said, his head tilting to attention, you think I'm lying? You think this is some kind of crap here, that I'm making up a story? Then just say it.

I didn't say a thing.

You think I'm running around? he said. I'm knocking my brains out to keep us in this $250,000 house we can't afford and can't sell and you're running tabs on me? Maybe we ought to have a discussion about that.

We're not going to have a discussion about anything, she said. He looks forty, she thought, and his gut is starting to swell. The sideburns are ragged and at night, the nights that he's next to me, he breathes like an old man, a sob in his throat. He's not going to last but who lasts? What stays? Ten years ago we made plans and every one of them worked out. I'm having trouble getting wet. AIDS is crossing the Huguenot line. The kids are no longer an excuse. We moved here expecting the usual, who was to know the joke was on us? I'm entitled to something too, she said, just think of that.

What does that mean? he said indifferently. He stood, gathered papers, stacked them, and leaned to open his briefcase. You trying to tell me something?

Nothing, she said, nothing at all. Make of it what you will.

Because if that's the deal, two can play you know. I don't have to get a heart attack at forty-two to keep you in a place like this. I can just let it go.

Forget it, she said. I didn't mean anything. It was just an expression. Pushing it, she thought. We're starting to push it now. It used to be easier; now we've got to get closer and closer to the bull.

Everything's an expression, he said. He opened the briefcase, inserted the papers, closed it with a snap. There's no time to discuss this now, he said, maybe later we ought to settle a few goddamned things. Maybe we'll sit down this weekend and talk.

I'll make an appointment, she said.

Enough, he said, enough of this. I'm out the door. You got something to say, maybe you write it down in words of one syllable, we fix it so a simple guy like me can see this. We're practical in the sales department, we only know what's in front of us. You got to spell it out.

Me and my imaginary friend, she said.

Imaginary friend? Is that what you call him now?

You'll be late for the bus, she said. You'll miss your connections and what will happen midday? He stared at her. You've got a schedule to meet, I mean, she said. In four years he won't be able to come, she thought. He'll be a heavy, barking lump next to me and I'll be counting the heartbeats, waiting for the hammer. That's what's going to happen. You bet it would have to be imaginary, she said.

He laughed, a strangulated groan. Too much, he said, you're too much for me. Always were. Always ahead of me. He leaned forward, kissed her cheek, his eyes flicking down indifferently, taking in her body, then moving away, all of him moving away, arching toward the wall and then the door. Keep it going, he said, just take a tip from me and keep it going. He reached toward the door.

Just like I do, he said and with a wink was gone.

She followed him, closed the heavy service door, sat on the stool, ran her feet in and around her slippers, looking at the clock. In her mind she ran the day forward, spun the hours, turned it until it was one in the afternoon and she would be in the Lenox waiting to be taken. She had worked it all out. But that still left hours, even figuring in the time at the bar and the arrangements to be made there. Too much time altogether. She thought of that.

She thought of it for a long time and of other things, the kids off at school, the difficult arc of the morning already getting passed. What do you think? she said to herself, what do you really think of this? Does it make any sense at all? Is this what we wanted?

Desolation, a voice said. That isn't what you wanted, that's what you've got. So you do the best you can. You make it up as you go along. That's the suburban way of life.

Well, there was nothing to say to that. There almost never was. What she could say would destroy the game. She kicked off her slippers and moved toward the stairs, ready to get dressed, ready to pull herself together. Again. Playing it out.

Two years before that, a Thursday in summer she had said, I can't go on this way anymore, Harry. Can you understand that? It's too much for me, it's not enough for me, it's a greyness, a vastness, I can't take it. I need something else. I can't die this way. She had run her hand on his thigh, felt the cooling, deadly torment of his inanition.

It's not just you, she said. It's everything. It's everybody.

We can work it out, he said. There are things we can do.

We can't do anything. I've thought it through. It's just the situation and it's too much. It's not enough, it's—

It's not just the two of us, he said. There are things to be done.

No shrinks, she said. No counselors. We've had enough of them. We're not getting anywhere.

I don't mean that, he said. There are other things. Things we can do on our own, things that will change.

Oh, Harry, she said, Harry, you have answers, but there *are* no answers, there are only plagues out there and darkness.

So we'll do something, he said, practically. He was a practical man. Because of the plagues, the risks. No one goes out there now if they can help it. I don't want to go out there and neither do you. So we have to work something out.

What? she said. What do you want? What's the answer?

He clutched her hand. We know all about it in the sales game, he said, and I can teach you.

Teach me what?

Masks, he said.

Masks? Halloween?

Repertory theater, he said. That's what we're going to have here. A little repertory theater. So get ready for the roles of your life.

Once she had loved him, she supposed. She must have loved him a lot. In deference to that, then, she laid back in the bed wide-eyed, listened to the tempo of his breathing as it picked up, touched him.

Okay, she said. Tell me more. I'm listening.

Yes, he said. Yes.

In the darkness, as he spoke, it was as if there were now another presence heaped under the bedclothes, an imaginary friend maybe, *her* imaginary friend listening.

He told her what he had in mind.

He sold her on it.

On the forty-eighth floor, she backed against the high window in the hotel room, her eyes fixed on the door, listening to the sound of the key turning. No, she said, no.

The man hobbling toward the door, half-dressed, turned, stared. No what? he said.

No more of this, she said. There's someone out there, she said. There's someone really out there with the key in the lock. We're in over our heads.

She could hear the key turning, turning. It encountered an obstruction, then suddenly it didn't and it was through. The door was moving.

The terror was clambering within her like an animal. He looks forty, she thought, and his gut is starting to swell. He's breathing like an old man. *Over our heads,* she said. I don't know what to do.

He looked at her, speechless. Wait a minute, he said. Now just wait—

The door was open. The man from the bar was there smiling, holding a gun now, pointing it. Fornicators, he said, I knew what you were up to. I have the key and I followed you here. Now you're going to pay. You disgust me.

She moved toward the window. Harry was rooted in place.

She looked at the priestly little man with the gun and sadly she looked at her husband, waiting now for whatever would happen.

Curtain, Harry, she said.

There's a passage in Higgins's *The Friends of Eddie Coyle* on marriage. "I got nothing to say about it," the guy says, "there's no way you can understand it unless you've been married; there's no way to explain it." Well, yes, there probably is—my metaphor of fifteen years ago was repertory theater, the donning of masks, the same old reliable faces beneath the inconstant, swooning trappings, but I got bored with this as explanation just about the time that this particular thread of insight seemed to unravel and here is the faithful editor, this book, and this tremulous story to give me a better idea: marriage as psychic vampirism. Of course.

But then again, of course (one hastens to say against the anticipated misunderstandings) everything is psychic vampirism, symbiosis, mutual exploitation; *life* is a form of psychic vampirism; we give unto and take back in different measure and sometimes are unwilling to admit the transaction, call it something else. But then again—and unless you been there, Eddie—there's no way that you can understand this, just no way that you are going to be able to grasp the issue.

"Folly for Three" in an earlier and murkier draft was written in tribute to Cornell Woolrich, whom I knew toward the end of his life and about whom too much has now been written (after many years of too little; "too much" is worse, speaking of vampirism); the story did not, in its Woolrichian mode, make a great deal of sense. Ellen Datlow's services in extracting from the murk the story that this wanted to be were remarkable and (old too late and too late smart) an education. Mutual dependency yet *again*, Eddie old pal.

Barry N. Malzberg

THE IMPALER
IN LOVE

Rick Wilber

Here's an honest-to-God traditional-type vampire—with a very untraditional urge.

1

Did we frighten your effete God
with that first fevered embrace
that so fed my need that I left you mortal?

You cried for me with pleading hands,
you sought my sudden entrance—
no coy flirtation, no shuttered portal,

there was only a hunger and your firm commands
until I filled your cup, accepted your innocence,
and repaid you with your life.

II

But now, but now—
the sun dies into a cobalt sea,
a reflected spear of its demise

aimed across horizon miles
to beach-edging pines where we stand
as small waves lap a tired shore.

An owl flies overhead on silent, death-hunt wings
to arrow across the narrow beach and bring
shell-stabbing talons to a scuttling crab—
the hermit's claw a feeble gesture of damned—
defiance before it is consumed.

You turn and sweetly smile and say:
"We can still be friends, I'm sure of it,"
and I can only nod and sigh
for what you cannot know of my demands.

I loved you, fragile thing,
and nearly shared it all.
Nearly.

III

I am blessed hard,
angry and hungry and hard to think of how it was
and could have been before your passion set
in this cooling sea of smiles and friendship and talk.

I kept you alive, your rosaried cross and Christ
and simple psalms no more redoubt against my skill
than the hermit's sad claw and crushed chitin.

I kept you alive, I fed from your passion
that sated my own as none had ever done.
I hid my truth to revel in your loins

while your hips thrust to mine
to give rise to desires long dismissed.
Your lips, your tongue defined

our mutual need, and order grew
from the dark chaos that has led me always.
And so I loved you.

I, the fool, loved you in your mortal guile
and set aside a millennium's lessons
for this false hope, all while

knowing it would turn to ruin.
I touched your pale perfection,
pierced your bold smile to enter
and bathe in your warm balm.

IV

But that, dear one, was in another time,
before this silent hour,
this sad and silent hour of mine,
came to you.

Your talk of friendship ends your life,
the cross you bore is lifted now,
your catholic taste has brought this strife
and blame to you.

This sun has set and the hermit has raised
its futile claw against a final consummation
that is, though long delayed, now yours
and mine, to finally share.

This poem began with the middle stanzas after I had watched a darkly beautiful sunset with my wife on a quiet beach in Barbados. We noticed, walking along the Caribbean shore of the beautiful island just as the sun disappeared, some gulls tearing at the partially eaten remnants of a crab at the water's edge. I had been startled several nights earlier by an owl swooping down over my head around midnight in my own backyard in Tampa. Those various scenes tumbled together into useful metaphors that connected with my thoughts on the consuming passions that mark vampirism.

I was determined to avoid the obvious traits and behaviors, the bats and fangs and wooden stakes and garlic. But I was equally committed to having some fun with the sexual drive and innuendo that permeates the vampire legends, so I let that sort of language run rampant. What would happen, I wondered, if a vampire fell in love with a good Catholic girl but she then broke his heart by offering friendship?

Rick Wilber

THE MOOSE CHURCH

Jonathan Carroll

Carroll often writes stories within stories—leading the reader into the middle of his characters' lives—and has the rare ability to pique the reader's interest so that one wants to know more about those characters outside the limits of the story. For example, I want to know more about the letter writer in "The Moose Church."

This is one of two stories in which dreaming takes on a sinister aspect.

*J*udy,
just returned from Sardinia where we'd planned to stay two weeks but ended up driving away after five days because it is one HIDEOUS island, dahling, let me tell you. I'm always suckered by books like *The Sea and Sardinia* or *The Colossos of Maroussi*, where famous writers describe how wonderful it was to be on wild and wooly islands forty years ago when the native women went golden topless and meals cost less than a pack of cigarettes. So, fool that I am, I read those books, pack my bag, and flea (intended) south. Only to see topless women all right—two-hundred-pound German frau/tanks from Bielefeld with bazooms so enormous they could windsurf on them if they only hoisted a sail, meals that cost more than my new car, and accommodations the likes of which you'd wish on your worst enemy. And then, because I have a limp memory, I always forget the sun in those southern climes is so deceptively hot that it fries you helpless in a quick few hours. Please witness my volcanic red face, thanks.

No, I am past forty now and consequently have every right to "Just Say No" to things like these trips from now on. When we were driving back, I said to Caitlin, Let's just go to the mountains for our next vacation. Then lo and behold, we came to an inn below the mountains near Graz, next to a small flickering brook, with the smell of woodsmoke and slight dung, red-and-white checked tablecloths, a bed upstairs that looked down on the brook through swaying chestnut trees, and there were chocolates wrapped in silver tinfoil on our pillows. There's no place like home, Toto.

While we were in Sardinia, we spent a lot of time in a café/bar that was the only nice thing about the place. It was called the Spin Out Bar and when the owners found out we were American, they treated us like heroes. One of them had been to New York years ago and kept a map of Manhattan pinned on the wall with red marks all over it to show anyone who came in where he'd been there.

At night the joint filled up and could be pretty rowdy, but besides the Nordic windsurfers and an overdose of fat people in floral prints, we met a number of interesting characters. Our favorites were a Dutch woman named Miep who worked in a sunglasses factory in Maastricht. Her companion was an Englishman named McGann and there, my friend, sits this story.

We couldn't figure out why Miep was in Sardinia in the first place because she said she didn't like a lot of sun and never went to the water. She was happy to leave it at that, but McGann thought it germane to add, "She reads a lot, you know." What does she read about? "Bees. She loves to study bees. Thinks we should study them because *they* know how to make a society work properly." Unfortunately, neither Caitlin nor my knowledge of bees extends beyond stings and various kinds of honey we have tasted, but Miep rarely said anything about her books or her bees. In the beginning Miep rarely said anything about anything, leaving it up to her friend to carry the conversation ball. Which he did with alarming gusto.

God knows, the English are good conversationalists and when they're funny they can have you on the floor every five minutes, but McGann talked too much. McGann never *stopped* talking. You got to the point where you'd just tune him out and look at his pretty, silent girlfriend. The sad part was, in between all his words lived an interesting man. He was a travel agent in London and had been to fascinating places—Bhutan, Patagonia, North Yemen. He also told half-good stories, but inevitably in the middle of one about the Silk Road or being trapped by a snowstorm in a Buddhist monastery you'd realize he'd already spewed so many extraneous, boring details that you'd stopped paying attention six sentences ago and were off in your own dream image of a snowbound monastery.

One day we went to the beach and stayed too long—both of us came home in wicked sunburns and bad moods. We complained and snapped at each other until Caitlin had the good idea of going to the bar for dinner because they were having a grill party and had been talking about it since we'd arrived. Grill parties are not my idea of nirvana, especially among strangers, but I knew if we stayed in our barren bungalow another hour we'd fight, so I agreed to go.

"Hello! There you two are. Miep thought you'd be coming so we saved you places. The food is really quite good. Try the chicken. Lord, look at your sunburns! Were you out all day? I remember the worst sunburn I ever had …" Was only part of McGann's greeting from across the room when we came in and walked over. We loaded up plates and went to sit with them.

As both the evening and McGann went on, my mood plunged. I didn't want to listen to him, didn't want to be on this burnt island, didn't relish the twenty-hour trip back home. Did I mention when we returned to the mainland on the overnight ferry there were no more cabins available, so we had to sleep on benches? We did.

Anyway, I could feel myself winding up for one hell of a temper tantrum. When I was three seconds away from throwing it all onto McGann and telling him he was the biggest bore I'd ever met and would he shut up, Miep turned to me and asked, "What was the strangest dream you ever had?" Taken aback both by the question, which was utterly out of left field, and because her boyfriend was in the middle of a ramble about suntan cream, I thought about it. I rarely remember my dreams. When I do they are either boring or unimaginatively sexy. The only strange one that came to mind was playing guitar naked in the back seat of a Dodge with Jimi Hendrix. Jimi was naked too and we must have played "Hey Joe" ten times before I woke up with a smile on my face and a real sadness that Hendrix was dead and I would never meet him. I relayed this to Miep who listened with head cupped in her hands. Then she asked Caitlin. She told that great dream about making the giant omelette for God and going all over the world trying to find enough eggs? Remember how we laughed at that?

After we answered, there was a big silence. Even McGann said nothing. I noticed he was looking at his girlfriend with an anxious, childlike expression on his face. As if he were waiting for her to begin whatever game was to follow.

"Dreams are how Ian and I met. I was in Heathrow waiting to fly back to Holland. He was sitting next to me and saw that I was reading an article on this 'Lucid Dreaming.' Do you know about it? You teach yourself to be conscious in your night dreams so you can manipulate and use them. We started talking about this idea and he made me very bored. Ian can be very boring. It is something you must get used to if you are going to be with him. I still have trouble, but it is a week now and I am better."

"A week? What do you mean? You've only been together that long?"

"Miep was coming back from a beekeepers' convention in Devon. After our conversation in the airport, she said she would come with me."

"Just like that? You came here with him instead of going home?" Caitlin not only believed this, she was enchanted. She believes fully in chance encounters, splendid accidents, and loving someone so much right off the bat you can learn to live with their glaring faults. I was more astonished that Miep'd come with him yet said openly what a bore he was. Was that how a love-at-first-sight bond was sealed: Yes, let's fly off together, darling, I love you madly and I'll try to get used to how boring you are.

"Yes. After Ian told me about his dreams, I asked if I could come. It was necessary for me."

I said to McGann, "Must have been some kind of powerful dream you had." He looked plain, pleasant, and capable but only in a small way—like an efficient postman who delivers your mail early, or the salesman in a liquor store who can rattle off the names of thirty different brands of beer. I assumed he was a good travel agent, up on his prices and brochures and a man who could choose a good vacation for someone who didn't have much money. But he wasn't impressive and he talked forever. What kind of dream *had* he had to convince this attractive and nicely mysterious Dutch woman to drop everything and accompany him to Sardinia?

"It wasn't much really. I dreamt I was working in an office, not where I do work but some other place, but nowhere special. A man walked in who I knew a long time ago but who died. He died of cancer maybe five years ago. I saw him and knew for sure that he had come back from the dead to see me. His name was Larry Birmingham. I never really liked this fellow. He was very loud and much too sure of himself. But there he was in my dream.

I looked up from my desk and said, 'Larry. It's you! You're back from the dead!' He was very calm and said yes, he'd come to see me. I asked if I could ask him questions about it. About death that is, of course. He smiled, a little too amusedly I realize now, and said yes. About this time in the dream, I think I *knew* I was dreaming, you know how that happens? But I thought go on, see what you can find out. So I asked him questions. What *is* death like? Should we be afraid? Is it anything like we expect . . . that sort of thing. He answered, but many of the answers were vaguely obscure and confusing. I'd ask again and he'd answer in a different way, which at first I thought was clearer, but in the end it wasn't—he had only stated the muddle differently. It wasn't much help, I'll tell you."

"Did you learn anything?"

Ian looked at Miep. Despite her aloofness and his ten-mile-long dialog it was very obvious that there was great closeness and regard between these two remarkably dissimilar people. It was a look of love to be sure, but a great deal more than that. More, a look that clearly said there were things they knew about each other already that went to the locus of their beings. Whether they'd known each other a short week or twenty years, the look contained everything we all hope for in our lives with others. She nodded her approval but after another moment, he said gently, "I . . . I'm afraid I can't tell you."

"Oh, Ian—" She reached across the table and touched her hand to his face. Imagine a laser line of light or heat going directly across that table, excluding everything but those two. That's what both Caitlin and I felt watching them. What was most surprising to me was it was the first time Miep had either talked or shown real feeling for her man. But there was suddenly so much feeling that it was embarrassing.

"Ian, you're right. I'm sorry. You're so right." She slipped back into her chair but continued looking at him. He turned to me and said, "I'm sorry to be rude, but you'll understand why I can't tell you anything when I'm finished.

"Excuse me, but before I go on, it's hard for me to tell this so I'm going to have another drink. Would anyone like a refill?"

None of us did so he got up and went to the bar. The table was silent while he was gone. Miep never stopped looking at him. Caitlin and I didn't know where to look until he returned.

"Right-O. Tanked up and am ready to go. You know what I was just thinking, up there at the bar? That I once drove though Austria and got a case of the giggles when I passed a sign for the town of Mooskirchen. I remember so well thinking to myself that a bonkers translation of that would be 'Moose Church.' Then I thought well why the hell not—people worship all kinds of things on this earth. Why couldn't there be a church to Mooses? Or rather, a religion to them. You know?

"I'm rattling on here, aren't I? It's because this is a terribly difficult story for me to tell. The funny thing is, when I'm finished you'll think I'm just as bonkers as my imagined worshipers at the Moose Church, eh, Miep? Won't they think I don't have all my bulbs screwed in?"

"If they understand, they will know you are a hero."

"Yes, well, folks, don't take Miep too seriously. She's quiet but very emotional about things sometimes. Let me go on and you can judge for yourself whether I'm crazy or, ha, ha, a hero.

"The morning after that first dream, I walked to the bathroom and started taking my pajamas off so I could wash up. I was shocked when I saw—"

"Don't tell them, Ian, show them! Show them so they will see for themselves!"

Slowly, shyly he began to pull his T-shirt up over his head. Caitlin saw it first and gasped. When I saw I guess I gasped too. From his left shoulder down to above his left nipple was a monstrously long and deep scar. It looked exactly like what my father had down the middle of his chest after open-heart surgery. One giant scar so wide and obscenely pink. His body's way of saying it would never forgive him for doing that to it.

"Oh, Ian, what happened?" Sweet Caitlin, the heart of the world, involuntarily reached out to touch him, comfort him. Realizing what she was doing, she pulled her hand back, but the look of sympathy framed her face.

"Nothing happened, Caitlin. I have never been hurt in my life. Never been in the hospital, never had an operation. I asked death some questions and when I woke the next morning this was here." He didn't wait for us to examine the scar more closely. The shirt was up and over his head quickly.

"I'm telling you, Ian, maybe it is a kind of gift."

"It's no gift, Miep, if it hurts terribly and I can't move my left arm very well anymore! The same with my foot *and* my hand."

"What are you talking about?"

Ian closed his eyes and tried once to continue. He couldn't and instead rocked up and down with his eyes closed.

Miep spoke. "The night before we met, he had another dream and the same thing happened: This Larry came back and Ian asked him more questions about death. But this time the answers were clearer, although not all of them. He woke up and he says he had begun to understand things that he didn't before. He believes that's why the scar on the inside of his hand is smaller—the more he understands of the dream, the more it leaves him alone. A few nights ago he had another but he woke with a big cut on his leg. Much bigger than the one on his hand."

Ian spoke again, but his voice was less. Softer and . . . deflated. "It will tell you anything you want to know, but then you have to understand it. If you don't . . . it does this to you so you'll be careful with your questions. The trouble is, once you've started, you can't stop asking. In the middle of my second dream I told Birmingham I wanted to stop; I was afraid. He said I couldn't. The ultimate game of 'Twenty Questions,' eh? Thank God Miep's here. Thank God she believed me! See, it makes me so much *weaker*. Maybe that's the worst part. After the dreams there are the scars, but even worse than that is I'm so much weaker and can't do anything about it. I can barely get out of the bed. Most of the time I'm better as the day goes on . . . but I know it's getting worse. And one day I won't . . . I know if Miep weren't here . . . Thank God for you, Miep."

I later convinced him to show us the scar on his hand, which was utterly unlike the one on his chest. This one was white and thin and looked years old. It went diagonally across his palm and I remember thinking from the first time we'd met how strangely he moved that hand, how much slower and clumsier it was. Now I knew why.

There's more to this, Judy. But what do you do in a situation like that? When half your brain thinks this is mad but the other half is shaking because *maybe-it's-real*. They asked us for nothing, although I doubt there was anything we could do. But after that night whenever I saw or thought of McGann, I liked him enormously. Whatever was wrong with the man, he was afflicted by something terrible. Either insanity or death dreams were clearly out to get him and he was a goner. But the man remained a bore. A good-natured, good-humored bore who, in the midst of his agony or whatever it was, remained wholly himself as I assume he'd always been. That's the only real courage. I mean, come on, none of us goes into burning buildings to save others. But watching a person face the worst with grace, uncomplainingly, grateful even for the love and help of others . . . That's it, as far as I'm concerned.

Two days later, Caitlin and I decided more or less on the spur of the moment to leave. We'd had enough and weren't getting any pleasure at all from the place. Our bags were packed and the bill was paid within an hour and a half. Neither of us like saying goodbye to people, and as you can imagine, we were spooked by McGann's story. It's not something anyone would be quick to believe, but if you were there that night and seen their faces, heard their voices and the conviction in them, you'd know why both of us were uncomfortable in their presence. But it happened that as we were walking out to the car, we ran right into Miep, who was coming toward the office in a hurry.

Something was clearly wrong. "Miep, are you all right?"

"All right? Oh, well, no. Ian is . . . Ian is not well." She was totally preoccupied and her eyes were going everywhere but to us. Then a light of memory came on in them and her whole being slowed. She remembered, I guess, what her man had told us the other night.

"He had another dream today, after he came home from the beach. He lay down and it was only a few minutes, but when he woke—" Instead of continuing, she drew a slow line across the lower part of her stomach. Both Caitlin and I jumped at that and asked what we could do. I think we both also started toward their bungalow, but Miep shouted, really shouted, "No!" and there was nothing we could do to convince her to let us help. If that were possible. More than that though, the thing that struck me hardest was her face. When she realized we weren't going to try and interfere, she looked over our shoulders toward their place, where Ian was, and the expression was both fear and radiance. Was it true? Was he really back there, scarred again by death, scarred again because he hadn't understood its answers to his questions? Who knows?

On the boat back to the mainland, I remembered what he had said that night about the Moose Church and how people should be allowed to worship whatever they want. *That* was the look on his girlfriend's face—the look of one in the presence of what they believe is both the truth and the answer to life. Or death.

Our Thoughts,
Ted

"The Moose Church" is a result of a terrible but rather interesting trip to Sardinia. I was so taken by the idea of the story that I decided to use it as the first part of the next novel I will be doing. As to the theme of vampirism, say whatever you will, the ultimate vampire is death.

Jonathan Carroll

MRS. RINALDI'S ANGEL

Thomas Ligotti

Ligotti is justly celebrated for his baroque journeys into the unconscious. This story is a little more straightforward and slightly less baroque in language, without, however, losing his unique voice.

Like Carroll's before it, this story, too, is about dreams, but here the dreamer is a collaborator despite himself, inadvertently causing great harm.

From time to time during my childhood, the striking dreams that I nightly experienced would become brutally vivid, causing me to awake screaming. The shouting done, I sank back into my bed in a state of superenervation resulting from the bodiless adventures imposed upon my slumbering self. Yet my body was surely affected by this nocturnal regimen, exercised harshly by visions both crystalline and confused. This activity, however immaterial, only served to drain my reserves of strength and in a few moments stole from me the benefits of a full night's sleep. Nevertheless, while I was deprived of the privilege of a natural rest, there may also have been some profit gained: the awful opulence of the dream, a rich and swollen world nourished by the exhaustion of the flesh. The world, in fact, *as such*. Any other realm seemed an absence by comparison, at best a chasm in the fertile graveyard of life.

Of course my parents did not share my feelings on this subject. "What is *wrong* with him," I heard my father bellow from far down the hallway, his voice full of reproach. Shortly afterward my mother was by my side. "They seem to be getting worse," she would say. Then on one occasion she whispered, "I think it's time we did something about this problem."

The tone of her voice told me that what she had in mind was not the doctor's appointment so often urged by my father. Hers was a more dubious quest for a curative, though one which no doubt also seemed more appropriate to my "suffering." My mother was always prone to the enticements of superstition, and my troubled dreams appeared to justify an indulgence in unorthodox measures. Her shining and solemn gaze betrayed her own dreams of trafficking with esoteric forces, of being on familiar terms with specialists in a secret universe, entrepreneurs of the intangible.

"Tomorrow your father is leaving early on business. You stay home from school, and then we'll go and visit a woman I know."

Late the following morning, my mother and I went to a house in one of the outlying neighborhoods of town and were graciously invited to be seated in the parlor of the long-widowed Mrs. Rinaldi. Perhaps it was only the fatigue my dreams had inflicted on me that made it so difficult to consolidate any lucid thoughts or feelings about the old woman and her remote house. Although the well-ordered room we occupied was flush with sunlight, this illumination somehow acted in a way of a wash over a watercolor painting, blurring the outline of things and subduing the clarity of surfaces. This obscurity was not dispersed even by the large and thickly shaded lamp Mrs. Rinaldi kept lighted beside the small divan on which she and my mother sat. I was close to them in an old but respectably upholstered armchair, and yet their forms refused to come into focus, just as everything else in that room resisted definition. How well I knew such surroundings, those deep interiors of dream where everything is saturated with unreality and more or less dissolves under a direct gaze. I could tell how neatly this particular interior was arranged—pictures perfectly straight and tight against the walls, well-dusted figurines arranged well upon open shelves, lace-fringed tablecovers set precisely in place, and delicate silk flowers in slim vases of colored glass. Yet there was something so fragile about the balance of these things, as if they were all susceptible to sudden derangement should there be some upset, no matter how subtle, in the secret system that held them together. This volatility seemed to extend to Mrs. Rinaldi herself, though in fact she may have been its source.

Casually examined, she appeared to present only the usual mysteries of old women who might be expected to speak with a heavy accent, whether or not they actually did so. She wore the carnal bulk and simple attire of a peasant race, and her calm manner indeed epitomized the peasant quietude of popular conception: her hands folded without tremor upon a wide lap and her eyes were mildly attentive. But those eyes were so pale, as was her complexion and gauzy hair. It was as if some great strain had depleted her, and was continually depleting her, of the strong coloring she once possessed, draining her powers and leaving her vulnerable to some tenuous onslaught. At any moment, during the time my mother was explaining the reason why we sought her help, Mrs. Rinaldi might have degenerated before our eyes, might have finally succumbed to spectral afflictions she had spent so many years fending off, both for her own sake and for the sake of others. And still she might have easily been mistaken for just another old woman whose tidy parlor displayed no object or image that would betray her most questionable and perilous occupation.

"Missus," she said to my mother, though her eyes were on me, "I would like to take your son into another room in this house. There I believe I may begin to help him."

My mother assented and Mrs. Rinaldi escorted me down a hallway to a room at the back of the house. The room reminded me of a little shop of some kind, one that kept its merchandise hidden in dark cabinets along the walls, in great chests upon the floor, boxes and cases of every sort piled here and there. Nothing except these receptacles, this array of multiform exteriors, was exposed to view. The only window was tightly shuttered and a bare light bulb hanging overhead served as the only illumination.

There was nowhere to sit, only empty floor space; Mrs. Rinaldi took my hand and stood me at the center of the room. After gazing rather sternly down at me for some moments, she proceeded to pace slowly around me.

"Do you know what dreams are?" she asked quietly, and then immediately began to answer her own question. "They are parasites—maggots of the mind and soul, feeding on the mind and soul as ordinary maggots feed on the body. And their feeding on the mind and soul in turn gnaws away at the body, which in turn again affects the mind and the soul, and so on until death. These things cannot be separated, nor can anything else. Because everything is terribly inseparable and affects everything else. Even the most alien things are connected together with everything else. And so if these dreams have no world of their own to nourish them, they may come into yours and possess it, exhaust it little by little each night. They use your world and use it up. They wear your face and the faces of things you know: things that are yours they use in ways that are theirs. And some persons are so easy for them to use, and they use them so hard. But they use everyone and have always used everyone, because they are from the old time, the time before all the worlds awoke from a long and helpless night. And these dreams, these things that are called dreams, are still working to throw us back into that great mad darkness, to exhaust each one of us in our lonely sleep, and to use up everyone until death. Little by little, night after night, they take us away from ourselves and from the truth of things. I myself know very well what this can be like and what the dreams can do to us. They make us dance to their strange illusions until we are too exhausted to live. And they have found in you, child, an easy partner for their horrible dancing."

With these words Mrs. Rinaldi not only revealed a side of herself quite different from the serene wise woman my mother had seen, but she also took me much deeper into things I had merely suspected until that day in the room where chests and strange boxes were piled up everywhere and great cabinets loomed along the walls, so many tightly closed doors and drawers and locked-up lids with so many things on the other side of them.

"Of course," she went on, "these dreams of yours cannot be wholly exorcised from your life, but only driven back so that they may do no *extraordinary* harm. They will still triumph in the end, denying us not just the restoration of nightly sleep. For ultimately they steal away the time that might have measured into immortality. They corrupt us in *every way*, abducting us from the ranks of angels we might have been or become, pure and calm and ever-lasting. It is because of them that we endure such a meager allotment of years, with all their foulness. This is all I can offer you, child, even if you may not understand what it means. For it is surely not meant that you should fall into the fullest corruption before your time."

Her speech concluded, Mrs. Rinaldi stood before me, massive and motionless, her breathing now a bit labored. I confess that her theories intrigued me as far as I could comprehend them, for at the time her statements regarding the meaning and mechanisms of dream appeared to be founded on somewhat questionable assumptions, unnecessarily outlandish in their departures from the oldest orthodoxies of creation. Nonetheless, I decided not to resist whatever applications she chose to make of her ideas. On her side, she was scrutinizing my small form with some intensity, engaged in what seemed a psychic sizing up of my presence, as if she were seriously unsure whether or not it was safe to move on to the next step with me.

Apparently resolving her doubts, she shuffled over to a tall cabinet, unlocked its door with a key she had taken from a sagging pocket in her dress, and from within removed two items: a slim decanter half-filled with a dark red liquid, presumably wine, and a shallow wide-mouthed drinking glass. Carrying these objects back to me, she put out her right hand, in which she held the glass, and said: "Take this and spit into it." After I had done this, she poured some of the wine into the glass and then replaced the decanter in its cabinet, which she locked once again. "Now kneel down on the floor," she ordered. "Don't let anything spill out of the glass, and don't get up until I tell you to do so. I'm going to turn out the light."

Even in total darkness, Mrs. Rinaldi maneuvered well about the room, her footsteps again moving away from me. I heard her opening another cabinet, or perhaps it was a large chest whose heavy lid she struggled to push back, its old hinges grinding in the darkness. A slight draft crossed the room, a brief drifting current of air without scent and neither warm nor cold. Mrs. Rinaldi then approached me, moving more slowly than she had before, as if bearing some weighty object. With a groan, she set it down, and I heard it scrape the floor inches from where I knelt, though I could not see what it was.

Suddenly a thin line of light scored the blackness, and I could see Mrs. Rinaldi's old finger slowly lifting the lid of a long low box from which the luminousness emanated. The glowing slit widened as the lid was drawn back farther, revealing a pale brilliance that seemed confined wholly within the box itself, casting not the least glimmer into the room. The source of this light was a kind of incandescent vapor that curled about in a way that seemed to draw the room's darkness into its lustrous realm, which appeared to extend beyond the boundaries of the visible and made the box before me look bottomless. But I felt the bottom for myself when the whispering voice of Mrs. Rinaldi instructed me to place the glass I was holding down into the box. So I offered the glass to that fluorescent mist, that churning vapor that was electrical in some way, scintillating with infinitesimal flashes of sharp light, sprinkled with shattered diamonds.

I expected to feel something as I put my hand in the shining box, easily setting the glass upon its shallow and quite solid bottom. But there was nothing at all to be felt, no sensation whatever—not even that of my own hand. There seemed to be a power to this prodigy, but it was a terribly quiescent power, a cataract of the purest light plummeting silently in the blackness of space. If it could have spoken it might have told, in a soft and reverberant voice, of the lonely peace of the planets, the uninhabited paradise of clouds, and an antiseptic infinity.

After I placed the glass of wine and spittle into the box, the light from within took on a rosy hue for just a moment, then resumed its glittering whiteness once again. It had taken the offering. Mrs. Rinaldi whispered "Amen," then carefully closed the lid upon the box, returning the room to blackness. I heard her replace the object in its tabernacle of storage, wherever that may have been. At last the lights came on.

"You can get up now," Mrs. Rinaldi said. "And wipe off your knees, they're a little dirty."

When I finished brushing off my pants I found that Mrs. Rinaldi was again scrutinizing me for telltale signs of some possible misunderstanding or perhaps misconduct that I might disclose to her. I imagined that she was about to say, "Do not ask what it was you saw in this room." But in actuality she said, "You will feel better now, but never try to guess what is in that box. Never seek to know more about it." She did not pause to hear any response I might have had to her command, for she was indeed a wise woman and knew that in matters such as these no casual oath of abstention can be trusted, all fine intentions notwithstanding.

As soon as we had left Mrs. Rinaldi's house, my mother asked me what had happened, and I described the ceremony in detail. Nevertheless, she remained at a loss for any simple estimate of what I had told her: While she expected that Mrs. Rinaldi's methods might be highly unusual, she also knew her own son's imagination. Still, she was obliged to keep faith with the arcane processes that she herself had set in motion. So after I recounted the incidents that took place in that room, my mother only nodded silently, perhaps bewilderedly.

I should document that for a certain period of time my mother's faith in Mrs. Rinaldi did not appear to have been misplaced. The very day of our visit to the old woman was for me the beginning of a unique phase of experience. Even my father noted the change in my nighttime habits, as well as a newfound characterology I exhibited throughout the day. "The boy does seem quieter now," he commented to my mother.

Indeed, I could feel myself approaching a serenity almost shameful in its expansiveness, one that submerged me in a placid routine of the most violent contrast to my former life. I slept straight through each night and barely ruffled my bedcovers. Not to claim that my sleep was left completely untouched by dreams. But these were no more than ripples on great becalmed waters, pathetic gestures of something that was trying to bestir the immobility of a vast and colorless world. A few figures might appear, tremulous as smoke, but they were the merest invalids of hallucination, lacking the strength to speak or raise a hand against my terrible peace.

My daydreams were actually more interesting, while still being incredibly vague and without tension. Sitting quietly in the classroom at school, I often gazed out the window at clouds and sunlight, watching the way the sunlight penetrated the clouds and the way the clouds were filled with both sunlight and shadows. Yet no images or ideas were aroused by this sight, as they had been before. Only a vacant meditation took place, a musing without subject matter. I could feel something trying to emerge in my imagination, some wild and colorful drama that was being kept far away from me, as far away as those clouds, remaining entirely vaporous and empty of either sense or sensation. And if I tried to draw any pictures in my notebook, allowing my hand all possible freedom (in order to find out if it could feel and remember what I could not), I found myself sketching over and over the same thing: boxes, boxes, boxes.

Nonetheless, I cannot say that I was unhappy during this time. My nightmares and everything associated with them had been bled from my system, drained away as I slept. I had been purified of tainted substances, sponged clean of strangely tinted stains on my mind and my soul. I felt the vapid joy of a lightened being, a kind of clarity that seemed in a way true and even virtuous. But this moratorium on every form of darkness could only last so long before the old impulses asserted themselves within me, moving out like a pack of famished wolves in search of the stuff that once fed them and would feed them again.

For a number of nights my dreams remained somewhat anemic and continued to present only the palest characters and scenes. Thus, they had been rendered too weak to use me as they had before, seizing, as they did, the contents of my life—my memories and emotions, all the paraphernalia of a private history—and working them in their way, giving form to things that had none of their own, and thereby exhausting my body and soul. Mrs. Rinaldi's theory of these parasites that have been called dreams was therefore accurate . . . as far as it went. But she had failed to consider, or perhaps refused to acknowledge, that the dreamer on his part draws something from the dream, gaining a store of experience otherwise impossible to obtain, hoarding the grotesque or banal enigmas of the night to try to fill out the great empty spaces of the day. And my dreams had ceased to perform this function, or at least were no longer adequate to my needs—that appetite I had discovered in myself for banqueting on the absurd and horrible, even the perfectly evil. It was this deprivation, I believe, that brought about the change in the nature of my dreaming.

Having such paltry sustenance on which to nourish my tastes—frail demons and insipid decors—I must have been thrown back upon my own consciousness . . . until finally I came into full awareness of my dreaming state, intensely lucid. Over the course of several nights, then, I noticed a new or formerly obscure phenomenon, something that existed in the distance of those bankrupt landscapes that I had started to explore. It was a kind of sickly mist that lingered about the horizon of each dream, exerting a definite magnetism, a tugging upon the austere scenes that it enveloped from all sides, even hovering high above like an animate sky, a celestial vault that glistened softly. Yet the dreams themselves were cast in the dullest tones and contained the most spare and dilapidated furnishings.

In the very last dream I had of this type, I was wandering amid a few widely scattered ruins that seemed to have risen from some undersea abyss, all soft and pallid from their dark confinement. Like the settings of the other dreams, this one seemed familiar, though incomplete, as if I were seeing the decayed remnants of something I might have known in waking life. For those were *not* time-eaten towers rising around me, and at my feet there were not sunken strongboxes crumbling like rotten flesh. Instead, these objects were the cabinets and cases I remembered from that room in Mrs. Rinaldi's house, except now this memory was degenerating, being

dragged away little by little, digested by that mist, which surrounded everything and nibbled at it. And the more closely I approached this mist, the
more decomposed the scenery of the dream became, until it was consumed
altogether and I could see nothing but that sparkling, swirling vapor.

It was only when I had entered this foggy void that the true sense of
dreams, the inherent dread of my visions, was restored to me. Here was a
sort of reservoir into which the depths of my dreams were being directed,
leaving only a shallow spillover that barely trickled through my nights. *Here,*
I say, without knowing really what place or plane of being it was: some
spectral venue, a vacant plot situated along the back street of sleep, an
outpost of the universe itself . . . or perhaps merely the inside of a box hidden
away in the house of an old woman, a box in which something exists in all
its insensible purity, a cloudy ether free of tainted forms and knowledge,
freely cleansing others with its sterile grace.

In any event, I sensed that the usual boundaries of my world of sleep
had extended into another realm. And it was here, I found, that the lost
dreams were fully alive *in their essence.* Consumed within that barren vapor,
which I had seen imbibe a mixture of my own saliva and the reddest wine,
they lived in exile from that multitude of unwitting hosts whose experiences
they used like a wardrobe for those eerie performances behind the curtain of
sleep, forcing the sleeper into the role of both player and witness in the alien
manipulations of his memories and emotions, the ungranted abduction of
his private history for the wreckless revels of these parasites called dreams.
But here, in that prison of glittering purity, they had been reduced to their
primordial state—dreams in abstraction, faceless and formless things from
the old time that a very old woman revealed to me. And although they had
neither face nor form, none of the multitudinous disguises in which I had
always known them, their presence was still quite palpable all around me,
bearing down upon the richly laden lucidity I had brought with me into a
place I did not belong.

A struggle evolved as that angelic mist—agent of my salvation—held at
bay the things that craved my mind and soul, my very consciousness. But
rather than join in that struggle, I gave myself up to this ravenous siege,
offering my awareness to what had none of its own, bestowing all the
treasures of my life on this wasteland of abstract dreams.

Then the infinite whiteness itself was flooded with the colors of countless faces and forms, a blank sky suddenly dense with rainbows, until *everything* was so saturated with revels and thick with frenzy that it took on the utter blackness of the old time. And in the blackness I awoke, screaming for all the world.

The next day I was standing on Mrs. Rinaldi's porch, watching as my mother repeatedly slammed the door knocker without being able to summon the old woman. But something told us she was nevertheless at home, a shadow that we saw pass nervously behind the front window. At last the door opened for us, but whoever opened it stayed on the other side, saying: "Missus, take your child home. There is nothing more that can be done. I made a mistake with him."

My mother protested the recurrence of my "sickness," taking a step inside the house and pulling me along with her. But Mrs. Rinaldi only said: "Do not come in here. It is not a fit place to visit, and I am not fit to be looked upon." From what I could observe of the parlor, it did seem that an essential change had occurred, as if the room's fragile balance had failed and the ever-threatening derangement of its order had finally been consummated. Everything in this interior seemed askew, distorted by some process of decay and twisted out of natural proportion. It was a room seen through a warped and strangely colored window.

And how much stranger this color appeared when Mrs. Rinaldi suddenly showed herself, and I saw that her once-pale eyes and sallow face had taken on the same tint, a greenish glaze as of something both rotten and reptilian. My mother was immediately silenced by this sight. "Now will you leave me?" she said. "Even for myself there is nothing I can do any longer. You know what I am saying, child. All those years the dreams had been kept away. But you have *consorted* with them, I know you did. I have made a mistake with you. You let my angel be poisoned by the dreams that you could not deny. It *was* an angel, did you know that? It was pure of all thinking and pure of all dreaming. And you are the one who made it think and dream and now it is dying. And it is dying not as an angel, but as a demon. Do you want to see what it is like now?" she said, gesturing toward a door that led into the cellar of her house. "Yes, it is down there because it is not the way it was and could not remain where it was. It crawled away with its own body, the body of a demon. And it has its own dreams, the dreams of a demon. It is dreaming and dying of its dreams. And I am dying too, because all the dreams have come back."

Mrs. Rinaldi then began to approach me, and the color of her eyes and her face seemed to deepen. That was when my mother grasped my arm to pull me quickly from the house. As we ran off I looked over my shoulder and saw the old woman raving in the open doorway, cursing me for a demon.

It was not long afterward that we learned of Mrs. Rinaldi's death. True to her own diagnosis, the parasites were upon her, although local gossip told that she had been suffering for years from a cancer of some kind. There was also evidence that another inhabitant of the house survived the old woman for a short time. As it happened, several of my schoolmates reported to me their investigations after dark at the house of the "old witch," a place that I myself was forbidden by my parents to go. So I cannot claim that I observed with my own eyes what crept along the floor of that moonlit house, "like a pile of filthy rags," said one boy.

But I did dream about this prodigy; I even dreamed about its dreams as they dragged every shining angelic particle of this being into the blackness of the old time. Then all my bad dreams abated after a while, just as they always had and always would, using my world only at intervals and gradually dissolving my life into theirs.

A few words on the death of the personal vampire. One of the noblest and most tragic figures of the imagination, the vampire has long been reduced to serving some allegorical function in various mundane contexts—psychology, sociology, politics, and so on. The vampire attained his stature through the emotion of fear of a fantastic evil, yet how utterly he has lost it all at the heavy hands of writers and critics whose ceaseless prying has exposed him too often to daylight, murdering his mystery with tabloid revelations as well as talky sessions of analysis.

But if the vampire no longer inspires the emotion he once did, perhaps it is partly his own fault. He lost his mystery entirely because he had so little of it to start. His nature and habits were always documented in detail, his ways and means a matter of public record. Too many laws lorded over him, and all laws belong to the natural world. Like his colleague the werewolf, he was too much a *known quantity*. His was a familiar, most of the time human body, and it was used like a whore by writers whose concerns were predominantly for the body and the everyday path in which it walks. Consequently, the vampire was stripped of all that made him alien to our ordinary selves, until finally he was transformed into merely the bad boy next door. He remained a menace, to be sure. But his focus shifted from the soul to the senses. This is how it is when a mysterious force is embodied in a human body, or in any form that is too well fixed. And a mystery explained is one robbed of its power.

Rest in peace, Nosferatu. None will ever take your place.

Thomas Ligotti

THE POOL PEOPLE

Melissa Mia Hall

Hall's story deals with an experience seldom written about from the victim's point of view—particularly in horror fiction. The protagonist has been so maimed emotionally that she has lost her sense of self.

1. THE POOL

The water's so blue it hurts my eyes. On a day like this you have to wear sunglasses or go blind. I'm wearing dark ones, old-fashioned Audrey Hepburn *Breakfast at Tiffany's* sunglasses. The glamorous, heavy-duty I-want-to-be-alone kind. And I'm alone. My cousin has gone to work and left me here by her pool. Her swimming pool. I'll be safe here. I can relax and take it easy. Get a tan on a body that hasn't known a tan since high school. Of course I know sunburns are dangerous. I've slathered my body with sunscreen. I smell like a dream of Hawaii.

This is my summer vacation.

And I'm sitting by the pool.

2. THE PEOPLE

I saw them for the first time in a dream. I'd fallen asleep in the sun. My eyelids bled pink light, then I opened my eyes and my eyeballs fell forward into my lap. I picked them up and put them back in and leaned forward, staring into the water. My hands gripped the side of the pool. The pebble-coarse side slid into smoothness. I touched the surface of the water with the palm of my hand. I felt the ripples. I thought, Molly, you're dreaming, and then I saw them, clear as day, the people. They sat at a table under the water, on the bottom. Fully clothed, they were, their hair streaming out from their heads like seaweed.

Like a show I saw or wanted to see at the Aquarena Watercade Extravaganza a long, long time ago, when I was little. How I loved the idea of people pretending they weren't really underwater, sucking secret oxygen.

And now, here they are again. Waving.

3. THE POOL MAN

It's too much sun, seeing people in a pool, waving. I was just remembering a TV commercial. And staring into the water. I should swim. The exercise would be good for me. I'd impress Cara Ann, too. She's so proud of this pool, this house, the lovely landscaping, the life she's made here, without Al.

She wants me to be happy. I open a book instead. The pages are too white. I move over to a circle of shade. I take a sip of tepid Coke. I need ice. I stand up and stretch, lady of supreme leisure.

"The gate was open—"

I drop my book. The intruder looks embarrassed. "Ms. Clovis was expecting me—"

My hand closes over the back of a wrought-iron chair. I can barely breathe. Every time I see them, I feel emptier, looser, gone. But now here is this man. I tighten inside, clench. All men are dangerous. I know that, I know.

He flashes an open billfold like he's from the FBI and stuffs it back into the back pocket of his baggy shorts. "I'm the pool man—at least for today. I'm helping out my big brother, Ben. He owns Sunside Pools—and he's in a bind and I told him, hey, bubba, I'll help you out. I owe him, see? So, just get back to whatever it was you were doing. I won't be long. Well, not too long. It's been a while. You're working on a tan—I see—I know, what tan?

Well, never mind, I'll get to work and you won't even know I'm here."

"Cara Ann forgot to tell me—"

She had left a note on the refrigerator I had forgotten to read. I thought it probably said something about what to fix for dinner or when she was coming home. I should've read it.

"I hope you're not planning on swimming. That'll have to wait, I'm afraid, while I do all this. But you can stay out here and keep me company."

He won't stop talking. I stare at him, still uneasy. He's not dressed in a uniform and he's too attractive to be trusted. He has a tan almost as dark as George Hamilton's, which cannot be too healthy, dark eyes, carelessly sexy. He tosses his longish hair back like Miss Piggy and keeps talking, about the weather, music, his favorite kind of food, baseball. He plays with his pool tools like a child.

"What's wrong?"

A fish does this, out of water, gasping. Slowly, I must breathe in and out, slowly. Suddenly there's a wet towel on my face. I push it off and meet the pool man's searching, too observant eyes.

"Lady, you fainted. I've seen that in old movies, but never in real life. Are you okay? Are you sick or something? Should I call Ms. Clovis? She works on that TV show—what is it? I could call her—"

"I'm fine, really."

"Are you sure?"

"No," I say, managing a smile. His white shirt is unbuttoned. He has dark hair on his chest. My head hurts. The white shirt has tiny black dots woven into the cloth. They appear to be moving.

"I think I'd better help you into the house where it's cool."

"Thanks—"

"Bergman, Pete, and you are—"

"Molly Woods."

"Nice to meet you, Molly." He says this with an expectant grin. He acts as if I am sharing some sort of secret joke, but then he sees I don't get it. He leads me into the house. I flop on the nearest chair and motion for him to go back outside. He overwhelms me with the scent of an aftershave mingled with sweat. He keeps looking at me with an expression that frightens me.

"I know, I may or may not be a killer." His hand rests on the sliding glass door. "Trust me, I'm not." He smiles again and his perfect white teeth amaze me. Everyone here has such perfect teeth. Self-consciously, I cover my mouth. My teeth need cleaning desperately.

The door slides shut. I watch him go about his business. He moves in slow motion, carefully. He pauses and considers each action he takes. Something's not right.

I go to the kitchen and get a knife. I sit in the den and watch him out the window. He better not come back in here. The steak knife stays in my lap. I call Cara Ann and ask when she'll be home. "Seven o'clock, like I told you, silly," she says, laughing. "Didn't you read my note?"

I go get the note after I hang up. I read it, keeping the knife always close at hand. It says nothing about a pool man coming.

I look outside and he's bending over the water. Around his neck is a thin gold necklace with a small disc. A tiny round flashlight. He sees something under the water. He stoops down but doesn't use the net. He just stares, shakes his head, and straightens up. He suddenly looks at the house. I know that he cannot see me, but it's as if he does. He smiles.

"I'm leaving!" he yells. "Till next time, Molly—!"

There won't be a next time. He's crazy. But I have the knife.

He comes to the sliding glass door. He knocks on it, still smiling. "Listen, Molly, if you swim, tomorrow, whenever, make sure and take the Polaris out." He points at that white machine thing with the long umbilical cord.

"I know—" I shout.

"And, hey, Molly—I hope you feel better." He seems sincere. "You want to come lock the gate after I leave?"

He doesn't see the knife. I stroke the handle. I'll put it in the pocket of my pink cover-up. I'll carry it with me. He has done nothing wrong.

I follow him out to the gate.

"You living here now?"

"Just visiting."

I glimpse the faint wrinkles at the corners of his eyes. I realize he's probably in his late thirties. Too old to be a pool man?

"You're not local. I could tell that."

I stroke the handle of the knife. I'm perfectly safe. He will not harm me. "No, I'm not. I'm from Tulsa, Oklahoma."

He suddenly leans forward and kisses my cheek. "Welcome to California," he says and the gate clangs shut.

I run back to the house. From the pool I hear strange voices and a bubbling sound. It's a fantasy, just a fantasy. It comes of vacationing. I am used to working and a normal life. Idle time and idle hands create insanity. You think too much. And when you think, you remember.

4. THE DREAM

The people in the water return to me. I know I'm dreaming, but I'm so happy to see them. I try to say hello, but bubbles come out of my mouth instead of words. I am underwater, too. I start to walk over, to sit down at the table with them. But there aren't any other chairs and it's awkward. I want to see them up close. I force my legs to move. Closer. The water keeps teasing me, pushing me back. Closer. They don't see me. They don't hear me. Then the man turns toward me and stares right through me. His hair is graying at the temples. The sunlit water twists it out straight. His forehead doesn't match the rest of his face. It's much paler, more inno-cent and exposed. His eyes widen suddenly, registering my presence. I frighten him. He quickly glances at the woman who has also seen me. She waves her hand. I try to say hello again, then I stop because I see blood, or probably red dye, issuing from her mouth. The woman loses her seat. Released from the chair, which had been holding her in with silky black ribbons, the woman rises through the water. Her legs are gleaming white. The thin white skirt also rises, a flower blossoming backward. The man's face turns upward, following her ascent.

I'm at the table now, looking at the empty chair.

There's a crash or a splash, something that makes the water rumble and stir. The woman has split the surface. She is gone. I sit down in the chair. I am naked. He's watching me, helpless, as the other ones laugh. They're watching me. Everyone sees I'm naked. Two hands come around from the back of the chair, or it is the chair. I think it is the chair. I can't breathe because it is squeezing me. The man's mouth screws up in pain. His chair has hands, too. He can't stop it. And the black ribbons swim around us like snakes. Water moccasins. They hiss, "Watch what we're going to do to her, Mr. Principal, watch us-ss-s." The bubbles keep escaping from my mouth. There is nothing I can say, but if I could, I would. The bubbles fly away, one after another, in a line, like laundry on a line drawn up and away by the wind. One of them I touch with my hand before it escapes; it is rainbow-hued and shining. My hands burn. The ropes twist. What will the children say. Will their eyes go round and spin into shame? Don't look. Don't see.

"It hurts!" I scream or I think loudly and he hears me but one of the other bubbles has settled over his face. It develops into a monarch butterfly.

The hands clutch my middle, the nails biting into my stomach.

"Let go of me—let go—" And then it's dark and I'm in another place, a bad place. But the water's still there, pushing down, and I do not see the table. I'm drowning. "Help me!" My scream melts into a coughing silence. The hands keep holding me down. "Let me go—" I hit the water and it's glass. I hit it but the glass will not break. Safety glass. "I'm not going to hurt you," the other voice says. I keep hitting till my hands hurt because I hurt. The hands hurt.

5. THE VACATION

"So, are you having a good time? You need to get out more, do stuff. This weekend I was thinking we could go up the coast or something. I have a friend who has this neat beach house. We could go up there, you know, really get away, watch the ocean."

I could do that. Cara Ann's face brightens when I smile at her. She's encouraged.

"Oh, God, I could use a vacation myself. Listen, at work yesterday, it was just horrible—horrible. It took all day—all because of Serena. Belts. I'm serious. She puts belts on everything she wears. I don't care if it's the most gorgeous suit in the world or the most delicate skirt. Belts, big red plastic belts or awful gold ones. She insists, the star insists. And who am I? Just the lowly costume supervisor. Sometimes, I know, it doesn't matter. And even sometimes the belts aren't so bad. But sometimes, it just makes me sick. To work so hard—" Cara Ann sighs and leans back on the couch.

I lose myself in the contemplation of belts. It's the after-diet-succeeds mania—look at how little my waist is—when you keep cinching the belt in tighter and tighter, regardless of how much it hurts or accentuates the faintest bulge.

"Maybe she lost a lot of weight lately. She's overcompensating." But red plastic?

"And the producer? He's no help. He says, Serena wants belts, she gets belts. I groan. Over a negligee? Won't the viewers think she's gone around the bend or something?"

"Well, maybe she has," I observe, picturing a red plastic belt around a pale pink satin teddy. I laugh. "Maybe her boyfriend has a thing about belts."

"I guess I hate feeling powerless. But it made me sick yesterday, I mean physically ill. I threw-up-my-tacos sick. I don't know, getting sick over a belt? What's wrong with this picture? It's not like I'm working to discover a cure for cancer."

I smooth my ponytail and look outside. The pool's turquoise water catches the fading sun. It is chemically clean and not crippled by an oil slick. But I would rather see the ocean.

Cara Ann notices my switch in attention. "So this pool man, did he have blond hair with faintly green tips and real narrow shoulders. Was his name J. G.? Say about nineteen or twenty?"

"No, he was a lot older and dark. He was slow, real slow, not retarded, but like he wasn't sure of what he was doing."

"Oh, yeah, really good-looking—white, white teeth—smile a lot? Talk a lot?"

"Well, yes."

"What was his name—?"

"Pete Bergman."

"Oh, wow—I knew it—that's P. C. Bergman—God, that Pete—what a kidder." She shakes her short bouncy blond hair and giggles.

"What's the joke?"

"He's an actor. Don't you—didn't you recognize him?"

"Should I?"

"He's on *Santa Fe Stories*—plays a continuing role."

"Oh." I remember the knife and how I was so frightened of him. My cheeks burn and I know I'm blushing, something I've never been able to control and Cara Ann laughs even harder.

"Well, it's not that funny—"

"He's good, I mean, really good. I guess he's practicing for something, researching a role. I know Ben, his brother. He owns Sunside Pools. He told me his little brother was slightly wacko. I met him at a party last year. When Ben started out, Pete actually worked for him, but that was a long time ago. It's too bad his career hasn't ever really taken off."

"But he's still working—"

"On *Santa Fe Stories?* Yes, but I heard his character might be killed off. The last time he left the soap was five years ago—his character got hit on the head by a jealous husband and he wandered off, thinking he was his evil twin brother Raven Blackfoot and Santa Fe never heard of him again till last year when he came back and had a car accident that restored his memory. Then he was Gavin Gold again."

"How do you keep up with all that?"

"VCR. I tape all the episodes on my bedroom set. I've watched that show since I was a kid. Habit and it's the best daytime soap on the tube, period."

Cara Ann fixes herself an iced tea and asks me if I want one.

"No, I'm okay. But tell me why—why do you really like it so much? I've never been able to get hooked on one."

"Continuity. With all the shit I've been through, I just like something that stays relatively the same. Throughout the divorce from Al, the job changes, moving, the custody battle over Teddy, when dad was sick, all the way through them I could watch the citizens of *Santa Fe Stories* and know basically, I was okay because their problems were always so ridiculous and awful that mine seemed to pale in comparison."

A reasonable conclusion. I feel like hugging Cara Ann. "Teddy will be back soon. You miss him, don't you?" Count on me to state the obvious. I should hug her, but I sit across the room from her, frozen. My problems are indistinct. I am in awe of her.

"Hey, this is your vacation, cousin, let's celebrate tonight. You want to?" She comes over to me and pinches me. "Let's go—and if Pete comes again, ask him if Gavin's brain tumor is going to pull the plug on him permanently."

"Are we going to take off this weekend, really—go up the coast?"

"I'll see if I can take some time off. That would be great," she says, but her eyes are suddenly distant and preoccupied. I see her measuring her waist with her hands. Belts. I realize she's just talking and that when it comes time to go, she'll probably have to beg off. She'll tell me I should take off on my own. That I shouldn't be afraid to drive up the coast by myself. She'll tell me about a bed-and-breakfast some friend owns. She'll tell me she'll meet me there a day later. But if I go, I'll have to go alone. And I won't.

I have been here one week.

I am still scared.

6. THE FEAR

The first thing you do, after some of the shock has worn away, is to deny it happened. Or you decided that whatever happened, happened for a reason, that somehow you did something to deserve it. But mostly, you push it way back under the bed or into the depths of a closet, somewhere that seldom gets cleaned out. I have pushed it as far away from me as I can, but it's still there.

This vacation is supposed to make me feel better, my own brand of therapy. Trying to save money, I suppose. Afraid if I went into therapy, real therapy, the doctor would keep asking me to come back until eventually he'd decide I would need to be admitted to some expensive clinic, that I'd agree and disappear from the rest of my life without a whisper. A safe thing to do.

I could do that. I'm just too tired. I'd like to go to sleep and never wake up.

My mother and father want me to straighten up, be an adult, especially since I'm over thirty. It's way past time. My father's not averse to the idea of psychiatric help but my mother warns me, "It would always be on your record." Maybe she's afraid at some point people will find out and I would thereafter turn into Mrs. Woods's poor loony girl, the one who started off so promising and ended up—well—disturbed.

But I can't get away from it. I don't know what to do. I can't really think about it. There's a wall there, a big, thick stone wall and I don't want it to tumble down on top of me. So I come here to recuperate and there is this pool.

Cara Ann has left me alone to sort things out. Again. She's very patient with me. I think I'm getting better. Maybe I will fix myself a thick chocolate milkshake. Lots of calories. But I can't, I'm just not hungry.

I called Dad last night and he told me an awful joke and I laughed till I cried. Then Cara Ann and I went to a concert of a saxophonist, a rather famous one you see on television from time to time, David Sanborn. But at one point, there was a song that bothered me. It was smoky sweet and trailing down the aisle toward me, it wrapped me up tight and then left, going back the way it had come. I asked Cara Ann what the name of the song was. She didn't know. She said she'd get some tapes for me and maybe we'd find it. But it's here now, the music's in my head.

And I'm looking at the pool.

I like water. Water soothes and refreshes the skin. Sit down in a shower and let it fall on the top of your head. Such freedom. And in a hot tub full of bubbles.

Bubbles.

I see some.

In the water over there.

My feet are in the water. Something dark is coming. Something seems to touch the balls of my feet. I get out of there quickly.

Shadows stretching up and forward. Shadow. Nothing there.

The pool people are still there. I know it. What if I submerge myself. In the water and below me their bodies would rise up to meet me and we would entwine, entangle, and sink down into shadow. Then later, we would float like dead fish in a polluted lake of green glass. Going nowhere. Have you ever noticed how sometimes toxic water glitters with rainbows?

I wish they would show themselves.

I sit down on a white deck chair and wipe the wetness off my legs. I haven't done any swimming in a long while. I used to be deathly afraid of the water since the time a dumb swimming instructor threw me off the high diving board and I almost drowned. What a guy—convinced that scare tactics should be included in lessons for six-year-olds. "Sink or swim!" was his rallying cry, I recall. So I decided to sink. Swimming at that point of my life was as alien an idea as flying.

Eventually, I did learn to swim. Maybe I should take a swim now. I have the beginnings of a healthy tan. I don't need to sunbathe anymore. I could use the exercise.

Maybe tomorrow. Right now I'm just too weak. I feel like an over-watered hanging basket, all the excess water draining out of the bottom, into the pool, into their breathless, sucking mouths.

7. THE ACTOR

"You really didn't know who I was?"

He sits across from me, sipping a glass of iced tea. A lemon wedge bobs in the melting ice and he smiles, again, intent upon some secret joke. Then he laughs. "You've really never seen my show? Or say, I've been in a movie or two. *A Kiss After Death* or *The House of Mirth*—that was on PBS. No? Oh—I know—I was on *Miami Vice* back a few years ago. I had a close-up with Don Johnson. I was a drug lord's bodyguard." Silence. "No? Well, you realize, of course, that this doesn't do much for my ego."

"I'm sorry, honestly, but Cara Ann tapes all of the episodes of *Santa Fe Stories* and I did watch a couple the other night. And you were good—you really seemed to have a handle on your character."

"It's a pile of crap, isn't it? I've been doing Gavin so long I'm thinking shit, maybe *I'm* the real evil twin brother, not Raven Blackfoot."

"Don't put yourself down—" He makes me uncomfortable—fidgeting with his teaspoon and jogging one leg up and down in a nervous, but not totally unattractive movement that makes me too aware of the muscles in his calves. I glance at the pool for solace. The water moves with the wind. "You should be proud of yourself, being a well-known actor and everything. I guess I should read *People* more. I used to watch *Entertainment Tonight* while I graded papers."

He smirks. "Once in a blue moon, right?"

I stare at him weakly. He wants me to flirt. I try a small smile. "It's been really special to meet you—even if it was under dubious circumstance." So, I am flirting. It's not too difficult. I'm wanting him to ask me out. I'd shock Cara Ann, have a date with a TV star. Do I feel stronger? The sun does not go through me.

I'm not floundering. It has not resurfaced. It is far away. Surely, I am stronger.

He brushes my hand. He's wearing a watch with a sporty plastic band instead of a Rolex. I find myself absurdly relieved. Now his hand drifts over mine. Does it show the time in other time zones?

I don't care. I'm glad he decided to drop by. He smiles. His hand caresses mine. Pressure.

"I felt really bad about the other day. Barging in—it's just something

I do sometimes. I mean, I've met Cara Ann and I thought it was her day off—it was a joke. I'm in a transitional phase of my career and I needed—"

I pull my hand away and he acts like it embarrasses him. He quickly grips his glass. "Yeah, Cara Ann told me that your character might be killed off, something about a brain tumor?"

He flinches as if I have slapped him. "Come time to move on, you move on," he says curtly. He makes a big deal out of checking the time. "Would you look at that? Duty calls—lunch with my agent. Guess I'd better run." The actor stands, half in and half out of the sun. I'm surprised someone like him would bother with some no-name teacher. Then I catch my self-depreciation and glare at the obscenely cheerful pool. I wonder if I should ask for his autograph? Mom might like it.

"Thanks for dropping by," I say stiffly, also standing. I hold my stomach in and hope I look attractive. "It was a nice surprise."

The pool people are back. Waving at me. Waving in streams of blood. I'm dizzy. I'm going to fall into the water and drown. I will fall; I can't stand still. My arms turn cartwheels. Head over heels, slipping, falling, going down. Gone under.

He catches me. We're sitting at the edge of the pool. He turns me around and studies me with concern. It's like he knows me, for God's sake. Like he's worried. What an actor—or I look really awful. "Should I call Cara Ann? A doctor?"

"I guess I'm just hungry. I'm sorry about that. I just lost my balance. Really, Mr. Bergman, I'm fine. I'll go heat up a frozen burrito in the micro-wave. I'll be really okay. This is *so* embarrassing—"

He looks away from me, into the pool. He frowns. "It's not that. It's not that at all." He glances at me. "Talk to me—tell me about it."

Talk to him? My head pounds.

We go inside and I tell a perfect stranger about it and the pool people. He is kind but distracted. He listens patiently and gives me the name of a local psychiatrist. He pities me. He leaves this time without smiling. He says he'll stop by again sometime and maybe we'll have dinner some evening if he can clear his schedule. I don't expect to ever see him again. His eyes are too troubled by the sight of me. I am too real.

And I have to go back to them. I have no choice. They need me.

8. THE MOVIE

Cara Ann has a date with a semifamous chef. She's giddy with happiness. She is certain he'll share the secret of his Double Chocolate Amaretto Mousse. He's Italian-German, a bizarre combination. His accent startles me when he comes to pick her up in his old white Jaguar. He kisses my hand and invites me to come to his restaurant with Cara Ann before I leave to go back home. I am delighted.

My cousin tells me not to wait up for her. As if I'm that stupid.

I go back to the TV in her bedroom and select a few movies to wade through.

I'm watching *Breakfast at Tiffany's* for the tenth time in my life. It's really late. I should go to bed. My eyelids are heavy. It's the scene where Holly is searching for Cat in the rain. I want to die. The rain keeps streaming into Holly's eyes and I start crying "Cat—Cat—" Then it's over but I'm still crying. I have lost something, too. But I can't find it. I will never find it.

I cry myself to sleep.

9. THE NIGHTMARE

He is underwater with them. Naked. He has been cut with a razor and the wounds gape open. The black ribbons are now bright red plastic belts and they curl around him. He sits at the table, his head back, the whites of his eyes trained on the watery blue sky and shrouded sun. The actor. And I cannot save him. He has been canceled.

And worse, I do not want to save myself. I sit next to him and slowly, but surely, every breath in my lungs escapes and rises to the surface without me. I know I no longer fight it. My pink legs stretch out before me. It's all over. Someone keeps telling me I'm a whore, a slut, a prostitute, and I realize it does not matter because I am dying.

In a dream you're not supposed to die. But I did.

And in that pool, Cara Ann's pool.

But I do not want to.

Die.

10. THE RESCUE

We went shopping on Melrose Avenue, Cara Ann and I did. We also hit the other major shopping areas and had a fine dinner at the chef's restaurant. We saw Cher or someone who looks just like her. I told Cara Ann it couldn't be Cher because she lives in New York and Cara Ann confided her showbiz sources had informed her that she was in town working on some hot movie deal. I think she just didn't want me to leave LA without seeing a really famous movie star, bigger than P. C. Bergman. Poor Pete.

I bought some clothes. And I'm going home soon, I think, or maybe I'll never go home. I am very unhappy because it's still there. This vacation has not done me a lot of good. I don't really remember anything about it. Not like I should. Maybe I never will. Maybe I shouldn't. I might stay another week. I might not teach this year.

I haven't heard from the actor, but Cara Ann heard from Ben that I made quite an impression. She didn't say what kind. She might've just said that to make me feel better. She is guilty about the time spent with the chef—Paulo or Paulie. Her little boy, Teddy, comes back next week. It might be nice to stay a little longer.

And it might not.

The weather continues warm. I wrote a postcard to Mom and Dad that actually said, "Wish you were here." What if they're on the next plane?

I'm going to swim today.

I'm wearing the expensive Norma Kamali swimsuit I bought on a whim and that will take me months to pay off. I'm in the shallow end. It's early morning and Cara Ann's gone to work. The air's too cool. My skin shows off a wonderful set of goose bumps. I wade deeper in. Then I see them, the pool people, and they see me. Only this time I hear them. Screaming. Someone has tied them to their chairs. Someone is raping the woman, or trying to. It's just a shadow. God, no, the man, the man is dead. He cannot help her. And look at the woman pushing at the shadow hands and now another shadow falls across her, holding her down with his feet. No one wants to rescue her. No one. But I can. She knows I can see her.

"I'm coming to save you! I'll save you—hold on, I'm coming—" I'll dive in. I can do it. She doesn't know how weak I am, how bloodless and thin.

My legs feel like two trembling towers of strawberry Jell-O. But I have to do it.

"Molly!" I turn and see Pete waving at me from the gate. It's locked. Now is not the time—he can't stop me. Idiot's trying to climb over the gate but I can't wait, there isn't time. I point at the pool people and I wade in deeper. I've got to take a good breath and plunge in. He's hurting her. He has one of her breasts; he's squeezing it hard. I can see it so plain. I can see no one cares. But I do.

"I'll tell—everyone will know what an ass you are. Let me go, you sorry bastard—" I'm in over my head and sinking. I'm going way down on butterfly wings laden with weights. I'm a butterfly in an astronaut's suit. I am drowning.

I could swim if I really wanted to. I could die, too. I have a choice. Why doesn't someone help?

"We're just going to fuck you, just like your boss does." They were just kids, bad boys in fake leather, with knives and hard cocks, sixteen, seventeen, eighteen. And I begged them to stop, to let me go. "Please, God, let me go, *please.*"

The water swallows me whole. Down at the bottom I see the table's gone; the chairs are gone. The pool people have at last abandoned me. I can rescue no one but myself. A knife in the water, plunging backward. My hand shoots up. Attention class. Any questions?

The man's hand grasps mine strongly. But I'm already climbing out of the pool.

"Are you okay?" he says.

And I kiss him. He touches my face. "You know who they were, don't you?" he says.

I nod.

"My students."

Assault as vampire.

To put the stake through the heart of any vampire, you must first know the identity of the vampire. Denial of assault is subtle and dangerous. The assault is given a sort of power both corrosive and sickening. In order for Molly to rescue herself, she had to first acknowledge what had happened. In doing so, she puts the stake through the vampire and frees herself to live again, no longer allowing the rapists to keep raping her, again, and again, and again.

I wrote this story for all of the Mollys out there and the men like Pete who try to understand them.

And also because butterflies cannot wear astronaut suits, nor should they have to.

Melissa Mia Hall

A WEEK IN
THE UNLIFE

David J. Schow

Schow's protagonist knows how to get rid of vampires. He's a media creation and has all the answers. . . .

1

When you stake a bloodsucker, the heart blood pumps out thick and black, the consistency of honey. I saw it make bubbles as it glurped out. The creature thrashed and squirmed and tried to pull out the stake—they always do, if you leave on their arms for the kill—but by the third whack it was, as Stoker might say, dispatched well and duly.

I lost count a long time ago. Doesn't matter. I no longer think of them as being even *former* human beings, and feel no anthropomorphic sympathy. In their eyes I see no tragedy, no romance, no seductive pulp appeal. Merely lust, rage at being outfoxed, and debased appetite, focused and sanguine.

People usually commit journals as legacy. So be it. Call me sentry, vigilante if you like. When they sleep their comatose sleep, I stalk and terminate them. When they walk, I hide. Better than they do.

They're really not as smart as popular fiction and films would lead you to believe. They do have cunning, an animalistic savvy. But I'm an experienced tracker; I know their spoor, the traces they leave, the way their presence charges the air. Things invisible or ephemeral to ordinary citizens, blackly obvious to me.

The journal is so you'll know, just in case my luck runs out.
Sundown. Nap time.

2

Naturally the police think of me as some sort of homicidal crackpot. That's a given; always has been for my predecessors. More watchers to evade. Caution comes reflexively to me these days. Police are slow and rational; they deal in the minutiae of a day-to-day world, deadly enough without the inclusion of bloodsuckers.

The police love to stop and search people. Fortunately for me, mallets and stakes and crosses and such are not yet illegal in this country. Lots of raised eyebrows and jokes and nudging but no actual arrests. When the time comes for them to recognize the plague that has descended upon their city, they will remember me, perhaps with grace.

My lot is friendless, solo. I know and expect such. It's okay.

City by city. I'm good at ferreting out the nests. To me, their kill patterns are like a flashing red light. The police only see presumed loonies, draw no linkages; they bust and imprison mortals and never see the light.

I am not foolhardy enough to leave bloodsuckers lying. Even though the mean corpus usually dissolves, the stakes might be discovered. Sometimes there is other residue. City dumpsters and sewers provide adequate and fitting disposal for the leftovers of my mission.

The enemy casualties.

I wish I could advise the authorities, work hand in hand with them. Too complicated. Too many variables. Not a good control situation. Bloodsuckers have a maddening knack for vanishing into crevices, even hairline splits in logic.

Rule: Trust no one.

3

A female one, today. Funny. There aren't as many of them as you might suppose.

She had courted a human lover, so she claimed, like Romeo and Juliet—she could only visit him at night, and only after feeding, because bloodsuckers too can get carried away by passion.

I think she was intimating that she was a physical lover of otherworldly skill; I think she was fighting hard to tempt me not to eliminate her by saying so.

She did not use her mouth to seduce mortal men. I drove the stake into her brain, through the mouth. She was of recent vintage and did not melt or vaporize. When I fucked her remains, I was surprised to find her warm inside, not cold, like a cadaver. Warm.

With some of them, the human warmth is longer in leaving. But it always goes.

4

I never met one before that gave up its existence without a struggle, but today I did, one that acted like he had been expecting me to wander along and relieve him of the burden of unlife. He did not deny what he was, nor attempt to trick me. He asked if he could talk a bit, before.

In a third-floor loft, the windows of which had been spray-painted flat black, he talked. Said he had always hated the taste of blood; said he preferred pineapple juice, or even coffee. He actually brewed a pot of coffee while we talked.

I allowed him to finish his cup before I put the ashwood length to his chest and drove deep and let his blackness gush. It dribbled, thinned by the coffee he had consumed.

5

Was thinking this afternoon perhaps I should start packing a Polaroid or some such, to keep a visual body count, just in case this journal becomes public record someday. It'd be good to have illustrations, proof. I was thinking of that line you hear overused in the movies. I'm sure you know it: *"But there's no such THING as a vampire!"* What a howler; ranks right up there alongside *"It's crazy—but it just might work!"* and *"We can't stop now for a lot of silly native superstitions!"*

Right; shoot cozy little memory snaps, in case they whizz to mist or drop apart to smoking goo. That bull about how you're not supposed to be able to record their images is from the movies, too. There's so much misleading information running loose that the bloodsuckers—the real ones—have no trouble at all moving through any urban center, *with impunity*, as they say on cop shows.

Maybe it would be a good idea to tape-record the sounds they make when they die. Videotape them begging not to be exterminated. That would bug the eyes of all those monster movie fans, you bet.

6

So many of them beleaguering this city, it's easy to feel outnumbered. Like I said, I've lost count.

Tonight might be a good window for moving on. Like them, I become vulnerable if I remain too long, and it's prudent operating procedure not to leave patterns or become predictable.

It's easy. I don't own much. Most of what I carry, I carry inside.

7

They pulled me over on Highway Ten, outbound, for a broken left tail-light. A datafax photo of me was clipped to the visor in the highway patrol car. The journal book itself has been taken as evidence, so for now it's a felt-tip and high-school notebook paper, which notes I hope to append to the journal proper later.

I have a cell with four bunks all to myself. The door is solid gray, with a food slot, unlike the barred cage of the bullpen. On the way back I noticed they had caught themselves a bloodsucker. Probably an accident; they probably don't even know what they have. There is no sunrise or sunset in the block, so if he gets out at night, they'll never know what happened. But I already know. Right now I will not say anything. I am exposed and at a disadvantage. The one I let slip today I can eliminate tenfold, next week.

8

New week. And I am vindicated at last.

I relaxed as soon as they showed me the photographs. How they managed documentation on the last few bloodsuckers I trapped, I have no idea. But I was relieved. Now I don't have to explain the journal—which, as you can see, they returned to me immediately. They had thousands of questions. They needed to know about the mallets, the stakes, the preferred method of killstrike. I cautioned them not to attempt a sweep-and-clear at night, when the enemy is stronger.

They paid serious attention this time, which made me feel much better. Now the fight can be mounted en masse.

They also let me know I wouldn't have to stay in the cell. Just some paperwork to clear, and I'm out among them again. One of the officials—not a cop, but a doctor—congratulated me on a stout job well done. He shook my hand, on behalf of all of them, he said, and mentioned writing a book on my work. This is exciting!

As per my request, the bloodsucker in the adjacent solitary cell was moved. I told them that to be really sure, they should use one of my stakes. It was simple vanity, really, on my part. I turn my stakes out of ashwood on a lathe. I made sure they knew I'd permit my stakes to be used as working models for the proper manufacture of all they would soon need.

When the guards come back I really must ask how they managed such crisp eight-by-tens of so many bloodsuckers. All those names and dates. First-class documentation.

I'm afraid I may be a bit envious.

This is a vampire story with no vampires in it.

From punk vampires to porn vampires to gay vampires to vampirism-as-AIDS, vampire fiction has become conventional, a category unto itself. As a genre it is by and large ultraconservative, moribund, demographic, derivative, totally safe, and utterly dull, dull, dull. Grave wavers who wet themselves over today's endlessly recycled bloodsucker might do well to exhume and rediscover the only two fundamental American vampire novels of this century—Richard Matheson's *I Am Legend* and Les Whitten's *Progeny of the Adder*. From them sprang, ultimately, the entire culture of pop vampirism as we know it today.

Distaste for such an adulterated gimmick as traditional vampirism played a big part in the creation of the above-mentioned books. It's the ultimate challenge: *Transcend me if you can.*

It is the oversaturation of vampire lore, and the trivialist's lust to accumulate ever more of it, that is itself a new form of vampirism.

The vampire hunter of unlife is a creature who feeds off *your* hunger to believe in vampires.

David J. Schow

LIFEBLOOD

Jack Womack

Womack, known for his science fiction novels, has only been writing short fiction in the last two years. His first story, also horror, was chosen for The Year's Best Fantasy & Horror: Fourth Annual Collection. *"Lifeblood" shows how the rituals of religious orthodoxy can be easily perverted to create one's own personal religion—deliberately or unconsciously. Judging from these two stories, Womack is an expert in the psychological obsessions that run our lives and hasten our deaths.*

"One of the Pre-Raphaelites, I forget which," the woman said, "buried a manuscript of his unpublished poems with his wife, or perhaps it was his sister, when she died. Several years later he decided he wanted to publish them after all, so he and his friends went to her grave one night and dug her up and retrieved them. Before they reburied her, he combed her hair."

The man and the woman met on Sunday afternoons at the pastry shop on Amsterdam below 111th Street. This particular afternoon, they were talking about love.

"I never realized theologians could be so romantic," he said.

"Those stories were never taught, you know," she said, laughing. "I had to find them, or rather they found me."

They'd been friends for years. They sat there, drinking coffee and sharing a slice of strudel, speaking with the ease and comfort that so rarely lovers, or even brothers and sisters, know.

"A woman I knew in graduate school died a couple of weeks ago," she said. "By the time I heard, the funeral was over. I should have gone."

"I'm sorry," he said. "She must not have been very old."

"Younger than me, actually. I've never told you about her. About what happened. I've always felt responsible for her falling in love."

"Romance, again—"

"It was such a long fall," she said.

"So tell me about it."

"The first time I met Leah was in October of my second year. She lived next door to my friend Alice, in an apartment building on Claremont. When I saw her there in the hall I remembered she was in the class I was taking on Dante. She was very thin and pale, and wore long-sleeved sweaters in the warmest weather. If I'd thought about her at all before then, it was only to wonder whether she was an anorexic or an addict, for I remembered that there were those who called her both. She was neither, in fact. She and Alice already knew each other, and she joined us that evening, and we talked."

"About what?"

"Nothing serious, as I recall. She'd transferred to Barnard from out west for her last two undergraduate years, and like Alice was in the comparative literature department. Leah was extremely intelligent, and so sweet as an angel, or such was the impression she found it impossible not to give. She was so talkative it was easy to tell how shy she truly was. Sometimes she'd say something in such a way, with such offhand yet careful phrasing, that I suspected she'd memorized a number of lines that could serve her well in any social situation, and repeated them as she'd had them told to her.

"Sometime before I left Alice's she went back to her place, to her studies, she said, though shortly afterward we heard her leave. When she'd gone I asked Alice when they'd met. She told me Leah had cut herself one morning, and needed help."

"Cut herself?" The waitress returned to refill their cups. The woman added cream to her coffee, lightening it until its color was so swarthy as her skin.

"She knocked on Alice's door, saying that she'd nicked her hand badly while slicing bread. She held a washcloth on the wound but couldn't get the bleeding to stop. Alice took a towel and wrapped it tightly around Leah's hand. Once the blood stopped Alice saw that it wasn't a deep cut, though she said it looked very frightening until she got used to seeing it.

"She asked Leah if she wanted to go to the hospital to make sure it didn't need stitches but she said it didn't, and that she had gauze in her apartment. Alice went back with her to make sure she'd be all right, for then as always Leah appeared so fragile that she might have broken beneath the gentlest touch.

"Her apartment was clean and neatly furnished, as if she used it only for storage. The bathroom, Alice said, was the coziest room in the place, and when she was telling me this she said she remembered how surprised she'd been to see how much gauze Leah had."

"So she might have been clumsy with knives," he said. "It could have happened before."

"Alice also said the only bread she saw in the kitchen was already sliced," she said. "My suspicions naturally arose. I liked Leah immediately, but for some time afterward the secret agent side of me emerged, and I found myself often attempting to draw theories from what few data I had, but nothing I could imagine seemed likely enough. She and I hit it off well, and we talked often before and after class, and the three of us started going to movies together, to those depressing middle European ones you're always teasing me about. She was so pleasant to be around, even when she was sad, and she seemed so often sad.

"Private, too, intensely private at times. She'd built any number of walls around herself, and only allowed one gate to open at a time. But she let us in, part of the way. Leah said she'd been raised a Catholic, but that now she was agnostic, like me. Perhaps she thought it would make me feel more comfortable; she was very sensitive to the beliefs of others. She told us she'd never gotten along with her family, and that was why she'd moved. Once she made an odd remark, or so we found it at the time, that babies should not be born of men and women, that parents' pain could forever after harm their children. She was safe in that regard, she told us; she could never have her own family to destroy. When we asked her to elaborate, she wouldn't.

"We were certain she was seeing someone. She often went out at night, Alice said, not returning until morning. At first we were rather worried about her, until we realized she always seemed all right upon her return, and that she had been going out for some time before we became concerned. Alice eventually saw the someone she saw. He was a good deal older, and from his bearing and unfashionable dress Alice inferred that he was a former professor of Leah's. She inferred as well that their relationship was more than academic, but Alice couldn't say how much more.

"We imagined that she was content, if not happy, with whatever she had.

"One morning after a discussion on the *Inferno* I noticed a red stain spreading along Leah's sweater cuff, and pointed it out to her. She was quite comfortable around me by then; I think in some ways more comfortable than she was around Alice, because I didn't live so nearby. Without thinking she rolled up her sleeve. Her arm was so thin, and her skin so translucent, that she looked as if she were starving. One of her cuts had reopened, and she bled."

"One of her cuts?"

"Woven into her arm were dozens of thin scars. Small ones, whiter than her skin." The woman replaced her cup within her saucer's basin, and set aside her fork. "She was deliberately cutting herself, you see."

"Why would she do such a thing?"

The woman offered no theory. "When Leah saw me staring at her arm she quickly pulled down her sleeve, and I felt so embarrassed, as if I'd come into her apartment with friends to surprise her, and found her in the bathroom, naked and sick. She behaved as if nothing were amiss, and left at once, saying she needed to talk to her adviser. I intended to mention it to Alice that evening, but never had the chance, because the three of us went out that night. We were taking her to a party because we thought it was good she should get out and meet new people. The most awful thing happened there. I mean that in both senses of the word."

"What was that?"

"Did you ever fall in love with someone at first sight, or watch as it happened to others?" The man shook his head. She sipped her coffee; some spilled onto the table as she lifted the cup to her mouth. "The only experience I could compare it to, not an exact comparison, would be a religious conversion."

"As when one joins a cult, I suppose."

"Not at all. In this there's one messiah, true, but only one apostle as well, and both participants slip in and out of both roles as the drama demands. The surrounding world becomes as gauze around them. Food, drink, sleep, all else is suddenly inessential to life. Nothing becomes so important as being with, and in some ways even attempting to become, the other person.

The desire that one blood might beat through two hearts can so swiftly overwhelm."

"I'm as glad I've never experienced it, then," he said, motioning to the waitress that they should receive more strudel. "You make it sound dreadfully obsessive."

"Have you ever heard the old belief that the soul is visible through the eyes?" she asked. "When two people meet and fall in love at first sight I think they do see one another's souls, and know even before they speak that their minds have at once become as one between them, that a true juncture exists. It's an easy enough step in most circumstances to conjoin the bodies, after that. But the last step is most difficult.

"If the souls themselves are enabled to merge, then an apostate such as myself could call it—well—not transubstantiation, I don't believe, but certainly impanation, where a union is affected without loss of respective substance. The triangle is given its point, in a sense. The trinity is complete."

"I gather this is something else you weren't told about in graduate school," he said.

"Call me romantic, if you'd like. Such love can bring the glow of paradise unto the world. But if something goes wrong, it can as easily turn on all the lights of hell. And something did go wrong."

"She met someone. A man?" The woman nodded. "What was he like?"

"From what little I saw, and from all I heard, he was very much like her. Sometimes I've wondered that if they'd only been more dissimilar they might still be together." For a moment the woman stared into the surface of her coffee; the waitress returned with their second helping. "Probably not. If they hadn't been so alike, would they have been so attracted as they were?"

"You're asking me?"

"No," she said. "What was he like? His name was Henry. He was a writer, though I never read anything he wrote. The time or two I'd seen him before he'd struck me as being even shyer than she was, and not nearly so adept at putting it to good use. I gathered he generally avoided social events like the plague. He was older in years than we were, but not by many, and in many ways I suspect that even Leah was truly older.

"They saw one another, and we didn't see them again the rest of the night, and by morning they were inseparable. When I say that even now I feel responsible for their getting together, I know I shouldn't, that it was nothing more than serendipity, but still—"

"You're too quick to blame," he said.

"Too slow, sometimes," she said. "But they were such lonely people after all, and when lonely people meet you can't help but hope they'll be happy."

"Were they happy?" he asked.

"Even coming into class Leah gave every impression of walking on clouds. Those friends of ours who knew Henry told us of the most marvelous transformations in his being, that his voice, his facial expressions, even the way he breathed, changed. So much becomes other so quickly in this sort of relationship. Even the sense of time is subverted, you see. A day may seem to hold a week, or a year. A month might feel no longer than a minute. When two people believe that they've known each other forever, after all, that their meeting itself was at some eternal point preordained, then what is time but something of which there's never enough?"

"Did they stay happy?"

"They wanted to, I'm sure," she said. "After the first few days they were but rarely seen in public together. Alice probably saw them more often than most, in truth, because he stayed at Leah's so often as she stayed at his place, or wherever else it was that she still sometimes stayed, for sometimes Alice would hear him leave, late at night, and then hear her leave soon after, and she'd know she was going to see the other man. That bothered Alice, but there were other aspects that troubled her more."

"Such as?"

"By the end of their first week together he had become so pale as Leah, and even in autumn a tan shouldn't fade so fast. Then, too, the walls in Alice's building weren't especially thick, and sometimes Alice heard more than she wished to hear. She was alone herself at the time, and of course even at the best of times one tries not to think of what your friends might do in bed, even if you truly want to know. Sometimes they were very noisy, and sometimes they weren't, and it was when they weren't that most disconcerted Alice."

"I don't understand—"

"Alice knew the layout of Leah's apartment and knew which of Leah's rooms abutted hers. Some nights as she lay in bed, Alice would imagine that they'd gone to sleep at last, and then realize that they hadn't, that they were in the bathroom. Each night Henry came over a pattern repeated itself.

From the midst of silence a low murmur would rise as if from a dream; a sound of pain followed, manifesting itself sometimes as a cry, sometimes as a moan. It never seemed to be Leah's voice that she heard, but then neither of them was loud, and Leah was undoubtedly more subdued because she was more used to it. Then all would be quiet again, until they returned to bed, seemingly with renewed vigor.

"One morning Alice took her trash to the basement. Leah'd already taken hers down, Alice saw, for she recognized a shopping bag she'd seen Leah come in with a day or so before. It was from a medical supply house, and it was filled with what Alice at first took to be red party streamers, disposed of as if after a Valentine's Day celebration. But this was just before Thanksgiving.

"After Thanksgiving I ran into Leah on Broadway, and I could tell she'd been crying, her eyes were so red they looked as if they'd been bleeding. I said let's go somewhere and talk, and she said she had to meet Henry in a little while but readily agreed to come with me, and we went to Café 112. I asked her what was upsetting her so. Do you know how sometimes strangers share with you the sort of revelations friends never share? It can happen, too, with people you know, so long as you don't know them well.

"As she talked to me she spoke in such a way that on one level nothing was said, while on another level all was revealed, or at least much more. She began telling me about the older man she saw, without letting slip any details other than that they'd been together a long time and that they'd met in the same way as she'd met Henry. As a mentor, she said, he'd helped her in innumerable ways, but as she continued to speak I perceived an aspect of their relationship that possibly neither of them saw. If theirs, too, had been love at first sight, and I don't know that it was, then their convergence hadn't quite been true; that perhaps with her compliance his mind took over a part of hers, or even replaced it entirely for a time, and thus it wasn't always Leah who spoke when her lips moved. If we stick with the metaphor I was using earlier, then I'd say that what occurred between them was more of an inadvertently forced consubstantiation.

"Too soon for him, too soon for Leah, he discovered she'd fallen in love with Henry, and he didn't take it well at all. She tried to explain to me as she'd tried to explain to him the realities she understood. He found her relationship with Henry disturbing enough in ways other than how it interfered with their own that he was having none of it. So one night she told him she'd been able to become closer to Henry in a way he was unable, or unwilling, to be.

"As she recalled how that upset him it upset her anew, and she pulled at her hair until she dislodged her barrette. It fell to the floor. I leaned down to pick it up for her, and when I did I saw that her socks had drooped over her ankles. Her legs were thin as her arms, and as laced with tiny white scars. They looked as if for years her nerves had been trying to break free of her skin, that they could no longer be rubbed raw."

The woman drank the rest of her coffee before continuing her tale. He watched her drink, forgetting to eat.

"Both made her better, she told me, and both made her worse, and she thought she knew who helped the most, or rather who hurt the least. But she had no idea how to tell the other of her decision, and so for the moment decided not to decide. The angles of the triangle seemed too perfect to disturb, but she said she knew they had to be. There was, you see, one more complication."

"What?"

"My period, she said. You've stopped having it? I asked, thinking at first I grasped the complications without her telling, unable to imagine that she could have ever been regular, thin as she was. I started, she said.

"What could I do? I took her hands—you can't imagine how cold they were—and held them, and sat with her awhile longer. I waited for her to say more, but surely she knew when she'd said enough. She looked at the clock on the wall and told me she needed to go meet Henry, who lived around the corner. As I walked along with her I felt as if I were accompanying a ghost as she commuted between the houses she haunted.

"Henry stood on the stoop of his building, awaiting her; she smiled so when she saw him, and, taking leave of me, ran to him. They were happy, and that was the most frightening thing of all. When he slipped his arms around her I saw the cuffs his bandages made.

"A day or so after that I went to Mexico with my parents for Christmas. When I returned I called Alice, to see what had happened in my absence. Much, she told me.

"Henry came over one night during the week before New Year's. Leah had stayed out Christmas Eve, but Alice had a hunch she hadn't been with

Henry. They didn't say much that she could hear through the wall, and she had somewhere to go herself, and so she left them to their devices. No one can say what happened after that. Maybe Leah related the decision she'd made to him that night, or maybe she already had; maybe she'd already told the one she needed to tell before coming over, and so took this night to celebrate. But something went wrong—immediately or ultimately, who knows—and he was cut too deeply, and didn't get help in time.

"When Alice came home the police were still there. They found Henry in the bathtub, she heard, though not from Leah. Leah sat in the hall, wrapping her arms around herself as if they were bandages, pressing her face against her knees until her legs were bloody. An older man stood in the hall, talking to the officials, and if you didn't know better you might have thought he knew every answer. Eventually he helped her to her feet, and walked with her, down the hall.

"Suicide, they called it, but Henry was no more suicidal than Leah."

The man lay down his fork, feeling hungry no longer. The waitress smiled as she walked by.

" 'No greater grief than to remember days of joy, when misery is at hand,'" she said.

"What's that from?" he asked.

"Canto Five of the *Inferno*," she said. "Poetry can so often help you get to sleep at night."

"What happened afterward?"

"Leah didn't come back to school the next semester," she said. "Possibly so that she wouldn't hear what anyone had to say, but I suspect she'd heard it all before. The next time I saw her was in the spring, here in the pastry shop. She sat by herself in the corner over there, seeming more translucent than before, almost as if, with her compliance or not, she was gradually fading away. I don't think she saw me at all, though I stood before her, and I never saw her again after that.

"Then a couple of weeks ago, she died. Alice found out that she was buried next to Henry, and we wondered about that for a time. It'd be nice to imagine that life can at least be fair to the dead."

"What did she die of?" he asked. "She didn't—"

The woman shook her head. "A virus, we heard. You know how malicious gossip can be. If her older friend retained possession over part of her mind, then I'm certain Henry carried much of her soul away with him. And what was left must have finally given out. Still, she surely did as she thought she had to do. Sometimes I think it's better to be alone, after all. It's safer."

"Check, please," he said; the waitress walked over, moving through the crowd. "But cutting herself like that. How could she have convinced them to go along—"

"I can't speak of the ways of courtship," she said, "but after accepting the trinity, you take communion."

Love slinks pink-footed and sleek,
Scurries through the soul's walls,
Eludes the traps set out to kill it,
At night bites the extremities till they bleed.

Jack Womack

REQUIEM

Melinda M. Snodgrass

What does it mean to be human? This question is one that has haunted SF and horror from H. G. Wells's half men in The Island of Dr. Moreau, *through John W. Campbell's alien shapeshifter in "Who Goes There?" The question of what is human is also central to much of Philip K. Dick's work, particularly his novel* Do Androids Dream of Electric Sheep?

The tortured characters in "Requiem" love and appreciate art, and perform music. But they are unable to create. In the context of this story, this alone is what keeps them from being fully human.

*D*own in the hall someone was enacting the final act of a French farce. *Probably Martin Fletcher,* Barnaby idly thought, using shunt level to avoid any bleed. *Their taste had always run to the absurd.* Main level was feeding properly, pain exploding from the tender flesh of his buttocks as the thin switch continued its steady rhythm. Beneath him Lucinda ground with her hips, timing each thrust to the beat of the tiny bamboo whip. He was nearing climax, and Mary increased the tempo of the whipping. He cursed his newly acquired belly. He felt like a barrel trying to balance on a particularly slippery log. Lucinda caught her legs about his back forcing him down atop her, and he groaned as the heavy meal he had eaten earlier in the evening shifted like a sliding load of ball bearings.

The warm moistness of her cunt closed about his penis squeezing, demanding, and with a white-hot rush he came even as Mary laid one final, triumphant, and very hard blow across his bare, red ass.

Lucinda's throaty sounds of pleasure were punctuated by screams, and bellowed French commands, and the sound of popping champagne corks.

Barnaby grimaced—*So overdone*—and rolled onto his back. And gave a yelp as his tender bottom hit the satin sheets. Lucinda propped herself on an elbow, raked back her long black hair with one hand, and grinned down at him. Her nipples formed rich coffee-colored circles against the tawny skin of her breasts.

"Performance tonight?"

"No, just a rehearsal."

"You must be tense. You don't usually call for the full treatment except for a performance."

He grabbed one swinging breast, and rubbed his thumb across the nipple. "Decided to treat myself."

She rolled away, consulted an ornate white-and-gold clock. "Hour's almost up."

"Do you have to be so cold-blooded? Can't you convince me that it's romance at work here?"

"You don't want romance, Barnaby, you want sluts. For romance you go home to that pretty wife of yours."

"She's frigid."

"Goodbye, Barnaby."

"She doesn't understand me."

"Leave the money on my desk, Barnaby."

"You don't love me."

"That's right, Barnaby."

A few minutes later, and he was out in the chill Santa Fe night. There were a few cars about jouncing and grinding through the monumental potholes that littered the streets like bomb craters. He stuck to the sidewalk, the tough buffalo grass brushing at his pants leg where it thrust through the cracks in the concrete. It wasn't far to the performance hall, and with a star-littered sky overhead, and a brisk wind carrying the scent of burning piñon to his nostrils, he was just as happy to walk.

It also allowed time for the blood to retreat from his inflamed buttocks. The touch of his undershorts against the swollen skin was agony, but it also managed to keep an erection shoving at his zipper. And if he took his time he would be able to sit and rehearse for three hours, serene and relaxed from Lucinda's and Mary's ministrations.

Another car lurched past, and its headlight swept across the mouth of an alley. It was like looking down a black throat with a trashed-out dumpster and several battered garbage cans thrust up like broken teeth. And in the midst of it two shadowy figures were locked in a desperate struggle. Harsh pants and faint whimpers drifted from the alley. Barnaby dug his hands into his coat pockets, hunched until his collar rode up around his ears, and hurried past. It was none of his affair. Had no part in his game. But there was a sick taste on the back of his tongue that lingered for several blocks, and had nothing to do with the cheap wine he had consumed with dinner.

Patricia and Peter were waiting. He muttered an apology for again being late, and seated himself at the baby grand. Peter, his violin tucked beneath his sharp chin, and his brown curls forming a halo about his head, had the look of a mad monk. Patricia was a different sort altogether. Her blue eyes seemed to focus on nothing, and with her long, straight blond hair hanging to her waist she looked like a lost flower child. But there was nothing innocent about the way she gripped her cello between her thin legs. Barnaby's erection bumped urgently against his zipper, and he wished she would stop wearing such short skirts to rehearsal.

Peter made a new mistake this night. So breathtaking in its audacity and creativity that Barnaby almost lost his count. The violinist muttered an apology, but he was staring at the notes with the adoration of an ascetic witnessing the kingdom of God. Patricia had formed a curtain with her hair. Barnaby couldn't read her reaction.

The final trembling chord hung in the air, and Barnaby dropped his hands into his lap. After twenty minutes of playing, and Peter's remarkable addition, he found that his ass had stopped hurting, and the flash of Patricia's pale thigh brought no answering response from his crotch.

"Shall we try it again?" he heard himself ask.

"Sure, and I'll try not to foul up this time."

"No problem."

Patricia shook back her hair, and eyed him, reading more from the innocent two-word remark than he had intended. Sensing perhaps his exultation. Behind her blue eyes lurked the somna, glaring, hostile, very suspicious.

The keys were slick beneath his fingers as they began again. This time it was perfect. Perfect as it was always perfect. As it would have been perfect the time before barring Peter's fascinating gaff. Perfect, soulless, and heartless. And the fault, Barnaby sadly concluded in time with the final chords, was not in the music.

Patricia didn't wait for any quiet banter. She packed her cello in short jerky motions that betrayed her agitation, ducked her head, and hurried from the studio.

"I shouldn't have done that," Peter said contritely.

"No, that's not true. It was magnificent." Barnaby hesitated, then dug out a handwritten score. "Would you mind?"

"Oh, Barnaby, you never give up."

"No."

An "A" hung in the air, then tuned and ready Peter sight-read swiftly and perfectly through the first page. He stopped, bow poised, double chins forming because of his pressure on the instrument.

"Well?"

"It's terrible. Just like the others."

"You see no improvement?"

He considered, replayed a phrase, frowned, caught his lower lip between his teeth. "Some." He dropped the violin to his knee. "Barnaby, why is it so important to you?"

"I don't know, but it is. Vitally important." He swung off the bench and paced the sterile room, shoes squeaking on the linoleum floor. "Sometimes when I'm playing I feel as if I'm on the verge of some great insight, some total understanding that will—"

"What I'm on is the verge of trouble." The snap of the locks on the case echoed off the dingy white walls. "You're a dangerous man to know, Barnaby. You incite a person to risk, and I've taken enough risks for one night."

But they didn't, and that was the problem. Life was a series of endlessly repeating patterns. The thoughts roiled like sullenly boiling poison; but buried deep on the shunt level, safe from any eavesdropping. He slid onto the bench, and ripped out a Mozart piano sonata. Wondering as he played why when using the same seven notes he produced soulless dreck, while Mozart had produced genius, magic. The magic went to work, drawing from deep within him a sensation that was odd and unpleasant and exhilarating all at once. A vise closing somewhere deep within himself.

With a sigh he dropped the lid, a sullen *bang* in the silent room, and left the recital hall.

He has several choices. A late post-rehearsal supper. Home—his mind shied violently from that. He knew what was waiting for him at home. Or Sal's.

Sal's filled with noise, and smoke, and male presence. The waitresses were male wet dreams incarnate. Cute, and buxom, and dumb as rocks. They made appropriate squealing noises when pinched or propositioned, and the rest of the time kept their mouths shut, and served drinks.

Sal, a tall, skinny Italian whose spade beard made him look like a rather befuddled Lucifer, was polishing glasses behind the bar. On the large TV, hung precariously on the wall, the Bears were slaughtering the Patriots at the Super Bowl. Groans, curses, shouted advice, rose from the knot of construction workers, cowboys, and truckers huddled at one corner of the bar.

"The usual?"

"Yeah."

Sal slopped whiskey into a shot glass, and Barnaby tipped it down.

"Neat whiskey will play hell with your liver."

"Well, now that would be a new experience. The descent into the gutter with redemption to follow."

"Hush." Dr. Antonio Garcia's thin, blue-veined hand closed about his upper arm, and forced him away from the bar. "Barnaby, my friend, you are very fey tonight." They settled into a red leather booth. "What troubles you, my friend?"

The score fluttered onto the table between them. The doctor prodded the pages with a cautious forefinger. "Music."

"Yeah, mine."

"Is it good?"

"No, it stinks. Like the piece before it, and the piece before that, and—"

"Why are you surprised?" The Spaniard sighed, and ran a hand across his beautiful white hair. It fell in long waves back from a high white forehead. Which made the darkness of his deepset brown eyes all the more compelling.

"Barnaby, my young friend. There are a million things in this world that we can do—"

"Perfectly," he interrupted bitterly.

"As you say, but art is not one of them. The blood of the somnas has thinned and our kind doesn't make music."

"Oh, we *make* music. Like we *make* ball games, and *make* wars, and *make* marriages, but we create nothing." Uneasy interest flared like a point of light from his passive watcher.

"That is not our function—"

"Our function is boredom."

"Not so. We are the vital link between our somnas, and reality. We provide experience, sensation, growth, challenge, but with the dangers filtered by our loyal bodies."

Antonio had assumed his erect tutorial position, finger upraised, his soft, deep voice exploring each word for the maximum effect. Intellectual smugness glowed on his face. For Barnaby this was merely one in an endless repeat of the good doctor's pet philosophy.

"Antonio, you remind me of the Jewish apologists of old time, 1930s. They continued to excuse, and explain Adolf Hitler even as they were led into the gas chamber."

"That is a disgusting analogy! We are not a despised minority being persecuted by our overlords. We are partners in a most unique and special relationship, and we should be grateful for our chance to serve. Without the development of the somna/piggyback relationship there would be no humans on Earth. That great history would have been snuffed out by the actions of a random, malignant virus. As it is we have preserved—"

"Which is my point! We 'preserve,' we experience, but we don't create. And I'm not even sure we're preserving all that well. Look at the fucking streets, the garbage collecting on the sidewalks. And who can blame them. It's a hell of a boring game to be a garbage collector or a member of a street crew. So we get to be doctors and lawyers, and conductors and composers and Indian chiefs. And for what? For What!"

"Barnaby, go home. These distempered freaks do you no good." Hostility and compassion flickered in the dark eyes as Antonio and the somna watched him.

As for himself a band of incandescent pain seemed to be tightening about his temples. With a gasp he crammed the pages into his pocket, and lurched from the booth.

"You'll feel better in the morning."

"Yeah . . . yeah, you're right. I've been working too hard. This opening concert . . . ha ha, burning the candle at both ends . . . ha ha." How easily the words of his role slipped from his tongue. How comforting to have the role to return to. If he didn't he would have to make one. For himself. All by himself.

Laura was waiting. The green shades on the brass student lamp threw a dim light across the darkened living room, and drew highlights from her short cap of light brown hair. Head bowed she sat curled in the corner of the sofa. The line of her neck was a curving song. But it seemed vulnerable, too. Pale and slender, bent like an autumn flower beneath a weight of winter ice. He experienced the same squeezing sensation he had felt during the Mozart. Slipped forward, and kissed her. The short hairs at the nape of her neck tickled his lips.

She flinched, jerked away. "Don't touch me."

He too recoiled from the acid that laced the words. "Laura, love."

"You slime! You son of a bitch!" She spat the words at him from behind the protection of the coffee table. Her voice held only hatred, but her body spoke of unendurable pain as she huddled in upon herself, arms wrapped protectively about her chest.

"What, what have I done? The first night I've been able to get home early, and you start screaming at me."

"You don't like it? Then go back to your bimbos!" She snatched a package of cigarettes from the mantel. It took her five tries to get it lit, and a part of Barnaby admired her ability to suppress her dexterity. It was perfect from the trembling fingers to the cords of her neck etched harshly beneath the fair skin as she sucked in the smoke. "For months I've suspected, but now I have the proof."

A manila envelope slapped onto the brick floor at his feet spilling its contents. Photos. Black and white, grainy, unfocused, but clearly recognizable. His face, looking bloated with the weight that had been laid on him, sheen of sweat, hair matted, eyes screwed tightly shut in ecstasy as Lucinda beat him. Shame lay like a bad taste on the back of his tongue.

"God damn it!" he roared. "I'm under a lot of pressure. And since you're so fucking frigid—"

"Bad choice of words there," she smirked. "Just because I'm not willing to behave like an animal."

"Don't finish. I know it by heart. I hear it every night in bed. *I'm an artist. The physical blunts the soul,*" he mimicked in cruel parody. "Well, if that's the case you ought to be a fucking angel by now."

She dealt him a ringing slap, and he caught her by the wrists, forced her in close. Her head thrashed trying to avoid the kiss that had little to do with love, and a great deal to do with violence.

They staggered about the room locked in this travesty of an embrace. There was a crash, and his soul cringed as a priceless Santa Clara Indian seed pot shattered on the bricks. Dismay loosened his grip, and Laura kneed him neatly in the balls. Pain like a red-hot poker shot from his groin through the top of his head. He collapsed with a keening cry, and held himself.

Laura began booting down the hall toward the bedroom, then froze, turned back, weariness and release etched on her delicate face. Barnaby still hurt. A lot. But the somnas were gone. Exhausted perhaps by the violence of their backs' emotions.

Slowly he rose, came into her arms, laid his head against her soft bosom, felt despair.

They had only a little time. A few seconds becoming minutes becoming (if they were lucky) hours. To spend any way they pleased. His mind stuttered and stopped; *a long walk in moonlight, conversation, playing a duet, making love.* They were like children in a toy store. A multiplicity of delights, joy at having the choice, pain at having to choose. As usual Laura settled the matter.

She slipped from his arms, entered the bedroom. He watched hungrily as her mincing, duck-footed dancer's walk carried her away from him. She would wait, and if there was enough time he would join her there. But now he had to work.

The score was tucked between the pages of a Mozart symphony. Camouflage, or was he hoping that genius somehow rubbed off? He spread the pages, stared wearily at the tiny ink strokes each representing so many hours of anguish. He was sick to death of notes. They haunted his every waking moment.

Why was he so driven? What did he hope to accomplish by this herculean task? To prove that Antonio, and the other philosophers of their age, were wrong? That creativity could exist? And what were the consequences if he were correct?

Worse, what were the consequences for *him* if he failed? Reality was rendered marginally bearable because of this dream. And if he tried and failed—what then? There was no way out. No way to simply say, "I'm tired, I've had enough. I won't go on." Of course he would go on—and on. He had no choice. But it would be an eternity of living with neither hope nor meaning.

He twirled the pen between his fingers. Measure 156. *Miserere.* Mercy. It was a prayer. Pen clenched between his teeth he played the preceding five measures. The notes hung trembling in the shadowy room. They formed a presence in the darkened room rich with the scent of pipe tobacco, Laura's perfume, and old wood lovingly polished with beeswax and lemon oil. *Were they any good?* No, that question could only freeze him. He repeated the phrase. Rediscovering its soul. Or was it his own?

He bent to the paper. *Treble clef—g, e, c—dotted quarter, sixteenth f, back to a.* The scratchings of a pen, the crackle of paper, the occasional fragmentary musical phrase. Forming a miraculous harmonious whole.

The lone time continued. Barnaby stretched feeling the vertebrae in his spine snapping one by one as he straightened. Carefully he returned the sheets to their hiding place, and buried the memory of his work in shunt level.

He realized, with a start, that while he was sitting and gaping mindlessly at the dull ivory keys of the piano Laura was waiting, and precious private moments were flitting past. He hurried from the study, down the long hall, hesitated before a closed, sealed door. Its twin lay across the hall. Duty warred with resentment. Duty won out. He opened the door into the blue-lit aquatic dimness. Gazed at the figure curled protectively about itself, floating, sleeping, dreaming. Elaborate machinery clicked and sighed measuring out life in tiny doses. The warmth, wash and ebb of a primal ocean, an eternal womb.

Resentment died to a dull ember, and he felt a wash of pity. He had long ago worn out love. He wondered what the somna would think of that admission? Perhaps be grateful that pity still remained. No, such an analysis was beyond it. That was reality, and the somna fed on dreams.

As did he.

He softly closed the door.

Under the goading of his very real personal demon his behavior went from bad to worse. Evenings after rehearsals and performances were spent in screaming battles with Laura. Little progress was made on the requiem for even when lone time occurred he was too exhausted and devastated to work.

He wondered if his watcher had somehow become aware of his secret life, and was using these emotional storms to destroy him. If so it had picked an excellent technique.

Laura opened in *Giselle.*

And the mad scene was unlike any ever seen before. She seemed to float about the stage as if madness had driven out the physical leaving only a fragile, hollow-eyed wraith whose expressive port de bras held a universe of loss, and betrayal. Barnaby ached for her for he *knew* she was dancing out her private anguish.

Behind her the corps de ballet went cleanly, sharply, perfectly through the choreography. It was a tour de force ballet perfection . . . and it held all the soul of a puppet show. Dancing automatons.

But that's because they are *automatons*, thought Barnaby, and felt a stir of fear and resentment from the somna. Molecular programs able to feel pain and pleasure, but unable to replicate themselves. Automatons.

And you're automatons too, he flashed at the conductor and orchestra all busily sawing and tooting and gesticulating away. And so are you, he told the audience, as he went slewing about in his seat. And you! And You! And YOU! He was half out of his seat, knee resting on the plush velvet seat cushion, knuckles whitening as he gripped the back of the chair. Around him people stirred, frowned, tittered, shifted nervously.

And so am I.

He collapsed back into his chair. Stared morosely at the stage. Sneered at the willies waltzing about that idiotic prince. Waited for the magic to come again, but Laura had lost whatever had earlier animated her. The final pas de deux could have been a course in weight training.

He had tried to talk about it at the reception afterward. But the people kept drifting away from him, like wraiths, phantoms . . . willies. He blundered about feeling large and gross, but *real* God damn it! Real! And they kept scattering.

"We're just not real." He was perched precariously on a chair, listing from side to side, and he couldn't remember how he got there. White, strained faces stared up at him, and he stretched out his hands, clutching feebly at the air. Trying to grip . . . what? "Don't any of you see it?" he cried. "Laura was real tonight. Oh, it was only for a minute or two, but she was *real*. We should be real like that . . . all of the time."

A hand closed about his wrist, holding him steady.

"Oh, hello, Dr. Garcia."

"Barnaby, stop it. You're upsetting everyone."

"Good. They *need* to be upset." He staggered, slithered off the chair, fell onto it with a hard bump. "I feel strange."

"You're drunk."

"No I'm not. I'm not really drunk. I'm—" He paused trying to think what he was . . . Doing.

"You need to stop thinking about this, Barnaby. You're damaging yourself."

"Good."

"Antonio, let me." Laura's hand was cool against his cheek.

"Laura, no," whispered the doctor. "You're not supposed to be here!"

"Who are you to know where I'm supposed to be?"

His finger thrust out accusingly. "You're ignoring instructions!"

"Yes, no, perhaps, maybe."

Barnaby couldn't tell if she was being facetious or if her neural-paths really were in disarray from this direct disobedience.

"Outrageous. This is atomistic behavior."

"Yes, no, perhaps, maybe," sang out Barnaby, but Laura's only response was a glance filled with blazing anger.

She got him home, dumped him unceremoniously on the couch, and went to check her somna. He sensed rather than heard her return. Huddled into the corner of the sofa, knees pulled to chest, he stared into the yawning pit of the corner fireplace.

"You're leaving."

"Yes."

"On instructions?"

"No." That brought him off the couch. There was again that viselike pressure in his chest, but this had nothing to do with joy. She seemed very small and fragile as she leaned against the doorjamb; a shadowy figure, arms wrapped protectively about her scrawny chest. "This has nothing to do with the soap opera, this is real."

"Why, why?" There seemed to be a swelling in his throat, and the words emerged as a harsh whisper as he forced them past the obstruction.

"I'm afraid."

"But tonight—"

"Was a mistake. I should never have done it. I'm sorry, Barnaby, I'm staying in the womb."

"And if I succeed?"

"You won't. It was a hopeless dream."

"All right, forget succeeding. " He gripped her shoulders. "If I finish it?"

"I'll come."

"And if I should succeed?" He enunciated carefully giving her a tiny shake between each word.

"Then it's a different world, isn't it?"

"Is it?"

"You haven't considered the ramifications."

"So Antonio says."

"Good luck, Barnaby." She stood on tiptoes, pressed a soft kiss onto the corner of his mouth.

He hadn't really thought she'd leave. But in the morning both she and her somna were gone. His somna probed, excitement flaring like tiny explosions at this newest twist, then slid back defeated, frustrated, confused by his lack of response.

Seated at the piano late one night, muffled beneath a weight of unhappiness, Barnaby realized that he was experiencing a true emotion. No posturing, no drama, no stirring speeches . . . just loss, and a grinding pain centered once more in the chest.

No wonder man's ancestors thought the heart was the center of all.

You could duplicate mind. Brilliance was easy. He was brilliant. But the heart of man, the soul of man—that was hard.

Laura took up with Rudolfo. The somna agitated, Rudolfo gloated, postured, challenged, Laura drooped. It could have been exciting. The growing rivalry, culminating in violence, the death of the philandering husband at the hands of the handsome, virtuous young lover. But Barnaby refused to play; walking away, focusing on his writing, and wondering if it might not have been a deliberate attempt to be rid of him. Enough damage, and reconstruction would have been necessary. And then he wouldn't be him anymore.

He stopped waiting for the lone times, and wrote whenever his public life gave him time at home. The somna was an angry presence, squatting like an outraged cat in the shadowed corners of a room. But it didn't interfere. Perhaps because after so long as a spectator it was incapable of self-initiated action. Or perhaps because it too believed he would fail.

Only one section remained. The Agnus Dei. He no longer needed the piano, the music ran incessantly through his mind. He also realized he couldn't pen those final phrases with the somna only feet away. As strange as it seemed, after lifetimes of interactive games, this was something that he needed to do alone.

He took out the car, and spent several minutes trying to remember the last time it had been driven. He wondered if in some other enclave, say Fez, a man was busy brushing the dust from his car, and reflecting about how long since it had been driven. The banality of the thought was somehow comforting.

In a few blocks he had left behind the inhabited sections of the city. But the houses continued to straggle across the piñon-covered hills, sad reminders of when Santa Fe had held seventy-five thousand busy, vibrant, productive souls. Now it held ten thousand somnas, and their faithful "backs." Or make that nine thousand nine hundred and ninety-nine. *This* "back" wasn't very fucking faithful.

He wound up the atrocious two-lane highway toward the old ski basin. Reached the pull off that afforded the finest view of the changing aspens in the autumn. No fall of gold spilled down the mountains at this time of year. Instead the bare grey/white trunks of the naked aspens thrust like bones into the dark green masses of the pines.

Barnaby arranged himself on a boulder, felt the bite of the cold stone through his trousers. Opened his portfolio, spread the pages, lifted his pen, poised; waiting for the fanfare, the applause, the breathless trembling gasp of amazement from the multitudes.

The wind sighed down the mountains, tossed the branches of the evergreens with a sound like a distant ocean, fluttered the pages, and passed touching his cheek like a chilly caress.

And he realized that for better or worse he was *alone.*

He was still sitting in frozen frightened stasis when a shower of stones and dirt came skittering down the cliff face on the opposite side of the road. A man followed using a brush and outcroppings with the practiced ease of the longtime mountain climber. He was a big man, with blue eyes that sparkled in a ruddy, wind-chapped face. It was a familiar face. He was the conqueror of Everest.

"Hallo," he said in that clipped, British public-school accent which always sounded fake to Barnaby.

"Hello."

"What are you about?"

"I'm completing a requiem mass," Barnaby replied lightly.

"Oh? Whose?"

"I don't know yet. Could be mine."

"Ah, ha ha, jolly good." E.H. tugged at the turtleneck. "Or mine. I'm tackling Everest next week, don't you know." The smile was back in place as he plowed manfully on with the script.

Barnaby folded his hands primly on the portfolio. "How many times does this make?"

"Uh . . . eh?" The smile faded.

"How many times?"

"Nine," came the sullen response.

"Doesn't it get boring?"

The genial facade was down. For an instant, Barnaby saw despair, and a desperate hunger writhe across the broad, handsome face. Then the mask was back, the somna raging behind the blue eyes.

An accusatory forefinger thrust out. "Y-y-you're damaged!"

Barnaby stood, clutching the portfolio to his chest. "No. What I am is scared. But it's okay." He smiled, considering, then added with wonder. "And

I'm not bored. I'm curious and anxious and alive. I'm about to take a risk. Thank you."

He sat, shook the pen to start the flow of ink. The notes flowed from his soul to the page. He was at peace.

It was absurdly easy to arrange. They were to perform the Verdi Requiem as the second half of the December concert. During intermission he quietly gathered up the Verdi, and replaced it with his. By the time the orchestra and chorus had noticed it was too late. Most of the looks he received were terrified or hostile, but Peter's lips skinned back a grin that was almost a grimace, and he gave Barnaby a brief thumbs-up signal.

No rehearsal was necessary. They went through rehearsals merely to maintain the charade, the vicarious enjoyment for the somnas.

But it wasn't perfect!

As section followed section errors crept in. Perhaps they were caused by disruption of the neural-paths because of this awful deviation from instruction. Whatever the cause they were there, and they did not detract, rather they added to the heartbreaking poignancy of the work.

The final minor chord hung like a cry in the still air of the auditorium. Barnaby bent double, clutching the podium with both hands in order to stay erect. The vise was back, squeezing at his chest, because *it had been so beautiful!*

There was no applause. The audience, orchestra, and chorus went stumbling, almost sleepwalking into the New Mexico night. They knew, because they could forget nothing, that the music they had heard and played and sung was original. After three hundred years of repetition a new voice had been heard.

A few were manic in their joy. Peter capering about with his violin in one hand and bow in the other chanting in a grotesque singsong.

"You did it. You did it. You did it."

Barnaby feared that he was damaged, and caught him by the shoulders. "Stop it!"

For a long moment he searched Peter's blue eyes, fearing and not understanding what he read there. "You did it," the violinist whispered again, and spinning from his grip skipped from the stage.

Thrusting his baton into his hip pocket Barnaby wandered about the empty stage gathering up scores. Then hesitated, not knowing what to do with them. Finally he paced to the edge of the stage, and let them fall, an ivory waterfall, onto the carpeted floor. His own master score he tucked beneath one arm, and slowly left the stage.

The green room added to his sense of eerie unreality. No chattering crowds, eager well wishers, flushed performers. A bottle of champagne shifted in its bucket, the rattle of the ice loud in the silent room.

Barnaby started back to the stage, but stopped, arrested by a shadowy hatted and coated figure in the darkened wing.

"*Do* you know what you did?" asked Dr. Antonio Garcia.

"Huh?"

"That young man," he gestured toward the empty stage where only moments before Peter had capered. "Seemed to think you had done it. I'm just wondering if you know what *it* is."

The ancient figure seemed to be holding itself with unnatural rigidity. Holding in . . . something.

"Stop being so fucking portentous." He lit a cigarette. "I wrote a requiem. I proved that 'backs' *can* create."

"Which means what?"

"Shit, I don't know." Smoke erupted in two sharp narrow lines from his nostrils. "That I'll write a symphony next?"

Antonio's lined face twisted with anger, quickly suppressed and controlled. "Why a requiem, Barnaby?"

"I don't know. Something meaningful there, you suppose?" A broad grin that brought no answering response from Antonio.

"Yes, Barnaby, there *is* something meaningful there." The words hissed out fueled by his suppressed violence. "You've done for us, you heedless fool. You've upset the balance. Expressed the discontent. You've given us choices. An hour ago our world was secure, our place in it established, defined. Now there is no guiding force."

Barnaby backed away until he came up against the shell. "You're somna," he began.

"Don't speak to me of that thing! You've ruined us! Ruined us! The entire world has changed, and you don't see it! God, what a moron. Well, I can't face your new world, Barnaby. But I can't go back," he muttered as he tottered toward the exit. "But I can't choose. Can't. Can't. Can't." The quavering voice faded, and Barnaby stood frozen with shock.

The somna was a huddled, frightened presence. Barnaby stepped into the icy night, and it stirred, uncoiling itself from the deepest recesses of his mind. It probed, urged, agitated.

"No," he said aloud, and the word was filled with weariness. "I'm not playing." It slunk back to cower and brood.

The streets were filled with disoriented "backs." Some still trying to play out their somnas' games, but it was like a one-handed man clapping. And Barnaby realized that the network that linked all the "backs" had brought them all the message of his requiem whether they had attended the concert or not. He once more thought of his imaginary counterpart in Fez, and wondered if he understood what had occurred.

Barnaby was starting to, and the understanding terrified him.

Laura was waiting at the house. Cowering on the doorstep. Lost waif. Her hands closed convulsively on his arm as he knelt beside her.

She tried to speak, but only inarticulate sounds emerged. He soothed her with hands and lips and voice. "I love you, Laura," he whispered against her hair.

He rose, stared down at her bowed head. *You've started this, Barnaby, you crazy fucker.*

So does that mean I have to end it? he wailed.

Yes!

I didn't know what I was doing. No answer. *I never meant, never intended . . .*

Choice.

He pressed Laura's shoulders, unlocked the door, walked in. Fear coiled through his mind. Burrowed, sought to hide. He gazed down at the floating somna. White and naked, muscles atrophied from decades of nonuse. For three hundred years they had dreamed life, and their faithful "backs" had experienced every endless nuance, sharing each sensation with their silent, insatiable parasites.

Choice.

Your time has passed. A monitor gave up its grip on flesh with a sticky pop. *It's not malice that motivates me. Just boredom.* The IV's slid from the skeletal arms, and hung like dying seaweed over the edges of the tank. *You've abdicated your right to humanity.*

The somna was writhing now. Wasted muscles jerking as it struggled against the onrush of death. The mouth opening and closing, thick syrupy nutrient bath rushing down the gasping throat.

It was awful, terrifying, and disgusting all at the same time. But he forced himself to watch to the end. After so many years with this silent watcher it was his final act of service. When the final agonized shudder ended he leaned down, and gently closed the staring eyes.

And now he knew that humanity had truly passed to them. He had fashioned and destroyed, created and killed.

It was a contradiction heretofore only achieved by humans.

Requiem was written because I was asked to edit an anthology of New Mexican science fiction authors, and the University of New Mexico Press insisted that I write a story as well. This kind of kick in the rear is required before I will write a short piece. I'm a novelist, and frankly stories intimidate me.

But having agreed to this task I had to find a tale to tell. I have several and very diverse areas in which I have a passionate interest. One is music—I studied opera at the Conservatory of Vienna. Another is the area of legal rights for artificially created entities—androids, robots, AI programs, etc. By wedding these two interests I suddenly found myself wrestling with the question of creativity. Can a robot innovate? Does an android have a soul? Can an AI program dream and desire?

The vampirism element wasn't a conscious decision. Again, I was grappling with the issues of ownership—human proprietorship of their creations—and it wasn't until the story was completed that I realized how truly horrific the floating, dreaming human beings actually were.

So that's the saga of "Requiem." Someday I'd like to go back and figure out what caused the virus that destroyed most of humanity. And how the "backs" built their new society. And if they killed all the humans. Hmmm, sounds like a novel. Guess I'm home again. Maybe I'll make another foray into short fiction next year—if somebody asks me to.

Melinda M. Snodgrass

INFIDEL

Thomas Tessier

I've been a fan of Tessier's since I read Finishing Touches, *a subtle novel of psychological suspense about the loss of innocence, which leads to corruption.*

In "Infidel," Tessier deals with the loss of faith, which—as an invitation allows a traditional vampire to enter one's house—here opens a door for despair to enter the soul.

"*A*nd how is me dear old friend Andy these days?"

"He's fine. He's in good health, and he said to tell you he plays golf at least once a week."

"Tsk." Monsignor Comerford shook his head in mock annoyance but couldn't keep from smiling. "It's a grand racket, the parish priest. Marry 'em and bury 'em, and count the weekly take. Tell Andy I said that, would you?"

"I will," Caroline replied.

"Did you know Andy and I were in college together in Dublin? University College. That was ages ago, of course."

"Yes, he told me that's where you met," Caroline said. "And UCD was where James Joyce went too, wasn't it?"

"That's right, Earlsfort Terrace. Great writer, Joyce," the monsignor added perfunctorily, as if he did not quite agree with his own statement. "A fine feel for the city back then, I'll say that much for him."

Caroline reached into her purse. "I took this snapshot of Father Andy a couple of weeks ago," she said as she passed it to the elderly priest.

"Ah, will you look at that chubby little bugger," Monsignor Comerford exclaimed with glee as he took the photograph. "He was always first at the table, now that I think back on it. Mind you, he never shied away from a gargle either, but you'd better not tell him I said *that*. He might worry about his image. Parish priests tend to fret about such things in America."

"You can keep it, Monsignor," Caroline said as he attempted to return the photograph. "It's for you."

"Thank you very much." He set the picture down on his desk, next to the letter of introduction that Father Andy had written for Caroline. "But let's skip that 'Monsignor' business, shall we? Gerry will do nicely." Caroline smiled and nodded. "Good. Now then, how long have you been in Rome?"

"Four days."

It came as a mild surprise for Caroline to be reminded that she was sitting in an office in Vatican City, not in a rectory in some leafy suburb of Dublin. Monsignor Comerford, she knew, had been stationed at the Vatican for nearly two decades, but he was still thoroughly Irish in his appearance, accent, and manner. The pink, well-scrubbed complexion, the curly white hair, the steady cascade of cigarette ash down the front of his black jacket, the gentle singsong voice—all seemed to belong more in a cluttered Georgian sitting room with peat blazing fragrantly in the fireplace and a big bottle of Powers on the sideboard than in this obscure corner of the papal bureaucracy. Caroline had no clear idea what the Monsignor *did* at the Vatican, but neither did Father Andy.

"And it says here—" tapping at the letter, "—you're a librarian. Is that right?"

"Yes," Caroline answered.

"Very good, and what exactly is it you'd like to do?"

"I'd love to spend some time just looking through the books, the archives. It probably sounds silly, but I've always dreamed of having a chance to explore the Vatican library. I love books and manuscripts, all forms of writing."

Caroline hoped he wouldn't ask if she had been to Trinity or the Bodelian or the Sorbonne, because she hadn't. How could she explain to the priest that it wasn't just books, but the Vatican itself that had drawn her? She really did dream of the Vatican—bizarre images of capture, of anonymous torture, of being trapped forever in an endless maze of barren hallways. Nothing was ever said, there were no signs, but somehow Caroline always knew that she was in the Vatican. At times she wondered if the recurring dreams were a form of sickness, but they never frightened her; on the contrary, she had come to feel almost comfortable with them.

"Is it the dirty books you're after?" Monsignor Comerford's eyes had turned steely. "We've a regular army of these so-called scholars who come trooping through here, most of them American I might add, and all they want to do is study the dirty books. Why we even keep them is beyond me, but nowadays destroying a book is almost a mortal sin. To some folks, anyway."

The monsignor was apparently finished, so Caroline answered his question. "No. History and the history of the faith are my favorite subjects." Faith, she thought, and the loss of it.

"Ah, that's a welcome change." The monsignor beamed at her. "If all the fine young women of the world felt that way, there'd be a lot less bother taking place."

There was a barb in the compliment, for Caroline noticed how the monsignor glanced at her unadorned ring finger. History and books were all well and good, but he believes I should be married and taking care of a bunch of babies, she thought. That was fine with her. Caroline might disagree with Monsignor Comerford as to what a woman should or should not do, but she was actually pleased that he was a priest from the old school. She hadn't come to the Vatican looking for trendiness or progressive attitudes. Her own faith had been blasted by the winds of modernism swirling through the Church in recent years.

"Well, you'd better get started," the monsignor said, rising from his seat. "You can have the rest of the afternoon, just get yourself back here by five. That's when I leave, and I wouldn't want you getting lost."

"Neither would I."

"And if you haven't had enough, you're more than welcome to come back tomorrow. There's so much of that clutter downstairs a person could spend years poking through it all, if he had nothing better to do with his life. And contrary to what you might have heard, none of it is off-limits." The priest paused, then winked at her. "Of course, it's not everyone that gets in."

Monsignor Comerford left Caroline with Father Vincenzo, who was apparently in charge of "the collection." A short, thin man who wore wire-rimmed glasses and spoke excellent English, Father Vincenzo showed her some of the noteworthy documents and volumes in the official library. Air-conditioned, computerized, it was a completely modern operation in a centuries-old setting. And yet, it was a good deal smaller than Caroline had expected. But then Father Vincenzo took her on a tour of the three main levels below ground, where one room grew out of another and the number of them ran into the dozens before she lost count. There were books and manuscripts and tottering heaps of papers piled on every inch of shelf space, from floor to ceiling. Tiny corridors appeared, and then abruptly ended. On the third and lowest level the floor was made up of large stone slabs, long since worn smooth. The rooms were small and boxy, and seemed to have been carved right out of the earth. The passageways were quite narrow and the only lights were strung along the low ceiling with electric cable.

There were no labels, no numbers, no signs, nothing at all to indicate order. If you wanted to find something, where would you start, Caroline wondered. But she was delighted, because she finally felt she had arrived where she was meant to be.

"These are the oldest stacks," Father Vincenzo explained. "Everything valuable or important has been removed, but otherwise it is not very organized."

"There's so much of it," Caroline said.

"Yes, it extends under most of Vatican City. The equivalent of two or three square blocks in New York City, I think." Then a smile formed at the corners of Father Vincenzo's mouth. "You are a book lover. This, I think, is what you came to see."

"Oh, yes, yes. I'm amazed. It's so much like I pictured it in my fantasies." The word seemed too personal, almost sexual in its intensity. Caroline felt her cheeks flush, and all she could do was add weakly, "But more so."

Father Vincenzo brought Caroline back to the stairs in order to show her how easy it was to find the way out, and then he left her alone to pursue her curiosity. She appreciated the fact that he didn't feel it necessary to warn her against damaging, copying, or tracing over anything.

Caroline wandered aimlessly for a while, stopping to look at one item or another, and then moving on. Her knowledge of French and Latin was excellent, and she had a smattering of Italian, but most of the pages on the third level were handwritten, and sooner or later the calligraphy defeated her. Caroline simply could not concentrate, her mind refused to focus. What am I doing here?

Somewhere in a far corner of the third level, Caroline found a battered footstool in one room. She sat down on it, and leaned back against a wall of large, leathery tomes. She was tired, and her feet ached, the usual tourist curse, but she felt very happy. Pennsylvania seemed a billion miles away. She let her eyes close for a moment, and she sucked in the musty air. To Caroline it was like a rare and delicious perfume.

Books were the center of her life, and it had been that way ever since she was a small child. She liked to believe that she could still remember fumbling to open her very first picture book of nursery rhymes—but Caroline knew that was probably more her fancy than an actual memory. Books were mysterious, frightening, thrilling, disturbing, uplifting, nurturing, endlessly available, and always accommodating. Caroline had dated many men over the years, but she had yet to find one who offered the same array of valuable qualities. Most of the time that didn't bother her. If you had to have something other than a relationship for the focal point of your life, what better than books?

Books, and belief. But belief was an increasingly elusive notion. For years it had been a natural part of Caroline's life, but lately it seemed irrelevant, or not even there. Nothing specific had happened to cause this change, yet it seemed as if the deep well of her faith had gradually evaporated to the point where it was now not much more than a thin, moist residue. But you can't control faith, anymore than you can choose your dreams.

Caroline stood up and resumed her wandering. In one large room she came across signs of fairly recent activity. There were stacks of bound papers on a table, many more on the floor around it. A prospectus announced the publication of the *Annals of the Propagation of the Faith* in five hundred volumes over a period of twenty years. Caroline knew that the *Annals* were regular reports to the Vatican from Catholic missionaries all over the world. It was a staggering thought. How many centuries of this tedious and obscure paperwork had accumulated by now? And yet, Caroline was sure that some of it must be quite fascinating. However, clipped to the prospectus was a laconic handwritten note, dated November, 1974, which stated that the project was abandoned because of the bankruptcy of the publisher. And of course the Vatican wouldn't squander its own funds on such an improbable commercial venture, Caroline thought, smiling as she left the room.

She walked until she came to the lowest (the floor had a way of gradually winding down into the earth) and most remote corner of the third level. Certainly this was where the overhead reach of electric cable and lights ended. About twenty feet away, just visible in the gloom, was a stone wall that marked the end of the passageway. The books and manuscripts, stacked from the floor to the ceiling on each side, were wedged together so tightly and had been undisturbed for so long that they appeared to have hardened into a solid mass, and Caroline was afraid she would damage them if she tried to remove any one item for scrutiny. She started to turn away, intending to make the long climb back up to the street level, but then she stopped, as she thought she noticed something odd about the far wall.

It was an optical illusion, aided by the feeble light. Yes, she realized, moving closer. There was not one wall, but two, at the end of the aisle. The outer wall, which came from the right, stopped just short of the stacks on the left, and the inner wall receded almost imperceptibly behind it. Caroline approached the gap, barely a foot wide, and peered around the corner.

Total darkness. She reached into it, and felt nothing but cool air. The passage continued. Caroline didn't know what she should do. She wanted to follow it, to find out where it went, but she had nothing to light her way. She could trip and tumble down a hole, or walk into a den of snakes or vermin— too many bad things could happen. Buy a flashlight and return tomorrow.

Yes, but first . . . Caroline slid her foot along the ground and edged herself behind the wall. Just a step or two, she promised, to see if it ends abruptly. Her outstretched hand bumped against something hard, not stone. A metal bar. Caroline gripped it and harsh rust flaked loose in her hand. It had to be a gate, which meant that the passage *did* go on. Caroline shook it firmly once, and the whole thing broke free. It was too heavy and unwieldy to control, so she shoved it away from her. The sound that came in the darkness told her that the gate had hit a wall and then slid down to the left. Firm ground, and a turn.

Caroline worked her way along the narrow passage. The wall swung back to the left, as expected. She moved cautiously around the turn, probing the air with her hand. Caroline stopped. This was as far as she could safely go without a light. She stared at the uniform blackness ahead of her. Beyond this point she could easily get lost in a maze of passageways. Okay, she thought, you found something interesting; come back tomorrow with a flashlight and a sack of bread crumbs.

Caroline hesitated, her mind dancing with possibilities. It could be a long-forgotten catacomb, or a burial chamber that held the mummified remains of ancient Romans. She might even discover some manuscripts that dated back two thousand years. She should discuss it with Father Vincenzo, and together they could organize a proper exploration. But even as Caroline considered this, she found it impossible to turn back. The priest's office was so far away, such an enormous climb—and Caroline felt too tired. The cumulative effects of travel and touring and the miles of walking had finally caught up with her. The dead air didn't help either. She would have to rest for a few minutes before leaving.

As she stood there, leaning against the wall, Caroline began to notice the quality of the darkness. You could say that it had no depth at all, or that its depth was endless. But it was not a perfect darkness, she realized. Somewhere in it, close by or off in the distance, there was—not light, but the subtlest texture of light. I must look like someone on drugs, Caroline thought as she stared ahead. Pupils dilated wide as drift nets to sweep any random photons across the threshold of visibility. I look like a freak, but that's okay because it's a freaky situation. Caroline felt dizzy and disoriented, as if she could no longer tell which way was up, and yet there was nothing she could do—except fall down, if that's what was going to happen—because she was just too tired, too damn tired to care. But she was not wrong. There was light, or something like it.

Caroline was aware of the fact that she was walking. Toward the light, into the dark, it didn't matter which. She felt oddly detached from what was happening, as if her body had decided to move and her mind was simply floating along with it. Probably no one still alive in the Vatican knew of this hidden area, Caroline thought dreamily. Which means, *No one in the world knows where I am now.* But that didn't frighten her. On the contrary, she felt caught up in something of real importance out on the boundary of faith and uncertainty, and dreams.

A suffusion of light infiltrated her right eye, knocking her off balance. It wasn't that strong, Caroline saw as she steadied herself and her eyes readjusted. It was a glow, a hazy cloud of cold light some distance away, too weak to illuminate this place. Yet it had confused her for a brief moment. Caroline crossed the intervening space and walked into the faint light. She looked at a flight of crude stairs that coiled down and away from her, deep into the chilly earth.

For just an instant Caroline's mind slid toward the idea of leaving, but just as quickly it skittered away. Her body had no strength for going back now. It was as if she were caught on an electric current that carried her only forward, and down. And so Caroline descended the wet and slippery steps, pressing her hands against the close walls and bending her head beneath the low rock ceiling. Count the number—but the numbers bounced around like a flock of billiard balls clicking in her brain, and the momentum of her descent increased rapidly, flooding her with apprehension, so she couldn't.

Almost brightness. Caroline's knees sagged as her feet hit bottom suddenly and there was nowhere to go. She had arrived in a small room, really nothing more than a landing. Then she saw the gate, another gate. No, it was a door. Through the bars, a square cell, empty but for the old man lying in the middle of the floor. A clutch of tattered rags. The man looked ancient. What light was this?

Ah, child.

—Who . . . are you?

The words formed in her mind but never escaped her lips. It didn't matter. The old man smiled, and felt, disturbingly, as if he somehow made Caroline's face smile with him.

Mani.

—What?

Caroline's brain swirled sickeningly, and it took an effort of the will to remain on her feet. The old man kept smiling that near-death smile. A sack of dead skin. But the smile, and those eyes, were very much alive. He moved slightly, the muted sound of dusty parchment rustling.

Ma-nee.

The first syllable prolonged, the second quite crisp despite the long vowel. Caroline shook her head slowly.

—No . . .

Manicheus, if you wish.

Impossible, Caroline thought. It was all wrong and she knew she should leave at once, but instead her body sank down on the wall until she was sitting on the bottom step.

—The holy man?

Paraclete. Yes.

—No. Manicheus died in A.D. 275.

Was put to death.

—As a heretic.

Yes, as a heretic.

The old man's laughter simmered uncomfortably in Caroline's brain. This is crazy, she thought, I'm hallucinating, the dreams are pushing up and breaking the surface.

No.

She struggled to recall what she knew of Manicheanism. It was one of many heretical sects that had sprung up in the early years of the Church, and perhaps the most dangerous. The Church had spared no effort to wipe out the Manicheans, although some of their beliefs still lingered on in the despair and cynicism that permeated so much of modern life. They claimed that the universe was made up of two equal forces, light (good) and dark (evil), in eternal conflict. God was good, but God did not reign supreme in this universe. If you put evil on a par with good, then all else is permanently diminished and faith becomes a matter of arbitrary choice. Human beings were just insignificant players in a cosmic struggle without beginning or end. So the gap between the Church and the Manicheans was a vast theological chasm that could never be bridged. But it was an issue of purely academic interest now, or at least it should be, Caroline thought.

—How could you be here?

They brought me back and locked me in this place.

—But why? Didn't they kill you?

Yes, but to them I was a heretic.

—I still don't understand.

The laughter came again, rippling through Caroline's mind in a very unpleasant sensation.

They believed that heretics return to this world, possessing terrible powers. The power to draw the lifeblood of faith out of other souls. To control the feeble human mind. That is why they burned heretics, and tore the bodies to pieces.

But that was another time, centuries ago, and now not even the Church believes in such things. Beliefs change, but do they ever matter?

The Pope had to see me, to see for himself that I really was dead, and so they brought me back from Persia.

—And put you down here and forgot about you?

Oh, they played with me awhile, using their knives and hot irons. Dry laughter, like whistling sand. *But then the old Pope dies, and yes, I was forgotten.*

—When did you last . . .

See someone? A charming young novice in the thirteenth century. I haven't been able to move from this spot in about perhaps three hundred years now. Easy to find souls, but not to bring them all the way into this place.

The old man was crazy, Caroline had no doubt. But whatever the truth about him might be, he obviously needed care, and maybe medical attention. He certainly did not belong down in a clammy dungeon. It was a miracle he wasn't already dead. He looked so frail and helpless, and there was such sadness in his eyes.

—I'll get help.

Don't leave me, child.

—What should I do?

The door. Come to me.

Caroline approached the cell door. The hinges looked as if they wouldn't budge. She put her hands around one of the bars in the center of the door, and shook it. The hinges held, but there was some give inside the lock. Caroline shook the door again and the corroded latch crumbled steadily beneath the pressure. Rusty flakes showered down to the floor. The hinges shrieked painfully as Caroline forced the door open.

The old man looked up hopefully as she slipped into the cell and went to him. She wasn't sure what to do next. He looked too weak and fragile to move.

Hold me.

Caroline sat down on the floor beside him, took him by the shoulders, and carefully lifted him up. His head lolled against her shoulder, then slid a little, resting over her heart, and he smiled gratefully. Caroline had no desire to move.

Touch me with your skin.

Caroline stroked his cheek lightly—it felt cool and dry, like one of the old manuscripts she had examined. Regardless of who he was or why he was there, the old man responded to her hand on his cheek. His eyes brightened and his features became more animated. He was certainly old, but so small and shrunken, like some lonely, withered child.

I need to be closer.

Caroline didn't understand. Her mind felt tired, lazy, and remarkably tranquil. She didn't want to move at all. She hugged the old man closer to her.

To your warmth.

Her mind couldn't follow a complete thought anymore. Nothing mattered but the moment, and her part in it. Caroline unbuttoned her blouse and the old man quickly pressed his face to her skin.

More.

Her bra was in the way. Caroline pulled it down, uncovering her breasts. The old man rubbed his face against them, burrowed between them, and then she felt his tongue, like fine sandpaper, seeking her nipple. Caroline was paralyzed with delirium, dazed with a sense of giving. It felt as if her body were a vessel full of precious liquid, a kind of inner sea of living warmth that was now flowing through her skin into him. But there was nothing to replace it, and Caroline's heart quickened with a sudden surge of useless alarm.

—Holy man . . .

Once.

—You brought me here?

In a way, yes.

—You spoke to me in dreams . . .

In dreams you spoke with yourself, and I am what you found.

—You took my faith . . .

What we let go was never there.

—Help me . . .

Become what you become, as I did.

—They were right . . .

Well, yes.

—You became . . .

What they made me.

—God help me . . .

And who is that, child?

Caroline reached up to touch her own cheek and was amazed to find that it already felt as cool and dry as onionskin. Too weak to move, Caroline rested her hand on the man's bony shoulder. She was vaguely aware that she ought to push him away. There was no muscle strength left in her arm. Then Caroline was unable even to remain sitting up, and she fell back flat on the floor. She felt so light there was no pain when her head hit the stone. The old man moved lower and rested his face in the warm softness of her belly. He left no mark on her, for the touch of her skin was enough. An image flickered across her mind—she was buried beneath a million books, and it was not an unpleasant experience. Then the books began to fall, tons of them raining silently down through the darkness, and Caroline fell with them, a fading ribbon of liquid heat that spun and swirled as she flew gloriously out of herself.

She wakes in darkness. Disoriented for a moment, she shoves the dead bones off her bare skin. Now she knows where she is and what comes next. She stands, buttons her blouse, and leaves. She knows the way. So much time has gone by. It's late, and she has a million things to do.

Dona Rintelman got me wondering about what might have been lost or forgotten in the recesses of the Vatican over the course of centuries. This story is for Dona, but it is emphatically *not* about her.

Any similarity between the hold that the world's religions exert on some of their believers, and the legendary power that vampires have over certain hapless human beings, is of course entirely in the mind of the observer. Things always look different from the inside.

Thomas Tessier

Do I Dare to
Eat a Peach?

Chelsea Quinn Yarbro

Tessier's story was about the human embodiment of a religious heresy as vampire. In Yarbro's classic, the State, represented by a few men, metaphorically takes on the characteristics of vampirism when it gives these men the power to brainwash Weybridge and drain him of his personality, his hope, and his will.

Weybridge had been burgled: someone—some *thing*—had broken in and ransacked his memories, leaving all that was familiar in chaos. It was almost impossible for him to restore order, and so he was not entirely sure how much had been lost.

Malpass offered him sympathy. "Look, David, we know you went through a lot. We know that you'd like the chance to put it all behind you. We want you to have that, but there are a few more things we have to get cleared up. You understand how it is."

"Yes," Weybridge said vaguely, hoping that, by agreeing, he might learn more. "You have your . . . your . . ."

"Responsibilities," Malpass finished for him. "Truth to tell, there are times I wish I didn't have them." He patted David on the shoulder. "You're being great about all this. I'll make sure it's in the report."

Weybridge wanted to ask what report it was, and for whom, but he could not bring himself to say the words. He simply nodded, as he had done so many times before. He opened his mouth, once, twice, then made a wave with one hand.

"We know how it is, old man," Malpass said as he scrutinized

Weybridge. "They worked you over, David. We know that. We don't blame you for what you did after that."

Weybridge nodded a few more times, his mind on other things. He eventually stared up at the ceiling. He wanted to tell Malpass and the others that he would rather be left alone, simply turned out and ignored, but that wasn't possible. He had hinted at it once, when they had first started talking to him, and the reaction had been incredulity. So Weybridge resigned himself to the long, unproductive wait.

In the evening, when Malpass was gone, Stone took his place. Stone was younger than Malpass, and lacked that air of sympathy the older man appeared to possess. He would stand by the door, his arms folded, his hair perfectly in place, his jaw shaved to shininess, and he would favor Weybridge with a contemptuous stare. Usually he had a few taunting remarks to make before relapsing into his cold, staring silence. Tonight was no different. "They should have left you where they found you. A man like you—you don't deserve to be saved."

Weybridge sighed. It was useless, he knew from experience, to try to tell Stone that he had no memory of the time he was . . . wherever it was he had been. "Why?" he asked wearily, hoping that some word, some revelation, no matter how disgusting, would give him a sense of what he had done.

"You know why. Treating the dead that way. I saw the photos. Men like you aren't worth the trouble to bring back. They should leave you to rot, after what you did." He shook his head. "We're wasting our time with you. Men like you—"

"I know. We should be left alone." He stared up at the glare of the ceiling light. "I agree."

Stone made a barking sound that should have been a laugh but wasn't. "Oh, no. Don't go pious on me now, Weybridge. You're in for a few more questions before they throw you back in the pond. One of these days you're going to get tired of the lies, and you'll tell us what you were doing, and who made you do it."

Weybridge shook his head slowly. His thin, hospital-issue pajamas made him chilly at night, and he found himself shivering. That reminded him of something from the past, a time when he had been cold, trembling, for days on end. But where it had happened and why eluded him. He leaned back on the pillows and tried to make his mind a blank, but still the fragments, disjointed and terrifying, were with him. He huddled under the covers, burrowing his head into the stacked pillows as if seeking for refuge. He wanted to ask Stone to turn the lights down, but he knew the young man would refuse. There was something about nightmares, and screams, but whether they were his own or someone else's, he was not sure.

"You had any rest since you got here, Weybridge?" Stone taunted him. "I'm surprised that you even bother to try. You have no right to sleep."

"Maybe," Weybridge muttered, dragging the sheet around his shoulders. "Maybe you're wrong, though."

"Fat chance," Stone scoffed, and made a point of looking away from him. "Fat fucking chance."

Weybridge lay back on his bed, his eyes half focused on the acoustical tile of the ceiling. If he squinted, he thought he could discern a pattern other than the simple regularity of perforations. There might be a message in the ceiling. There might be a clue.

Stone stayed on duty, silent for most of his shift, but favoring Weybridge with an occasional sneer. He smoked his long, thin dark cigarettes and dropped the ashes onto the floor. The only time he changed his attitude was when the nurse came in to give Weybridge yet another injection. Then he winked lasciviously and tried to pat her ass as she left the room.

"You shouldn't bother her," Weybridge said, his tongue unwieldy as wet flannel. "She . . . she doesn't want—"

"She doesn't want to have to deal with someone like you," Stone informed him.

Weybridge sighed. "I hope . . ." He stopped, knowing that he had left hope behind, back in the same place his memories were.

Malpass was back soon after Stone left, and he radiated his usual air of sympathy. "We've been going over your early reports, David, and so far, there's nothing . . . irregular about them. Whatever happened must have occurred in the last sixteen months. That's something, isn't it."

"Sure," Weybridge said, waiting for the orderly to bring him his breakfast.

"So we've narrowed down the time. That means we can concentrate on your work in that sixteen-month period, and perhaps get a lead on when you were . . ." He made a gesture of regret and reached out to pat Weybridge on the shoulder.

"When I was turned," Weybridge said harshly. "That's what you're looking for. You want to know how much damage I did before you got me back, don't you?"

"Of course that's a factor," Malpass allowed. "But there are other operatives who might be subjected to the same things that have happened to you. We do know that they are not all pharmacological. There were other aspects involved." He cleared his throat and looked toward the Venetian blind that covered the window. It was almost closed, so that very little light from outside penetrated the room.

"That's interesting, I guess," Weybridge said, unable to think of anything else to say.

"It is," Malpass insisted with his unflagging good humor. "You took quite a risk in letting us bring you back. We're pretty sure the other side didn't want you to be . . . recovered."

"Good for me." Weybridge laced his hands behind his head. "And when you find out—*if* you find out—what then? What becomes of me once you dredge up the truth? Or doesn't that matter?"

"Of *course* it matters," Malpass said, his eyes flicking uneasily toward a spot on the wall. "We look after our own, David."

"But I'm not really your own anymore, am I?" He did not bother to look at Malpass, so that the other man would not have to work so hard to lie.

"Deep down, we know you are," Malpass hedged. "You're proving it right now, by your cooperation."

"Cooperation?" Weybridge burst out. "Is that what you think this is? I was dragged back here, tranked out of my mind, and hustled from place to place in sealed vans like something smuggled through customs. No one asked me if I wanted to be here, or if I wanted you to unravel whatever is left of my mind. Cut the crap, Malpass. You want to get the last of the marrow before you throw the bones out." It was the most Weybridge had said at one time since his return, and it startled Malpass.

"David, I can understand why you're upset, especially considering all you've gone through. But believe me, I'm deeply interested in your welfare. I certainly wouldn't countenance any more abuse where you're concerned." He smiled, showing his very perfect, very expensive teeth. "Anyone who's been through what you've been through—"

"You don't know what it was. Neither do I," Weybridge reminded him.

"—would have every reason to be bitter. I don't blame you for that," Malpass went on as if nothing had been said. "You know that you have been—"

"No, I don't know!" Weybridge turned on him, half rising in his bed. "I haven't any idea! That's the problem. I have scraps here and there, but nothing certain, and nothing that's entirely real. You call me David, and that might be my first name, but I don't remember it, and it doesn't sound familiar. For all I know, I'm not home at all, or this might not be my home. For all I know, I never got away from where I was and this is just another part of the . . . the experiment."

Malpass did not answer at once. He paced the length of the room, then turned and came back toward the head of the bed. "I didn't know you were so troubled," he said finally, his eyes lowered as if in church. "I'll tell your doctors that you need extra care today."

"You mean more drugs," Weybridge sighed. "It might work. Who knows?"

"Listen, David," Malpass said with great sincerity, "we're relying on you in this. We can't get you straight again without your help, and that isn't always easy for you to give, I know."

Weybridge closed his eyes. He had a brief impression of a man in a uniform that he did not recognize, saying something in precisely that same tone of commiseration and concern that Malpass was using now. For some reason, the sound of it made him want to vomit, and his appetite disappeared.

"Is something wrong, David?" Malpass asked, his voice sounding as if he were a very long way off. "David?"

"It's nothing," he muttered, trying to get the older man to go away. "I . . . didn't sleep well."

"The lights?" Malpass guessed, then went on. "We've told you why they're necessary for the time being. Once your memory starts coming back, then you can have the lights off at night. It will be safe then."

"Will it?" Weybridge said. "If you say so."

Malpass assumed a look of long-suffering patience. "You're not being reasonable this morning, David."

"According to your reports, I don't have any reason, period." That much he believed, and wished that he did not. He longed for a sense of his own past, of a childhood and friends and family. What if I am an orphan, or the victim of abuse? he asked himself, and decided that he would rather have such painful memories than none at all.

"What's on your mind, David?"

"Nothing," he insisted. There were more of the broken images shifting at the back of his mind, most of them senseless, and those that were coherent were terrifying. He had the impression of a man—himself?—kneeling beside a shattered body, pausing to cut off the ears and nose of the corpse. Had he done that? Had he seen someone do that? Had he been told about it? He couldn't be sure, and that was the most frightening thing of all.

"Tell me about it," Malpass offered. "Let me help you, David."

It was all he could do to keep from yelling that his name was not David. But if it was not, what was it? What could he tell them to take the place of David?

"You look terrible. What is it?" Malpass bent over him, his middle-aged features creased with anxiety. "Is there anything you can tell me?"

Weybridge struck out with his arm, narrowly missing Malpass. "Leave me alone!"

"All right. All right." Malpass stepped back, holding up his hands placatingly. "You need rest, David. I'll see that you get it. I'll send someone in to you."

"NO!" Weybridge shouted. He did not want any more drugs. There had been too much in his bloodstream already. He had the impression that there had been a time when his veins had been hooked up to tubes, and through the tubes, all sorts of things had run into his body. He thought that he must have been wounded, or . . . A light truck overturned and burst into flame as a few men crawled away from it. Had he been one of the men? Where had the accident occurred? He put his hands to his head and pressed, as if that might force his mind to squeeze out the things he needed to know.

Malpass had retreated to the door and was signaling someone in the hallway. "Just a little while, David. You hang on," he urged Weybridge. "We'll take care of you."

Weybridge pulled one of his pillows over his face in an attempt to blot out what was left there. Gouts of flame, shouts and cries in the night. Bodies riven with bullets. Where were they? *Who* were they? Why did Weybridge remember them, if he did remember them?

Another nurse, this one older and more massive, came barreling through the door, a steel tray in her hand. "You calm down there," she ordered Weybridge so abruptly that his fear grew sharper.

There was a chill on his arm and a prick that warmed him, and shortly suffused through him, turning his world from hard-edged to soft, and making his memories—what there were of them—as entrancing as the boardwalk attractions of loop-the-loop and the carousel.

Later that day, when Weybridge babbled himself half awake, they brought him food, and did what they could to coax him to eat it.

"You're very thin, Mr. Weybridge," the head nurse said in a tone that was more appropriate for an eight-year-old than a man in his late thirties.

"I'm hungry," Weybridge protested. "I *am*. But . . ." He stared at the plate and had to swallow hard against the bile at the back of his throat. "I don't know what's the matter."

"Sometimes drugs will do this," the head nurse said, disapproval in her tone and posture.

"You're the ones keeping me on drugs," he reminded her nastily. "You don't know what—"

The head nurse paid no attention to him. She continued to bustle about the room, playing at putting things in order. "Now, we're not to lie in bed all day. Doctor says that we can get up this afternoon for a while, and walk a bit."

"Oh, can *we?*" Weybridge asked with spite. "What else can *we* do?"

"Mr. Weybridge," the head nurse reproached him. "We're simply trying to help you. If you just lie there, then there's very little we can do. You can see that, can't you?"

"What happened to the *we* all of a sudden?" He wanted to argue with her, but lacked the energy. It was so useless that he almost wished he could laugh.

"That's better; you'll improve as long as you keep your sense of humor." She came back to the foot of his bed and patted his foot through the thin blankets. "That's the first step, a sense of humor."

"Sure." How hopeless it seemed, and he could not find out why.

By the time Malpass came back, Weybridge had enough control of himself that he was able to take the man's kind solicitations without becoming angry with him.

"You're going to get better, David," Malpass promised. "We'll be able to debrief you and then you can get away from all this. If you cooperate, we'll make sure you'll have all the protections you'll need."

"Why would I need protections?" And what kind of protections? he added to himself.

Malpass hesitated, plainly weighing his answer. "We don't yet know just how much you did while you were with the other side. There are probably men who would like to eliminate you, men from their side as well as ours. If we put you under our protection, then your chances of survival increase, don't you see that?" He stared toward the window. "It would be easier if we could be certain that you're not . . . programmed for anything, but so far, we can't tell what is real memory and what is . . . random."

"That's a nice word for it: random." Weybridge leaned back against the pillows and tried to appear calm. "Do you have any better idea of what happened?"

"You were in prison for a while, or you believe you were in prison, in a very dark cell, apparently with someone, but there's no way to tell who that person was, or if it's your imagination that there was someone there." He coughed. "And we can't be sure that you were in prison at all."

Weybridge sighed.

"You have to understand, David, that when there are such states as yours, we . . . well, we simply have to . . . to sort out so much that sometimes it—"

"—it's impossible," Weybridge finished for him. "Which means that I could be here for the rest of my life. Doesn't it?"

Malpass shrugged. "It's too early to be thinking about that possibility."

"But it *is* a possibility," Weybridge persisted.

"Well, it's remote, but . . . well." He cleared his throat. "When we have a more complete evaluation, we'll talk about it again."

"And in the meantime?"

"Oh," Malpass said with patently false optimism, "we'll continue to carry on the treatment. Speaking of treatment," he went on, deftly avoiding more questions, "I understand you're going to be allowed to walk today. They want you to work up an appetite, and you need the exercise in any case."

"The head nurse said something about that," Weybridge responded in a dampening way.

"Excellent. *Ex*cellent! We'll tell headquarters that you're improving. That will please the Old Man. You know what he can be like when there's trouble with an operative in the field." He rubbed his hands together and looked at Weybridge expectantly.

"No, I don't know anything about the Old Man. I don't know anything about headquarters. I don't recall being an operative. That's what I'm being treated for, remember?" He smashed his left arm against the bed for emphasis, but it made very little sound and most of the impact was absorbed by the softness.

"Calm down, calm down, David," Malpass urged, once again speaking as if to an invalid. "I forgot myself, that's all. Don't let it trouble you, please."

"Why not?" Weybridge demanded suspiciously. "Wouldn't it trouble you if you couldn't remember who you were or what you'd done?"

"Of *course* it would," Malpass said, even more soothingly. "And I'd want to get to the bottom of it as soon as possible."

"And you think I don't?" Weybridge asked, his voice rising.

"David, David, you're overreacting. I didn't mean to imply that you aren't doing everything you can to . . . recover. You're exhausted, that's part of it." He reached out to pat Weybridge's shoulder. "I hear you still aren't eating."

The surge of nausea was so sudden that Weybridge bent violently against it. "No," he panted when he felt it was safe to open his mouth.

"The nurses are worried about you. They can give you more IV's, but they all think you'd do better if you . . ." He smiled, making an effort to encourage Weybridge.

"I . . . can't," Weybridge said thickly, trying not to think of food at all.

"Why?" Malpass asked, sharpness in his tone now. "Can't you tell me why?"

Weybridge shook his head, bewildered. "I don't know. I wish I did." Really? he asked himself. Do you really want to know what it is about food that horrifies you so? Or would you rather remain ignorant? That would be better, perhaps.

"You've got to eat sometime, David," Malpass insisted.

"Not yet," Weybridge said with desperation. "I need time."

"All right," Malpass allowed. "We'll schedule the IV for three more days. But I want you to consent to a few more hours of therapy every day, all right?" He did not wait for an answer. "You have to get to the bottom of this, David. You can't go on this way forever, can you?"

"I suppose not," Weybridge said, fighting an irrational desire to crawl under the bed and huddle there. Where had he done that before? He couldn't remember.

"I'll set it up." Malpass started toward the door. "The Old Man is anxious to find out what happened to you. We have other men who could be in danger."

"I understand," Weybridge said, not entirely certain that he did. What if he was not an agent at all? What if that was a part of his manufactured memories? Or what if he was still in the hands of the other side—what then? The headache that had been lurking at the back of his eyes came around to the front of his head with ferocious intensity.

"We're all watching you, David," Malpass assured him as he let himself out of the white-painted room.

Stone regarded Weybridge with scorn when he heard about the increased therapy sessions. "Taking the easy way, aren't you, you bastard?" He lit a cigarette and glowered at Weybridge.

"It doesn't feel easy to me," Weybridge replied, hoping that he did not sound as cowardly as he feared he did.

"That's a crock of warm piss," Stone declared, folding his arms and directing his gaze at the window. "Anyone does what you did, there's no reason to coddle them."

It was so tempting to beg Stone to tell him what it was he was supposed to have done, but Weybridge could not bring himself to demean himself to that hostile man. "I'm not being coddled."

"According to who?" Stone scoffed, then refused to speak again, blowing smoke toward the ceiling while Weybridge dozed between unrecallable nightmares.

The therapist was a small, olive-skinned gnome named Cleeve. He visited Weybridge just as the head nurse was trying to coax him out of bed to do his required walking. "Out for your constitutional, eh, Mr. Weybridge?" His eyes were dark and glossy, like fur or crushed velvet.

"We're going to walk twice around the nurses' station," the head nurse answered for him. "It's doctor's orders."

Weybridge teetered on his feet, feeling like a kid on stilts for the first time.

Dear God, had he ever walked on stilts? He did not know. The effort of a few steps made him light-headed, and he reached out for Cleeve's shoulder to steady himself. "Sorry," he muttered as he tried to get his balance.

"Think nothing of it, Mr. Weybridge," Cleeve told him in a cordial tone. "All part of the service, I give you my word." He peered up at Weybridge, his features glowing with curiosity. "They've had you on drugs?"

"You know they have," Weybridge said a little wildly. His pulse was starting to hammer in his neck.

Cleeve nodded several times. "It might be as well to take you off some of them. So many drugs can be disorienting, can't they?" He stared at the head nurse. "Who should I speak to about Mr. Weybridge's drugs? I need to know before we start therapy, and perhaps we should arrange a . . . new approach."

The head nurse favored Cleeve with an irritated glance. "You'd have to talk to Mr. Malpass about that."

"Ay, yes, the ubiquitous Mr. Malpass," Cleeve said with relish. "I will do that at once."

Weybridge was concentrating on staying erect as he shuffled first one foot forward, and then the other. His nerves jangled with every move and his feet were as sore as if he were walking on heated gravel. "I don't think I can—"

Both the head nurse and Cleeve turned to Weybridge at once. "Now, don't get discouraged," the head nurse said, smiling triumphantly that she had been able to speak first. "You can take hold of my arm if you think you're going to fall."

Weybridge put all his attention on walking and managed a few more steps; then vertigo overwhelmed him and he collapsed suddenly, mewing as he fell.

"I'll help you up, Mr. Weybridge," Cleeve said, bending down with care. "You appear to be very weak."

"Yes, I suppose I am," Weybridge responded vaguely. He could not rid himself of the conviction that he had to get to cover, that he was too exposed, that there were enemies all around him who would tear him to pieces if he did not find cover. Who were the enemies? What was he remembering?

Cleeve took Weybridge by the elbow and started to lever him into a sitting position, but was stopped by the head nurse. "Now, we don't want to indulge ourselves, do we? It would be better if we stood up on our own."

"That's a little unrealistic," Cleeve protested. "Look at him, woman— he's half starved and spaced out on the chemicals you've been pouring into him."

Hearing this, Weybridge huddled against the wall, arms and knees gathered tightly against his chest. He did not want to think about what had gone into him. The very idea made him cringe. He swallowed hard twice and fanned his hands to cover his eyes.

"They're necessary," the head nurse said brusquely. "Until we know what's happened to this man...."

Cleeve shook his head. "You mustn't mistake his condition for the refusal of an enemy. From what I have been told, this man is one of our operatives, yet everyone is behaving as if he were a spy or a traitor." He steadied Weybridge with his arm. "When it's certain that he's been turned, then we can do what must be done, but not yet."

The head nurse folded her arms, all of her good humor and condescension gone. "I have my orders."

"And so do I," Cleeve said mildly. "Mr. Weybridge, I'm going to help you back to bed, and then I want to arrange to have a little interview with you. Do you understand what I'm saying?"

It was an effort to nod, but Weybridge managed it; his head wobbled on the end of his neck. "I want . . . to talk to . . . someone." He coughed and felt himself tremble for the strength it cost him.

"Good. I'll return in an hour or so. Be patient." Cleeve gave a signal to the head nurse. "Get him back into bed and arrange for an IV. I don't think he's going to be able to eat yet."

The head nurse glared at Cleeve. "You'll take responsibility for him, then? I warn you, I won't be left covering for you if you're wrong."

What were they arguing about? Weybridge asked himself as he listened to them wrangle. What was there to be responsible for? What had he done? Why wouldn't anyone tell him what he was supposed to have done? He lifted one listless hand. "Please . . ."

Neither Cleeve nor the head nurse paid him any heed. "You'll have to tell Malpass what you're doing. He might not approve."

Cleeve smiled benignly. "I intend to. As I intend to ask for permission to remove Mr. Weybridge from this wing of the hospital. I think we can do more with him in my ward." He turned toward Weybridge. "Don't worry. We'll sort everything out."

"What...?" Weybridge asked, frowning. He felt very tired, and his body ached in every joint. He supposed he was suffering from malnutrition, but there was more to it than that. Even as the questions rose again, his mind shied away from them. There was so much he could not understand, and no one wished to explain it to him. He pulled himself back onto the bed, pressing his face into the pillow, and nearly gagging on the carrion smell that rose in his nostrils. He retched, gasping for air.

"That's enough of that," the head nurse said with unpleasant satisfaction. "When Mr. Malpass takes me off this case, I'll stop giving him drugs, but for the time being, it's sedation as usual. Or do you want to argue about it, Mr. Cleeve?"

Weybridge was sprawled on the bed, his face clammy and his pulse very rapid. His face was gaunt, his body skeletal. He was like something from deep underwater dragged up into the light of day. "I... I..."

Cleeve sighed. "I'm not going to oppose you, Nurse. Not yet. Once I talk to Mr. Malpass, however—"

The head nurse tossed her head. "We'll see when that happens. Now you leave this patient to me." She gave her attention to Weybridge. "We're too worn out, aren't we?"

Weybridge hated the way she spoke to him but had not strength enough to protest. He waited for the prick in his arm and the warm bliss that came with it. There was that brief respite, between waking and stupor, when he felt all the unknown burdens lifted from his shoulders. That never lasted long—once again, Weybridge felt himself caught in a morass of anguish he did not comprehend.

The walls were thick, slimy stone, and they stank of urine and rats. His own body was filthy and scabbed, his teeth rattled in his head and his hair was falling out. He shambled through that little space, maddened by fear and boredom. Someone else cowered in the darkness, another prisoner—was he a prisoner?—whose?—why?—or someone sent to torment him. He squinted in an effort to see who it was, but it was not possible to penetrate the shadows. He thrashed on his clean, white bed, believing himself in that dreadful cell—if he had been there at all.

Malpass was standing over Weybridge when he woke with a shout.

"Something, David? Are you remembering?"

"I ..." Weybridge shook his head weakly, trying to recapture the images of his dreams, but they eluded him. "You ..." He had seen Malpass' face in the dream, or a face that was similar. He had no idea if the memory was valid, or the dream.

"We're having a little meeting about you this morning, David," Malpass said heartily. "We're reviewing your case. The Old Man is coming to hear what we have to say."

Weybridge could think of nothing to say. He moved his head up and down, hoping Malpass would go on.

"Cleeve wants you over in his division. He thinks he can get at the truth faster with those suspension tanks of his and the cold wraps. We'd rather keep you here on drugs, at least until you begin to ... clarify your thoughts. However, it will be up to the Old Man to decide." He gave Weybridge's shoulder another one of his amiable pats. "We'll keep you posted. Don't worry about that. You concentrate on getting your memory in working order."

There was a fleeting impression of another promise, from another man—or was it Malpass?—that winked and was gone, leaving Weybridge more disoriented than before. Who was the man he had seen, or thought he had seen? What had he done? Or was it simply more of the confusion that he suffered? "How soon will you know?"

"Soon," Malpass said, smiling. "Today, tomorrow. They're going to put you on IV for a while this morning. This evening, they want you to try eating again."

"I can't," Weybridge said at once. "No food." He was sick with hunger; he could not endure the thought of food. "I can't."

"The head nurse will look after you," Malpass went on, blithe as a kinder-garten teacher. "We're going to take Stone off for this evening, and Cleeve will stay with you. He wants a chance to talk to you, to study your reactions."

"Cleeve?" Weybridge repeated.

"He saw you yesterday," Malpass reminded him sympathetically, his face creasing into a mask of good-hearted concern. "You remember speaking with Cleeve, don't you?"

"Yes," Weybridge said, ready to weep with vexation. "I haven't forgotten. It's the other things that are gone."

"Well, possibly," Malpass allowed. "You don't seem to recall coming here. Or have you?"

"I . . ." Had there been an ambulance? A plane? He was pretty sure he had been in a plane, but was it coming here, or had there been a plane earlier, before he had done—whatever it was he had done? Had he flown then? He was certain that he could recall looking down from a great height—that was something. He tried to pursue the image without success.

"Don't work so hard, you only make it more difficult," Malpass admonished him. "You don't need that extra stress right now. If you get frustrated, you won't be able to think clearly about your treatment and getting better."

"I don't think clearly in any case, frustrated or not," Weybridge said with great bitterness.

"We're trying to do something about that, aren't we?" Malpass said, smiling once again. "You're in the best hands, you're getting the finest care. In time, it will come back. You can be sure of that."

"Can I? And what if it doesn't?" Weybridge demanded.

"David, David, you mustn't think this way. You'll straighten it all out, one way or another," Malpass said, moving away from Weybridge. "I'll drop in later, to see how you're doing. Don't let yourself get depressed, if you can help it. We're all pulling for you." With a wave, he was gone, and Weybridge longed for a door he could close, to keep them all out.

There was a new nurse that afternoon, a woman in her mid-thirties, not too attractive but not too plain, who regarded him with curiosity. She took his temperature, blood pressure, and pulse, then offered to give him a sponge bath.

"I'll take a shower later," he lied. He did not like the feeling of water on his skin, though why this should be, he was unable to say. He knew he was a fastidious person and the smell of his unwashed skin was faintly repulsive.

"It might be better if you let me do this for you," she said unflappably. "As long as you're hooked up to that IV, you should really keep your arm out of water. It won't take long. And I can give you a massage afterward." She sounded efficient and impersonal, but Weybridge could not bear the thought of her touching him.

"No thanks," he said, breathing a little faster. What was making him panic?

"Let me give it a try. Dr. Cleeve suggested that we give it a try. What do you think? Can we do your feet? If that's not too bad, we'll try the legs. That's reasonable, isn't it?"

Both of them knew it was, and so he nodded, feeling sweat on his body. "Go slow," he warned her, dreading what she would do. "If I . . ."

She paid no attention to him. "I realize that you're not used to having a woman bathe you, but after all, your mother did, and this isn't much different, is it?" She had gone into the bathroom while speaking and was running water into a large, square, stainless-steel bowl. "I'll make it warm but not hot. And I'll use the unscented soap. I've got a real sponge, by the way, and you'll like it. Think about what it can be like with a big, soft sponge and warm water."

The very mention of it made him queasy, but he swallowed hard against the sensation. "Fine," he panted.

The nurse continued to get the water ready for him. "You might not think that you'll like it at first, but you will. I've done work with other . . . troubled patients and in this case, you're easy to deal with. You don't make any unreasonable demands or behave badly." She was coming back to him now, carrying the pan of soapy water. "It won't be so hard. I promise." She flipped back his covers, nodding at his scrawny legs. "Feet first, okay?"

He did not trust himself to answer her; he gestured his resignation.

"Left foot first. That's like marching, isn't it?" She laughed as she reached out, taking his ankle in her hand. "The water is warm, just as I said it would be." She lifted the sponge—it was a real sponge, not one of the plastic ones—and dribbled the water over his foot.

Weybridge shrieked as if he had been scalded, and jerked away from her. "No!"

"What's wrong?" she asked, remaining calm.

"I . . . I can't take it. I don't know why, but I can't." He felt his heart pounding against his ribs as he gasped for air. "I can't," he repeated.

"It's just water, Mr. Weybridge," the nurse pointed out. "With a little soap in it."

"I know," he said, trying to sound as reasonable as possible. "But I can't."

"The way you can't eat, either?" she asked, curious and concerned. "What is it about water? Or food, for that matter?"

"I wish I knew," he sighed, feeling his heartbeat return to a steady, barely discerned thumping.

"Can't you figure it out?" She moved the pan of bath water aside. "Can you tell me anything about it, Mr. Weybridge?"

He shook his head. "I wish I could. I wish I could tell someone what it was. I might be able to get rid of it if I knew what it was." His eyes filled with tears and he turned away from her in shame.

"Why would food and water do this to you?" she mused, not addressing him directly, yet encouraging him.

"There was . . . something that happened. I don't . . . remember, but it's there. I know it's there." He brought his hands to his face so that he would not have to let her see his expression. He had a quick vision—perhaps not quite a vision, but an image—of a man with a large knife peeling the skin off someone's—his?—foot, grinning at the screams and maddened profanities his victim hurled at him. Weybridge's skin crawled, and after a short time, he pulled his foot out of the nurse's hands. "I can't," he whispered. "I'm sorry. It's not you. I just can't."

"But . . ." she began, then nodded. "All right, Mr. Weybridge. Maybe we can take care of it another time. It would be sensible to tend to this, don't you think?"

"Sure," he said, relieved that he had postponed the ordeal for a little while.

"What's the matter, though? Can you tell me?" Her expression was curious, without the morbid fascination he had seen in the eyes of Malpass and Cleeve.

"I wish I could. I wish I knew what was happening to me. I wish I . . . I wish it were over, all over." He clasped his hands together as if in desperate prayer. "I've tried and tried and tried to figure it out. I have what are probably memories of doing something terrible, something so ghastly that I don't want to think about it, ever. But I don't know what it was, really, or if it ever really happened, or if it did, it happened to me. There are times I'm sure it was someone else and that I've merely . . . eavesdropped on it. And other times, I *know* I did it, whatever it is, and . . . there are only bits and pieces left in my mind, but they're enough." It was strangely comforting to say these things to her. "I've heard that murderers want to confess, most of them. I'm willing to confess anything, just to know for sure what happened, and maybe, why."

The nurse looked at him, not critically but with deep compassion. "They're speculating on what's real and what isn't: the doctors and the . . .

others here. Some of them think you've blocked out your trauma, and others believe that you're the victim of an induced psychosis. What do you think?"

"I don't know what to think. It's driving me crazy, not knowing." He said this quite calmly, and for that reason, if no other, was all the more convincing.

"Do you want to talk about it—I mean, do you want me to stick around for a while and try to sort out what went on when you were—" She stopped herself suddenly and her face flushed.

"Are you under orders?" Weybridge asked. "Are you doing this because they told you to?"

"Partly," she said after a moment. "I shouldn't tell you anything, but . . . they're all using you, and it troubles me. I want to think that you're doing your best to get to the bottom of your . . . your lapses. I don't like the way that Malpass keeps glad-handing you, or the way Cleeve treats you like a lab animal." She had taken hold of the thin cotton spread and now was twisting the fabric, almost unconsciously.

"Are they doing that?" Weybridge asked, not really surprised to learn it.

"They are," she said.

Weybridge nodded slowly, wondering if this kind nurse was just another ploy on Malpass' or Cleeve's part to try to delve into his missing past. He wavered between resentment and hope, and finally said, "Which of you is supposed to be Rasputin and which is supposed to be the saint? That's the usual way, isn't it? One of you convinces the poor slob you're interrogating that you're on his side and the other one is the bad guy, and by pretending to be the guy's friend, you get him to open up." He slammed his fists down onto the bed, secretly horrified at how little strength he had. "Well, I wish I could open up, to any of you. I wish I could say everything, but I can't. Don't you understand that, any of you? I can't. I don't remember." There were only those repugnant, terrifying flashes that came into his mind, never for very long, never with any explanation, but always there, and always genuine, and always leaving him so enervated and repelled that he wanted to be sick, and undoubtedly would have been, had he anything left in his stomach to give up. "God, I don't even know for certain that we're all on the same side."

"Of course we are, David," the nurse protested.

"You'd say that, no matter what," Weybridge muttered. "You'd claim to be my friend, you'd make me want to confide in you, and all the time it would be a setup, and you'd be bleeding me dry, getting ready to put me on the dust heap when you're through with me. Or maybe you want to turn me, or maybe I turned, and you're with my old side, trying to find out how much I revealed to the others. Or maybe you think I was turned, and you're trying to find out."

"What makes you think you were active in espionage?" the nurse said to him. "You're talking like someone who had been an operative. Were you?"

"How the hell do I know?" Weybridge shot back. "Everyone here acts as if I was some kind of spy or intelligence agent or something like that. I've been assuming that I was."

"Suppose you weren't?" She stared at him. "Suppose it was something else entirely."

"Like what?" Weybridge demanded.

The door opened and Malpass stepped into the room. "Hello, David. How's it going?"

The nurse gave Malpass a quick, guilty look. "I was trying to give Mr. Weybridge a massage," she said.

"I see," Malpass said with sinister cordiality. "What kind of luck are you having?"

"It seems to bother him so . . ." She got off the bed and smoothed the covers over his feet.

"Well." Malpass shook his head. "Tomorrow might be better. There are several things we're going to try to get done this evening, and it would be better if you had a little nap first, David." He motioned to the nurse to leave and watched her until she was out of the room. "Did she bother you, David?"

"She was nice to talk to," Weybridge said with a neutral tone, suddenly anxious to keep the nurse out of trouble. Whatever she was, she was the only person he had met who had been genuinely—or appeared to be genuinely—interested in him as a person.

"That's good to know. It's fine that you're talking to someone," Malpass said, smiling more broadly than before.

"You'll make sure she doesn't get in trouble for talking to me, won't you?"

Malpass' eyebrows rose. "Why, David, what makes you think that she'd be in trouble for a thing like that?"

Weybridge frowned. "I don't know. You're all so . . . secretive, and . . . odd about what you want out of me."

"David, David," Malpass said, shaking his head. "You're letting your imagination run away with you. Why would we want to do such a thing to you? You're sounding like you regard us as your jailers, not as your doctors. We want you to improve. No one wants that more than we do. But can't you see—your attitude is making everyone's job more difficult, including your own. You're letting your dreams and fears take over, and that causes all sorts of problems for us. If I could find a way to convince you that you're creating chimeras . . ."

"You'd what?" Weybridge asked when Malpass did not go on.

Malpass made a dismissing gesture. "I'd be delighted, for one thing. We all would be." He cocked his head to the side. "You believe me, don't you?"

Weybridge shrugged. "Should I?"

"Of course you should," Malpass assured him. "God, David, you'd think that you were being held in prison, the way you're responding. That's not the case at all. You know it's not."

"Do I?"

"Well, think about it, man," Malpass said expansively. "You're being taken care of as thoroughly as we're able. We want you to get better, to get well and be independent. I think everyone here is pulling for you, and . . . well, David they are all very concerned for you. Everyone hopes that you'll be over this . . . . problem soon." He gave Weybridge his most sincere look. "You're a very special case, and we all want to see you get well, entirely well."

"Un-huh," Weybridge said, looking away from Malpass. "And what will happen to me when I get well? Where will I go?"

"Back home, I would guess," Malpass said, trying to give this assertion an enthusiastic ring.

"Back home," Weybridge echoed. Where was that? What was his home like? "Where do . . . did I live?"

"You mean, you don't remember?" Malpass asked, apparently shocked by this question.

"Not really. I wouldn't be asking if I did," he said testily. "And don't coddle me with your answers. That won't help me at all." He folded his arms, taking care not to press on the IV needle taped just below his elbow.

"Well, you live in a small city about . . . oh, eight hundred miles from here. It's on a river. The countryside is rolling hills. The city has a very large textile industry, and most of the agricultural land in the immediate area is devoted to sheep ranching. There's also a good-sized university. You were an assistant professor there for four years. Do you remember any of this?" Malpass asked. "You're frowning."

Weybridge tried to recall such a place and found nothing in his mind that had anything to do with a small city near a river, or a university. "What did I teach?"

"Physics" was Malpass' swift answer. "Astrophysics. You were lured into the private sector to help develop hardware for space exploration. You were considered to be very good at your work."

"Then, how in hell did I end up here?" Weybridge demanded, his voice shrill with desperation.

"That's what we'd all like to know," Malpass said, doing his best to sound comforting. "Your ... affliction is a real challenge to us all."

"When did I become an intelligence agent, if I was teaching and then doing space research in industry? What was the name of the university where I taught? What city did I live in? What company did I go to work for? Who was my boss?"

"Whoah there, David," Malpass said, reaching out and placing his thick hand on Weybridge's shoulder. "One thing at a time. First, the Old Man has decided that, for the time being, we're not going to give you too many names. It would be distracting, and you might use the information to create ... false memories for yourself based on the names instead of your recollections. You can see the sense in that, surely."

"I suppose so," Weybridge said sullenly. "But what the fuck does that leave me?"

"In time, we hope it will restore your memories. We want that to happen, all of us." He gripped a little tighter, giving Weybridge's shoulder a comradely shake, doing his best to buck his charge up. "When you can name your university, the head of your department, then we'll know we're getting somewhere."

"Why did I become an agent? Or did I?" He had not intended to ask this aloud, but the words were out before he could stop them. "Is this some kind of ruse?"

"Of course not," Malpass declared.

"You'd say that whether it was or not," Weybridge sighed. "And there's not any way I can prove the contrary." He lowered his head. "The bodies. Where were they? Whose were they?"

"What bodies, David?" Malpass asked, becoming even more solicitous.

"The ones I see in my dreams. The ones with . . . pieces missing. There are some in cells and some in . . . trenches, I guess. It's . . . not very clear." He felt the sweat on his body, and smelled his fear.

"Can you tell me more about them?" Malpass urged. "What do you remember?"

Hands on the ground, just hands, with palms mutilated; a torso with the striations of ropes still crossing the chest; a child's body, three days dead and bloated; scraps of skin the color of clay sticking to rusty chains; a man on a wet stone floor, his back and buttocks crosshatched with blood-crusted weals; a woman, hideously mutilated and abused, lying on her side, legs pulled up against her chest, waiting for death: the impressions fled as quickly as they came. "Not very much," Weybridge answered, blinking as if to banish what he had seen.

"Tell me," Malpass insisted. "You've got to tell me, David. The Old Man has been asking about your ordeal, and if I can give him something— anything—he might decide to . . ." He did not go on.

"To what?" Weybridge asked. "Or can't you tell me that, either?"

"I . . . haven't been given permission," Malpass said in an under voice. "I'll need to get it if I'm going to explain what it is the Old Man needs to know."

This was the first time Weybridge had ever seen Malpass display an emotion akin to fear, and in spite of himself, he was curious. "Why should the Old Man care what I remember? He has me where he wants me, doesn't he?"

"Well, sure, but we don't want you to have to remain here indefinitely," Malpass said uneasily, attempting to make a recovery. "We're all . . . doing our best for you."

Weybridge shook his head. "That's not enough, Malpass. You're holding back too much. I don't want to say anything more until you're a little more forthcoming with me." It was exciting to defy Malpass, so Weybridge added, "I want the lights out at night. I need sleep."

"I'll see if it can be arranged," Malpass hedged, moving away from the bed, where Weybridge sat. "I'll let you know what we decide."

What had he said? Weybridge wondered. What had caused the change in the affable Mr. Malpass? He could not find the answer, though it was obvious that something he had triggered disturbed the man profoundly. "Is there something you'd like to tell me, Malpass? You seem distraught."

"I'm . . . fine, David. You're probably tired. I'll let you have a little time to yourself, before they bring you your supper."

Was it Weybridge's imagination, or was there a trace of malice in Malpass' tone of voice? He watched Malpass retreat to the door and hover there, his hand on the latch. "What is it?"

"Nothing," Malpass said fervently.

"I'm interested in what it is the Old Man wants to know. Find out if you can tell me. Maybe we can all work together if you're not so secretive with me." He was almost light-headed with satisfaction as he saw the door close behind Malpass.

The afternoon hours dragged by; Weybridge remained in solitude, the IV unit by his bed his only company. He would have liked to have something to read, but this had been refused when he asked the first time, and Weybridge had not renewed his request. He lay back against the skimpy pillows and stared up at the ceiling, trying to make patterns and pictures of the play of light and shadow there.

About sunset, Dr. Cleeve entered the room, his pursed mouth giving him the look of an overstuffed bag with a hole in it. "I see you are alone," he said.

"Is that unusual?" Weybridge asked angrily. "Did you think someone else would be here?"

"Under the circumstances, yes, I did." Dr. Cleeve said with great meaning. "The Old Man isn't satisfied with your progress. He's about ready to give up on you, and so is Malpass."

"Give up on me? How? Why?" In spite of himself, he felt worried by this announcement.

"You're not telling them what they want to know, what they need to know. They think you've been turned and that you're simply playing with them to gain your new masters some time."

"That's not true!" Weybridge protested, trying to get to his feet. "It's not possible! I don't know what I did, I don't know why I'm here, I don't even know who you are, or who I am. What do I have to do to make you believe that?" His pulse throbbed in his head and his eyes ached. There were the images, the memories of so much horror that he could not to bear to look at them directly, but that proved it—didn't it?—that he was not deceiving them.

"Mr. Weybridge," Dr. Cleeve soothed. "You're overwrought. I can understand how that would be, but clearly you can see that you are not on very firm ground." He reached over and patted Weybridge's arm, just below the place where the IV needles were taped. "I see that your veins are holding up fairly well. That's something. A man in your condition should be glad that we do not yet have to cut down for a vein."

"It . . ." There was a fleeting vision of arms and legs, tattered remnants of bodies floating on a sluggish current, catching against river reeds, piling up, then drifting on.

"What is it, Mr. Weybridge?" Dr. Cleeve asked intently. "What is happening to you now?"

Weybridge shook his head. "I . . . it's gone now. It's nothing." He felt the sweat on his forehead and his ribs, and he could smell it, hating the odor for its human aliveness.

"Mr. Weybridge," Dr. Cleeve said, folding his arms and regarding Weybridge through his thick glasses, "are you willing to let me try an . . . experiment?"

"How do you mean, 'an experiment'?" Weybridge asked, suspicious in the depths of his desperation.

"There are ways that we can . . . accelerate your mind. We could find out what had truly happened to you, and what you have done. The danger is that if you have been turned, we will know about it, unquestionably, and you will have to face the consequences of your act, but the waiting would certainly be over." He studied Weybridge with increasing interest. "It would not be difficult to do, simply a bit more risky than what we have been doing up till now."

"And what is the risk?" Weybridge asked, wishing he knew more about Dr. Cleeve—any of them—so that he could judge why the man had made this offer.

"Well, if the suppressed memories are traumatic enough, you could become psychotic." He spread his hands in wide mute appeal. "You could still become psychotic just going on the way you are. It may, in fact, be that you are already psychotic. There's really no way of knowing without taking certain risks, and this, at least, would end the suspense, so to speak." He tried to smile in a way that would reassure Weybridge, but the strange, toothy unpursing of his mouth was not reassuring.

"I'll have to think about it," Weybridge hedged.

"Let me suggest that you do it very quickly. The Old Man is anxious to have your case resolved, and his way would most certainly do you permanent damage." Dr. Cleeve watched Weybridge closely. "If you have not already done permanent damage."

"And we won't know that until we try one of the techniques, right?" Weybridge ventured, his tone so cynical that even he was startled by the sound of it.

"It is the one sure way." Dr. Cleeve paused a moment. "It may not be that you have any choice."

"And it is really out of my hands in any case, isn't it?" He sighed. "If I say yes to you, or if I wait until the others, the Old Man—whoever he is— makes up his mind to put my brain through the chemical wringer. Which might have been done already. Did you ever think of that?"

"Oh, most certainly we've thought of it. It seems very likely that there has been some . . . tampering. We've said that from the first, as you recall." He smacked his fleshy palms together. "Well. I'll let you have a little time to yourself. But try to reach a decision soon, Mr. Weybridge. The Old Man is impatient, as you may remember."

"I don't know who the Old Man is. He's just a name people keep using around here," Weybridge said, too resigned to object to what Dr. Cleeve said to him.

"You claim that's the case. That's how the Old Man sees it. He thinks that you're buying time, as I said. He thinks that this is all a very clever ploy and that you're doing everything you can to keep us from following up on your case." He shrugged. "I don't know what the truth of the matter is, but I want to find it out. Don't you?" This last was a careful inquiry, the most genuine question the man had asked since he'd come into the room.

"You won't believe it, but I do," Weybridge said, feeling himself grow tired simply with speaking. He had reiterated the same thing so often that it was no longer making much sense to him. "I have to know what really happened to me, and who I am."

"Yes; I can see that," Dr. Cleeve said with an emotion that approached enthusiasm. "You think about it tonight. This isn't the kind of thing to rush into, no matter how urgent it may appear."

As Weybridge leaned back against the pillows, he was feeling slightly faint, and he answered less cautiously than he might have under other circumstances. "If it gets us answers, do whatever you have to do."

"Oh, we will, Mr. Weybridge," Dr. Cleeve assured him as the door closed on him.

There were dreams and fragments of dreams that hounded Weybridge through the night. He was left with eyes that felt as if sand had been rubbed into the lids and a taste in his mouth that drove what little appetite he possessed away from him, replacing it with repugnance.

Malpass did not come to visit him until midday, and when he arrived, he looked uncharacteristically harried. "You're having quite a time of it with us, aren't you, David?" he asked without his usual friendly preamble.

"I've done easier things, I think." He tried to smile at the other man, but could not force his face to cooperate. "I wish you'd tell me what's going on around here."

"The Old Man wants to take you off the IV unit and see if a few days on no rations will bring you around. I've asked him to give me a few more days with you, but I don't know if he's going to allow it. Three of our operatives were killed yesterday, and he's convinced you can tell him how their covers were blown."

"It wasn't me," Weybridge said firmly, and even as he spoke, he wondered if some of those drastic images stored in his mind where the memories had been might be associated with the loss of the other operatives.

"The Old Man doesn't believe that. He thinks you're still following orders." Malpass licked his lips furtively, then forced them into a half smile that reflected goodwill. "You've got to understand, David. The Old Man simply doesn't buy your story. We've all tried to convince him that you're probably nothing more than a pawn, someone who's been set up to distract us, but that isn't making any headway with the Old Man. He's pissed about the other operatives, you see, and he wants someone's head on the block. If it isn't yours, it may have to be mine, and frankly, I'd rather it was yours." This admission came out in a hurry, as if he hoped that in saying it quickly, he would disguise its meaning.

"And you want this over with, don't you, Malpass?" Weybridge asked, feeling much more tired than he thought it was possible to be. "I want it over with too."

"Then you'll agree? You'll let them question you again, with drugs so we're sure you're telling us the truth?" He sounded as eager as a schoolboy asking for a day without classes.

"Probably," he said. "I have to think it over. You're going to have to muck about in my mind, and that's happened once already. I don't want to be one of those miserable vegetables that you water from time to time."

Malpass laughed as if he thought this caution was very witty. "I don't blame you for thinking it over, David. You're the kind who has to be sure, and that's good, that's good. We'll all be easier in our minds when the questions have been answered."

"Will we? That's assuming you find out what you want to know, and that it's still worth your while to keep me alive. There are times I wonder if you're on my side or the other side—whoever my side and the other side may be—and if anything you're telling me is true. If you were on the other side, what better way to get me to spill my guts to you than to convince me that you're on my side and that you're afraid I've been turned. You say you're testing me, but it might not be true."

"David, you're paranoid," Malpass said sternly. "You're letting your fears run away with you. Why would we go through something this elaborate if we weren't on your side? What would be the purpose?"

"Maybe you want to turn me, and this is as good a way as any to do it. Maybe I've got information you haven't been able to get out of me yet. Maybe you're going to program me to work for you, and you started out with privation and torture, and now that I'm all disoriented, you're going to put on the finishing touches with a good scramble of my brain." He sighed. "Or maybe all that has already happened and you're going to see what I wrecked for you. And then what? You might decide that it's too risky to let it be known that you've found out what happened, and so you'll decide to lock me up or turn me into some kind of zombie or just let me die."

"You're getting morbid," Malpass blustered, no longer looking at Weybridge. "I'm going to have to warn the Old Man that you've been brooding."

"Wouldn't you brood, in my position?" Weybridge countered, his face desolate.

"Well, anyone would," Malpass said, reverting to his role as chief sympathizer. "Have you been able to have a meal yet?"

The familiar cold filled him. "No," Weybridge said softly. "I . . . can't."

"That'll be one of the things we'll work on, then," Malpass promised. "There's got to be some reason for it, don't you think? David, you're not going to believe this, but I truly hope that you come through this perfectly."

"No more than I do," Weybridge said without mirth. "I'm tired of all the doubts and the secrecy." And the terrible visions of broken and abused bodies, of the panic that gripped him without warning and without reason, of the dread he felt when shown a plate of food.

"Excellent," Malpass said, rubbing his hands together once, as if warming them. "We'll get ready, so when you make up your mind we can get started."

"You're convinced that I'll consent. Or will you do it no matter what I decide?" Weybridge said recklessly, and saw the flicker in Malpass's eyes. "You're going to do it no matter what, aren't you?"

"I'll talk to you in the morning, David," Malpass said, beating a hasty retreat.

There were dreams that night, hideous, incomplete things with incomprehensible images of the most malicious carnage. Weybridge tossed in his bed, and willed himself awake twice, only to hear the insidious whispers buzz around him more fiercely. His eyes ached and his throat was dry.

Dr. Cleeve was the first to visit him in the morning. He sidled up to Weybridge's bed and poked at him. "Well? Do you think you will be able to help me?"

"If you can help me," Weybridge answered, too exhausted to do much more than nod.

"What about Malpass? Are you going to put him off, or are you going to convince him that my way is the right one?" The tip of his nose moved when he spoke; Weybridge had never noticed that before.

"I . . . I'll have to talk to him." He moved his arms gingerly, taking care to test himself. "I want to do what's best."

"Of course you do," Dr Cleeve declared. "And we've already discussed that, haven't we?" His eyes gloated, though the tone of his voice remained the same. "You and I will be able to persuade the rest of them. Then you'll be rid of your troubles and you can go about your life again instead of remaining here."

"Will I?" Weybridge had not meant to ask this aloud, but once the words were out, he felt relieved. "Or am I speeding up the end?"

"We won't know that until we know what's been done to you, Mr. Weybridge," said Dr. Cleeve. "I'll have a little talk with Malpass and we'll arrange matters."

"When?" Weybridge asked, dreading the answer.

"Tomorrow morning, I should think," he replied, hitching his shoulders to show his doubt.

"And then?" Weybridge continued.

"We don't know yet, Mr. Weybridge. It will depend on how much you have been . . . interfered with." He was not like Malpass, not inclined to lessen the blows. "If there is extensive damage, it will be difficult to repair it. It's one of the risks you take in techniques like this."

Weybridge nodded, swallowing hard.

"Malpass will doubtless have a few things to say to you about the tests. Keep in mind that he is not a medical expert and his first loyalty is to the Old Man."

"Where is your first loyalty?" Weybridge could not help asking.

"Why, to the country, of course. I am not a political man." He cleared his throat. "I hope you won't repeat this to Malpass; he is suspicious of me as it is."

"Why is that?"

"There are many reasons, most of them personal," Dr. Cleeve said smoothly. "We can discuss them later, if you like, when you're more . . . yourself."

Weybridge closed his eyes. "Shit."

"I have a great deal to do, Mr. Weybridge. Is there anything else you would like to know?" Dr. Cleeve was plainly impatient to be gone.

"One thing: how long have I been here?"

"Oh, five or six weeks, I suppose. I wasn't brought in at first. Only when they realized that they needed my sort of help. . . . That was sixteen days ago, when you had recovered from the worst of your wounds but still could or would not eat." He waited. "Is that all, Mr. Weybridge?"

"Sure," he sighed.

"Then, we'll make the arrangements," Dr. Cleeve said, closing the door before Weybridge could think of another question.

He was wakened that night—out of a fearful dream that he would not let himself examine too closely—by the nurse who had been kind enough to be interested in him and had tried to rub his feet. He stared at her, trying to make out her features through the last images of the dream, so that at first he had the impression that she had been attacked, her mouth and nostrils torn and her eyes blackened.

"Mr. Weybridge," the nurse whispered again, with greater urgency.

"What is it?" he asked, whispering too, and wondering how much the concealed devices in the room could hear.

"They told me . . . they're planning to try to probe your memory. Did you know that?" The worry in her face was clear to him now that he saw her without the other image superimposed on her face.

"Yes, that's what they've—we've decided."

"You agreed?" She was incredulous.

"What else can I do?" He felt, even as he asked, that he had erred in giving his permission. "Why?"

"They didn't tell you, did they? about the aftereffects of the drugs, did they? Do you know that you can lose your memory entirely?"

"I've already lost most of it," Weybridge said, trying to make light of her objections.

"It can turn you into a vegetable, something that lies in a bed with machines to make the body work, a thing they bury when it begins to smell bad." She obviously intended to shock him with this statement, and in a way she succeeded.

"You don't know anything about that," Weybridge said heatedly. "You haven't seen bodies lying unburied in an open grave in a field where the humidity makes everything ripe, including the bodies." He coughed, trying to think where that memory came from. "You haven't been locked in a stone-walled room with five other people, no latrine and not enough food to go around."

"Is that what happened to you?" she asked, aghast at what she heard.

"Yes," he said, with less certainty.

"Did it?"

"I think so. I remember it, pieces of it, anyway." He rubbed his face, feeling his beard scratch against the palms of his hands. Under his fingers, his features were gaunt.

"They'll force you to remember it all, if it happened," she warned him. "Don't you understand? They'll throw you away like used tissue paper when they're done. They don't care what happens to you after they find out what you know. Truly, they won't bother to see you're cared for." She reached out and took him by the shoulders. "If you want to stay in one piece, you've got to get away from here before they go to work on you. Otherwise, you'll be . . . nothing when they're through with you, and no one will care."

"Does anyone care now?" he wondered aloud. "I don't know of anyone."

"Your family, your friends, someone must be worried about you. This place is bad enough without thinking that . . ." Her voice trailed off.

"And where is this place? If I got out, where would I be? Don't you see, I have no idea of who these people are, really, or where we are or what it's like outside. No one has told me and I don't remember. Even if I got out, I would have no place to go, and no one to stay with, and nothing to offer." His despair returned tenfold as he said these things.

"I'll find someone to take care of you until you remember," she promised him, her eyes fierce with intent.

"And feed me?" he asked ironically. "Do you have a friend with an IV unit?"

"Once you're out of here—" she began.

"Once I'm out of here, I'll be at the mercy of . . . everything. Where are we? Where would I have to go for the Old Man—whoever he is—not to find me and bring me back? It might be worse out there." He shivered. "I don't think I can manage. If I could get out, I don't think I'd be able to get very far before they brought me back."

"We're near a river. We're about fifteen miles from the capital, and—"

"What capital is that?" Weybridge inquired politely. "I don't know which capital you mean."

"*Our* capital, of course," she insisted. "You can get that far, can't you? There are names I could give you, people who would hide you for a while, until you make up your mind what you want to do about . . . everything."

"I don't know about the capital," Weybridge repeated.

"You *lived* there, for heaven's sake. Your records show that you lived there for ten years. You remember that much, don't you?" She was becoming irritated with him. "Don't you have any memory of that time at all?"

"I . . . don't think so." He looked at her strangely. "And for all I know, my records are false. I might not have been here ever, and it could be that I haven't done any of the things I think I have."

"Well, letting them fill you up with chemicals isn't going to help you find out. You'll just get used up." She took his hand and pulled on it with force. "Mr. Weybridge, I can't wait forever for you to make up your mind. If they found out I came in to see you and tried to get you to leave, I'd be in a lot of trouble. You understand that, don't you?"

"I can see that it might be possible." He tugged his hand, but she would not release it. "Nurse, I don't want to go away from here, not yet, not until I can get some idea of who I am and what I did. Not until I can *eat*."

"But you will be able to if you leave. You're being manipulated, Mr. Weybridge. David. They're doing things to you so that you can't eat, so you'll have to stay here. If only you'd get away from here, you'd find out fast enough that you're all right. You'd be able to remember what really happened and know what was . . . programmed into you. They don't care what comes of their little experiments, and they're not going to give a damn if you go catatonic or starve to death or anything else. That's the way they've been treating agents that they have questions about." She paused. "I have to leave pretty soon. It's too risky for me to remain here. They'll catch me and then they'll . . ." She turned away, her eyes moving nervously toward the door.

Weybridge closed his eyes, but the dreadful images did not fade. There were three naked figures, two of them women, twitching on a stone floor. They were all fouled with blood and vomit and excrement, and the movements and sounds they made were no longer entirely human. "I've been thinking," he said remotely, his throat sour and dry, "that I've been going on the assumption that all the pieces of things I remember, all the horrors, were done to me. But I can't find more than three scars on my body, and if it happened, I'd be crosshatched and maimed. I've thought that perhaps I *did* those things to others, that I was the one causing the horror, not its victim. Do you think that's possible? Do you think I finally had enough and wouldn't let myself do anything more?" This time when he pulled on his hand, she let him go.

"I can't stay, Weybridge. If you haven't got sense enough to come with me, there's nothing I can do to change your mind. You want to let them do this to you, I can't stop you." She got off his bed, her eyes distraught though she was able to maintain an unruffled expression. "After today, you won't have the chance to change your mind. Remember that."

"Along with everything else." He looked at her steadily. "If you get into trouble because of me, I want you to know that I'm sorry. If I'm right, I've already caused enough grief. I don't know if it's necessary or possible for you to forgive me, but I hope you will."

The nurse edged toward the door, but she made one last try. "They might have given you false memories. They're doing a lot of experiments that way. Or you could be someone else, an agent from the other side, and they're trying to get information out of you before they send you back with a mind like pudding." She folded her arms, her hands straining on her elbows. "You'd be giving in to them for no reason. Hostages, after awhile, try to believe that their captors have a good reason to be holding them. That could be what you're feeling right now."

"Nurse, I appreciate everything. I do." He sighed. "But whether you're right or not, it doesn't change anything, does it? I can't manage away from this . . . hospital. I'd be worse than a baby, and anyone who helped me would be putting themselves in danger for nothing. And if you're trying to get me back to the other side, who's to say that I'm one of theirs? Perhaps they want me to do more than has already been done."

She opened the door a crack and peered out into the hall. "I've got to leave, Weybridge."

"I know," he said, filled with great tranquility. "Be careful."

"You, too," she answered. And then she was gone.

Weybridge lay back against the pillows, his emaciated features composed and peaceful as he waited for the needles and the chemicals and oblivion.

Short stories are experiments, at least when I write them. I've said that before and it's still true. So here are a few notes on this particular experiment.

Amnesia and related memory failure have always intrigued me. How much of a personality is, in fact, memory? And what happens when memory is damaged or manipulated? How much of personal integrity is a product of conditioning and experience, and how much is bred in the bone?

In this story another factor that interested me was the predatory feeling many helpers have toward their helpees. There is no consensus about who Weybridge really is or what he has actually done, and only his assumption that he was the one perpetrating the terrible acts he may or may not remember gives him the serenity to face oblivion. Everyone else has a personal agenda where Weybridge is concerned; Weybridge, without real knowledge of himself, has no such agenda. For him, it is easier to face extinction than self-knowledge.

There's probably a lesson in there somewhere.

Chelsea Quinn Yarbro

TRUE LOVE

K.W. Jeter

K. W. Jeter's short stories are more explosive than his novels—perhaps because of their compression. He writes about archetypical relationships (in Alien Sex, *a young man's first sexual experience with a prostitute; in* A Whisper of Blood, *the daughter-father relationship) and gives them a horrific twist.*

By perverting normal relationships—those between adult and child and father and daughter—Jeter creates another shocker.

*T*he brown leaves covered the sidewalk, but hadn't yet been trodden into thin leather. She held the boy's hand to keep him from slipping and falling. He tugged at her grip, wanting to race ahead and kick the damp stacks drifting over the curbs. The leaves smelled of wet and dirt, and left skeleton prints on the cement.

"Now—be careful," she told the boy. What was his name? She couldn't remember. There were so many things she couldn't forget.... Maybe her head had filled up, and there was no more room for anything else. The mounded leaves, slick with the drizzling rain. Her father scratching at the door, the word when there had been words in his mouth, the little word that used to be her name.... The boy's name; what was it? She couldn't remember.

The boy had tugged her arm around to the side, not trying to run now, but stopping to press his other hand against one of the trees whose empty branches tangled the sky.

"You don't want to do that." She pulled but he dug in, gripping the tree trunk. "It's all dirty." His red mitten was speckled with crumbling bark. A red strand of unraveled wool dangled from his wrist.

You do want to . . . That was her father's voice inside her head. The old voice, the long-ago one with words. She could have, if she'd wanted to—she'd done it before—she could've recited a list of sentences, like a poem, all the things her father had ever said to her with the word *want* in them.

"There's something up there."

She looked where the boy pointed, his arm jutting up straight, the mitten a red flag at the end. On one of the wet branches, a squirrel gazed down at her, then darted off, its tail spiked with drops of rain.

The boy stared openmouthed where the squirrel had disappeared. The boy's upper lip was shiny with snot, and there was a glaze of it on the back of one mitten, and the sleeve of the cheap nylon snow jacket. She shuddered, looking at the wet on the boy's pug face. He wasn't beautiful, not like the one before, the one with the angel lashes and the china and peach skin.

"Come on." She had to bite her lip to fight the shudder, to make it go away, before she could take the boy's hand again. "It's gone now. See? It's all gone." She squeezed the mitten's damp wool in her own gloved hand. "We have to go, too. Aren't you hungry?" She smiled at him, the cold stiffening her face, as though the skin might crack.

The boy looked up at her, distrust in the small eyes. "Where's my mother?"

She knelt down in front of the boy and zipped the jacket under his chin. "Well, that's where we're going, isn't it?" There were people across the street, just people walking, a man and a woman she'd seen from the corner of her eye. But she couldn't tell if they were looking over here, watching her and the boy. She brushed a dead leaf off the boy's shoulder. "We're going to find your mother. We're going to where she is."

She hated lying, even the lies she had told before. All the things she told the boy, and the ones before him, were lies. Everything her father had ever told her had been the truth, and that was no good, either.

Her knees ached when she stood up. The cold and damp had seeped into her bones. She squeezed the boy's hand. "Don't you want to go to where your mother is?"

Now his face was all confused. He looked away from her, down the long street, and she was afraid that he would cry out to the people who were walking there. But they were already gone—she hadn't seen where. Maybe they had turned and gone up the steps into one of the narrow-fronted houses that were jammed so tight against each other.

"And you're hungry, aren't you? Your mother has cake there for you. I know she does. You want that, don't you?"

How old was he? *His name, his name* . . . How big, how small was what she really meant. If he wouldn't move, tugging out of her grasp, wouldn't come with her . . . She wanted to pick him up, to be done with saying stupid things to his stupid little face, its smear of snot and its red pig nose. Just pick him up and carry him like a wet sack, the arms with the red-mittened hands caught tight against her breast. Carry him home and not have to say anything, not have to tell lies and smile . . .

She had tried that once and it hadn't worked. Once when there hadn't been any other little boy that she could find, and the one she had found wouldn't come with her, wouldn't come and it had been getting dark, yet it had been all light around her, she had been trapped in the bright blue-white circle from a street lamp overhead. And the boy had started crying, because she had been shouting at him, shouting for him to shut up and stop crying and come with her. She had picked him up, but he'd been too big and heavy for her, his weight squirming in her arms, the little hard fists striking her neck, the bawling mouth right up against one ear. Until she'd had to let him go and he'd fallen to the ground, scrambled to his feet and run off, crying and screaming so loud that other people—she had known they were there, she'd felt them even if she couldn't see them—had turned and looked at her. She'd scurried away and then started running herself, her heart pounding in her throat. Even on the bus she'd caught, she'd known the others were looking at her, even pointing at her and whispering to each other. How could they have known? Until she'd felt a chill kiss under the collar of her blouse, and she'd touched the side of her face and her fingers had come away touched with red. The boy's little fist, or a low branch clawing at her as she'd run by . . . The tissue in her purse had been a wet bright rag by the time she'd reached home.

That had been a bad time. The little boy had run away, and she'd been too frightened to try again, scared of people watching when it had gotten so dark, so dark that she couldn't see them looking at her. She'd had to go home to where her father was waiting. And even though he couldn't say the words anymore, to say what he wanted, she knew. One or the other, and the little boy had run away.

She'd stood naked in her bathroom, the tiny one at the back of the house, her face wet with the splashed cold water. She'd raised her arm high over her head, standing on tiptoe so she could see in the clouded mirror over the sink. A bruise under one breast—the little boy had kicked her; that must've been where she'd got it, though she couldn't remember feeling it. Her father couldn't have done that, though her ribs beneath the discolored skin ached with a familiar pain. He wasn't strong enough, not anymore....

"Where are we?"

The boy's voice—this one, the little boy whose mittened hand she held in her own—brought her back. They were both walking, his hand reaching up to hers, and the streetlights had come on in the growing dark.

"This isn't my street. I don't live here."

"I know. It's okay." She didn't know where they were. She was lost. The narrow, brick-fronted houses came up so close to the street, the bare trees making spider shadows on the sidewalk. Light spilled from the windows above them. She looked up and saw a human shape moving behind a steam-misted glass, someone making dinner in her kitchen. Or taking a shower, the hot water sluicing around the bare feet on white porcelain. The houses would be all warm inside, heated and sealed against the black winter. The people—maybe the couple she had seen walking before, on the other side of another street—they could go naked if they wanted. They were taking a shower together, the man standing behind her, nuzzling her wet neck, hands cupped under her breasts, the smell of soap and wet towels. The steaming water would still be raining on them when he'd lay her down, they'd curl together in the hard nest of the tub, she'd have to bring her knees up against her breasts, or he'd sit her on the edge, the shower curtain clinging wet to her back, and he'd stand in front of her, the way her father did but it wouldn't be her father. She'd fill her mouth with him and he'd smell like soap and not that other sour smell of sweat and old dirt that scraped grey in her fingernails from his skin ...

The boy pressed close to her side, and she squeezed his hand to tell him that it was all right. He was afraid of the dark and the street he'd never been on before. She was the grown-up, like his mother, and he clung to her now. The fist around her heart unclenched a little. Everything would be easier; she'd find their way home. To where her father was waiting, and she'd have the boy with her this time.

Bright and color rippled on the damp sidewalk ahead of them. The noise of traffic—they'd come out of the houses and dark lanes. She even knew where they were. She recognized the signs, a laundromat with free dry, an Italian restaurant with its menu taped to the window. She'd seen them from the bus she rode sometimes.

Over the heads of the people on the crowded street, she saw the big shape coming, even brighter inside, and heard the hissing of its brakes. Tugging the boy behind her, she hurried to the corner. He trotted obediently to keep up.

The house was as warm inside as other people's houses were. She left the heat on all the time so her father wouldn't get cold. She'd found him once curled up on the floor of the kitchen—the pilot light on the basement furnace had gone out, and ice had already formed on the inside of the windows. There'd been a pool of cold urine beneath him, and his skin felt loose and clammy. He'd stared over his shoulder, his mouth sagging open, while she'd rubbed him beneath the blankets of his bed, to warm him with her own palms.

Warm . . . He had kissed her once—it was one of the things she couldn't forget—when she had been a little girl and he had been as big as the night. His eyes had burned with the wild rigor of his hunt, the world's dark he'd held in his iron hands. The kiss had tasted of salt, a warm thing. Long ago, and she still remembered.

She took off the boy's jacket in the hallway. Her shoes and his small rubber boots made muddy stains on the thin carpet runner. Her knees were so stiff now that she couldn't bend down; she had the boy stand up on the wooden bench against the wall, so she could work the jacket's zipper and snaps.

"Where's my mother?" Coming in to the house's warmth from the cold street had made his nose run again. He sniffed wetly.

"She'll be here in a minute." She pushed the open jacket back from the boy's shoulders. "Let's get all ready for her, and then we can have that cake."

The boy had just a T-shirt on underneath the jacket, and it was torn and dirty, with a yellow stain over some cartoon character's face. The boy's unwashed smell blossomed in the close hallway air, a smell of forgotten laundry and milk gone off. She wanted that to make her feel better. The boy's mother was a bad mother. Not like that other boy's mother, the one three or four times ago. She remembered standing by the greasy fire in the backyard, turning that boy's clothing over in her hands, all of it clean-smelling, freshly washed. Inside the collar of the boy's shirt, and in the waistband of the corduroy trousers, little initials had been hand-stitched, his initials. That was what she'd do if she'd had a child of her own; she would love him that much. Not like this poor ragged thing. Nobody loved this little boy, not really, and that made it all right. She'd told herself that before.

"What's that?" He looked up toward the hallway's ceiling.

She pulled his T-shirt up, exposing his pink round belly. His hair stood up—it was dirty, too—when she pulled the shirt off over his head.

"Nothing." She smoothed his hair down with her palm. "It's nothing." She didn't know if she'd heard anything or not. She'd heard all the house's sounds for so long—they were all her father—that they were the same as silence to her. Or a great roaring hurricane that battered her into a corner, her arms over her head to try to protect herself. It was the same.

She dropped the T-shirt on top of the rubber boots, then unbuttoned the boy's trousers and pulled them down. Dirty grey underwear, the elastic sagging loose. The little boys things *(little . . . not like . . .)* made the shape of a tiny fist inside the stained cotton. *(Great roaring hurricane) (Arms over her head)* She slipped the underpants down.

The boy wiggled. He rubbed his mouth and nose with the back of his hand, smearing the shiny snot around. "What're you doing?"

"Oh, you're so cold." She looked into his dull eyes, away from the little naked parts. "You're freezing. Wouldn't a nice hot bath . . . wouldn't that be nice? Yes. Then you'd be all toasty warm, and I'd wrap you up in a great big fluffy towel. That'd be lovely. You don't want to catch cold, do you?"

He sniffled. "Cake."

"Then you'd have your cake. All you want."

His face screwed up red and ugly. "No. I want it now!" His shout bounced against the walls. The underpants were a grey rag around his ankles, and his hand a fist now, squeezing against the corner of his mouth.

She slapped him. There was no one to see them. The boy's eyes went round, and he made a gulping, swallowing noise inside his throat. But he stopped crying. The fist around her heart tightened, because she knew this was something he was already used to.

"Come on." She could hear her own voice, tight and angry, the way her father's had been when it still had words. She tugged the underpants away from the boy's feet. "Stop being stupid."

She led him, his hand locked inside hers, up the stairs. Suddenly, halfway up, he started tugging, trying to pull his hand away.

"Stop it!" She knelt down and grabbed his bare shoulders, clenching them tight. "Stop it!" She shook him, so that his head snapped back and forth.

His face was wet with tears, and his eyes looked up. He cringed away from something up there, rather than from her. Between her own panting breaths, she heard her father moving around.

"It's nothing!" Her voice screamed raw from her throat. "Don't be stupid!"

She jerked at his arm, but he wouldn't move; he cowered into the angle of the stairs. He howled when she slapped him, then cried openmouthed as she kept on hitting him, the marks of her hand jumping up red on his shoulder blades and ribs.

She stopped, straightening up and gasping to catch her breath. The naked little boy curled at her feet, his legs drawn up, face hidden in the crook of his arm. The blood rushing in her head roared, the sound of a battering wind. The saliva under her tongue tasted thick with salt.

For a moment she thought he was still crying, little soft animal sounds, then she knew it was coming from up above. From her father's room. She stood for a moment, head tilted back, looking up toward the sounds. Her hair had come loose from its knot, and hung down the side of her face and along her back.

"Come on . . ." She kept her voice softer. She reached down and took the boy's hand. But he wouldn't stand up. He hung limp, sniffling and shaking his head.

She had to pick him up. She cradled him in her arms—he didn't feel heavy at all—and carried him the rest of the way up the stairs.

Her father was a huddled shape under the blankets. He'd heard them coming, and had gotten back into the bed before she'd opened the door.

She knew that was what he'd done. A long time ago, when he'd first become this way—when she'd first made herself realize that he was old—she had tried tying him to the bed, knotting a soft cord around his bone-thin ankle and then to one of the heavy carved lion's paws underneath. But he'd fretted and tugged so at the cord, picking at the knot with his yellow finger-nails until they'd cracked and bled, and the ankle's skin had chafed raw. She'd untied him, and taken to nailing his door shut, the nails bent so she just had to turn them to go in and out. At night, she had lain awake in her room and listened to him scratching at the inside of his door.

Then that had stopped. He'd learned that she was taking care of him. The scratching had stopped, and she'd even left the nails turned back, and he didn't try to get out.

She sat the little boy at the edge of the bed. The boy was silent now, sucking his thumb, his face smeared wet with tears.

"Daddy?" She pulled the blanket down a few inches, exposing the brown-spotted pink of his skull, the few strands of hair, tarnished silver.

"Daddy—I brought somebody to see you."

In the nest of the blanket and sour-smelling sheets, her father's head turned. His yellow-tinged eyes looked up at her. His face was parchment that had been crumpled into a ball and then smoothed out again. Parchment so thin that the bone and the shape of his teeth—the ones he had left, in back—could be seen through it.

"Look." She tugged, lifted the little boy farther up onto the bed. So her father could see.

The eyes under the dark hood of the blanket shifted, darting a sudden eager gaze from her face to the pink softness of the little boy.

"Come here." She spoke to the boy now. His legs and bottom slid on the blanket as she pulled him, her hands under his arms, until he sat on the middle of the bed, against the lanky, muffled shape of her father. "See, there's nothing to be afraid of. It's just nice and warm."

The shape under the blanket moved, crawling a few inches up to the turned-back edge.

The boy was broken, he had been this way a long time, it was why she'd picked him out and he'd come with her. Nobody loved him, not really, and that made it all right. He didn't fight as she laid him down, his head on the crumpled pillow, face close to her father's.

A thing of twigs and paper, her father's hand, slid from beneath the blanket. It cupped the back of the boy's head, tightening and drawing the boy close, as though for a kiss.

The boy struggled then, a sudden fluttering panic. His small hands pushed against her father's shoulders, and he cried, a whimpering noise that made her father's face darken with his wordless anger. That made her father strong, and he reared up from the bed, his mouth stretching open, tendons of clouded spit thinning to string. He wrapped his arms around the little boy, his grey flesh squeezing the pink bundle tight.

The boy's whimpering became the sound of his gasping breath. Her father pressed his open mouth against the side of the boy's neck. The jaws under the translucent skin worked, wetting the boy's throat with white-specked saliva.

Another cry broke out, tearing at her ears. She wanted to cover them with her hands and run from the room. And keep running, into all the dark streets around the house. Never stopping, until her breath was fire that burned away her heart. The cry was her father's; it sobbed with rage and frustration, a thing bigger than hunger, desire, bigger than the battering wind that shouted her name. He rolled his face away from the boy's wet neck, the ancient face like a child's now, mouth curved in an upside-down U, tongue thrusting against the toothless gums in front. His tears broke, wetting the ravines of his face.

He couldn't do it, he couldn't feed himself. She knew, it had been that way the last time, and before. But every time, hope made her forget, at least enough to try the old way. The way it had been years ago.

She couldn't bear the sound of her father's crying, and the little boy's fearful whimper. She knew how to stop it. On the table beside the bed was the knife she'd brought up from the kitchen—that had also been a long time ago—and had left there. Her hand reached out and curled around the smooth-worn wood. Her thumb slid across the sharp metal edge.

She brought her lips to the boy's ear, whispering to him. "Don't be afraid, it's all right . . ." The boy squirmed away from her, but she caught him fast, hugging his unclothed body against her breast. "It's all right, it's all right . . ." He saw the knife blade, and started to cry out. But she already had its point at his pink throat, and the cry leaked red, a drop, then a smearing line as the metal sank and cut.

The red bloomed on the sheets, the grey flooded to shiny wet. The boy's small hands beat against her, then fluttered, trembled, fell back, fists opening to stained flowers.

He didn't fight her now, he was a limp form in her embrace, but suddenly he weighed so much and her hands slipped on the soft skin that had been pink before and now shone darker and brighter. She gripped the boy tighter, her fingers parallel to his ribs, and lifted him. She brought the bubbling mouth, the red one that she had pulled the knife from, up to her father's parted lips.

The blood spilled over her father's gums and trickled out the corners of his mouth. The tendons in his neck stretched and tightened, as though they might tear his paper flesh. His throat worked, trying to swallow, but nothing happened. His eyes opened wider, spiderwebs of red traced around the yellow. He whimpered, the anger turning to fear. Trapped in the thing of sticks his body had become, he scrabbled his spotted hands at her face, reaching past the boy between them.

She knew what had to be done. The same as she'd done before. Her father's bent, ragged nails scraped across her cheek as she turned away from him. She nuzzled her face down close to the little boy's neck. She closed her eyes so there was only the wet and heat pulsing against her lips. She opened her mouth and drank, her tongue weighted with the dancing, coiling salt.

She didn't swallow, though her mouth had become full. Her breath halted, she raised her face from the boy's neck and the wound surging less with every shared motion of their hearts. A trickle of the warmth caught in her mouth leaked to her chin.

A baby bird in its nest . . . a naked thing of skin and fragile bone . . . She had found one once, on the sidewalk in front of the house, a tiny creature fallen from one of the branches above. Even as she had reached down, the tip of her finger an inch away from the wobbling, blue-veined head, the beak had opened, demanding to be fed . . .

The creature's hunger had frightened her, and she'd kicked it out into the gutter, where she wouldn't have to see it anymore. That had been a baby bird.

This was her father. She kept her eyes closed as she brought herself down to him, but she could still see the mouth opening wide, the pink gums, the tongue in its socket of bubbled spit. She lowered her face to his, and let the lips seal upon her own. She opened her mouth, and let the warmth uncoil, an infinitely soft creature moving over her own tongue, falling into his hunger.

The little boy's blood welled in her father's mouth. For a moment it was in both their mouths, a wet place shared by their tongues, his breath turning with hers. She felt the trembling, a shiver against the hinges of her jaw as his throat clenched, trying to swallow. She had to help even more, it had been this way the last time as well; she pressed her lips harder against her father's mouth, as her tongue rolled against the narrow arch of her teeth. The warmth in their mouths broke and pushed past the knot in her father's throat. He managed to swallow, and she felt the last of the blood flow out of her mouth, into his and then gone.

She fed him twice more, each mouthful easier. Between them, the little boy lay still, beautiful in his quiet.

The boy's throat had paled, and she had to draw deep for more. The sheets were cold against her hands as she pushed herself away from him.

Her father was still hungry, but stronger now. His face rose to meet hers, and the force of his kiss pressed against her open lips.

The blood uncoiled in that dark space again, and something else. She felt his tongue thrust forward to touch hers, a warm thing cradled in warmth and the sliding wet. Her throat clenched now. She couldn't breathe, and the smell of his sweat and hunger pressed in the tight space behind her eyes.

His hands had grown strong now, too. The weak flutter had died, the palms reddening as the little boy had become white and empty. One of her father's hands tugged her blouse loose from the waistband of her skirt, and she felt the thing of bone and yellowed paper smear the sheet's wet on her skin. Her father's hand stroked across her ribs and fastened on her breast, a red print on the white cotton bra. He squeezed and it hurt, her breath was inside his hand and blood and the taste of his mouth, the dark swallowing that pulled her into him, beat a pulsing fist inside her forehead.

She pushed both her hands against him, but he was big now and she was a little girl again, she was that pale unmoving thing rocking in his arms, playing at being dead. She was already falling, she could raise her knees in the dark wet embrace of the bed, she could wrap herself around the little blind thing at the center of her breasts, that just breathed and stayed quiet, and that even he couldn't touch, had never been able to touch . . . the little boy was there, his angel face bright and singing, her ears deafened, battered by that song that light that falling upward into clouds of glory where her mother in Sunday robes reached for her, her mother smiling though she had no face she couldn't remember her mother's face—

She shoved against her father, hard enough to break away from him, his ragged fingernails drawing three red lines that stung and wept under her bra. She fell backward off the bed, her elbow hard against the floor, sending numb electricity to her wrist.

Another shape slid from the edge of the bed and sprawled over her lap. The little boy, naked and red wet, made a soft, flopping doll. She pushed it away from herself and scrambled to her feet.

The bed shone. From its dark center, the depth of the blanket's hood, her father looked out at her.

She found the doorknob in her hands behind her back. Her blouse clung to her ribs, and had started to turn cold in the room's shuttered air. The door scraped her spine as she stepped backward into the hallway. Then she turned and ran for the bathroom at the far end, an old sour taste swelling in her throat.

In the dark, between the streetlights' blue islands, she could feel the leaves under her feet. They slid away, damp things, silent; she had to walk carefully to keep from falling.

There was work to be done back at the house. She'd do it later. She would have to change the sheets, as she always did afterward, and wash the stained ones. She used the old claw-footed bathtub, kneeling by its side, the smell of soap and bleach stinging her nose, her fingers working in the pink water. He let her come in and make the bed, and never tried to say anything to her, just watching her with his blank and wordless eyes, his hungers, all of them, over for a while.

And there were the other jobs to be done, the messier ones. Getting rid of things. She'd have to take the car, the old Plymouth with the rusting fenders, out of the garage. And drive to that far place she knew, where these things were never found. She would come back as the sun was rising, and there would be mud on the hem of her skirt. She'd be tired, and ready to sleep.

She could do all that later. She'd been brave and strong, and had already done the hardest jobs; she could allow herself this small indulgence.

The cold night wrapped around her. She pressed her chin down into the knot of the scarf she'd tied over her hair. The collar of her coat had patches where the fur had worn away. The coat had been her mother's, and had been old the first time she'd worn it. A scent of powder, lavender and tea roses, still clung to the heavy cloth.

At the end of the block ahead of her, the Presbyterian church hid the stars at the bottom of the sky. She could see the big stained-glass window, Jesus with one hand on his staff and the other cupped to the muzzle of a lamb, even though there were no lights on in the church itself. The light spilling over the sidewalk came from the meeting room in the basement.

She went down the bare concrete steps, hand gripping the iron rail. And into the light and warmth, the collective sense of people in a room, their soft breathing, the damp-wool smell of their winter coats.

Where she hung her coat up, with the others near the door, a mimeographed paper on the bulletin board held the names for the altar flowers rotation. Sign-ups to chaperone the youth group's Christmas party. A glossy leaflet, unfolded and tacked, with pledges for a mission in Belize. Her name wasn't anywhere on the different pieces of paper. She didn't belong to the church. They probably wouldn't have wanted her, if they'd known. Known everything. She only came here for the weekly support group.

There was a speaker tonight, a woman up at the front of the room, talking, one hand gesturing while the other touched the music stand the church gave them to use as a podium.

She let the speaker's words flutter past as she sat down in one of the metal folding chairs at the side of the room; halfway down the rows, so she only had to turn her head a bit to see who else had come tonight. She had already counted close to twenty-four. There were the usuals, the faces she saw every week. A couple, a man and a woman who always held hands while they sat and listened, who she assumed were married; they nodded and smiled at her, a fellow regular. At the end of the row was somebody she hadn't seen before, a young man who sat hunched forward, the steam from a Styrofoam cup of coffee rising into his face. She could tell that he was just starting, that this was a new world for him; he didn't look happy.

None of them ever did, even when they smiled and spoke in their bright loud voices, when they said hello and hugged each other near the table with the coffee urn and the cookies on the paper plates.

They had another word for why they were here, a word that made it sound like a disease, just a disease, something you could catch like a cold or even a broken arm. Instead of it being time itself, and old age, and the grey things their parents had become. Time curled outside the church, like a black dog waiting where the steps became the sidewalk, waiting to go home with them again. Where the ones who had known their names looked at them now with empty eyes and did not remember.

She sat back in the folding chair, her hands folded in her lap. The woman at the front of the room had the same bright, relentless voice. She closed her eyes and listened to it.

The woman had a message. There was always a message, it was why people came here. The woman told the people in the room that they had been chosen to receive a great blessing, one that most people weren't strong enough for. A chance to show what love is. A few years of grief and pain and sadness and trouble, of diapering and spoon-feeding and talking cheerily to something that had your father or your mother's face, but wasn't them at all, not anymore. And then it would be over.

That was a small price to pay, a small burden to carry. The woman told them that, the same thing they'd been told before. A few years to show their love. For these things that had been their parents. They'd be transfigured by the experience. Made into saints, the ones who'd shown their courage and steadfastness on that sad battlefield.

She sat and listened to the woman talking. The woman didn't know—none of them ever did—but she knew. What none of them ever would.

She looked around at the others in the room, the couple holding hands, the young man staring into the dregs of his coffee. Her burden, her blessing, was greater than theirs, and so was her love. Even now, she felt sorry for them. They would be released someday. But not her. For them, there would be a few tears, and then their love, their small love, would be over.

She kept her eyes closed, and let herself walk near the edge of sleep, of dreaming, in this warm place bound by winter. She smiled.

She knew that love wasn't over in a few sad years. Or in centuries. She knew that love never died. She knew that her love—real love, true love—was forever.

Stories, when they work, if they work at all, are like lit matches dropped down a well. You don't really see anything except, for a moment, how deep and dark the well is.

I don't know what this story means, other than that it's a story about love and happiness. I don't have much more to say about it, except . . .

1. The words *victim* and *victimizer* are not easily defined. People who do have easy definitions for those words are lying to you, for reasons of their own; and

2. Martyrdom is a seductive endeavor, but then, it should be.

After that, there's only silence.

K. W. Jeter

HOME BY THE SEA

Pat Cadigan

Cadigan has written at least two other terrific vampire stories—"My Brother's Keeper" and "The Power and the Passion." Like Jeter's, this one packs a wallop and you won't soon forget it.

There was no horizon line out on the water.

"Limbo ocean. Man, did we hate this when I was a commercial fisherman," said a man sitting at the table to my left. "Worse than fog. You never knew where you were."

I sneaked a look at him and his companions. The genial voice came from a face you'd have expected to find on a wanted poster of a Middle Eastern terrorist, but the intonations were vaguely Germanic. The three American women with him were all of a type, possibly related. A very normal-looking group, with no unusual piercings or marks. I wondered how long they'd been in Scheveningen.

I slumped down in my chair, closed my eyes, and lifted my face to where I thought the sun should be. It was so overcast, there wasn't even a hot spot in the sky. Nonetheless, the promenade was crowded, people wandering up and down aimlessly, perhaps pretending, as I was, that they were on vacation. It was equally crowded at night, when everyone came to watch the stars go out.

Of course *we're on vacation*, a woman had said last night at another of the strange parties that kept congealing in ruined hotel lobbies and galleries. This had been one of the fancier places, ceilings in the stratosphere and lots of great, big ornate windows so we could look out anytime and see the stars die. *It's an* enforced *vacation. Actually, it's the world that's gone on vacation.*

No, that's not it, someone else had said in an impeccable British accent. It always surprised me to hear one, though I don't know why; England wasn't that far away. *What it is, is that the universe has quit its job.*

Best description yet, I'd decided. *The universe has quit its job.*

"Hey, Jess." I heard Jim plop down in the chair next to me. "Look what I found."

I opened my eyes. He was holding a fan of glossy postcards like a winning poker hand. Scheveningen and The Hague as they had been. I took them from him, looked carefully at each one. If you didn't know any better, you'd have thought it had been a happy world, just from looking at these.

"Where'd you find them?"

"Up a ways," he said, gesturing vaguely over his shoulder. He went *up a ways* a lot now, scavenging bits of this and that, bringing them to me as if they were small, priceless treasures. Perhaps they were—souvenirs of a lost civilization. Being of the why-bother school now, myself, I preferred to vegetate in a chair. "Kid with a whole pile of them. I traded him that can of beer I found." He stroked his beard with splayed fingers. "Maybe he can trade it for something useful. And if he can't, maybe he can fill a water pistol with it."

What would be useful, now that the universe had quit its job? I thought of making a list on the back of one of the postcards. Clothing. Shelter. Something to keep you occupied while you waited for the last star to go out—a jigsawpuzzle, perhaps. But Jim never showed up with one of those, and I wasn't ambitious enough to go looking myself.

My old hard-driving career persona would have viewed that with some irony. But now I could finally appreciate that being so driven could not have changed anything. Ultimately, you pounded your fist against the universe and then found you hadn't made so much as a dent, let alone reshaped it. Oddly enough, that knowledge gave me peace.

Peace seemed to have settled all around me. Holland, or at least this part of Holland, was quiet. All radio and TV communications seemed to be permanently disrupted—the rest of the world might have been burning, for all we knew, and we'd just happened to end up in a trouble-free zone. Sheerly by accident, thanks to a special our travel agency had been running at the time. We joked about it: *How did you happen to come to Holland? Oh, we had a coupon.*

A kid walked by with a boombox blaring an all-too-familiar song about the end of the world as we know it and feeling fine. The reaction from the people sitting at the tables was spontaneous and unanimous. They began throwing things at him, fragments of bricks, cups, cans, plastic bottles, whatever was handy, yelling in a multitude of languages for him to beat it.

The kid laughed loudly, yelled an obscenity in Dutch, and ran away up the promenade, clutching his boombox to his front. Mission accomplished, the tourists had been cheesed off again. The man at the next table had half risen out of his chair and now sat down again, grinning sheepishly. "All I was gonna do was ask him where he found batteries that work. I'd really like to listen to my CD player." He caught my eye and shrugged. "It's not like I could hurt him, right?"

Jim was paying no attention. He had his left hand on the table, palm up, studiously drawing the edge of one of the postcards across the pad below his thumb, making deep, slanted cuts.

"I wish you wouldn't do that," I said.

"Fascinating. Really fascinating." He traced each cut with a finger. "No pain, no pain at all. No blood and no pain. I just can't get over that."

I looked toward the horizonless ocean. From where I was sitting, I had a clear view of the tower on the circular pier several hundred feet from the beach, and of the woman who had hanged herself from the railing near the top. Her nude body rotated in a leisurely way, testifying to the planet's own continuing rotation. As I watched, she raised one arm and waved to someone on the shore.

"Well," I said, "what did you expect at the end of the world?"

"You really shouldn't deface yourself," I said as we strolled back to the hotel where we were squatting. If you could really call it a hotel—there was no charge to stay there, no service, and no amenities. "I know it doesn't hurt, but it doesn't heal, either. Now you've got permanent hash marks, and besides not being terribly attractive, they'll probably catch on everything."

Jim sighed. "I know. I get bored."

"Right." I laughed. "For the last twenty years, you've been telling me I should learn how to stop and smell the roses and now *you're* the one who's complaining about having nothing to do."

"After you've smelled a rose for long enough, it loses its scent. Then you have to find a different flower."

"Well, self-mutilation *is* different, I'll give you that." We passed a young guy dressed in leather with an irregular-shaped fragment of mirror embedded in his forehead. "Though maybe not as different as it used to be, since it seems to be catching on. What do you suppose *he's* smelling?"

Jim didn't answer. We reached the circular drive that dead-ended the street in front of our hotel, which had gone from motorcycle parking lot to motorcycle graveyard. On impulse, I took Jim's hand in my own as we crossed the drive. "I suppose it's the nature of the end of time or whatever this is, and the world never was a terribly orderly place. But nothing makes sense anymore. Why do we still have day and night? Why does the earth keep turning?"

"Winding down," Jim said absently. "No reason why the whole thing should go at once." He stopped short in the middle of the sidewalk in front of the hotel. "Listen."

There was a distant metallic crashing noise, heavy wheels on rails. "Just the trams running again. That's something else—why does the power work in some places and not in others?"

"What?" Jim blinked at me, then glanced in the general direction of the tram yard. "Oh, that. Not what I meant. Something I've been wondering lately"—there was a clatter as a tram went by on the cross street "—why we never got married."

Speaking of things that didn't seem important anymore—it wasn't the first time the subject had come up. We'd talked about it on and off through the years, but after eighteen years together, the matter had lost any urgency it might have had, if it had ever had any. Now, under a blank sky in front of a luxury hotel where the guests had become squatters, it seemed to be the least of the shadow-things my life had been full of, like status and career and material comforts. I could have been a primitive tribeswoman hoarding shiny stones for all the real difference those things had ever made. They'd given me nothing beyond some momentary delight; if anything, they'd actually taken more from me, in terms of the effort I'd had to put into acquiring them, caring for them, keeping them tidy and intact. Especially the status and the career. And they sure hadn't stopped the world from ending, no more than our being married would have.

But I was so certain of what Jim wanted to hear that I could practically feel the words arranging themselves in the air between us, just waiting for me to provide the voice. *Well, dear, let's just hunt up a cleric and get married right now.* Add sound and stir till thickened. Then—

Then what? It wasn't like we actually had a future anymore, together or singly. The ocean didn't even have a horizon.

"I think we *are* married," I said. "I think any two people seeing the world to its conclusion together are married in a way that didn't exist until now."

It should have been the right thing to say. Instead, I sounded like a politician explaining how a tax increase wasn't really a tax increase after all. After two decades, I could do better than some saccharine weasel words, end of the world or no.

Say it, then. The other thing, what he's waiting for. What difference does it make? The question I had to answer first, maybe the question Jim was really asking.

The edges of the cuts he'd made in his hand moved against my skin. They felt like the gills of an underwater creature out of its element, seeking to be put back in.

No pain at all. No blood and no pain.

It's not like I could hurt him, right?

Right. It's the end of the world as we know it, and I feel nothing. So we can go ahead now, do all those things that used to be so dangerous. Self-mutilation, bonding rituals, any old hazard at all.

Jim's eyes were like glass.

"Better get into the lobby now if you want to see it."

It was the Ghost of Lifetimes Past; that was what Jim and I had been calling her. She stood a respectful distance from us, a painfully thin blond woman in a dirty white tutu and pink satin ballet shoes. The most jarring thing about her was not her silly outfit, or the way she kept popping up anywhere and everywhere, but that face—she had the deep creases of someone who had lived seventy very difficult years. Around the edge of her chin and jawbone, the skin had a peculiar strained look, as if it were being tightened and stretched somehow.

"The crucifixion," she said, and gave a small, lilting giggle. "They're probably going to take him down soon, so if you want a look, you'd better hurry." Her gaze drifted past us and she moved off, as if she'd heard someone calling her.

"You in the mood for a crucifixion?" I said lightly. It was a relief to have anything as a distraction.

"Not if we can possibly avoid it."

But there was no way we could. Pushing our way through the small crowd in the lobby, we couldn't help seeing it. I vaguely recognized the man nailed directly to the wall—one of the erstwhile millionaires from the suites on the top floor. He was naked except for a wide silk scarf around his hips and a studded collar or belt cinched wrong side out around his head in lieu of a crown of thorns. No blood, of course, but he was doing his best to look as if he were in pain.

"God," I whispered to Jim, "I hope it's not a trend."

He blew out a short, disgusted breath. "I'm going upstairs."

Somehow, I had the feeling that it wasn't really the crucifixion he was so disgusted with. I meant to follow him but suddenly I felt as nailed in place as the would-be Christ. Not that I had any real desire to stand there and stare at this freak show, but it held me all the same. All that Catholic school-ing in my youth, I thought, finally catching up with me after all these years, activating a dormant taste for human sacrifice.

Ersatz-Christ looked around, gritting his teeth. "You're supposed to mock me," he said, the matter-of-fact tone more shocking than the spikes in his forearms. "It won't work unless you mock me."

"You're a day late and a few quarts low," someone in the crowd said. "It won't work unless you shed blood, either."

The crucified man winced. "Shit."

There was a roar of laughter.

"For some reason, that never occurs to them. About the blood."

I looked up at the man who had spoken. He smiled down at me, his angular face cheerfully apologetic. I couldn't remember having seen him around before.

"This is the third one I've seen," he said, jerking his head at the man on the wall. The straight black hair fell briefly over one eye and he tossed it back. "A grand gesture that ultimately means nothing. Don't you find it rather annoying, people who suddenly make those grand risky gestures only after there isn't a hope in the hell of it mattering? Banning the aerosol can after there's already a hole in the ozone layer, seeking alternate sources of power after nuclear reactors have already gone into operation. It's humanity's fatal flaw—locking the barn after the horse has fled. The only creature in the universe who displays such behavior."

I couldn't place his accent or, for that matter, determine if he actually had an accent—I was getting tone-deaf in that respect. He didn't look American, but that meant nothing. All the Americans were getting a European cast as they adopted the local face.

"The universe?" I said. "You must be exceptionally well traveled."

He laughed heartily, annoying ersatz-Christ and what sympathizers he had left. We moved out of the group, toward the unoccupied front desk. "The universe we know of, then. Which, for all intents and purposes, might as well be all the universe there is."

I shrugged. "There's something wrong with that statement, but I'm no longer compulsive enough to pick out what it is. But it might be comforting to know that if there is a more intelligent species somewhere, its foibles are greater than ours, too."

"Comforting?" He laughed again. "It would seem that in the absence of pain, no comfort is necessary." He paused, as if waiting for me to challenge him on that, and then stuck out his hand. "I'm Sandor."

"Jess." The warmth of his unmarked, uncut hand was a mild shock. Fluctuations in body temperatures were as nonexistent as blood in these nontimes. Which would only stand to reason, since blood flow governed skin temperature. Everyone was the same temperature now, but whether that was something feverish or as cold as a tomb was impossible to tell with no variation. Perhaps I just hadn't been touching the right people.

"Odd, isn't it," he said, politely disengaging his hand from mine. I felt a rush of embarrassment. "They wanted to investigate it at the hospital, but I wouldn't let them. Do you know, at the hospital, people are offering themselves for exploratory surgery and vivisection? And the doctors who have a stomach for such things take them willingly. Yes. They cut them open, these people, and explore their insides. Sometimes they remove internal organs and sew the people up again to see how they manage without them. They manage fine. And there is no blood, no blood anywhere, just a peculiar watery substance that pools in the body cavity.

"And hidden away in the hospital, there is a doctor who has removed a woman's head. Her body is inactive, of course, but it does not rot. The head functions, though without air to blow through the vocal cords, it's silent. It watches him, they say, and he talks to it. They say he is trying to get the head to communicate with him in tongue-clicks, but it won't cooperate. *She* won't cooperate, if you prefer. And then there's the children's ward and the nursery where they keep the babies. These babies—"

"*Stop* it," I said.

He looked dazed, as if I'd slapped him.

"Are you insane?"

Now he gave me a wary smile. "Does sanity even come into it?"

"I mean . . . well, we just met."

"Ah, how thoughtless of me."

I started to turn away.

That strangely warm hand was on my arm. "I do mean it. It *was* thoughtless, pouring all that out on someone I don't know. And a stranger here as well. It must be hard for you, all this and so far from home."

"Oh, I don't know." I glanced at the crucified man. "It's all so weird, I think maybe I'd just as soon not see it happen anyplace familiar. I don't really like to think about what it must be like back home." I jerked my thumb at the man nailed to the wall. "Like, I'd rather that be some total stranger than one of my neighbors."

"Yes, I can see that. Though it must be a little easier to be with someone you're close to, as well." He looked down for a moment. "I saw you come in with your companion."

I gave him points for perception—most people assumed Jim was my husband. "Are you from here?" I asked.

"No. As I'm sure you could tell."

"Not really. Is Sandor a Polish name?"

He shrugged. "Could be. But I'm not from there, either."

There was a minor commotion as the police came in, or rather, some people dressed in police uniforms. Scheveningen was maintaining a loose local government—God knew why, force of habit, perhaps—with a volunteer uniformed cadre that seemed to work primarily as moderators or referees, mostly for the foreigners. They pushed easily through the thinning crowd and started to remove the crucified man from the wall, ignoring his protests that he wasn't finished, or it wasn't finished, or something.

"*Ite missa est,*" I said, watching. "Go, the Mass is over. Or something like that."

"You remember the Latin rite. I'm impressed."

"Some things hang on." I winced at the sound of ersatz-Christ's forearm breaking. "That sounded awful, even if it didn't hurt."

"It won't heal, either. Just goes on looking terrible. Inconvenient, too. At the hospital, they have—" He stopped. "Sorry. As you said, some things hang on."

"What do you suppose they'll do with him?" I asked as they took him out. "It's not like it's worth putting him in jail or anything."

"The hospital. It's where they take all the mutilation cases bad enough that they can't move around on their own. If they want mutilation, they can have plenty there, under better conditions, for better reasons, where no one has to see them."

Finally, I understood. "Did you work there long?"

"Volunteered," he said, after a moment of hesitation. "There are no employees anymore, just volunteers. A way to keep busy. I left—" He shrugged. "Sitting ducks."

"Pardon?"

"That's the expression in English, isn't it? For people who leave themselves open to harm? In this case, literally open."

"If it doesn't hurt and it doesn't kill them, and this is the end of it all as we know it," I said slowly, "how can they be leaving themselves open to harm?"

"A matter of differing cultural perspectives." He smiled.

I smiled back. "You never told me what culture you were from."

"I think you could say that we're all from here now. Or might as well be. There's an old saying that you are from the place where you die, not where you were born."

"I've never heard that one. And nobody's dying at the moment."

"But nothing happens. No matter what happens, nothing happens. Isn't that a description of a dying world? But perhaps you don't see it that way. And if you don't, then perhaps *you* aren't dying yet. Do you think if you cut yourself, you might bleed? Is it that belief that keeps *you* from mutilating yourself, or someone else? Do you even wonder about that?"

I looked from side to side. "I feel like I'm under siege here."

He laughed. "But *don't* you wonder? Why there aren't people running through the streets in an orgy of destruction, smashing windows and cars and each other? And themselves."

"Offhand, I'd say there just doesn't seem to be much point to it." I took a step back from him.

"Exactly. No point. No reward, no punishment, no pleasure, no pain. The family of humanity has stopped bickering, world peace at last. Do you think if humans had known what it would take to bring about world peace, that they'd have worked a lot harder for it?"

"Do you really think it's like this everywhere in the world?" I said, casually moving back another step.

"Don't you?" He spread his hands. "Can't you feel it?"

"Actually, I don't feel much." I shrugged. "Excuse me, I'm going to go catch up on my reading."

"Wait." He grabbed my arm and I jumped. "I'm sorry," he said, letting go almost immediately. "I suppose I'm wrong about there being no pleasure and pain. I'd forgotten about the pleasure of being able to talk to someone. Of sharing thoughts, if you'll pardon the expression."

I smiled. "Yeah. See you around." I shook his hand again, more to confirm what I'd felt when he'd grabbed my arm than out of courtesy, and found I'd been right. His skin definitely felt cooler. Maybe *he* was the one who wasn't dying and I had sucked whatever real life he had out of him.

Only the weird survive, I thought, and went upstairs.

No matter what happens, nothing happens. Jim was curled up on the bed, motionless. The silence in the room was darkening. Sleep canceled the breathing habit, if "sleep" it actually was. There were no dreams, nothing much like rest—more like being a machine that had been switched off. Another end-of-the-world absurdity.

At least I hadn't walked in to find him slicing himself up with a razor, I thought, going over to the pile of books on the nightstand. Whatever had possessed me to think that I would wait out the end of the world by catching up with my reading had drained away with my ambition. If I touched any of the books now, it was just to shift them around. Some-times, when I looked at the covers, the words on them didn't always make sense right away, as if my ability to read was doing a slow fade along with everything else.

I didn't touch the books now as I stretched out on the bed next to Jim. He still didn't move. On the day—if "day" is the word for it—the world had ended, we'd be in this room, in this bed, lying side by side the way we were now. I am certain that we both came awake at the same moment, or came to might be a better way to put it. Went from unconscious to conscious was the way it felt, because I didn't wake up the way I usually did, slowly, groggily, and wanting nothing more than to roll over and go back to sleep for several more hours. I had never woken up well, as if my body had always been fighting the busy life my mind had imposed on it. But that "day," I was abruptly awake without transition, staring at the ceiling, and deep down I just *knew*.

There was no surprise in me, no regret, and no resistance. It was that certainty: *Time's up.* More than something I knew, it was something I *was*. Over, finished, done, used up . . . but not quite gone, as a bottle is not gone though emptied of its contents. I thought of Jim Morrison singing "The End," and felt some slight amusement that in the real end, it hadn't been anywhere near so dramatic. Just . . . *time's up.*

And when I'd finally said, "Jim . . . ?" he'd answered, "Uh-huh. I've got it, too." And so had everyone else.

I raised up on one elbow and looked at him without thinking anything. After awhile, still not thinking anything, I pulled at his shirt and rolled him over.

Sex at the end of the world was as pointless as anything else, or as impossible as bleeding, depending on your point of view, I guess. The bodies didn't function; the minds didn't care. I felt some mild regret about that, and about the fact that all I *could* feel was mild regret.

But it was still possible to show affection—or to engage in pointless foreplay—and take a certain comfort in the contact. We hadn't been much for that in this no-time winding-down. Maybe passion had only been some long, pleasant dream that had ended with everything else. I slipped my hand under Jim's shirt.

His unmoving chest was cadaver-cold.

That's it, I thought, *now we're dying for real.* There was a fearful relief in the idea that I wouldn't have to worry about him mutilating himself any further.

Jim's eyes snapped open and he stared down at my hand still splayed on his stomach, as if it were some kind of alien, deformed starfish that had crawled out of the woodwork onto his torso.

"You're warm," he said, frowning.

And like that, I was lost in the memory of what it was to feel passion for another human being. What it was to *want*, emotions become physical reactions, flesh waking from calm to a level of response where the edge between pleasure and pain thinned to the wisp of a nerve ending.

I rolled off the bed and went into the bathroom. Behind me, I heard Jim rolling over again. Evidently he didn't want to know about my sudden change in temperature if I didn't want to tell him. A disposable razor sat abandoned on the counter near the sink. If I took it and ran my fingertip along the blade, would I see the blood well up in a bright, uneven bead? I didn't want to know, either.

The exploding star was a fiery blue-white flower against the black sky. Its light fell on the upturned faces of the crowd on the promenade, turning them milky for a few moments before it faded.

"Better than fireworks," I heard someone say.

"Ridiculous," said someone else. "Some kind of trick. The stars are thousands and millions of light-years away from us. If we see them exploding now, it means the universe actually ended millions of years ago and we're just now catching up with it."

"Then no wonder we never made any contact with life on other planets," said the first voice. "Doesn't *that* make sense? If the universe has been unraveling for the last million years, all extraterrestrial life was gone by the time we got the technology to search for it."

I looked around to see who was speaking and saw her immediately. The Ghost of Lifetimes Past was standing just outside the group, alone as usual, watching the people instead of the stars. She caught my eye before I could look away and put her fingertips to her mouth in a coy way, as if to stifle a discreet giggle. Then she turned and went up the promenade, tutu flouncing a little, as an orange starburst blossomed in the west.

If Jim had come out with me, I thought, weaving my way through the crowd, I probably wouldn't have been doing something as stupid as following this obviously loony woman. But he had remained on the bed, unmoving, long after it had gotten dark, and I hadn't disturbed him again. I had sat near the window with a book in my lap and told myself I was reading, not just staring until I got tired of seeing the same arrangement of words and turning a page, while I felt myself fade. It had been a very distinct sensation, what I might have felt if I had been awake when the world had ended.

The Ghost of Lifetimes Past didn't look back once but I was sure she knew I was following her, just as I knew she had meant for me to follow her, all the way to the Kurhaus. Even from a distance, I could see that the lights were on. Another party; what was it about the end of the world that seemed to cry out for parties? Perhaps it was some kind of misplaced huddling instinct.

I passed a man sitting on a broken brick wall, boredly hammering four-inch nails into his chest, if we hung notes on them, I thought, and sent him strolling up and down the promenade, we could have a sort of postal service-cum-newspaper. Hear ye, hear ye, the world is still dead. Or undead. Nondead. Universe still unemployed after quitting old job. Or was it, really?

The Ghost flounced across the rear courtyard of the Kurhaus without pausing, her ballet shoes going scritch-scritch on the pavement. Light spilled out from the tall windows, making giant, elongated lozenges of brightness on the stone. One level up, I could see people peering out the galleria windows at the sky. When the sun went, I thought suddenly, would we all finally go with it, or would it just leave us to watch cosmic fireworks in endless night?

They made me think of birds on a nature preserve, the people wandering around in the lobby. Birds in their best plumage and their best wounds. A young, black-haired guy in a pricey designer gown moved across the scuffed dusty floor several yards ahead of me, the two chandelier crystals stuck into his forehead above the eyebrows, catching the light. Diaphanous scarves fluttered from holes in his shoulder blades. Trick or treat, I thought. Or maybe it was All Souls' Day, every day.

At the bar island, someone had used the bottles on the surrounding shelves for target practice and the broken glass still lay everywhere like a scattering of jewels. I saw a woman idly pick up a shard lying on the bar and take a bite out of it, as if it were a potato chip. A man in white tie and tails was stretched out on the floor on his stomach, looking around and making notes on a stenographer's pad. I wandered over to see what he was writing, but it was all unreadable symbols, part shorthand, part hieroglyphics.

There was a clatter behind me. Some people were righting one of the overturned cocktail tables and pulling up what undamaged chairs they could find. It was the group that had been sitting near me on the promenade that day, the man and his three women companions, all of them chattering away to each other as if nothing was out of the ordinary. They were still unmarked and seemed oblivious to the freak show going on around them—I half expected the man to go to the bar and try to order. Or maybe someone would sweep up some broken glass and bring it to them on a tray. Happy Hour is here, complimentary hors d'oeuvres.

The Ghost reappeared on the other side of the bar. She looked worse, if that were possible, as if walking through the place had depleted her. A tall man on her left was speaking to her as he ran a finger along the wasted line of her chin while a man on her right was displaying the filigree of cuts he'd made all over his stomach, pulling the skin out and displaying it like a lace bib. The skin was losing its elasticity; it sagged over the waistband of his white satin pajama pants. The layer of muscle underneath showed through in dark brown.

I turned back to the group I'd seen on the promenade, still in their invisible bubble of normalcy. The man caught sight of me and smiled a greeting without a pause in what he was saying. Maybe I was supposed to choose, I thought suddenly; join the freaks or join the normalcy. And yet I had the feeling that if I chose the latter, I'd get wedged in among them somehow and never get back to Jim.

They were all staring at me questioningly now and something in those mild gazes made me think I was being measured. One of the women leaned into the group and said something; it was the signal for their intangible boundary to go back up again. Either I'd kept them waiting too long, or they didn't like what they saw, but the rejection was as obvious as if there had been a sign over their heads.

I started for the side door, intending to get out as fast as I could, and stopped short. The boy standing near the entrance to the casino might have been the same one who'd had the boombox, or not—it was hard to tell, there were so many good-looking blond boys here—but the man he was talking to was unmistakably Jim. He hadn't bothered to change his rumpled clothes or even to comb his hair, which was still flat on one side from the way he'd been lying on the bed.

Jim was doing most of the talking. The kid's expression was all studied diffidence, but he was listening carefully all the same. Jim showed him his hand and the kid took it, touching the cuts and nodding. After a few moments, he put his arm around Jim's shoulders and, still holding his hand, led him around the front of the closed, silent elevator doors to the stairs. I watched them go up together.

"Do you wonder what that was all about?"

I didn't turn around to look at him. "Well. Sandor Whoever from Wherever. The man who can still raise the mercury on a thermometer while the rest of us have settled at room temperature. If you start talking about interesting things people are doing in the hospital, I might take a swing at you."

He chuckled. "That's the spirit. Next question: Do you wonder how they get the power on in some places when it won't work in others?"

"In a way."

"Do you want to find out?"

I nodded.

He didn't touch me even in a casual way until we reached his room on the fourth floor. It was the first time I'd ever been higher than the galleria level. The lights in the hallway shone dimly, glowing with what little power was left from whatever was keeping the lobby lit up, and his hand was like fire as he pulled me out of the hallway and into the room.

His body was a layer of softness over hard muscle. I tore his clothing to get at it; he didn't mind. Bursts of light from the outside gave me fleeting snapshots of his face. No matter what I did, he had the same expression of calm acceptance. Perhaps out of habit, covering the secret of his warmth—if the rest of us pod creatures knew he was the last (?) living thing on earth, what might we not do for this feeling of life he could arouse?

Already, his flesh wasn't as warm as it had been. That was me, I thought, pushing him down on the bed. I was taking it from him and I couldn't help it. Or perhaps it was just something inherent in the nature of being alive, that it would migrate to anyplace it was not.

Even so, even as he went from hot to cool, he lost nothing. Receptive, responsive, accommodating—in the silent lightning of dying stars, calm and accepting, but not passive. I was leading in this pas de deux, but he seemed to know how and where almost before I did, and was ready for it.

And now I could feel *how* it was happening, the way the life in his body was leached away into my own un-alive flesh. I was taking it from him. The act of *taking* is a distinctive one; no one who had ever taken anything had taken it quite like I took Sandor.

He gave himself up without resistance, and yet *give up* was not what he was doing, unless it was possible to surrender aggressively. It was as if I wanted him because his purpose was to be wanted, and he had been waiting for me, for someone to provide the wanting, to want him to death. Ersatz-Christ in the lobby had had it wrong, it never could have worked. Humans didn't sacrifice themselves, they were sacrificed to; they didn't give, they were alive only in the act of taking—

Somehow, even with my head on fire, I pulled away from him. He flowed with the movement like a storm tide. I fought the tangle of sheets and cold flesh against warm, and the violence felt almost as good as the sex. If I couldn't fuck him to death, I'd settle for beating his head in, I thought dimly. We rolled off the bed onto the carpet and I scrambled away to the bathroom and slammed the door.

"Is there something wrong?" The puzzlement in his voice was so sincere I wanted to vomit.

"*Stop it.*"

"Stop what?"

"Why did you let me do that to you?"

He might have laughed. "Did *you* do something to me?"

A weak pain fluttered through my belly. There was a wetness on my thighs.

"Turn on the light," he said. "You can now, you know. It'll work for you, now that you're living."

I flipped the switch. The sudden brightness was blinding. Turning away from the lights over the sink, I saw myself in the full-length mirror on the door. The wetness on my thighs was blood.

My blood? Or his?

The pain in my belly came again.

"Jess?"

"Get away. Let me get dressed and get out of here. I don't want this."

"Let me in."

"No. If you come near me, I'll take more from you."

Now he did laugh. "What is it you think *you* took?"

"Life. Whatever's left. You're alive and I'm one of the fading ones. I'll make you fade, too."

"That's an interesting theory. Is that what you think happened?"

"Somehow you're still really alive. Like the earth still turns, like there are still stars. Figures we wouldn't all fade away at once, us people. Some of us would still be alive. Maybe as long as there are still stars, there'll still be some people alive." The sound of my laughter in the small room was harsh and ugly. "So romantic. As long as there are stars in the sky, that's how long you'll be here for me. Go away. I don't want to hurt you."

"And what *will* you do?" he asked. "Go back to your bloodless room and your bloodless man, resume your bloodless wait to see what the end will be? It's all nothing without the risk, isn't it? When there's nothing to lose, there's really nothing at all. Isn't that right?"

The lock snapped and the door swung open. He stood there holding on to either side of the doorway. The stark hunger in the angular features had made his face into a predator's mask, intent, voracious, without mercy. I backed up a step, but there was nowhere to go.

He lunged at me and caught me under the arms, lifting me to eye level. "You silly cow," he whispered, and his breath smelled like meat. "*I* didn't get cooler, *you* just got *warmer*."

He shoved me away. I hit the wall and slid down. The pain in my shoulders and back was exquisite, not really pain but pure sensation, the un-alive, undead nerve endings frenzied with it. I wanted him to do it again, I wanted him to hit me, or caress me, or cut me, or do anything that would make me *feel*. Pain or pleasure, whatever there was, I wanted to live through it, get lost in it, die of it, and, if I had to die of it, take him with me.

He stood over me with the barest of smiles. "Starting to understand now?"

I pushed myself up, my hands slipping and sticking on the tiled wall.

"Yeah." He nodded. "I think maybe you are. I think you're definitely starting to get it." He backed to the sink and slid a razor blade off the counter. "How about this?" He held the blade between two fingers, moving it back and forth so it caught the light. "Always good for a thrill. Your bloodless man understands that well enough already. Like so many others. Where do you think he goes when he takes his little walks up the promenade, what do you think he does when he leaves you to sit watching the hanging woman twist and turn on the end of her rope?" He laughed and popped the blade into his mouth, closing his eyes with ecstasy. Then he bared his teeth; the blood ran over his lower lip onto his chin and dripped down onto his chest.

"Come on," he said, the razor blade showing between his teeth. "Come *kiss* me."

I wasn't sure that I leaped at him as much as the life in him pulled me by that hunger for sensation. He caught me easily, holding me away for a few teasing seconds before letting our bodies collide.

The feeling was an explosion that rushed outward from me, and as it did, I finally did understand, mostly that I hadn't had it right at all, but it was too late to do anything about it. The only mercy he showed was to let the light go out again.

Or maybe that wasn't mercy. Maybe that was only what happened when he drained it all out of me and back into himself, every bit of pain and pleasure and being alive.

He kept the razor blade between his teeth for the whole time. It went everywhere, but he never did kiss me.

The room was so quiet, I thought he'd left. I got up from where I'd been lying, half in and half out of the bathroom, thinking I'd find my clothes and go away now, wondering how long I'd be able to hide the damage from Jim—if damage it was, since I no longer felt anything—wondering if I would end up in the hospital, if there was already a bed with my name on it, or whether I'd be just another exotic for nightly sessions at the Kurhaus.

"Just one more thing," he said quietly. I froze in the act of taking a step toward the bed. He was standing by the open window, looking out at the street.

"What's the matter?" I said. "Aren't I dead enough yet?"

He laughed, and now it was a soft, almost compassionate sound, the predator pitying the prey. "I just want to show you something."

"No."

He dragged me to the window and forced my head out. "See it anyway, this one time. A favor, because I'm so well pleased." He pulled my head back to make me look up at the sky. A night sky, very flat, very black, featureless, without a cloud and with no stars, none at all.

"A magic lantern show, yes," he said, as though I'd spoken. "*We* put the signs and wonders in the sky for you. So you wouldn't see *this*."

He forced my head down, digging his fingers more deeply into my hair. Below, in the courtyard, people wandered among a random arrangement of cylindrical things without seeing them. They were pale things, silent, unmoving; long, ropy extensions stretched out from the base of each one, sinking into the pavement like cables, except even in the dim light, I could see how they pulsed.

While I watched, a split appeared in the nearest one. The creature that pushed its way out to stand and stretch itself in the courtyard was naked, vaguely female-looking, but not quite human. It rubbed its hands over the surface of the cylinder, and then over itself. I pulled away.

"You see, that's the other thing about your kind besides your tendency toward too little, too late," he said conversationally as I dressed. If I tucked my shirt into my pants I could keep myself together a little better. "You miss things. You're blind. All of you. Otherwise, you'd have seen us before now. We've always been here, waiting for our time with you. If even one of you had seen us, you might have escaped us. Perhaps even destroyed us. Instead, you all went on with your lives. And now we're going on with them." He paused, maybe waiting for me to say something. I didn't even look at him as I wrapped my shirt around the ruin of my torso. "Don't worry. What I just showed you, you'll never see again. Perhaps by the time you get home, you'll even have forgotten that you saw anything."

He turned back to the window. "See you around the promenade."

"First time's the worst."

The Ghost of Lifetimes Past fell into step beside me as I walked back along the promenade. She was definitely looking worse, wilted and eaten away. "After that," she added, "it's the natural order of things."

"I don't know you," I said.

"I know you. We all know each other, after. Go home to your husband now and he'll know you, too."

"I'm not married."

"Sure." She smiled at me, her face breaking into a mass of lines and seams. "It could be worse, you know. They like to watch it waste me, they like to watch it creep through me and eat me alive. They pour life into us, they loan it to us, you could say, and then they take it back with a great deal of interest. And fascination. They feed on us, and we feed on them, but considering what they are, we're actually feeding on ourselves. And maybe a time will come that will really be the end. After all, how long can we make ourselves last?"

She veered away suddenly, disappearing down a staircase that led to one of the abandoned restaurants closer to the waterline.

As I passed the tower, the hanging woman waved a greeting. There would be no horizon line on the ocean again today.

I had thought Jim would know as soon as he saw me, but I didn't know what I expected him to do. He watched me from where he lay on the bed with his arms behind his head. Through the thin material of his shirt, I could see how he'd been split from below his collarbone down to his navel. It seems to be a favorite pattern of incision with them, or maybe they really have no imagination to speak of.

He still said nothing as I took a book from the stack on the nightstand and sat down in the chair by the window, positioning myself with my back to the room. The words on the pages looked funny, symbols for something I no longer knew anything about.

The mattress creaked as Jim got up and I heard him changing his clothes. I didn't want to look—after all, it wouldn't matter what I saw—and still not wanting to, I put the unreadable book aside and turned around.

The incision was actually very crude, as if it had been done with a jagged shard of glass. I wanted to feel bad at the sight, I wanted to feel sorry and sad and angry at the destruction, I wanted of feel the urge to rush to him and offer comfort. But as Sandor had pointed out, in the absence of pain, no comfort was necessary.

Abruptly, Jim shrugged and finished dressing, and I realized he'd been waiting for something, maybe for me to show him my own. But I had no desire to do that yet.

"I'm going for a walk up the promenade," he said, heading for the door. "You can come if you want." He didn't look back for a response.

"Do you think," I heard myself say just before he stepped out into the hall, "they're everywhere? Or if we could just get home somehow . . ."

"Jess." He almost smiled. "We *are* home."

I followed him at a distance. He didn't wait for me, walking along briskly but unhurriedly, and I didn't try to catch up with him. The sky seemed darker and duller, the sounds of the people on the promenade quieter, more muffled. The trams didn't run.

I stayed out until dark. The dying-stars show was especially spectacular, and I watched it until Sandor finally got around to coming back for me.

I was sitting on the promenade in Scheveningen on a cloudy day at the end of August. There was no horizon line on the ocean. I started thinking about vampires at the end of the world—vampires because I was sitting next to Ellen Datlow, with whom I share a fascination with vampirism and the many forms it can take, and the end of the world because of the peculiar way sky and sea melted together without even a hint of demarcation, as if there were really nothing out there. Would vampires show up at the end of it all, I wondered, and if so, what kind? Suppose the vampires were the ones who were really alive and the people were the living dead?

Sitting around thinking odd thoughts in various locations is a strange thing to do, I guess, but it's a living.

Pat Cadigan

THE RAGTHORN

Robert Holdstock and Garry Kilworth

This may be the most traditional of the stories in the anthology, not for its vampire, which isn't at all traditional, but in its richness of detail. This novelette is a mystery, a historically accurate study, and a classic quest story. A lovely yet chilling grace note with which to culminate this book.

> Quhen thow art ded and laid in layme
> And Raggtre rut thi ribbis ar
> Thow art than brocht to thi lang hayme
> Than grett agayn warldis dignite
>
> *Unknown* (c. A.D. 1360)

September 11, 1978

I am placing this entry at the beginning of my edited journal for reasons that will become apparent. Time is very short for me now, and there are matters that must be briefly explained. I am back at the cottage in Scarfell, the stone house in which I was born and which has always been at the centre of my life. I have been here for some years and am finally ready to do what must be done. Edward Pottifer is with me—good God-fearing man that he is—and it will be he who closes this journal and he alone who will decide upon its fate.

The moment is *very* close. I have acquired a set of dental pincers with which to perform the final part of the ritual. Pottifer has seen into my mouth—an experience that clearly disturbed him, no doubt because of its intimacy—and he knows which teeth to pull and which to leave. After the inspection he muttered that he is more used to pulling rose thorns from fingers than molars from jaws. He asked me if he might keep the teeth as souvenirs and I said he could, but he should look after them carefully.

I cannot pretend that I am not frightened. I have edited my life's journal severely. I have taken out all that does not relate forcefully to my discovery. Many journeys to foreign parts have gone, and many accounts of irrelevant discovery and strange encounters. Not even Pottifer will know where they are. I leave for immediate posterity only this bare account in Pottifer's creased and soil-engrimed hands.

Judge my work by this account, or judge my sanity. When this deed is done I shall be certain of one thing: that in whatever form I shall have become, I will be beyond judgement. I shall walk away, leaving all behind, and not look back.

Time had been kinder to Scarfell Cottage than perhaps it deserves. It has been, for much of its existence, an abandoned place, a neglected shrine. When I finally came back to it, years after my mother's death, its wood had rotted, its interior decoration had decayed, but thick cob walls—two feet of good Yorkshire stone—had proved too strong for the ferocious northern winters. The house had been renovated with difficulty, but the precious stone lintel over the doorway—the beginning of my quest—was thankfully intact and undamaged. The house of my childhood became habitable again, twenty years after I left it.

From the tiny study where I write, the view into Scardale is as eerie and entrancing as it ever was. The valley is a sinuous, silent place, its steep slopes broken by monolithic black rocks and stunted trees that grow from the green at sharp, wind-shaped angles. There are no inhabited dwellings here, no fields. The only movement is the grey flow of cloud shadow and the flash of sunlight on the thin stream. In the far distance, remote at the end of the valley, the tower of a church: a place for which I have no use.

And of course—all this is seen through the branches of the tree. The *ragthorn*. The terrible tree.

It grows fast. Each day it seems to strain from the earth, stretching an inch or two into the storm skies, struggling for life. Its roots have spread farther across the grounds around the cottage and taken a firmer grip upon the dry stone wall at the garden's end; to this it seems to clasp as it teeters over the steep drop to the dale. There is such menace in its aspect, as if it is stretching its hard knotty form, ready to snatch at any passing life.

It guards the entrance to the valley. It is a rare tree, neither hawthorn nor blackthorn, but some ancient form of plant life, with a history more exotic than the Glastonbury thorn. Even its roots have thorns upon them. The roots themselves spread below the ground like those of a wild rose, throwing out suckers in a circle about the twisted bole: a thousand spikes forming a palisade around the trunk and thrusting inches above the earth. I have seen no bird try to feed upon the tiny berries that it produces in mid-winter. In the summer its bark has a terrible smell. To go close to the tree induces dizziness. Its thorns when broken curl up after a few minutes, like tiny live creatures.

How I hated that tree as a child. How my mother hated it! We were only stopped from destroying it by the enormity of the task, since such had been tried before and it was found that every single piece of root had to be removed from the ground to prevent it growing again. And soon after leaving Scarfell Cottage as a young man, I became glad of the tree's defensive nature—I began to long to see the thorn again.

To begin with however, it was the stone lintel that fascinated me: the strange slab over the doorway, with its faint alien markings. I first traced those markings when I was ten years old and imagined that I could discern letters among the symbols. When I was seventeen and returned to the cottage from boarding school for a holiday, I realised for the first time that they were cuneiform, the wedge-shaped characters that depict the ancient languages of Sumeria and Babylon.

I tried to translate them, but of course failed. It certainly occurred to me to approach the British Museum—after all my great-uncle Alexander had worked at that noble institution for many years—but those were full days and I was an impatient youth. My study was demanding. I was to be an archaeologist, following in the family tradition, and no doubt I imagined that there would be time enough in the future to discover the meaning of the Sumerian script.

At that time all I knew of my ancestor William Alexander was that he was a great-uncle, on my father's side, who had built the cottage in the dales in 1880, immediately on his return from the Middle East. Although the details of what he had been doing in the Bible lands were obscure, I knew he had spent many years there, and also that he had been shot in the back during an Arab uprising; a wound he survived.

There is a story that my mother told me, handed down through the generations. The details are smudged by the retelling, but it relates how William Alexander came to Scarfell, leading a great black-and-white Shire horse hauling a brewer's dray. On the dray were the stones with which he would begin to build Scarfell Cottage, on land he had acquired. He walked straight through the village with not a word to a soul, led the horse and cart slowly up the steep hill to the valley edge, took a spade, dug a pit, and filled it with dry wood. He set light to the wood and kept the fire going for four days. In all that time he remained in the open, either staring out across the valley or tending the fire. He didn't eat. He didn't drink. There was no tree there at the time. When at last the fire died down he paid every man in the village a few shillings to help with the building of a small stone cottage. And one of the stones to be set—he told them—was a family tombstone whose faded letters could still be seen on its faces. This was placed as the lintel to the door.

Tombstone indeed! The letters on that grey-faced obelisk had been marked there four thousand years before, and it had a value beyond measure. Lashed to the deck of a cargo vessel, carried across the Mediterranean, through the Straits of Gibraltar, the Bay of Biscay, the obelisk had arrived in England (coincidentally) at the time Cleopatra's Needle was expected. The confused Customs officers had waved it through, believing it to be a companion piece to the much larger Egyptian obelisk.

This then is all I need to say, save to add that three years after the building of the cottage the locals noticed a tree of unfamiliar shape growing from the pit where the fire had burned that night. The growth of the tree had been phenomenally fast; it had appeared in the few short months of one winter.

The rest of the account is extracted from my journal. Judge me upon it. Judge my sanity. There are many questions to which there seem no answers. Who, or what, guided me to previously hidden information during the years? My uncle's ghost perhaps? The ghost of something considerably more ancient? Or even the spirit of the tree itself, though what would be its motive? There are too many coincidences for there *not* to have been some divine, some spiritual presence at work. But who? And perhaps the answer is: *no person at all,* rather a force of destiny for which we have no words in our language.

August 7, 1958

I have been at Tel Enkish for four days now, frustrated by Professor Legmeshu's refusal to allow me onto the site of the excavation. It is clear, however, that a truly astonishing discovery is emerging.

Tel Enkish seems to be the site of an early Sumerian temple to a four-part god, or man-god, with many of the attributes of Gilgamesh. From the small town of Miktah, a mile away, little can be seen but a permanent dust cloud over the low, dry hills, and the steady stream of battered trucks and carts that plough back and forth between the dump site and the excavation itself. All the signs are that there is something very big going on. Iraqi officials are here in number. Also the children of the region have flocked to Tel Enkish from miles around the site. They beg, they pester, they demand work on what is now known as "The Great Tomb." They are unaware that as a visitor I have no authority myself.

August 9, 1958

I have at last been to the site. I have seen the shrine that William Alexander uncovered eighty years ago. I have never in my life been so affected by the presence of the monumental past in the corroded ruins of the present.

My frantic messages were at last acknowledged, this morning at eight. Legmeshu, it seems, has only just made the connection between me and William Alexander. At midday, a dust-covered British Wolesley came for me. The middle-aged woman who drove it turned out to be Legmeshu's American wife. She asked me, "Have you brought the stone?" and looked around my small room as if I might have been hiding it below the wardrobe or something. She was angry when I explained that I had brought only my transcription of the glyphs on the weathered rock. She quizzed as to where the stone was now located, and I refused to answer.

"Come with me," she snapped, and led the way to the car. We drove through the jostling crowds in silence. Over the nearest rise we passed through barbed-wire fencing and checkpoints not unlike those to be found in army camps. Iraqi guards peered into the vehicle, but on seeing Dr. Legmeshu waved us on. There was a sense of great agitation in the air. Everyone seemed tense and excited.

The site itself is in a crater of the tel, the mound on which the temple had been built and over which later generations of buildings in mud had been added. In the fashion of the notorious archaeologist Woolley, the top layer of the tel had been blasted away to expose the remains of the civilisation that had flourished there in the third millennium B.C. It had not been Legmeshu who had been so destructive, but my ancestor, Alexander.

As I feasted my eyes on the beautifully preserved building, she waited impatiently. She told me that the temple was from the period associated with Gilgamesh the King. It was made of refined mud-brick, and had been covered with a weatherproof skin of burnt brick set in bitumen.

"Where had the Alexander stone been set?" I asked, and she pointed to the centre of the ruins. "They had created a megalith structure at the very heart of the temple. The stone that your relative stole was the keystone. This is why you *must* return it. We cannot allow ..." She broke off and looked at me angrily. If she had been about to make a threat, she had thought better of it.

Her attitude led me to expect the worst from the male Dr. Legmeshu, but I am delighted to say that he could not have been more charming. I found him in the tent, poring over a set of inscriptions that had been traced out on paper. He was leaning on a large slab of rock and when I looked more closely I saw that it was identical to the lintel at Scarfell Cottage.

He was fascinated by the route I had taken in discovering him. The Iraqi government had made formal representation to the British government, five years before, for the return of the "Tel Enkish Stone" to its natural site. Unlike Elgin Marbles, which the British Museum regarded as their right to keep safe, no official in London had ever heard of the Tel Enkish Stone.

The argument had waged within those same "scenes" for years, and had finally been taken up by the press. A picture of one of the other Tel Enkish stones had caught my attention, along with the headline: WHERE IS THE ALEXANDER STONE? some keen reporter had obviously done his research to the point where he had made the connection.

The museum by that time had established that the stone had been removed by Professor Alexander, who they understood had retired to an unknown location after returning from the Middle East in the late 1890s. The Iraqi government believed none of this of course, thinking that the British Museum had the stone hidden, and relations were soured between the two countries for some years afterwards.

I have told Legmeshu that the stone lies in a quarry, the location of which I shall make known to the museum on my return to the United Kingdom. He has accepted this.

The story of those events, eighty years before, is difficult to ascertain. Alexander had worked on the site with Legmeshu's own great-grandfather. The two men had been close friends, and had made the astonishing discovery of the megaliths at the heart of the mud-brick temple together. There had been eight stones arranged in a circle, standing vertically. Four stones had lain across their tops. A mini Stonehenge. And in the centre, four altars, three to known gods, one . . . one that defied explanation.

"No trace of those altars remain," Legmeshu told me over tea. "But my great-grandfather's notes are quite clear. There were three altars to the three phases of the Hunter God: the youth, the king, the wise ancient. But to whom the fourth altar was dedicated . . . ?" He shrugged. "A goddess perhaps? Or the king reborn? My relative left only speculation."

There had been a difference of opinion during that first excavation; a fight; and a death. Apart from what I have written here, the record is blank, save for a folk memory from the inhabitants of Scarfell concerning a tree that grew one winter—a black and evil-looking thorn.

Legmeshu snatched my copy of the Scarfell inscription. He ran his eyes over the signs, the cuneiform script that seemed as familiar to him as was my own alphabet to me. "This is not all of it," he said after a long while. I had realised some time before that the fourth surface of the stone, flush with the brickwork between door and ceiling, had characters on it like the other three. They could not be read of course without demolishing the cottage, which I had not been prepared to do at the time. I told Legmeshu that the fourth side had been exposed over a long period to the toxic air of a northern English factory town and the characters had been all but erased.

He seemed beside himself with fury for a moment. "What a destructive and stupid thing to do, to leave the stone in such a place. It *must* be returned! It *must* be rescued!"

"Of course," I said. "I intend to do so on my return to England. I have only just located the stone myself, after years of studying my great-uncle's notes ..."

He seemed mollified by this. I have no intention of giving up the whereabouts of the stone however. I lie without shame. I feel obsessively protective towards the stone ... towards the cottage, and yes, in my adulthood, towards the tree. Somehow they are linked through my great-uncle and to remove or destroy any one of them would be like smashing the Rosetta Stone with a sledge hammer.

Legmeshu seemed to come to a sudden decision, saying, "Follow me," and led me down to the site itself. We came at last to the wide tarpaulin that covered the centre of the temple.

It was an area of mystical energy. I could sense the presence of invisible power. It had an immediate and lasting effect on me. I began to shake. Even as I write—hours after the experience—my hand is unsteady. As I stood there I was in the far past. Fingers of time brushed through my hair; the breath of the dead blew gently against my face. Sounds, smells, touches ... and an overwhelming, awe-inspiring *presence*—silently watching me.

Legmeshu seemed entirely unaware of these things.

His voice brought me back to the present. He was pointing to the small concrete markers that now showed where the stones had stood, in a circle about twenty feet in diameter. On the floor, clearly outlined in the dry mud, were the twisting impressions of roots.

"It was open to the sky," Legmeshu said. "In the centre of the stones a tree had been grown, quite a large tree by the looks of it. The four altars were oriented east-west. We think there may have been a mud-filled pit below the trunk of the tree, to support its growth."

"And the purpose of the place?" I asked. Legmeshu smiled at me and passed me a small book. I opened it and saw that he had written out the translations from each stone. The particle content of the Alexander stone had just been added and I studied the stilted English. Almost immediately I was aware of what I was reading.

Legmeshu's breathless, "It includes much of the original epic that has been lost, and earlier forms of the rest. It is a momentous find!" was quite unnecessary. I was lost in words:

And behold the waters of the Flood were gone. The mud covered the land as a cloak which stifles. Gilgamesh waited on a hill and saw Utnapishtim, Boatman of the Flood, rise from the plain of mud and beckon. "Gilgamesh I shall reveal to you a secret thing, a mystery of the gods. Hark my words. There is a tree that grows from fire under the water, under the mud. It has a thorn prick, a rose blade on every twig. It will wound your hands, but if you can grasp it, then you will be holding that which can restore youth to a man. Its name is Old Man Who Would Be Young." "How deep is the mud?" Lord Gilgamesh asked. "Seven days and seven nights," answered the Boatman, and Gilgamesh drew breath and swam into the blackness.

When he had cut Old Man Who Would Be Young he swam again to the surface of the mud. Utnapishtim sent a woman with golden tresses to clean and annoint the body of the kingly man. And Gilgamesh possessed her for seven days and seven nights in a fury of triumph, and not for one moment did he let go of Old Man Who Would Be Young. And when the child was born, Utnapishtim gave it at once to Old Man Who Would Be Young, so that the first berry appeared on the branches. "Now it will grow," the Boatman said. "And I have told you of the temple you must build and the manner of annointing the flesh."

Now Gilgamesh departed for high-walled Uruk, and when the thorns of Old Man Who Would Be Young pricked his thumbs he was increased of power. And he denied all the old men their touch of the tree, so that their youth was denied them. But when the time came, Gilgamesh alone would place Old Man Who Would Be Young in the proper way, and lie with it in an embrace of seven days and seven nights.

Here then, carved in stone, was a version of the immortality tale of The Epic of Gilgamesh that was quite unlike the story from the clay tablets. And it was an *earlier* version, Legmeshu was quite adamant, a cruder form, with hints of the magic ritual that the later version appears to have lost.

"The stone came from Egypt," Legmeshu said. "This place functioned as a ritual site of enormous importance for perhaps two hundred years. The secret plant seems to have been a thorn, which would account for the pattern of roots on the mud there. I believe this place celebrated immortality. And the fourth altar may be representational: the risen life. So we have Youth, King, Magus, and again Youth."

Legmeshu spoke, but his words became just sounds. He seemed more interested in archaeology than in the astonishing *literary* discovery. To him, legends are only part of the story of the people; they are one more tool, or one more part of the machine that is archaeology. He wants the words intact, as much as he wants the stone intact, but I realise now that he has not been affected by the *meaning* of the words, neither their literal interpretation nor what they imply about culture and ritual in the earliest of civilised times.

Quite clearly my great-uncle was! What other reason could there have been for his dragging away one of the stones—the key stone—and raising, too, a strange and gloomy tree. Did he find the seed of a familiar thorn that in the time of Babylon was known as Old Man Who Would Be Young?

The key! It tells of the growth from fire of a tree. It tells of the child who must be given to the growing sapling. And what other salient information lies on the hidden face of the lintel, awaiting discovery?

August 10, 1958

I can stay here no longer. I wish to return to the site at Tel Enkish but I have received word that the Iraqis are unhappy that I "own" the stone. The time has come to slip away from this country. For a while, anyway. I leave so much unfinished; I leave so many questions unanswered.

June 14, 1965

I had almost come to believe that my supernatural encounter at Tel Enkish was no more than imagination; whimsy. The intervening years have been very barren and very frustrating. (Legmeshu has finally ceased to hound me for the stone, but I still watch my back whenever I am in the Near or Middle East.) Now, something has turned up and I have flown to Cairo from Jerusalem (via Cyprus).

It began two months ago. I was in Jerusalem, initiating the project for which Cambridge has at last agreed to fund me: namely, to identify and discover that true symbolic and mythological meaning of the type of tree that provided the Crown of Thorns at Christ's execution. (A briar wreath, a coif of knotted thistles, a halo of thorn tree twigs? From what species of shrub or tree?) The reference to the "resurrecting thorn" in the work of the unknown writer of Gilgamesh has haunted me for years. Of all the world's great resurrections, Christ's is the most famous. I am increasingly obsessed with the true manner of that raising, and the Crown of Thorns is a teasing symbol, a provocative invitation that came to me while staring at the ragthorn through the window of Scarfell Cottage.

One afternoon, in the university library canteen, a noisy crowded place, I overheard a conversation.

The two men were behind me, speaking in awkward English, obviously a second language to them both. One of them was an Israeli diplomat I recognised; the other was an Arab. I guessed from the dialect of his occasional exclamations in his first language, that he was Egyptian. Their conversation was hushed, but I could hear it quite clearly, and soon became intrigued.

The Egyptian said, "Some diving men, with the tanks on the back—not professional men—tourist. They are swim near Pharos Island, where sunk the old light warnings for ships . . ."

The Israeli took a moment to work out what was being said.

"Light warnings? Light*house.* The Pharos lighthouse?"

The Egyptian said excitedly, "Yes, yes! By ancient city Alexandria. Yes. Find some very old jar. Very old. Thousands years. No sea get into jar. Papers inside. Old papers. Old before coming of Roman peoples. Many more jars in sea, so I am told."

Their voices dropped even lower and I found it was hard to catch what was being said. All I could determine was that the Israeli government are interested in any scroll that relates to its own culture. Naturally, they are prepared to pay a great deal of money and the Egyptian was busy lining his own pockets by bringing this information to the attention of the Israeli Ministry of Culture.

The thought occurred to me immediately: Might there be something in the jars that relates to the *thorn?*

It has been years since Tel Enkish, but once again I have a feeling of fate unfolding: of being watched by the silent past. I am convinced there is something in Cairo for *me.*

June 19, 1965

My contact here is Abdullah Rashid. He is well known to the professors at the University in Jerusalem and has "supplied" objects and information to them for some years.

Professor Berenstein in Jerusalem is a friend of mine and kindly arranged the surreptitious meeting with this man who is in a position to inspect and copy the contents of the jars. This morning, after "checking my credentials," Abdullah came to my hotel. Over breakfast he explained that five of the ancient jars had already been taken from the water and two of them opened in controlled conditions. He is cagey about this knowledge of the contents, but has remarked, cryptically, that he believes there *is* a reference to some thorn tree amongst the first papers to be removed and examined.

The discovery is, as I knew, being kept under tight wraps, and Abdullah was surprised and impressed that I managed to hear about the parchments. It is the intention of the Egyptians to translate the documents and plays themselves, and take full credit before releasing the finds to the world at large. Hence, people like Abdullah are making a great deal of money leaking facsimiles of the parchments.

This is what Abdullah has told me: The discovery so far is of several documents that survived the fire in the Library of Alexandria two thousand years ago. The belief is that before the rioting crowd managed to penetrate the library, strip its shelves, and set the place alight, a number of soldiers loaded saddlebags with whatever the librarians could select to save, and rode from the city to a galley, which pulled offshore. Here, forty glazed amphorae were filled with manuscripts and sealed with wax, linen, more wax, and finally corked with clay. For some reason the jars were thrown overboard near the lighthouse. Perhaps the crew suddenly found themselves in danger and unable to set sail? Nothing more is known of this. Certainly the intention would have been to recover the vessels, once the danger was past, but it must be surmised that there were no survivors who knew of the whereabouts of the jars, or even that they existed. Seawater rotted the rope nets holding them together and then currents carried some of the jars out into the Mediterranean, and stretched them in a line towards Cyprus.

June 20, 1965

Today we saw the recovery operation at work. The shores of Alexandria are always bustling with small craft, mostly feluccas similar to that in which we serenely approached the island. We blended well, since I had dressed in local fashion. It was calm on the blue waters, but the sun bore down on us with unrelenting pressure and its effects have made me quite dizzy. We sailed to Pharos Island, to the northern point, and watched a large rusty dredger assist a team of divers in bringing up the precious artifacts.

Eventually we received our reward. We saw one of the amphorae winched from the water. It was long and slender, encrusted with limpets and barnacles, and dripped a particularly silky, dark green weed, which hung from the bullet-blunt jar like a beard. A crab of gigantic size dangled from this furze by one claw, as if reluctant to release the treasure that had for so long been the property of the ocean.

I asked Abdullah where the amphora would now be taken. He told me, "To the museum." There it would be opened in controlled conditions.

"Is there no chance I could witness the opening?"

He shook his head and laughed. He told me that only certain government ministers and professors would be there. And some technical assistants, who were highly trusted.

Again the laughter as he prodded his chest.

"People like me," he said.

Abdullah's work would be to photograph the opening of the jars, at each stage, then any contents, page by page. Facsimilies would be made from the photographs.

"These facsimilies would be for sale?"

"Not officially of course"—he smiled—"but all things are negotiable, yes?"

June 23, 1965

Abdullah was here, but the news is not good. He has been unable to obtain copies yet, not just for me but for others, as he must not be caught compromising his position at the museum. He has photographed several manuscripts so far.

It is a mixed bag, apparently, and includes two pieces by Plato, a play by Flatus called *Servius Pompus*, and twenty pages of a manuscript by Julius Caesar, entitled *His Secret Dialogues with the Priests of Gaul on the Nature of their Magic and Rituals.*

The final piece of parchment contains an even more exquisite original hand: that (it is believed) of Homer himself. It is a fragment of his *Iliad*, and consists of half of the Death of Hector, all the Funeral of Patroclus, and a third or so of the Funeral Games. It is a manifestly ancient hand, and the

Egyptians are quite convinced that it *is* the writings of Homer, adding weight to the argument that Homer was one man, and not a collective of writers.

All of this would be enough to excite me beyond tolerance, but Abdullah, aware of the nature of my search, has now told me something that holds me breathless in anticipation: that the *Iliad* fragment contains reference to a "blood thorn."

That is the facsimile I want. I have told him that no matter what else he obtains, he *must* get that fragment of unknown Homer. My enthusiasm has no doubt put up the price of those lines of verse, but I am sure I am being skillfully teased into such a state by Abdullah. He could probably produce the goods now, but is jigging the price up with his procrastination, pretending he is being watched too closely. I can play the game too, and have let him see me packing my suitcase, and looking anxiously at my diary.

October 1, 1965

I am back at the cottage in Scarfell, the place of my birth. I have come here because I *feel* I have been summoned home. I have been at Cambridge for most of the summer, but the voice of something dark, something omnipresent, has called me here ... home to the cottage, to the wild valley, to the tree.

I have translated much that Abdullah was able to sell me. And indeed, the documents make fascinating reading.

The "new" play by Titus Maccius Plautus (200 B.C.) is hilarious. *Servius Pompus* is completely typical, dealing with a common legionary in Fabius' army who is convinced he is of noble birth, and treats his comrades like dirt. His ultimate discovery that he is slave-born earns him a permanent position: on a cart, collecting the dung left behind by Hannibal's elephants.

The fragment of Caesar is most atypical however and very strange, detailing as it does the legendary and magic matter of the Celtic inhabitants of Europe, and there is a fascinating revelation concerning the coded language that existed within the arrangement of the stones on the landscape.

All that is for another paper. For the moment, it is the Homeric verse that excites me, for in this fragment of the epic cycle of the Greeks on the shores of Asia Minor there is a reference to the resurrection that confirms me in two beliefs: that there has been a deliberate effort to obliterate this knowledge from the world, and that someone—or some *thing*—is guiding my search to build again that knowledge from the clues I am gradually discovering.

The autumn day is dark as I write this, with huge columns of thunderous cloud drifting over Scarfell from the west. I am working by lamplight. I am chilled to the bone. The great rugged face of the fell surrounds me, and the solitary thorn—black against the darkness—seems to lean towards me through the small leaded windows that show its sinister form. That tree has known eternity. I sense now that it has seen me learn of Achilles, and *his* unsure use of the ancient magic.

Here then is my crude translation of the passage of the *Iliad* that is relevant. It is from the "Funeral of Patroclus," Achilles' great friend. While Achilles sulked in his tent, during the siege of Troy, Patroclus donned the man's armour and fought in his place, only to be killed by the Trojan hero Hector. After Patroclus's body had been burned on the funeral pyre ...

> ... then they gathered the noble dust of their comrade
> And with ashes from the fire filled a golden vase.
> And the vase was double-sealed with fat
> Then placed reverently in the hut of the gallant Patroclus,
> And those who saw it there laid soft linens
> Over the gold tomb, as a mark of respect.
> Now the divine Achilles fashioned the barrow for his friend.
> A ring of stone was laid upon the earth of the shore
> And clear spring water was sprinkled amongst the stones.
> Then rich dark soil was carried from the fields and piled upon the stones.
> Until it was higher than the storm-soaked cedar.
> Prince Achilles walked about the barrow of Patroclus
> And wept upon the fertile ground which held his friend
> While Nestor, son of Neleus, was sent a Dream from Heaven.
> The Dream Messenger came from Zeus, the Cloud-compeller
> Whose words reached the ears of the excellent Achilles
> Who pulled the blood thorn from the wall of Troy
> And placed the thorn tree on the tear-soaked mound.
> In its branches he placed the sword and shield of Patroclus
> And in so doing pierced his own flesh with the thorn,
> Offering lifeblood as his blood for life.

Here, the fragment returns to the story content as we know it: the funeral games for Patroclus and the final reckoning between Achilles and the Trojan champion, Hector. My translation leaves a great deal to be desired. The *metre* of Homer's verse in the original seems very crude, not at all as we have become used to it, and perhaps later generations than Homer have "cleaned up" the old man's act, as it were. But there is power in the words, and an odd obsession with "earth." When Homer wrote them, I am sure he was powered by the magic of Zeus, a magic that Achilles had attempted to invoke.

Poor Achilles. I believe I understand his error. The whole ritual of the burial, of course, was intended to *bring Patrodus back to life!*

His mistake was in following the normal Mycenaean custom of burning the body of his friend upon the pyre. Patroclus never rose again. He couldn't. It is apparent to me that Zeus tried to warn him *not* to follow custom, *not* to place the body of his friend upon the burning faggots, because several lines previously (as the body of Patroclus was laid upon the pyre), Homer had written:

> *Now in the honouring of Patroclus there was unkind delay,*
> No fire would take upon the wood below the hero.
> *Then the excellent Achilles walked about the pyre and mourned anew*
> *But through his grief-eyes he saw the answer to the fire*
> *And raised his arms and prayed to all the winds*
> *And offered splendid sacrifice to the two gods*
> *Boreas from the North and Zephyr of the Western Gale.*
> *He made them rich libations from a golden cup*
> *And implored them blow among the kindling*
> *So that the honouring fire* might grow in strength and honoured ash be
>   made of brave Patroclus.

No fire would take and Achilles failed to see the chance that his god was offering him. Zeus was keeping the wind from the flames, but seeing his warnings go unheeded, he turned away from Achilles in a passing pique.

Nothing else in this fragment seems to relate to the subject of the thorn, or its means of operation. Abdullah has promised to send me more material when and if he can, but since nothing has arrived for several months, already

I suspect that the knowledge of the lost amphorae and their precious contents is being suppressed.

What can I learn from Homer? That there was a genuine belief in the power of the *thorn* to raise the dead? That some "pricking of the flesh" is important? Achilles pricks his arm: his blood for life. But this is not the only life hinted at in the two references I have so far found: a child was given to the tree, according to the Gilgamesh fragment. I feel the darkness closing in.

March 11, 1970

The stone lintel is *bound* to the tree! Bonded to it. Tied! It is a frightening thought. This morning I tried to dislodge the stone from its position, scraping at the cement that binds it to the rest of the coarse stone of the cottage. I discovered that the ragthorn's roots are *in the house itself!* It is clear to me now that my great-uncle had a far better understanding of the importance of the tree and stone than I have so far imagined. Why did he drag back the Gilgamesh stone to England? Why did he embed it in the way he did: as part of a door, part of a house. Is the "doorway" symbolic? A divide through which one passes from one world to another? Obviously the hidden side of the lintel contains words of great importance, words that he decided had to be concealed from the curious eyes of his contemporaries.

The stone is not a tomb's marker, it is the tomb itself: the tomb of lost knowledge!

All this has occurred to me recently and this morning I began to extract the lintel from its resting place. I used proper tools and a great deal of brute strength. Imagine my surprise when I discovered that I was scraping through *plant tissue!* A thorny root stabbed out at me, then hung there, quivering and slowly curling. It has frightened me deeply. The whole lintel is covered and protected—on its hidden face—by an extension from the ragthorn that grows at the end of the garden, a menacing and evil presence. I could sever the root to the cottage, but I feel a chill of fear on each occasion that I ponder this possibility. Even now, as I write, I feel I am drawing a terrible darkness closer.

The tree has come to inhabit the house itself. There is a thick tendril of dark root running along the wall in the kitchen.

The chimney stack is webbed with tree roots. I lifted a floorboard and a thin tendril of the ragthorn jerked away from the sudden light. The floor is covered with tiny feelers.

Webbed in tree. And all centering on the stone lintel, the ancient monolith.

No wonder I feel watched. Was it my uncle's doing? Or was he merely obeying the instructions of a more sinister authority?

September 22, 1970

I have received a message from the British Museum, forwarded from my rooms in Cambridge by my research assistant, David Wilkins. He alone knows where I live. He is an able student, a keen researcher, and I have confided in him to a considerable degree. On my behalf he is searching the dusty archives of Cambridge for other references to the "ragthorn" or to resurrection. I am convinced that many such references must exist, and that it is a part of my new purpose to elicit them, and to use them.

"Has the museum any record of William Alexander, or any knowledge of the whereabouts of his papers?" I had asked in 1967, without result.

The new letter reads quite simply thus: "We have remembered your earlier enquiry concerning the effects, records, papers, and letters of William Alexander and are pleased to inform you that a small string-bound, wax-sealed file has been discovered, a fragment of his known effects that has clearly been overlooked during the process of reinstatement of said effects to the rightful owner. We would be most pleased to offer you the opportunity to break the seal on this file, and to review the contents, prior to discussing a mutually suitable arrangement for their final disposal."

September 25, 1970

I wonder now whether or not William Alexander *intended* this file to be discovered. I would like to think that in his aging bones, he felt someone coming behind, a soul-mate, a follower, who would become as entranced with his work as he was himself. Considering what I believe now, however, I think it more likely that he intended at some time to recover the file in person, and perhaps *after* most people believed him gone.

Today I have spoken to my great-uncle. Or rather . . . he has spoken to me. He is as close to me now, as I sit here in my room in the Bonnington Hotel writing these notes, as close to me as if he were here in person. He has left a fragment of his work, a teasing, thrilling fragment.

What did he do with the rest of his papers? I wonder.

The man was born in 1832. There is no record of his death. The year is 1970. It is autumn. I tremble to think of this, but I wonder if a man, born before the reign of Victoria had begun, is still walking abroad, still soaking up the rain and the wind and the sun of the England that birthed him, or of the Bible lands that so captured his heart.

This is a summary, then, of the day's events and discoveries:

This morning I entered the labyrinthine heart of the British Museum: those deep dark corridors and rooms that have been burrowed into the bruised London clay below the building. I was conducted to a small book-lined room, heavy with history, heady with the smell of parchment and manuscript. A man of sober demeanor and middle age received us. He had been working under a single pool of desk lamplight, imprisoned by it like some frugal monk. On my arrival he favoured me with room lighting, so that his desk was no longer a captive of the lamp. He was, despite his dour looks, a cheerful soul, and was as delighted by his discovery of William Alexander as I would become of my discovery of his remaining notes. Alexander, it seems, was an old rogue. He had a formidable reputation. He was known as an eccentric man, of extravagant tastes, and frontiers-man's manners. He had shocked the denizens of the nineteenth-century archaeological establishment with his rough Yorkshire speech, his out-landish manners. If it were not for the fact that he produced priceless historical artifacts from lands closed to most Europeans, he might have been ostracized by society from the outset.

He had, it seemed, collected his papers and belongings from his private offices in the deep recesses of the museum, on the 15th March, 1878. His departure had been quite typical of the man. He had placed his files and books upon a handcart and hauled it, clattering, up the levels, dragging it through the reading room disturbing everyone present, through the wide foyer, and out into the day, having caused more than one jowl in the establishment to quiver with indignation. He used to tell my mother, with a hearty chuckle, that if the Victorians were good at one thing, it was displaying indignation.

On passing the Chief Curator on the steps outside, he reached into a bag, drew out a vase of exquisite Egyptian design, and passed it over. When opened, within the neck of the previously sealed vase was a perfectly preserved red rose, its scent a fleeting moment of an ancient summer day, instantly lost as the flower became dust.

Not on the cart that day, however, were thirty sheets of paper, loosely bound between two stiff pieces of cardboard (marked with his initials) and tied with string. He had placed a red wax seal across each of the round edges of the sheaf. On being handed the package, I slit the seals and cut through the formidable string knot with my penknife: shades of an Alexander who lived long before William.

Most of the sheets in the folio are blank. I shall summarise the puzzling contents of the rest.

Sheet 21. This consists of the single word: REVELATION!

Sheet 22. This is written in a more precise hand, but clearly William Alexander's. It reads: "The Bard too! The knowledge passed down as far as ELZBTH 1st. Who censored it? Who changed the text? Two references are clear, but there must be more. There *must* be. Too sweet a myth for WAS to ignore. P—— has discovered lost folio, but spirited it away." (Two sheets covered with numbers and letters: a code of some sort?)

Sheet 25. This is headed "The Dream of the Rood." It is one of two sheets that clearly relates to the "thorn" and "resurrection." The margin of this sheet is peppered with words from the Anglo-Saxon language, but the main body of Alexander's text reads like this: *"Sige-beam."* This means Victory tree? The runic character "thorn" is used more prolifically in the alliterative half-lines than seems usual around this point in the poem's body. Then the word *swefna:* "of dreams." Then there are the words *syllicre treow:* "wonderful tree." This phrase is enclosed by the rune "thorn." A dream tree, a tree of victory (victory over death?) *surrounded and protected by thorns.*

"Yes." *The tree of everlasting life.* The tree is the *rood,* of course, the symbol of Christ's cross. But surely "tree" is meant in another sense too? A literal sense. Then, to confirm this, the phrase in the poem "adorned with coverings." Perhaps this means more than it says? Perhaps strips of material? *Rags?*

"I am certain that the message here is the *ragthorn tree.*"

This is the only note on *The Dream of the Rood* in my great-uncle's file, but it proves that *some* albeit cryptic references to the ragthorn remain extant, since this text can be read in any school edition of the poem.

It is clear that an abiding and darker myth concerning the return to life of a soul "buried beneath a tree" has been imposed upon the Christianity of the author (who probably wrote the "Rood" in the eighth century). But was the ragthorn at that time a tangible shrub that could be plucked, planted, and left to resurrect the corpse of the thane or lord buried below? Or was it already a myth by that time in Old England?

The last sheet contains two fascinating pieces of Middle English poetry, dating from the late 1300's, I would think, as one of them is the last stanza of Chaucer's famous poem *The House of Fame*, believed to be unfinished. It is clear that the poem *was* completed, but the last few lines removed, either by Chaucer himself, or by orders of his patron:

Alexander, who must have discovered the parchment, though it is not part of his file, had this to say:

"It is Chaucer's script, no doubt about it. The parchment page is faded, the ink has spread, but I am certain this is the original. Other editions omit the final four lines. Here they are, following the *known* ending:

> *Atte laste y saugh a man,*
> *Which that y (nevene) nat ne kan*
> *But he seemed for to be*
> *A man of gret auctorite . . .* (here the known MS ends)
> *Loo! how straungely spak thys wyght*
> *How* ragethorn *trees sal sithe the night,*
> *How deeth sal fro the body slynke*
> *When doun besyde the rote it synke.*

To put those last few lines into more familiar language: Lo, this man spoke of strange things, of ragthorn trees scything away the darkness and how death will creep away from the body if it is buried beneath the ragthorn's roots.

Finally, a single stanza from an English religious lyric, which my uncle found at the same time:

Upon thys mount I fand a tree
Wat gif agayne my soule to me!
Wen erthe toe erthe of mortual note
And ssulen wormes feste in thi throte
My nayle-stanged soule will sterte upriss
On ssulen wormes and erthe to piss.

(On this hill I found a tree
which gave me back my (soul)—
While the world might take note of mortality
And sullen worms feast on *your* throat,
My thorn-pierced body will rise up
To treat the worms and the world with contempt.

This, then, concludes my listing of the sheets bound into what I shall call "The Alexander Folio." How much further in his quest my great-uncle managed to journey is hard to know, but he certainly discovered more than have I. What fire must have burned within him. What a fever of discovery!

How death shall from the body slink when down beside the root it sinks. . . .

That tree. That terrifying tree. It is the route to and from the Underworld for a man who is reluctant to die, who wishes to remain . . . *immortal.*

October 13, 1971

I am being directed, or drawn, towards new discoveries. Is it my greatuncle? Or the tree? If it is William Alexander, then he must be dead, for the spirit of a living man would not work this way. It is only spirits that have been freed from mortality that can guide the living.

This leaves me wondering about whether Alexander attempted immortality—and *failed.*

I suspect that if I searched the grounds of Scarfell Cottage carefully, or dug below the walls, into the space below the tree, I believe I would find his bones. Is he here, urging me to finish what he could not, whispering to me: Do it right, do it right? Or . . . am I influenced by something else, some other spiritual presence?

I can only conclude that if not he, then the ragthorn is my guide. This would beg the question: Why? Why would the thorn wish me to find the clues to its secret power over life and death, its unnatural, no, *supernatural,* force? Unless—and my heart races at the thought—*unless I am its chosen disciple!* Gilgamesh was chosen. No doubt others after him, with Alexander the last. It is possible to fail. Of course it is possible to fail. But I intend to understand, thoroughly, what is expected of me, and succeed where Alexander did not.

A low mist, thick and blunt-nosed, winds through the valley like a soft sentient beast, sniffing amongst the mosses and rocks and leaving damp crags and stunted hawthorns dripping with moisture. Its restlessness finds its way into my spirit. I find writing difficult. There is a feeling on the land of a permanent, mist-ridden dusk. I pace the house, constantly going outside to stare at the ragthorn, perched like some black-armoured mythical bird upon the crumbling drystone wall.

Even inside the house, my eyes continually stray to the lintel, to the evidence of the tree that has it in its tendrilous grasp. My work lies scattered around the house. I am possessed by a desire to leave the place. But I cannot. I have not heard from Wilkins for months. It is a year since I have opened the Alexander folio. Something *must* happen soon. Something must happen.

April 10, 1972

The tree has grown. For the first time in years the ragthorn shows signs of growth, twig tips extending, roots inching farther across the garden, extending below the house itself. It is coming into bud, and it seems to shake, even when there are no winds.

September 17, 1972

An odd fragment has come to light as I worked in Cambridge, searching for the Shakespearean folio owned and hidden by Lionel Pervis (the P—— of the Alexander folio), who I have discovered was my uncle's contemporary. The fragment is a further piece of Middle English, perhaps once part of a collection of Sacred Songs. This fragment, a faded vellum sheet pressed between the pages of a copy of the second edition of *Paradise Lost,* may once have belonged to Milton himself. Certainly, this edition of his book has annotations in his own hand, still clear despite his blindness. One is tempted to wonder whether the dying man was clutching at a truth whose greatness had only been hinted at. He had perhaps discovered this obscure and frightening stanza from a hymn and kept it as an odd symbol of hope and resurrection.

Quhen thow art ded and laid in layme
And Raggtre rut this ribbis ar
Thow art than brocht to thi lang hayme
Than grett agayn warldis dignite.

When you are dead and buried in lime
And the roots of the Ragthorn form your ribs
You will then be brought back to your home
To greet the world again with dignity.

November 22, 1974

I have at last found a fragment of the lost folio of *Hamlet,* but not from my searches at Cambridge! It was here all the time, in the Alexander papers. One of the apparently blank sheets is not blank at all. I would not have discovered the fact but for a coincidence of dropping the sheets onto the floor and gathering them by the dim light of the hurricane lamp. The shadowy signs of word-impressions caught my attention immediately. The marks were shallow, the merest denting of the heavy paper from the rapidly scrawled writing on the now-lost top sheet. But the impressions were enough for me to use a fine powder of lead, and a wash of light oil, to bring out the words fully.

Clearly, Alexander was privileged to hear the relevant passage from *Hamlet,* from the original prompt copy of the play, and wrote them down. Lionel Pervis would not part with the whole folio itself, and perhaps it is now destroyed.

(Even as I write these words I feel apprehensive. I am certain, those years ago, that I carefully examined these blank sheets and found nothing. I know I tested for secret ink. I *know* that. I would surely have noticed signs of overwriting.)

The fragment of *Hamlet* makes fascinating reading, and tells me much about the method: the actual means by which the process of burial and rebirth must be achieved.

Here is Alexander's account of the discovery, and his copy of the scene that some hand, later, had eliminated from the versions of Shakespeare's play that have come down to us:

> Pervis is a difficult man to talk to. His career is in ruins and he is an embittered man. He has confirmed certain thoughts, however. Added valuable insight. In summary: The most reliable text of *Hamlet* is to be found in the Second Quarto. However, no editor would dismiss entirely the text that appears in the First Folio, though scholars have proved that the First Folio was derived from a corrupt copy of the prompt-book, used at the Globe Theatre.
>
> Pervis' brother is a barrister of repute, in Lincoln's Inn Fields. Was present during the discovery of a hidden room in the cellars of his firm's building, which had been walled up and forgotten. A mountain of documents was discovered in that room, among them several pages of a manuscript of great interest to Shakespearean scholars. Pervis (the barrister) sent these to his brother, in order for the Shakespearean actor to assess their worth in academic terms and asked what monetary value they might have. Pervis (the actor) claimed never to have received the papers and was taken to court by his brother and, though he could not be convicted on the evidence, was widely believed to have stolen the manuscript. It ruined his life and his career.
>
> Pervis later claimed to have been "given" a copy of the manuscript, though it is fairly certain he sold the original to a private collector who will have it now, in some safe in Zurich. Pervis would not release the copy to anyone, but insisted that the new version must first be heard from him, playing Hamlet's ghost at the Old Vic. Victorian society was scandalised and he was refused and demands were made upon him, which sent him into retreat, somewhere in Wales. It was there I managed to track him down. He was by that time a bitter old man. He knew of me, of my reputation for scandalising the society that he believed had dealt him meanly, and with a certain amount of gold was persuaded to part with lines of the text, including reference to the burial place of Hamlet's father, beneath the roots of an *exotic thorn tree*.

(From Act I, Scene V)
Ghost: Thus was I sleeping by a brother's hand,
*   Of life, of crown, of queen at once dispatched,*
*   Cut off even in the blossoms of my sin,*
*   Unhouseled, disappointed, unaneled,*

No reck'ning made, but sent to my account
With all my imperfections on my head.
Aye, quarters to the four winds pointed right
Below the 'bracing ragthorne's needled limbs,
Yet by ironic touch my flesh immured,
Base metal traitoring this but perfect tomb.
O, horrible! O, horrible! Most horrible!
If thou has nature in thee bear it not,
Let not the royal bed of Denmark be
A couch for luxury and damned incest . . .
But howsoever thou pursues this act,
Taint not thy mind, nor let thy soul contrive
Against thy mother aught—leave her to heaven,
And to those thorns that in her bosom lodge
To prick and sting her.
Fare thee well at once,
The glow-worm shows the matin to be near
And 'gins to pale his uneffecutal fire,
To where my bones lie compassed.
Thus to thee
Adieu, adieu, adieu, remember me.
(The ghost vanishes)

I have read this speech fifty times now, and still the words thrill me. Since William Alexander had seen this verse, he must surely have seen the clear indications of *method*, the method of burial beneath the ragthorn's "root vault."

"*Quarters to the four winds pointed right . . .*" The body positioned so that it formed a star, confirmed by that later line: "*where my bones lie compassed.*" Obviously not a *set* of compasses, because the angles on such instruments are variable. It has to be the four main points of the magnetic compass: north, south, east, and west.

Then also that warning, not to take metal into the grave.

Yet by ironic *touch my flesh immured,*
Base metal traitoring this but perfect tomb . . ."

But for the metal, the tomb would have been perfect. (For the raising of the dead?) *Ironic touch.* That play on *irony* and the metal *iron.* Perhaps he had been buried in full armour, or an amulet, whatever, the metal touched his body and imprisoned it within the roots of the ragthorn. The miracle could not take place. Metal had negated the power of wood, a living substance.

I am this much closer to an understanding.

March 18, 1976

My great-uncle is buried beneath the ragthorn. I say this without evidence of bones, or even a final letter from the strange man himself, but I sense it as surely as I feel the tree feeds from the stone.

This afternoon, with a trusted local man called Edward Pottifer, I excavated into the hillside beyond the drystone wall, where the valley slope begins to drop away steeply towards the stream. The ragthorn's roots have reached here too, but it soon became clear where Alexander himself had dug below the tree to make his tomb. We cleared the turf and found that he had blocked the passage with rubble, capping it with two slabs of slate. He must have had help, someone like Pottifer perhaps, because he could not have back-filled the passage himself. I suppose there is no record of his death because he knew it had to be that way. If a man took his body and buried it beneath that tree, it would have been done in the dead of night, in the utmost secrecy, for the church, the locals, and the authorities would surely have forbidden such a burial.

He knew the method, and yet I feel that he failed.

He is still there. I'm afraid to dig into the ragthorn root mass. I am afraid of what I shall find. If he failed, what did he do wrong? The question has enormous importance for me, since I have no wish to repeat his failure.

I am ill. The illness will worsen.

April 12, 1976

I have been studying the evidence, and the manner and nature of the burial is becoming clearer. At Cambridge, Wilkins has sought out all the different meanings of the various key words and I am increasingly convinced that I have a firm knowledge of just *how* the body must be placed in the encompassing, protective cage of roots. The orientation of the body must be north—south, with the arms raised as in a cross to the east and west. There must be no metal upon or within it. The armour is stripped away, the weapons are removed. Metal is counter to the notion of resurrection, and thus I have left instructions that my back teeth are to be removed when I am dead.

May 1, 1976

In preparation for that *time* when it comes, I have now—with the help of Pottifer—dug a passage several feet long into the side of the hill, below the ragthorn. I have finally taken the same route as that followed by William Alexander, but a hundred years has compacted the earth well, and it is no easy task. That we are on the right track is confirmed only by the mixture of slate that appears in the soil, and the fact that the thorn *allows* our excavation to continue in this direction. We press on, striking up, away from the bedrock. We did attempt other passages at first, but with every foot in the *wrong* direction there was a battle to be made with the protecting thorny roots. They snagged at our flesh and pulled at our hair, until we had to abandon those first diggings. The tree knows where it wants to put me.

May 3, 1976

I have found the remains of an infant! Thank God Pottifer was not with me at the time, for it would have shaken him badly. There is a reference in the passage from Gilgamesh: *"and when the child was born, Utnapishtim gave it at once to Old Man Who Would Be Young, and the first berry appeared on the branches."* William Alexander planted this particular shoot or cutting of the tree and would have needed a similar offering. The thought horrifies me, that some mother in a nearby village, or some passing gypsy family, lost their newborn child one Victorian night.

May 10, 1976

Pottifer has made the breakthrough. He came scuttling out of the hole, his face black with earth, his fingers bloody from his encounters with sharp slate and wild thorns.

"Bones!" he cried. "Bones, Professor. I've found bones. Dear God in heaven, I touched one."

He stared at his hand as if it might have been tainted. I crawled into the passage and edged along to the place where he had found my great-uncle. The earth here was looser. The cage of roots was behind me and I could feel into what seemed to be a soft soil. It was possible to work my hands through and touch the dismembered bones and the ribs of the man who lay there. Every bone was wrapped around with the fibrous wormlike rootlets of the tree.

I became very disturbed. I was invading a place that should have been inviolate, and felt that I was an unwelcome intruder into this earthy domain.

My great-uncle had failed to attain resurrection. He had done some-thing wrong and now, I swear, the tree has his soul. It had sucked his spirit from his body to strengthen itself, perhaps to extend its root system, its power over the surrounding landscape? Was this the price of failure, to become the spiritual slave of the tree? Or am I just full of wild imaginings?

Whatever, the embrace of those roots is not a loving one, but one of possession. It is a cruel grip. The tree had hung on to the ash urn of Patroclus because the bones must not be burned. It had not released the flesh of Hamlet's father because there was metal on the body. But *I* am determined to triumph.

When I touched my ancestor's skull, I drew back sharply, then probed again. There were no teeth in the jaws. The skeleton was also oriented correctly, north, south, east, and west.

It was as I withdrew my probing hand from the soft-filled earth chamber that my fingers touched something cold and hard. I noted where it lay, that it was at the top of the leg, close to the spine, and clutched it and drew it out.

Edward Pottifer stared at the iron ball in my hand. "That's from an old gun," he said, and at once I remembered the story of my great-uncle's skirmish in the Middle East. Yes. He had been shot and close to death. They had operated on him in the field, but then transported him, delirious, to a hospital in Cyprus, where he recovered. He must have been under the impression that the bullet was removed from his body at that first operation. Of course, his back would have pained him at times, but old wounds do that, without iron in them. That must have been it, for he surely wouldn't have taken the chance, not after finding the method in *Hamlet*.

I did not mean to laugh. It was not disrespect, but relief. He had carried that iron ball into the grave with him. He had removed his teeth, perhaps gold-filled, but not the bullet.

I spoke carefully and succinctly to Edward Pottifer. I told him my teeth were to be removed at death. That my body was to be stripped and *no* metal, not even a cross around my neck, was to be buried with me. My body would be a cross. I marked clearly where my head was to be placed, and how my arms should be raised to the sides. "I will give you a compass. There must not be the slightest deviation."

He stared at me for a long time, his young face showing the anguish he felt. "When do you expect that might be, sir?" he asked me. I assured him that it would not be immediately, but that I was in my fifties now, and a very ill man. I told him to come every day to the house, to make sure I was still alive, and to become familiar with me, and less afraid of me. And of course, I would pay him well for his services. Work was not easy to find in the dale, and the temptations of this offer were too strong for him: I have my grave-digger, and I know he can be trusted.

December 24, 1976

As I write this I am experiencing a sense of profound awe. Young Wilkins is here, and he is frightened and shocked. He arrived at the cottage last night, an hour or so before I was ready to retire. I had not expected him. He had travelled from London that afternoon, and had decided not to tele-phone me from the station. I understand his reasons for coming without forewarning.

I wonder what it must have felt like for him to be picking through the decaying fragments of several old parchments—brought to Cambridge by Abdullah Rashid, who subsequently vanished!—separating by tweezers and pallet knife those shards of some ancient writer's records that showed any legible writing at all; how it must have felt to be sorting and searching, eyes feasting upon the forgotten words . . . and then to find John the Divine himself!

The writing is fragmentary. The state of ruination of the scrolls is appalling. The Arab traders had already cut each precious document into forty pieces, thinking that by so doing they would increase forty-fold the value of their find. And they were struck by the Hand of Calamity as surely, as certainly, as if Jehovah himself had taken control of their fate. All of them are now imprisoned. Abdullah Rashid is now an exile (perhaps even dead?). Yet he was compelled to come to England, to seek me out . . . to bring his last "gift" (he asked for nothing in return) before disappearing into the night.

I was fated to discover these parchments.

It is the last reference of the ragthorn that I shall discover. No more is needed. It is a fragment that has given me *courage*.

At last I understand my great-uncle's reference to REVELATION! He had heard of the lost passage from Revelations of St. John the Divine. Perhaps he saw them? It was enough for him too. Revelation! Triumph!

Oddly, the references to resurrection are not what has frightened Wilkins. If he is afraid it is because he feels that too many of his beliefs are being threatened. He has been sobered by the encounter. But he saw the words "thorn" and "rag" and has brought to me my final, most conclusive proof that there is indeed a lost and forgotten mechanism for the resurrection of the dead, nature's alchemy, nature's embrace, a technique that defies science. No scientist will accept the revivification of the flesh under the influence of thorn, and root, and cold clammy earth. Why should they? But it happened! It has been recorded throughout history; it had begun, perhaps, in ancient Sumeria. There have been deliberate attempts to lose, to deny the fact . . . folios have been scratched out, poems obliterated, classics rewritten . . . the words of the ancients have been edited dutifully, perhaps by frightened servants not of God, but of *dogma* that preaches only the resurrection of the *soul* . . .

Oh, the irony! Oh, the pleasure at what St. John the Divine has told me.

It was all there for us to see, all the symbols, all the truths. The wooden cross, which He himself fashioned in His carpenter's shop, ready for the moment of His thricefold death, drowned, stabbed, and hanged on the tree.

The Crown of Thorns, His mastery over the forest.

The immortal wood, the tree of life, the regenerating forest—of course it can shelter and protect the mortal flesh. There is in the tree a symbol, a reality too powerful for monks with quill pens to dare to fight, to challenge. So they cut it out, they *excised* it. In this way cutting out the soul of John, they cut out the heart from the past.

"He that dies by the wood shall live by the wood."

Perhaps I have the original copy of the parchment, the *only* copy remaining? It was found in a jar, in the hills of Turkestan, and had come into the possession of Abdullah . . . and had done so because it was *meant* to find its way into my hands.

For now I shall record in the journal only part of what St. John said. It is from Chapter 10 of the Revelations. It might have preceded verse 3. It is my great hope. It has confirmed my faith in the rightness of what I shall achieve. A miracle occurred in the house of Lazarus.

And I looked into the Light, and Lo, I saw Him command a thorn tree to spring from the roof of the house of Lazarus. And the tree had seven branches and on each branch there were seven times seven thorns. And below the house seven roots formed a cradle around the dead man, and raised him up so that again his face was in the light.

So cometh the power of the Lord into all living things.

And again He cried: That ye might rise anew and laugh in the face of Death, and blow the dust from thy lungs in the eyes of Death, so that ye can look on Hell's face *and scorn the fires and rage upon the flames and* rise thee up.

And Lo, I saw how the thorn withered and died and the Angel of the Lord flew from its dust.

And He cried out in the voice of the Immortal King:

The Lord is in all things and He is in the One Tree.

He that dies by the wood shall live by the wood.

He that dies by the thorn shall live again by the thorn.

April 15, 1978

Pottifer was here. I sent him to the tree, to begin to clear the chamber. The pain in my chest is greater than I can bear sometimes. I must refuse the sensible remedy of moving to London, to be closer to the hospital that can relieve such things, and extend my life, even though they cannot cure me.

Pottifer is very calm. We have kept the secret from the village and not even his family knows. He has managed to clear the root chamber whilst keeping the failed bones of my ancestor undisturbed below a thin layer of soil. As long as I am within that quivering cage of thorns I shall succeed. I shall live again.

There is a great danger, however. I believe now that the tree took William Alexander, body and soul, for its own. Perhaps that is its exacted compensation for the failure of its disciples, to possess *all* that remains, not just the flesh, but the spirit also?

I *know* I have it right, and I can depend on Pottifer, completely, just as my great-uncle must have depended on such a man. Pottifer is devoted to me, and obeys me implicitly.

September 11, 1978 (extract)

The moment is very close. I have now acquired a set of dental pincers with which to perform the final part of the ritual. Pottifer has seen into my mouth and knows which teeth to pull.

September 20, 1978

Pottifer is with me. I am certainly going. How vigorously the body clings to life, even when the mind is urging it to relax in peace. There is no longer any pain. Perhaps the closeness of death banishes such mortal agonies. I can hardly move, and writing is now an effort of will. This will be the final entry in my journal. Pottifer is very sad. I admire him. I have come to like him very much. His great concern is to get my body into the chamber before the *rigor* of death stiffens my limbs. I have told him to relax. He has plenty of time. Even so, he need wait only a few hours for the rigor to pass. I have though of everything. I have missed no point, no subtlety. When I am gone, Pottifer will end this journal and wait for one year and one day before returning to Scarfell Cottage. These papers, I am sure, will not be there. They will be in my own hands. If they *are* still in evidence, Pottifer is to send them to young Wilkins, but I am absolutely certain that I will be here to decide their fate, just as I have decided my own.

Adieu, or rather *au revoir.*

September 21

This is Pottifer. The docter told me to rite this when he was gone. I berried him as he told me to, and no dificulties. He said there must be no mistakes and spoke on the tree saying it sucked men dry of there souls who make mistakes. His last words to me were Pottifer I must face Hell and look on its face like Saint John tells. He seemed very fearfull. I give him a kiss and said a prayre. He shouted out in pain. You do not understand I must first look on Hells face he shouted you must berry me face down.

I said to him, you are a good man docter, and you shall *not* face Hell. You shall face Heaven as you diserve. Saint John does not need your penance. Do not be fearful of Hell. You are to good and if you come back I shall be your good friend and welcome you straight.

Then he died. His fists were clenched

He is in the earth now and all that I have is his teeth, God bless him. I wanted to put a cross but the thorns have grown to much and there is green on tree and I do not like to medle to much since there is more growth and very fast. No one has seen the tree so green and florished for a long wile not since that time in the last centry so the tales go.

P.S.

This is Pottifer agen. I have got some thing more to say. Some thing odd has hapened. It is more that one year and one day. The docter is still in the ground. I was in the pub and a man came in and asked for a drink. He said he was the royal poet. I think he said his name was John Betcherman. He had been walking near Scarfell and had seen the tree. He had felt some thing very strange about the place he said. A strong vision of death. Some-one screaming. He was upset. He asked about the cottage but I said nothing. He wrote a poem down and left it on the table. He said there I have exercised this terrible place and you have this and be done with it. Then he left. Here is the poem. It makes me feel sad to read it.

On a hill in highland regions
Stands an aged, thorny tree
Roots that riot, run in legions
Through the scattered scrub and scree:
Boughs that lap and lock and lace
Choke the sunlight from that place.

Deep below its tangled traces
Rots the corpse of one unknown
Gripped by roots whose gnarled embraces
Crush the skull and crack the bone.
Needled fingers clutch the crown
Late, too late to turn facedown.

There were these two British writers, one lived in the country, the other in the city. The country writer loved to visit the city and partake of brandy and Greek kebabs in the local hostelry. The city writer liked to visit the country and guzzle ale and barbecued steak under the apple trees. The two writers needed an excuse for these indulgences, and so they invented one, and this excuse was called "collaborating on a story" . . . It soon emerged that the story was to be about a legendary tree, which they both vaguely recalled from the tales their grandfathers used to tell them of mystery and myth. Soon they were delving with suppressed excitement into old documents at the British Museum and began to come up with some frightening discoveries.

The first of these finds was in studying the original text, in Anglo-Saxon, of the Old English poem "The Dream of the Rood." The marrying of the "tree" (crucifixion cross) and the "thorn" (a runic character) was too elaborately regular to be an accident of metre or alliterative language. Other discoveries followed, and the story gradually surfaced, like a dark secret from its burial mound.

The tall, hairy-faced writer, his eyes shining in the near darkness of the British Museum at five o'clock on a winter's evening, said, "We've got something here, mate." The short, clean-shaven writer, his hands full of trembling documents, answered with true English understatement, "You're not wrong, mate." So between them they began writing the history of the terrible "ragthorn tree."

Then again, they could have invented the whole thing, like these bloody storytellers do. As their old grandfathers used to say, "Why spoil a good story by sticking to the truth?"

Robert Holdstock
Garry Kilworth

CONTRIBUTORS'
NOTES

LEONID NIKOLAYEVICH ANDREYEV

Thanks to Maxim Gorky's introduction to Russian literary society, Andreyev became one of the best-selling authors in Russia during the first few years of the twentieth century. He disliked the Bolshevik regime as much as he had disliked the czarist regime, as reflected in his plays *He Who Gets Slapped* and *Life of Man,* the latter earning him first an attack by the Russian church for blasphemy and later by the communist party for "petit bourgeois negativism." His work was banned for decades after that in the U.S.S.R. In his later years, and after three suicide attempts, he left Russia for Finland, where he died in 1919.

SCOTT BAKER

Scott Baker lives in Southern California. In 1982 he won the Prix Apollo for Best SF Novel published that year in France (*Symbiote's Crown,* Berkley, 1978). In 1984 he was nominated for the World Fantasy Award for his infamous novelette *The Lurking Duck,* and in 1985 he won the World Fantasy Award for his short story, "Still Life With Scorpion."

In 1986 and 1987, Tor published his novels *Firedance* and *Drink the Fire From the Flames,* the first and second books in the Ashlu Cycle, a work about Babylonian shamanism.

EDWARD BRYANT

Edward Bryant was born in New York and reared on a cattle ranch in southern Wyoming. He now lives in Denver. Early in his career he wrote science fiction, winning two Nebula Awards, but he's now better known for his horror fiction. His horror books include *The Baku* and *Fetish*.

PAT CADIGAN

Pat Cadigan was born in New York, grew up in Massachusetts, spent most of her adult life in the Kansas City area, and now lives in London, in the UK. She has won the Arthur C. Clarke Award twice for her novels, *Synners* and *Fools*, as well as the Locus Award for best short story—"Angel"—and best collection—*Patterns*. Although her novel-length work to date is exclusively science fiction, a good percentage of her shorter fiction has been fantasy and horror. Now that she lives in London, she expects to write a lot more in those genres as she wanders through some of the older and more shadowy places, particularly in North London where she lives with her son Rob and her husband, the Original Chris Fowler (not to be confused with the author of *Roofworld*).

JONATHAN CARROLL

Jonathan Carroll is the author of several acclaimed novels, including *Voice of Our Shadow, Bones of the Moon, From the Teeth of Angels, After Silence, Black Cocktail, Outside the Dog Museum, A Child Across the Sky, Kissing the Beehive, The Marriage of Sticks, The Wooden Sea, Glass Soup*, and *The Ghost in Love*. He has won the World Fantasy Award for his story "Friend's Best Man" and his short fiction as been collected in *The Panic Hand*.

From the publication of his first novel *Land of Laughs*, Carroll has been delighting readers with his memorable characters and his overflowing imagination. He has the ability to swerve unerringly between science fiction, fantasy, and horror—often.

SUSAN CASPER

Susan Casper is a native Philadelphian who attended Temple University and recently retired from the bureaucracy of the Commonwealth of Pennsylvania to write full time. Her fiction has appeared in *Playboy, Isaac Asimov's Science Fiction Magazine, The Magazine of Fantasy & Science Fiction,* and *Amazing,* as well as most other science fiction and fantasy magazines and several anthologies, including the prestigious *In the Fields of Fire* (Jack Dann and Jeanne Van Buren Dann, editors). She has collaborated with Gardner Dozois in editing an anthology entitled *Ripper!*

SUZY MCKEE CHARNAS

Suzy McKee Charnas is a born-and-raised New Yorker. After two years in Nigeria with the Peace Corps, she taught in private school in New York and then worked with a high school drug-abuse treatment program. In 1969 she married, and moved to New Mexico, where she began writing fiction full-time.

Her first novel, *Walk to the End of the World* (1974), was a Campbell award finalist. The cycle of four books that sprang from *Walk* ended in 1999 with *The Conqueror's Child,* which won the James P. Tiptree Award. Her SF and fantasy books and stories have also won the Hugo award, the Nebula award, and the Mythopoeic award for young-adult fantasy. Her play *Vampire Dreams* has been staged several times, and a collection of her stories and essays, *Stagestruck Vampires,* was published in 2004.

She lectures and teaches about SF, fantasy, and vampires whenever she gets the chance to, most recently in a writing workshop at the University of New Mexico. Her website is at www.suzymckeecharnas.com.

JACK DANN

Jack Dann is a multiple-award winning author who has written or edited over seventy books, including the international bestseller *The Memory Cathedral; The Man Who Melted; The Silent,* a novel of the Civil War; *The Rebel: An Imagined Life of James Dean;* and a number of short story collections: *Timetipping,*

Jubilee, Visitations, The Fiction Factory, and *Promised Land,* a companion volume to *The Rebel.* Dann lives in Australia on a farm overlooking the sea and "commutes" back and forth to Los Angeles and New York.

GARDNER DOZOIS

Gardner Dozois was the editor of *Asimov's Science Fiction* magazine for almost twenty years, and is still the editor of the annual anthology series *The Year's Best Science Fiction.* He has won fifteen Hugo Awards and thirty-one Locus Awards for his editing, and two Nebula Awards and a Sidewise Award for his own writing. He is the author or editor of over a hundred books.

S.N. DYER

S.N. Dyer is the author, under various names, of a novel, sixty short stories, and a few cartoons; also, the loser of several writing awards. The author has been cursed by ownership of three inattentive, ungrateful rescued cats.

HARLAN ELLISON®

Harlan Ellison® has been called "one of the great living American short story writers" by the *Washington Post.* He has won the Hugo Award 8 ½ times, the Nebula Award three times, the Edgar Allan Poe Award of the Mystery Writers of America twice, the Georges Méliès fantasy film award twice, and was awarded the Silver Pen for Journalism by P.E.N. He won the first Bram Stoker Award of the Horror Writers of America for Best Collection for his thirty-five-year retrospective, *The Essential Ellison.* Recent collections include *Angry Candy* and *Slippage.* He is a recipient of the Life Achievement Award of World Fantasy Convention and the Horror Writers Association and the Living Legend Award of the International Horror Guild. He has also been named a Grand Master by the Science Fiction Writers of America.

Joe Haldeman

Joe Haldeman has written about two dozen novels and appears in about twenty languages. His novels *The Forever War* and *Forever Peace* won both the Nebula and Hugo Awards. He's won five Nebulas and five Hugos all together, and three times the Rhysling Award for science fiction poetry.

He also paints and plays guitar, both as a devoted amateur, and bicycles whenever the weather allows. He and his wife Gay bicycled across America, 3,050 miles, from Florida to California a few years back. When he can, he seeks out dark skies for his 12" telescope.

He teaches writing as a professor at Massachusetts Institute of Technology every fall semester.

His most recent novels are *Camouflage*, which won the Nebula and Tiptree Awards, *Old Twentieth, The Accidental Time Machine*, and *Marsbound*.

Melissa Mia Hall

Melissa Mia Hall's short fiction's been published in various format and languages for over twenty years, most recently in *The Mammoth Book of Extreme Fantasy, Front Lines, Baen's Universe* website (a collaboration with Joe R. Lansdale), *Retro Pulp Tales* ed. by Joe R. Lansdale, and *Cross Plains Universe*. She edited and contributed to the anthology *Wild Women*. Her story, "Psychofemmes" was reprinted in *The Year's 25 Finest Crime and Mystery Stories* in 1998.

A veteran book industry journalist and fiction author, Hall's critical work appears in *Publishers Weekly*, various newspapers and online venues, in non-fiction books such as *Icons of Horror and the Supernatural*, edited by S.T. Joshi, and *Supernatural Literature of the World*, edited by S.T. Joshi and Stefan Dziemianowicz, and most recently in *The Book of Lists—Horror: An All-New Collection of Spine-Tingling, Hair-Raising Blood-Curdling Fun and Facts* compiled by Amy Wallace, Scott Bradley, and Del Howison.

ROBERT HOLDSTOCK

Robert Holdstock is the author of several novels and collections, including his 'Mythago' Cycle: *The Bone Forest, Lavondyss, The Hollowing, Gate of Ivory,* and *Mythago Wood,* which received the World Fantasy Award in 1985 and was aptly hailed by Alan Garner as "a new expression of the British genius for true fantasy." His more recent work is 'The Merlin Codex': *Celtika, The Iron Grail,* and *The Broken Kings.* Holdstock was born in rural Kent but has made London his home for a quarter of a century.

HARVEY JACOBS

Harvey Jacobs' latest novel is *Side Effects,* a pharmaceutical fable. His last novel, *American Goliath,* based on the true story of the Cardiff Giant scam, was a World Fantasy Award finalist. Earlier works include the novels *Beautiful Soup, The Juror,* and *Summer On A Mountain Of Spices,* and the short story collections *My Rose & My Glove* and *The Egg of the Glak.* His stories have appeared in many anthologies (including several edited by Ellen Datlow) and many magazines in the U. S. and abroad including *New Worlds, The Magazine of Fantasy & Science Fiction, Omni, Esquire,* and *Playboy,* He lives and works in Sag Harbor, New York.

K.W. JETER

K. W. Jeter was born in Los Angeles in 1950. He has written some very edgy novels, including *Dr. Adder, The Glass Hammer,* and *Infernal Devices.* He has also had a number of short stories published. His work defies classification.

GARRY KILWORTH

Garry Kilworth has been writing short stories for thirty-five years now and is still fired with enthusiasm for the medium. In 2006 PS Publishing brought out his collection *Moby Jack and Other Tall Tales* which covers ten years of stories. The same publisher will be bringing out *Tales From The Fragrant Harbour,* a collection of original general fiction stories written while the author lived in Hong Kong, paired with a collection of fantastical tales also penned in the same location. The first half will be subtitled "Once-Told Tales" and the second section "Twice-Told Tales" (thanks to Nathaniel Hawthorne, much admired). Garry Kilworth lives in England some of the time and in various other countries the rest of the year.

KATHE KOJA

Kathe Koja writes novels for adults and for young people (sometimes the same books). She lives in the Detroit area with her husband, artist Rick Lieder, and their cats.

TANITH LEE

Tanith Lee was born in 1947 in North London, England, didn't learn to read until she was eight, and started to write when she was nine. "Having," she says, "virtually wrecked, single-handed, the catering world with her waitressing, the Library system with her library-assistance and all types of shops with her mishandling of everything, she was set free into the world of professional writing in 1975 by DAW Books."

Tanith Lee lives with her husband John Kaiine by the sea in Great Britain and is a prolific writer of fantasy, science fiction, and horror. Her most recent books are the those in the adult fantasy Trilogy: *LIONWOLF: Cast A Bright Shadow, Here In Cold Hell,* and *No Flame But Mine;* the three young adult novels: *Piratica, Piratica 2,* and *Piratica 3;* and *Metallic Love,* (the sequel to her adult SF novel *The Silver Metal Lover*). She is currently working on a dark adult fantasy whose title she will only reveal as *A. T. C. O. T. C*, while researching for an even darker work concerning a rabid parallel Bronze Age of violence and sorcery.

FRITZ LEIBER

Fritz Leiber is the author of such classic novels as *Conjure Wife*, *The Big Time* and *Gather, Darkness!* as well as numerous short stories, including the Hugo and Nebula Award winner "Gonna Roll the Bones," which was first published in *Dangerous Visions*. He is credited with coining the descriptive term "sword and sorcery," and created the memorable characters Fafhrd and Gray Mouser to populate his heroic-fantasy adventures. *The Knight and Knave of Swords* comprises the seventh and final novel of that series.

THOMAS LIGOTTI

Thomas Ligotti is recognized as a contemporary master in the genre of horror fiction and his work has been compared to that of classic horror writers Edgar Allan Poe and H. P. Lovecraft.

He has received several awards, including the Horror Writers Association Bram Stoker award for his collection *The Nightmare Factory* and short novel *My Work Is Not Yet Done*.

Ligotti's latest collection of stories is *Teatro Grottesco*, published by Durtro Press. A short film of his story "The Frolic" is available on a DVD. In addition, a graphic novel based on works from Ligotti's 1996 collection *The Nightmare Factory* was released in 2007, with a second volume scheduled to appear in 2008.